Lyn Andrews is one of the UK's top one hundred best-selling authors, reaching No. 1 on the *Sunday Times* paperback bestseller list. Born and brought up in Liverpool, she is the daughter of a policeman who also married a policeman. After becoming the mother of triplets, she took some time off from her writing whilst she raised her children. Shortlisted for the Romantic Novelists' Association Award in 1993, she has now written twenty-two hugely successful novels. Lyn Andrews divides her time between Merseyside and Ireland.

The Ties That Bind

and

Liverpool Songbird

Lyn Andrews

<u>headline</u>

THE TIES THAT BIND first published in Great Britain in 1999
by HEADLINE BOOK PUBLISHING

LIVERPOOL SONGBIRD first published in Great Britain in 1996
by HEADLINE BOOK PUBLISHING

First published in this omnibus edition in 2005
by HEADLINE BOOK PUBLISHING

A HEADLINE paperback

10 9 8 7 6 5 4 3 2 1

ISBN 0 7553 2662 8

Typeset in Times by Avon DataSet Ltd,
Bidford-on-Avon, Warwickshire

Printed and bound in Great Britain by
Mackays of Chatham plc, Chatham, Kent

Headline's policy is to use papers that are natural, renewable and
recyclable products and made from wood grown in sustainable
forests. The logging and manufacturing processes are expected to
conform to the environmental regulations of the country of origin.

HEADLINE BOOK PUBLISHING
A division of Hodder Headline
338 Euston Road
London NW1 3BH

www.headline.co.uk
www.hodderheadline.com

The Ties That Bind

For Gordon Crabb, my extremely talented illustrator, who brings my characters to life, visually, in almost the exact images I have of them in my mind. My grateful thanks, Gordon.

And for my hairdresser Roy Searle, who not only makes sure I'm perfectly 'coiffed' each week, but listens to my moans and complaints with patience and good humour, and has proved invaluable for advice and information.

PART I

Chapter One

1937

'Mam says they've done a moonlight flit from the Holy Land.'

Nessie Harrison, aged ten years and two months, imparted this piece of news with immense satisfaction. But the three figures sitting on the low wall that ran around the tannery didn't receive it in the manner she'd expected. The tannery, owned by J. Smush Ltd, wasn't an obvious venue for their gatherings. It stank atrociously in summer and wasn't much better in winter; the residents of Naylor Street never really got used to the smell.

But, despite its drawbacks, it had always been a sort of meeting place. *Their* meeting place. They'd congregated there winter and summer when they'd had time to spare, although during that awkward stage of their development, the transition between childhood and youth, meetings had become fewer. There had been awkwardness, on all their parts, as they realised that they weren't just kids any more. Somehow, almost overnight it seemed, they'd grown up and street games and other such pastimes were no longer shared with the same enthusiasm. But still they would meet sporadically, and now, as before, the wall of Mr Smush's premises was a place that Nessie, the bane of her elder sister Elizabeth's life, was strenuously excluded from.

3

Elizabeth and Nessie's parents, Delia and Jack Harrison, owned the corner shop situated at the junction of Naylor Street and Gladstone Street. They were open all hours and sold everything from bread to coal. It provided them with a comfortable if far from luxurious living, but Delia Harrison had the good fortune to have a very well-off sister in America who had no children of her own and who was very generous where her two nieces were concerned. All the money she sent to her sister Delia was earmarked for the girls' education. Delia wanted something far, far better for her daughters than a shop or factory job. So Elizabeth was being taught by the nuns at the Convent of Notre Dame in Everton Valley, and Nessie would follow her when she was eleven.

At fourteen Elizabeth was quite tall although she constantly bemoaned the fact that she had inherited her mother Delia's 'bonny' figure. Her eyes were Elizabeth's most attractive feature, large and deep blue in colour, but in Delia's view her daughter's hair was her 'crowning glory', a thick deep chestnut mass that reached her shoulders in natural waves. Delia was sure her striking daughter ought to be able to make something of herself.

'How does your mam know they've done a flit?' Mike Flynn asked Nessie.

He was a tall, well-built lad of almost fifteen, with dark brown hair and brown eyes. One of the noisy, boisterous, obstreperous Flynn family who lived in number ten, Naylor Street, he was very interested in the family who were moving in next door. The house had been empty for a few weeks which was unusual but then the Piercesons themselves had been unusual. No one in the street had been sorry when they'd left. Mr Pierceson and his sons spent more time in

4

Walton Jail than they did at home and Mrs Pierceson and her elder daughter hardly left the snug in the Unicorn. The younger ones had been left to run wild. He was quite amazed that his own mam hadn't already found out about the new family. She usually did. There wasn't much that went on in Naylor Street that Eileen Flynn didn't know about. She spent most of her day standing on the doorstep, jangling, leaving, as Delia Harrison often remarked, her house like a junk shop and an untidy one at that.

'She knows 'cos someone told her.' Nessie's voice was full of defiance.

'Like who, exactly?' Ginny Greely demanded. Like her widowed mother, Ginny always liked a bit of gossip. Her hazel eyes had already taken in everything Nessie was wearing and she was envious. She herself had no knitted hat to cover her lank, dark ash-coloured hair, no woollen mitts for her chapped hands and no warm scarf. She pulled her thin brown coat closer to her body, crossed her arms and tucked her fingers beneath her armpits. Her hands were so cold they were numb. Frost was already beginning to glisten on window-panes, doorsteps and cobbles, as well as on the roofs. If the houses were warm then in the morning the lacy patterns of ice on the window-panes were pretty, but Ginny's house was never that warm. Often there was ice on the inside of the glass too. Still, in a few days it would be Christmas and they were all looking forward to the holiday.

Earlier that day Ginny, Mike and their friend Johnny Doyle had left school for good, all of them fortunate enough to have jobs to go to. They'd arranged to meet by the factory wall to talk about their futures and their plans, and Elizabeth, the only one of them staying on at school, had also joined them.

Ginny was going to work in Birrel's Fishmonger's, two doors down from the Harrisons' shop, but she wasn't very happy about it.

'Mam, I *hate* fish! You know I *hate* fish! They're so slimy.' She'd shivered. 'It will be a cold, wet, horrible job.' Then she'd thought about having to cut off the heads with their glassy, staring dead eyes, and the tails and fins. And she'd have to learn how to gut them. It made her feel sick to think about it. She'd have to wear a white coat and a turban over her hair. The coat wouldn't stay clean for very long. She'd seen the state of Mr Birrel's at the end of the day.

'You'll go and you'll be grateful for it. I had to stand Jerry Birrel at least a dozen pints of best bitter before he agreed to take you on, milady,' had been the firm reply from Mabel, her mother.

For Mike Flynn it would be up at the crack of dawn and down to the Salthouse Dock to shovel coal into sacks for Dawson's Coal Merchant's who, along with all the others, had their allocated stock dumped in mountainous piles on to the dockside from the cargo holds. It was a dirty, back-breaking job, but the only one he could find. He had no rich relatives in America nor a barmaid mother who had a little influence with certain customers.

For Johnny Doyle, for whom the three were still waiting, it was the Merchant Navy. He'd signed on as a bellboy on Cunard's *Ascania*. He would make his first trip in the New Year.

'Well, has the cat got your tongue, Nessie?' Elizabeth probed. 'Who told Mam they'd done a flit from the Holy Land? You're sure you're not telling us stories again?'

'She *did* say it!' Nessie shot back at her sister. 'She *did*! Honest to God!'

' "Honest to God" and "the Holy Land". She's a real scream, isn't she?' Ginny said drily.

Elizabeth and Mike both laughed. The Holy Land was the name given to an area in the Dingle in the south end of the city, where the streets were all named after biblical characters: David, Isaac, Jacob and Moses Streets. Like Scotland Road and its immediate neighbourhood, the area depended heavily on the docks, the shipping and all the service industries for employment and, also like Scotland Road, the housing was substandard: old, inadequate and in some cases a very real danger to life and limb. Like their counterparts in Scotland Road, the women in the Dingle fought a daily battle against dirt, disease and poverty.

'Oh, get home, Nessie, and leave me in peace,' Elizabeth dismissed her sister scornfully. 'You made it up. Mrs Flynn would have known, she always does. Get home, you're a bloody pain, always trailing after me.'

Nessie glared at her sister. 'It's true and I'll tell Mam you swore, Lizzie Harrison.'

'And you'll get belted when I tell Mam you called me "Lizzie",' Elizabeth retorted, 'and Ginny and Mike will back me up.'

Delia Harrison had always insisted that her elder daughter be addressed by her full Christian name at all times. Elizabeth was Elizabeth. Not Liz or Lizzie, Bess or Bessie, or even Beth. Elizabeth herself wouldn't have minded being called Beth at all but her mam was adamant. They had 'standards' to keep up, she always maintained firmly in her 'Sunday voice', as Elizabeth called it. Elizabeth had never understood why her younger sister was addressed by a derivative of her full Christian name. When she'd protested that it wasn't fair, her mam would reply, 'You're the eldest, you have more sense and I expect more from you.' Just what 'more' was, exactly, she didn't know.

Nessie stuck out her tongue, knowing her moment of glory had passed. Only Mike Flynn had shown any real interest in the new family who had moved into number twelve that day.

'If you don't get home now you'll not get over the doorstep for the rest of the week,' Elizabeth reminded Nessie. Delia insisted her younger daughter be in by half past seven at the very latest.

As if on cue the door of the Harrisons' shop opened and Delia's strident voice was heard along the length of the street.

'Nessie! Nessie, it's turned half past and I want you in this house in one minute flat!'

'See!' Elizabeth said smugly, pushing a strand of hair that had escaped from her beret out of her eyes.

Nessie pursed her lips and glared at them all.

'Vanessa Harrison, get in here this minute or your da will come and get you, and then God help you, milady!'

Nessie turned away, annoyance and apprehension in her eyes. When her mam used her full and, in her own opinion, far too fancy Christian name, she knew she was in trouble. Although she didn't know it, Nessie's opinion of her name was shared by most of the neighbours. As Eileen Flynn always said, it was just Delia Harrison's way of showing off.

As Nessie trailed reluctantly down Naylor Street, Elizabeth looked after her in despair. 'She's a little horror! If I *had* to have a sister why couldn't I have got a decent one, not one like her?' she complained bitterly.

'I've got two of them, so stop moaning,' Mike Flynn muttered gloomily.

Ginny decided it was time to change the subject.

'Where's Johnny? He's late!'

'Oh, you know what his da's like. Even though he has the pub he's all holier than thou. He doesn't think Johnny should mix with the likes of us, especially now he's got the best job of us all,' Mike replied.

'At least he's being *allowed* to get a job. *I've* got to go back to flaming school. But I'm not going to stay there for another four flaming years followed by God knows how long at teacher-training college. I don't care how much she carries on! I *hate* that place! I *hate* flaming kids and I can't think of anything worse than having to teach them. Look at our Nessie! Imagine having a classful like *her*!' Elizabeth kicked her heels against the wall in frustration. 'I wish Aunty Margaret would stop sending money. I don't mind the clothes she sends, they're usually great, it's just the money. It only encourages Mam to get more airs and graces and we have enough rules and regulations already. We live over and at the back of a shop off Scottie Road, for God's sake, and they want me to be a *teacher*! And when our Nessie starts at the convent I'll still be there! Oh, I'll die of mortification, I'll just die!'

Elizabeth's litany of complaints stopped as Johnny Doyle arrived, panting. He was a wiry lad, the 'greyhound breed' was how his father described him. It didn't matter how much he ate, he never seemed to gain any weight. His hair was fine, blond and unruly and was always falling in his eyes. Pushing it back had become a habit. He sat down on the wall next to Mike.

'I thought I'd never get out. He's had me moving crates from the cellar to the yard ever since I got home from school! Thank God he's safely in the bar now and your mam is in the saloon, Ginny, laughing and joking as usual.'

Ginny shrugged. Her mother was a barmaid for both Eddie Doyle in the Globe and in another local pub, the Unicorn. It was hard to make ends meet but somehow her mam did it – just. Thankfully she was easy-going and hadn't become bitter and sour about being a widow with a child to bring up. In fact sometimes she was too easy-going. She liked a drink herself, did Mabel Greely, or May as she was always called. On occasions people made cutting remarks but they rolled off May like water off a duck's back.

'What did your Nessie want?' asked Johnny. 'I saw her legging it off home and your mam was standing on the shop step with a face like thunder.'

'Oh, some nonsense about the family moving into number twelve.'

'What?' Johnny didn't want to miss anything interesting about them.

'She said they'd done a moonlight from the Holy Land.'

'They must really be in a mess,' Ginny interrupted. 'I wonder how they can afford the rent here if they're so skint that they had to move across the city?'

'How do I know? How do I know our Nessie was even telling the truth? She's a nasty little cat. She loves causing trouble.' Elizabeth stared glumly at the ground. 'Things at home wouldn't be so bad if there were more of us. If I had brothers.'

'You're dead lucky that there *aren't* more of you. Our house is like a lunatic asylum most of the time,' Mike retorted.

With only Jack and Delia, Elizabeth and Nessie to share three bedrooms, a big kitchen that doubled as a sitting room, a scullery, and a privy and wash house in the yard, the Harrisons lived in luxury compared to Mike's family. The Flynns were crowded into a two-up, two-down terrace house you could hardly swing a cat in.

Sick of Nessie, Elizabeth changed the subject. 'When exactly do you sail, Johnny?'

'On New Year's Eve, would you believe! I'll miss all the "do's",' he stated morosely.

'You'll get a good send-off though. You'll be half-deafened by the noise from all the other ships in the river and the docks. It always sounds great, and with all the church bells ringing too.'

'I know. It won't be the same though, will it? I'll be running around, dressed up in that daft uniform, all buttons and gold braid and that flaming hat! It looks like a biscuit tin stuck on my head.'

'Have you got all your gear then?' Mike asked.

'Yeah. Mam took me down to Greenberg's in Park Lane and got me kitted out *and* she had to pay for it all. They don't provide uniforms for the likes of us. God! I'll feel such a flaming fool.'

'Look on the bright side. No one will know you – the passengers anyway. And you'll get tips as well as wages.'

'Half the crew will know me, though. I'll be skitted soft.'

'Well, I wouldn't mind being skitted soft to see big places like New York, be given three good meals a day, be paid *and* get tips,' said Mike. 'It's better than shovelling coal all day, out in all flaming weathers.' Like Ginny he wasn't looking forward to starting work. Still, he'd have money of his own, even after he'd turned up his keep to his mam, and money of his own was something he'd never had very much of before. If he'd wanted to go to the pictures he'd had to collect empty jam jars for Mrs Harrison and run errands and the like. Once, when as a lad he'd had the money for the pictures but no boots or even a pair of cut-down trousers, he'd stood in the yard and cried until Brenda, his eldest sister, had found a big safety pin and had pinned the back tails of his shirt to the front ones so he could go. When he remembered such hard and humiliating times, filling coal sacks and having a wage of his own began to look good.

'Will you be seasick?' Ginny asked Johnny, although it was more of a deliberation than a question.

'God, I hope not. I'd have half the neighbourhood splitting their sides.'

'I bet half the neighbourhood were sick to start with,' Ginny sniffed. 'Mary Malloy from William Henry Street said their Norman is sick every single trip and he's been going to sea for nearly nine years. It's nothing to be ashamed of.'

'You're not sick on the ferry, so why should you be sick on a ship of that size?' Elizabeth said flatly. She was bored and you could see your breath it was so cold. The lads had their hands in their jacket pockets, the collars of their jackets turned up and their caps pulled down over their ears.

Ginny's coat was almost threadbare. She had no stockings, just a pair of old, broken-down shoes. She was shivering uncontrollably.

Elizabeth took off her scarf and gloves. 'Here, put them on, you're perished.'

Ginny wrapped the knitted scarf over her head and around her neck. 'Thanks.'

'You'd better keep them.'

'I can't. What'll your mam say?'

Elizabeth shrugged. 'I'll say I lost them. Left them in the cloakroom at school. She didn't see me when I came out and I've got more, Ginny.'

'If you're sure . . .'

'I am. Now, shall we go and see if our Nessie was right about the new neighbours?'

'Well, we've got to walk home, so there's no harm in having a look. Are you two coming?' Ginny asked.

Mike and Johnny exchanged glances. There was nothing else interesting on offer, so they nodded and followed the girls.

Number twelve, Naylor Street had the dubious benefit of having a lamppost outside. True, its light brightened the front rooms of the house so there was no need to use the gas light, but it was also frequently used as a meeting place as well as for cricket stumps in summer and one half of a football goalpost in winter, its twin being on the other side of the road. If someone managed to get an old tyre and some rope then it was used as a swing but that usually didn't last long. Some spoilsport adult always took it down. There was no money to spare for toys and games so the local kids had to devise them and utilise what they could find.

The lads considered themselves very lucky that Johnny Doyle had a proper football – a casey – and so were the envy of all the other boys in the surrounding streets. Until then they, like everyone else, had had to use a ball made up of rags.

Number twelve was the same as all the other houses in

the street: old, decrepit, soot-blackened, its windows like sightless eyes. The steps were worn and crumbling, but unlike all the other houses, the windows were dirty, their sills and the doorsteps untouched by scrubbing brush or donkey stone.

'It doesn't look as though there's anyone in there at all,' Ginny speculated in a loud whisper.

'There is. Look.' Elizabeth pointed to a bundle of what looked like rags that had been left on the top step. The door was ajar.

'Well, go on then, knock,' Mike urged.

'There's no sign of life *anywhere*,' Johnny pointed out. 'And that could just be a bundle left by . . . anyone.'

'Oh, you two are the living end,' Elizabeth said impatiently as she quickly went up the steps and rapped hard with the dull, pitted knocker. The door itself was sagging on its hinges and most of the dark brown paint had peeled off long ago. Once she'd knocked, however, she did retreat to her place on the pavement beside her friends.

They all heard the whispering, then the sound of footsteps coming down the lobby and finally a shape appeared in the doorway. The streetlight illuminated the figure and they could see that it was a girl. One about their own age too, Elizabeth surmised.

She was first to speak. 'We . . . we've only come to see if we can . . . help, like? We heard you've just moved in today.'

The girl came down the steps and they could see her more clearly. She was small and slightly built. Her black hair was cut short, her eyebrows slanted outwards and upwards like a bird's wing and, with her blue eyes, fringed with dark lashes, her pert button of a nose and pale skin, she had an almost

14

elfin look about her, Elizabeth thought. She also looked afraid.

'There's no reason to be frightened, honestly. I meant it. We just came to help. What's your name?'

The girl hesitated, her glance sweeping over the little group. 'Theresa, but everyone calls me Tessa. Tessa O'Leary.'

'I'm Elizabeth Harrison. Mam and Dad have the corner shop. This is Ginny Greely. She and her mam live in number fifteen. Mike Flynn lives next door in number ten. They're a noisy lot, always rowing and fighting.' Elizabeth's words were tempered by her smile.

Mike grinned. 'Only when me da has spent most of the housekeeping in the pub.'

'And this is Johnny Doyle. His da has the pub, the Globe. Have you got any brothers and sisters?' Elizabeth's tone was friendly. 'I've got a nasty little cat of a sister and Mike's got two older sisters and—'

'Our Harold who's nine and is a holy terror,' Mike finished for her.

Tessa seemed to relax a little. 'I've got two brothers. Our Colin, he's sixteen, and our Jimmy, he's nine too, like your Harold. I had two sisters but they died when they were just babies. There's Mam and Da, of course.'

Elizabeth was bursting to ask if they had really done a moonlight and why, but she curbed her curiosity.

'Have you got a job? I mean, we . . . well, those three have just left school. Today, in fact. As for me, I'm stuck in flaming school. I'll tell you about it sometime.'

Tessa shook her head. 'No. I've no job . . . yet.'

'What about your brother and your da?' Johnny asked.

'Well, Da works on the docks, when he can, and . . . and

15

. . . our Colin is sort of . . . looking.' What she didn't say was that Colin had just been released from Borstal for stealing. It wasn't the first time and it was one of the reasons they'd moved. But it wasn't the most important reason.

'Oh, he'll get something, Tessa,' Elizabeth said brightly. She liked Tessa O'Leary, she decided, there was just something about the girl that made her warm to her.

'I know you don't really need them, what with the lamppost an' all, but why aren't there any lights on?' Ginny asked.

Tessa became hesitant. 'We . . . we don't—'

'Have any money for the gas meter?' Mike interrupted. 'It's the same in our house. Sometimes we have to sit in the dark or Mam lights some candles while we go and cadge a few coppers.'

Tessa smiled. A genuine smile, full of relief. She seemed thankful they weren't the only ones in the street to be so hard up.

'I'll go and see what I can get out of my old feller,' Johnny offered, thinking he'd have to endure a lecture about lending money to strangers. But they had no light, for God's sake. Even his da, who claimed to be so religious, so Christian, couldn't refuse such a request.

'Do you want me to bring this in for you?' Mike pointed to the bundle.

'No, I don't want you to bring anything in! I want you to mind your own flaming business! Tessa, get in here!'

They all took a step backwards as Mary O'Leary appeared in the doorway and glared down at them.

'We . . . we . . . was only trying to help,' Mike said.

'Well, we don't need your help, so clear off the lot of you,' she snapped.

Tessa bit her lip.

'We *were* only trying to help, Mrs O'Leary. Everyone around here helps one another,' Elizabeth said in a firm but polite tone.

Mary O'Leary eyed her with open hostility. 'A right hardfaced little madam, aren't you?'

'No, I'm not, and if you want credit from my mam you'd better not speak to her in the same tone of voice!'

Tessa gazed pleadingly at Elizabeth.

Any more of this and her mam's temper, which was very short these days, would be vented on her for not getting rid of them as she'd been told to do, never mind standing holding a conversation with them.

'Oh, you must be from the shop then.' Mary hated having to be polite to the girl, but she'd already sent Richie, her idle, useless wastrel of a husband, down to see what he could scrounge out of the shopkeeper. She was too tired, too worried, too heartsore to go herself. It would be bad enough having to face the neighbours and their questioning in the days to come.

'Yes, I am,' Elizabeth said quietly.

'And I suppose the rest of you came sneaking around just to get a look at us too.' Mary couldn't hold back her mounting irritation.

'I told you, Mrs O'Leary, we just came to offer our help.'

She'd had enough. 'Clear off! I don't need you all cluttering up my doorstep at this time of night. Haven't you got homes to go to? Tessa, gerrin!'

She turned away and Tessa picked up the bundle.

Elizabeth laid a hand on her arm. 'We're sorry, really we are.'

'I know, but, well . . . she's had a hard time lately and she always has a temper at the best of times.'

'It goes with the name, I suppose,' Elizabeth smiled. 'You know, Irish.'

'Oh, aye, half of Liverpool has got Irish blood in them. My mam and da included,' Johnny said. He felt sorry for the girl.

Tessa smiled. 'I know.'

'Well, if you do need anything . . .' Elizabeth offered.

'Thanks. I'd better go in or she'll kill me.'

When the door had closed they all looked at one another.

'God, isn't she just a bitch!' Ginny exclaimed.

'I know mine's got a temper, but I wouldn't fancy having *that* one for a mam. Oh, I can see some fireworks ahead. My mam won't put up with *that*, especially as they'll be living next door,' Mike said.

'And we didn't find out much at all, except that she's got two brothers,' said Elizabeth. 'But I liked her. Maybe if she comes into the shop or I see her on the street I'll find out more.'

'Your mam will get more out of her than you will,' Mike said sagely, nodding his head.

Elizabeth grinned in agreement. 'Probably. And she'll show her the door if she carries on like that in future!'

The four of them continued down the street, strangely cheered by the prospect of the excitement to come.

18

Chapter Two

Tessa leaned her back against the door, the bundle clutched in her arms, tears not far away. They had been nice, really nice. Especially Elizabeth from the shop. She hoped Elizabeth's mother would be just as understanding. She had had nothing to eat since last night and she felt faint with hunger and cold.

It was the cold that had affected her the most. Hunger was always with her lately. She was so cold even her bones were aching and she knew she must look awful. She had no coat or hat, not even a shawl. The other girl – Ginny – had had a coat on. It was old and thin, but it was a coat. The navy blue skirt and grey jumper were all she had in the way of protection from the icy weather. But at least they had a roof of sorts over their heads. It had taken Mam a full week to find this house. For seven long days she'd walked the streets in this area, traipsing all the way over here so that they could be well away from the Dingle.

These days she could do nothing right, as far as her mam was concerned. Things had never been easy in Isaac Street, but everyone there had been more or less in the same boat. She thought back over her childhood. It hadn't been unhappy. Mam had been strict with them over clothes and boots. She'd never had a single piece of clothing that was new, but she'd never complained. What use was there in doing that? Da worked on the docks, like most of the men in the street, but not often enough, so her mam had always said. Still, what furniture and pots and pans and crockery they did have were treated with great care. Mam had been strict about that too. The last few weeks had been terrible, really terrible, but today had been the worst day of her life. The tears began to roll slowly down her cheeks.

'Tessa, bring that thing in here!' Mary's voice echoed through the dark, empty house.

Tessa didn't want to go into the kitchen where Colin had lit and placed a single candle on the shelf over the range. Half of all their troubles had come about because of him. Oh, there were times when she wished him to the other end of the earth or even dead. She knew that was sinful but she couldn't help it.

He just wasn't the same as everyone else in the family. Where he got his badness from she didn't know. Even her mam's lectures and belts had had no effect. Da didn't seem to be too bothered about any of them and left Mam to deal with their escapades, but Colin's behaviour was worse than that.

'Tessa, did you hear me?' Mary called.

'Yes, Mam. I'm coming.'

The kitchen seemed cavernous. The corners were very dark and the flickering flame threw feeble shadows, but as her eyes became accustomed to the gloom she could see her mother sitting on an orange box, her shoulders humped and her head in her hands as if to protect herself from the harsh reality of her life. Colin sat on an empty upturned paint tin. Of young Jimmy, there was no sign.

'Where's our Jimmy?' Tessa put the bundle on the dirty, scuffed lino floor.

Mary raised her head. 'God knows! And God knows I don't care either. I . . . I . . . never thought I'd see the day when we'd be forced to live like this.' Worry and exhaustion made her look haggard. Deep lines showed on her forehead and around her eyes and mouth. She looked sixty, not forty-six. In her eyes there was utter despair. Tessa went over to her.

'Da will get *something*, Mam.' She turned to her brother. 'And *he* can get himself out, find our Jimmy, and the pair of them can go and pick up rubbish. Anything at all that will burn.'

Colin scowled at her but she ignored him. There was always *someone* nagging him. Making him do things he didn't want to do. He'd had nothing all his life and as he'd got older the unfairness of it all had made him angry and hard. His da had been no example – he was weak and had no ambition whatsoever. His mam ignored him most of the time; she looked on him as a failure but she'd never given him any help or encouragement. All she was interested in was keeping the flaming house clean and worrying what the neighbours were thinking. What the hell! 'Give a dog a bad name' so that saying went, he didn't care. So what if he pinched anything he could get his hands on? Those he stole from could more than afford it. And in Borstal he'd learned that petty thieving was a waste of time. If you were going to steal, then pinch something that would fetch pounds rather than pennies, or take money in the first place. He was biding his time. He'd find out more about the people in this area of Liverpool, then he'd work out the best way to steal enough to get out of this dump.

'One of those lads has gone to try to get us a few coppers

for the gas. It'll be all right, Mam, we can use the gas ring then and I'll make us all a cup of tea.'

'Oh, this is a nice start, isn't it? Forced to take charity from strangers.'

'They won't mind, Mam. The one who lives next door said they're always running around to beg for pennies for the gas.'

'A nice lot they must be then!' Mary snapped. Oh, she could kill Richie and Colin. She had nothing, not a single thing to show for twenty-four years of marriage. She had no money to make a home in this house, nor any interest in doing so. It was too shabby, far worse than the one she'd had in Isaac Street.

She'd been so proud of that little house. At first they'd had only the essentials but she'd scrubbed the bare boards in all the rooms and down the stairs every single Wednesday. A scrubbing brush, a bar of carbolic soap and a bucket of hot water were all you needed, she'd often joked with her neighbours. Poverty was no excuse for dirt, that had been her motto.

Gradually, she'd acquired things. All bought second-hand, but washed down and polished. She'd had lino and rag rugs in all the rooms. Her windows had always shone; her curtains were always clean.

'I see Mary's step-dashing again' was an often-heard remark and she'd taken it as a great compliment.

Now she had nothing. Nothing at all. Not even a chair to sit on, let alone a bed to rest her aching head. Suddenly the kitchen door burst open and Jimmy arrived, scruffy and dirty as usual. A few months ago he wouldn't have dared to get into that state.

'There's some lad waiting at the front door. He said he had come to see our Tessa.'

'Look at the state of you, you little hooligan!' Tessa snapped. She sincerely hoped her mam wasn't going to tell her to go and shut the door in the face of whoever it was on the doorstep. 'You and your useless brother can go out and look for rubbish or there'll be no fire! Get out the back way, there should be plenty of stuff in the jigger and people won't see you doing it.' Even now she was considerate of her mam's pride. 'I'll go and see who . . . who it is at the front.'

Before her mother could reply she left the room and walked down the lobby.

It was Johnny Doyle who stood on the step.

'Here, I managed to get sixpence out of my da and that's no easy thing, I'll tell you! He's not called "Moneybags" around here for nothing, although "Scrooge" would suit him better.'

'Oh thanks, that's great. I mean it. I'll pay you back when . . .'

'You don't need to. It's a gift, a pressie, like.'

Tessa nodded with gratitude.

'Well, don't forget, Tessa, if any of us can help you've only got to shout.'

'Thanks. Thanks again, Johnny,' she replied, shyly. He seemed very kind.

As he turned to go she caught sight of her father wandering slowly down the road. She prayed he had been to the shop and not the pub. All the money they had left after the rent had been paid was ten shillings, and that to keep a family on for God alone knew how long. There were so many things they needed, but food and a fire were priorities.

They'd all have to get jobs and quickly. Mam had sold her wedding ring and the one her own mother – Tessa's grand-mother – had left. Oh, they'd been in the pawnshop more often than on her mam's finger, but she knew it had broken her mam's heart to have to sell them. If Da had spent the money Mam had given him for food on drink, much as she loved him, she would kill him herself. He was never violent or abusive when drunk. Just the opposite: laughing and joking and falling over things. He'd give you the world, except he'd just spent his wages.

'What did you get, Da?' she asked as he came within earshot.

'Bread, dripping, tea, some spuds an' a bundle of chips for the fire,' Richie answered, handing half his purchases to a relieved Tessa. The woman in the shop hadn't been very co-operative until her husband had come out and urged her to put it on the slate. He looked a decent feller but you could see who wore the trousers in that house. Richie had managed to evade the woman's questions as to why they'd moved across the city by asking about work, and her husband had given him the name of one of the blockermen at this end of the eight miles of docks. He was very grateful. It wasn't that he didn't like work; he did, and he worked hard. He was just good-natured and liked a few pints with the lads. It was a habit that had grown steadily over the years as he had realised how shrewish, bad-tempered and nagging his wife had become. She started the minute he set foot in the door. He knew he would never get out again to go for a drink, so he didn't go home. Why, after a hard day's work, a man had to put up with continual complaints and unfair criticism of his character he didn't know. It was better to have a laugh and a joke and maybe even a bit of a gamble in pleasant company than to endure Mary on top note.

'Well, I've got sixpence for the gas meter so we can have some tea with bread an' dripping. Then I'll boil the potatoes. I've told those two to get out and see what they can find to start a fire.'

Tessa forced herself to smile as she entered the kitchen.

'I told you things would be all right, Mam. Look, I've sixpence for the gas and Da's managed to get a few bits. We can have a drink, a butty and some spuds each.'

Mary looked up and glared at her husband. 'We haven't got a kettle. We haven't got a teapot or cups and plates, not any more.'

'Oh, Jesus, Mary and Joseph! I've said I'm sorry. For God's sake don't start again!'

The light of battle filled Mary's eyes. 'Again! I've hardly started on you, Richie O'Leary! We had a decent home, one it took me years to get together. You could have got regular work if you'd tried, but no. Now look at us, it's all gone, every last bit of it!'

Tessa went into the lobby and put the sixpence in the meter under the stairs. Oh, they were going to start again. Would it never end? The yelling, the accusations, the never-ending bitterness that had made her mam old before her time. She went back into the kitchen and, with a match dug out of her da's pocket, lit the gas jet. It had no glass mantle but it did light the place up. The sight of the room in all its dingy, dirty dampness made her bite her lip and fight down the despair that rose up in her.

Colin came back through the scullery with a handful of sticks, pieces of paper, and some orange peel.

'Where's our Jimmy?' Tessa asked him.

'I told him to keep looking. I'd had enough. It's freezing out there. It's not much better in here!' he added.

Tessa rounded on him. 'You idle, useless—'

'Tessa, that's enough, girl. It's been a bad day for everyone.' Richie stopped the tirade of insults and sat down on the paint tin.

'There's not even a decent chair to sit on, is there?' Mary said waspishly. 'Never mind beds or even mattresses.'

Richie looked down at his scuffed and battered boots. When had things gone so very wrong? A year ago, maybe two. He'd just let things slide. He'd let himself get deeper and deeper in debt. And he'd never worried about it until last summer. Oh, he could murder a pint but there'd be no ale for him tonight, or any other night as far as he could see.

'Get back to your brother,' Mary demanded of her eldest son. 'Go on, or there'll be nothing to eat for you, meladdo.'

Sulkily Colin went out, slamming the back door, the sound of which made Mary jump.

'That lad will be the death of me. If he starts again, I'll swing for him. It's your fault, Richie. You've been too soft with him. You were *always* too soft with him!'

'God, Mary, give it a rest!'

Tessa stood in the doorway, an old pan in her hand. She'd found it under the sink. It was so old that the previous occupants had obviously thought it not worth taking with them, wherever it was they'd gone. But it was all she could find. She bent her head and began to cry quietly. The only kind of drinking vessel was one empty and rather dirty jam jar.

Mary looked across at her daughter and then her husband.

'I'll never forgive you, Richie O'Leary, until my dying day!'

Her husband refused to meet her furious gaze. 'Well, that's no surprise, is it?' he shrugged. 'God knows why I ever married you. Why come home from work to be greeted by a list of complaints? I'd sooner stay in the pub.'

Mary's eyes flashed with anger. 'Why I ever married *you*, I don't know. You've always been a drunken waster! Sneaking like thieves in the darkness away from Isaac Street, to get away from people you owed money to! When I think of all the years of hard work that went into making that house into some sort of decent home and then to have both the bailiffs and Mogsey Doran on the doorstep at once to clear the house and leave us nothing. Thrown out in the road we'd have been if we hadn't come here to this . . . this midden!'

She paused, overcome by tears, then, compelled by her rage, went on, 'You still owe money to Mogsey Doran and God help you if he and his cronies find us! And as for *him*, your precious son who was thieving from everyone! Oh, God, the shame. Mother of God, the shame of it!' Mary began to cry again. It had all been too much to cope with. Colin's first sojourn in Borstal had brought her the sympathy of her friends and neighbours. 'Easy led, Mary. No real badness in him, luv. He'll learn a hard lesson in there, girl.' The second time they weren't as charitable and then . . . then everything had been taken from her.

Instantly Tessa went to her side. 'Mam! Mam, don't get all upset again, please! Things will be fine now. Da, me and our Colin will get work. Jimmy can get some sort of job before or after school and Saturday. We'll soon have things back to . . . normal.' Things would never, ever be 'normal' again, she thought, but she had to try to cheer her mam up.

'We'll all go out in the morning early and see what we can get. There's lots of factories at this end of the city.'

'And the feller in the shop said to try and see Albert Brown down at number two Husskinson Dock,' Richie added half-heartedly, wondering if the men were decent blokes to work with.

'You can take my useless brother with you, Da,' Tessa said cuttingly.

Mary's sobs diminished. Her anger was spent; without the energy it had generated she felt weak. Oh, if only she could crawl into a warm bed like the one the bailiffs had taken yesterday, with a stone waterbottle or a brick or oven-shelf wrapped in a piece of cloth, but there were no beds, no waterbottles, no comforts at all. However, she tried to smile and look interested in Tessa's words. Her only surviving daughter was a good girl. She always tried to help as much as she could. She'd even gone up to the Riverside Station at the Pier Head with a tray of little silver-coloured brooches she'd bought for tuppence a dozen and had tried to sell them for sixpence each to the passengers arriving and departing on the boat trains. She'd managed to earn a bit of money before the policeman had stopped her for not having a trader's licence. Mary was always sorry after she'd vented her anger and frustration on Tessa's head. Tessa was the only one in the family who tried to help.

If her other baby daughters had survived, the workload would have been more than halved. Fresh tears stung her eyes. Even after all these years she missed them. She could remember their smiles, their first tottering steps. It was a pain that would never go away.

And the present was just as painful as the past. It'd be

the bare boards they'd have to sleep on tonight and they'd all be fully dressed or they'd freeze. She felt as though she were standing on the edge of a deep abyss and that if she stepped forward she would fall. Fall into oblivion. She wanted to fall. With all her heart she really wanted to let go and fall, but she knew she couldn't even do that. If nothing else there were Tessa and Jimmy to think of. She couldn't care less about the other two, her elder son and her husband. For better or worse, she'd vowed all those long years ago. Well, she'd certainly not had the 'better'. She dropped her head hopelessly into her hands once more as Tessa put the pan on the gas ring.

Chapter Three

The lads and their father all slept badly but neither Tessa nor her mother closed their eyes all night.

She had to get work soon. She just *had* to, Tessa told herself over and over again. But what kind of work? She'd just left school and she wasn't trained to do anything, not even to be a kitchenmaid or maid of all work. All that was on offer was shop work, if she was lucky enough to get it – or factory work, which was more likely. But would *anyone* employ her looking the way she did?

The bit of fire, which hadn't given much heat in the first place, had died. They hadn't kept the gas light lit for long. The gas supply had to be saved for heating water on the single ring.

She was so cold she wondered if she would wake up in the morning if she went to sleep. That fear was added to all the others and she had cried quietly for most of the night.

Mary wondered bitterly how Richie and Colin could sleep. Jimmy was excluded by his age from worrying about all the troubles that beset them. She just prayed that they would get jobs. Anything, anything at all. Even if only Richie got work it would be something. She tried to get comfortable on the hard floor but she was cold, so very, very cold. It was the worst night she'd had to endure in her entire life.

She was sorry she had spoken the way she had to the little group that had come to help, but what could they *do*? And they would have told their parents. She had already unwittingly made enemies when she needed friendship desperately. She had her pride, she told herself, but pride wouldn't fill empty stomachs or keep a fire in the range.

She knew Tessa was awake; every now and then she'd hear a half-stifled sob and the sound tore at Mary's heart.

When the fingers of cold grey daylight slipped in through the fly-speckled window-pane Mary gave up the battle for sleep, and with a groan got to her knees.

Tessa was instantly on her feet and placed her hands gently on her mother's shoulders. 'Lie back, Mam, I'll make us a cup of tea.'

'What with, girl?'

Mary's face was grey and her hair was tangled with strands sticking out like straw in a haystack.

'We'll use the old tea leaves, unless someone has thrown them out,' Tessa whispered.

'No one would be as stupid as that, not even your da. What will you use for heat?'

'The gas ring. We must have some gas left.'

Mary nodded and lay down again. 'Just don't wake your da or the other two, not yet.'

There was enough gas left to boil the pan of water. The leaves had lost their flavour but Tessa poured the hot water over them, then added a bit of condensed milk.

She did her best not to let any of it spill as she poured it into the jam jar. It was too precious to waste. She handed the jar to Mary. 'Here, Mam, this'll warm you up.'

'I'll just have half, luv, you have the other. I know you've been awake all night.'

'I'll use the rest of the gas to heat the water to rinse out the jam jar and get a bit of a wash. I want to start off early.'

Mary raised herself on one elbow and then sat up. She pulled her blouse out of her skirt and began to tear at it. Eventually the coarse fabric ripped and she handed the piece to Tessa.

'Use that, Tessa, until we get proper . . . things.'

As she took the piece of what was now a rag Tessa choked on a sob. What had things come to? They were the poorest of the poor. She knew how humiliating it had all been for her mam, but somehow tearing that scrap from her blouse had made Tessa's heart ache more than anything else. Poor Mam. Poor, poor Mam. How she'd suffered these last few days.

Tessa didn't feel much better after rubbing the cloth over her face and hands. Her clothes were creased and wrinkled and her hair was a mess. Thankfully she'd managed to keep her comb and brush by hiding them from the bailiffs under her shapeless jumper, but there was no mirror for her to see the end result. She just had to hope she looked a bit tidy.

When she went back into the kitchen her da and Jimmy were awake.

'Do I look all right, Mam?'

'You do, Tessa.' It was her da that answered, getting stiffly to his feet. Jimmy was rubbing the sleep out of his eyes.

'I'm making an early start, Da.'

'I will myself. Get down there to the stands and see this Albert Brown bloke.'

'Wake that lazy little no-mark,' Mary instructed her husband. 'I'll have to try and do *something* to this place and keep my eye on meladdo here.'

Richie poked Colin with the toe of his boot. 'Get up. It's

time to go and look for work, lad. We'll get chucked out of here if we don't pay next week's rent. They don't give you a week free just because it's Christmas.'

Colin reluctantly got to his feet, a look of resentment in his eyes.

As Tessa opened the front door she looked up and down the street. It was not yet fully daylight but lights shone from most upstairs windows, including the ones over the shop. She thought about Elizabeth and wondered how she'd slept. In a warm, clean bed, with sheets, thick fleecy blankets and a heavy quilt, no doubt, she thought enviously.

If Elizabeth was up at all, she'd come down to a warm kitchen and very probably a hot breakfast. 'It looks as though we're not early enough, Tessa,' Richie said as he closed the front door behind them both.

'Oh, don't say that, Da, please! We've *got* to get work today.'

'Well, at least I've got a reference of sorts, but I suppose I'll have to wait on the stands like everyone else.'

Tessa nodded. It was the way the dockers were employed. Picked at random by the bowler-hatted foremen, or blockers as they were called, men fought for half a day's work. It had always been like that for as long as anyone could remember. It wasn't right, but it wasn't about to be changed. There were too many men chasing too few jobs. The employers had the upper hand.

Tessa and Richie both nodded and said, 'Good morning,' to Delia Harrison who was opening her shop. The blinds were already up and she'd turned the sign on the door over to the side that said 'Open'.

Delia nodded back, thinking how pale and scruffy the girl

34

looked. She sighed. There were hundreds of girls like that in this city – and adults too. She hoped they would have a successful day. It was partly a charitable hope but it was a shrewd one too. They would be customers when they had jobs and money.

God alone knew what they had now. No one had seen any furniture arrive, unless they'd brought it with them in the early hours of yesterday morning. All the man had asked for were a few bits, not enough to feed five people – Elizabeth had told her how big the family was when she'd come in – *and* he'd asked her to put it on the slate, something she certainly hadn't been prepared to do until Jack had intervened. She just hoped she wouldn't regret it.

There was no money for tram or bus fares so Tessa and Richie walked along Scotland Road together for a short time, before Tessa bade her father goodbye and good luck.

She intended to start with the shops. The morning was cold but it looked as though it would stay fine; she was thankful that there was no wind or rain. All she had on for warmth was the old grey jumper and navy skirt and she'd be soaked to the skin if it rained. If her clothes got wet she had no way of drying them.

Two hours later she'd worked her way down to the junction of Scotland Road and Boundary Street. She'd had no success at all in any of the shops.

'Even if it's only until after Christmas, sir,' or 'madam,' she'd pleaded with all the shopkeepers, but to no avail. Any extra staff had already been engaged. She was just too late. She leaned despondently against a wall, staring at the dock estate and the factories stretching away ahead of her. Beyond them flowed the cold waters of the Mersey. All the buildings were soot-blackened, including the three famous ones that dominated the Pier Head and were known to sailors the world over. She was hungry and so cold her lips were blue.

''Ere, girl, cum an' warm yer 'ands,' a kindly gateman called to her from his dockside hut.

'Ta ever so much.' Her fingers were so numb that as the warmth from the brazier penetrated them she could have cried. 'I'm looking for work, you see.'

'You've no coat or hat or stockings.'

'I know. Things are ... bad. Really bad.'

'Bad all over, luv.'

'Do you know where I should start first? The factories, I mean.'

'You'll have to walk back. Bibby's, Silcock's, Tate's, the match factory, the BA,' he rattled them off.

'What's that?'

He scrutinised her face. 'Where've you come from, girl, that you don't know it's short for the British and American Tobacco factory?'

'The Dingle.' She didn't want to tell him the exact address or the creditors might find them.

He pursed his lips. It was one of the oddities in this city. The north end didn't know what the south end was doing and vice versa.

'I'd better get on my way.'

'Aye, you'd better. Good luck, girl.'

She smiled at him and began to walk as briskly as her tired legs would let her, along Vauxhall Road. Perhaps she would have more luck at the factories.

* * *

Colin had lingered in the house for as long as possible until his mam had yelled at him and virtually shoved him out of the door. There'd been no breakfast, just a few swigs of half-cold tea.

He certainly had no intention of tramping the streets looking for work. There were too many doing that already. He stopped in front of Pegram's Grocer's and gazed into the window. There were boxes and tins of just about everything you could think of. It was Christmas and the shops were well stocked. Outside the butcher's hung rows and rows of plucked turkeys and capons. It would be no hardship just to reach up and snatch one, but if he took it home he'd have to explain how he got it and they'd all have to share it. He moved on, stopping outside Skillicorn's bakery. The smell of fresh bread made him feel faint. No perfume in the world could match that of bread still hot from the oven.

He looked around cautiously. There wasn't a copper in sight, nor many shoppers either. Just delivery carts and lorries and their drivers. A tram trundled along, its trolley sparking on the icy cables. A bus rattled over the cobbles behind it. Some shopkeepers were just opening up and he made up his mind. He pulled his cap down over his forehead. No one knew him around here. He went inside.

'What'll it be then?' the plump middle-aged woman asked him pleasantly, glad to have a customer. She didn't seem at all suspicious, not even of the way he was dressed, but then probably most of her customers looked like him, Colin thought. Shabby and down-at-heel.

'Give us a large white tin and half a dozen of them soft rolls, missus, please.'

She bustled about putting the bread and rolls into brown

paper bags. He looked around. He was still the only customer.

'That'll be sixpence.'

He took the bags off the counter, shoved them under his jacket and ran out, the woman's shrieks loud in his ears. He didn't stop running until he turned into Kew Street where there was a piece of wasteland. He squatted down on his haunches and began with the rolls. Even though there was nothing to put in them they tasted like manna from heaven. The loaf would last him all day. At least *he* wouldn't go hungry tonight. And if he got the chance to nick an overcoat he would. He'd tell Mam someone had taken pity on him when he'd gone asking for work.

He wandered around the area familiarising himself, noting where the food and clothing shops were, and the pawnbrokers and the shops called 'cannies' or 'canteens' which were little more than a piece of wooden board jammed into the doorway of someone's house. They sold ready-cooked food to take home or eat on the street. He noted too the police stations: Rose Hill, Athol Street, St Anne Street. He'd give them a wide berth. He stopped and spoke to a group of men and boys who lingered on the street corner. They were like himself, unemployed, some from choice, others because they had simply despaired of ever getting a job.

'Try the Labour Exchange. Yer just might get lucky,' one man advised. Colin thanked him but had no intention of going down the 'Labour' – they asked all kinds of questions.

He wondered why his mam didn't go on the Parish, but of course you more or less had to beg for Parish Relief and he knew she wouldn't. By mid-afternoon he was cold and fed up. He'd managed to snatch a battered purse from an old woman. It contained a thruppenny bit and a penny. Not much, he thought, but enough to get him a couple of pies from Reigler's. He dared not show his face in Skillicorn's again. He cut through the back entries and, at the junction of Titchfield Street and Tatlock Street, he unexpectedly came across a pitch and toss game.

Gambling in any form always interested him; he took after his da in that respect.

'Any chance of gettin' in on it, lad?' he asked a spotty youth dressed in the uniform of the poor: old, greasy jacket, moleskin trousers, broken-down boots and a once-white muffler wrapped around the neck.

'How much 'ave yer got?' one of the older men asked, casting a suspicious glance over him.

'Fourpence.'

'Ever played before?'

'Nope. Never seen it played before either,' Colin lied.

The smirk on the man's face told him what to expect but inwardly he smiled too. If this lot thought he was a fool they were soon going to find out otherwise.

The rules were explained and he put on a puzzled expression. He'd lose a couple of times, just to lull their suspicions, and then . . .

An hour later he walked away with one shilling and sixpence and the promise that he'd return tomorrow so they could try and win it back. He had no intention of going back and none of going home either. He'd get a hot meal from one of the cannies, then he'd wander along to Champion Whates lodging house and get a decent bed for the night – after he'd got some sort of coat. There were many advantages of not being known in a neighbourhood but he'd have to watch his step. Too much thieving and illegal gambling and his face and name would soon be common knowledge.

For Richie things hadn't been too bad either. He'd asked one of the men on the stand to point out Albert Brown and then he'd gone over and had a word with him.

'So, how come you aren't going down to the south end, the Coburn and the Brunswick and Herculaneum docks?' he'd been asked after saying they'd moved from the Dingle.

'Not much work down there, boss.'

The blockerman looked him up and down then nodded slowly.

'You'll have to go on the stand like everyone else.'

'I know, boss.'

He'd joined the others, they were all blowing on their hands and stamping their feet for, even though the sun was out and the sky a clear blue, it was freezing. Tomorrow was Christmas Eve and everyone desperately wanted work. There must have been between fifty and sixty men and Albert Brown called out the names of only thirty. But Richie's had been amongst them. The other men melted away, shoulders slumped with disappointment, desperation in their eyes. They'd be back at lunchtime to see if they could get half a day at least.

'You get down with that lot to number two Husskinson. There's two freighters in. One with pig iron, the other with fruit – and I don't want any boxes broken "accidentally" either. I'll check.'

''E come over on a razor boat, did that feller. There's no 'Arry Freemans with 'im around,' the middle-aged man walking beside Richie muttered.

Richie knew what he meant. There would be nothing free

this morning. Obviously Albert Brown kept a check on the stevedores who were in charge of the cargoes. But it was a docker's prerogative to get *something* and they all knew the ways and means.

The morning had gone quickly as the pig iron was unloaded and stacked on the dockside. Liverpool dockers were the quickest in the world – when they chose to be. At dinnertime he again took his position on the stand and was picked once more.

'It's a cargo of Irish confetti,' the blockerman informed the gang he'd picked and then divided into two groups.

'Bloody stone chippings!' Richie muttered.

His words caught the attention of the man standing next to him. 'Yer a birrof a day-old chick, aren't yer? I 'aven't seen yer around 'ere before,' his companion said.

'Just moved from over the water,' Richie lied. 'Not much work over there.'

'In the one-eyed city?'

'Aye, Birkenhead.'

'Couldn't yer get work at Laird's?'

'No, they'll only take on skilled, semi-skilled and their own for labouring,' Richie answered. It was partly true. Cammell Laird's was the big shipbuilders on the other bank of the Mersey and most of their labourers lived in Birkenhead.

'Bloody typical!'

'I . . . I was hopin' to get a bit of 'Arry Freemans, like, what with it being Christmas an' all.' Richie's expression was hopeful.

His fellow docker looked quizzically at him. 'You a minesweeper then?'

'What if I am? Everyone here is on the lookout to pinch

some food. What's the *City of Benares* carryin' then?'

'Fruit. You 'eard 'im. Oranges probably, an' maybe bananas.'

'I've never even seen one, let alone 'ad one to eat.'

'Overrated, lad, I 'ad one once. Broke it off a big 'and of them and ate it. Not much to it. Couple of mouthfuls an' it's gone. Not much taste either. Can't understand all the fuss. And yer get some bloody big spiders in them too. Big, black, hairy ones. Give yer the screamin' shits they would. An' they're poisonous.' He shuddered at the recollection.

'I don't like the sound of that but I wouldn't mind a couple of oranges for the kids, like.'

'Well, sling yer hook so it'll break open a crate and we'll all have some. Take no notice of yer blockerman. 'E says that every time the cargo's food or drink. 'E gets 'is share, believe me, an' the Paddy Kellys, though they'd have their tongues ripped out before they'd admit it. They'd lose their bloody jobs. Aye, an' soft jobs they are too.'

Richie nodded. Some of the dock police were all right, others were not. Too zealous in their jobs by far was the general opinion.

He'd worked hard all day and his back felt as if it was breaking, but he was going home with pockets full of oranges and his wage for the day. They usually didn't get the pay owing to them until Fridays but Christmas week was different. Surely that would keep Mary from her eternal moaning. He'd even go straight home now too, but not tomorrow. It was Christmas Eve tomorrow; everyone finished at dinnertime and there were more than enough ale houses to pick from along the Dock Road. She couldn't complain. A man was entitled to a drink on Christmas Eve, wasn't he?

Chapter Four

The pale winter sunlight that filtered in through the window
made things look even worse, Mary thought. She glanced
around the kitchen. There was a large patch of damp above
the window, a sign of broken guttering. The ceiling was
almost as dark and brown as the door. The skirting boards
had all been ripped out and probably used as firewood. She
couldn't blame the previous tenants for that, last night she
would have done the same thing herself. The kitchen door
didn't fit properly, and whenever it was opened or closed it
made a scraping noise that went straight through her. There
were two uncovered gas jets on the wall; she'd get oil lamps,
they were far cheaper and were less of a fire hazard than
candles.

There wasn't any use at all in even going and looking at
the front downstairs room. In fact she was almost certain
that the floorboards in there had also been burned as a means
of heating. Desperate people did desperate things. She
remembered someone commenting about it yesterday. Dear
God, was it only yesterday? She'd have to complain and go
on complaining to the landlord to get the floorboards
replaced and it would be years, if ever, before she got any
furniture for the room.

The range was in desperate need of a good clean with a
wire brush and then blackleading. The floor needed scrubbing, the windows needed cleaning. All the walls and the

ceiling needed a coat of whitewash with lime added to deter the bugs. That was just one room and she had neither the heart nor the energy to do it. The state of the scullery didn't bear thinking about. Furthermore she had no brushes, buckets, Jeyes Fluid, nor even a bit of soap. There was no food either.

All she had left in her purse was ten shillings and she knew no one in this neighbourhood at all that she could borrow from until Richie got paid, *if* he got paid.

She'd just have to muster up what was left of her courage and go to the corner shop. Richie had said they were all right and she didn't blame the woman for refusing credit until her husband intervened. She wouldn't give credit to anyone looking like Richie, and a total stranger, if she had the good fortune to own a shop. It was going to be awful. It hurt her pride but she'd have to put her pride in her pocket.

She tidied her hair with Tessa's brush, tucked her blouse into her skirt and pulled on the second-hand black coat she'd had for over six years. Even the colour had faded, she thought, looking at it with distaste. The only brand-new dress she'd ever had in her life had been her wedding dress and she'd quickly sold that along with her veil and headdress to furnish her first home.

There was no need to close the front door behind her, they had nothing, absolutely nothing to steal. She blinked rapidly as she went from the gloom of the lobby into the sunlit street. She looked up and down the street and wrinkled her nose at the smell permeating the air. Obviously it was a tannery. Nothing else smelled like that.

Mary walked slowly, she was so nervous. She greeted pleasantly those women on their knees scrubbing their steps, something she'd done herself so often. They'd all answered with a smile but she could feel their eyes boring into her back and knew their curiosity was overwhelming.

When she reached Harrison's she could see that there were two other customers beside herself: a big blowsy-looking woman with an old shawl around her shoulders, and a thin one with a mass of dark hair that was obviously curled with tongs or curling pins. There was a hint of humour in her eyes and she was quite well dressed – for the area. They broke off their conversation as she approached the counter.

'Morning. It's Mrs O'Leary, isn't it?' Delia hoped she sounded business-like but friendly and helpful. The woman looked awful – it wasn't just her clothes.

Mary nodded.

'Our Elizabeth told me she called on you with her friends, like, and of course your husband came down for a few bits and pieces.'

Again Mary nodded. Oh, this was so hard. She knew that she and her family would have been discussed by half the street and that speculation was rife.

'I . . . I'll be paying for them when he gets home from work.'

''As 'e got a job then?' Eileen Flynn asked companionably, pulling the shawl around herself and leaning on the counter. She had some good news but it would keep. All this would provide an interesting topic of conversation for a week.

'He's gone down to see that blockerman Mr Harrison recommended and I . . . we're very grateful for your help.'

May Greely laughed. 'No doubt I'll meet him over the next two days. They all finish up in the pub eventually.'

Mary could have hit her. There was always someone like her ready with the snide remarks.

Delia gave May a warning look.

'No doubt he will. It's Christmas after all,' Mary answered sharply.

'What can I get you, Mrs O'Leary?' Delia asked.

'A large loaf, a pound of dripping, a quarter of tea, tuppence worth of sugar and a couple of bacon rashers . . . oh, and a small bag of coal.' She could have gone on and on with a list of the things she really needed, but this was all she could afford.

In silence her purchases were weighed out, wrapped and then Delia looked questioningly at her.

'I'll pay now for these, Mrs Harrison. I don't like to run up a bill.'

'Very wise, most people put *everything* on the slate and have half a dozen excuses for not paying.' She looked pointedly at Eileen Flynn, who ignored her.

'Well, thank you and it was nice to meet you, Mrs . . . er . . .'

'Flynn,' Eileen supplied. 'You're my next-door neighbour, so pop in any time and don't be afraid to ask for the loan of anything.'

'And I'm Mrs Mabel Greely. May to my friends. I'm a widow.'

'Aye, and a merry one too,' Delia muttered under her breath. 'And it's Mrs Delia Harrison.'

'Mary. Mary O'Leary. That's me. Richie you've met. Our Colin is sixteen and our Tessa is fourteen and me youngest, Jimmy, is nine.'

'Well, luv, I just 'ope he isn't the little tearaway my

youngest is. Yer need eyes in the back of yer 'ead to keep up with 'im, 'aven't yer, May?'

'Never a truer word, Eileen, never a truer word. I'm fortunate that I have only our Ginny and I've never had much trouble with her. Her da died when she was only five. I've been on my own since then. She's startin' Birrel's after Christmas an' you should have heard the complaints! You'd think jobs grew on trees.'

'They don't want to work at all, kids these days. I'm sick of tellin' our 'Arold ter get himself something, even if it's only fetchin' and carryin' from Great Homer Street market on Saturdays. Lazy little get he is!'

Mary didn't want to linger, but what else could she do without seeming very rude and stand-offish? She smiled, and quickly said, 'I've sent our Jimmy out today with the same instructions. I'll have to see about him going to school after the holiday.' Then she gathered up her purchases, including the coal, which nearly creased her, and nodded her thanks. She made her way slowly to the door and the street beyond.

'Maybe we should help her,' Delia said. 'She was staggering under the weight of that coal.'

Eileen ignored her. 'Well, that's fine, isn't it?' she commented sharply. 'A few bits an' pieces an' then off she goes with her nose in the bloody air.'

Delia sighed. 'Well, she got what she came for. Just what was it you wanted yourself, Eileen?'

'A tin of conny onny, a few carrots, an onion and five pound of spuds.'

'Blind scouse again?' Delia commented.

'Yes, I'll swing for that bloody useless husband of mine

yet. I said, "Yes, it's Christmas, but everyone starts celebrating it on Christmas Eve, not two flaming weeks before!"
I've not 'ad a full week's wage offen him for best part of a
month an' me tryin'—' Eileen halted her tirade. Both Delia
and May had heard it all before, many times, and her
dissatisfaction with Frank Flynn certainly wasn't what she'd
come here to announce, particularly as her audience had
increased by two sets of unsympathetic ears: Maisie Keegan
and Katie Collins, who had just come into the shop.

Delia, however, thought she was expected to enquire.

'And you trying to what, Eileen?'

Eileen straightened her shoulders and jerked up her many
chins. 'Our Brenda's getting wed after New Year an' I'm
trying to save up a bit ter give her a good "do".'

'Is it that feller with a face like a wet week from Breck
Road?' Katie Collins asked, folding her arms over her grubby
print wrapover pinafore.

Eileen glared at her. ' 'Is name is Thomas Kinsella an' 'e's
as decent and 'ard-working a feller as you'd wish to meet.
'E's on the trams. A good steady job with a regular wage.
Not like some I could mention.' Eileen knew that Katie
Collins's husband was fond of a drink too. 'He lives with his
mam an' our Brenda says the 'ouse is a little palace.'

'So, she'll be going to live with him and his ma then?'
May asked.

Eileen nodded.

'I wouldn't fancy starting out like that. Is the owld one a
bit of a tartar then?' Katie Collins asked.

'She is not! Our Brenda's dead lucky. I had to start off
with Frank's mam and she still 'ad five kids at 'ome. We
couldn't stay with me mam, God rest 'er, she had eight!'

Delia shook her head. No wonder Eileen's house resembled a junk shop: it was all she'd ever known, having grown up in a two-up two-down in Athol Street with eight brothers and sisters and her parents.

'Where'll the wedding be – St Anthony's, I take it?' Delia queried, shovelling the potatoes from one of the large scuttle-shaped metal bins and emptying them into the canvas bag Eileen held out.

'Yes. It's her parish, remember. Mind you, there's holy murder goin' on over the bridesmaids.'

'Why?' May asked. Everyone was now engrossed in the news: time, shopping and other chores forgotten.

'Well, she said she won't 'ave no little ones. They're a flaming nuisance. So that's upset her little cousins. She's just 'aving 'er mates from work. "And what about yer own sister? What's wrong with our Maureen?" I said.' Eileen looked around with satisfaction. Everyone was riveted, even Delia. 'Do you know what she said to me?'

'No, we're not flaming mind-readers,' Katie Collins replied acidly.

' "Our Maureen is too wild! She runs the streets with them terrible common girls from Paul Street." 'Ave yer ever 'eard anything like it?'

'So, what did you say then? What did your Maureen say?'

'Our Maureen didn't say anything, because I told 'er I'd wear meself out giving her a good 'iding if she didn't behave.' Eileen drew herself up with importance. '*I* said to our Brenda that if she wasn't going ter 'ave her own sister then she wasn't getting no wedding out of Frank and me. Old Ma Kinsella and her precious Thomas could cough up for the whole "do".'

'How did that go down?' May asked. There were always arguments at weddings and funerals, but this was priceless.

'Like a stone in the canal. So, she's 'aving our Maureen and them two mates. I've got to find the flaming money for our Maureen's dress and I'll 'ave to rig our 'Arold out, let alone meself!'

'Don't get all upset over that yet, Eileen, luv. We'll all help out. You've got that nice cream straw hat, Delia.'

'You're very generous at lending other people's clothes, May Greely.'

'Ah, don't go getting a cob on, Delia. Where in the name of God is she going to find the money for new clothes for herself?' Maisie Keegan intervened.

'She can make her flaming husband work harder, sign the pledge and go to the Temperance Society instead of lining Eddie Doyle's pockets. I know how much he spends,' May said flatly.

'You would!' Eileen retorted.

'All right, don't let's have a bust-up over it, you know we'll all help out, Eileen,' Delia promised.

'Ta. I knew I could count on you. I couldn't 'ave better friends an' neighbours. You've got to give them a bit of a send-off.'

'It's a pity that others don't take the same attitude,' Delia said before trying to get her customers organised: it was nearly dinnertime and her feet were already killing her. At least the wedding would be something to look forward to in the New Year.

Dusk was falling rapidly as Tessa dejectedly headed for home. She was so exhausted she could hardly place one foot in front of the other. Hunger made her light-headed and the tears that had fallen so frequently this last couple of days blurred her vision once more. She'd tried everywhere and everywhere it was the same story. No jobs going at the moment. Try again after Christmas. After Christmas. They'd all be dead of cold by then. They were half-starved already. She was even beyond caring whether her da and Colin had got work.

In a daze she stepped into the road and a lorry swerved and narrowly missed her. The driver cursed her loudly, while the driver of a horse and cart shook his fist at her. Scotland Road was always busy, but more so with Christmas approaching. She was pulled back on to the pavement where she looked vaguely and without recognition at her rescuer.

'Tessa! Tessa, you were nearly run over! You were nearly killed!' Elizabeth cried.

Overwhelmed by disappointment and despair, Tessa began to cry in earnest.

Elizabeth put her arm around her shoulder. 'You're frozen! Have you had anything to eat?'

Tessa shook her head. 'I . . . I've been everywhere for a job. I've not had time and I'm so cold, and so tired, and . . .' she sobbed.

'Here, put this on.' Elizabeth shrugged off her navy blue woollen coat and wrapped Tessa in it.

'You're . . . you're in uniform.'

'I know. I've been to school. Every other school finished yesterday. *We* have to stay on.' She shivered as the cold air cut through her navy blue serge dress with its long sleeves and cream Peter Pan collar and cuffs. She wore fawn lisle stockings, brown shoes and her velour hat with its badge emblazoned with a sprig of lily of the valley and the words 'Notre Dame' in gold lettering above it.

'You're coming home with me.'

'I can't, your mam . . . my mam . . .'

'I said, you *are* coming home with me. At least you can have something to eat and get warm before you go home.'

Tessa let herself be guided along Scotland Road and down Naylor Street.

Elizabeth pushed open the shop door, thankful there were no customers. Her mam was brushing the floor. 'I found her wandering along the road, Mam. She's so cold, hungry and tired that she's almost dead on her feet. She stepped out in front of a lorry and nearly got herself killed.'

'Mother of God, girl, you're in a terrible state. Take her into the kitchen, Elizabeth, I'll be in in a minute. How long has she been out?'

'Since this morning, or so I gather. She's not even got a coat or a shawl!'

Jack Harrison looked up in surprise as Elizabeth steered Tessa into the kitchen. He'd just finished his tea.

'I think Mam will want you to go out into the shop, Da.'

Jack folded his newspaper and got to his feet.

Delia came through a second later.

'Right. Elizabeth, go upstairs and bring down the quilt off your bed while I get something hot down her. Nessie, fetch me a pan and put the kettle on and I *don't* want to hear a single word of complaint. Do as you're told.'

Nessie pulled a face behind her mother's back but went to carry out Delia's instructions. In a couple of minutes Tessa was swaddled in the heavy patchwork quilt, sitting by the range sipping hot sweet tea while Delia stirred a pan of soup and Elizabeth cut slices of bread.

'Your mam was in the shop this morning.' Delia fussed around Tessa, folding the quilt back so she could place the tray with the bowl of soup and slices of bread on Tessa's lap. 'She insisted on paying for the few things she bought and said as soon as your dad got home from work she'd pay for the rest.'

'Mam ... Mam's got her pride.' Tessa's eyes were still full of tears, but now they were tears of pure gratitude. Oh, it was heaven to be warm again and to be having nourishing food.

'So, why have you finished up here in Naylor Street in that filthy old house that should be condemned? Even the Piercesons, and a right gang of hooligans they were too, wouldn't stay put there!'

Tessa didn't want to tell them the reason. Mam would kill her if she did, but they'd been so good to her. She looked up at Elizabeth imploringly.

'Mam, can't that wait?' Elizabeth intervened. 'You can see she's upset now.'

Delia nodded. 'Perhaps I should go and see your mam, let her know where you are. It's dark and she'll be worried.'

'No! Please, no! I ... she'll ...'

'Mam?' Elizabeth pleaded again.

Delia sighed. Obviously things were very bad but the girl was afraid to tell her.

'Well then, will you let Elizabeth take you home once you've got that down you?'

'Of course she will,' Elizabeth forestalled Tessa's reply. She was determined to see just how the family were living. She stood a better chance of finding out than her mam did.

A quarter of an hour later, wearing an old coat of Elizabeth's, a pair of knitted mittens on her hands, and a tam-o'-shanter over her hair, Tessa walked the short distance up the road with Elizabeth. 'I feel so much better now. Thanks, thanks, Elizabeth.'

'Oh, that's OK. I couldn't have left you to go and get yourself killed, now could I?'

'I just didn't know where I was or what I was doing.'

'I could see that. Anyway, what are friends for – and we *are* friends, aren't we?'

'Yes, please. I . . . I've never had a real friend before. Not someone like you.'

'I've only had Ginny from this street, but she's not close. It's all because I have to go to that flaming school. I've no real friends around here and I get skitted something awful because of the uniform.'

'What's the matter with it?'

'It's awful! It's really *awful*, especially the hat. I think they picked the worst style possible. I get kids from Major Lester's school next door yelling after me: "Ay, girl, lend us yer hat, we're havin' soup ternight!" I daresn't take it off or there'd be holy flaming murder from the nuns. I swear they stand in the very top rooms and watch us. You can see right down Royal Street and Everton Valley from up there. Our Assembly Hall's up there. We can only go there to the big hall when we're fourteen. I'll go after Christmas.' Tessa finally managed a smile as Elizabeth pulled a mock-unhappy face.

They had reached number twelve and, as on the previous night, everywhere was in darkness.

'Thanks for bringing me home. I'd better get in now, 'cos she *will* be worried.'

'I'm coming with you and don't start an argument. Mam is always calling me a bossy boots so complaining will only be a waste of breath.'

There was nothing Tessa could do.

Elizabeth followed her down the dark lobby. The place was freezing cold. When Tessa opened the kitchen door Elizabeth gasped aloud at the sight that met her eyes. Mrs O'Leary was sitting on an upturned paint tin, her arms wrapped around her body. A young lad was kneeling by her, his head in her lap. Tessa's da was hunched up on the floor by the small fire that was struggling to burn in the range.

As Mary looked up, horrified to see their visitor, Tessa exclaimed, 'I'm sorry, Mam! Oh, what else could I do? They've been so good to me. I was lost and cold and hungry, they took me in . . .' Tessa was once more in tears.

'She was nearly killed, Mrs O'Leary. She stepped out into the main road.' Pity filled Elizabeth's heart. They had nothing. Absolutely *nothing*.

Mary got stiffly to her feet. 'That's all right, Tessa, luv.'

'But I haven't got a job, Mam. All day I've been looking.'

'That's all right too. Your da has. I don't know where our Colin is.' She shot her daughter a warning look.

Tessa nodded.

'We'll be just fine now, girl,' Mary said to Elizabeth. 'Thanks for looking after her. Thank your mam for me. I'm much obliged.'

Elizabeth just stared at her. Tessa's mam looked exhausted. She shrugged. 'I'll do that, Mrs O'Leary. Goodnight then.'

'Goodnight. Can you let yourself out, Elizabeth?' Tessa asked quietly.

'What do you think I am? Not safe to be let loose?'

Elizabeth smiled but inwardly she was horrified. Oh, the Flynns, the Greelys, the Keegans, the Collinses and the others were all hard up but at least they had *some* furniture. The O'Learys didn't have a scrap.

Chapter Five

When she heard the front door close Tessa squatted down beside her mother. Tessa's eyes were bright with tears and her bottom lip trembled as her spirits plummeted again. 'Her mam said you'd been in the shop today.'

'I had to go and get some bits, we desperately needed coal.'

'And that's the last of it, isn't it?' Tessa looked hopelessly at the dying embers in the range. They were losing their glow and their heat; the room would soon become cold again. 'Did you carry it all back yourself?'

'Of course I did. There was no one else to do it.'

'I told her to leave things like that to our Colin,' Richie put in.

'Where is he?' Tessa asked.

'I don't know, luv. He went out this morning to look for work. I've not seen him since.'

'Oh, he'll be all right, Mam. He's always looks after himself. I just hope he doesn't start—'

'He won't,' Richie said grimly.

'Jimmy went out too but he couldn't get anything. Not a single thing and he *did* try. But things are bound to look up soon.'

'I know they will, Mam,' Tessa agreed but without much conviction in her voice. Colin and Jimmy and herself had all tried and failed. This was going to be a Christmas she would never forget – but for all the wrong reasons.

Last year had been worse than all the previous years, but at least there had been a good fire to heat the room, they'd all had a decent meal, and some kind of gift, mainly home-made things. This year she knew there would be nothing.

Elizabeth shut the scullery door behind her and went into the kitchen.

'Well, how *are* things up there?' Delia asked.

Elizabeth shook her head. 'Oh, Mam! It's terrible. They've got nothing at all. There's not even a chair, Mrs O'Leary was sitting on an upturned paint tin!'

Delia looked concerned. 'Mother of God! Was there not a single stick of furniture of any kind?'

'No, not one. And there were no lights on and the fire was going out.'

'So why have they come here to live?' Nessie butted in.

'Little pigs have big ears! It's nothing to do with you, Nessie, and it's about time you went to bed and be thankful you've a bed to lie on at all!' her mother snapped.

As Nessie flounced from the room Delia turned her attention once more to the plight of the O'Leary family. Of course the fire would be dying by now, Mary had only bought a small bag and that was this morning – hours ago now. 'I would have thought they'd have some furniture.' Delia looked at her husband questioningly.

'It would be the bailiffs, I expect. They take everything, leave you with only the clothes you stand up in. It's not their fault, it's just a job to them. But that family must be up to their eyes in debt. No wonder they did a flit.'

Jack wondered just how much they owed. Some people made a real mess of their lives. Usually it all stemmed from the fact that the man couldn't get regular employment and so, once they'd sold or pawned everything they could, they inevitably got behind with the rent. It was a downward spiral. He didn't condemn them; there but for the grace of God he could have gone.

'Now I can see why the poor woman looks so ill. The worry, shame and despair of it all would kill you.'

Jack looked speculatively at his wife. 'He looked to be a decent sort, but maybe it was drink and gambling.'

'Drink and gambling and you say he's a *decent sort*! To get into such debt that he's reduced his family to the state they're in now? I certainly don't call that "decent", Jack Harrison!'

'Well, Frank Flynn is almost as bad, Delia.'

'God, don't I know it, but Eileen's never let him get so bad that they'll be turned out on to the street. She's stood at the dock gates and waited to relieve him of his wages before today. Oh, and their Brenda is getting married in the New Year,' she added as an afterthought.

'So who's paying for that?'

'They are, if she can keep Frank out of the pub, and I suppose Brenda's ma-in-law will help out. She can't be short, that lad of hers has a good job on the trams. But what are we going to do about the O'Learys, Jack? We can't leave them like that, especially over Christmas.'

Jack Harrison was thinking the same thing. He'd felt sorry for the man when he'd come into the shop last night. He had a hangdog, confused sort of look about him, as though he were out of his depth with nowhere to turn.

'She's very proud, Mam,' Elizabeth said. 'She's trying to put a brave face on everything.'

'That's all well and good, but if she doesn't get some help soon she'll be in her grave, dead from cold, worry and starvation.' Delia looked thoughtful while Elizabeth watched her closely. She knew her Mam was trying to work something out.

'I'm going to buy a half-hundredweight of coal,' Delia said firmly. 'They need to keep warm and have something to cook with. We'll get them some food too. They must have some kind of Christmas dinner. I couldn't sit down to ours with a clear conscience if we don't help. Do you know if they have *any* money at all?'

'Only a few shillings, Mam.'

'Well, that won't buy much in the way of furniture,' Jack stated flatly.

'Well, we can't take up a collection from the neighbours. Most of them are not much better off themselves – and, besides, she'd go mad. I know if it were me, I would, and she said her husband had work. I hope she's right.'

'Mam, what about Hennessy's? They could get stuff from there, pay what they can now and the rest later.'

'A few shillings won't go far with that old miser and he wouldn't give them anything without some kind of reassurance that he'd get the rest of his money.' Delia was scathing in her reference to the local pawnbroker. There were literally hundreds of pawnshops in the area but Hennessy's was closest.

'Da, if I go down now, maybe I can persuade them, or one of them, to go and see what Mr Hennessy will give them. It mightn't be so bad if I go,' Elizabeth suggested.

'She's got a point, Delia.'

'Yes, yes, I think that might just work, Elizabeth, but it's too late now, he'll be closed.'

'I'll go first thing in the morning.' She just hoped Mrs O'Leary could be persuaded.

Next morning she was up at seven a.m. and at eight she rapped gently on the door of number twelve. Her mam and da had been up in the early hours of the morning. For them it would be a long and very busy day that wouldn't be over until eight p.m. when her mam closed the shop door for good. Dad had gone to the market and Mam was stocking up the shelves, the counter and even the floor until there was hardly any room to turn around, let alone to stand and serve in. However, when Nessie had pointed this out she got a clip around the ear plus an order to 'do *something* useful' from her already harassed mother.

Number twelve looked awful: grim and sort of dead. That was something Elizabeth had never really noticed before.

It was Tessa who opened the door to her.

'Tessa, you look almost as bad as you did yesterday.'

'I know. Come in, we've had another terrible night.' Tessa was thinking how clean, neat and well cared for Elizabeth looked. 'Our Colin didn't come home at all and Mam has been worried sick. As if she hasn't enough to worry about. I told her not to get upset. He can look after himself and he's selfish through and through.'

Elizabeth's brow furrowed in a frown. 'Are you *sure* he can look after himself? He's only sixteen.'

'I'm dead sure.' Tessa hesitated. 'If . . . if I tell you

61

something, will you keep it a secret from *everyone*?' she whispered.

'I swear. Cross my heart and hope to die.' Elizabeth crossed herself.

'He . . . he's been in trouble with the scuffers – twice.'

Elizabeth's eyes were wide with astonishment. 'What for?' she hissed.

'Stealing. He's been in Borstal twice. That's why I'm not worried about him. In fact we'd all be better off if he was kept in Borstal for ever.'

'I can see now why your mam won't tell anyone why you've moved here.'

'Oh, it's not only him. Da . . . Da . . . likes a pint and then he starts gambling and—'

'He's not on his own then. Him next door to you is as bad.' Elizabeth jerked her head towards the Flynns' house.

'We . . . we owe everyone, even the moneylender.'

'Oh, God!' That really was bad, Elizabeth knew. If they didn't get their money back moneylenders quite often got violent, and the interest they charged was extortionate.

'Tessa!' Mary's voice echoed in the empty house.

'It's only me, Mrs O'Leary. It's Elizabeth. I came to see how Tessa is.'

Elizabeth followed Tessa into the dismal room.

'And you too, of course,' she finished politely.

'That was good of you. Mr O'Leary has gone to get a half-day on the docks, he'll be in later. Tell your mam I . . . I'm sorry I didn't come in last night to pay what I owe.'

'That's all right. She doesn't mind.'

'She seemed a fair enough woman.'

'She is and so are the rest of us, except our Nessie and

you'd have to be a saint to put up with *her*.' Elizabeth paused, planning just how she would bring up the subject of furniture.

'I can't ask you to sit down . . .' Tessa said apologetically.

'It doesn't matter. I've not come for a long visit, but . . . well, perhaps Tessa and me can go down to see Mr Hennessy. He has stuff that's, well, quite cheap.'

Mary looked down at her cold work-roughened hands. The girl must have told her parents everything last night. 'Is he a second-hand dealer or a—?'

'Pawnbroker,' Elizabeth furnished the answer.

Mary shook her head. There still wasn't enough money. Food and warmth were her priorities.

'I don't think what we have will stretch that far,' she answered dejectedly, choosing her words carefully.

'Oh, that's no problem. He'll let you have things on spec and then you can pay later on. When you get on your feet, like. After Christmas. Mr O'Leary's got fairly steady work, hasn't he?'

'Yes. Yes, I suppose he has, thanks to your da, if a job on the docks can be called "steady".'

For the first time in days Tessa saw a glimmer of hope in her mother's eyes. 'Shall we go down, Mam? Elizabeth and me?'

'I'll come with you. I can see things for myself and get what we need.'

Elizabeth exchanged a look full of relief with her new-found friend. Tessa already had on the old coat that Delia had insisted she keep. She'd slept in it.

When they arrived at Mr Hennessy's cluttered and none-too-clean establishment, Elizabeth thought she detected a look of anticipation in the pawnbroker's shrewd grey eyes and wondered whether her da had been down already to see him after coming home from the market. Her mam would have told him the plan.

'This is Mrs O'Leary and Tessa, they've just moved here and they need some things.'

'What sort of "things"?'

Mary thought hard. If she could just get the bare essentials it would be a start.

'A table and chairs or a couple of benches. Three mattresses and some blankets and a couple of pans, a kettle and some dishes. That's it for now.'

'Do you want flock mattresses or donkey's breakfasts?' He was alluding to the ones filled with straw.

'Straw,' Mary answered in a clipped, business-like tone of voice. She pushed the thought of being so destitute they even had to make do with straw to the back of her mind.

'I think we can manage that. How much have you got to put down?'

'Five . . . six shillings. I know it's not much.' That would only leave her with what Richie had brought home, which had to be put aside to save for next week's rent, and she still owed Delia Harrison money for the bits Richie had bought.

Elizabeth was surprised that the man didn't pull a face and start whining that he wasn't a rich man and he had a business to run and a family to look after, even though everyone in the area knew he lived with his ageing mother. It made her certain that her da had got to him first.

'Right. I'll sort it all out and I'll bring it up on the handcart meself, free of charge.'

Elizabeth raised her eyes to the ceiling. Free of charge! You'd wait a long time for something 'free' from him.

Mary handed him the money. 'And when will you need the rest?'

'By the end of January, at the latest.' He was quick enough to answer, Elizabeth thought.

'I can manage that,' Mary said with great relief. By then, with steady work, they would be well on their way to having the basic necessities again.

Elizabeth indicated a thick knitted black shawl. 'Why don't you throw in that out of the goodness of your heart, Mr Hennessy? It is Christmas Eve.' Tessa had to have something other than that old coat.

The man gave her a nasty look but passed the shawl over to Tessa who wrapped it around herself thankfully.

'If looks could kill I'd be dropping dead!' said Elizabeth cheerfully after they had closed the door of the pawnbroker's behind them. 'The old miser, he's as bad as Johnny Doyle's da.'

'He's the one who has the pub? The Globe?'

'Right. But he won't let anyone run up more than half a crown on the slate and he knows who can pay and who can't.'

This piece of information cheered Mary up for a few minutes before she remembered that there was a pub on every corner of every road, or so it seemed.

When they got back to the house it was to find young Jimmy staring at an assortment of items placed in the middle of the room.

'Where did they come from?' Mary demanded.

'I don't know, Mam. I was out playin' in the street with Harold Flynn an' some other lads. Someone's got a real casey but he wouldn't lend it to us. Harold Flynn said he just might get one for Christmas though an' wouldn't that be great?'

'And pigs might fly and wouldn't *that* be great?' Elizabeth replied.

'And the yard is full of coal, Mam.'

'Stop telling lies, Jimmy.'

Mary went quickly out through the scullery and stood wide-eyed with surprise at the small mountain of coal that had been dumped beside the ashcan. It was anthracite too, the best-grade coal, and it must have cost a pretty penny.

The mop, brush, bucket, soap, 'Aunt Sally' liquid soap and Jeyes Fluid must have come from the Harrisons' shop, but the pile of old but clean pieces of towels and sheets Delia must have rooted out of her airing cupboard and cut up. The woman must instinctively have known that she was a clean person who would have been horrified at the state of the place she'd moved to. She was deeply touched, so grateful that tears pricked her eyes. People were good in this part of the city too, she thought, even making sure the gifts of coal and cleaning stuff were delivered when she was out of the house and therefore couldn't refuse to accept them. If Colin and Richie stayed on the straight and narrow, surely she could maintain her dignity, even earn respect from these neighbours who had been so very generous and thoughtful?

'I'll give you a hand. I've nothing else to do,' Elizabeth offered.

'Won't your parents need you to help out in the shop?'

'No. They say I'm more of a hindrance than a help and our Nessie's even worse. I'm used to cleaning and Mam is teaching me to cook. We have cookery lessons at school.'

'She goes to the Convent at Everton Valley,' Tessa informed her mam.

Mary just nodded. That cost money and it was money she herself wouldn't have spent on educating a girl. All they did was get married and have a family, so why waste hard-earned money? She just prayed that when Tessa married it would not bring her the same heartache her own marriage had.

The rest of the morning and early afternoon was spent in trying to scrub the grime off the walls and floor. It really needed a coat of paint, Elizabeth thought as she cleaned the kitchen window with soap, water and old newspaper to make them shine. Tessa was hard at work with a pad of wire wool, cleaning the dirt and rust off the iron range.

When Mr Hennessy finally brought the things they'd bought, the lobby and kitchen floors were clean, as were those in the two bedrooms upstairs. All the windows had been cleaned even though there were no curtains for any of them. A good fire was roaring in the grate and a pan of potatoes was boiling on the hob. Every inch of the scullery including its earthenware sink and single cold-water tap had been scrubbed with Jeyes Fluid and the cleaning utensils were now stored neatly under it.

'They must have been a dirty lot, the old tenants,' Mary had commented.

'Oh, they were. The Piercesons. They were really awful. In and out of Walton Jail by the minute. Everyone was glad to see the back of them,' Elizabeth informed her as she went down the lobby struggling with a straw-stuffed mattress.

Mary had gone very pale.

'It's all right, Mam, no one knows,' Tessa hissed. She

knew Elizabeth wouldn't break her promise.

'Anyone at home?' a man's voice called from the front step.

'What is it?' Mary demanded. The man was clutching a large cardboard box to his chest.

'Found this on your doorstep, missus. Here, I wouldn't go leaving stuff around for anyone to walk off with. Happy Christmas!' He dumped the box on the floor and had gone before anyone could say a word.

'Who . . . what . . . ?' Mary was confused.

'Mam was going to put together a few things for you,' Elizabeth said quietly.

'But she's already given us so much – I can't—' Mary caught sight of her daughter and younger son's expressions. They had worked so hard. Her pride would have to take second place to their needs this time. 'Let's open it and see what's inside.'

Elizabeth helped Mary to carry the box into the kitchen and Tessa and Jimmy Oh'd and Ah'd over the ham shank, the pudding, the oranges, the butter, the jam, the tea and the slab of fruit cake. That was something they'd never had before. Mary sat down at the table and covered her face with her hands so the children would not see her tears.

'Mam! Mam, are you feeling poorly?' Tessa shook her mother's shoulder gently.

Mary looked up. 'No. No, Tessa, luv. Someone up there is looking after us. We'll all go to church in the morning and remember the Harrisons in our prayers.' She smiled gratefully at Elizabeth.

They were stacking the groceries on the shelf in the scullery when the kitchen door opened and Colin came in.

'Hello, Mam! The place looks great now! But who in the name of God bought all this bloody food?'

'Don't you use language like that under my roof! Where have you been all night?' Mary demanded.

'Oh, around. It wasn't much use coming home to an empty house with no job.'

Tessa glared at him. *He* wouldn't have walked the streets as she'd done, or slept rough. He'd been somewhere warm and he'd probably had meals too.

'So where did you get the overcoat from then?' Tessa demanded suspiciously.

Colin had anticipated this question. 'From a feller who felt sorry for me at one of the places I went to for a job.' He stared at his sister, defying her to challenge him. She couldn't and neither could his mam, not in front of the girl from the shop.

'Just don't think you're staying here, idling your time away. Get down to the market – any market – and see if there's any fetching and carrying to be done.' Mary held his gaze.

'Where's me da?'

'Where you should be, at work.'

'They don't work after dinner on Christmas Eve an' it's after three.'

Tessa could have hit him. Why did he always have to go and upset Mam?

'I said go and find *something* to do and keep out of . . . mischief,' Mary said in a tone that brooked no argument.

Colin shrugged and left the kitchen. He wasn't old enough to go into a pub but he knew where he could get his hands on a few bottles of beer. 'Mam, me da's home!' he shouted from the lobby.

The sound of a loud, tuneless voice came to their ears, singing a version of 'We Wish You a Merry Christmas'.

Mary looked at Tessa. 'Tessa, will you go and get him . . . inside.' Despair fell like a heavy cloak over her shoulders. Richie hadn't changed. He was drunk – again.

As Johnny Doyle alighted from a tram and began to walk home along a crowded Scotland Road he slowly found himself grinding to a halt. Obviously there must be a fight or some other kind of disturbance that was holding everyone up. It was nothing new on Christmas Eve, he thought. He'd just have to wait. He still hadn't got his mam a present yet but he'd left it late on purpose. Many of the pawnshops reduced their prices on Christmas Eve. When this lot had been sorted out he intended to call into Cookson's. His reverie was broken by a movement of the crowd and he saw a lad fighting his way through, lashing out at everyone in his path. So that's what the hold-up was, a petty thief. He was amazed however to see Colin O'Leary dash past him. Instinctively he'd leant back, out of Colin's way – he hardly knew the lad but he'd not thought of him as being a thief. Those couple of seconds were enough for Colin to break free of the crowd before Johnny could do anything to stop him. Well, there was a policeman in pursuit, Johnny thought, and he shrugged and walked on in the direction of the pawnshop.

When he emerged, delighted that he'd got his mam a nice pair of earrings at a price that hadn't left him penniless, he began to walk home. It was dark now and cold and he turned the collar of his jacket up and bent his head against the wind. He turned into Naylor Street with the intention of calling on Mike but was distracted by the screams and pleadings of a young girl. It was little Patsy Sullivan from number sixteen, an undernourished five-year-old. She was sobbing and trying to reach up to grab something, just what he couldn't see. But he couldn't mistake Patsy's tormentor. It was Colin O'Leary.

Colin had been relieved and delighted to have given the scuffer the slip. The fact that everywhere was crowded and the policeman too was fairly new to the area had worked in his favour. He'd leaned against the wall of the jigger to get his breath back. God, he hated this bloody place, he'd thought. It was worse than the one he'd come from. Then he'd walked around the corner into the street and had heard a child singing. He didn't know who she was but she was dirty, scruffy and as thin as a rake. She was singing to something she'd had wrapped up in a rag. A doll, he'd surmised, but maybe not. The likes of her wouldn't have a doll, she didn't even have a coat. She epitomised the whole neighbourhood, he'd thought savagely.

'Shurrup, you sound like a bloody cat out on the tiles,' he'd snarled.

The child had glared up at him and then he'd seen what she was nursing. It *was* a cat, well, a kitten, and like her it was half-starved, dirty and verminous.

'I'll give you something to sing about!' he'd cried and snatched the animal from her. It mewed with pain at being roughly handled and then swung up and down by the scruff of its neck.

'Give it back ter me! Give it back, 'e's me friend, like!' Patsy had yelled at him.

He'd laughed and had started to torment her, ignoring her frantic pleadings and tears. Then, suddenly, a hand closed around his wrist in a vice-like grip. Colin dropped the kitten with a squawk of pain.

'You're not only a thief, you're a bloody coward as well!' Johnny yelled at Colin. 'Kids and helpless animals!' Little Patsy immediately picked up the mewling kitten and fled.

Johnny caught Colin by the lapels of his coat. 'Listen you, I'm only going to say this once! Around here we don't thieve from shops and we don't torment kids or animals. I'll put your eye in a sling if I see or hear you've been at it again and you can be sure that all the lads and fellers in this street will be watching you too. Now clear off!' Johnny released Colin, aiming a swipe at the lad's head just to emphasise his point.

Colin slunk down the street, hating their new home more than ever.

Chapter Six

As her husband slept off the effects of his afternoon celebrations and the loss thereby of his morning's wages, Mary, aided by Tessa, tried not to show her bitter disappointment at his conduct. They had both really thought he'd turned over a new leaf.

After they'd put him to bed they sat down beside the fire in the kitchen. The room was still dingy and sparsely furnished but at least now it was warm. The flickering flames gave an illusion of cheerfulness.

'I wish I had something to give you, Tessa – aye, and our Jimmy too. Poor lad, he'll be the only one in the street who'll get nothing.'

'I don't think he will. An apple, an orange and a new penny is all a lot of kids will get. As for me – I understand.'

'I wish I understood your da.'

'Oh, Mam, don't let's think about it. Has he got any money left? A threepenny bit or a silver sixpence?'

'I'll have a look in his pockets, but I doubt it.'

Mary took Richie's jacket from the back of the chair. He'd gone to bed in the rest of his clothes.

'There's nothing. Just bits of loose tobacco and string. Wait . . .' She searched more thoroughly. 'There's something in the lining, I'm sure. It's torn in a few places.' She drew out the coin and placed it in Tessa's hand.

'It's a silver threepenny bit, Mam!'

Mary smiled. 'We'll give it to our Jimmy, with an orange.'

Tessa smiled too. 'He's no sock to hang up so we'll put it on the table and tell him Santa couldn't find his sock. He'll be made up.'

'What about you?'

Tessa got up and put her arms around her mother. 'I've got you, and we've furniture, food and a fire. That's enough for me.'

Mary kissed her on the cheek. 'You're a good girl, Tessa. I don't know what I'd do without you.'

'Come on, Mam, let's go to bed.'

Mary nodded. 'If straw was good enough for Him in that manger, it's good enough for us.'

Tessa was so relieved that there was something soft to sleep on and some blankets and the shawl and Elizabeth's old coat to cover her that she didn't mind sharing the donkey's breakfast with her mother. Colin, Da and Jimmy shared the other bedroom. Jimmy had his own mattress, much to Colin's annoyance. His da was out for the count and took up most of their mattress.

Mary lay with her eyes tightly closed. The room was quite bright owing to the streetlamp and the fact that they had no curtains. She thanked God for all the blessings that had come her way in the last two days, but although physically exhausted, she found it difficult to sleep. She could not get comfortable at all and just when she was starting to doze off a dull, dragging pain would start and waken her. She did not know what it was and it frightened her.

Tessa too was finding it hard to sleep. She'd been so optimistic that morning. Oh, how could Da be so thoughtless after everything they'd been through? He just didn't seem able to pass a pub without going in. Just what was so special about them she didn't know – apart from the beer. Many of them were terrible. Dirty sawdust on the floor, the bar counter awash with spilt beer, the stink of ale, stale tobacco and sweat. At least that was the impression she got when she passed. Da simply ignored the results of his weakness. Well, this would have to stop. She determined that, first thing tomorrow, when the chance arose, she was going to try as she'd never done before to make him see what was plainly under his nose.

Christmas Day dawned bright, clear and very, very frosty. The O'Learys all tidied themselves as best they could and went to church. Tessa saw Elizabeth and her family immediately. Mrs Harrison was wearing a very smart dark green coat and a matching green felt hat; Elizabeth wore her best navy blue coat and a new light blue hat and she had a small fur muff to tuck her hands into. It was suspended around her neck by a length of cord and was obviously a Christmas present.

Tessa noticed that all the Flynns were there too, and from the slightly greenish-grey tinge of his skin and the puffiness around his eyes, Mr Flynn looked as if he had a monumental hangover. Mrs Flynn and Brenda's grim expressions gave credence to her assumption. She and her mam had also heard part of the row that had gone on next door late last night. The walls were so thin you could hear everything. Her mam had raised her eyes to the ceiling but knew just how her neighbour felt.

Ginny Greely was there too, with May, who was wearing a fancy red and black hat which really didn't go very well with her brown coat.

Johnny Doyle and his two brothers, all well scrubbed, their hair plastered down, sat beside their sanctimonious-looking father and pale, washed-out, plain little mother. She constantly darted furtive and, Tessa thought, frightened glances at her husband and her sons.

The O'Learys all looked shabby beside their neighbours, but that didn't bother Colin; he was bored. His mind was wandering from the service to ways of making money. All he had to look forward to today was the Christmas dinner, even though it was only ham and not turkey or goose or capon. But if he wanted to get his hands on anything else, he'd have to be dead careful from now on. Even his da was being watchful where once he'd turned a blind eye to Colin's escapades.

But Da was a fool, spending hard-earned money on beer and horses and pitch and toss. *He* wasn't going to make the same mistakes. He wanted more out of life than a few hours' enjoyment, a hangover, then more hard graft. How Da put up with Mam and her eternal nagging and complaining Colin didn't know. And Tessa was getting as bad.

When the service was over and they'd shaken hands with the parish priest and wished the Season's Greetings to all their neighbours they set off for home. The pavements were slippery and Tessa linked her arm through her father's and made sure they gradually fell back until they were out of earshot.

Jimmy had been telling his mam how he was going to spend the money Santa had left him.

'It's going to be a Happy Christmas after all,' Richie said amiably.

'It is but oh, Da, it's only because of the goodness of the

neighbours. Why did you go and spend your wages? I thought—'

'Ah, come on, Tessa, luv, don't you start on about that too. I had enough of it from your mam and it's Christmas. Frank Flynn was in a worse state than me. I saw him hanging on to a lamppost.'

Tessa sighed. 'Da, I'm worried about Mam, really worried. She's had the move to cope with, not to mention our Colin. She's still upset. She . . . we both thought that now you'd be, well, more thoughtful. No one minds you having a couple of pints, Da,' she hurried on before he could stop her. 'But what if our Colin or me don't get jobs? I don't think *he's* even tried.'

'That's a bit unfair, Tessa. He promised me he'd turned over a new leaf. And of course you'll get a job, luv. You're bright, clean and tidy, always on time, never poorly—'

'But all I'm fit for is factory work and I tried everywhere!'

'You'll get something soon, Tessa, and so will our Colin. Unless someone finds out he's been to Borstal.'

'Do you believe him?'

Richie shrugged. 'I'll wait and see.'

Tessa took a deep breath. 'Will you promise me something, Da?' she asked, looking earnestly up into his face.

'What?'

'That you'll try harder in the future to just keep it to a pint before you come home and . . . and no gambling, please?'

His expression changed. 'It's not your place to be asking me things like that, girl.'

'I know it's not, but, Da, look at us! We didn't have much before, and we still owe money, but now we're the poorest of the poor.'

Richie felt guilty. He didn't intentionally go out of his way to spend his wages, it just sort of happened.

'Please? Please, Da? It would mean so much to us . . . all of us,' Tessa pleaded. 'Especially me,' she added. She'd always been his favourite.

Richie was silent for a minute then he slowly nodded. 'Just a pint, Tessa.'

'Promise? Really, really promise?'

'I *really* promise.'

She smiled up at him, some of her fears alleviated. She prayed he did mean it. But how many times had his promises been made and broken?

They'd all had their dinner and her mam and da were sitting dozing by the fire. Colin had gone out with a muttered excuse but she really didn't care where he'd gone. Jimmy had gone in to see Harold Flynn and, judging from the noise next door, all the previous night's animosity had been abandoned. There were shrieks of laughter from Eileen and her daughters and bellowing from Frank and Mike. She was wondering just what she could do and was relieved when she heard the doorknocker. She went to open the door to Elizabeth.

'Mam said if you're as bored as me you can come down to our house for an hour or two. She's fed up with me mooching around and our Nessie is being a pain, as usual, even though she got nearly everything she asked for. If I'd had my way she'd have got nothing, she's just greedy and selfish.'

'Just like our Colin.'

'What's he done?

'Nothing. He's gone out.'

'Well, are you coming?'

Tessa ran down the lobby into the kitchen, told her sleepy-eyed mother where she was going and snatched up her shawl.

'How's your mam? Did you have a good dinner?' Delia asked. Jack was asleep in his comfy winged armchair.

'She's having a doze and the dinner was really great.'

Delia smiled and looked across at her husband. 'They're all the same, aren't they? It's *us* who do the shopping and the cooking and the serving and *they* all go to sleep. Go on – you can go up to your bedroom, Elizabeth, and maybe I'll have a quick doze before I start on the dishes.'

'Leave them, we'll do them. I did ours so Mam could have a rest.'

'It's a pity my two don't think like you, Tessa.'

'What did you have to go and say that for? There's piles and piles of dishes! I think she's used every pan and dish we own,' Elizabeth said when they were at the top of the stairs and therefore out of earshot.

'Because your mam's been so good to us, and you and your da too.'

Elizabeth shrugged and opened the door to her room.

'You've got a *fire* in your bedroom!' Tessa was incredulous.

'I only have one on special occasions like now, or when I'm sick or when it really is very, very cold.'

'Oh, isn't it all . . . great!' Tessa gasped.

'I suppose it is.' Elizabeth had never given much thought to it before. 'Didn't you have things like this when you lived in Isaac Street?'

'No. I had some things. A bed, of course. A chest of drawers, a stool and curtains and rag rugs, but you've got . . .

everything.' Tessa looked in amazement at the neatly made single bed with its bright patchwork quilt. She gazed at the highly polished wardrobe in which she supposed Elizabeth had lots of clothes, and at the dressing table on the top of which there was a set of little glass bowls, a trinket box and a ring stand placed on crocheted mats. A stool covered in pink chintz was pushed into the knee hole of the dressing table. The curtains were made of the same material and there was even wallpaper. It had a white background with little springs of pink and blue flowers all over it. Tessa had never known anyone who had wallpaper in the downstairs rooms let alone the bedrooms. There were two pictures on the wall and a small silver-framed mirror.

'Do you want to see the awful uniform we have to wear in summer?' Elizabeth asked. 'You've seen the winter thing.'

'You have a different one for summer?' Tessa said, sitting down on the dressing-table stool Elizabeth had pulled out and placed near the fireplace.

'Well, we'd be roasted alive in that thick scratchy serge.' Elizabeth delved into the wardrobe and threw a blue dress and then a blazer on the bed. Tessa caught a glimpse of several other dresses and blouses. Elizabeth held up the dress. 'It's like a rag!' It was cornflower-blue rayon with short puffed sleeves and a cream Peter Pan collar with, at the centre, a narrow blue bow.

'What's wrong with it?' Tessa wouldn't have minded it.

'I'm *fourteen*, not four! It's like something you'd dress a toddler in. And I once had the bow cut off.'

'Why?' Tessa demanded.

'It undoes.' Elizabeth demonstrated by a sharp tug on the loose ends. 'And I was chewing these ends. Up comes Sister

Imelda and fishes out a pair of scissors hanging on a long black ribbon – they have all kinds of things hidden in those long skirts – and cuts the bow off. "Elizabeth Harrison, if you choose to ruin a perfectly good piece of material, you can do without it!" she says, all huffy-like. Mam wasn't half mad. She had to make another one.'

'Don't you get hot in that?' Tessa pointed to the navy blue blazer lying on the bed. The badge on the breast pocket was the same as the hat badge.

'Yes, and we can't take it off either. We have white socks, brown sandals, and white gloves which are always getting dirty and lost. Mam says I must use them as dusters or handkerchiefs, they're so filthy. And then the hat.'

'Another soup dish?' Tessa laughed.

Elizabeth grimaced. 'It's just as bad. Same shape but it's Panama straw. If it gets wet it's ruined – it goes all limp and soggy. So the last time it rained I took it off and pushed it into my satchel. Mam was furious.'

'Why?'

'Because it was ruined just the same. It was all out of shape and she had to buy another one. I didn't get out of the house for a week for that and I'm not allowed to keep it in here. I think it's under lock and key.' Elizabeth laughed.

'Do you really hate it there? It sounds like fun.'

'Fun! It's nothing like fun! I'm a misfit, you see. The rest of them come from really well-off homes. They all speak with posh accents, so I don't fit in even though Mam pays extra for elocution lessons. It's a waste of time. I just *can't* speak like that! It's all so . . . false. I forget and start dropping my aitches. She pays for piano lessons too and we haven't even got a piano! It's all to impress Aunty Margaret in New Jersey.'

'So what do you want to do when you leave there?'

'I don't really know. I think . . . I think . . . I'd like to work in Woolies. Just imagine seeing all the things they sell!'

'Do you think they'll let you?'

'Not a chance. Mam would make me take the veil first. But I know this much, I'm not staying on. I'm leaving when I'm sixteen.'

'At least you'll have had a good education. You can have a pick of jobs. I can't even get one.'

Elizabeth looked at her closely and then bit her lip.

'What's the matter?'

'Nothing. Before we broke up, I heard Sister Julie saying she needed some help. Some domestic help. She's about a hundred but she sees that everywhere is kept clean. You have to kneel in a corner and say a whole decade of the rosary if you so much as drop a tiny bit of paper on the floor!'

'Aren't there younger nuns who could help?'

'Oh, they do. You're nearly always tripping over one of them polishing floors. There's miles and miles of polished wood floors. That's why we have indoor shoes and outdoor shoes. Another daft idea.'

'Not if you're the nun who has to polish them.'

Elizabeth was deliberating. 'There must be *something* they need *someone* to do. I'll ask Mam if she'll come with me to ask Mother Superior if they have some work for you.'

'Me?'

'Yes. You need a job, don't you, and it would be better than working in one of those terrible factories.'

Tessa looked flabbergasted. 'Work in a convent? Me?'

'Why not? You go to church, you're hard-working, you won't be cheeky or "impudent", as they say, you need a job to help your mam get a decent home together, what more deserving case could there be?'

'Will you really do that? Ask your mam too?'

'Of course. If you get something you wouldn't be able to speak to me, of course.'

Hope had taken hold of Tessa. Imagine working in a convent. It would be clean, warm, quiet. Everything a factory job wouldn't be. And she'd be able to see Elizabeth, even if she couldn't talk to her. Maybe they could travel to and from home together. Maybe the new year would really be the start of something new. Something better.

Chapter Seven

Tessa would never forget the day she stood before Mother Superior in the parlour of the Convent. True to her word Mrs Harrison, urged on by Elizabeth's pleadings, had written to make enquiries. She had given Tessa's circumstances and a brief character reference. It had to be brief: she hardly knew the girl, but she was moved by her plight. The reply had come back that if Mrs Harrison would bring the young girl for inspection and interview on Monday 10 January her suitability as a 'lay domestic' would be considered.

'You can't go looking like a rag bag. Oh, God! I didn't mean to say something like that.' Elizabeth clapped her hand over her mouth. It was one of her failings. She always went in with both feet, opening her mouth before she thought about what she was going to say.

Tessa looked down at the creased and none-too-clean navy blue skirt and her shapeless grey jumper, which was already thin on the elbows and cuffs.

'I know what you mean. I *do* look like a walking rag bag,' she replied ruefully.

'I'll lend you something,' Elizabeth offered firmly.

'Nothing too good, Elizabeth, please,' Delia called from the scullery where she was washing up, up to her elbows in soap suds and greasy plates. She did feel genuinely sorry for Tessa, for the whole family in fact, although there was something she didn't like about the eldest boy. Just what it was she couldn't put her finger on. But it wouldn't do for Elizabeth to make a bosom friend out of the girl. It was a friendship that would do her daughter no good at all. Elizabeth's future was mapped out, even though when it was mentioned her daughter pressed her lips together tightly and that stubborn look came into her eyes.

Once upstairs Elizabeth delved into her wardrobe and took out a very dark blue skirt and a cream blouse she had always hated. 'Here, this might do.'

'Don't you think this will look too . . . good?' Tessa said, holding the blouse up. It was a warm winceyette material.

'No. Not if you wear the coat I gave you over it. You'll look tidy, but, well . . .'

'As poor as a church mouse.' Tessa smiled ruefully.

'You'll have to wear stockings or socks or something.'

'I think socks would be better.'

Elizabeth rummaged in the top drawer of the chest and brought out a pair of off-white socks that would have been destined for the rag man anyway when the spring clear-out came around and summer uniform day arrived, which was usually in May and usually on the coldest day of the month.

'Oh, Mrs Harrison, I'm terrified!' Tessa said as they arrived outside the Convent.

Delia looked down at her. She was a rather pretty girl: fine-boned and dainty. With some flesh on her bones, the right clothes, and her hair cut decently, she would be very pretty.

'Don't worry, you'll be fine. Just answer truthfully and in a quiet polite voice,' Delia advised, pressing the doorbell, the loud clanging of which echoed around the hall inside.

Tessa stood on the top step, her stomach turning over

with nerves, looking up at the beautiful glass fanlight over the imposing door with its knocker, brass plate and handle shining in the pale, frosty early-morning sun.

The door was opened and a small, elderly nun looked at them questioningly.

'I'm Mrs Delia Harrison. My daughter is a pupil here. This is Tessa, Theresa O'Leary. Mother Superior is expecting us.'

Delia herself felt nervous. The interior of the hall was unnerving. It was painted a dark green colour and the walls were adorned with holy pictures. The floor was covered with black and white chequered tiles and there were four wide polished mahogany doors, one of which the little nun guided them to. She knocked quietly, entered and then returned. 'Mother Frances says you are to go in.'

Delia took a deep breath. She had only ever been in this inner sanctum once before. It was daunting to a woman of the working class.

Tessa was shaking. She looked down at the tiled floor. There wasn't a speck of dirt or a single crack on it.

A middle-aged nun looked at them over her glasses. 'Please sit, Mrs Harrison.' Delia's letter was on the desk in front of her.

Delia sat nervously on the edge of an upright chair and Tessa stood at her side. 'Thank you, Mother.'

Mother Superior glanced at the letter, and then at the large painting of their foundress, Blessed Mère Julie, which hung over the elegant fireplace. She folded her hands piously.

'So, this is the young girl?'

'Yes, Mother. This is Theresa O'Leary.'

'Well, Theresa, why do you want to come and work here?'

Tessa looked up. Elizabeth had prepared her for this.

'Look demure, or at the floor, stand still and don't fidget. Just tell her, plainly.'

'We . . . we have just had to move from the Dingle, Mother. We are almost destitute. I would take any kind of a job and before Christmas I really *did* try. I went to every shop and factory.' She didn't miss the slight shudder that shook the woman's shoulders at the word 'factory'. 'But Elizabeth – Miss Harrison – suggested I come to you for . . . help.'

'Exactly what happened to put your family in a state of destitution?'

The girl looked downtrodden, pale and under-nourished and yet she spoke well. 'Destitute' was a word she had obviously learned for the occasion – she had probably been coached by Elizabeth Harrison: a stubborn and often impudent girl who was just not the right type for a school like this.

'My father. He works very hard when he can, but some days there isn't any work. He is a docker, and he has . . . weaknesses.' That was what Elizabeth had told her to say.

'Weaknesses?'

Tessa took a deep breath. 'He . . . he likes a drink, Mother, and . . . he gambles.'

'Indeed.'

The frosty tone made Tessa look down into the eyes of the seated nun whose plump, rounded features gave no clue to her character. Tessa hoped her own eyes were honest and pleading.

'But now he's turned over a new leaf and we all want to get back to the hard-working, simple and clean life we used to have. That's why I need work. Please, Mother, he really has made a new start.'

The nun turned her glance to Delia, who nodded.

'I believe your younger daughter . . . ?'

'Vanessa,' Delia supplied.

'. . . is also destined for a superior education. She will come to us?'

'Yes. Yes, definitely, Mother. When she's eleven. She's ten at the moment.'

Mother Superior didn't reply for a few seconds. She was weighing up the prospect of another paying pupil against the cost of taking this shabbily dressed girl into the kitchens.

'Very well. You can start in the kitchens when term begins on Monday. You will be assisting Sister Augustine. You'll work from seven a.m. to five-thirty p.m. and we will pay you five shillings and sixpence a week.'

It wasn't much, Tessa thought, but it was better than nothing.

Delia stood up and placed a hand on Tessa's shoulder. They certainly weren't delving into their coffers, she thought, but she smiled. 'Thank you, Mother. That is very generous.'

'Thank you. I'll work hard and never be late,' Tessa added.

The nun nodded her head and stood up. The interview was over.

Elizabeth made her repeat every single word, and couldn't believe that Tessa had taken no notice of her surroundings with the exception of the hall and that there was carpet on the floor in the parlour.

'I was relying on you. I've only been in there myself once

and then I was scared even to open my mouth, let alone gaze around the room.'

'You were scared and you expected *me* to have noticed everything! Elizabeth, I was quaking!'

'We're never allowed near *their* rooms. They're not paying you much. When do you start?'

'When you go back. I have to be there for seven o'clock, so I'll have to leave about a quarter past six.'

'Oh, that's a pain. I wanted to walk with you.'

'I finish at half past five.'

'I'll wait for you. I'll dawdle around inside as much as I can, then I'll wait outside the back gate.'

'You'll be frozen, it's an hour and a half.'

'I don't mind,' Elizabeth said cheerfully. 'Just as long as you take notice of *everything*!'

It was with real pleasure for once that Tessa walked down the lobby of number twelve. At last she had some good news. The kitchen door was half open and she could see her mother sitting at the table peeling potatoes. She'd laid a sheet of old newspaper on the table top. It and the peelings would be burned: putting them into the ashcan would be a sheer waste. They would augment the precious coal.

'Mam! Mam! I got it! I got a job working in the kitchens for five and six a week!'

Mary stood up. 'Glory be to God!'

'I know it's not much and it's less than I could get in a factory but it's clean and warm and I won't mind what I do. Elizabeth is going to wait for me when she finishes school and we can come home together.'

Mary looked into her daughter's dancing dark eyes. 'She's a kind-hearted girl, is Elizabeth, even if her mam's got some fancy ideas. It will do you good, Tessa, to have someone of your own age. You never really had many friends in Isaac Street, did you?'

'No, I didn't, Mam, and Elizabeth is sort of special.'

'Well, she would be with all the money that comes from the rich aunt in America,' Colin said cuttingly.

'It wouldn't hurt *you* to shift yourself, meladdo, and get some kind of a job.'

'Mam, I've told you I'm trying.'

'Oh, you're that all right! You're very "trying",' Tessa snapped at him. She didn't know what he did during the day, but he always came home in the evening obviously well fed. Where he got the meals from she didn't know.

'Give me your old jumper and skirt and I'll wash them through. You'll have to have something clean to start with. At least they can't object to that. You won't be dressed up.'

'But these are Elizabeth's clothes, Mam.'

'I don't think she'll mind you keeping them until I can get your own things washed and dried.' Mary smiled. 'With you and your da both in work regular like, we'll soon be able to buy things and have a decent home again. Maybe there'll even be some spare for clothes . . .'

It was a dark wind- and rain-lashed morning as Tessa set out for work. She had been going to wear her one and only coat, but she had nothing to cover her head, so Mary insisted she put on her shawl; it would at least keep her hair dry.

'See you this evening, Mam,' she said, kissing Mary on the cheek. Her mother stood at the door, heedless of the cold and damp, and watched her walk up the street, her head bent against the weather.

If only she felt better, Mary thought. The pains she'd felt the night before Christmas had become more or less continuous. If only she had more energy, she'd go and get some bit of a job too. She could go cleaning offices – a lot of women did that, usually in the early morning or late evening. There was a small army of them and they all had kids who needed feeding and clothing. But she was always so tired these days and she knew the dragging pains were beginning to show in her face.

Colin took up his usual vantage post on the corner of Scotland Road and Chaucer Street. There was a branch of the Liverpool Savings Bank on the opposite corner. It was a large, imposing building, with tall chimneys and a turret like those on castles. It was two storeys high and its name was painted in gold lettering on the side. He'd watched the place for almost a week now: counting the customers in and out; noting what time they were busy and when they were quiet; what time the staff arrived; what time they left; and when they went out for their lunch.

They'd have hundreds of pounds in their tills, maybe even thousands. He'd also made a note of when the money arrived. It was carried in a big black box by a single man, accompanied by one police constable.

He'd make a proper job of this one. He'd considered taking a partner, it would have been useful, but whom did he know? Whom could he trust around here? Besides, he would have to split the money in half. That was what really settled the matter. He'd wait his chance. In a couple of weeks, when he was absolutely certain of the best possible time. Probably after the money had been delivered and before the rush just before they closed their doors at half past three in the afternoon, he thought. Then he'd be away from this dirty, poverty-stricken hole of a city for good. He'd go to New York on one of those big liners that were always either tied up at the Landing Stage or in one of the docks that his da worked on.

Colin never stole from the shops now in case the shop-keepers remembered him when the police came asking about the bank raid. He usually took the overhead railways back to the Dingle and got a morning's or afternoon's work on the docks down there. There were men who knew him, of course, but he didn't worry about the risk. He earned just enough to get by. Sometimes it was more when he got a couple of full days consecutively. But he was sick of both his mam's and Tessa's questions and jibes. At least Da wasn't always nagging him.

Elizabeth hung around the back door to the Convent. She'd idled her time away as best she could but by four-thirty she could delay no longer. It was freezing and she hoped Tessa wouldn't be long. She walked up and down just to keep a bit warm. She was perplexed about something her mam had said this morning before she left.

'Elizabeth, I know Tessa is a quiet, well-behaved girl, and I don't mind you being friends, but I just don't want you to consider her as your . . . *only* friend.'

'She *is* my only friend. Hardly anyone around here speaks to me because I have to go to that awful school.'

'It is *not* an awful school. You are getting the best

education that money can buy. Anyway, you're still friendly with Ginny, aren't you?'

'Yes, but it's sort of . . . different.'

'You know how hard both your da and me work to keep you there. Even with your aunt's help it's not always easy. There's books, uniform, extra lessons—'

'I know, Mam. So why can't I leave and go to St Anthony's or St Sylvester's?'

If she'd gone to a local school like everyone else, she, like them, would have left by now.

'You will *not* be leaving the Convent. We all want much much better things for you. Your life will take a different turn from Tessa's, that's why I'm telling you not to make such a fuss of her. We've helped her family get settled, and we've helped get her a job, now leave it at that.'

Elizabeth had shaken her head and had left for school. There was going to be a terrible row one of these days, she knew it – she just *knew* it – because she was determined not to be forced to do something she would hate. When she set her mind to something so important, she could be immovable.

The Convent's back door opened. Tessa slipped out. 'I'm sorry, have you been here long? I've no real idea of the time. I have to wait to be dismissed.' She wrapped her shawl around her and over her head and linked arms with her friend.

'No, not really. I've been thinking about something. Well?'

'What?'

'You promised to tell me *everything*! Were they horrible? The nuns, I mean. Did they come popping up behind you, and frightening the daylights out of you? They're always doing that to me. You feel guilty and you haven't even *done* anything.'

'You sound as if you hate them.'

'No, I don't *hate* them, but all the things we do there, like elocution, etiquette, embroidery and walking properly, don't seem to be of much use to the likes of me.'

'Are you still determined to leave at sixteen?'

'Yes. Two more years. Eight terms more. God, it doesn't bear thinking about. Oh, I'm such a misery! I know, we'll go and see Ginny or Mike and find out as much as we can about Brenda Flynn's wedding. Come on, let's run. There's a tram coming. You can tell me everything on the way.'

'I haven't got any money.'

'I have, come on.' Elizabeth grabbed Tessa's hand and they ran laughing towards the tram stop, heedless of the cold and damp. Elizabeth was determined to ignore her mam's instructions about getting too friendly with Tessa. The ties that bound them already would be hard to sever.

After telling her mam about her first day over her tea of blind scouse (with dripping butties to follow), Tessa wrapped herself in her shawl and walked down the road towards the tannery.

Elizabeth had told her of this meeting place but she was apprehensive. Perhaps they wouldn't want her to be included in their little group. But as soon as she caught sight of Elizabeth she relaxed.

'You've been ages!' Elizabeth complained.

'I'm sorry but I had things to tell Mam.' Tessa seated herself on the low wall.

'What's it like, working there?' Ginny asked.

'Not bad at all. It's clean and warm and they gave me something to eat.'

'I wish I could have landed a job like that.' Ginny looked pointedly at Elizabeth, who ignored her. 'I'm frozen to the bone when I get home and if I complain all I get is an ear-bashing from Mam. She doesn't have to put up with the cold when she's at work and—'

'We all know you don't like it, Ginny,' Mike Flynn interrupted.

'How can you like stinking of fish all day? I told Mam I never, ever want to eat fish again.'

'What did she say? Doesn't old Birrel give you anything to bring home?' Mike asked.

'Of course he does. Anything that's a day old. But I just can't eat it. It sticks in my throat and I gag. All I can think about is gutting it.' Ginny shivered and looked even paler.

'I'll be glad when it's March. I hate the winter,' Elizabeth said, fully aware that she was the one most protected against it.

'I can't say I'd like to be Johnny. I bet he's seasick. Out there in the middle of the Atlantic, rolling and pitching all day and night. God, it must be awful,' Mike said, pulling a face.

'How about you? What's your job like?' Elizabeth asked.

'I shovel coal all flaming day. My back feels as if it's broken by the end of it, but at least it keeps me from freezing. Half an hour for dinner we get, that's all, and a round of bread and dripping is all Mam gives me. She's saving up.'

'That's why we came down here tonight. How are things going for the Big Day?'

Mike grimaced and shoved his hands deeper into his

pockets. 'Down the drain, that's how they're going. Mam and our Brenda do nothing but row and fight. At least me da can get out and go to the pub.'

'You just said they were saving up, so where does he get the money from?' Ginny demanded.

'Mam's always asking the same question, but at the top of her voice. Probably the whole street can hear her.'

'Has your Brenda sorted out the bridesmaids yet?' Elizabeth asked. The outcome of that row was eagerly awaited by every woman in the street.

'Oh, aye, but half the family's not speaking to the other half. I couldn't care less meself. You're all coming, aren't you? Johnny is – he'll be home just in time.'

'Of course we'll all come,' Ginny answered.

'The whole street and half the neighbourhood will come. Any excuse for a knees-up,' Elizabeth laughed.

'Us too?' Tessa said timidly.

'Yeah. Your mam and da, your Colin and Jimmy.'

'It'll be great. There hasn't been a "do" around here for ages,' Ginny said enthusiastically.

'That's because of the last one, Nancy Deegan's,' Mike said.

'What happened then?' Tessa enquired.

'It got a bit out of hand, like. Her da said the fella she'd married wasn't up to much and that she certainly wasn't getting a bargain in him and his entire family. There was murder – everyone pitched in, the women too. The scuffers had to be called. The bridegroom and the bride's father spend the night in Rose Hill nick. It was dead funny seeing the pair of them being hauled up the street and the sergeant telling the rest of them to get home, or he'd nick the lot of them.'

'I bet the bride didn't think it "dead funny".'

'No, neither did her mam or her ma-in-law.'

'There won't be anything like that, will there?' Tessa asked timidly.

'Fat chance. *He's* flaming teetotal. A right miserable sod he is. I don't know what she sees in him.'

'I do. She's got the chance to get away from you lot and when the old girl dies they'll have the house to themselves. A whole house to themselves! It must be like heaven,' Ginny marvelled.

'There's only you and your mam living over there,' Mike stated.

'Don't forget the lot that have upstairs and if we had a cellar there'd be another lot in that. As it is they're up and down the stairs like yo-yos. The kids are always fighting and screaming and she's always yelling at them and him too. It's just what you need when you get home cold and tired. At the weekends you usually have to step over him in the lobby. Out for the count. Paralytic drunk. Me mam just laughs.'

'Well, if he drinks in the Globe or the Unicorn she won't mind how drunk he gets, it pays her wages and therefore the rent,' Elizabeth said philosophically. 'I hope it doesn't rain on the day, or worse, snow,' she added.

'Is she walking to the church?' Ginny asked.

'Well, Mam wants her to have a hackney with a horse and so does she, but me da says it's a waste of money and she can walk like everyone else does. She says she isn't *like* "everyone else" and she'll thank him to remember that she's getting out of a slum and into a decent area. That caused another row.'

Elizabeth laughed. 'Oh, you're always making a joke of

things.' His family were the noisiest in the street but she liked Mike's sense of fun.

Mike rolled his eyes and grinned. 'Well, if you didn't laugh at the carry-on, you'd cry or go completely round the bend.'

'But you make it sound like a circus.'

'It is. Bloody Fred Karno's is what it is!' Mike replied, still grinning broadly.

Chapter Eight

Had she heard her son's remarks Eileen Flynn would have agreed wholeheartedly. She was getting no help from anyone. All Brenda did was moan. All Maureen and young Harold did was torment her and more often than not Frank took refuge in the pub on his way home from work. Lately she'd taken again to going to meet him down at the docks. It was humiliating for both Frank and herself but she didn't care. At least that way she got most of his wages, though there were still shouting matches when he eventually arrived home. He upbraided her for showing him up before his work- and drinking-mates. She'd yell back that it was bad enough feeding and clothing them all, never mind forking out for a wedding.

'The way he's goin' I'll be pawnin' me own wedding ring to pay for the "do",' Eileen complained loudly to Mary and May when she met them in the shop.

They murmured their sympathy, particularly Mary who wondered if she should use the same tactics with Richie – though he had been much more thoughtful about his drinking lately. Quite suddenly a pain, like a red hot knife stabbing her, tore into her abdomen. Mary cried out and gripped the counter.

'Mother of God! She's goin' ter faint, Delia! May, get a stool or something and be quick!' Eileen held Mary's sagging body from falling to the floor.

Delia ran through into her kitchen, grabbed a three-legged stool and a glass of water and informed her startled husband, who was unloading the stock he'd brought earlier that morning from the warehouse, that she might need him in the shop.

'Have yer got any smellin' salts, Delia? She's a terrible colour,' Eileen yelled.

Mary was beginning to come round as May and Eileen lowered her on to the stool. She was confused. What was happening to her? She made an attempt to get to her feet.

'You sit down there, luv, you're not well at all.'

'I'll be fine. Just give me a few minutes.'

Delia shook her head. 'You won't be fine at all. You look like death warmed up. Come on, I'll take you into the kitchen, Jack will see to the shop.'

'No! No, really, I'm great now. I ... I've been getting these little turns since Christmas.'

'That was not a "little turn". I thought you'd gone unconscious, out like a light.'

'I thought yer were a gonner, meself!' Eileen added.

Delia and May both glared at her.

'God! A mouth like the Mersey tunnel!' May muttered to Delia.

Mary had now struggled to her feet, and insisted she was well enough to get home alone.

'Well, you go and lie down when you get back. Make yourself a cuppa first then get straight off to bed,' Delia advised as Mary left the shop.

'That woman needs a doctor. I've noticed how poorly she's been looking lately,' Delia said.

'That's as may be, but she certainly didn't want to go into your kitchen,' sniffed Eileen.

'What's wrong with my kitchen, may I ask?' Delia demanded.

'Oh, for God's sake, Delia, don't go off the deep end. She didn't mean that there was *anything* wrong with your kitchen. It's cleaner and tidier and a damned sight warmer than mine or Bucket-gob's here.'

'And 'aven't you gorra nice way of puttin' things, May Greely!'

Delia sighed. These days Eileen was as quarrelsome out of her house as she was in it.

'I'm not having a repeat performance of Nancy Deegan's wedding,' Brenda Flynn said firmly as she sorted through the pile of ironing which for one reason or another her mam never quite got round to doing. These days, Brenda would pick out her own clothes and iron them and Maureen did the same. The ironing board always seemed to be up and the irons left at the foot of the range.

'That was all the family's fault. Shockin' it was. Even Father Walsh couldn't do nothing with them. I'm not having a performance like that either. You can have a good do without all that fighting and arguing.'

'Everyone rows at weddings,' Maureen said as she experimented with a lead pencil to see if she could shape her eyebrows with it. She wanted a real one from Woolies but her mam had gone mad when she'd mentioned it and called her a painted hussy.

'Not at this one,' Brenda replied, attacking the collar of her best blouse with the flat iron. She would be glad to get out of this house. The place was always a tip and meals were always either half cold or burned to a crisp. Her soon-to-be mother-in-law had been horrified to learn that she couldn't even bake; all she'd been able to say by way of an excuse was that her mam had never baked and therefore had never taught her. She'd promised Thomas that she would learn from his mam and that she'd do all the heavy housework. It would be a real pleasure to see good furniture well cared for and floors polished, to have sheets on the bed and a bedspread and eiderdown. All the latter were luxuries she'd never known. She was certainly not going to have a life like her mam had had, she'd vowed to herself.

'I still don't really like that blue colour,' Maureen complained about the dress she would have to wear.

Brenda glared at her.

'Don't start that again, milady,' Eileen warned, wagging her forefinger at her daughter.

'It's February now, why couldn't we have something bright and cheerful, like red or orange or emerald green?'

'Oh, yes, red and orange would be great, wouldn't it?' Brenda answered sarcastically. 'In red you'd all look like tarts, orange you'd all look like something from the Orange Lodge.'

'And green is bad luck,' Eileen finished. 'That blue is very nice, Brenda, take no notice of 'er.'

'I'm not. It's *my* wedding and they'll wear what *I* want and if you don't like it, Maureen, then you know what you can do.'

'Jesus, Mary and Joseph, don't start on that again, Brenda – and you, milady, keep yer lip buttoned up.'

Brenda turned her attention to the other important matter. 'Mam, have you spoken to Da about the carriage?'

'I 'ave. 'E says you can walk. You can show off the frock

from Blackler's that cost four weeks' wages. 'E said you've got more money than sense.'

'I'll freeze!' Brenda protested.

'We'll all flaming well freeze. At least your dress has got long sleeves,' Maureen added.

'If I 'ear one more complaint from you, Maureen Flynn, you'll get a go-along with the back of me 'and,' Eileen threatened.

She'd be glad when all this was over. She had a permanent headache and Frank was no help at all. She often thought of saying to hell with the lot of them and going and joining him in the pub.

'At least you'll be warm, Mam. You'll have a coat and that hat of Mrs Harrison's.'

'That's more for decoration than anything else. It won't keep me warm. I 'ope to God it's not blowing a gale.'

'I'll buy a couple of hat pins,' Brenda said firmly. 'And I hope Da stays sober.'

Eileen raised her eyes to the ceiling. That would be asking too much. She'd have a hard enough time keeping him sober before they even got to the church. It wasn't unusual for the father of the bride, the bridegroom, best man and groom's father, plus most of the male guests, to be found propping up the bar, having a quick bevvy to give themselves Dutch courage before the service. But there'd be none of that from the groom and best man, who was a friend of Thomas's and also teetotal. After the ceremony she just couldn't care less.

Elizabeth, Ginny and Tessa had a meeting in Elizabeth's bedroom to discuss their outfits.

'I've got nothing but the things you gave me,' Tessa said

ruefully after Elizabeth had showed them her dress that had been bought specially for the occasion. It was a deep rose-pink Viyella with a white roll collar and long sleeves.

'I haven't got much choice either,' Ginny added.

'All right, just what have you got, Ginny?'

'A navy skirt, a brown one and a grey one. The grey is the smartest.'

'Well, I've got a grey jumper and a really nice bright pink scarf that you could sort of drape around the neck. You could get some pink ribbon and make an Alice band. That would brighten it up. And I'll do your hair.'

Ginny's hair was fine and a sort of mousy-fair colour. It never looked properly clean because all she had to wash it with was soap. Elizabeth made up her mind to get a sachet of Sta Blonde and use that. She'd dry it and then curl the ends with the tongs. She was good at things like that. She hadn't meant it at all when she'd told Tessa she would like to work in Woolworth's; what she really wanted to do was be a hairdresser, but she hadn't a cat in hell's chance of that.

'Now you, Tessa. You can wear my cream blouse and Ginny's brown skirt. You could get a piece of narrow brown ribbon and I'll make a bow that you can tie under the collar. Brown and cream go really well.'

'Would that be all right, Ginny? About your skirt, I mean?' Ginny nodded.

'What about my hair?'

Elizabeth looked quizzically at her friend. 'Will you let me cut it?'

'God! I wouldn't let you loose with a pair of scissors on my hair, Elizabeth Harrison!' Ginny cried.

Tessa looked uncertain.

'It's already short, so there's not much that can go wrong.'

Ginny sucked in her breath and shook her head.

Tessa made up her mind. 'Oh, all right. Just promise to be careful.'

'I promise. Stay there while I go and get Mam's scissors.'

Soon Elizabeth reappeared with a pair of scissors in one hand and towel and dustpan and brush in the other. 'Mam says I've got to clean up and if I snatch you bald she'll kill me. She will too.'

Tessa sat on the dressing-table stool with the towel around her shoulders while Elizabeth, with more confidence than she felt, snipped away.

'It does look better,' Ginny said tentatively.

'Of course it does. She's got a natural wave in it.'

'Oh, I won't end up with a head full of waves and curls, will I? I might lose my job if they think I'm ... sort of flighty.'

'Stop worrying about them. Tell them it's the St Joan of Arc cut. They can't complain about that.'

'Who was she?' Ginny asked.

'Oh, she was French and had her hair cut short so she looked like a boy and fought with the soldiers against us. So the history book says.'

'What happened?' Tessa's mind for the moment had been diverted.

Elizabeth tutted impatiently. 'She was burned at the stake because she said she kept hearing voices in her head. They thought she was a witch or mad or both, something like that.' Elizabeth stood back and ran a critical eye over her handiwork.

'So who won then?' Ginny pressed.

'We did, of course. Right, now you can turn around.'

Tessa swivelled round on the stool to see her reflection in the dressing-table mirror. 'Oh!' she exclaimed.

'Oh, don't tell me you hate it?'

'No! No, I think it's great! What do you think, Ginny?' It looked so much better, Tessa thought. It had shape and style. Elizabeth certainly had a gift.

'It's much better than it was,' Ginny replied.

'So now will you let me cut your fringe, Ginny Greely? It's always in your eyes and makes you look like a shaggy dog.'

So Ginny submitted to Elizabeth's scissors while Tessa watched closely.

'What would we do without her, Ginny?' Tessa asked, patting her own hair.

'Look a mess, I suppose. But she's terrible bossy.'

Elizabeth flicked the towel at Ginny and they all laughed.

Tessa ran home to show off her new hairstyle to her mam, who was as impressed with Elizabeth's skill as Tessa and Ginny had been.

'I wonder if she could do anything with mine?' Mary knew her own hair was badly in need of attention. Suddenly she leaned forward, clutched her stomach and cried out.

Horrified, Tessa was on her feet. 'Oh, Mam! Mam! Let me go and get Mrs Harrison, or even Mrs Flynn from next door!' she pleaded. Her mam looked terrible. Her face was as grey as her hair and she looked old, so old.

'No! No, Tessa! It'll pass. It always does.'

Tessa bit her lip. She couldn't have failed to notice how her mam had been looking ever more exhausted since Christmas, but Mary had refused to talk about it. Delia had told her about Mam's 'little turn' in the shop, but Mary had shrugged that off too. And there was no money for a doctor even if her mam could be persuaded to see one. She resolved to talk to her da about it.

Richie, however, really didn't think Mary was ill enough for a doctor. 'I know she's not well but sometimes, well, sometimes she just uses it to sort of get at me. To make me feel guilty.'

Tessa was horrified. 'Oh, Da! That's a terrible thing to say! I *do* think she should see a doctor and so does Mrs Harrison.'

'She's fine, honestly. And where would we find the money, Tessa, luv?'

She nodded but she was unconvinced. If only he didn't waste so much money, she thought, there would be a possibility to save up.

Johnny Doyle returned from his first trip two days before the wedding. As soon as he could get away from home, he joined his friends who had gathered at the tannery when they heard he was back.

'I bet you were sick.'

'I bloody wasn't, Mike.'

'Oh, the lies some people tell,' Elizabeth jeered.

'I *wasn't*. A born sailor, so the Chief Steward said. They call him a "Three Ringer" because of the three gold bands on his uniform sleeve. *That* feller is as sharp as a razor and knows all the antics that go on. And you wouldn't believe what half of them get up to,' Johnny said with pride. It was true: to his own amazement he hadn't been sick.

'You've only got to see the state of the stokers *before* they sail.' Mike knew a lot of them, they lived locally. They were all members of Cunard's 'Black Gangs'.

'Was the weather really bad? What were the passengers like?' Elizabeth pressed.

'Most of them were sick and stayed in their bunks all day. The weather was terrible, we were thrown all over the place. One waiter had a broken arm, a steward had a broken leg, and I was dead scared, I'll tell you. God! You wouldn't believe it. Enormous waves came crashing down and all the decks were under water. I just prayed the ship would come up again and she did. Time after time. The noise was frightening. It was as if the sea was deliberately trying to . . . to crush us.'

'I wouldn't fancy that much,' Tessa said hesitantly. She still felt shy among the old friends. She hardly knew Johnny, although he'd been so kind their first day in Naylor Street, and he had greeted her warmly today.

Johnny smiled at her. He really did like her. It was hard to believe she had a brother like Colin. They were as different as chalk and cheese. 'You don't have to worry about me, Tessa.'

She became confused. 'I . . . I didn't mean . . . it like that. Well, I did, in a way, I . . .' She fell silent and her cheeks began to burn. Sometimes she was such a fool.

Johnny pretended not to notice. 'There was a lot of damage. Half the lifeboats had gone and the deckchairs had been swept away. The rails were all twisted and so was the monkey island.'

'What's that when it's at home?'

'Don't you know *anything* about ships, Mike? It's part of the bridge. Not the wheelhouse, but the bits that stick out so the Old Man can see the sides of the ship when you dock.'

'Oh, never mind all that! What was New York like?' Elizabeth demanded impatiently.

'Great! Absolutely great! The buildings are so tall and close together but there's a huge park in the middle. That statue they've got – Liberty – is enormous. You can climb up inside it. And the bridges – well, I didn't think we'd get under the Verrazano-Narrows bridge. It's the first one, after that there's two more. But there's people of every colour and religion and it seemed as if all the hustle and bustle went on day and night!'

'Our Brenda's wedding won't seem much fun after all that,' Mike said enviously.

'It will! I'm all in favour of any kind of "do". They won't let me have a bloody drop of *anything*. I'm too young. And they won't let me into the Pig and Whistle either.'

Everyone laughed. It was a term they all knew. The crew bar on all ships was called the 'Pig and Whistle'.

They'd all trooped up to St Anthony's on the Saturday morning early, so as to get there before the bridal party.

None of the girls wore the outfits they would wear that evening, but Ginny's hair had a lovely shine on it, Tessa noticed, and her own hairstyle had drawn compliments from her da and even from Colin.

Brenda had in the end got her own way over the carriage and Eileen was looking very smart in Delia's hat and coat over a blue and cream check dress she'd got second-hand from O'Dwyer's on Great Homer Street.

She was quite proud of her efforts. They were all turned out neatly if not grandly. Frank wore his good suit, returned from the pawnbroker's for the occasion. It would go back there on Monday morning, as would Mike's suit and Harold's Norfolk jacket. They hadn't let her down. Frank had been shadowed all morning by Maureen in all her finery, much to their mutual annoyance.

'Don't you let yer da out of yer sight for a second!' had been Eileen's exact instruction as she'd removed the curling papers she'd lost a lot of sleep over the previous night.

As the first triumphant notes of the organ thundered out the Bridal March from *Lohengrin* everyone turned to look at the bride.

'Doesn't she look gorgeous!' Ginny hissed to Tessa. If and when she got married it was something like this she wanted.

Brenda did look radiant. The dress was of plain white satin with the high neck and long sleeves the church demanded, but it was trimmed around the neck, cuffs and train with lace. She had a wreath of wax orange blossom on her head that held in place the full-length tulle veil.

'Would you look at the gob on their Maureen,' Johnny Doyle whispered to Tessa.

'She hates the dress – well, the colour anyway. She wanted to wear red.'

'She would. She'd be all powder, lipstick and rouge if her mam hadn't stopped her,' Ginny added in a loud whisper.

'What time are you coming round tonight?' Elizabeth asked.

'Dunno really. As soon after seven as possible.'

'Is your mam going?' Ginny asked Johnny.

'No. I think she wanted to but Da's got a cob on.'

'Why?'

'Because they won't all be in the pub putting money

in his till. And they weren't in today.'

'I should think not. Who on earth starts drinking at this time of day?' Elizabeth said indignantly.

'I don't know what he's got to moan about. Half the guests will be in there this afternoon. They should have weddings later, it's murder hanging around all afternoon. The fellers either go to the pub or a football match and all the owld women drink port and lemon and pull everyone to bits,' Ginny added.

'I'll call for you both at half past seven,' Elizabeth said firmly.

'Mam might want us all to go together, us being new, like,' Tessa said.

'My mam won't mind me coming with you.'

'Neither will mine,' Ginny added.

'Besides, it will mean I can get away from our Nessie.'

'Are the younger kids going too?' Tessa was surprised.

'Yes. No one dares leave them at home. God knows what they'd get up to. At least if they're at the "do" everyone can see that they're behaving.'

'It's usually the grown-ups who don't behave. The kids are all right.'

'Except for the time Harold Flynn and Bertie Miller ate all the ice cream and were as sick as pigs. Serves them right.'

'I heard their mams battered the pair of them next day after they'd got over their hangovers,' Johnny laughed.

Delia turned around. 'Will you lot kindly remember where you are, jangling away like that! It's a disgrace.'

They all looked very nice, so Mary told them when Elizabeth

and Ginny called. She'd never seen Tessa looking so smart. She knew she herself looked dowdy, as did Richie and young Jimmy. Only Colin looked decent, in a shirt, tie, trousers and sports jacket. Where he'd got them she didn't know. She didn't want to know either.

'You behave yourselves, all of you. We're newcomers, remember, and people have been very good to us. I don't want anyone pointing a finger and saying what a disgrace we are,' she'd instructed all of them.

The party was already in full swing and had spilled out into the street, but Elizabeth pushed her way down the Flynns' lobby to the kitchen followed by the others.

'What a crush!' Ginny complained.

'I know. It's murder,' Mike added.

'What's it like in the back yard?' Elizabeth asked.

'Just as bad,' came the despondent reply.

'Well, I don't fancy standing up all night,' Ginny stated.

'Aren't you going to have a bit of a whirl around the floor then?' Colin asked. This looked like a good 'do' and there had hardly been many exciting occasions of late.

'Whirl! Around what floor?' Tessa demanded.

'Don't be such a misery. Enjoy yourself,' he answered before pushing his way to where the beer was, followed by his father.

'We could sit on the stairs,' Elizabeth suggested.

'The kids are there,' Johnny pointed out.

'Well, we'll shift them.'

Clutching glasses of beer that Mike had managed to get for them, they cleared the younger children off the stairs.

Nessie, who wore a huge red bow of satin ribbon in her hair, glared at her sister when told to move. The stairs were a good vantage point. She protested vehemently, but the protest wasn't taken up by the others.

'And you look like a chocolate box with that enormous bow in your hair!' was Elizabeth's parting shot, after Nessie said she looked a mess in her frock.

Tessa sipped her drink and then pulled a face. 'It's horrible.'

'I know. Mike, why couldn't you get us some sherry instead of ale?'

'Because me mam and Aunty Hilda and Aunty Madge finished all that off this afternoon. They're all half-cut now but me mam says that after all the arguing and worry she's going to enjoy the bloody party.'

'I thought your mam and Aunty Madge had had a row,' Elizabeth said.

'That's all over now.'

Elizabeth grinned at him. 'How you put up with your family I'll never know. You're so easy-going, you just take everything in your stride, you never seem to get annoyed.'

Mike shrugged. 'What's the point of getting a cob on over things? There are enough rows as it is.'

'Laugh and the world laughs with you, cry and you cry alone.'

'You've always got some saying or other.'

It was Elizabeth's turn to shrug. 'It's having to go to that terrible school. I wish I had your attitude, it would help me cope with trailing up there every day.'

'Where's the happy couple?' Ginny asked, peering around.

'In the parlour with the ma-in-law, and you should see the gobs on all three of them. The sooner they all get to Breck Road the better. Even me da's given up on them.'

'Why?' Tessa asked.

''Cos he's out for the count. Blind paralytic drunk,' Mike laughed.

'Oh, that's great, isn't it,' Elizabeth said scathingly.

'Well, are you going to have a dance, Elizabeth?' Johnny Doyle asked.

'We'll be crushed to death.'

'I'll make some room.'

'It won't matter much because Arnold Roberts plays everything at the same speed.'

Tessa laughed. 'Where did they get the piano?'

'It's on loan from a blockerman. I just hope he gets it back in one piece or me da will be out of favour, not to say a job.'

Colin had returned and sat down on the stair next to Ginny. He'd managed to swig two bottles of stout and was feeling confident. What's more, little Ginny Greely looked very attractive. He didn't know what she'd done to herself – he'd hardly noticed her before.

'You look nice tonight, Ginny.'

'Thanks. You don't look bad yourself.' Ginny sipped the bitter drink again. She really didn't know him very well.

'That's terrible stuff for a girl to drink.'

'I know, but it seems there's nothing else.'

'Well, put it down and come and have a dance. We can get to know each other better, like.'

Ginny felt shy and not like her usual self at all as she followed him.

Tessa watched him. Ginny was far too nice and far too trusting for Colin, but there was nothing she could do.

Elizabeth arrived back with Johnny, her face flushed. 'It's

terrible! I haven't got a single toe that hasn't been trodden on.'

'Mainly by me. Come on, Tessa, will you chance it?'

'If you want swollen feet then go on,' Elizabeth laughed.

Tessa let Johnny lead her into the parlour where Brenda and her new husband, plus a grim-faced elderly woman, sat stiff as ramrods in chairs that were equally upright. They all had faces like thunder, but their presence didn't seem to be dampening the merriment that was going on around them. In the mêlée she caught sight and sound of Eileen Flynn, propped up against the piano singing 'A Nice Cup of Tea' discordantly.

'I don't think my mam will approve of that,' Tessa shouted over the din.

'What?' Johnny asked.

'The state of Mrs Flynn.'

'Then she won't approve of your da, he's in more or less the same state. Of course, *she's* been at it all afternoon!'

Tessa bit her lip. Some of her exuberance had gone as she thought about her mam. Despite Richie's reassurance, she was still afraid there was something seriously wrong.

'It is a wedding, Tessa. Everyone's come to enjoy themselves. Relax!'

Tessa smiled. She did feel at ease with Johnny now. 'I will! But Ginny looks as if she's enjoying it a bit too much. Our Colin's up to something. He's not to be trusted.'

Ginny *was* enjoying herself. She'd never met anyone like Colin O'Leary before. He was so sure of himself. He'd told her *he* wasn't going to be living here hard up all his life. She'd never met a lad with ambition and plans for the future before.

'Will you come out with me, Ginny?'

She was taken aback. 'Out?'

'Yeah, on a date? We could go to the pictures.'

Ginny flushed and felt a little light-headed. She'd never had a date before and she wasn't very sure what her mam would say.

'I'd . . . I'd like to but I'll have to ask Mam.'

'Is she here?'

'Yes. She got off work early.'

'Then let's ask her.' And taking a flustered and blushing Ginny by the hand he went in search of May Greely.

He found her in the kitchen laughing and joking with a group of men.

'Mrs Greely, can we have a word, please?' Colin smiled at her. He could see no objection: her own reputation wasn't unblemished.

'Who are you?' May demanded.

'I'm Colin O'Leary, Tessa's brother, and I've come to ask you if I can take Ginny to the pictures one night in the week?'

May was startled. 'She's only fourteen.' Then, seeing the protest in her daughter's eyes, added, 'Nearly fifteen.'

'I'm sixteen, nearly seventeen, and I'll take good care of her.'

May shrugged and then laughed. 'Oh, go on then. The pair of you are still wet behind the ears.'

'Oh, thanks, Mam! Thanks, I—'

Ginny's words were drowned by a terrible screeching and screaming.

'Holy Mother of God! What's that? What's Delia doing, for God's sake?'

'I'm trying to separate these young hooligans, that's what I'm trying to do, May, and I'd appreciate some help!'

The noise level dropped considerably.

'I can't believe it. Just look at the mess this little madam has made of Harold's face. I think they've been drinking everyone's dregs.'

Nessie and Harold were yelling and kicking and punching like a pair of small furies and both Harold and Jimmy's faces bore the scratches from Nessie's fingernails.

Mary pushed her way through the crowd and took her son by the ear. She was mortified. Not only was her husband barely able to stand, her younger son was fighting like a tearaway. Now what would people think of them? She caught hold of Jimmy by the front of his shirt and slapped him hard across the face.

Harold and Nessie had been dragged apart but Nessie was still screaming until Delia used the same tactic on her daughter.

'Where's your da?' Delia demanded of Harold.

'He's no use, Mrs Harrison,' Ginny informed her.

Delia looked at Mary and saw understanding in the woman's eyes.

'Right. Home, milady, right now. And you can think yourself lucky your da doesn't take off his belt and use it on you all the way back. Elizabeth, get your coat.'

'Ah, Mam, that's not fair! She's the one in trouble, not me.'

Delia was furious. 'I said, get your coat! Do I have to fetch your father to you too?'

Tessa was at her mother's side. 'I'll take him home, Mam,' she offered, looking sympathetically at her friend.

'Thanks, luv, but I'll see to him myself. As for your da . . . he can sleep on the step for all I care.'

'You just can't trust any of them not to make a show of you, can you? Get out of that door, the pair of you,' Delia said grimly. Nessie was in for a hiding when she got her home.

Mary nodded her heartfelt agreement. God knows where Colin was or what he was up to, but she didn't care. She had enough on her hands already with Richie drunk and Jimmy now bawling his eyes out.

''Bye, Tessa,' Elizabeth said. After Mam had finished with Nessie, her sister was going to get a belt from her too; she'd ruined the night.

''Bye.' Tessa turned to look for her friends but couldn't see them so they left, leaving Colin slightly subdued and Mike Flynn wondering where he could sleep with the house still crowded out and both his parents now unconscious. He wished he could go home with Elizabeth. It always seemed so peaceful in their house. It was tidy and organised and no one shouted or yelled, except in extreme cases, and it had to be very extreme indeed for Delia to raise her voice. She'd demonstrated that tonight. She'd dealt with all the fuss quickly and calmly. He looked wistfully at the door through which Jack and Delia had led their children. Oh, yes, it would be great to go home with them.

Chapter Nine

By March it was clear, even to Richie O'Leary, that his wife was seriously ill. All through the winter months of January and February, since she had confessed to the pains, she had seemed to get thinner and thinner. Quite often she couldn't stand the pain she was in and would cry out loud or grip the table or sink so tightly that her knuckles would be white. Her face was that of an old, old woman, drawn, haggard, lined; her eyes looked enormous, ringed with dark shadows.

Tessa had easily slipped into the well-ordered routine at the Convent and had even earned praise from Sister Augustine, always a force to be reckoned with. But it was to Sister Bernadette, the other nun with whom she worked in the kitchens, that she confided her worries, one day when they were both sitting at the big scrubbed table, peeling vegetables, surrounded by pans and enamelled bowls.

'I'm watching her fade away before my eyes,' Tessa said with desperation.

'Then you must get a doctor in to see her, Tessa.'

'We haven't got any money for doctors. There's the rent, the gas, the coal and that's before food and clothes, cleaning stuff and bits of furniture. There's only Da's wages and mine. He's being really great. He's keeping his promises. He only has one pint of beer a day, two on Saturdays.'

'Then you must try to find a few pence a week. You can have all the money in the world, but if you haven't got your health, then you have nothing. Apart from your faith in Jesus Christ.' Sister Bernadette reached over and patted Tessa's hand.

'She just wouldn't see a doctor. She'd go mad if I even mentioned it.'

'In this case I think you will find that the end justifies the means. Don't take no for an answer, Tessa. It's for her own good. She does her best for all of you – isn't it better for *you* to risk a little bit of wrath for *her* good?'

'Yes, you're right. I'll start saving and our Jimmy can go collecting empty jam jars and lemonade bottles and we'll add that to the rest.' She wished she'd made the decision sooner.

'She's right,' Tessa said to Elizabeth as they walked to the bottom of Everton Valley, Tessa with the folds of her shawl held tightly to her face, Elizabeth clutching her school hat for the wind was strong and blustery.

'Just don't tell her until the doctor arrives on the front step. She can't tell him to go away then, can she?' Elizabeth suggested.

'I wouldn't put it past her, she's so stubborn. Oh, Elizabeth, she's so pale and thin.'

'I know. Mam's worried too. She was only saying the other day that she looks like two eyes on a stick. Come in with me first, before you go home, and we'll see what my mam can suggest.'

Tessa nodded. She was really very, very worried about her mam. It seemed a huge effort for her to even lift a pan, let alone tackle the washing and ironing. Either Jimmy, Colin or herself brought the coal bucket in, for that was completely beyond her strength.

They didn't get as far as the shop, for young Jimmy came running at full belt down the street, his face ashen, his eyes wide with fright.

'Jimmy! Jimmy, what's the matter?'

'It's Mam ... Mam ...' he panted, clutching at Tessa's shawl. His shoulders were heaving with his efforts.

Tessa caught hold of him and steadied him. 'What's the matter with Mam?'

'She ... she ... was just putting the kettle on when ... I ... got in. I was next door, but she had to keep sitting down ... and then ...'

Tessa shook him. 'Then *what*?'

'She ... she ... sort of crumpled in a heap and fell on the floor. I ... I ... can't wake her up, Tessa.' He burst into tears but they were ignored.

'You go in and see to her, I'm going for Mam!' Elizabeth instructed before breaking into a run.

Tessa ran inside and found Mary, just as Jimmy had said, lying unconscious on the floor.

Instantly she was on her knees beside her mother and gently shook her shoulders. 'Oh, Mam! Mam! Wake up! Tell me what's wrong! Tell me what's the matter, please?' she begged. She heard her younger brother's sobs but she took no notice, her own eyes were full of tears. Oh, why couldn't Mam hear her? Why didn't she open her eyes? She was cradling Mary's head in her lap, the tears streaming down her cheeks, when Delia Harrison and Eileen Flynn arrived simultaneously, Eileen alerted by Tessa's cries and Jimmy's sobs heard clearly through the wall.

'Oh, Mother of God! What's up with her?' Eileen demanded of Tessa.

'I don't know. Jimmy said she just crumpled up and fell on the floor. I can't make her hear me!'

'Eileen, help me get her on to the sofa,' Delia instructed.

The two women, assisted by Tessa and Elizabeth, who had followed her mother, managed to lift Mary's inert form on to the old leather sofa that was Mary's latest acquisition from Hennessy's.

'Why won't she wake up?' Tessa demanded frantically.

Eileen and Delia exchanged glances.

'God, she's nothing but a bag of bones!' Eileen said worriedly. 'I never realised. I just *never* realised.'

'Elizabeth, go back home, take five shillings out of my purse and go round to Dr Duncan and tell him he's needed urgently, very urgently.'

Elizabeth ran.

'Maybe we should call for an ambulance?'

'No! If she's anything like me, I'd sooner suffer in me own 'ome than go into a hospital. I've never known anyone yet who came out alive. Usually it's feet first from *those* places.' Eileen shivered.

'They're not *that* bad,' Delia said swiftly, noticing Tessa's appalled expression, 'but we'll wait and see what Dr Duncan says.'

Gently Delia examined Mary's head to see if she had struck it on something as she'd fallen but there was nothing to indicate that she had: no cuts or bruising on her temples.

'Have you got a blanket, Tessa?'

'Yes, there's one on our bed.'

'Is it . . . decent?' Delia asked. The poor woman would be mortified if, when the doctor arrived, all she had to cover her was an old coat. Doctors were very respected, not to say revered.

'It's not too bad.'

'Then go on up and get it, child.'

When Tessa had gone Delia shook her head. 'Whatever it is, I don't think she's long for this world. We've both seen enough of disease and death not to recognise the signs.'

Eileen crossed herself. 'Oh, God luv her, the life she's had. Terrible, terrible 'ard. Worse than me even and that's saying something. And she was always tryin' to provide a good 'ome for them all. Every single thing she has in this poor 'ome is cleaned and scrubbed and polished. There's some kind of 'ot meal on the table for them and 'er washin' is a sight for sore eyes. Always step-dashin' an' all. What do you think it is?'

'I know it's not consumption: in the short time I've known her I've never heard her cough and she doesn't have that sort of "look" about her.'

'Do you think it's, you know, women's trouble?' Eileen patted her stomach.

'I don't know, Eileen, but it's serious. As you said, God help her, she's been dragging herself around since Christmas, getting steadily worse. At least she's managed to get a few more things around her.' Delia glanced about the kitchen. 'Not much in the way of comforts, mind, but she was getting there, bit by bit.'

'She'd have got there sooner if *he'd* stayed off the ale completely and that young no-mark had got himself some work. Steady work, I mean.'

'I know. But Richie's not bad. In fact I quite like him. He's easy-going, always pleasant. There's no harm in him.

He's just . . . thoughtless. I don't think he really *thinks* about anything.'

'I know, I've got one the same at home.'

'Tessa's the only one who really worries about Mary.'

They both cut short their deliberations as Tessa came back with the blanket, a fairly thick but coarse grey Army one.

Delia tucked it around Mary. Earlier, Eileen had rolled up Tessa's shawl to make a pillow.

'Will Dr Duncan come out?' Tessa asked, gnawing at her bottom lip.

'Of course he will. He's not like some I could name who won't set foot in a house in this neighbourhood. *You* have to go to *them* and they still look down their noses at you,' Delia answered firmly. She had a lot of faith in Dr Duncan.

'I wish she would just open her eyes, even for a second.'

'Well, she's not banged her head or anything like that, we've looked,' Delia answered reassuringly. 'Go and stand at the door, Tessa.'

Glad of *something* to do, Tessa left the room.

The minutes dragged. They were interminable, Tessa thought as she stood peering down the street. Why was he taking so long? It wasn't all *that* far away.

At last she saw the car turn into the street, accompanied by a small group of scruffy young boys, half of them barefoot.

Elizabeth jumped out and yelled at the entourage and they all scuttled away, then stopped and continued to watch from a safe distance.

'Oh, you've been ages,' Tessa said, gripping Elizabeth's arm while Dr Duncan got out of the car.

'I ran as fast as I could. I couldn't even speak when I got there.'

'I'm sorry, it's just that I'm *so* worried.'

'I know. Come on, let's go into the kitchen.'

The two girls went in, followed by the doctor.

'She's unconscious, Doctor, and I don't know for how long,' Delia informed him.

'Right. The first thing we have to do, Mrs Harrison, is to get rid of everyone except yourself and . . .' He looked around at the small group. Elizabeth and Eileen he knew; the young lad he didn't.

'Me! Please, Doctor? Can I stay?' Tessa begged.

'Tessa is her only daughter, and she's been a great help to her mother,' Delia added.

'Very well. But the rest of you must leave.'

Eileen took Jimmy's hand. 'Come on, lad, you an' our 'Arold can 'ave a sugar butty in our 'ouse and wait for your da to get 'ome.'

'Elizabeth, go on home and help your da and see that our Nessie does her homework. I know she does it after tea but I think tea will be late tonight.'

With a sympathetic glance at Tessa, Elizabeth left.

Dr Duncan then took Mary's claw-like hand, checking her pulse. He eased her eyelids up gently to reveal unseeing eyes.

'Mrs Harrison, could you and the young girl take off her jumper and skirt?'

Gently, Tessa did so while Delia supported Mary. Dr Duncan had taken a stethoscope from his black leather Gladstone bag. As his gaze travelled over Mary's form he shook his head and sighed deeply. He knew he had been called for far too late. In fact, even if he'd been called much sooner there would have been nothing he could do for the poor woman, except to ease the pain. It was cancer. It didn't matter exactly where it had struck first, now she was riddled with it.

'What is it . . . please?' Tessa begged.

He looked up at Delia then Tessa. 'I won't tell you a pack of lies, child. Your mother is ill. Very ill.'

'Is there . . . nothing you can do?'

'I'm afraid not. All I can do is give you some medicine to ease the pain. God help us, the poor woman must have been in agony,' he muttered under his breath. Delia put her arm around Tessa's shoulders. It was best to know, she thought.

'How long?' she asked.

'Not very long, I'm afraid. Her condition must have been deteriorating for some time.'

'Days? Weeks? Months?' Delia pressed.

'Weeks, I'd say. You know I'm not a person who believes in euphemisms or false hopes, Mrs Harrison.'

'Will she . . . will she wake up?' Tessa asked timidly.

He nodded and smiled sympathetically at the girl. Death was no stranger in these hard streets. 'She will, though the medicine will make her sleep for most of the time. But you'll be able to talk to her and on her "good" days – and there will be a few – she'll be able to speak.'

'She . . . she . . . she's going to die?'

Delia held Tessa tightly, her own tears not far away. 'I'm afraid so, luv. You've known – you've seen how much pain she was in.'

Tessa couldn't take it in. She'd known Mam was in terrible pain, but she'd thought that once the doctor had seen her, he would know what was wrong and would then be able to cure her. Now . . . now Mam was going to die. She was going to leave them and there was nothing anyone could do.

As Delia showed the doctor to his car, Tessa knelt down beside her mother and took one of Mary's work-roughened hands and held it to her cheek. She couldn't speak. She felt as though a hand had gripped her throat, she could barely swallow and hardly breathe. Her mam . . . her lovely mam who had suffered so much was . . . dying.

She looked up as Delia returned, accompanied by Richie.

'Tessa, luv, go on down to our Elizabeth. I have to talk to your da.'

'No! No! I'm not leaving her.'

'Tessa, luv, go on. Everything will be . . . settled.' She could hardly say 'all right'.

With great reluctance Tessa stood up and turned away. Her da looked stupefied, she thought, as she passed him.

'I . . . I . . . can't believe it, Delia. I knew she was sick, but—'

'Didn't you even *think* she should see a doctor?'

'She's been like this for ages.' Richie looked down at his wife. He was completely dumbfounded.

'All the more reason. What will you do?'

'Me? Do? I . . . I . . . ?' He was floundering. He couldn't even think straight. What would they do without her? What would *he* do without her? She was the one who held them together through good times and bad. She was the strong one, not him. This couldn't be happening.

'Oh, you're a lot of use, Richie, aren't you?' Delia said sharply. He might be pleasant but he must always have been pretty useless, judging from his behaviour since they moved here and Mary's own words about her husband's failings. She knew he was the reason they were here in the first place.

'I don't know what to do,' he pleaded.

Suddenly she felt sorry for him. He genuinely didn't know and she realised that he had never done so.

'We'll work something out, Richie. We'll all take turns in nursing her. Tessa will have to go on working up there at the Convent.'

'Why?'

'Because you need the money,' Delia answered, but it wasn't the main reason. If she stayed at home, Tessa would just become a drudge, a skivvy at their beck and call, and for a girl as young as she was that just wasn't fair. Oh, she knew there were hundreds like her, struggling to bring up children, keeping families together, but how they suffered for it. They lost an education, and therefore any chance of a decent job. There was little opportunity for a social life and they were thereby denied a chance to be courted. She liked Tessa – in her place, of course – although the girl wouldn't amount to much. All Tessa could expect was to continue in the Convent, meet someone decent and get married. It wasn't what Delia planned for Elizabeth, but Tessa deserved her chance. Delia wouldn't turn her back on Tessa's plight, not when time was so short and there were enough people to help out.

'Eileen Flynn, myself, May Greely, Tessa, and some of the other neighbours will work out a plan, so that no one really suffers at this . . . difficult time.'

Richie just stared at her blankly.

Delia lost her patience. 'Oh, get up to the pub, for God's sake. You're more of a hindrance than a help. Just give Eileen a knock, she's got your Jimmy. Where is the other one? Your Colin?'

Richie just shook his head. He had no idea, nor did he care.

'God help her, what a shower of useless layabouts she's had to put up with. Your Tessa is the only one of you with any go about her.'

Silently, his shoulders sagging, Richie turned away.

Chapter Ten

Delia had called a meeting of all the neighbours and, once the evening meal was over and the dishes washed and put away, one by one they arrived and all crowded into her kitchen. Those earliest to arrive seated themselves on the sofa, armchairs and straight-backed chairs that Delia had placed around the room. The latecomers had to stand. Both Elizabeth and Nessie had been sent to bed, Elizabeth under protest.

'I'm going on fifteen, I'm not a kid, like she is. Why can't I stay up? There must be *something* I can do.'

'If there is then I'll tell you in the morning. I don't want to hear any complaints or moans or tantrums, I've enough on my mind without you two making things worse. Get up those stairs, the pair of you.'

Delia had been very firm and so they both went off in a huff, Elizabeth because, in her opinion, she had been treated unfairly. This concerned Tessa and Tessa was her friend and would need all the help she could get now. It was awful for poor Tessa; she herself couldn't even begin to imagine what she would do if it had been her own mam who was lying in bed, dying.

Nessie too was feeling very disgruntled. It wasn't as if she would go up and down the street blabbing about it. It was too serious for that. It must be really terrible for some strange doctor to come and tell you your mam was going to die.

Still, she took consolation from the fact that Elizabeth had been excluded too.

'Most of you will have heard the bad news about Mrs O'Leary . . . Mary. For those that haven't: the poor woman is dying. She's been ill since Christmas but never admitted it.'

Maisie Keegan was the first to speak after Delia had passed round cups of tea. 'We don't really know 'er very well, do we? She kept 'erself to 'erself.'

'I suppose we don't, but put yourself in her place, Maisie. The poor woman is dying. She must be worried sick about her kids. She can't keep the home going either.'

'What's wrong with their Tessa? She doesn't seem to do very much up there with the nuns,' Katie Collins complained. She still carried a grudge against Tessa, for her daughter Alice could have done with a job like that. The money wasn't good, but there were perks and it gave you a bit of status, not working in a factory or shop.

Delia glared at her. 'Well, this is a nice way of going on, I must say. Very Christian of you, Katie Collins, when we all took turns seeing to *your* mam when you had to go out to work to keep a roof over your head and food on the table.' Delia's tone was scathing and Katie Collins looked uncomfortable.

Then Delia went on, brisk and business-like: 'She'll need someone to see to her throughout the day and later on I think through the night as well. Then there's all the other things. Tessa can get herself and the rest of them out to work and school and then when she comes home from work herself she can see to the evening meal.'

'I'll go in in the mornings and maybe later on in the evening and Jimmy can come 'ome from school with our

'Arold and stay until bedtime,' Eileen offered.

'I don't mind doing the washing,' Maisie Keegan added. 'And there will be quite a bit of that.'

'Not *that* much, Maisie, there's no sheets or anything like that, but I suppose that's a blessing in a way. We'd better start now and save the newspapers. She'll need to lie on them – later on, like.'

'I'll take a turn with you, Delia,' Katie Collins offered grudgingly, 'in the afternoons.'

'I'll give Eileen a bit of help in the mornings. I'm at work all evening,' May Greely offered. 'And when it's time, later on, I'll come in for a few hours when I finish at work, say until two in the morning.'

'I'll see to it that there's enough food and heat, it's the least I can do,' Delia stated.

'What about that useless lad of hers? I don't know what he does for a job, but he never seems to be at home and he never seems to want for much either.'

'God knows what he does, Maisie, she'd never say, but he'll have to pull his weight from now on. I'll deal with him.'

'What about 'er 'usband?' Maisie asked.

Delia sighed. 'He's as much use as a wet *Echo*. He's just . . . lost. Doesn't know what to do or say. I sent him up to the pub in the end.'

'And what use would that be?' Katie Collins demanded, looking pointedly at May.

'He's out from under Tessa's feet,' Delia shot back.

May got up. 'Well, I'd best get back up there myself. The old skinflint said an hour and he'll dock it out of my wages.' She would have liked to have stayed on and gossiped as sometimes she went for days without seeing her neighbours.

She was sorry for the poor woman but she knew Delia was right about Richie. He wouldn't be able to cope very well, left to his own devices. It would be Tessa who would carry the heavy burden alone if they didn't help out.

They all began to finish their tea and get their things together.

'There's one thing we haven't talked about.'

'And what's that, Katie?' Delia asked sharply. She'd never had much time for the woman. She was a trouble-maker.

'Where the money's going to come from to bury 'er?'

Everyone, except May, sat down again. It was the greatest humiliation of all for the deceased to be buried in a pauper's grave.

'Do we have to talk about it now?' May asked.

'I think we do.' Delia spoke for them all.

May sighed. 'Look, I'll *have* to be going, but whatever you decide include me in it.' She buttoned up her coat and left them to it.

'What are we going ter do? She won't be in no Burial Club, coming 'ere with not a stick of furniture even.'

Delia had been thinking rapidly. The whole cost couldn't be borne by the neighbours. 'I'll go to all the businesses. Birrel's, the pub, Rooney's Greengrocer's up on the corner, and see what I can get out of them. After all, where would they be without us?'

'Eddie Doyle should cough up a fair bit, the amount of money Richie O'Leary has spent in that pub. Bevvied as the landlord's cat half the time, 'e used ter be,' Eileen said.

'That feller wouldn't give yer the sniff of the barmaid's apron,' added Katie.

'And then we'll all have to chip in, like. I know most of you are hard up—'

'Hard up! Giz a laugh, Delia!' Maisie interrupted. 'Hardly a penny ter bless yerself with in our 'ouse. My feller's as bad as your Frank, Eileen.'

'Well, give me what you can,' Delia urged.

'Make sure you tell 'er who's gone up ter the alehouse.'

'I will, Katie,' Delia said firmly, getting to her feet. The conflab was over. She'd known they would all help out.

Richie had gone into the Globe and straight to the bar, but he was so confused that he couldn't order his usual. In fact he couldn't speak.

'What's up with you?' Eddie Doyle asked. He was a dour man with very little humour. In fact a lot of the time his customers wondered why they went there. The excuse was that it was nearby, close enough for some of them to stagger the few yards home. Eddie Doyle was a man who said 'the towel's on' and meant it.

Richie could only shake his head.

'Yer'd better give 'im a drop of the Pope's phone number,' Frank Flynn said with concern. In the short time he'd known Richie, he'd never seen his next-door neighbour in such a state.

'Tharrell do! I'll thank you not to be making jokes about His Holiness in the alehouse. And I'm not dishing out glasses of the best Vat 69 whisky unless someone's going to pay for it.'

'An' yer call yerself a good Catholic? Near eating the flaming altar rails on a Sunday an' first inter confession on a Saturday,' Frank Flynn remarked cuttingly.

'The feller's in shock, yer can see that. Give 'im a drop of the crater,' Billy Keegan instructed. 'I'll pay!' He slapped down the money on the bar counter and Eddie Doyle measured the whisky into a small glass.

'Get that down yer, lad,' Billy urged. Richie's hand was shaking as he picked up the glass and drained it in one go.

'So, what's up with yer?' Frank asked.

'It's . . . the wife.'

'Jesus, yer not goin' ter start bloody moanin' about 'er. We come 'ere ter get away from them,' Mick Collins objected.

'She's . . . she's . . . dying.'

There was silence and Frank indicated to Eddie Doyle that more whisky was required. This time there was no request for payment. Eddie Doyle was as shocked as the rest of them.

'How? When? What with?' Mick Collins asked. Richie drank the contents of the glass more slowly this time.

'Delia Harrison sent for the doctor. He . . . he took one look at her and said . . . it was only weeks . . . she had left. Some sort of growth . . . some disease, I can't remember its name . . . has been eating away at her. Oh, Jesus Christ Almighty, and I thought she was just moaning, trying to get sympathy. Trying to make me feel guilty! I didn't know! I just didn't know!'

'How could you?' Eddie Doyle asked with more compassion in his voice than any of them had ever heard before.

'I *should* have listened to her. I should have *thought* more. She's lost so much weight, there's not a pick on her! I didn't stop to think about that even.'

'If we all took that attitude, Richie, we'd go round the flaming bend.'

'That's not much bloody comfort, is it?' Billy Keegan retorted.

Richie continued to shake his head in disbelief.

'Don't worry too much about it, lad, the women are dead good when things like this happen. They'll get themselves organised. Look after her, see to the 'ouse, things like that. And if yer 'aven't got the price of a bevvy, we'll all stand yer a pint.' God knows yer going ter need it, Frank Flynn said under his breath.

Elizabeth was sitting with Tessa in the kitchen. When the neighbours had left she'd begged Delia to let her go. 'Mam, please? It must be awful for her. She'll be on her own and terribly upset, I know how much she loves her mam. She's been worried for ages.'

'All right, but don't be too long. I know it's been a shock but she's got work in the morning and you've got school.'

'Do we both *have* to go? I mean, what will people think?'

'They won't *think* anything. In fact it's the best place for both of you. You can offer up your prayers for Mrs O'Leary and the nuns will too. I'll write a note for Mother Superior, you can pass it in.'

Mary had been moved to her bed and Jimmy was staying next door at Eileen's. Mary had come round for a few minutes, long enough for Delia to give her the medicine and for Tessa to tell her things were being looked after.

'I don't want to leave her on her own, and she will be if I go to work.'

'She won't be on her own, Tessa. Mam will organise

everything. She's good at organising people,' Elizabeth answered glumly.

'It's all so . . . confusing. I can't think straight. So much has happened so soon. What about Da and Jimmy and *him*?'

'I told you, Mam will see to everything.'

'Where will I sleep?' Tessa's eyes were pleading and full of tears.

'With your mam. Look, I'll ask Mam if I can bring my quilt up, make things warmer and more . . . cheerful for you both. And some pillows too.'

'Oh, Elizabeth, I'm glad we came here, what would have happened if I didn't have you, your mam and . . . everyone?'

'Don't think like that. Do you still have donkey's breakfasts?'

Tessa nodded.

'Not for much longer. I'll tell Mam you need a proper mattress and a proper bed,' she added generously. She knew her mam and da wouldn't mind the expense. You couldn't leave the poor woman on a straw mattress on the hard, cold floor.

They both jumped as the front door slammed and Colin came into the room, looking very pleased with himself. He'd bought a suit and a shirt with the money he'd won in a pitch and toss game and then he'd been tipped off about a horse. The odds were good and he'd given Bert Meadows, who was a bookie's runner, half a crown to win. It was a dead cert and he'd won a couple of pounds. He had actually been into the Liverpool Savings Bank, to get his bearings: how far from the door the counter was; how many people – staff and customers – were inside at the time; how much time he'd need to grab the money; and just how far he would have to run before he would be safe.

He'd asked the teller with a serious look on his face how you went about opening a bank account. Of course his request had been met with a supercilious smile and a dismissive reply but that didn't matter, he'd achieved his object.

'Where have *you* been?' Elizabeth asked coldly. 'It's nine o'clock.'

'What's up with you two? You've got gobs on you that would stop the Liver clock.'

'If you're interested, your mam is very ill. The doctor's been—' Elizabeth answered.

'Mam's . . . Mam's . . . dying. A . . . a few . . . weeks. That's all.' Sobs again choked Tessa.

Colin looked incredulously at them both. Mam! Dying! In a few weeks! He was shocked to the core. Although he was utterly selfish and there had been many a yelling match between them, and hidings too, deep down he did love his mam.

'She . . . she can't be. She's not old . . .'

'You don't have to be old. Your sisters died, didn't they?' Elizabeth snapped.

Tessa wiped her eyes. 'Why should you care anyway? All you ever did was bring her shame and heartache just like Da did.'

'Where is Da?'

'Where he usually is, in the flaming pub,' Elizabeth answered cuttingly. She didn't like Colin O'Leary at all.

'Does he . . . does he know?'

'Of course he does. He was in such a state that Mam lost patience and sent him up there.'

'I'll go and bring him home,' Colin said quietly, ignoring Elizabeth's ill-concealed dislike of him.

'Aren't you even going up to see her?' Tessa asked.

Colin shook his head. 'She . . . she wouldn't want to . . . to see me.'

'At least you got that one right. Anyway, she's asleep now, so you can clear off and do what you like. Just make sure that you bring some money into the house so she won't have to worry about that.'

'I already do.' Colin glared at Elizabeth. Bossy little upstart.

Tessa raised her head from Elizabeth's shoulder. 'You bring it in but you keep most of it.'

'Oh, clear off!' Elizabeth was exasperated. 'Can't you see you're just upsetting everyone? Go and get your da home. If he can stand, that is. God knows why Mam sent him to the pub. The last thing Tessa and your mam need is a drunk on their hands.'

Colin needed no second telling. Mam was the only person in the family he cared a fig about, the rest of them could go to hell for all he cared.

'Mornin', luv, 'ow are yer?' Eileen bustled in through the scullery.

Tessa smiled weakly. The kitchen was in chaos. There were newspapers on the table as well as half a loaf going stale, a bottle of sterilised milk, and last night's cups and mugs. Clothes were draped over the back of the sofa and a pile of ironing occupied the cushions. Mam would go mad if she could see it.

'I'll go on up, Tessa, luv. See if there's anything she needs.

You get yourself out, I'll see to yer da and meladdo. Our Maureen is getting the other two ready for school.'

'Our Colin isn't here. I . . . I don't know where he is. He was supposed to go and bring Da home from the pub but Da came home on his own and Colin didn't come back.'

'Well, 'e's no loss. 'Ow's yer da?'

'He's got a hangover.'

'Tell me something I don't already know, luv. Frank said 'alf the fellers in the pub were buyin 'im beer and even whisky, but Frank said 'e *was* in a terrible state over yer poor mam.'

Tessa just nodded as Eileen took herself off upstairs. She had had a bad night lying next to her mother on the straw-stuffed mattress. Through the everlasting hours of darkness, listening to her mother's shallow breathing, she'd wondered how she would feel trying to sleep when her mam was no longer here. It was beyond imagining. Mam had always been there. Oh, she'd scolded and doled out punishment but she'd also calmed and cared for them too.

How much sleep would she ever get in the future? She would have to lie there night after night, in close physical contact, knowing that by the day Mam was getting weaker, until . . . And then what? How could she ever sleep in this room? She'd be alone. She didn't even have a sister she could share with. As the hours had dragged by the tears ran down her cheeks and she'd fought not to break into sobs which would disturb her mother.

When she heard Eileen call out her name her heart lurched and she panicked. She took the stairs two at a time.

'Oh, what's the matter?' she gasped. 'Is she . . .?'

'She's awake. She wants ter speak ter you, luv.'

Tessa knelt, then crouched down beside Mary. She looked even more pale and drawn than ever and she was obviously trying to fight the drug-induced sleep that had engulfed her.

'Mam! Mam, it's me, Tessa. How are you feeling now?'

'Tired. So tired . . .'

'It's the medicine the doctor left, Mam. You have to try and sleep, then you won't have any pain. Everything is being taken care of. You're not . . . not to worry.' Her voice was harsh with raw emotion.

Mary nodded. 'Tessa . . . Tessa . . .' She tried to reach out for her daughter's hand.

Tessa caught it and clasped it between her own. 'What, Mam? What is it?'

'Promise me . . . promise you'll make something out . . . out of yourself.'

Tessa was confused. This wasn't what she had expected and it sounded as though her Mam *knew*. 'Like what, Mam? I'm fine at the Convent, they're good to me.'

Mary managed to continue, 'I . . . know . . . but you . . . you're still only a . . . skivvy.'

What did her mother want? What exactly was she asking of her? Tessa searched her mind for some job, some occupation that would please Mary.

'Would . . . would a job in one of those posh shops in Bold Street do?'

'No. You . . . can . . . do better.' Mary's breathing was irregular.

'What about a stewardess on one of those big ships, would that be good enough?'

Mary managed a brief smile. 'It would, Tessa. Promise.'

'I promise, Mam.'

'Go . . . go . . . to work . . . luv.'

As Tessa stood up slowly, loath to leave her mother, she turned to Eileen and shrugged. 'What else could I say?' she whispered.

'Not much, but you've just promised to aim too high, girl. Hell will freeze over before a slummy like you will be taken on by one of that lot.'

But as Tessa went downstairs she made a decision. She would try. She would do almost anything to keep that promise.

Chapter Eleven

The tender, pale green leaves were opening on the trees in all the city parks the day Mary O'Leary passed away. It was a day Tessa would always remember. Life had been running so smoothly, she thought, and that had lulled her into a sense of false optimism. She hadn't wanted to think very deeply about the day her mam would die. She had pushed it to the back of her mind. Mam was ill in bed but, thanks to all the neighbours, Tessa was able to go to work. She was out of the house. For a while, at least, she'd been able to occupy herself with something other than her mother's pain.

Prayers were said every day by the nuns and pupils for Mary. Not that she should recover, but to ease her suffering and ensure her place in heaven, the latter being stressed all the time. Tessa *knew* her mam's place in heaven was assured. Mary O'Leary had done nothing bad in all her life. The money that was still owed was her da's responsibility. He'd been the one to waste it, not her mam. As the weeks passed, even all the prayers had become a normal thing.

It was Eileen who found her. Mary was barely breathing and Eileen had sent Kenneth Keegan, one of the younger Keegan boys who was off school with mumps, for the parish priest. Before he'd left the presbytery, Father Walsh had telephoned Mother Superior to send Tessa home. She'd run all the way down Everton Valley and halfway along Scotland Road before she jumped on a tram. For the rest of the way the tram seemed to crawl along, stopping every few minutes, and the same words went round and round her head: 'Don't let her have died before I get home, Lord! Oh, please, please let me be in time.'

As she entered the house there was no sign of anyone. Richie was at work, she presumed Colin was too and Jimmy was at school. But the house wasn't deserted. Eileen and Delia were both with the priest, who had just finished administering the Last Rites.

'Come here to me, Tessa,' Eileen said. She placed an arm around Tessa as the girl sat gingerly on the edge of the bed that Delia had insisted on buying.

'Is she . . . can she . . .'

'She's not dead, child, but we can only assume that she can hear us,' Father Walsh said as he folded his purple stole.

'Mam? Mam, can you hear me? It's Tessa.' Her voice was low but pleading.

There was no movement of Mary's eyelids; no sound, no matter how faint, from her lips. Tessa clasped her mother's hand tightly. 'Mam, if you can hear me, squeeze my hand.' They all waited but there wasn't even the slightest pressure on Tessa's fingers.

'Mam! Mam, I promise I'll make something of myself and I'll look after Da and the other two—' Her voice broke and the tears she had been fighting back now started to flow without restraint.

Mary's eyes half opened for a second.

'Oh, Mam! Say something, please?' Tessa begged.

Mary's eyes closed and from her throat came a strange sound, one Tessa had never heard before, but which the others had heard many times.

'She ... she's gone, luv,' Delia said quietly, placing a hand on Tessa's shoulder. 'She's out of her pain now. You go on down with Father Walsh, your da will need you and so will your brothers.'

'That no-mark Colin doesn't deserve anything special, he can look after himself,' Eileen muttered, crossing herself. Delia did the same and wondered just how Tessa was going to fulfil her promise to amount to something and look after her father and brothers.

As Tessa walked into the kitchen they all turned to look at her but she couldn't see any of them clearly, tears blinded her.

'Da ... Mam's ... gone,' she managed to stutter before pulling Jimmy to her and holding him close. With a cry, Richie got up and stumbled towards the stairs but Colin didn't follow him. He simply hadn't taken it in.

It was a dream world, Tessa thought. Nothing was real, not even Jimmy's sobs or the silent tears of her father, or Colin's almost blank, uncaring expression. Not the neighbours coming in to help out or pay their respects.

Her mam was laid out in the parlour, a room they had never used. Sheets had been hung around the walls and Delia had supplied a pair of curtains that were permanently closed, all of which hid the damp patches and rotten wood. Four candles burned in their brass holders at the top and the foot of the coffin. Delia had told her she was not to worry about paying for a funeral. She had collected enough to give Mary a decent burial. It was something that Tessa hadn't even thought about.

She slept fitfully, alone in the bed now. At first she hadn't wanted even to go inside the room again but Delia had insisted.

'Would she be happy with you sleeping on a straw mattress on the bare boards? No, she would not. Tessa, you are the only one in the entire family who gave her any support and help and consideration.'

'But Da . . . ?' she'd queried. 'Won't Da want the bed?'

Delia ignored her. He hadn't done much to provide for them. He'd left Mary to see to everything. Why should he be offered preferential treatment in the form of a proper bed now? One she herself had bought?

'It's *his* duty now to see that you all pull together.' She was thinking of Colin.

'But you know what he's like, Mam did everything.'

'I know, but he'll just have to pull himself together and get on with it,' had been Delia's firm reply.

Delia and Eileen had insisted that she go back to work too. Between them, with May, Maisie Keegan and Katie Collins, they would arrange everything and keep up the routine of housework, shopping and cooking until after the funeral.

Masses were said daily in the Convent chapel for her mam, but Tessa felt that Mam, who was undoubtedly in heaven, would have preferred the prayers to be said for those she'd left behind and who were grieving for her. Her work didn't allow her to dwell too much on things and that was another blessing, so Eileen and Delia said.

Jimmy would be all right, once the ordeal of the funeral was over. He'd miss his mam, but less than herself, Da and Colin. He'd spent the last weeks virtually living with Eileen and, as Eileen said, 'Kids get over things quicker than we do and she's been ill for a bit. He got used to that.'

Da, after the first few days, hadn't touched a drop of either beer or spirits and for that she'd been thankful, but he seemed to be totally lost. He couldn't concentrate for very long or make decisions. It was as if he'd been at sea in a ship in rough weather and had now lost his sheet-anchor.

'Da, you *have* to try. I know it's not easy but we *all* miss her. We *all* leaned on her for help and advice. Now you've got to *try*, Da!' she'd implored. Richie had only shaken his head and looked more confused. What did Tessa expect of him? What was she suggesting? Oh, maybe in time he would understand and get used to Mary not being here.

He was riddled with guilt. He'd taken no notice of her when she'd become ill. He hadn't listened to Tessa. He should have had more sense. He should never have got in the financial mess in the first place. He should have curbed his drinking. She'd struggled along all these years, keeping a clean and decent home, food on the table, clothes on their backs, boots on their feet, and he'd just let her struggle and worry, while he . . . he'd been no help. He was useless.

Apart from her problems with Richie, Tessa now seemed to argue with Colin every day. Nothing would change him.

'You're going to have to take some of the responsibility now.' Tessa confronted him one morning before he disappeared God knew where, as usual. 'You've seen the state of Da. He can't cope.'

'Well, neither can I,' he replied.

'You can *and* you're the oldest.'

He'd become annoyed. 'I . . . I miss her too, Tessa.'

'*You!* You only ever think of yourself. Look at all the worry you caused her. All that could have started . . . things off,' she'd replied cuttingly.

'Don't put the blame for Mam's illness on me, Tessa. Me da was as bad.'

'At least he didn't go thieving and get caught – twice! You never cared for Mam!'

'I did. In my own way.'

'Well, your way was a funny way of showing it.'

'Listen, Tessa, don't go pointing the finger at me.'

'You're going to have to sort yourself out now. Get some decent work and bring some money in to help me keep a home going.'

He'd turned his back on her and stormed down the lobby, furious, for he'd spoken the truth. In his own way he *had* cared for his mam, but he wasn't going to go down to the docks and sweat and strive for a few pounds a week and then have to give most of it to Tessa. No way. He'd have money soon, plenty of money. Enough to buy Ginny Greely fancy clothes so they could go to the smart places in town without her showing him up. He was quite fond of Ginny. She wasn't demanding and she was in awe of him. She didn't make sarcastic remarks when he told her that soon he'd earn a small fortune and they could live the high life, maybe even leave Liverpool and go to America. She didn't ask questions as to where this money was coming from. He knew that Tessa and particularly Elizabeth Harrison disapproved of him taking Ginny out, but her mam didn't seem to mind and she was the one who really counted.

The sun shone brightly and the sky was blue on the day the horse-drawn hearse stood outside number twelve, Naylor Street. The black plumes on the black bridles barely moved. There wasn't even a breath of wind. It should be grey and cold and windy, Tessa thought miserably. It wasn't a day for sunshine at all.

They would follow the hearse on foot along Scotland Road to the church for the funeral mass and then Mary would be buried in the churchyard.

Tessa wore a grey skirt and a black jacket. It was really one of Elizabeth's blazers. Delia had unpicked the badge and had it dyed by Johnson's. Tessa also wore one of Elizabeth's hats – minus the school insignia – trimmed with a band of black grosgrain ribbon. Her da and Colin had no formal mourning clothes but each wore a black armband on their jacket sleeve. Jimmy had one too and a new dark grey herringbone tweed cap, purchased by Delia. Those neighbours who could attend did so and all along Scotland Road, as the procession passed, men and boys removed their caps and women crossed themselves or stood with eyes downcast. Although they had never known Mary O'Leary it was the custom. Richie walked alone at the front of the cortège, followed by Colin, Tessa and Jimmy. She had her arm around the bewildered youngster and was having a hard time to keep her own tears back at the sound of his pathetic, gulping sobs.

Once at the church, she was barely aware of the service. Father Walsh's voice seemed faint and far away. The faces of the neighbours blurred into a single mass. It was only when they finally stood outside before the open grave that she realised the finality of it. Mam was dead. Dead!

The soil pressed into her hand by the priest felt cold and damp and she shivered even though the sun was warm on her face. Father Walsh's words were still indistinct, as were the sobs of her brother and father. The only thing that seemed real was the cold earth in her hand: soil she must now throw on top of her mam's coffin. The noise it made was the most awful sound she'd ever heard. Her heart was breaking.

She didn't remember much of the walk back and, once in the house, Delia, Eileen and May Greely took over, passing cups of tea and ham sandwiches to the mourners. To Tessa it seemed as though the house was bursting with them, and there were so many she didn't really know.

'Why the hell don't they all go home? All they've come for is the food,' Colin muttered to Tessa.

Delia heard him. 'That's a nice thing to say, I'm sure. Many people have had the decency to give up a few hours' pay or gone out of their way to show some respect for your mam! If you ask me, apart from Tessa, Mary's well out of it for the rest of you,' she snapped.

Elizabeth, who had been given time off school, glared at Colin. Her heart went out to her best friend. During the mass she'd tried to understand how Tessa must be suffering, but despite her lively imagination she just couldn't conceive how she would feel if it were her mam. She'd sat at Tessa's side once they'd got back to the house.

'Mam's right. Don't take any notice of *him*, Tessa!'

Tessa turned to her. 'What am I going to do now?'

'The same as you've always done. Tomorrow you'll all be back at work and Jimmy will be at school. Don't worry, Tessa, if you need any help, just ask. Ask me. You know I won't let you down. And take no notice of that lot up there when they start going on about God's mercy and Purgatory and things like that. I don't think they really *know* what it's like to be feeling lost and unhappy. They don't live like we do. They don't live in the *real* world.'

Tessa squeezed her hand, but still wondered if in the months ahead she would cope.

* * *

She did cope. As the weeks went by the neighbours gradually left her to manage things. It wasn't that they didn't care any more; they would always be there if she needed them. But the time had come for her to take over. Yet she missed her mam so much still. Many were the times when she let herself into the house and shouted, 'Mam, I'm home,' or turned suddenly to address her mother before she realised that Mary was no longer there for her to share her troubles or her moments of happiness.

It was late in the afternoon on a warm day in early July and she and Elizabeth were walking home. School had finished for the summer, but Elizabeth still went to meet Tessa from work and tried to cheer her friend up. Tessa saw him standing looking up and down the road and she grabbed Elizabeth's arm.

'Oh, God!'

'What's the matter?' Elizabeth asked, breaking off from a litany of complaints about Sister Imelda who was the bane of her life and who had given her so much homework for the holidays that she got a headache just *thinking* about it.

'It's him. It's Mogsey Doran.'

'Who's he when he's at home?'

'The moneylender. He . . . he's found us.'

'Oh, Holy Mother of God! Quick, round the back into the jigger.' Elizabeth virtually pushed Tessa into the entry.

'What will I do? If he sees Da, then—'

'We'll just have to make sure that he doesn't see any of you. Run down the jigger to our back yard while I walk down the street and get a good look at him.'

'But what can you do?' Tessa panicked.

'I'll have to wait and see. Is your Jimmy in with the Flynns?'

'Yes, but he'll be playing out with Harold and the rest of the kids.'

'If I see him I'll shove him into Eileen's house and tell him to stay there. Go on, run.'

Tessa needed no further telling.

Elizabeth began to walk slowly down the street. There were kids outside but they were further down by the tannery end. She hoped that was far enough away, because she couldn't draw attention to Jimmy by chasing him up the street to Eileen's house. She herself felt a bit afraid of the big, rough-looking man who was still standing looking up and down the street.

'Are you looking for someone?' she asked, praying her nervousness didn't show.

'Who are you?' he asked suspiciously.

'My mam and da have the shop. Who are you?'

He ignored her question. 'Do you know anyone called O'Leary?'

She made a great show of trying to think before she finally shook her head. 'Not O'Leary. There's a family in the next street called O'Dwyer.'

'No, it's definitely O'Leary. Richie, wife and three kids, two lads and a girl.' He didn't say that it was Colin he'd recognised in the Dingle and whom he had followed until the lad had disappeared down the back jiggers where he'd lost sight of him. But he now knew they were living somewhere around here.

'Well, I don't know anyone called O'Leary around here and nearly *everyone* comes into the shop at some time,' Elizabeth replied, trying to control her startled expression. She'd just seen her mam run from the shop and yank Jimmy

156

away from his friends and back inside. She sighed with relief as they disappeared from sight before the man looked back down the street. Tessa must have told Mam.

'Well, I *know* they're around this area, so I'll just wait.'

Elizabeth took a deep breath. 'You'll have to mind that the scuffers don't see you and arrest you for loitering. They're always walking around in pairs round here. A real pain, they are.'

He glared at her and turned away. He was certain the hardfaced little bitch knew *something*. He leaned his back on the lamppost. He could wait.

Elizabeth had to force herself not to break into a run but saunter down the street as she always did. She even pretended to jump from flag to flag to avoid the cracks.

'What in the name of God do you think you're doing?' Delia asked when she got home.

'That feller *is* the moneylender and he looks dead tough. He asked for the O'Learys and I said I'd never heard of anyone of that name living around here but he's going to just hang around. I told him to be careful he didn't get arrested for loitering.'

Delia cast her eyes to heaven. One of these days Elizabeth's tongue would get her into serious trouble. Still, she'd shown some guts.

'What time does your da get in, Tessa? And Colin?'

'Colin never comes in at the same time every day, but Da ... he's usually home by seven,' Tessa replied. 'Quite often he walks half the way to save on the fare to buy his tobacco for his cigarettes.'

Delia looked perturbed. 'I'll just have a word with your da, Elizabeth. Stay there, all of you.'

When Delia had apprised her husband of the situation, he looked grim. 'I'll go round all the men in the street that are home from work.' He knew the type of moneylender Mogsey Doran was and Richie and his family had had enough to contend with over the last few months.

Those men that were in followed him to the pub, and he left messages with the wives of those who weren't. He'd had a good look at Mogsey Doran and had even exchanged a few words with him. The conversation had been more or less the same as the one Mogsey had had with Elizabeth but Mogsey had nevertheless decided to look in the pub himself. Young Kenneth Keegan had been posted at one end of Naylor Street and Harold Flynn at the other. They had strict instructions to tell Richie and Colin to get inside the house fast and stay there until someone went to inform them of what was happening. As more and more of the men slipped into the pub Eddie Doyle realised that something was up and asked the stranger point blank what he was doing in this area.

'I'm lookin' for a feller named O'Leary. He owes me money.'

'Can't help there, mate.' Eddie Doyle looked around. 'Anyone else know anything about this feller O'Leary?'

Heads were shaken and Mogsey scrutinised all their faces. There was something going on here, he thought. You didn't get fellers in such numbers in the pub this early. Most of them were still in their working clothes.

'Well, I think I might just hang around outside and wait and see who passes, like.' And before anyone could stop him he left.

'Christ Almighty! Get after him. If he catches sight of Richie or Colin or even Tessa . . .' Jack Harrison cried and there was a mass exodus of the patrons of the Globe. Jack, who was first out, was horrified to see Richie walking slowly, head bent, up the street. He'd skin Harold Flynn alive for not warning him!

'I've caught up with you at last, O'Leary!' Mogsey Doran bellowed down the street.

Richie looked up and stopped dead in his tracks, the colour draining from his face. Oh, God! What was he going to do now? Mogsey'd found them. He hadn't given much thought to the moneylender lately. He'd felt as though he'd given him the slip entirely. The group of men, now joined by some of the women, instantly surrounded Richie.

'You've no business round here, so sling yer bleedin' hook!' Frank Flynn shouted, elbowing his way towards the moneylender.

'He owes me. He owes me, it's all legal, like,' Mogsey shouted back.

'Legal my flaming arse! Go an' tell that to the scuffers in Athol Street station, you'll see just how bloody "legal" it is!' Jack Harrison said mockingly.

Mogsey glared at him and then at Richie. 'I'm tellin' you, O'Leary, I want me money an' if I don't get it—'

Frank Flynn was a big man. He grabbed Mogsey by the lapels of his jacket, lifting him off his feet. 'Yer'll do what? You so much as put yer nose around the bloody corner or gerr anyone else ter come round 'ere and I'll break yer bleeding neck. I don't care 'ow big yer think yer are, sod off – and don't come back or you'll effing well finish up under the Landin' Stage. It'll be effing months before they find yer an' even then yer own mother wouldn't recognise yer! Bugger off!' Frank's last words were bellowed in Mogsey's face and he shrank back.

Frank released him and, after looking at the grim, unyielding faces of those who surrounded him, Mogsey straightened his jacket and turned and walked away, seething with anger inside. A gang of young lads followed him, shouting abuse, until they were called back by their parents. Harold got a belt from his father for not doing the job he'd been sent to do.

'Jesus! Thanks! He'd have killed me but for you.' Richie meant every word and he was so grateful that he shook all their hands in turn.

'You'll hear no more from that feller. He knows he'll get a good kicking if he bothers you, and the undertow at the Landing Stage is very strong, he'd be gone in seconds,' Jack said grimly.

'Thanks, lads. Thanks again.'

'You don't owe anyone else, do yer, Richie?' Frank asked.

'No. I must have been mad to have got involved with him. Thank God Mary wasn't alive to see him.'

Jack looked puzzled. 'How do you think he found you?'

'I don't know.'

'I do,' May suddenly announced and they all turned towards her.

'I've a mate who's seen your lad, Colin, hanging around the Dingle quite a few times. It wouldn't have been hard to follow him. I don't suppose Tessa or Jimmy ever go down there, and neither do you.'

'I'll bloody kill him!' Richie exploded.

'I'd find out just what that lad of yours is up to if I were you,' Jack suggested.

'Come on, Richie, we'll go back to the pub. You need a drink down you. I'll pay,' May offered and gradually the crowd moved away as Richie followed her back to the Globe.

Chapter Twelve

They saw nothing more of Mogsey Doran and for that they were all grateful.

That night Tessa stayed with Elizabeth.

'Mam, she's terrified that that Mogsey feller will come back in the middle of the night,' Elizabeth had pleaded.

Delia had agreed. The girl had enough to contend with and she'd been coping very well of late. But her estimation of Richie O'Leary had taken a steep dive.

'I'm glad that Mary isn't here. How she ever put up with him, I'll never know. He's useless. He's weak, he's a spendthrift—'

'All right, Delia, luv, we know his failings, but that won't stop us from looking out for him and the kids if that shark comes back.'

'Don't go saying things like that, Jack. Tessa and young Jimmy are scared.' Jimmy as usual had gone to Eileen's to stay.

That night Richie, urged on by May – who always seemed to be in and out of number twelve these days – had a serious talk with Colin.

'What the bloody hell do you think you're playing at? That feller would have broken my neck, and yours too, if it hadn't been for the fellers in the street.'

Colin scowled back at his father and May. 'How come I always get the blame? Nothing is ever our Tessa or Jimmy's

161

fault. No, I'm the one who always gets the blame when things go wrong.'

'You get the blame because you usually deserve it,' May answered. 'I've seen you hanging around in town, particularly around Lime Street Station and the Riverside Station. Looking for easy pickings, were you? For people too busy with seeing to their luggage that they might not notice a handbag or a wallet that was just waiting to be nicked? And you've been back down the Dingle. That's why it's your fault. That Doran feller saw you an' followed you. He'll have seen what you're up to. I'd watch my step if I were you, Colin, he'd shop you to the scuffers without a second thought. He'd think he would be paying you back.'

'What's it all to do with you?' Colin demanded.

'Don't be so bloody hardfaced!' Richie said sharply.

'I'm not. She's got no right to be saying things like that – accusing me of pinching bags and wallets!'

Richie glared at his son. It sounded as though Colin was up to his old tricks again. 'You are hardfaced. Don't you speak to May like that.'

Colin looked speculatively at his father. So, that was the way the wind blew, he thought. 'It's "May" now, is it?' There was a note of sarcasm in his voice.

'Listen here, you thieving little toe-rag, what yer da and me do is none of yer business. We're friends, that's all,' May said cuttingly.

Colin laughed. 'Oh aye, pull the other one, it's got bells on! Ouch!' he cried as Richie's hand caught him across the side of the head.

'You'll have some respect! *I* pay the rent, so *I'll* have whoever I like in here. And May's been kindness itself over the months. You should be grateful, meladdo!'

'If you don't buck your ideas up soon and show some respect, I'll put a stop to you taking our Ginny out!' May added. 'She's easy led, but I'm not. Her da wasn't a bit like you and if you don't come up to my expectations then I'll put a stop to your gallop where our Ginny is concerned.' May's voice was firm. From now on she'd watch him like a hawk. She'd never really liked him but Ginny did. He was the first lad she'd ever gone out with and he did make a fuss of her, but Ginny was naïve. She'd believe everything he told her. She herself wouldn't believe the daylight out of him from now on.

Colin stormed out, slamming the front door behind him. The bloody cheek of her. She was nothing but a slut. A loud, common barmaid who could drink and swear and laugh at the risqué jokes with all the men in the neighbourhood. Mam would be turning in her grave if she knew someone like May Greely was in and out of the house that she had struggled so hard to make halfway decent and in which she'd died.

He was about to cross over the road, making his way to Ginny's, when he saw her coming up the street.

She looked concerned. 'Colin, what's the matter? You look dead narked. Who's been having a go at you?'

'I am upset, Ginny. I've just had a right ear-bashing from me da and your mam.'

Ginny looked incredulous. As far as she knew Colin hadn't crossed her mam in any way. 'From Mam? What for?'

'Oh, come on, let's have a bit of a walk. I'm that mad I can't stand still and I *hate* this bloody street. You can't do anything without someone making remarks or accusations.'

She'd never known him to be so angry before. Oh, he was impatient sometimes, and he was often moody, but she took no notice of his moods. They usually didn't last long. She tucked her arm through his. 'So, what did Mam say to you, Col?'

'That if I didn't buck my ideas up she'll stop me seeing you.'

Ginny stopped and looked at him quizzically. 'Buck your ideas up? What does she mean by that?'

'How do I know? Get some kind of boring, useless job that pays buttons, I suppose.'

'You don't want to do that, Col. You'd be just like all the other lads around here, except for Johnny Doyle that is.'

She didn't know just *what* Colin did all day but he seemed to get by. She sensed that he didn't want her to ask point blank. She supposed he lived by his wits, for he was sharp and clever, and he was never short of money.

Some of his anger left him. He had her support at least. 'They were both blaming me for that Mogsey Doran coming here looking for me da.'

She looked up at him. 'That wasn't your fault.'

'According to your mam it was. She said he'd seen me around. What am I meant to do? Stay here all day, not going anywhere?'

'That's not fair! How were you to know *he'd* see you? You're not some kind of mind-reader! And why shouldn't you go into town or anywhere else anyway?'

'It's not *me* who owes that feller money, it's Da.'

'Of course it's not you, you wouldn't be that daft. Maybe I shouldn't say it but I often think your da lives in a world of his own. He seems to be able to just . . . well, ignore things, hoping they'll go away.'

Colin nodded and they walked hand in hand along the

main road towards the tram stop. They'd get the tram to Lester Gardens, it was only a few stops.

'Have you noticed that your mam and me da are always in and out of each other's pockets these days?'

Ginny pondered the question, then she nodded. 'They are, now I come to think about it.'

'I said as much and got roared at.'

'Do you think they . . . well . . .?'

'Will get married?'

'Mam likes a drink and a bit of a flirt but that's all. It's years and years since me da died and she's never really bothered with anyone.'

'She's never been livin' over the brush, like?'

'No! She never brings anyone home. I've never had a string of "Uncles", if that's what you mean.'

Colin sniffed, disappointed.

They got off at the bottom of Royal Street outside the Astoria Cinema where sometimes they went to see a film. The little park was set back off the busy road and was nearly always deserted. It was sandwiched between two streets of largely commercial buildings and always looked a bit neglected. There wasn't much grass; it consisted of gravel pathways with mainly evergreen shrubs interspersed with the smaller summer bedding plants. There were a couple of arbours with wooden benches. Ginny sat down on a bench obscured by a large rose bush that had been left to go back to briar. She liked Colin O'Leary very much. He treated her so well. He was always buying her little things, taking her out to places most of the other lads she knew wouldn't dream of going. And, again unlike them, he had plans. Plans which seemed to include her too.

Ginny glanced sideways at him. He was a handsome lad and she was well aware that she looked like a mousy little slip of a thing. She would never be pretty, let alone a raving beauty. She felt very honoured that he'd chosen her even though he could have had his pick of the girls. When she encountered the flirtatious and often openly brazen glances cast in his direction by other girls, she felt jealous because nearly all of them were more attractive than herself. Maybe she would look a little bit pretty if she had the right clothes and the right hairstyle. She didn't have Tessa's big dark eyes and waving dark hair, or Elizabeth's mop of really beautiful hair and her education, but Colin seemed to like her the way she was. Maybe that in itself was appealing to him: that no one else seemed to want her. She pushed that thought from her mind as he put his arm around her and drew her close to him.

He did still like her, in fact in some ways she was great, Colin thought, but he was getting restless. She never made any demands on him. But just because he confided in her, in a vague sort of way, of course, didn't mean he had any intention of becoming seriously involved or of marrying her or anything. He wanted someone with Tessa's looks and Elizabeth's education as a wife, but with the submissiveness of Ginny. When he found that combination, and he was certain he would eventually, then he'd get married and not before. But, he wondered, was his da thinking of marriage? He certainly didn't want to have to put up with calling a floosie of a barmaid 'Mam'. He had loved his mam, in his own way, and wouldn't put up with a replacement, yet she had never understood how he felt about the rotten hand fate had dealt him. She'd slaved all her life for what they'd had and was as honest as the day was long. His philosophy, on the other hand, was to take everything that came your way, by fair means or foul. No, Mam had never understood that.

His da was useless. He'd always needed someone to make decisions. He'd always shied away from responsibility. Another thought came to mind. If his da did marry May Greely then Ginny would become his stepsister and that would put paid to any hopes she might have of ever marrying him. He'd be in the clear on that one and without him even having to tell her.

Elizabeth and Tessa were sitting on the steps of number twelve. 'We're going to have to say something to her,' Elizabeth said firmly. They had been discussing Ginny and Colin.

'What? If I tell her what a little rat he is she'll never believe me. I'm his sister, for God's sake,' Tessa replied.

'Exactly. You know him better than anyone, better than your da even.'

Tessa liked Ginny and she didn't want her to get hurt. She was an inoffensive girl and she was obviously smitten by Colin's attentions. 'Do you think I should say something about . . . well, you know?' she asked.

Elizabeth pondered this. 'She'd get a cob on if she found out that I've known all along and she hasn't. And she might go and ask your da or even tell her mam and get her to ask if it's true.'

'That would be worse, in fact it would be terrible. Her mam would go mad. Easy-going or not, *that* would put the fat in the fire and *everyone* would get to know. May Greely isn't known for keeping her mouth shut.'

'Shut up, here comes Ginny,' Tessa whispered.

'You look pleased with yourself, Ginny,' Elizabeth said, drawing her skirt aside so Ginny could sit down on the warm step too.

'Where've you been?' Tessa asked.

'Only to Lester Gardens with your Colin. He's really annoyed with my mam and your da, Tessa.'

Elizabeth and Tessa exchanged wary glances.

'What over?' Elizabeth demanded.

'Oh, the usual stuff, all about him "bucking his ideas up". Mam told him it was his fault that that Mogsey feller had found you here – as if it could have been! – and gave him the length of her tongue.'

'I'm glad she did. Maybe he'll take some notice of her. He just ignores everyone else,' Tessa said crossly.

'Honestly, you're always making him out to be some sort of hooligan,' Ginny replied indignantly.

Again there was a furtive glance between the two friends.

'He is. He always has been. He does exactly what he likes. He never considers anyone else at all and believe me I *know* what I'm talking about.'

Ginny jerked up her chin defiantly. 'You don't know *everything* about him just because he's your brother. He's . . . different when he's with me.'

'How different?' Tessa demanded.

'Well, he never goes on and on about things like work and jobs and money.'

'He always seems to have enough to take you out, Ginny, but where does he get it? We don't know. Mam often said he'd end his days in Walton Jail, and I think she was right.'

Ginny bristled with indignation but Elizabeth managed to head off the torrent of defensive words that she could see were bubbling up on the other girl's lips.

'Ginny, it's because we're your friends that we care about you. We're just pointing out that maybe you shouldn't believe everything he tells you.'

'Why not?' Ginny demanded hotly. In her opinion they weren't acting much like friends.

'Because . . .' Tessa paused. Should she tell Ginny or not? No, she couldn't. She just shrugged.

'You see?' Ginny said triumphantly. 'I *know* he's not a hooligan, far from it. He . . . he's different with me. And he's got plans, big plans for the future.'

'What plans?' Tessa cried. Oh, God, he wasn't going to start again, please, she thought.

'Plans for the future. *He* doesn't want to spend all his life in some dead-end job, always counting the pennies. No, he wants to be *someone*. Have a better life and . . . and he wants me to be part of it.'

Tessa looked helplessly at Elizabeth. This sounded ominously familiar.

Elizabeth shrugged. 'He's not about to do any of that without an education, is he? I mean, businessmen have to have certain standards. It's all talk, just wishful thinking.'

'It's not!' Ginny retorted, her cheeks beginning to grow pinker.

'It is, Ginny. He's always been like that, full of big plans, but they're only in his head. He . . . he'll never amount to much,' Tessa added.

Ginny got up, her hazel eyes cold with anger.

Elizabeth grabbed at her arm. 'Ginny, we don't want you to get hurt. We *do* care about you. We're *not* making all this up. Tessa's his sister, she sees him every day of her life.'

'Well, I'm not listening to *anything* either of you say. You're a nasty spiteful cat, Tessa O'Leary, and you . . . you're just jealous, Elizabeth Harrison.'

Elizabeth let out a whoop of laughter. 'Me! Me, jealous! What in God's name have I got to be jealous about? I can't stand him, the slimy little toe-rag! Sorry, Tessa.'

'There's no need to apologise to me for our Colin. Look, Ginny, we really don't want to fight with you. We just don't want to see you get hurt.'

'I won't because *he* won't hurt *me*!' Ginny said before flouncing across the road to her own house.

At half past two the following day Colin took up his position across the road from the Liverpool Savings Bank. Today was the day. It had all been perfectly planned but he felt as though there was sweat standing out on every pore in his body. He was certain that people were looking at him strangely. Then he pulled himself together. No one was looking at him at all. Why should they? He was no different from many people on the street and they were all absorbed in their own problems. Even the two old shawlies on the next corner were engrossed in their gossiping.

He counted the minutes in his head and dead on time the money arrived. He balled his fists in his pockets. He had to stay calm. That was the secret. Calm, unruffled and unhurried, as though it was a thing he did every day of his life.

The cashier and the attendant police officer departed and once they had gone out of sight he crossed the road, slowly. This was it. Everything depended on the next few minutes. All the things he wanted, everything he'd dreamed about was just minutes away. His chance to make a new life, in a new country where no one knew him, where he was certain he could make even more money. Jesus, it was no use carrying on thinking like that: it was undermining his confidence and his nonchalant appearance.

Colin pushed open the heavy wooden door. He looked around once, then made his way to the highly polished mahogany counter. The bank was empty, just as he'd reckoned. He had to force himself to walk slowly and not glance around all the time, or look uneasy or furtive. God, but it took some nerve. He was sweating profusely and he was certain that any minute now he'd wet himself with sheer fright.

The teller was shuffling paper and barely glanced up at him until the untidily written note was pushed across the counter. Colin grasped the short thick piece of wood that was in his pocket – it was in fact a catapult – and moved it slightly so that in the confines of his jacket it resembled the barrel of a gun.

The eyes that now met his own were wide with terror and the teller began to grab all the notes in the drawer. It seemed to take ages. Now his whole body was shaking, something he fought to control as the seconds dragged by.

'Get a bloody move on!' he hissed at the pale-faced young man.

The contents of the drawer, including some golden guineas, were stuffed into a canvas bag. No one seemed to have noticed what was going on. He snatched it and moved on to the next teller. A woman. He'd only left himself time to get money from two. It would be enough. Any more and the whole place would erupt.

With trembling hands he shoved the note under the woman's nose but wasn't prepared for the outcome. She began to scream at the top of her voice and was joined by the first teller, who shouted, 'Thief! Thief! Thief!'

The door of the bank opened and a rotund man he'd never seen before came in. Colin's nerve broke and, dropping the bag, he turned and ran, shoving aside the bewildered customer.

Their shouts followed him as he ran down Scotland Road towards Byrom Street. He knocked people aside without a thought, terrified that any minute a policeman would confront him.

By the time he reached the Technical College he could go no further. He was exhausted. He was shaking and sweating, gasping for breath, and to make matters worse he had wet himself in sheer terror. He sat down on the steps that led up to the main door of the College and dropped his head in his hands. Jesus Christ! What a bloody useless failure he was! For a few minutes he'd had a couple of hundred pounds in his grasp. If that bloody woman hadn't started yelling he would never have lost his nerve. If he'd picked another cashier, he'd have got clear away with two bags. Now he had nothing, except the determination to try again. He hadn't gone through all the weeks of waiting and watching and planning to waste it as he had just done. So much for his fine plans. But he would wait. He had plenty of time on his hands.

PART II

Chapter Thirteen

1939

The months of January and February of 1939 were bitterly cold. Winter held the city in an icy grip and took its toll of lives; the young, the old, the infirm and the poor suffered particularly. Moreover, dark clouds were hanging over Europe and the first rumblings of war evoked a sense of dread in those who had fought and survived the Great War – the war to end all wars as it had come to be known. Spain was in the throes of civil war, the Royal Air Force were taking delivery of four hundred planes a month and air-raid shelters were being distributed to the residents of houses in London. But all this was of little importance to Richie and his family.

In number twelve, Naylor Street the house was so desperately cold that no matter how high the fire in the range was banked up with slack to keep it going through the night, by morning there would be ice on the inside of the kitchen window.

Upstairs, although now there were proper beds with blankets and quilts, they all slept in old jumpers, cardigans, socks and woollen long johns – even Tessa wore them.

She was always first up and as she raked out the ashes and reset the fire she shivered uncontrollably, although she wore her heavy shawl over her clothes.

It took her only seconds to dress. She kept all their clothes on a rack above the range to save them from becoming frozen stiff. Still, by the time her da and the lads came down it was to a warm room with a dish of hot porridge on the table. She made it the previous night and left it on the hob so it wouldn't be stone cold.

They did have more in the way of comforts than they'd had a year ago, for Richie kept his daily consumption of ale to two glasses per evening and often it was May Greely who paid for the second one. She felt sorry for Richie. He was still looking to someone else to find solutions to his problems. If she was honest, May realised it wasn't a wife he needed, it was a mother, but maybe that was why she was fond of him.

She had taught Tessa the very basic skills of patching and darning, something that Mary had never found time to do, for she had always insisted on doing such tasks herself.

May also kept an eye on Colin, who, after a few more rows with herself and Richie, seemed to have settled down. He'd got a job as a labourer in a big haulage company in Vauxhall Road. It didn't pay very much and he had to turn a third of it up to Tessa but he was fed up going looking for casual work at the docks, north or south. He wanted a regular sum of money and it would help lull suspicions at home.

He hadn't given up the idea of a second attempt at robbing a bank, but whenever he did think about it, he'd remember the sheer terror of his first try.

He was always complaining to Ginny about the shortage of money. It meant they couldn't go out to the pictures or the music hall as much but she didn't mind. Her feelings for

Colin had grown month by month, something her mam did not view with approval or pleasure.

'Mam, I'm nearly sixteen. I've been working in that flaming shop for over a year now and you know how I hate it.'

'I don't see what your job has to do with anything, *and* you're still only a bit of a kid to me, *and* I still don't trust him. I just hope you aren't letting him take liberties with you, because if he is—'

'Mam! He'd never do anything like that! What kind of a girl do you think I am?' Ginny had interrupted, but with guilt as she thought of the times when she had let him take exactly the kind of liberties her Mam was talking about. But she loved him and he loved her so where was the harm in it? She'd never let him make love to her properly, she was too scared of getting pregnant.

'I would hope you're a sensible girl. A lad never marries a girl who lets him have his own way, no matter how much he says he loves you.'

'Well, I *don't* let him "have his own way" so can we please drop the subject?'

Tessa and Elizabeth also kept a watchful eye on their friend.

'Do you think he'll ever get her an engagement ring?' Elizabeth asked as she and Tessa walked down Everton Valley, muffled to the eyes in scarves and hats. Tessa now had a good thick warm coat in a dark grey herringbone tweed. She'd got a cheque from Sturla's department store in Great Homer Street and she paid off the debt at ninepence a week. Delia had given her a scarf, hat and mitts that had been knitted for Elizabeth, who was always losing such things.

177

'Hardly anyone has an engagement ring. They're lucky to have a wedding ring and often that spends more time in the pawnbroker's than on their finger.'

'Well, has he said anything to her?'

'Like what?'

'Oh, honestly, Tessa O'Leary, you are so aggravating sometimes, you know very well what I mean!'

Tessa laughed. 'If you meant has he said he loves her and that he'll marry her – one day – then Ginny is out of luck. It may look like he's settled down, on the surface, but I know him. He's got something on his mind; he's just biding his time. I wish she'd meet someone else. She's not bad-looking now. You keep her hair nice and she's got some decent clothes but no, she hangs on to him.'

'Well, it's no use us trying to prise her away from him, it always ends up in a fight.' Elizabeth decided to change the subject: 'What did they give you today?'

Tessa was carrying a wicker basket covered with an old but clean piece of material. She used it to carry her bits and pieces around and also to bring home anything Sister Bernadette gave her in the way of food.

'A big jar of thick pea soup. I had some for my dinner and it's great. It's got pieces of ham in it.'

Elizabeth pulled a face. 'I know, we had it too.'

'You're really finicky with your food, do you know that? I'm always amazed your mam lets you get away with it. She never lets your Nessie leave things or refuse to eat something she doesn't like the look of, let alone even taste.'

'And speaking of our Nessie, what's she still doing hanging round the tram stop?'

Tessa followed Elizabeth's gaze and saw Nessie, now in

the uniform of the Convent, standing at the tram stop looking decidedly put out and fed up.

'What's up with you? Why aren't you home by now?' Elizabeth demanded.

Nessie had just started her first term and her elder sister avoided her like the plague. 'There's no trams running. I've been here ages and I'm frozen stiff.'

'How do you know the trams have stopped?' Elizabeth demanded.

'Because there haven't been any. Sometimes you're so stupid.'

Elizabeth made a swipe at her but Nessie jumped out of reach.

Tessa intervened. 'Oh, stop it, you two, or you'll both be reported and then there'll be trouble. Maybe the cold and ice have done something to the wires.'

'I've never known that to happen before. They only stop when it's really foggy.'

Tessa shrugged. 'I suppose we'll have to walk home.'

'It's just a pity *she* didn't think of that ages ago, instead of hanging around for non-existent trams. And you've got a cheek to call me stupid, Nessie Harrison! Mam'll probably have half the street out looking for you, so you'll catch it when you get home,' she finished with some satisfaction.

Nessie broke away from them and began to walk quickly along Kirkdale Road.

'I've never known anyone like you two. You're always fighting.'

'Brenda and Maureen Flynn were always half killing each other when they were younger. Oh, I meant to tell you, she's going to have a baby. Mrs Flynn came in to tell Mam last night. She's made up she's going to be a grandma, or a nin as she said. Mam hates that word.'

'Why?'

'How do I know? You know Mam – she's got some funny ways. She said it sounds "common". Dad said it comes from the Welsh word for grandmother, *Nine*, but Mam only said she didn't care where it came from—'

Their conversation was interrupted by the unmistakable rattling and rumbling of a tram.

'Honestly, Nessie, you're a real pain *and* you tell lies. What's that behind us? A flaming horse and cart?'

Nessie turned back as Elizabeth started to wave her school scarf wildly and the tram slowed down.

'Mister, will you tell *her* that the trams haven't been running!' Nessie demanded of the driver.

'You're right, girl. There was a dispute at the Spellow Lane depot. It's all over now, storm in a teacup, but there's been no trams for over two hours.'

'See!' Nessie cried triumphantly.

'Oh, get a move on, you're holding everyone up. Pay your fare, sit down and shut up!'

Tessa tugged at her friend's sleeve. 'Elizabeth, leave her alone, everyone's looking at us and the pair of you will be reported for making a show of yourselves and your uniforms. You know what they're like back there. I'm sure they have spies on every tram and bus.'

Elizabeth paid both their fares and they moved down the tram, past Nessie, who just scowled at her sister, and continued to sulk until they all got off at the top of Edgar Street. Then she walked ahead of them, head down and hands in her pockets until she collided with a man.

'Sorry,' she mumbled from the depths of her scarf.

'Are them two behind you your sisters?'

Nessie looked up. She didn't know him and she didn't like the look of him. He was big. Very big.

'One of them is my sister, the one in the uniform.'

'Who's the other one?' he demanded.

'What do you want to know for?'

'That's my business,' he snapped.

'She's just a friend. Her name's Tessa. Tessa O'Leary.'

'Thanks, kid, now push off home,' he replied.

Nessie had walked away but before she reached the corner of Edgar Street and Fontenoy Street, she heard Elizabeth's screams. She turned swiftly but was then rooted to the spot with fear. The man she'd just spoken to had hold of Tessa by the shoulders. She was fighting back with all her strength but Nessie could see it was useless. He was dragging her towards the entry between Naylor Street and Oriel Street. Elizabeth was lying on the pavement, holding her right arm.

'Nessie! Nessie! Go and tell Da! Find a scuffer! He's taking Tessa away and I think he's broken my arm! Go on, Nessie! Run! Run!'

Nessie took to her heels, her face white with shock.

Despite the terrible pain in her arm, Elizabeth managed to get to her feet. She looked around for help but there was no one. Where was he taking Tessa? Who was he? She got up, wincing in pain, and slowly began to follow them down the entry between the two streets.

She could still hear Tessa's cries but they were much fainter and muffled. The only light there was came from the upstairs windows of the houses. The bottom windows were obscured by the back walls. She peered into the gloom, trying to count the number of houses, hoping to see where Tessa was being taken, but she began to feel dizzy and leaned against the wall. She had to get home! She just *had* to tell someone. He might beat Tessa or assault her or, she shivered, even kill her. What was it he'd shouted at her before he sent her sprawling? Something about someone called 'Doran'.

She could hardly put one foot in front of the other, the pain was making her feel so ill. Her progress was slow but as she turned into Naylor Street she saw someone running towards her and she burst into tears.

'Elizabeth! Elizabeth, are you hurt? Who was it? Where's Tessa?' Jack Harrison was panting.

'Oh, Da! My arm! I think it's broken and I feel . . .'

Her father lifted her gently and carried her the rest of the way to where Delia stood on the shop step waiting anxiously.

'Is she all right, Jack? What's been going on?' Nessie had come tearing into the shop screaming that a man was half killing Tessa and Elizabeth and it had been a few minutes before either herself or Jack had managed to get any sense out of her.

'She says she thinks her arm is broken. She's shocked and sick with the pain.'

Delia whipped off her shop coat. 'I'll get her to Stanley Hospital right now. I'll get a taxi.'

'Mam! Mam, he took Tessa!' Elizabeth cried.

Jack squatted down on his haunches. 'Tell me what happened – slowly, Elizabeth, slowly.'

He listened in silence to his daughter's sobbing explanation, then he got up. 'It's someone connected with Mogsey Doran!'

'Oh, Holy Mother of God! I thought we'd seen the last of him!'

'So did I. If his bloody mate harms a hair of that girl's head I'll kill him myself.'

'Elizabeth, did you see where he took her?'

'The ninth house down Oriel Street. Oh, please, please, Da, go and help Tessa! Go now! Right now, in case anything happens!'

'Delia, can you see to her? Get her to hospital and back?'

'Yes. What are *you* going to do, Jack?'

'Round up everyone in the street and go and get Tessa back,' he replied grimly. Before this night was over Mogsey Doran would be missing one friend and would be on the receiving end of such a beating that if he survived he'd be crippled for life.

Soon Delia's kitchen was crowded with grim-faced men and lads of all ages. They had their own code of morals, their own way of handing out justice. To snatch a young girl like Tessa literally off the street and then drag her to some house and do God alone knew what to her, just because her father owed a few pounds, came high on their list of crimes requiring violent retribution.

'So you reckon it's number nine, Jack?' Frank Flynn asked.

Jack nodded. Richie was sitting white-faced and rigid with fear for his daughter. He'd thought all that was behind them. Nothing had been heard from Mogsey since that last time he'd shown his face in Naylor Street. Now he'd got Tessa, his lovely, caring, hard-working Tessa.

'Right then, you lot come with me, the rest of you go with Frank. You go to the back door, we'll go to the front,' Jack instructed.

183

'What if the bastard's got a lookout?' Mick Collins asked.

'He's right, Jack. This has all been carefully planned. He'd be a bloody fool not to have someone, a couple of kids maybe, to watch the street and the entry,' Frank Flynn replied.

'Then we'll go first, Frank. I'll take the street, you take the jigger. Then the rest of you follow, in twos or threes if necessary. Does anyone know anyone who lives in Oriel Street?'

'No one really well,' Billy Keegan answered. 'Fred Jessup sometimes comes into the Globe. I only know him to nod to. Do you think Doran might have planted some of his cronies in the street?'

'No. There might be another couple of fellers with him tonight but we'd have heard if half the street had new lodgers. You know what the women are like for jangling.'

'Do you think that Mogsey feller will be with this bloke?' Billy asked.

'I don't know but my guess is that he won't. Too bloody yellow-bellied to come himself after last time. But if he's not, then we'll all have to go down to the Holy Land. Mind, I expect there'll be more than one thug holed up there.'

'We don't want no trouble with the scuffers, Jack,' Mick Collins warned.

'There won't be, but if the worst comes to the worst we'll drag whoever's involved into Rose Hill nick. When they know what's happened they'll turn a blind eye to any "injuries". I think they call it "Resisting Arrest", and they'll add a few of their own "injuries". One way or another they'll get what's coming. I hope Doran paid them well.'

'What about . . . him?' Frank Flynn enquired in a low voice, jerking his head in Richie's direction.

Jack shook his head. 'Leave him here until we get back. Where's that no-mark of a bloody son of his?'

'God knows. Whoever knows when that lad's at home or what he's up to?' Billy answered scathingly.

'What am I supposed to be up to?' Colin asked, pushing his way through the group towards his father. There'd been no one in the house when he'd arrived home and he'd gone to see Eileen, who had told him he'd better get along to the Harrisons' as something had happened to Tessa.

'God, 'e's like the bloody Scarlet Pimpernel, comes an' goes an' yer never see nor 'ear him,' Frank remarked.

'Mogsey Doran's hard case snatched your Tessa on her way home. He's holed up in number nine, Oriel Street. We're just going to get her.'

Even Colin was stunned.

'Look at the gob on him. He's goin' ter be as useful as his bloody da,' Billy said.

'Stay here and see to your da, lad. Delia's gone to the hospital with our Elizabeth. That feller broke her arm when she tried to help Tessa. Nessie! Nessie! Come down here and make some hot sweet tea for Mr O'Leary and his lad,' Jack cried from the bottom of the stairs.

A white-faced and still shaking Nessie crept down in time to see them all leave. Oh, this was terrible! Terrible! They'd never believe her at school. At that thought some of the fear and shock left her and a gleam appeared in her eyes. If, or rather, when they got Tessa back she'd have a great tale to tell, particularly to that Patricia Armstrong who was so snooty. And all because she'd stood patiently, if stupidly, waiting for a tram to come along.

* * *

185

At the top of Oriel Street Jack met a police sergeant and constable. The street was almost deserted. As he walked towards them he saw small groups of men appear from the bottom of the road. They either leaned against the corners of the intersecting streets or stopped and stood under the streetlamps, ostensibly discussing something important.

'Evening, Officers,' Jack greeted them both politely.

'Good evening, sir. Anything we can help you with?' the sergeant asked.

'Not really, thanks. You're new, I haven't seen you before.'

'Been here a couple of months. We were called to a disturbance.'

'What kind of "disturbance"?' Jack asked.

'The non-existent kind. The house where it was supposed to be was in darkness – not a sound from inside and not a soul to be seen either.'

Jack shook his head. 'Bad that. Wasting police time.'

'I pointed that out to the neighbour who made the complaint.' He looked up and down the street. 'Well, don't let us detain you. A bit of business, is it?'

Jack nodded.

'Right then, Constable, let's be on our way.'

They know, Jack thought. They damned well know that we're up to something. They couldn't have helped notice the number of men who had suddenly appeared.

The pair were well out of sight by the time the others joined him.

'Better make it quick. God knows what they're doing to that girl. Someone complained about a disturbance.'

'What did those two say?' Frank asked.

'Nothing much. They know something is going on. Let's

get a move on. It must have been Tessa screaming that the neighbour complained about.'

'Fine bloody carry-on! What's up with the fellers in this street that they hear a girl screaming and do nothing except call in the bloody scuffers? I'll bloody break every bone in his body if he's laid a finger on that girl,' Frank growled, thinking of his own daughter Maureen.

Tessa was huddled up on the floor in a corner of the dark kitchen, sobbing quietly. She had never been so afraid in her life. When she'd been dragged in and flung across the floor she'd got up and had flown at her captor like a vixen, screaming as loud as she could and using her feet, nails and teeth. Then a pain had exploded in her head as a blow sent her reeling and she'd crawled into the corner. She could feel her lip swelling and taste the saltiness of her blood. The whole side of her face was throbbing but the pain was the least of her worries. What were they going to do with her? Who were they? There was more than one man, she'd heard them talking. Then there had come a loud hammering on the front door. She'd tried to get up and shout but a large hand smelling of dirt and tobacco had almost suffocated her. Eventually after the hammering had brought no results the hand was removed and she had been kicked back to the corner. Her only hope was Elizabeth, but as she'd fought and kicked she'd seen her friend sent sprawling and heard her screams of agony. She remembered that Nessie had been walking ahead. Would Nessie have run home? She would certainly tell her mam and dad that Elizabeth was hurt. Would Elizabeth be able to tell them where she was? She didn't really know herself. It had all happened so quickly that she couldn't remember how long it had been before she'd been thrown into this house. Oh, Mam! Mam! If you can hear me, help me! Please, Mam! Don't let them hurt me! Let Elizabeth have got home! She repeated the words silently over and over again.

She didn't know how long she'd been there – an hour, two, three? – when she heard the roar and the crash of the back door as it was kicked open. She tried to scream and flatten herself further against the wall. Now what? Oh, Holy Mother, what was going to happen to her now?

'She's in here!' Frank Flynn roared and simultaneously she heard the shouts and the splintering of wood as the front door received the same treatment as the back.

Then she was lifted gently.

'Tessa, luv, are you hurt?'

She broke down helplessly as she recognised Jack Harrison's voice. She was safe. They'd come to find her.

'All right now, luv, it's all over. We've a bit of business to attend to here, then I'll take you home.'

She sat on the floor with her hands over her ears as the whole house erupted into a cacophony of shouts, curses, yells and screams of pain, then she was being lifted gently up in a pair of strong arms.

'Take her home, Frank. Our Delia should be back from the hospital by now and if I meet any scuffers it might be awkward to explain why we're carrying the poor kid home.'

Frank nodded. Their work here was finished. All the men were drifting out through the back door and down the jigger.

Jack closed the front door as best he could and thought how strange it was that there were no other doors open or people out on their steps to see what was going on. It was also rare to find an unoccupied house in this area. Probably the occupants had been paid to 'go on a bit of a trip'. Maybe all the neighbours had been threatened – but that was unlikely to have much effect in this area and someone *had* complained to the police.

He rubbed his right hand ruefully. His knuckles were skinned and his shoulder was aching but it was nothing to the state those three were in. He smiled with grim satisfaction. Doran had been fool enough to come too. He probably intended to send word to Richie, demanding his money for Tessa's safe return. Well, he'd send no one any kind of message now. Frank Flynn had stamped on both his hands as he'd sprawled on the floor. Mick Collins had finished the job with a heavy and well-aimed kick of his booted foot to the spine. Doran might never walk again and he doubted that the other two would either. They hadn't put up much of a fight, realising that the odds were against them. They were both lying sprawled in the lobby.

He saw the two policemen as he reached the top of the street.

'Finished your "bit of business"?' the sergeant asked pleasantly, his gaze taking in the state of Jack's clothing and the beginnings of a black eye.

'Yes, that's right, thanks. All accounted for.'

'Anything we can do?'

'Send for an ambulance. I think there's someone in number nine who might need one.'

The sergeant nodded slowly but the constable looked perturbed. 'An ambulance? Sarge, hadn't we better—'

'No, lad. There's nothing to worry about. When you've been on the job for as long as I have you know about these things. It's just letting yourself in for a mountain of paperwork. Inquiries, statements, interviewing the entire street and getting no co-operation or thanks.' He addressed Jack again. 'I presume the "patient" won't be pressing charges?'

'I can safely say he won't. None of them will.'

'More than one.'

'Right. Well, goodnight again.'

Jack nodded and walked on. On his own the young constable could have made things very awkward for them. Thank God the older man knew the way things were done around here. They looked after their own.

Delia was back with a very subdued Nessie and a worried Elizabeth whose arm was in plaster up to her elbow.

'It's her wrist. It will take time to heal. What happened?'

Both Richie and Colin got to their feet.

'Where is she? What have they done to her?' Richie pleaded. All the time he'd sat there alone, save for a very quiet and subdued Colin, he'd prayed that Tessa would come back unhurt. He was riddled with guilt and fear. It was all his fault and he'd never forgive himself ever. If . . . if anything had happened to her he'd fling himself into the river. He should have done without his beer and his smokes, walked to and from work, in fact anything that would save money to pay off that bloody loan. He felt numb, he couldn't bear to think what was happening to Tessa.

Colin had felt afraid too. More trouble. It was all his da ever seemed to do – cause trouble that he didn't seem to be able to sort out. He'd left it for all the other fellers in the street to attend to. He'd never really had much respect for his father and now his opinion of Richie sank even lower.

'It's all right, Delia, luv, Tessa's fine. She's got a cut lip and a very sore face and she's been through a terrible ordeal, but she'll get over it. I doubt whether those three will.'

'Three!' Delia cried.

'Aye, Doran himself and two hard cases. All on their way to hospital by now, I shouldn't wonder.'

'Jack, did anyone see you . . . any of you?'

'No. I think the neighbours knew something and stayed out of sight.' He didn't tell her about the police, that would really have worried her.

Elizabeth got up off the sofa, tears in her eyes, as Frank Flynn carried Tessa in.

'Oh, Tessa, luv!' Richie cried.

'She's not too bad, Richie. Shock, a cut lip, a bruised face.'

'I'm going for Dr Duncan,' Delia announced, snatching her coat from the hook on the wall.

'I don't think there's any need for that, luv. There's nothing broken. I'm certain of it.'

'Oh, Tessa, Tessa, I'm sorry. I'm sorry, luv! It's all my fault!' Richie took her in his arms and buried his face in her hair to hide his tears.

Tessa managed a smile as she hugged him. 'It's not your fault, Da . . . It's all over now.'

'It is. None of them can walk. This time we did the job properly. We should have done it the first time.'

'Well, let's not start on that, Jack. Let me see to her, she's staying here tonight. She can share our bed with Elizabeth. I'll double up with Nessie and you can have Elizabeth's bed.'

Delia knew that Tessa and Elizabeth would both draw comfort from each other and she herself would be there on hand should Nessie wake up with nightmares. This was something to give an adult nightmares, let alone an eleven-year-old child.

Chapter Fourteen

It would take some time for Tessa to get over her injuries and her fright. She was so exhausted by her ordeal that as soon as she'd lain her head on the pillow in Delia and Jack's warm and comfortable bed, she was asleep. Both she and Elizabeth had been given hot sweet tea with a drop of whisky in it. It helped dull the aches and pains.

Delia went herself to see Mother Superior to explain why Elizabeth would not be in school for quite a while and why Tessa wouldn't be back at work until the beginning of the following week. She'd had the doctor out to both of them, despite all their protestations, although there wasn't much he could tell her that she didn't already know: that it would take time for both of them to get over it.

To his questions about how the girls had sustained their injuries she'd replied that they had both been fooling around and had slipped on the icy cobbles and had fallen heavily and awkwardly. Knowing that if he suspected any foul play he would report it to the police, she made a great show of being furious that girls of their age had been acting like five-year-olds.

He advised an aspirin from time to time for the pain both in Elizabeth's arm and Tessa's bruised face and cut lip.

'That was five shillings wasted. He only told me what I already knew, that they were shocked and hurt,' she told Eileen later that day.

'I don't know why you put up with that feller, I don't. Five shillings just to come out and see them! 'E's got a nerve.'

'I suppose it's his professional opinion you have to pay for, and his time.'

'Some professional opinion! Doling out aspirins!' Eileen had remarked before getting back to the subject that engrossed the entire street: Tessa's abductors. 'Them moneylenders should all be horsewhipped and flung in Walton Jail. Taking advantage of people's troubles! Do you remember that one from Paul Street – Molly Kirkbride? She was in such a state that she borrowed four pounds off one of them and do you know 'ow much she actually paid back? Nearly twenty and it took 'er years. 'Im out of work, 'er with five kids an' her ma-in-law living with them. I tell you, Delia, they all need bloody 'orsewhipping!'

'Well, at least that lot got what was coming. Now, what can I get you?'

Mother Superior did not view the situation with sympathy, nor could she understand why a woman like Delia Harrison and her family had got mixed up with the likes of the O'Learys. She was a shrewd woman and not a sight nor sound escaped her. Brief snatches of conversation from both the kitchen and the classroom had enabled her to sum up the situation.

The girl, Tessa, worked diligently, was quiet and biddable, always punctual and grateful for any help. She was also devout – but she was still a common little slummy. And of course the Harrisons, who now had two daughters at the school, were not the usual type of parents who sent their daughters here. They were working-class and nearly every other pupil's parents were professional people or had a private income.

'You do realise, Mrs Harrison, that this is a crucial time for Elizabeth,' she stressed. 'She will be taking her exams this year and the results are very, very important if she's to go into the lower sixth form.'

'Oh, I do realise that, Mother. I'll make sure that the time she is off will not be wasted. She will study. Would it be at all possible for books to be sent home? Vanessa could bring them and take back the completed work.'

The woman was determined at least, the nun thought. 'I think that can be arranged. But how will she be able to cope with the written work?'

Delia thought for a minute. 'Would it be acceptable if she . . . read it out and either myself or my husband were to actually write it down for her?'

'You mean dictation? It's highly irregular.'

'I realise that but as you've just said, Mother, this is an important time for Elizabeth.'

The nun pressed the fingertips of both hands together and pursed her lips. 'You would have to sign to say that it is completely Elizabeth's work. That there has been no assistance with grammar, spelling or input from any other person.'

Delia flushed a little. Just what kind of parents did the nun think her daughter had: cheats?

'Of course. We wouldn't have it any other way,' she replied with a cold edge to her voice.

All the way home it irritated her. There was always the same attitude and it boiled down to the fact that the nun just didn't want the daughters of shopkeepers and the like in her precious school. Well, next time she wrote to Margaret she'd tell her. Her sister had been widowed for fifteen years and Lars Van Holste had been a rich man. She'd met him on the ship carrying her to New York and had been married a month later. Everyone in the family had been utterly surprised. Margaret wasn't a beauty but she had a certain attraction and a lively personality. Over the years, in her letters, Delia had come to realise that her sister was a very shrewd woman. Not calculating and unfeeling, but she kept an eye on her finances and watched her shares carefully. Oh, Margaret would write to Mother Superior, pointing out that her nieces should have the best education and treatment that money could buy, and if Notre Dame couldn't or wouldn't supply that graciously, then there were other establishments that most certainly would.

She was still annoyed when she got home. Jack was in the shop, which was empty.

'Sometimes I don't know how I keep my temper with that woman. I *know* she's taken Holy Orders but she's such a snob! I thought pride came high up on the list of the seven deadly sins.'

'It does. What did she say to upset you?'

'Nothing. Well, not in so many words. It's just her attitude. Come through while I put the kettle on, we'll hear the bell if we have a customer. I'm frozen.'

Both Tessa and Elizabeth were in the kitchen. 'What did the old dragon say?' Elizabeth asked her mother.

'That will do from you, milady! You just remember she's a nun and deserves respect.' Under her breath she asked God to forgive her for her hypocrisy. 'You are to do your schoolwork at home and either your da or me will write out the answers. It's all been arranged. You've got to pass your exams or your aunt will not be very pleased and neither will I. Oh, damn! There's the shop bell. You can make your da and me a cup of tea.'

'How can I?' Elizabeth asked.

'I'll do it,' Tessa offered. 'And I'll bring it out to you, Mrs Harrison.'

Delia nodded her thanks as she donned her shop coat and followed her husband through the door. It was the lunchtime rush. There were not many people around here who could shop for a week all at the same time. They shopped from day to day or even meal to meal.

'I thought I was going to get out of doing any work.'

'Don't be daft. You didn't honestly think they'd let you sit around all day reading those love stories you've always got your head in?'

'Well, I didn't think I'd have to do homework. I'll have to know it all really well if one of them is going to write it out for me. I wonder how she managed to get them to agree to that?'

'It doesn't matter how.' Tessa filled the teapot and left the tea to brew. 'You're going to have to tell them soon about not wanting to stay at school.'

'I know, but I'll have to take my exams just the same. I can't leave without *anything*.'

'Well, I don't envy you. Why don't you want to be a teacher? It's a really good job. It's a profession. Just think how terrified everyone is of their teachers.'

'I know but I'm fed up with school! I really *hate* it and I don't like kids at all. I can't help that. I'd make a terrible teacher and ruin God knows how many kids' educations.'

'Well, you're going to have to say all that to your mam and da.'

Elizabeth pulled a rueful face and let her breath out slowly. 'I know. Maybe I'd better tell them tonight. Will you stay with me?'

'What good would that do? I can't say anything to help because I think you're mad to pass up a chance like that.'

'I know, but just *be* there. That will help.'

Tessa nodded. 'Oh, all right then. But I'd better pour the tea and then go back home. The fire will be almost out by now and if it is I'll have a terrible time getting it going again.'

All afternoon Elizabeth rehearsed what she was going to say but no matter how she put it, she knew it wouldn't make things any better. She had to steel herself for an almighty row, but one she fully intended to win because she had very different plans for her future.

Nessie came home laden with text books and exercise books.

'It's all written on a piece of paper and I'm to take back the Geography and Maths tomorrow,' she informed her sister with some satisfaction. She'd been the centre of attention all lunchtime and at breaks too. Everyone wanted to hear every detail and for once she felt important and confident.

Of course she didn't tell them about what her da and the others had done, she told them it was the police, guided by Elizabeth's information, who had found Tessa and brought her home. Nessie was far from stupid.

Elizabeth groaned. 'I'd forgotten that flaming Geography test. I can never get the trade winds right and what use is it anyway? I'm never likely to go anywhere near the southern hemisphere or even the Equator.'

'Well, it's got to be done by morning,' Nessie replied firmly.

'Go and get Tessa for me will you, Nessie?'

'What for? She certainly won't know anything about winds of any kind and besides, it's nearly teatime.'

'I'd forgotten that. Just go and ask her to come down straight after tea.'

'What will you give me?' Nessie demanded.

'I'll give you a clout with this plaster on my arm. Go on, Mam won't mind.'

Nessie went off in a huff, slamming the scullery door behind her.

When the meal was served Elizabeth hardly ate anything. Delia didn't press her or complain, thinking she was still in shock. She pushed the food around on her plate, her stomach churning. But she *had* to do it, she just *had* to.

She usually helped her mam to clear away and wash up but now all she could do was clear the table with her left hand. She jumped nervously as she heard Tessa's voice in the shop.

'Is everything all right at home, Tessa?' Delia asked as she folded the tablecloth and put it into one of the drawers of the dresser.

'Yes, thanks. They've all had their tea and I've washed up. Our Jimmy's gone next door, as usual, and our Colin's gone out, as usual. Mrs Greely called on her way to work.'

Delia raised her eyebrows. 'As usual!'

'Is your hand still hurting?' Tessa asked Elizabeth.

'It sort of throbs. Does your mouth hurt?'

'Only when I try to smile.' Tessa sat down on the sofa beside Elizabeth and jabbed her friend in the ribs with her elbow.

Elizabeth took a deep breath. Her whole future would be decided in the next half-hour.

'Mam, sit down. There's something I want to say to you.'

Delia looked at her quizzically. 'What?'

'Sit down, please.'

'Holy Mother of God, is it that bad?'

'I suppose it is, in a way. I . . . after . . . after my exams I'm not going back to school and I don't care how much you rant and rave, Mam, I mean it. I don't want to become a teacher. I'd be terrible. I'd ruin all the kids' lives and that wouldn't be fair. In fact it would be almost a crime and definitely a sin.'

Delia's eyes narrowed. She was taken aback but she should have seen this coming.

'I think this is something your father should hear. I'll be back.'

As she went into the shop Elizabeth looked pleadingly at Tessa.

'There's nothing I can say,' Tessa hissed.

When Delia returned with Jack in tow, Elizabeth's resolve wavered. They both looked very grim.

'So, what's all this your mother's just told me?' Jack demanded.

'Da, I know it's not what you want for me, what anyone wants for me . . .'

'No, it isn't, and especially not your Aunty Margaret! Do you realise just how much money has been spent on educating you? It runs into hundreds of pounds and you want to throw it all away.'

'Mam, I don't want to throw it all away! I *will* have qualifications.'

'And just what, may I ask, do you intend to do for a job?'

'I . . . I want to be a hairdresser!'

'A *what*?' Delia could hardly believe her ears.

'A hairdresser. All properly trained with an apprenticeship. You know I'm good at it, Mam.'

'I don't care how good you are at it, you are *not* going to be a hairdresser!' Delia shouted, then thought fleetingly of exactly what her neighbours and customers would say.

'Well, I'm *not* going back to school either!' Elizabeth yelled back.

Tessa cringed.

'She's got books, Mam,' said Nessie triumphantly. 'I've seen her with *The Art and Craft of Hairdressing*. She hides it in the bottom of her wardrobe. Under that box she's got her Communion dress in.'

'You sly sneaking little tell-tale, Nessie!' Elizabeth yelled.

'Nessie, that will be enough! Take your own homework upstairs and don't come down until we've sorted this out,' Jack said in a voice that brooked no argument.

'Oh, what am I to do with her, Jack? A hairdresser? A *hairdresser* of all things, for God's sake! We had such plans for her. What am I going to tell our Margaret?' Delia clasped her hands as if in supplication.

'Elizabeth, for the last time I'm telling you that you *will* continue your education.'

'I *won't*, Da! I *won't* do it! I'm not going back there. I'll leave home, run away, before I'll go back. And I'll keep running away no matter how many times I'm brought back. I . . . I'll even go to a House of Correction for Girls! I *will*!'

Elizabeth was near to tears but she meant what she said.

Jack looked at her and knew she wasn't just bluffing or making idle threats. She could be very, very stubborn at times.

Delia sat down at the table, covering her eyes with her hands. What had got into Elizabeth? She knew, she'd always known what was planned for her. Maybe it had something to do with Tessa. She wondered if she should have allowed the friendship to develop. But she'd thought that if Elizabeth went on to Teacher Training College the gulf between them would widen and they would grow apart. She didn't think that Tessa had deliberately tried to manipulate Elizabeth, if anything it would be the opposite way round; she knew her daughter. Oh, things were such a mess. The events of the last few days had been bad enough, and now this!

There was silence in the room, broken only by the ticking of the clock on the dresser. Tessa twisted her hands helplessly and Elizabeth held her breath.

At last her father spoke. 'If you are so determined that you would leave your home and shame us by being placed in an institution for wayward girls, then perhaps some enquiries should be made about an apprenticeship.'

'Jack, are you mad?' Delia cried.

He shook his head and gestured to her to remain calm and silent.

Elizabeth seized the opportunity. 'I'd be so grateful, Da, really I would. It's . . . it's my whole life I'm thinking of and I *have* thought about it, hard.'

'She . . . she does have talent . . .' Tessa said quietly and hesitantly.

Jack nodded curtly.

'What am I going to say to our Margaret, just tell me that? After all she's done! After all the money she's sent! Hundreds of pounds! And that ungrateful niece of hers has thrown it all back in her face!'

'Tell her the truth, Delia. You never know. Perhaps, in time, Elizabeth might have her own salon. Nessie might be the one who becomes a teacher, who knows?'

It was Delia's turn to shake her head. He'd taken Elizabeth's side. She didn't understand him or his thinking. Apprenticeships; salons; Nessie being a teacher. Nessie wasn't half as clever as Elizabeth, she had to work so much harder and Elizabeth was throwing everything away!

'Elizabeth,' Jack went on, 'I want your solemn word that you'll work hard for these exams. That you'll matriculate with good marks.'

A great wave of relief and gratitude surged through Elizabeth. 'Oh, Da, I *will*! I promise I'll do really well. Do you . . . do you mean it about an apprenticeship?'

'Well, if it's what you really want I suppose I do. But one slip-up, one set of bad marks and it's back you'll go into the lower sixth.'

Delia groaned and gave up the fight. She was seething inside and she'd give Jack a piece of her mind when the girls were in bed.

Sensing that her presence was adding to the friction between her parents Elizabeth went back to Tessa's house.

'I did it! I really did it!' she cried as she plumped herself down on the sofa. The house was empty; Tessa's da had gone to the pub.

'I never expected you'd be allowed to be a hairdresser. Wasn't your da great?'

'Oh yes, though I bet he's getting the length of Mam's tongue now. He knew I meant it, you see.'

Tessa was incredulous. 'Would you *really* have left home? Run away?'

'Of course I would. Da knew that. And I'd keep on running away until I got my own way. I'd *hate* to have to go to some terrible institution but I'd have gone.'

'You are the most determined, stubborn and often stupid person I've ever met, Elizabeth Harrison.'

'I know but now perhaps I'll get a bit of peace. It looks as though our Nessie's future will be concentrated on from today.'

'You've got what you wanted,' Tessa said wistfully. 'I won't be so lucky.'

'Why not? I'll help you, and you can ask Sister Bernadette too. You're always saying she's a real lady. She'll teach you manners and how to speak to people and things like that.'

'But wouldn't I need some qualifications? I haven't got any.'

Elizabeth turned her attention to Tessa's plight. 'I can't see them wanting much. I mean, all stewardesses do is look after people and you can do that. You've been looking after the family ever since your mam died. Why don't you go and ask at the shipping offices just what you'll need – when you feel better, that is?'

'Will you come with me? I'd be terrified.'

'Of course. You helped me and what are friends for?'

Tessa felt hopeful, really hopeful now. Sister Bernadette would teach her the things she would need to know and what Elizabeth had said about looking after people was true. If she got a good reference from the Convent that would surely be as good as a qualification.

* * *

Delia was still tight-lipped and fuming but she had agreed to write to the large hairdressing establishments to see how much an apprenticeship would cost. Two days later Tessa and Elizabeth both got the tram into town.

It was a clear but windy day and Elizabeth held on to her hat with her left hand. Her right arm was in a sling and her coat was buttoned over it. Tessa looked neat and tidy in her grey coat and red scarf, mittens and tam-o'-shanter.

'Which one shall we start with?' Elizabeth had asked.

They'd made a list of the most likely shipping lines who carried passengers and therefore stewardesses: Cunard, Canadian Pacific and Elder Dempster Line. They'd also looked up in the atlas just where the ships of those lines sailed to. Cunard went to New York and sometimes cruised around the West Indies. Canadian Pacific sailed to Canada, Australia and the Far East, and Elder Dempster plied to and from the west coast of Africa. The latter was also the 'mail' shipping line.

'Elder Dempster. They're not as big as the others. I might stand more of a chance with them.'

They got off the tram outside the Town Hall and walked down Water Street. India Buildings was at the bottom of the road, part of it facing the Pier Head.

The offices of the Elder Dempster Steam Ship Company were on the second floor and they climbed the stairs, shunning the lift. As Tessa said, she was scared enough already and she'd never been in a lift in her life. When they reached their destination Elizabeth pushed open the door that led to the reception area.

'Go on, just ask them plainly. I'll wait here.'

Tessa looked very nervous and bit her lip.

'Stop that! Look confident,' Elizabeth hissed.

Tessa made her way to the polished counter where a middle-aged man was writing in a large, heavy book. 'Yes, miss, can I help?' he asked genially.

'I . . . I . . . hope so, sir.'

'If it's about the next ship bound for Dakar I can give you an itinerary.'

'No, no, it's . . . nothing like that. I . . . I want to be a stewardess and I'd like . . . to . . . know . . .' Her nerves got the better of her and she fell silent.

He smiled at her. 'How old are you?'

'Sixteen, sir. I've worked in a convent for a year so I'm used to hard work and I've looked after my family since my mam died.'

'It's not that. You can't go away to sea until you're at least eighteen. Twenty-one with some companies.'

'Oh.' Tessa was disappointed.

'Come back when you're a couple of years older and I'm sure we can do something.'

She nodded her thanks, turned away and walked to where Elizabeth was waiting.

'Well?'

'I can't go yet.'

'What do you mean – yet?'

'I'm not old enough. I've got to be at least eighteen.'

'That's not fair! They take lads on at fourteen and sixteen – look at Johnny, he's been with Cunard for over a year now.'

'Well, that's what he said.'

'Oh, typical! One rule for them and another for us.'

'Oh, Elizabeth, get off your soap box.' Tessa was

disappointed and dejected. It had taken so much courage just to come and ask.

Once outside they walked back down Water Street to the Pier Head.

As usual the river was busy. There were ships tied up at the Landing Stage, the ferries were criss-crossing the choppy grey water, the dredgers moved slowly up and down and there were ships anchored mid-river, waiting to come alongside the Stage.

Tessa sighed as she stood, hands on the railings, looking towards the estuary.

'Don't be disappointed, Tessa, you've got two years to learn all kinds of things. Sister Bernardette and even Sister Augustine would help you. I'm sure when you're eighteen they'll take you on at once.'

'Do you think so, really?'

'I *do*.'

Tessa didn't reply. She looked pensive. I'll do it, Mam. I really will. You'll be proud of me, I swear it. I'll keep my promise, she said to herself. When she at last turned away there were tears in her eyes. Could a girl from the slums really get on in life? Could an ignorant girl like her who had come to Naylor Street in rags rise one day to the position of Chief Stewardess?

Chapter Fifteen

Delia had a shop full; it was late on a typically showery April afternoon and this was the teatime rush. Jack hadn't been feeling too well all day and she'd made him rest as much as possible. There was little Elizabeth could do to help her, with her arm still in plaster, and besides, she had a great deal of reading and learning by rote to do.

'Right, who's next?' she asked briskly, although she felt far from business-like. She'd been on her feet more or less since seven that morning and her back, feet and calves were aching. She also had the beginnings of a headache and wondered if she was sickening for something. Both she and Jack worked very hard. The only day she had off was Sunday and quite often people came to the back door asking for whatever it was they'd run out of. She looked questioningly at those nearest the counter.

'Well, I am but you go before me, Maisie, your feller gets 'ome before mine,' Katie Collins said generously. She'd had a bad week and money was very tight but she didn't want Maisie Keegan to see the few bits she could afford. She didn't mind the other customers knowing, not even Eileen Flynn, but Maisie had a mouth like the Mersey tunnel and it would be all around the parish that Mick Collins had drunk the housekeeping again.

'I'll 'ave a quarter of boiled 'am, Delia, luv, an' 'alf a pound of them tomatoes.'

'Boiled 'am on a Thursday? 'Ave yer come into some money then, Maisie?' Eileen asked.

'No, but I'm goin' ter our Rita's ternight, 'er feller is due 'ome from sea an' yer know what she's like at 'ousework. That feller of 'ers is dead fussy. Always goin' on about clutter, an' not puttin' things away, an' beds not made proper, like. Yer can't 'alf tell 'e's a flamin' steward. Do yer know what the latest trick is?' Maisie stopped to make sure everyone was giving their full attention. Delia sighed heavily. It was no use trying to rush Maisie.

'Well, go on then, Maisie, girl, we 'aven't got all night,' Eileen urged.

Maisie straightened her shoulders and patted her hair, well satisfied by the look of avid curiosity on her neighbours' faces. 'He won't 'ave no crusts on the butties!'

'Why not?' Katie demanded.

''As ter 'ave them all cut off. 'E says it ain't "proper" to 'ave them on "sandwiches" – if yer please.'

'It's a flaming sin that! Wasting good food,' Eileen remarked – with some justification, Delia thought.

'I've got to say I agree with you. Working as a first-class steward with Cunard has gone to his head.'

'That's just what I said ter our Rita. "Rita," I said, "tell 'im that iffen 'e wants ter carry on like that yer want more of an allotment left yer." But she won't. 'E 'as 'er demented when 'e's on leave, she's always glad ter see the back of 'im an' I can't say I blame 'er. So I'm goin' ter give 'er an 'and, like. But I can't leave my lot without something ter eat.'

Privately, Delia thought that a quarter of boiled ham and a few tomatoes wasn't much to leave for a man and his two sons when they got in from work and that Maisie should leave her sister to cope with her husband and the odd ways he had.

'Mick was saying that the news isn't too good,' Katie Collins said conversationally.

'What news?' Eileen demanded.

'That feller with the funny name, you know, the Minister for War. 'E was on the wireless.'

'You 'aven't gorra wireless.'

'I'm tellin' yer what some feller what's got a wireless set said ter Mick,' Katie said sharply in reply to Maisie's comment.

'Oh, God help us all! Tell me it's not going to start all over again,' Delia said, looking around the shop. There was a momentary lull; all the women present had lost fathers, uncles, brothers and cousins in the last war. Delia herself had lost both her older brothers in the mass slaughter that had been the battle of the Somme.

'At least that fightin' in Spain is over.' Maisie broke the silence. 'That's *good* news anyway.' She cast a disparaging glance at Katie. Everyone knew that war was drawing closer but no one wanted to think about it.

'Well, the government have said that the Territorial Army is goin' ter be doubled and there are more arms factories to be built an' trainin' camps and 'undreds of thousands of uniforms made, an' the Corporation is givin' out air-raid shelters ter nearly everyone, except us,' said Katie.

'Why not us?' Maisie asked indignantly.

'Because we 'aven't got anywhere ter put them. They won't fit into a yard, you've got to 'ave a birrof a garden.'

'What are we supposed to do then?' Eileen was just as indignant.

'We're ter go to municipal shelters, so they say, or cellars, if you've got one.'

'God, them 'ouses that 'ave got cellars 'ave families livin' in them! You'd be crushed to bits.'

''E also said they were goin' ter ev— evacuate all the kids.' Katie stumbled with the unfamiliar word.

'If I were you, Katie, I'd be telling Mick not to be taking so much notice of the wireless or wasting his money on flaming newspapers. We don't *want* another war and we don't want to hear about that Hitler or the other one, the Italian feller that's got up like a toy soldier with all that gold braid on his uniform – Mussolini. We've enough on our plates to cope with. Is that it, Maisie, or is there anything else?' Delia finished.

'No, that's all, luv.'

'One and fivepence, then. Do you want it on the slate?'

'If you don't mind, Delia. 'E gets paid termorrer, I'll settle up then.'

Delia reached under the counter and brought out a large book. She opened it at the page that read 'Keegan. Number 16' and added the amount to the one already owing.

'Now, Katie, it's you and we'd better get a move on.'

When things eventually quietened down Delia breathed a sigh of relief and went through into the kitchen where Elizabeth was reading a book. Jack was there too, looking as if he was in for a heavy cold or a dose of bronchitis.

'I'm worn out. Why do they always have to come in together? Can't they stagger it a bit? And Maisie Keegan was full of herself as usual. Some tale about their Rita and her husband. Katie Collins was full of her usual doom and gloom too.'

'Oh, aye, what is it now?'

'Mick has been listening to someone's wireless and reading things out to her from the paper too by the sound of it.' Delia put the kettle on the gas ring.

'What things?'

'Things I don't want to know about. Arms factories, training camps, air-raid shelters.'

Elizabeth looked up. 'Is there going to be a war, Mam?'

'I hope not. Dear God, I hope not. You've never been through one, I have.' Elizabeth followed her mother's gaze to the photographs of her dead uncles on the dresser.

Jack shook his head. It was growing more and more likely. He'd read that eighty thousand air-raid shelters were being distributed each week. If the bombing of innocent civilians was likely, as had happened in Spain, then they'd need them all. And if those two maniac dictators were power-mad and determined to get themselves Empires, like Britain had, then who knew where it would end?

'Well, thank God we've no sons and that you're too old, Jack.'

'That's just what a feller wants to hear when he's feeling like death warmed up,' Jack said mournfully.

Delia shook her head as she made the tea but before she could even pour it out the shop bell rang tinnily.

'Oh, blast! Elizabeth, do you think you can see who it is while I get a few sips of tea?'

'Mam, I'm supposed to be learning this.'

'I'll go, Mam. I'll come and tell you who it is and what they want. It can't be *that* hard to weigh out sugar and tea and stuff,' Nessie offered, thinking of the pile of homework she herself had to do and how best to postpone it.

'All right, Nessie. I suppose you can manage. I'll be out in five minutes.'

Nessie found May Greely in the shop.

'It's all right, Nessie, there's nothing I need. I've come to see your mam.'

'Oh,' Nessie replied rather dejectedly. 'You'd better come through.'

Delia was surprised. 'May! What's wrong? Why aren't you on your way to work?'

'I am. I told him I wouldn't be in until five. There's something I want to tell you. Do you think Elizabeth could go to Tessa's? Our Ginny's over there.'

'Of course she can if it's that important.'

'It is.'

Delia looked at her closely. It didn't look like trouble, May didn't seem upset.

'Nessie, will you go back out into the shop, please? Elizabeth, put that away and go to Tessa's.'

Both Elizabeth and Nessie looked startled and very curious.

'You keep as near to the door as you can, Nessie. See what you can hear,' Elizabeth whispered once they were into the shop. 'Mam, what time am I supposed to come back?' she shouted.

'In half an hour,' came the muffled reply.

Nessie could hardly contain her curiosity. 'I wonder what's up?'

'I don't know, just keep listening and hope no one comes in and wants serving,' Elizabeth answered.

For once they were of the same mind and there wasn't an argument.

When Elizabeth walked into Tessa's kitchen she stopped dead. Tessa and Ginny were sitting on the sofa; both were pale and looked dazed.

'What's up with you two?'

'I . . . I just don't believe it,' Ginny said, shaking her head.

'Believe what?' Elizabeth demanded.

'Da . . . Da's going to—'

'Marry my mam,' Ginny interrupted Tessa.

Elizabeth's mouth formed an 'O' of surprise. She was speechless.

'They told us just before Da went out and Mrs Greely went to . . .' Tessa also shook her head in disbelief. It still hadn't really sunk in.

Elizabeth had regained her composure. 'So that's what your mam wanted to talk to my mam about, Ginny. I got chased along here and our Nessie is minding the shop.'

'How could he? How could he, Elizabeth? Mam . . . Mam's only been dead a year!' Tessa cried.

Elizabeth pulled a small stool from its place by the range and sat in front of the two disbelieving girls. 'Didn't you notice anything?' she asked.

'Like what?' Ginny asked.

'Well, I suppose like them . . . going out?'

'She's always in and out of here all day and night. How were we supposed to know?' Ginny answered.

Elizabeth was still trying to take it in herself and she wondered how her mam and da were taking this piece of news. 'You won't have to call her "Mam", will you?'

Tessa couldn't reply to this at all. There was no one who could take her mam's place, least of all May Greely.

'Will I have to call him "Da"?' Ginny asked. She hadn't thought of that aspect of it. It was so long ago since her own da had died that it would be difficult to think of Richie O'Leary as 'Da'.

'Oh, who knows *anything*! Oh, why? Why did he have to do it? It was all right the way . . . things were.' Tessa broke down in tears. She just couldn't comprehend why her father had to marry anyone. Didn't he care about all the years he'd spent with Mam? About all the hard work and sacrifices Mam had made? He'd been lost and heartbroken, just as she'd been, at losing Mam. So how could he change so quickly? How could he forget so quickly?

Elizabeth was trying to think of things to say to cheer both Tessa and Ginny up. 'Well, look at it like this, you'll both be better off. You can share all the housework and shopping and cooking. Your Jimmy is always next door and Colin is always out – somewhere – and there'll be more money coming in, and your mam can bring all your stuff over here. You *are* going to live here, Ginny, aren't you?'

'Yes. That's why they told us together, like.'

'Does Colin know?'

Tessa nodded. 'He didn't say anything. He just slammed out.'

'So, what's new? What about Jimmy?'

Tessa's tears had stopped. 'I don't think he really understood. All he wanted to know was did it mean he'd have to stop going next door to Harold.'

'So, when is it going to be then?'

'They didn't say.'

'It won't be too long, Mam said the sooner the better to give the owld biddies less to talk about.'

Tessa burst into tears again. 'I . . . I don't think I'm going to be able to . . . face people. What will I say?'

'Why do you have to say anything? Let them jangle,' Elizabeth replied firmly.

'You know what they're all like around here,' Ginny wailed, feeling just as upset and confused as Tessa.

'Well, if you don't say anything and just look as if you're not upset at all they'll soon get fed up and start on something else.'

'I don't think I can do that! It . . . it will hurt too much. It will look as though I've forgotten all about my mam already and I *haven't*.'

'No, it won't, Tessa. People *do* know how much you loved your mam and how much you miss her. If anyone asks me or our Nessie, that's what I'll tell them. That you'll never forget your mam but you understand about your da and Mrs Greely.'

'Will I have to change my name?' Ginny asked, wiping her eyes. She was getting used to the situation already. Elizabeth was at least talking sense.

'How should I know? I don't think so anyway. And do the same as Tessa if anyone is hardfaced enough to ask you outright what you think. If you both put on brave faces it will be "much ado about nothing",' Elizabeth finished, remembering her Shakespeare from her English Literature lessons.

Tessa was still dabbing at her eyes but Ginny looked much happier until Colin barged into the kitchen. 'I thought *you'd* be here, Elizabeth Harrison. There's no show without Punch,' he snapped.

Elizabeth glared at him and got to her feet. She was almost as tall as him. 'I was sent here by your future stepmother.'

217

'With the mouth on her I'll bet we're the talk of the neighbourhood by now.'

'Oh, that's rich coming from you, Colin O'Leary. The whole street has got you taped,' Elizabeth replied sarcastically.

Colin ignored her. 'Ginny, will you come for a walk with me? We're not going to get any peace and privacy here. Da's gone off to the pub to announce the happy event. Everyone will be buying him ale and *she'll* be lapping up all the attention.'

As they left Tessa dissolved into tears again and Elizabeth put her arm around her, scowling at Colin's retreating back, but Tessa knew her brother was just as appalled as she was by the news. He'd never had much time for May; by the look of it, he'd have less from now on. For once in their lives they both felt the same way.

Delia felt quite taken aback herself. It was the last thing she'd expected but she was glad May had come and told her before the street gossips got wind of it – and they would. Nothing got past them; the walls were so thin you could hear almost everything that was going on in your neighbours' homes.

'I'm pleased for you both. When is it to be?'

'The end of the month. We've been to see Father Walsh and it's not going to be anything big or showy. Neither of us are spring chickens by a long chalk. In fact you'd be a long time looking at a chicken before you'd think of me,' May laughed.

They'd decided that their feelings for each other had grown and would continue to grow and so it made sense for them to get married. She'd been a widow for years and Richie had left a decent interval after Mary's death.

'We're just going to have family and a couple of friends. Maybe have a bit of a meal out somewhere. That'll be the best way to keep some of the gossip down. Oh, I know tongues will be wagging but it's all above board, we've nothing to hide.'

Delia nodded. May was good company and she was still a good-looking woman, attributes that made her popular with the customers of the pubs she worked in.

'Will you be giving up work?'

'I'll have to give up one of them, probably the Globe. I mean, it's not going to look right me serving me own husband. Eddie Doyle's not going to be happy but I earn more working in the Unicorn. You know what a flaming skinflint Eddie is. And talking of him, I'd better be making a move.'

'Well, we both wish you every happiness, May, you've been a widow for a long time and it's not easy for a woman on her own,' Jack said sincerely. He liked May Greely.

'And thanks for coming to let us know personally before it becomes public knowledge. What about the kids?' Delia added.

May shrugged. 'Colin just slammed out and I left our Ginny and Tessa looking as though they'd been hit by a steamroller, but they'll get used to the idea. They'll have to.'

As Delia closed the door behind May she looked at Jack quizzically.

'Well, that's a turn-up for the book. Didn't you suspect anything?' he asked.

'No, I didn't. Well, if I'm really truthful I did suspect that something was going on but it certainly had nothing to do with marriage. God forgive me for such uncharitable thoughts.'

Jack grinned. 'At least she came and told us. In half an hour the street will be up! There'll be women hanging over the yard walls as far down as the tannery. It's the best piece of gossip since Richie moved here.'

Delia looked concerned. 'I wonder how Tessa's taking it? She worshipped her mam and it is only a year since the poor woman was buried.'

'What about Ginny?'

'I think she'll be all right. In fact I think Richie will come off best. More money, more help, and someone to make the decisions. You know how utterly hopeless he is, Jack. Oh, don't get me wrong, I like him, but you've got to admit he's not much use dealing with trouble or making decisions. But I suppose most of the men in this street would be useless if they were widowed. Look at Frank Flynn and Mick Collins – couldn't organise anything to save their lives. No, I think they'll be good for each other. She's easy-going but she can get strict with the kids. She'll stand no nonsense from them. She'll also watch that Richie doesn't drink too much or get into debt again. I'll say this for her, she's always been a good manager. Apart from a couple of port and lemons I've never known her to waste money or get into debt and that's unusual around here, especially for a widow. And she's never . . . well, tried to earn money by "other means".'

'You know, Delia, you really surprise me sometimes. You must have *thought* about May going on the streets to earn a living to mention it at all.'

Delia became flustered. 'Nearly every woman in the street

must have *thought* about it, Jack. That's not saying one thinks she *would*. No, give her her due, she's always stayed respectable.'

Nessie, who had hardly been able to hear anything because she'd had two customers in, caught the end of the discussion. If she could, she'd wheedle it all out of Elizabeth because Mam certainly wouldn't tell *her* all the ins and outs, not by the look on her face. She was annoyed about *something* because her cheeks were pink and her lips were pursed up as if she'd been sucking a lemon.

'Well, aren't you going to say anything, Ginny?' Colin asked as they walked to the tram stop. They always went to Lester Gardens these days, weather permitting.

'What do you want me to say, Col?'

'I dunno.' He, like Tessa, was shocked and disgusted. He knew what May Greely wanted, beside the obvious. She'd been fed up managing on her own all these years. She wanted security, more money, a whole house instead of a couple of rooms. He'd never liked her and he knew the feeling was mutual. But when he thought of the two of them occupying that bed, the bed Delia Harrison had bought and in which his mam had died, it turned his stomach. She'd manipulated his da and like a fool his da had fallen for her tricks. There was however a good side to it and one he was thankful for.

'I suppose it will be a bit strange, like, to start with. But as Elizabeth said, we'll share all the housework and the washing, ironing and things like that. There'll be more money coming in so we'll stand a good chance of keeping more of our wages and then we'll be able to go out again, Col, like we used to do and have more things . . . special things, like.'

Although he was working, Colin always said they couldn't afford 'treats', as he called going out to specific places. He was saving up, he'd told her once when she'd got really upset about it. She thought he was saving up for a ring for her, so she'd not complained any further.

'But we won't be able to, Ginny.'

She looked up at him. 'Why? Don't you love me any more?' Tears sprang to her eyes and her bottom lip began to tremble.

'I do, Ginny, but don't you see? We'll be family. We'll be related.'

She was still mystified. 'Yes, but . . .?'

God, but she was thick, he thought, and she was looking at him in that stupid way she had.

'We'll be stepbrother and stepsister. We'll never be able to be together, to get married, like. It's not allowed and not only by the church.'

The realisation hit her as though she'd been punched in the stomach. 'Not . . . not . . . get married?'

'No. *I* don't want them to get married, Ginny, and that's the truth.' It was, he thought. For once he wasn't lying. 'I don't see why they can't keep things as they are.'

Ginny's eyes were now full of tears. 'Did . . . did you say that? Oh, talk to your da, Col, please. Make him see he's not being . . . fair, and I'll tell Mam I . . . I . . . love you and want to marry you but if she's marrying your da then . . .' She broke down in sobs and he put his arm around her.

'It won't do any good, Ginny. You know your mam, she's determined, and Da . . . well, nothing I could say would change *his* mind. He's not much time for me and neither has your mam. I'm sorry, Ginny, but we'll just have to treat each other as brother and sister, there's nothing else we can do.'

This was terrible! She'd not given that side of it a thought, but Mam was ruining their lives and Colin didn't seem to be bothered. Ginny struggled free of his grip and began to run. She didn't know where she was going to – even if she went to the ends of the earth it wouldn't help. She loved him and now he'd been snatched away from her and it wasn't right! How could they do this to her?

Chapter Sixteen

Ginny was inconsolable. She walked the streets in a daze, barely seeing anything through a mist of tears. When she returned home it was late, very late. May had just come in herself but she had not been worried by her daughter's absence, thinking Ginny was still over with Tessa.

'Ginny! What's the matter with you? You look terrible. I know it was a bit of a shock, luv, but your da's been dead for years. I can understand Tessa being upset, she only lost her mam last year, but there's no need for you to get yourself into this state. We'll all get on like a house on fire, you wait and see.'

'I don't care about anyone being dead! Or about getting on,' Ginny sobbed.

'Oh, come here to me, luv. I'd no idea you'd get so upset.'

As May tried to put an arm around her daughter, Ginny shied away. 'You've ruined my future, Mam! You've ruined it and you don't care.'

May wondered what on earth had got into her daughter. She'd never seen her so upset. And what did she mean by 'ruined'? 'What do you mean by that, Ginny?'

Ginny tried to fight down her sobs. 'Colin and me, that's what I mean. We'll be stepbrother and stepsister.'

May was still mystified. 'So?'

'We'll never be able to get married, that's what I mean! And it's all your fault, Mam!'

'Ginny Greely, you're far too young to be thinking of things like that!' This aspect hadn't even occurred to May.

'I don't mean now! When we were older! I love him and he loves me and you've *ruined* our lives!'

May was perturbed. 'Ginny, luv, pull yourself together. He's the only lad you've been out with and you're far too young even to know what love is.' She doubted that Colin O'Leary was capable of loving anyone other than himself.

'I'm not! I'm not!' Ginny protested. *She* knew how she felt, Mam didn't.

May pushed her gently down on the sofa. 'Ginny, now you just listen to me. You're only sixteen. You've got your whole life ahead of you. You'll have plenty of fellers wanting to take you out and one who will, eventually, love you, *really* love you, and want to marry you. Colin O'Leary isn't the only lad on earth.' She tried to be lighthearted, to lift Ginny's spirits. 'Fellers are like trams, there's always another one coming along. Now, stop that crying and go to bed, you've had a long and upsetting evening.'

Ginny wasn't placated and her Mam's flippant attitude only made her more angry and upset. 'I don't *want* another lad. I just want Colin! Oh, I'll never forgive you for this, Mam! How can I live under the same roof as him and just stop loving him? I'll be seeing him every day of my life and I won't be able to stand it! I *won't*!'

'Oh, Ginny, wipe your eyes. If I'd have known you were going to get this upset I'd have told you on your own, not with Tessa and *him*.' But Ginny refused to be comforted and ran from the room, leaving May staring after her and genuinely concerned.

This was something she hadn't known about: that Ginny

hoped one day to marry Colin O'Leary. That was something she certainly didn't want to happen. She'd not even guessed that Ginny was so fond of him. She disliked and distrusted the lad: he was trouble with a capital 'T'. He'd had poor Mary demented, long before they'd moved here, or so she had heard. She didn't know exactly what he'd done but there had been speculation long before she'd seen him lurking around railway stations. Well, she was determined that he wasn't going to have her demented too.

Mary, God rest her, had been so ill that she'd had enough to contend with. Thank God she'd never lived to see all the trouble there had been with Mogsey Doran. But she, May, was fit and well able to cope with Colin and his antics.

Perhaps seeing him every day would open Ginny's eyes to just what he was really like. Maybe the saying 'familiarity breeds contempt' would prove true. She certainly hoped so.

She sighed heavily and took off her shoes. She could hear Ginny sobbing in the other room. She put the kettle on as she always did: that last cup of tea helped her to unwind. Well, both Ginny and Colin would just have to make the best of it because Jack Harrison was right. She'd been on her own for too long, Richie genuinely seemed to love her and she was very fond of him. She didn't love him the way she'd loved Harry, Ginny's da. And she could never block out the memory of that terrible day when they'd come to tell her he'd fallen into the almost empty hold of the cargo ship *Liberty* and was dead. He'd broken his neck and back and died instantaneously, the blockerman had said. But that had been when she'd been a young woman with a five-year-old child.

She'd just have to leave Ginny to get over the forthcoming marriage. She'd be there on hand if Ginny wanted her, but the best thing she could do was let time resolve the situation. 'Time is a great healer', she always said.

Tessa had hardly slept all night, she was so upset. What made it worse was the fact that after *they* were married they would sleep in this very bed. She and Ginny would have to share the front downstairs room, Colin and Jimmy would stay where they were and Da and . . . *she* would have this room where her poor mam had died. She'd never get used to it – ever.

After work she'd gone to see Elizabeth. She'd not wanted to go straight home.

Delia shook her head when she saw the girl's wan face, the dark eyes reddened from weeping. She was obviously taking it hard and Delia could understand why.

'I didn't get much sleep last night,' Tessa admitted in response to Elizabeth's queries when they were alone in the kitchen.

'I don't think Ginny did either. Mam was saying to Da that she's really upset and that it was surprising. Then she said that Ginny had had a row with her mam last night because she won't ever be able to marry your Colin as they'll be related. Just why she wants to marry *him* I don't know. She could get lots of fellers.'

'I know. Maybe living in the same house will put her off. She'll see what he's really like.'

'If she wants to see, that is. Mam's always saying, "There's none so blind as those who don't want to see".'

'Oh, I don't even want to go home now, Elizabeth. I've lost all heart. I don't care whether there's a meal ready for them or not, or if they've got clean clothes, or . . . anything.'

Seeing Tessa so lost and miserable, Elizabeth racked her brains for something to take her mind off things. She lowered her voice: 'Mam's started to write to hairdressing salons.' At last Tessa looked interested, she thought with some relief.

'Which ones?'

'Hill's and Marcel's. They're both in Bold Street. She said seeing as I'd got my own way I might as well do the thing properly and try for an upper-class salon. I'll be the best-educated apprentice they've ever had. She's still not speaking to me. She's furious. She's tried about six times to write to Aunty Margaret and each time she's finished by tearing up the letter and throwing it in the fire. Da says she'll come round but I don't think she'll ever forgive me.'

'You'll just have to show her, and your aunty, that you were right.'

'I know. I intend to be the best, or at least *one* of the best hairdressers in Liverpool. I'll go to all the competitions and things like that and win prizes. I'll need people to practise on though.'

'Well, there's me and Ginny and maybe Doreen Keegan and Alice Collins.'

'Oh, Alice'll let me. Anything to look smart and fashionable without it costing a penny. She's just like her mam, is that one.'

'When do you think you'll be able to start?'

'Working, you mean?'

'Yes.'

'After I leave in the summer.'

'You can practise on us though long before that.'

'Yes. I can do both yours and Ginny's hair for the . . .

229

wedding! Oh, God! I'm sorry, Tessa! I never think. I just never bloody think!'

'I don't even want to go to that,' Tessa said with the hint of a sob in her voice again.

'I know, but you'll have to.'

'Our Colin won't. He never does anything if it doesn't suit him.'

Elizabeth quickly changed the subject. 'I think Mam is going to make sure that our Nessie does as she's told from now on. I heard her telling Da that she wasn't going to go through all this again with Nessie.'

'Do you think Nessie will be a teacher?'

'It doesn't look as though she's much choice. But she won't mind that – she'd make a good one. She's bossy and full of herself *and* she'd think she was going one better than me. But she's got years yet, anything could happen. She might even end up as a nun! Wouldn't that be a laugh?'

'Would your mam like that?'

'No – it would be wasting all that money again.'

'But nuns do teach.'

'I know. Don't I have to put up with them all day? But you don't need an expensive education to be a nun. All you have to know are the Latin prayers and responses to the mass.' Elizabeth blithely dismissed all the other and more serious aspects of taking Holy Orders.

Delia had written to the two top salons in Liverpool and in due course she received replies. An apprenticeship would cost two guineas and all equipment and overalls were to be purchased by the apprentice.

'More money!' Delia said irately.

'It's not as expensive as school, Mam,' Elizabeth said coaxingly.

Delia ignored her. She still wasn't reconciled to the prospect of jibes and sly comments from customers like Katie Collins and Maisie Keegan.

'You are to present yourself on Thursday evening at six-thirty at Hill's and at Marcel's on Friday at seven p.m.'

'Will you come with me?' Elizabeth could hardly contain her joy, but she didn't want to show it openly. Mam was still upset.

'Well, I can't let you go on your own. You'll put your foot in your manners for certain if I'm not there to watch you.'

'Mam, I wouldn't do anything like that! I'm not stupid!'

'Well, that's debatable. You'd better get out the clothes you want to wear and make sure they're clean and pressed.' Delia folded both letters and put them behind the clock on the mantel.

When her mother had gone back into the shop Elizabeth reached up and took them down and read them for herself. A little shiver of happiness ran though her.

Oh, she'd show them all. She meant what she'd said. She *would* be the best *and* she'd have her own salon one day. Then perhaps Mam would be proud of her. She really wanted her to be. She didn't care if Nessie did become a teacher, but it was very important to her that both her mam and her aunt be proud of her. But as she hugged the letters to her chest she found some of her natural self-confidence and assertiveness had deserted her.

It was a long time since the five of them had all gathered by the tannery wall, but Johnny was home so they'd agreed to

231

meet. These days they didn't see nearly as much of each other as they used to.

'You two don't look very happy. Mike told me the news,' Johnny greeted Tessa and Ginny cheerfully.

'Did you have to start off like that?' Elizabeth said. Her right arm was still in a sling but there were only a couple more weeks to go and then the plaster would come off and she'd have to go back to school.

'Well, it's *news* to me. What's your mam going to do, Ginny?'

'Apart from ruining my life, you mean?'

Johnny patted her arm sympathetically while Mike looked down at his boots. The whole street was divided over this wedding. Some people thought it would be the best thing for both Richie and May, and Mike's own mam was of this group. Others, like Katie Collins for one, thought it was a disgrace, Mary having been dead for only a year. The usual 'decent' interval was two years. They said May was just looking for someone to ease her burdens; she wasn't getting any younger and no one liked a barmaid who was growing old. It wasn't good for business. 'No one loves a fairy when she's forty!' was the way Katie Collins had described it.

'She's going to leave work – well, your da's pub anyway,' Ginny went on, sitting on the wall beside Johnny.

'Oh, that'll please him no end! Your mam's a good barmaid. He won't get another one unless he's willing to cough up more money. I can't say I blame her. The older he grows the more miserable he gets. He drags Mam down to Our Lady of the Angels in Fox Street now. They have a novena every Tuesday night.'

'What's he praying for?' Elizabeth asked.

'I don't know but I think Mam's praying that he'll stop being such a flaming misery and actually treat her better. He uses and speaks to her just like a skivvy. One of these days I'm going to tell him a few home truths. He's not going to like it, but he deserves it and Mam deserves better. She only gets one night out, once a fortnight, and that's to the Union of Catholic Mothers. And only one new outfit a year when he must be minted!'

'Let us know when this row is going to be and we'll all go into hiding,' Mike joked, but he felt sorry for Mrs Doyle. She was so quiet and inoffensive.

'So, will you be home for the wedding?' Elizabeth asked. 'No.'

'I wish I wasn't,' Tessa said miserably and Ginny nodded.

'It's on the last Saturday in the month and it's only going to be quiet, so Mam said.' Elizabeth paused and fiddled with the knot at the back of her neck that held the sling in place. 'Mam's going. They were both invited but they can't close the shop, not on a Saturday morning. I asked could I go instead, to support Tessa and Ginny, like, but they said no.'

'I'm to have a new costume. Well, the first costume I've ever had – the first "new" *anything* I've had.'

'And so am I,' Ginny added. For once she'd look smart and grown-up and it would be such a waste. She didn't know how she was going to stand in church in the same pew as Colin and listen to Father Walsh ask the questions and receive the answers that would separate her from Colin for ever.

She'd even wondered whether, when it came to the part where the priest said, 'If any person here present knows of any consanguinity, affinity or spiritual relationship speak now or for ever hold your peace,' she could cry out and say

233

that it wasn't right, it wasn't fair. But she couldn't do that. There was no reason why they shouldn't get married. It was going to be awful.

'You'll look great, both of you. Just like the "bloods" I have to look after.'

'The what?'

'The "bloods". It's slang for passengers, although there don't seem to be many on the next trip.'

'Why?' Elizabeth asked.

'The news, dope! It looks as if there's going to be another war and you can't help people remembering what happened to the *Lusitania*.'

They'd all heard of the tragedy of the Cunarder that had been sunk in May 1915 by a torpedo with the loss of 1,198 lives, mainly those of women and children.

'What will you do if there is a war?' Mike asked.

Johnny shrugged. 'Join the Royal Navy, I suppose. I can't see anyone wanting to cross the Atlantic. It'll be full of U-boats. What about you?'

'Probably Royal Navy too.'

'You're too young, both of you. Your birthday is on the same day,' Elizabeth reminded them.

'We'll be seventeen after Christmas and besides, we can lie about our ages. They did in the last one,' Johnny replied defensively.

'Yes, and look what happened then. Thousands of lads of sixteen and seventeen were killed. I bet they won't let *that* happen again. Anyway, no one wants to think about war,' Elizabeth dismissed the subject.

'Tell that to that Hitler feller,' Johnny said firmly. 'I heard you aren't going back to school after the next holidays.'

'I'm not. How do you know anyway? Mam's told no one.'

Johnny looked at Mike and winked.

'Oh, I should have known,' Elizabeth said resignedly. 'Your Mam, Mike.'

'She heard it from Flo Conway who lives—'

'Next door to us,' Elizabeth finished. So, the news was already out. Her mam would be furious. 'I'm going to be a hairdresser.'

Johnny looked at her with open scepticism. 'You're bloody mad, do you know that, Elizabeth? A cushy job as a teacher, all that time off, bossing all those kids around and good money and security.'

'That's just it. The bit about the kids. I hate them and I'd have no patience with them. You know how our Nessie gets on my nerves and she's grown-up compared to the ones I'd have to teach.'

'She's got to go for an interview at two places in Bold Street,' Tessa informed them.

Mike looked amazed. 'God, we're going up in the world. Bold Street!'

'Mam said if I'm going to do it I might as well do it properly.'

Mike's respect for Elizabeth increased. She'd always been different to the other girls in the street because she came from a well-off family, by his mam's standards anyway. But her independence was part of the reason he liked her. She could be a bit of a 'madcap' at times but she knew her own mind and was certainly determined. 'It must have taken a lot of guts to tell them,' he said admiringly.

'It did. There was murder. She's still giving me the cold-shoulder treatment.'

'But you got your own way in the end. You always do, Elizabeth Harrison,' Mike said with a grin.

'I wish I did,' groaned Ginny. 'No matter how I'd carry on, it wouldn't make any difference. Mam's going to marry Tessa's da and that's that. Everything between Colin and me will be over.'

'I didn't think there was anything much between you,' Johnny commented.

'There is . . . was,' she corrected herself.

'I've told you, Ginny, you're better off without him. You can do better,' Tessa said firmly and was rewarded by a glare of hostility from Ginny.

'Oh, this looks as if it's shaping up for a battle royal,' Mike said.

'It's not. Things will work out.' Elizabeth frowned at him. 'Anyway, Johnny, you ought to talk more to Tessa about the "bloods". She wants to be a stewardess.'

'The best of luck, Tessa, but if there's a war there won't be any passengers to look after,' Johnny pointed out.

'Oh, trust you, Johnny Doyle! You're full of enthusiasm and good news!' Elizabeth said sarcastically. 'That's just what she wanted to know, I'm sure. Anyway, there's nothing definite about any war, it's all talk.'

Tessa slid off the wall. She was going home. Things were bad enough without hearing that her dream might never ever be possible.

Johnny followed her. 'Tessa! Tessa! I'm sorry.'

She smiled sadly at him. 'What for? I know you didn't mean to disappoint me.'

'I didn't, honestly. Do you really want to be a stewardess?'

Tessa nodded.

'They work awfully hard. Everyone thinks they have the time of their lives, off seeing the world, but you have to make a special trip to see *anything*. Docks are the same the world over. In rough weather you have to dance attendance on your "bloods". Most of them are sick. It's really not a lot of fun, Tessa.'

'It doesn't sound it. But I'm not afraid of hard work or cleaning up after people. It's what I've been doing for years.'

Johnny was contrite. 'I *have* put you off. I can tell by your voice. I'm so sorry, Tessa.'

'You haven't. It's . . . it's something I promised Mam I'd do.'

'Well, if . . . when the time comes, if there's anything I can do to help, you will ask?'

'Thanks, Johnny. I'd be glad of any help.'

He smiled and pushed his hair away from his forehead.

It was a habit she liked, it made him seem sort of appealing. But she couldn't tell him that, could she?

On the Thursday evening Elizabeth was ready. She'd dressed with care, helped by Nessie, for although the plaster had come off, her wrist was still very sore. She finished her outfit off with a small pillbox hat and was thrilled to be wearing her first pair of nylon stockings. She'd spent ages making sure the seams were straight but she felt and looked so 'grown up' she was certain no one would take her for a schoolgirl.

Her mam looked smart too, she thought, in her two-piece costume in brown and cream dogstooth check. She certainly wasn't going to that place looking as though she hadn't two halfpennies to rub together, she'd told Jack firmly. 'You always look so smart when you're dressed up, Delia,' he'd replied encouragingly, knowing how much she was hating the idea of this interview. No matter how well established and well known the salon was she just didn't want Elizabeth to go to work there. She was very, very disappointed in her elder daughter.

All the way into town on the tram Elizabeth was nervous. What if they decided she wasn't hairdresser material? What if they were terribly posh and objected to the way she spoke? All the elocution lessons had helped but she still had an unmistakable scouse accent. She began to wind the strap of her shoulder bag around her wrist.

'Stop that, for heaven's sake. I know you're nervous, and so you should be, but stop fidgeting,' Delia snapped.

Hill's was the kind of place where once you opened the glass door you felt as though you were stepping into another world. The atmosphere was hushed, almost as if you were in church, Elizabeth thought.

The Art Deco-style reception area was carpeted and the desk was behind a frosted glass panel which had, as its centrepiece, the figure of a dancing lady. On either side were glass cabinets containing cosmetics and perfumes in very fancy bottles. Beyond that was a small area where clients could sit and browse through magazines while waiting to be summoned to one of the enclosed cubicles. Two of them had the doors open and a young girl was on her hands and knees washing the marble-effect linoleum. Elizabeth caught sight of a washbasin, a comfortable chair and footstool and mirrors surrounded by lights. Everyone she could see wore pink overalls with the shop's monogram embroidered in gold on the pocket.

A well-groomed young woman was sitting at the reception desk, her blonde hair dressed in a very complicated style of upswept curls and waves. What make-up she wore was lightly applied and her fingernails were painted with pink polish.

'May I help?'

'I . . . we . . . have an appointment to see Miss Mercer.'

The receptionist consulted her appointment book. 'You must be Mrs Harrison and Miss Harrison. Would you care to wait while I inform Miss Mercer of your arrival?'

Delia nodded and looked around her. Who could afford to come to somewhere as utterly luxurious as this, just to have your hair done? She felt almost as nervous as Elizabeth.

The receptionist returned. 'Would you follow me, please?'

They were led to a small cubicle which looked like all the rest except that there was a desk and two chairs and a small index file.

Miss Mercer was small and dark-haired and, again, immaculately turned out. Elizabeth would be like a fish out of water here, Delia thought, hopefully.

'Please sit down, Mrs Harrison.' Miss Mercer indicated a chair.

'Now, Miss Harrison – Elizabeth – would you like to tell me why you wish to become a hairdresser?' the manageress asked in a soft but firm voice.

Elizabeth swallowed hard. She'd prepared herself for this. 'It is something I enjoy and I don't want to sound arrogant, Miss Mercer, but I do seem to have . . . well, a flair for it. I practise on my friends.'

The manageress looked enquiringly at Delia who nodded her head.

'Well, that's important. You realise that you will be indentured for three years as an apprentice, and then two more years as an improver?'

'Yes, Miss Mercer,' Elizabeth replied quietly.

'You will have a thorough grounding in all aspects of hairdressing but you will have to work very long hours.'

'I don't mind hard work at all and I *will* be learning all the time. I really do want to be a good hairdresser.'

Miss Mercer looked closely at mother and daughter. 'You agree to all this, Mrs Harrison? I can assure you that she will receive the best training.'

Delia again nodded. She just couldn't say the words 'I agree'. They stuck in her throat.

'I see you are still at school. And a very good one too. When would you be able to start, should we offer you an apprenticeship?'

'When I finish in July.'

'*After* she has matriculated and with above-average marks.' Delia was determined to show the woman that she wasn't getting an unqualified, ignorant slip of a girl. There couldn't be many girls with expensive private educations who were hairdressers.

Miss Mercer smiled. 'Then I will be in touch very shortly and perhaps one Saturday you could come in, just for the morning, so I can see how you shape. Of course you will only observe, but there are other duties apprentices must do.'

Elizabeth lost some of her nervousness. It wasn't absolutely sure but it looked as if she would be offered an apprenticeship.

Miss Mercer rose and accompanied them as far as the reception desk. Once outside, Delia breathed a sigh of relief.

She'd felt almost panic-stricken in there. She hoped it hadn't shown.

'Well, at least we will know just what we are facing when we go to Marcel's tomorrow. You'd think they were doing you a great favour by taking you on, when it's the other way around. *We're* the ones who are paying, not them.'

'Do you think after we've been to Marcel's we could go and have a look at the kind of things I'll need to have?' Elizabeth asked. She still felt as though she were walking on a cloud.

'You can. I'm far too busy to be traipsing around hair-dressing wholesalers.'

Some of Elizabeth's euphoria disappeared. She'd got what she wanted but obviously Mam wasn't going to give her her blessing. If she achieved her ambition and got that appren-ticeship, would she be losing her close relationship with Mam? She couldn't suppress a tinge of sadness at the thought.

They went through the same ritual at Marcel's the follow-ing evening and again Elizabeth got the impression they were willing to take her on. If she was offered an apprentice-ship by both Hill's and Marcel's how would she choose? She knew she couldn't ask her mam. Mam wanted nothing to do with it. She had liked Miss Knowles and the decor was very plush, even more so than at Hill's. But Marcel's staff seemed friendlier; two of the younger girls had actually smiled at her, as had the receptionist, and the salon was bigger. She'd have to discuss it with Tessa.

Although May had said it was to be a quiet wedding, there was nothing she could do to stop half the women in the street attending the service in St Anthony's Church on Saturday 29

April. Those who genuinely wished Richie and May good luck and happiness cast supercilious glances at those who did not.

'Hypocrites, the lot of them!' Eileen Flynn had whispered to the woman sitting beside her.

Delia had been invited officially and had even agreed to stand for May, although she wouldn't hear of the title matron of honour being used. Frank Flynn agreed to be best man for Richie and, as he'd said to Eileen, 'Thank God they 'ad the sense not to ask those two girls to be bridesmaids and that Colin to be best man.'

'She's not that stupid, isn't May Greely,' Eileen had replied. In her opinion May really wasn't getting much of a bargain in Richie O'Leary, but still, it was her life.

The bride wore a dress of crêpe de Chine with a cream background covered all over with pale blue flowers. A large picture hat, more fashionable in the early thirties, covered her dark hair in which there wasn't a hint of grey, and she carried a small bouquet of spring flowers.

Elizabeth, who had come despite her mother's instructions, sat in the very back pew. She thought May looked nice – a bit too fussy, perhaps, but all right – and both Tessa and Ginny looked great. She'd already seen their outfits and she'd done both their hair last night. Her wrist was now almost completely healed and she found that the more she used it the less stiff it became.

Alice Collins was sitting next to Elizabeth. 'Ginny Greely looks almost pretty,' she remarked.

'What do you mean, "almost"?' Elizabeth demanded.

'Well, you've got to agree she's never looked as nice before.'

'That's because I washed and set her hair. I did Tessa's too,' she whispered back.

Alice looked interested. 'Do you think you could do something with mine? I couldn't pay you though,' she added quickly.

Elizabeth nodded. 'Of course I could.' The more practice she got the better. 'Doesn't that colour suit Tessa?' she added and Alice craned her neck to get a better view.

Elizabeth had accompanied Tessa and Ginny to buy the outfits. They'd gone to T. J. Hughes's in London Road. Tessa's was a bright pink two-piece with a fitted jacket which showed off her small waist. Ginny had chosen, with her help, a cornflower blue dress and jacket. 'It suits your colouring, Ginny,' Elizabeth had urged as Ginny had shilly-shallied over it. 'You've got shoes and a bag, all you need is a small white hat. We should get one in C & A and it won't be expensive,' she'd advised.

'It does,' Alice said, knowing if there was any more conversation, albeit whispered, they would both be in trouble.

Elizabeth felt so sorry for Tessa and Ginny. She knew Tessa would be thinking of her mam and Ginny would be torturing herself over Colin. At least they hadn't had to share the same pew, something she had pointed out last night to Ginny's relief. He sat with Jimmy on the left-hand side of the church while Ginny and Delia and May's sister-in-law from her first marriage sat on the right side. But the ceremony was still going to be an ordeal for them, and then they would have to get through not only the rest of the day but the rest of their lives as well.

Chapter Seventeen

Elizabeth was weary when she got off the tram. This August had been so hot and humid that she'd welcome some cooler days, which hopefully would come with the start of the new month. Tessa was waiting for her, for although they came home from opposite directions Tessa had insisted on it.

'You used to wait for me for over an hour, winter and summer, so I'm going to wait for you,' she'd replied firmly to Elizabeth's arguments. 'You look worn out.'

'I am. I never expected it to be *such* hard work – and it's so boring.'

'Don't go saying that to your mam.'

'I won't, but honestly, Tessa, I seem to spend more time sweeping up, washing floors and cleaning mirrors than I do watching and learning. All that stuff, which cost Mam a small fortune, and I only get to hold the hairpins, if I'm lucky. At this rate it'll be years before they'll let me cut *anyone's* hair.'

Delia had thought the list was endless when she'd gone with Elizabeth to Osborne and Garret, the wholesalers, the week before Elizabeth started at Hill's. She'd been a little disappointed not to be offered a place at Marcel's, but at least it made the decision for her. She had had her results and had indeed matriculated with very good marks. But that fact hadn't made her mam very happy. 'It's the waste, the sheer waste I can't forgive, Jack,' she'd heard her mam say the day after. So she didn't view the list of equipment in a favourable light. Two pairs of scissors were required, never to be used on anything except hair. That had been stressed emphatically. Then there were thinning scissors and an open 'cut throat' razor, also to be used for thinning and tapering, but not for a very long time. In the hands of an apprentice a razor was a lethal weapon, so Miss Mercer had said. The list continued with two steel combs, one 'light', one 'heavy'; a tail comb; clippers; two sets of waving irons, medium size 'B' or 'C'; and – to their surprise – even four coloured hairnets.

'I would have thought they'd have enough of their own,' Delia had remarked caustically. Finally there were her three pink overalls. Why she needed three God alone knew, Delia had commented.

'And there's so much to learn. It takes ages to pin curl and wave and the setting lotion they use is like glue, it leaves your fingers all sticky. Then there's all the different perms, and how to wind them: hot, tepid and cold perms, and those Callinan perms which look horrendous. You have to sit there for hours with your hair wound around these curlers attached to a machine that looks like something from another planet. I couldn't *stand* all that. Thank God I don't need a perm. And then there's Marcel waving with the heated irons.'

'I thought that was a kind of perm,' Tessa remarked.

'So did I, but it's not. It's all done with waving irons and like everything else, it takes hours. It's not as . . . glamorous . . . as I'd thought.'

'It'll be worth it though, in the end I mean,' Tessa tried to cheer Elizabeth up.

'I suppose so, but at the end of days like this I really do

wonder. Maybe I should have been a manicurist, at least they get to sit down.'

'Oh, stop moaning. Look how well you did Alice's hair. She was made up. Even her mam said she hardly recognised her.'

Elizabeth had cut Alice Collins's shoulder-length brown hair to just the level of her ears and had waved it, fixing the waves with clips until it was dry and then showing Alice how to brush it out and pin curl it so it would hold the style.

'I'm sorry to go on so, Tessa, but I've no one else to tell. Mam doesn't even want to know what I do all day.'

Tessa frowned. 'Is she still that bad?'

'Yes. I just don't talk to her about it now. Da's OK but he doesn't really understand anything I tell him.'

'What about Nessie?'

'Oh, she's interested even though she tries to hide it. Now she and Mam have decided she's to be the teacher in the family, she's so smug I could kill her.'

Tessa shook her head. Nessie wasn't half as bad as Elizabeth painted her. With a bit of effort on both sides the open hostility between them could be avoided. They were sisters after all.

When they arrived back at the shop Delia came through from the kitchen and smiled at Tessa. It was a smile that held little real warmth for she partially blamed Tessa for Elizabeth's change of career. If she'd wanted to, surely Tessa could have persuaded Elizabeth that hairdressing was not a wonderful career. Tessa's opinions carried a lot of weight with Elizabeth.

'I'll have to get straight back. I've things to do and everyone will be wanting their tea.'

Elizabeth nodded. Her friend had to run a house as well as work at the Convent. Tessa made her look spoilt and lazy, so she resolved not to complain about her lot any more.

Ginny was sitting, just staring into space, when Tessa got home – as she seemed to be every evening when Tessa returned. Things had been very strained at number twelve after Ginny and her mam had moved in with Richie, but over the months they all seemed to have settled down, except Colin and, because of his presence, Ginny. She seemed to have become quieter and more withdrawn.

In truth, Ginny was finding life utterly miserable. She hated her job at Birrel's but lacked the energy to look for anything better. Then there was Colin. She saw him every morning and for at least some part of the evening, although he went out quite a lot, and even more so at weekends. At first she wondered if he went out so much because he couldn't stand to be in the same room as her and not be able to hold her or kiss her. But if he was he gave no sign of it. And they were almost never alone so it was impossible to say anything about how *she* felt.

All through the summer on her Wednesday afternoons off, she'd sat at home reading *True Romance* or wandered into town to buy something. She now had quite a few nice outfits but she never went anywhere to wear them. Before her mam's marriage Colin sometimes used to meet her in town. How he'd managed to get the time off she didn't know, and after some coaxing he'd bought her a few little trinkets and sometimes they'd gone for tea in the Kardomah Café in Bold Street. Now life wasn't worth living; it was an effort just to get through every day. She couldn't talk to either her mam or Tessa about it because they didn't like him and were glad to see them lead separate lives.

The following Wednesday evening, Ginny found herself alone in the stifling kitchen. Tessa and Colin were out; Jimmy was next door; her mam was working and Richie (or Uncle Richie as she now had to call him) had gone to the pub. Ginny looked around her at the clutter and mess. She and Tessa and Mam were supposed to split the housework between them, but her mam never seemed to do anything at all. She didn't get up early, saying she worked late. She didn't go shopping, she sent either Ginny or Tessa. She did do a bit of the ironing, but that seemed to consist only of her own and Richie's things which left the bulk of it to Tessa and herself. She cooked, but never washed up. She never baked, Tessa did that. Her mam had shown her how to and Tessa had tried to teach Ginny but she couldn't be bothered to learn. She hated cooking. You spent hours preparing, boiling, roasting, baking, and it was all gone in about five minutes. Ginny rubbed her eyes. If she stayed in here for another night she'd go mad.

She went into the front room that she shared with Tessa and brushed her hair in the way Elizabeth had shown her. She was quite pretty, she thought, looking at her reflection in the mirror. Surely he must see *something* attractive in her? Taking her cardigan from the pile of neatly folded clothes on top of the ottoman, she left the house, closing the front door behind her.

She had no real idea of where she was going or what she would do. Should she go to the Pier Head and go for a sail on the ferry? On her own, with no one to share the trip with? No. Should she go into town to the cinema? Again she'd be on her own. There seemed to be nothing she would feel happy and comfortable doing on her own. Happy! she thought bitterly. She'd never be happy again.

Eventually she caught a tram. She'd go and sit in Lester Gardens. It wouldn't help, in fact it would only make her feel more miserable, but she couldn't help herself. She'd been so happy when she'd sat there with him all those times. But there would be very few people there and no one would notice if she indulged in a few tears: weeping for the love she'd lost through her mam's selfishness. Mam *was* selfish – and thoughtless, telling her that Colin wasn't right for her and comparing him with a tram! Well, so far there hadn't been anyone else and she doubted there ever would be.

When she got off at her stop she walked the few yards to the little park. It was a lovely evening, warm but no longer sticky. The flowerbeds were a riot of colour and she could smell the sweet perfume of the roses and night-scented stocks. The evening would have been just perfect, she reflected, if only . . .

She heard a girl's laughter but took no notice until she heard the boy laugh too. The colour drained from her cheeks and she clapped a hand over her mouth to stop herself from crying out. He was *here*! He had brought someone else to *their* park! Oh, why had she come here? If she hadn't she would never have known. But just *who* was with him? She made up her mind to confront him.

Colin was sitting on their bench, his arm around a very attractive but flashily dressed girl who was still laughing. Her thick mass of black curled hair was held back with bright red plastic slides that matched the colour of the dress she wore. Her fingernails were painted red too.

Vera Morley from Blackstock Street! She was known in

the entire neighbourhood to be little more than a common tart. Ginny's heart dropped like a stone and she couldn't help herself. She ran forward yelling, 'I hate you, Colin O'Leary! I *hate* you! Taking up with . . . *her*! She's just a slut! And you brought her . . . *here*!'

The smile vanished from his face. He was surprised and annoyed. 'Ginny, what's the matter with you? Have you followed me?' She had no claim on him. The bloody cheek of her. He could take out whoever he liked, he didn't have to ask *her* permission. He and Vera stood up, Vera with a mocking smile in her eyes and her red lips curled with contempt. It just increased Ginny's fury.

'No! I . . . I came here for some peace. How could you like her? She's a common, dirty little tart! She's had more fellers than hot dinners! Everyone knows about *her*!'

Vera, stung by these accusations, flew at Ginny screaming and trying to rake Ginny's face with her fingernails. 'You lying little bitch! You're just jealous because you look a bloody mess! Because it's *me* he likes to take out! *Me* who knows how to give him a good time. You're just a miserable, ugly little kid. He likes proper girls. Girls who don't keep moaning and following him around.'

Her words made Ginny tremble with fury and she grabbed Vera's hair and pulled with all her strength. Vera screamed in agony as a whole handful was wrenched out.

Colin decided it was time he intervened. He caught Ginny by her own hair and dragged her away from Vera.

'Stop it! Stop it! Get home, you bloody nuisance! Vera's right, you're a miserable, plain little kid. Just you wait until I tell your mam about you, although *she's* nothing but a bloody floosie herself. Go on, get home!'

Ginny broke free and started to run towards the gates. Colin made no move to stop her, instead he turned his attention to Vera who was sitting on the bench crying more with anger than pain.

'Take no notice of her! She's a nasty little bitch. I have to live under the same roof and believe me I know what she's—' The rest of his comforting words were interrupted by the screeching of tyres, the high-pitched neighing of a frightened horse, the rumble of wheels on the cobbles and then the shouts of angry men and the shrieks of horrified women.

'Oh my God! What's she done?' Colin covered the few yards to the park gates in seconds and was just in time to see a young policeman hanging on to the bridle of a carthorse for dear life to stop it bolting. The driver was shouting at it and yanking the reins back with all his strength. A lorry was turned broadside on to the on-coming traffic and the driver was jumping down from its cab. On the cobbles between the tram lines he could see a figure lying stretched out and recognised with sickening certainty that it was Ginny. She must have run straight out into the road. He forgot all about Vera Morley. If Ginny was dead then he'd be for it both from her mam and his da and most of the neighbours too. None of them liked him and he knew why. Johnny had told everyone about what he'd done on Christmas Eve. The Doyle boy had been right when he'd said that no one stole either from each other or the shops – they seemed to take a pride in the fact, which Colin found hard to understand. And surely no one could get angry over a bit of fun with a scruffy kid and a mangy kitten, but again it seemed as though they had.

'Ginny! Ginny!' he cried, pushing his way through the small group of people that had already collected. He dropped on to his knees beside her and lifted her head. She was breathing.

'Do you know who she is, the silly little bitch?' the lorry driver asked, bending down.

'Yes, she's my stepsister.'

The policeman and carter had got the horse under control and, wiping his brow with his handkerchief, the constable joined Colin and the lorry driver.

'She ran straight out in front of me, there was nothing I could do! She didn't even bloody look. Right out and hit the bonnet. I swear it, Officer.' The man was very shaken.

'It's all right, I saw what happened and it could have been a lot worse if that flaming animal had bolted.'

'It's his stepsister.' The man inclined his head towards Colin.

'So what happened?' the constable demanded, lifting Ginny's limp hand and feeling for a pulse.

'We had a row. She followed me here, then she just ran off . . . and . . . and before I could stop her she'd gone and then I heard the . . . the noise.'

'Well, she's breathing and she's got a steady pulse but I'll call an ambulance.'

The traffic was now at a standstill and the crowd was getting bigger. Two more policemen arrived. One began to direct the traffic and the other dispersed the crowd, except for the two witnesses, and started to take statements from the shaken carter and lorry driver.

Colin felt numb. Ginny was still unconscious.

'Where's the ambulance? What's the hold-up?' he demanded of the first policeman.

'It's on its way. Don't try to move her at all. She might

have a broken arm or leg or shoulder.'

Colin tried again to revive her. 'Ginny! Ginny, it's me, Colin. I'm sorry, Ginny, really I am.' There was still no response and he just knelt there dazed until at last they heard the clanging of the ambulance bell and it was waved through by the officer on point duty.

She was examined gently and her eyelids fluttered open.

'Ginny! Ginny, are you all right?' Colin cried.

'Don't try and sit up, girl, take it easy,' the ambulance driver said quietly. 'Now, luv, can you move your arms and legs?'

Ginny raised them, wondering where she was and what had happened to her.

'Good. Nothing broken. Now, does your head hurt? Do you feel sick?'

'It . . . it hurts here.' Ginny put her hand to the side of her head. 'But I don't feel sick. What happened? I want my mam.'

'It's all right, Ginny, I'm here. I'll help take care of you,' Colin promised. Relief was washing over him. Thank God she wasn't badly hurt.

With his help and that of the driver and constable she got into the ambulance.

'We're going to take you to Stanley Hospital, luv, just to make sure you're all right,' the second ambulance man told her.

Ginny was still dazed and unable to understand why she had to go to hospital and why Colin was with her and looked so worried. She closed her eyes. Her head really did hurt so she'd think about all that later.

'Where do you live, lad?' the ambulance man asked.

'Naylor Street. Are you *sure* she's not badly hurt?'

'There's nothing broken but she might be concussed. She took a nasty fall. She was lucky she didn't end up under the wheels of the lorry or the hooves of that horse. Those damned animals have caused more deaths and injuries than I can count. One sudden noise and they're away like an arrow from a bow, trampling everyone and everything in their path and quite often killing their driver. They should bring in a law that says they should have ear muffs as well as blinkers.'

Colin wasn't paying any attention, his eyes were fixed on Ginny's inert form.

'Listen, son, I think when we arrive at the hospital you'd better go home and tell someone what happened. If she needs any kind of operation they'll have to give their consent and be there.'

Colin nodded, his heart lurching sickeningly. He'd not thought of that.

When he at last arrived home everyone was in and Jimmy was in bed.

'Holy Mother of God! What's up with you?' May cried, thinking she'd never seen him in such a state. He looked terrible.

'It's Ginny. She . . . she's in hospital.'

'In *hospital*! Why? What happened?' May demanded.

'If you've done anything to hurt her I'll kill you, I swear I will!' Tessa cried.

'I didn't do *anything* to her! I had a date and she . . . she followed me. We had a row and she ran off, straight into the middle of the main road.'

May crossed herself and sank down in an armchair.

'Where did they take her?' Tessa demanded.

'Stanley Hospital. It's all right, I went with her. She's not badly hurt. She banged her head. The ambulance feller said you'd better go along there just in case. It wasn't my fault! She . . . she just ran!'

'She would if she saw you with someone else! You know how much she thinks of you. She's stupid where you're concerned,' Tessa yelled at him.

'I can't help that!' Colin cried defensively. 'She knows there's nothing I can do . . . now.'

'You wouldn't have done anything even if she hadn't become your stepsister! You don't love her. What did you say to her to make her run off like that?'

'I didn't say *anything*, Tessa. God's truth!'

'Liar! I know you and I know Ginny. It's *your* fault!'

'It's not!'

'For the love of God, stop fighting! I'm going up there.' May picked up her bag.

'I'm coming with you. She's my friend as well as my stepsister,' Tessa stated, snatching up her own shoulder bag. They departed quickly, leaving Colin with Richie. The two men were upset and shaken.

'You'd better make amends, lad, if she's not hurt, otherwise May will have your hide!' Richie said with foreboding. 'Trouble should be your middle name!'

When they arrived at the hospital May and Tessa were shown into a side ward by a sister whose apron crackled with starch as she walked. She hadn't been very co-operative about letting them in to see Ginny at this time of night until May had become angry and said she wasn't leaving the hospital until she'd seen her daughter and that even if they called the police she wouldn't be moved.

'I'm her *mother*, for God's sake! Haven't you got *any* pity in you?'

Ginny was lying in the iron-framed bed with a bandage around her head. Her face was almost as white as the bandage.

May gently patted her hand. 'Ginny, luv, it's me. It's your mam.'

Ginny opened her eyes. 'Oh, Mam! Mam! I'm sorry.'

'There's nothing for you to be sorry for, luv.'

'No, there isn't,' Tessa added, bending and kissing Ginny on the cheek.

'I . . . I remember running out. I couldn't see.'

'Don't upset yourself. You've got to rest, that sister said so and she's a tartar, believe me. You were very lucky, thank God, just a bit of concussion, that's what she said was wrong with you. But, luv, you could have been killed.' May was in a state of shock herself. Ginny looked so pale that she could be mistaken for a corpse.

Tessa took Ginny's hand. 'What did he say to you? Did our Colin upset you?'

'I don't remember. I don't even remember going . . . anywhere.'

'But he was with you in the ambulance!' May urged. She'd kill him if Ginny didn't get better.

Ginny tried to shake her head but winced in pain. 'No. No . . . I don't think he upset me. He was very worried about me.'

Tessa exchanged glances with May.

Ginny began to cry. 'Oh, Mam!'

'Ginny, stop that, luv, it's only going to make you feel worse. You'll be coming home tomorrow, but only if you don't upset yourself. Sleep now and get well.'

Obviously getting Ginny to remember what had happened before she'd run into the road was something they might never achieve, Tessa thought. But she was determined to find out who her brother's 'date' had been and, by the look on her face, she'd get all the help she needed from May.

Chapter Eighteen

Ginny came home the following afternoon. She was still pale and shaken but at least she hadn't been seriously hurt and for that they all thanked God.

'How is she?' Tessa asked the minute she got in from work.

'She's slept a lot but that won't do her any harm. Will you keep your eye on her while I'm at work, Tessa? I don't want her to get upset or excited.'

May was combing her hair in front of the mirror that was on the mantelshelf, but she looked concerned. 'I've been down to see Jimmy Birrel. She's not going into work tomorrow.'

'Of course I will. Can I go in and see her?'

'Of course, luv, it's your room as well, but if she's asleep, leave her.'

'I will.' May was genuinely worried, Tessa thought as she opened the door of the room that she and Ginny shared. The curtains were drawn and had been all day and the room was stifling; she'd have to have a window open later.

Ginny was awake. 'How are you now?' Tessa asked, taking off her linen jacket and hanging it on the knob of the brass bedstead.

'I don't feel too bad but Mam won't let me get up or have the window open and it's boiling hot.'

'Well, she's right about staying in bed, but we'll have the

window open, that's if the noise outside won't bother you?'

'No. There's not much noise anyway.'

Tessa drew back the curtains and pulled the sash window up, then drew one of the curtains halfway over to keep the sun out of Ginny's eyes.

'Don't complain too much, Ginny, about lying in bed all day. Make the most of it.' She smiled, sat down on the edge of the bed and took Ginny's hand. 'Do you remember anything . . . anything more, I mean?'

'No. I've tried to but I just get more confused and then my head aches. I do remember running out of the park and that I was crying, that's why I didn't see the lorry or the horse and cart. The next thing I remember was when I came round I was lying on the cobbles and my head was in Colin's lap and he was holding my hand and looking very worried.'

'Can you remember what he said to you?'

'Not really. He kept saying he was sorry and that I was to lie still. Then I remember an ambulance and a policeman and then the hospital and then you and Mam. That's all, Tessa.'

Tessa squeezed her hand. 'Well, don't try to remember any more, things may come back bit by bit if you don't force them. Ginny, you could have been killed. Your mam was terribly upset; we all were.'

'I know, I'm sorry, Tessa.' Ginny still looked pale.

'Well, you won't be going in to work tomorrow, your mam won't hear of it. She's been to see Mr Birrel.'

Ginny managed a weak smile. 'It's almost worth it to get away from all that stinking fish.'

Tessa smiled back. 'You know how partial your mam is to a nice bit of haddock.'

Ginny squeezed Tessa's hand. 'He really was upset, Tessa. Colin, I mean. So he must still love me.'

Tessa sighed. She was going to get to the bottom of this. 'I suppose he does,' she answered, getting up. 'You lie there and rest, I'll bring you something in to eat.'

Ginny smiled and closed her eyes. She really couldn't remember why she'd dashed out into the road like that. But Colin *had* been there and *must* still love her.

'She still can't remember anything before she ran out,' Tessa informed May.

'I know and I don't want to press her.'

'Well, I'm going to find out. He was at the back of it, I'm sure.'

'I wouldn't argue with you about that, Tessa. Will you see what he has to say for himself? I've got to go to work now.'

'I will,' she answered firmly.

May left and Tessa began to prepare the evening meal.

When he arrived home Colin did look worried, Tessa thought. He also looked guilty. Young Jimmy was next door and wouldn't be back until bedtime and Da wasn't home yet.

'Right. Now you can tell me what really happened. Just what did you do or say to Ginny that made her so upset that she was nearly killed?'

'What has she told you?' Colin asked defensively. All day he'd been worried that she would remember and that he'd be in for it when he got home.

'Never mind that. What did you do? Don't tell me you're not responsible, I know you too well.'

'Like I told you, I had a date and Ginny must have followed me. I told her to go home and leave me in peace. I'm a free man, she's got no claim on me.'

'And that made her run out? Who were you with?'

'Does it matter?'

'If it's part of the reason why Ginny is lying in there now, yes, it does.'

Colin hedged. He went into the scullery ostensibly to wash his hands but Tessa followed him.

'Don't you walk away from me, Colin O'Leary! Who was it?' she demanded.

'God, Tessa, you're like a dog with a bloody bone! If you must know it was Vera Morley from Blackstock Street. I've taken her out a few times, but she had nothing to do with what . . . what Ginny did.'

'Oh, what do you take me for? I didn't come over on the last boat! Vera Morley! She's not much better than the Maggie Mays on Lime Street. In fact she's worse. At least they are open about it and they get paid – or does *she* get paid too?'

Colin's face went scarlet. 'Trust you to think like that!'

'You know, for once I'm glad that Mam's dead. At least she doesn't have to face the fact that you've been carrying on with *that* one. But you haven't answered my question. Did you or she say anything to upset Ginny?'

Colin became irate. 'I've told you, Tessa, no one said anything!'

She didn't believe him. Later she'd go and see Vera Morley and find out the truth.

Colin hadn't made any move to go out after his meal. He just sat reading, or pretending to read, the *Evening Echo*, but he did look up in concern when Tessa announced she was going out.

'Where to?' he demanded.

'To see Elizabeth. Any objections?' she snapped.

He returned to the sports page.

'How is Ginny? I heard about the accident,' Delia asked when Tessa came into her kitchen.

'She's going to be all right. A couple of days in bed and she'll be back at work.'

'What possessed her to do such a thing?'

'I don't know, but I'm going to find out.'

'Isn't that her mother's responsibility?'

'She's gone to work.'

Delia raised her eyebrows, but went into the shop without saying anything.

'What happened?' Elizabeth asked. She'd been full of curiosity all day, ever since Eileen had told her the news as she'd walked up the street to the tram stop. Eileen, of course, had heard everything through the walls and had taken up her position on her front step as early as she could to inform anyone who passed by.

'She can't remember, but it's something to do with our Colin and that Vera Morley!'

'Vera Morley! God, she's like the station bike!'

'Hush, your mam will hear you! I *know*! I'm going to see her – will you come with me?'

'Of course, but don't tell Mam or she'll have ten blue fits!'

'Where are you going? You said you'd help me with my Latin,' Nessie asked as she came downstairs.

'I said I *might* help you, and where I go is my business,' Elizabeth answered.

'She won't be long, Nessie, and then she'll help you.' Tessa pushed Elizabeth towards the door. There was no use antagonising Nessie for no justifiable reason. She'd started to grow up and out of some of her less attractive character traits.

'I wonder what she looks like?' Elizabeth mused as they walked along Vauxhall Road to Blackstock Street. It wasn't the quickest way, but it was more direct.

'Haven't you ever seen her?' Tessa looked incredulous.

'No and I've lived here longer than you have.'

'She looks what she is.'

'Oh, this will be great!'

'No, it won't, Elizabeth! I don't want to even speak to her but I'm going to find out the truth for Ginny's sake.'

They walked the rest of the way in silence.

Blackstock Street was similar in character to Naylor Street: the houses were the same, the crowd of scruffy kids playing in the road or the gutter was the same. They asked what number house Vera Morley lived in.

'Number ten and I wish to God she'd clear off out of this street,' was the reply.

The house didn't look all that bad, Tessa thought. The windows and curtains weren't very clean but that wasn't unusual. The front door was closed and that *was* unusual, especially as it was a warm night.

Elizabeth hammered loudly on the knocker and they both waited. They'd wait all night if they had to, Tessa thought determinedly. Eventually the door was opened by a girl of about seven who wore only a pair of grubby, grey-looking knickers and whose dark brown hair was matted and very probably verminous. 'Is your Vera in?' Tessa asked.

'Who wants ter know?'

'You hardfaced little madam, get in there and ask her to come out here,' Elizabeth demanded. The child disappeared and eventually they heard footsteps on the bare boards of the lobby and Vera appeared in the doorway.

Elizabeth was taking in every detail. It was the first time she'd ever seen anyone who was called a tart. The girl was a couple of years older than herself, she judged. Her thick black hair was pinned up with fancy combs. She wore powder and rouge. Her eyebrows were plucked and pencilled and her mouth was a red gash out of which a cigarette protruded. She wore a grubby purple satin dressing gown that had multicoloured flowers embroidered on it and which clashed horribly with her red lips and nails.

'Who the 'ell are you?' she asked.

'I'm Ginny Greely's stepsister, Colin is my brother, and I want to know just what was said to make poor Ginny run into the road,' Tessa demanded angrily.

'Who bloody cares!' Vera blew smoke rings and watched them rise.

Tessa was infuriated and snatched the cigarette from her mouth and threw it into the gutter. '*I* bloody care!'

''Ere, they cost money,' Vera cried belligerently.

Elizabeth weighed in. She felt like smacking the girl hard across the face. 'So? We're not leaving until you've told us.'

Vera crossed her arms over her bosom and leaned against the doorframe and looked bored. 'I was out with yer brother, we were 'avin' a laugh an' a joke in Lester Park when she appeared. She must 'ave followed 'im. Then she starts screamin' an' yellin' and callin' me names. Well, I wasn't standin' for that, not from the likes of 'er. He told her to sod off an' leave us in peace an' then she went for me. Dragged a whole 'andful of 'air out me 'ead, the little bitch! I told 'er she was an ugly little kid who didn't know what fellers like

Colin want and he agreed. He said she was a bloody nuisance! Then off she goes.' Vera shrugged, drew a cigarette packet from her pocket and lit another Woodbine.

Tessa was livid. 'She's *not* an ugly little kid! She's a quiet, pretty, good girl! Too good for the likes of him!'

Vera shrugged. ''Er sort are two a penny around 'ere.'

'And your sort are paid in pennies!' Tessa shot back.

This annoyed Vera. 'Bugger off! Go on, clear off! It's nothin' ter do with me!'

Elizabeth, who was very sarcastic when she chose to be, and who was an expert in the art of the studied insult, after all her battles with Nessie, looked Vera up and down slowly and appraisingly. Then she turned to her friend, a serious, speculative expression on her face.

'Would you say she was worth a sixpence, Tessa, or would that be too much? I mean, she's not very clean and possibly not even attractive under all that make-up. She probably doesn't have a bath very often, so she must stink to high heaven. No, on second thoughts you're right. About tuppence is all I'd say she's worth. Of course, you'd have to see a doctor afterwards in case you'd caught anything, that would be more expense.'

'You . . . you toffee-nosed little cow!' Vera screamed at Elizabeth before slamming the door in their faces.

Elizabeth grinned. 'Well, she didn't like *that* much, did she?'

'Sometimes I think you should be on the stage, Elizabeth Harrison. I really do. You certainly knew how to deal with her.'

'It's a gift,' Elizabeth replied airily. 'Now, what are we going to do about your Colin and poor Ginny?'

Tessa looked thoughtful as they walked back up the street. The woman who'd given them the number of the Morleys' house was standing on her doorstep, a toddler asleep in her arms and another clinging to her skirt.

'Whatever it was yer said to 'er, girl, it took 'er down a peg or two. I've never seen 'er with a gob on like that!'

'Just a few home truths,' Elizabeth answered, and they walked on.

'Are we going to tell Ginny what those two said?' Tessa asked.

'We can't. I really don't think we should, unless she remembers herself.'

Tessa nodded her agreement. Elizabeth was making sense. May, when they told her about their visit to Vera, agreed too.

'But what about Da and our Colin?' Tessa asked.

'You leave both of them to me, Tessa, luv! I'll skin that little sod alive! Vera bloody Morley instead of our Ginny!'

'But she can only remember good things about him,' Tessa reminded her stepmother.

'Let her go on thinking that, but I'm going to make sure that *he* stays away from her in future. Oh, I wish to God she'd find someone else, I really do!'

'So do I,' Tessa said with equal passion.

Colin had sat in the kitchen for the whole time that Tessa was out. If she did find out the truth from Vera there'd be murder. May had never liked him and now she'd be livid. He had to get away from here. But where to? He didn't have much money. He'd spent most of it on Vera and he hadn't got his money's worth either.

His thoughts turned again to the Liverpool Savings Bank.

Should he try again? He knew where he'd gone wrong last time. He'd have to try a different branch, they'd be certain to remember his face. There was a branch in County Road, he'd go there. He'd go through all the watching and waiting again, but at least he knew which was the right day to go. This time he wouldn't be greedy. He'd just approach one teller. He couldn't take the risk of failing. Then he'd be away from here. A new life, that's what he needed, a new life in a new country. But he'd better make it soon. He was aware, as were all the men he knew, that war was imminent and that if it was declared then travel to America would stop. He'd go tomorrow and give the place the once-over, then by the end of next week, on Friday, he'd make his move.

After she'd left Tessa, Elizabeth bumped into Mike Flynn, quite literally. They were both walking with heads down, lost in thought.

'God, you gave me a fright!'

'And you gave me one too,' she answered. 'Where are you going?'

'To see your da actually. Where have you been?'

'To Blackstock Street with Tessa.'

'What for?'

Elizabeth told him.

'He's a bloody little creep. There's no one around here who likes him.'

'I know. I just hope Ginny sees some sense, but if she can't remember anything she'll go on thinking he was her knight in shining armour, kneeling on the cobbles beside her, all worried and concerned. And that's something no one wants!'

Delia was surprised to see Elizabeth come in with Mike Flynn.

'Elizabeth, how's Ginny?'

'OK, Mam.'

'Is there anything wrong in your house, Mike? You look serious.'

'No, everything's great. I've come to see Mr Harrison, if that's all right with you?'

'Of course it is, go on through. I'm just going to tidy up this place and lock up.'

'Do you want me to stay or shall I go upstairs?' asked Elizabeth.

'No, I don't mind you staying.'

Jack had just made himself a cup of cocoa.

'Now here's a surprise. You've not come on the cadge, have you, Mike?' he half-joked.

'No, I've come to ask you for some advice. My da's hopeless. All he's interested in is beer, fags, horses and greyhounds. The thing is, Mr Harrison, I've been working down the Salthouse Dock for Dawson's for nearly two years and I'm sick of it. I'm not qualified for anything else, anything that pays well and that's interesting, that is.'

Jack nodded. The lad's only alternatives were the docks and a dead-end job like the one he had.

'And we all know that there's going to be another war, but I'm too young for the services.'

'Oh, don't say that!' Elizabeth cried.

One look from her father silenced her.

'To have a trade is to have a future, lad, but before you can get a trade you've got to serve an apprenticeship, just like milady here. The pay is buttons and the hours are long.'

'At least he'd get some pay. All I get are "expenses".'

'Don't let's bring that up, Elizabeth, please,' Jack said firmly. 'The only thing I can suggest is that you go to evening classes.'

'But they don't have them for things like, well, engineering.'

'Of course they do, lad. Get yourself along to the Mechanics Institute and have a word with someone there. They'll be able to tell you what's on offer. You'll have to have patience though, you'll have to stick with Dawson's for a few years yet.'

Mike got up. 'I won't mind that so much if I know there is going to be a better job at the end of it. Thanks. Thanks, Mr Harrison, you've been a big help.'

Jack shook his hand. Mike was a good lad and he wished him well. He hadn't had much of a life up to now.

Elizabeth got up and went to the back door with him as her mother came in from the shop.

'What did he want?' Delia asked Jack. Mike Flynn didn't usually come into the shop.

'To ask advice about getting a decent job, eventually.'

Delia raised her eyebrows. 'Well, he's the only one in that family with any nous but I'll be surprised if he gets anywhere with his attitude.'

'What attitude?'

'Always clowning around, making stupid jokes about people. In fact turning everything into a joke. I can't see an employer putting up with that for long.'

Jack shook his head and picked up his newspaper. Sometimes with his Delia it was better just to keep quiet.

* * *

'What made you think about doing something else, Mike?' Elizabeth asked, leaning against the doorframe.

'Tessa and her plans to be a stewardess, I suppose. And I do want to get on in life. I don't want to finish up like Da.'

'You mean married with a gang of kids all squashed into a two-up, two-down?'

'Well, I hadn't thought that far ahead. I just mean that I want more than beer and fags and gambling.'

'Good for you.'

Mike looked abashed. Somehow this talk about the future had changed things between them. He didn't know how or why, but it had. 'Elizabeth, if I get on to a class, would you . . . well, would you help me, like?'

She looked interested. 'With homework, you mean? I'll try, but some of the things you'll be doing will be all . . . well, sort of technical and I'm useless at anything like that. I couldn't even master Algebra or Geometry.'

'I can't see it being all that technical to start with.'

'I suppose you're right. Yes, I'll be glad to help you, Mike.'

He shuffled his feet and twisted his cap in his hands. 'Can I ask you something else?'

'Of course.'

He was trying to frame the words.

'Well, what's up with you?'

'I'm trying to think how to say this.'

She was bemused. 'Say what?'

'Will you . . . will you come out with me, Elizabeth? To the pictures?'

She was taken aback and began to blush. She'd never really thought about him like *that*.

271

'If you don't want to, it doesn't matter.'

'Oh, I do! I mean . . . I'd like that.'

'When? This weekend?'

'Could we make it next? Mam's got plans this Sunday, and Saturday is our busiest day and I'm always completely worn out by the time I get home. Half the time I fall asleep in the chair.'

'All right, Sunday week, then. I'll look in the *Echo* at what's on in town. Will it be OK with your mam and dad?' he queried.

It wouldn't, she knew that. Well, with her da maybe, but definitely not her mam.

'Maybe we should wait a bit before telling them. Mam still hasn't really forgiven me for leaving school.' She certainly didn't want to make any more trouble.

He nodded. He understood exactly how Delia would feel, that he definitely wasn't good enough for her elder daughter.

'I'll be seeing you down by the tannery next week sometime. We'll fix it up then.'

She nodded. 'I'd better go in now.'

'See you, Elizabeth,' Mike said as he walked down the yard. It had been a really great evening for him. Now he had some hopes of being able to better himself and he'd finally plucked up the courage to ask Elizabeth out and she'd neither laughed at him or refused.

'What were you two talking about out there?' Delia asked. She still didn't like Elizabeth hanging around with one of the Flynns.

'Oh, nothing much. I'm going to help him when he starts at that Mechanics place.'

Delia looked shrewdly at her daughter. 'Just you see that

you don't let me down again, Elizabeth.'

'Mam! How long have I known him? Since we were babies! I've known Johnny Doyle for that long too, but I don't intend to marry either of them!'

'I sincerely hope not! Now, isn't it time you saw to your own homework?'

Elizabeth fetched her books but somehow she couldn't concentrate on *Therapeutic Treatments for the Hair and Scalp*. Fancy Mike asking *me* out, she thought. It was really a surprise. They'd been friends for years, as she'd told her mam, but now it seemed as though friendship was being turned into something else, and she didn't feel at all unhappy about it. Quite the reverse.

Chapter Nineteen

By the following Friday Colin knew as much as he needed to know about the routine of the bank. He'd not been to work all week, although he'd gone out and returned at his usual time. Things at home were very strained. No one was speaking to him, except Ginny, and every time she spoke directly to him either Tessa or May would interrupt and change the subject. Besides, he couldn't stand Ginny gazing at him like a moonstruck calf.

He was so confident of success that this time he'd packed a small bag with his few possessions and had hidden it under the bed. Cleaning under the beds was something that only Tessa did and she only ever did it at weekends. Ginny and May never cleaned that thoroughly.

As he stood outside Frost's, a small department store opposite the bank, he felt again all the nervousness and tension he'd suffered the last time. But his whole future depended on the next five minutes and he was determined not to let his nerves get the better of him.

He crossed the road slowly and opened the door. The decor was much the same as the Scotland Road branch and he quickly appraised the two tellers who were entering sums of money in large books. He decided to go for the elder of the two. Just as he'd done before he shoved the note towards the teller and gestured with the catapult in his pocket.

The eyes that met his were full of fear. 'I . . . I'm

sorry but . . . but there's not much here.'

Colin began to panic. 'Where the bleeding hell is it, then? It only arrived fifteen minutes ago, I watched the feller bring it!'

'In the safe.'

'Then go and bloody get it and be quick.' He again pointed the stick in his pocket towards the older man. Then he gestured at the younger teller: 'You! Don't you make a move or I'll use this bloody gun!'

The young teller was rooted to the spot. Colin felt the sweat spring out of every pore in his body. He paced up and down, his eyes darting from the young teller to the door and back again. The elderly man returned after what seemed to Colin a lifetime. Every minute he'd expected a customer to come in, just like last time.

'It . . . it's all there.' Two canvas bags were placed on the counter. Colin snatched them up, shoved them inside his jacket and ran out. Once on County Road he walked quickly away. County Road was intersected with narrow streets of red-brick terraced houses. He'd use these streets and the back entries, avoiding the main road, until he reached the junction with Spellow Lane, then he'd get a bus or a tram home. There was always one waiting. It was a sort of terminus, a halfway stop between Aintree and Fazakerley and town.

A number 22 tram was waiting and he paid his fare and went up the narrow stairs to the upper deck. He needed a cigarette to calm his nerves. He fumbled in his pocket and drew out a battered carton of Woodbines. There was only one left and as he lit it he thought from now on he would be able to afford expensive cigarettes, not Woodies, *and* he'd have a proper lighter and not a box of Pilot matches.

He felt elated. His nervousness disappeared and he felt an enormous sense of relief. Two bags! *Two* bags! There was obviously more on Fridays because people wanted money for the weekend and the banks were closed on Saturdays. He must have hundreds of pounds. His fingers itched to count it and he could hardly wait to get home.

When Colin finally reached his stop he went down the back jigger to Naylor Street and was relieved to find the house was empty. May was out. He went up to the bedroom and emptied the contents of both bags on the bed. The crisp new notes seemed to cover it entirely. He picked up a five-pound note. He'd never even seen one of the large white notes before. He crumpled it up in his hand and the sensation this gave him was something he'd never experienced before either. He stood for a few minutes looking at the money. He was rich! He was rich beyond his wildest dreams! He pulled himself together and stuffed it back into the bags, then, pulling his bag from under the bed, he put both the smaller canvas ones with all the notes inside, except the one he had crumpled. That one he put in his pocket. Now he'd head for the Cunard Building and the first ship out of Liverpool bound for America.

He looked around at the shabby room. He was well out of it, he thought. The place was not much better than a doss house. He left without a second glance, closing the yard door behind him, and walked down the entry with a spring in his step.

On his way to the Pier Head he stopped off in Church Street and bought a suit, three shirts and two ties in Hepworth's. He also went to Lewis's and bought pyjamas, a dressing gown, new underwear, shoes and socks, toilet requisites, a trilby hat and a large suitcase. In the changing room, he took out three more five-pound notes, to pay not only for his purchases but his fare. He couldn't go scrabbling around in his case for money. In the Gentlemen's toilets he put on his new clothes and set the trilby at what he thought to be a rakish angle. He left his old clothes there. Then, full of confidence and elation, he set off for the Cunard Building, the middle one of the famous trio on the waterfront.

When he arrived and the clerk looked at him with respect, he felt like a new person.

'Yes, sir? May I be of assistance?'

'I have to go to New York and I'm in a hurry. Business, you understand,' he added.

'You're in luck, the *Ascania* is due to sail at five o'clock. You'll just have time to embark. I presume you have your official documents?'

Colin panicked but then decided to bluff it out. 'Of course I have. I wouldn't be here otherwise.'

The clerk nodded. 'United States Immigration are very strict. Now, what class will you be travelling?'

'Second class, please.'

'Return?'

'Yes.' There was no use arousing suspicions by asking for a one-way ticket.

'That will be twelve guineas please, sir.'

Colin counted out the notes and coins and waited for his change and the ticket.

'*Bon voyage*, sir!' the clerk said pleasantly.

Once outside he crossed the open cobbled space, his hand shaking as he looked at the piece of printed card. This was his ticket to the future. But something was nagging at him. There was something he'd forgotten, he was certain. Then the realisation struck him like a blow to the stomach. Johnny Doyle sailed on the *Ascania*! He stopped dead. God! What was he going to do now? Think, that's what he'd have to do. He crossed to the tram terminus and sat on a wooden bench. If he waited for another ship he was taking a terrible risk of getting caught. Then he could be looking at ten years in jail. What if he went to London or Southampton? You could quite easily lose yourself in London or catch another ship from Southampton but it would take time and time was one thing he didn't have. No, he couldn't stand that. He'd have to risk it. If Johnny saw him he'd have to make up some story, but if he stayed in his cabin all day, just venturing out for meals, he may never see hide nor hair of Johnny. He worked mainly in the first-class sections of the ship. There wasn't a choice. He'd have to go because he certainly couldn't stay.

As usual the Landing Stage was busy. There were passengers and their families and friends; luggage being loaded; last-minute supplies being taken on board; the tugs already alongside and an official of the Cunard Line waiting at the bottom of the gangway for tickets.

Once on board he found his way to his cabin, guided by a steward. The ship was full and the companionways seemed to be crowded with people. Some were sitting on their luggage.

The steward looked harassed. 'Over-booked again! It always happens, every trip. I don't know what they do in those offices. You'd think they'd have enough sense not to give a cabin to two different sets of passengers! Well, the Purser's Office can sort it out. Here we are, sir.' He fumbled with a key, muttering about 'unnecessary *bon voyage* parties and flaming kids running riot', and opened the door.

Once inside Colin looked around. There was every comfort here, he thought, but it wasn't as grand as first class would be. He could afford first class but that would have drawn attention to himself and he would have needed a trunk full of fancy clothes which he'd never wear again. To him this small carpeted cabin and its bunk, made up with crisp white sheets and heavy white counterpane with the Cunard emblem embossed on it, its porcelain washbasin and thick white fluffy towels was sheer luxury.

He opened his case and unpacked his few belongings into the highly polished wardrobe, thinking he should have bought more shirts and trousers. Still, he could buy them in New York. He sat down on the bunk. New York! He'd only ever heard stories about it. How big it was, how tall the sky-scrapers were. How modern everything was. How it teemed with people of all creeds and colours and how you could still make fortunes there if you were lucky. Oh, he'd get on in New York all right.

He took the two canvas bags out of his case and then placed them on the floor and counted the money. He was set up for life. It had been his lucky day. He put most of the notes back into the bags and stuffed them under the mattress. He wished he could go up on deck to join the crowds and watch as they pulled away and sailed downriver towards the estuary, leaving Liverpool and his old life behind, but he couldn't risk it. He did experience a surge of excitement as he heard the three loud blasts of the ship's steam whistle and then the answering ones of the tugs, the ferries and the other ships on the river, and felt the deck beneath his feet begin to move. He climbed up on the bunk and looked out of the porthole: the *Ascania* was being pulled out into the river and he could see almost as far as the lighthouse on Perch Rock. He was on his way.

When there was no sign of Colin by ten o'clock that night Ginny began to worry. May was at work, Richie had just come back from his nightly visit to the Globe and Tessa was engrossed in a book.

'Something must have happened to him! He's always in from work about six or half past.'

Tessa looked up. 'Don't worry about him, Ginny. He used to stay out all night when Mam was alive, when we first came here. He'll come to no harm, believe me.'

But Ginny wasn't satisfied and by eleven o'clock she had convinced them that something must have happened to him.

'Oh, Ginny, for heaven's sake, go and look and see if his things are in the bedroom, if it will calm you down,' May said impatiently. She was tired and she certainly didn't really care where the lad was.

Ginny went upstairs and returned looking even more worried.

'Well?' May demanded.

'Everything has gone. He's left. He's run off. Come and see.'

Reluctantly Tessa and May followed a tearful Ginny back upstairs and after checking the chest of drawers and the old sea chest they looked at each other.

'So, the bird has flown. I wonder where to?' May said without much interest.

'Well, I'll be honest, I can't say I'm that bothered. He can

281

look after himself and he may be up to his eyes in ...
something. That wouldn't surprise me either,' Tessa said.

May nodded her agreement and then began to try to
comfort her daughter, who had dissolved into tears.

'Ginny, he won't be gone long. He'll be back. He's done
this before,' Tessa tried to reassure her friend.

'Who knows what gets into fellers' heads, luv? Some just
can't settle for long in one place, but they come back, usually
when they're broke and hungry. He'll be back, luv, you wait
and see.'

Ginny wiped her eyes but didn't reply. She wasn't convinced. She knew she wouldn't get much sleep tonight, she
was so worried.

On Saturday morning the *Daily Post* was full of the
robbery. It had been an audacious crime, committed by
someone who had 'nerves of steel', so the newspaper
commented. The police had a good description of the thief
who had got away with all the bank's takings and the money
that had only arrived fifteen minutes earlier. It was a
professional job, well planned and carried out with speed
and efficiency. They were looking for a tall, well-built lad of
about nineteen to twenty-one, with dark hair.

'Well, that covers most of the lads in the city,' Richie
commented dryly.

'I thought you said they had a good description?' May said.

'I did. It says so here.'

'Well, I don't call that good.'

'It says the teller would recognise him again—'

'They've got to catch him first,' May interrupted. 'Do
you think your precious son will put in an appearance today?'
she asked sarcastically.

'I've no idea. You know what he's like.'

'I do,' May replied. It wouldn't bother her if he never crossed this doorstep again. It would give everyone a bit of peace and quiet, and maybe Ginny would begin to see him in a different light.

By Saturday night the *Ascania* had left Cobh in County Cork behind and was steaming out into the Atlantic. Colin was bored sick. He saw only the steward, there was nothing to do at all except count his money and even that pleasure was waning. He'd tried to make plans but that didn't work either as he had no idea what he really wanted to do, or what was on offer in the huge country he was bound for. When he went for his meals he got glimpses of the public rooms and they looked so interesting and inviting that he began to think of venturing out. If he had to stay in that cabin for another five days he'd go mad. After all, the ship was full. Maybe he'd been over-cautious. If he just went for a quick wander round, not stay out for too long, there wouldn't be much of a risk in that. He'd mingle with the crowds, act casually and do nothing that would single him out for attention. He'd be all right.

He was very cautious at first, continually glancing around to see if anyone was watching him, until he realised he must look very furtive. He leaned on the rail of the Promenade Deck, lit a cigarette and looked down at the grey-green water that slid by, broken only by the white spray of the ship's bow wave. What was the matter with him? He looked like everyone else. Why on earth should he worry?

Next morning after breakfast he wandered along to the Library and Gentlemen's Smoking Room, which was furnished with cane and wicker chairs and tables and potted plants and pictures of oriental scenes. He relished his cigarette; he was a 'Gentleman' now. Then he strolled along the Boat Deck, looking out at the waters of the Atlantic that surrounded them and would do so for the next four days and three nights, breathing the damp salty air and thinking of just what he would do without 'official documents' when they reached their destination. He'd have to devise some form of dodging U. S. Immigration Officials. He had his return ticket, he was 'on business': maybe he'd accuse the steward of stealing his documents. That was a possibility. The problem would keep his mind occupied for most of the journey. He pulled his hat further down to make sure it didn't blow away, stuffed his hands in his pockets and walked on, totally engrossed.

Johnny Doyle had been told by the Chief Steward to make certain that all the chairs and rugs had been put out on the Promenade Deck as the deck steward was 'indisposed'. Johnny had had to hide a grin. 'Indisposed' meant either drunk or hungover: no wonder the Chief Steward had a face like thunder.

He was walking along with an armful of thick tartan rugs, for it was always chilly on the Atlantic, whatever time of year it was: the speed of the ship generated wind. He happened to glance down to the Boat Deck, then he stopped and leaned over the rail. It couldn't be! It couldn't possibly be! It was just someone who looked like him!

At that moment Colin decided to light a cigarette and stopped and fumbled in his pocket for his Senior Service cigarettes and lighter.

Johnny let out his breath slowly. It *was* him. It was Colin O'Leary. What the hell was he doing on board? No good, that was for certain. Just where had he got the money from? He detested Colin O'Leary – he'd never forgotten his wanton cruelty to that poor little girl – but what about Tessa? If she learned that he had shopped her brother, and in so doing brought more shame on the family, how would she react? He struggled with his conscience for a while until he made up his mind. O'Leary must have committed a serious, possibly violent crime to be running to the other side of the world and he knew that Tessa would almost certainly understand. He deposited the rugs on the nearest chair and walked away, heading for the Purser's Office to study the Passenger Manifest. If it *was* Colin, then he'd find some way of searching his cabin.

It was no hardship to find Colin's name and cabin number. Second class too, he thought. He went to find the steward.

'It'd be more than my job's worth to give you a key to 108. What do you want it for?' Taffy Williams asked.

'I've got some suspicions about the feller who's in there.'

'What sort of suspicions?'

'He's someone I know. He lives in our street and has a job as a labourer, so how come he can afford a second-class cabin?'

Taffy pondered this for a moment. 'OK, boyo, I can't give you the key but I can come with you. He's not on my section, it's Paddy Mahr's bit along here, but he's gone to see what he can scrounge from his pantry lad.'

They both looked around quickly then the Welshman opened the door.

'He hasn't got much in the way of gear, has he?' Taffy

said disparagingly as Johnny searched the small wardrobe.

'Where else would he hide something?'

'Under the mattress on the bunk. They all do it, they think it's safe. It's the first place anyone looks if they're out to pinch something.'

Taffy yanked up the mattress while Johnny searched underneath. His fingers closed over something.

'I've got it.'

'What is it?'

'A canvas bag – no, two by the feel of it, and they're full of something.'

The bags were pulled out.

Johnny was stunned. 'Bloody hell! He's robbed a bloody bank! Look at the lettering. *Liverpool Savings Bank.*' Johnny looked inside one bag. 'It's stuffed with money!'

'Then we'd better take it to the Three-Ringer. I'll take it and say I found it while doing the bunk. I'll have to say I was helping Paddy out. Returning a favour, see.'

'God, I knew he was crafty and light-fingered but I'd no idea he was into big stuff like this! Perhaps you should tell his nibs I know him.'

'OK. Wait for the summons then.'

'I'll be up on the Prom Deck, where I'm supposed to be.'

Johnny still couldn't believe it. Colin O'Leary, robbing a bloody bank! He had some guts, he'd say that for him.

Fifteen minutes later the 'indisposed' deck steward appeared to summon Johnny to the Chief Steward's office. He was surprised to see both Taffy and Colin already there, and as soon as Colin clapped eyes on him the colour drained from his face.

286

'Right, Doyle, do you know this feller?'

'Yes, sir. His name's Colin O'Leary, he lives in the same street as me.'

'And what does he do for a job?'

'He's a labourer for Mathew's Haulage in Vauxhall Road, sir.'

'I told you, I *won* the money on a horse,' Colin interrupted, recovering his wits. 'Well, on a couple of horses. I had a good day!'

'It would have to have been a whole herd of bloody horses, and why is it in these bags marked "the property of the Liverpool Savings Bank"?'

'That's what the bookie gave it me in, I swear to God!'

'Taffy, go to the Purser and ask if *Mr* O'Leary has lodged his passport and visa with him, and then find the Master-at-arms.'

'I . . . I didn't have time to get them. I . . . I decided on the spur of the moment to get away from Liverpool! Start a new life. We live in a slum.' He glared at Johnny, furious with him and with himself. Why, oh why had he gone wandering around the ship?

'Well, you're going back to Liverpool. The Master-at-arms is on his way. You'll be locked in your cabin for the rest of the voyage *and* for the return trip, then you'll be handed over to the Liverpool City Police and you can tell them that fairy tale. I've heard better excuses from a bevvied pantry lad!'

'I knew you'd come a cropper one day, O'Leary,' Johnny said to Colin as the Master-at-arms and the Assistant Purser came to take him away. Then Johnny thought of Tessa. Oh, life wasn't fair at all for some people. She'd had the moonlight flit, her mam's illness and death, her da's marriage to May and now this. He knew she'd cope, just as she'd coped with all the rest – Johnny had great admiration for her resilience – but this time she'd hardly be able to hold her head up with the shame of what her brother had done. He only wished there were something he could do to help.

On Sunday morning Elizabeth dressed with more care than usual for mass and hoped her Mam hadn't noticed. Mike was bound to be there with the rest of his family. They'd arranged their date for tonight and she could hardly wait.

Although it was a beautiful sunny September morning everyone seemed very preoccupied and apprehensive.

'I know that the prayers at mass this morning will be more fervent,' Delia said to Jack as she adjusted her hat to the right angle, but not with the care and attention she usually gave it.

'Bound to be, luv. We'll know before dinnertime the outcome of that Ultimatum but I can't see that little butcher backing down. They were bloody brave, those poor sods in Poland. Cavalry against artillery. There was no way they could win.'

Elizabeth looked at her parents with mounting apprehension. She knew, as did the rest of the entire city and country, that if there was no reply to the Ultimatum by eleven o'clock then there was only one course open to them. War.

Father Walsh's sermon that morning was all about the evil that was spreading over the world and the terror, death and destruction that Satan in the guise of Herr Hitler was responsible for. They prayed hard for the poor brave people of Poland and for those who had died trying to stem the might of the German army. There was no talk of 'praying for peace' now, Elizabeth thought, as there had been every Sunday for months. She closed her eyes tightly and tried to envisage just what the future would bring, but she couldn't.

Eddie Doyle, his timid little wife and two younger sons were waiting after mass and gathered a group of their neighbours and customers together.

'Do you all want to come back with me? We've a wireless set. There'll be no drink served, though. Not at a time like this.'

'I would 'ave thought we'd all *need* a drink at a time like this,' Frank Flynn said.

Eddie ignored him and led the group out on to Scotland Road.

It was a quarter to eleven when they were all finally settled in the saloon bar and the big Bakelite wireless set had been carried in and placed on the bar counter next to the handles of the beer pump, which were covered with a clean teacloth that Eddie obviously had no intention of removing.

Elizabeth had manoeuvred herself through the group until she was near to Mike and they exchanged glances of foreboding.

At five to eleven Eddie Doyle fiddled with the knobs and the wireless crackled into life. There wasn't a sound in the room as the tired, sad voice of Mr Chamberlain, the Prime Minister, told them that 'peace in our time' was over and that 'this country is now at war with Germany. We are ready.'

All the older women were crying silently. Delia hid her face against Jack's shoulder, remembering the terrible day when all those telegrams had been delivered in Liverpool, two of which had informed her that both her brothers were dead. Even now, twenty-two years later, she could still hear her mam's heartrending cries. The older men too looked drawn and worried. They had so many memories, all of them bitter, of brothers, cousins, mates who'd not been so lucky as themselves. Only in the young men and lads was there a total lack of understanding.

'For the love of God, Eddie, take that bloody teacloth off! I never thought I'd live to see it happen all over again.' Jack Harrison spoke for everyone.

'And this time it won't just be the soldiers and sailors,' Frank Flynn added. His words brought back all they had read about the bombing of civilians in Spain.

'All right, but get the kids out of here.'

All the younger element left their parents inside, glad to escape that doom-laden atmosphere.

Ginny, Tessa, Elizabeth and Mike huddled together.

'I'm scared stiff already,' Ginny said timidly.

'We all are. We don't know what to expect. It's not the same just *reading* about it in the newspapers. It . . . Things will happen to *us*,' Elizabeth added quietly.

Alice Collins joined them. 'Have you heard anything about your Colin yet?' she asked Tessa.

'No, and I've more important things on my mind,' Tessa replied, refusing to meet Ginny's gaze.

'Oh, God!' Tessa cried.

'What?' Elizabeth demanded.

'Johnny! Johnny Doyle. He sailed on Friday. What if the Germans start attacking shipping straightaway?'

'They won't have reached America yet, but they'll be safe enough,' Mike tried to reassure her, while wondering just how safe the ship would be on the return trip.

The group began to drift away to their homes and Mike turned to Elizabeth.

'What about tonight? It said in the paper last night that they'd close all the cinemas and theatres, if war was declared.'

She was disappointed. It would have been a distraction.

'We'll just go for a walk, everyone will be so upset they won't notice.'

'I know. Da fought in the last one and he won't say a word about it, not even when he's bevvied, and that's a miracle in itself.'

Elizabeth nodded her understanding. It was going to be an awful day. The King was going to speak on the wireless tonight, so they'd said. Kids had already been evacuated, air-raid shelters had been provided and gas masks – hideous things – had to be carried all the time. Her mam had been hoarding food for months, even though they'd been told not to.

'Will we still go to work?'

'I suppose so,' Mike answered.

Elizabeth looked up at him. 'Promise me something, Mike.'

'What?'

'That you won't lie about your age and join up!'

'Don't you want me to go?'

'No, not yet. Not until you're . . . old enough. Please?'

He took her hand. 'I promise.'

'You'd better not let your mam see you holding hands,' Tessa said quietly with a lilt of amusement in her voice. Observant as ever, she had noticed how Elizabeth and Mike's friendly relationship had changed recently.

'You're right.' Reluctantly Elizabeth slid her fingers from his.

The rest of the day was indeed awful, spent in nervous

speculation about the future. But they had no inkling of what the war might really mean to them until a couple of days later.

'Now what?' Mike asked, as Kenny Keegan came running towards the tannery wall where the four friends had gathered once again. 'What's up, Kenny?'

'It's just come through an' Mr Doyle's dead worried and Mrs Doyle's crying,' the lad panted.

'What for?' Elizabeth demanded.

'One of them German U-boats sunk the *Athenia* on Monday!'

'Oh my God!' Tessa cried, clasping her hands tightly.

'She was going back to Glasgow an' . . . an' they don't think that anyone is left alive.'

Tessa grabbed hold of Elizabeth's arm. 'Johnny's out there too! If they can sink one ship so soon, what chance do any of them have of making it back?'

'Oh, Tessa, don't think like that!' Elizabeth pleaded.

'No, don't. They'll be all right. The *Ascania*'s bigger and faster and they'll do a quick turnaround and run for home. He'll come back, Tessa. He will!' Mike was trying to convince himself as much as Tessa.

Tessa just nodded, and there were tears in her eyes.

'I never thought you cared about him . . . like that,' Elizabeth said as they turned the corner into Naylor Street.

'I . . . I do.'

Elizabeth gave her friend's hand a squeeze. What would happen to them all in the days, months and even years ahead? she wondered. Would the life they knew change beyond all recognition?

Chapter Twenty

The news of the sinking of the *Athenia* reached the *Ascania* by means of wireless telegraphy, and the Captain ordered the rest of the journey to be made at Full Ahead. He just prayed that the weather would hold.

Although sworn to secrecy so as not to worry the passengers, the crew had been told and emergency lifeboat drill ordered each night after midnight. All lights that could possibly be extinguished were put out. There was an air of fear on board now that hadn't been there on Friday when they'd sailed.

As Colin wasn't classed as a passenger any longer, the steward, Paddy Mahr, decided to inform his 'prisoner', who in his opinion was a surly little sod, of the situation.

'And how are you in yourself this morning?' he asked as he brought in the breakfast tray.

Colin just scowled at him.

'Wouldn't you think it was a grand day, looking out there?' He inclined his head in the direction of the porthole. 'But won't we all be glad when we're back home? Even you, me young bucko.'

'What kind of bloody stupid remark is that to make?' Colin said acidly.

'Sure, it's far from stupid. The crew and passengers of the *Athenia* would gladly swap places with us all. Wasn't she sunk by a torpedo on Monday? A hundred and fourteen souls went down with her, God rest them all.' The steward crossed himself.

Colin looked at him in amazement. 'Why?'

'Oh, it's "why", is it now? Because war was declared on Sunday morning and here we are stuck in the middle of the ocean with God alone knows what lurking down there.'

The terrible reality of their position dawned on Colin. They were easy prey. The *Ascania* was a merchant ship, she had no guns or depth charges. Was it better to reach Liverpool and ultimately Walton Jail or sit here never knowing if he'd end up being drowned?

'Now that'll give you something to keep your mind occupied. It's saying some prayers I'd be doing if I were you.'

Johnny was scared too. 'What kind of a chance do you think we'll have?' he asked the Second Steward, who'd called him in to give him a pep talk. The Chief Steward had summoned them all, in groups, and informed them of the situation, but as Johnny was so young – in fact the youngest crew member – he'd asked his second-in-command to reassure the lad.

'Good. The Atlantic's a big ocean and it's the most treacherous. When we reach New York we'll do a fast turn-round and the Captain will order Full Ahead for the whole way home. At twenty-nine knots we'll outstrip any U-boat, but we won't be sailing again with passengers. Every merchantman will be commandeered now by the Government for convoy duty.'

Johnny nodded, feeling better now. He didn't really mind not sailing again with passengers and he was too young for the Royal Navy.

'So, it's fingers crossed and pray to God the weather stays good. Get off now, lad, and try not too look so worried. The last thing we want is for the passengers to suspect something's up. Time enough for them to worry when we reach port.'

After a fortnight with no news, everyone in number twelve, Naylor Street was concerned about Colin. Ginny was frantic.

'I know something's happened to him! I just *know* it!'

'Well, I have to admit that he's never stayed away for so long,' Tessa said.

'Do you think we should inform the police?' May asked Richie.

Richie looked serious. 'Give him until tomorrow night. We know he intended going somewhere, he took everything with him. Maybe he's gone to look for work in London.'

'That wouldn't surprise me, him not telling us, I mean,' Tessa added.

'You're right, Tessa, he's probably got a job and a room down there.'

'And he wouldn't bother to write to us to stop us worrying,' May added. 'I don't think he's come to any harm, Ginny, luv.'

'But he never said a word to me! He didn't even say goodbye.'

'Maybe he didn't want to upset you, luv,' May said soothingly as she exchanged glances with Tessa.

'He wouldn't have gone and joined the Army, would he?' Ginny asked tearfully.

'I doubt that very much,' May answered. King and Country would be the last things on his mind, she thought.

But Ginny wouldn't be pacified. She *knew* something had happened to him. She was certain he would never have deliberately gone for so long without telling her, even though he'd been distant the week before he'd disappeared. He'd taken her to hospital after her accident though, hadn't he? That must mean something. But she still couldn't remember what had happened before she'd been knocked down.

Richie, urged on by Ginny and Tessa, who was more concerned for Ginny than her brother, finally agreed to go to the police.

'I know he's eighteen but that doesn't alter things,' May said as she gave his jacket a brush-down. 'Go, and let us get a bit of peace from milady in there,' she whispered.

They were all surprised by the loud hammering on the front door.

'Oh, maybe he's back! He's come back!' Ginny cried, making for the door.

Tessa caught her arm. 'Ginny, why would he be knocking on the front door? He'd come in the back way or just open the front door, he's got a key.'

The hopeful light in Ginny's eyes dimmed. Tessa was right. A feeling of dread settled over her again. It was increased as a uniformed police sergeant accompanied by a burly man in a serge suit and bowler hat came into the kitchen, followed by Richie.

'Oh my God!' May cried.

'Am I right in saying that one Colin O'Leary resides here?' the sergeant stated, referring to his notebook while the calm but penetrating gaze of the CID man swept the room and all their faces.

'Yes. What's happened?' Richie replied.

'Oh, what's happened to him?' Ginny begged tearfully. She was certain they'd come to tell them that something terrible had happened to poor Colin.

'We've had a message from the Master-at-arms on the *Ascania*, due into Liverpool tomorrow, that they have a Colin O'Leary on board, under lock and key. He's suspected of robbing a branch of the Liverpool Savings Bank, although he claims' – the CID man pulled a piece of paper from his pocket – 'that he won the money he has in his possession on a couple of horse races and the bookie's runner gave it to him in the bags marked with the bank's name.' He stopped and glanced at the faces of the four people in the kitchen, noting their expressions.

'He claims that he was with a "Ginny Greely" at the time of the raid.'

Ginny sat down slowly at the table. This wasn't happening. Colin wouldn't do something like rob a bank! But why was he on a ship? Where had he been going? Why hadn't he told her? And why had he said he'd been with her? None of it made any sense to her. Colin just *wouldn't* do something as terrible as that. He *must* be telling the truth about winning it. Oh, she wished he was here so she could ask him.

'Are you Miss Ginny Greely?' the sergeant asked.

May was instantly by her daughter's side. She was as stunned as the rest of them, but Ginny looked as though she were about to faint.

'Yes, she is, and I'm her mam.'

'Well, were you with him on the afternoon of Friday the first of September?'

Ginny broke down in tears. 'I . . . I . . . can't remember! I . . . can't remember *anything*, Mam.'

'Come on now, luv, don't get upset. We all know you were at work, or did you take time off?' May asked.

'I . . . I . . . Oh, Mam!' Ginny became incoherent. Until she saw him, *actually saw* him, she didn't know what to think or say. If he'd been falsely accused she'd stand by him, but was he innocent?

'She's not going to be much help. She had a bad accident not so long ago and it's affected her memory,' May informed them.

'How convenient,' the CID man said with heavy sarcasm.

'Go and check the records in Stanley Hospital if you don't believe it,' May said.

'You know he's been in trouble before? Borstal – twice. Now it looks as if he's graduated to bigger things.'

'Oh, Holy Mother of God!' May cried while Richie looked sheepish and Tessa sat down on the sofa and covered her face with her hands. Oh, this was terrible! She certainly didn't believe Colin's trumped-up explanation and neither would her da.

'Why didn't you tell me?' May demanded.

'I . . . I . . . thought he'd learned his lesson and I didn't want to upset you, May,' Richie replied guiltily. He really should have told her.

'Upset me! Upset me! Do you think I'd have let him take our Ginny out if I'd known that?'

'All right, that's enough. You can sort all that out between yourselves later.'

'When will he be home?' Richie asked them.

'Tomorrow morning. He'll be taken into custody as soon as they dock and probably go to the Main Bridewell in Dale Street.'

'Can we see him?' Richie asked.

'I don't want to see him ever again!' Tessa cried bitterly.

'You can, if he wants to see you. I imagine he will because he won't see you for a long time after that. He'll get eight years in Walton, if he's lucky. A hundred and fifty quid is a lot of money, as well as possessing a gun.'

'A gun!' May shrieked.

'Or what we assume was a gun.' He wasn't going to tell them that no one had actually seen it.

'Well, we'll leave you in peace now to carry on the argument, but we'll see you tomorrow, particularly you, Miss Greely. Be down at the Bridewell by half past eleven.'

No one made a move to escort the two men to the front door, they were all too shocked.

When the front door slammed Tessa broke the silence. 'Oh, I *hate* him! I really *hate* him! How could he do this to us?'

'And why did you never tell me he'd been in Borstal, Richie?' May demanded angrily.

'May, would you have married me . . . taken all of us on, if you'd known that?' Richie pleaded.

'I certainly wouldn't have had *him* under the same roof as the rest of us but I'd have still married you. But we'll talk about that later, when we're on our own.' She nodded towards the two shaken girls.

'How are we going to hold our heads up now?' Tessa exclaimed, her cheeks pink with anger. Then she turned to her stepsister. 'Oh, Ginny, please stop crying. Maybe now you'll see what he's really like. He's lying, he's robbed that bank all right and now he's using you to try to get himself off the hook.'

Ginny couldn't stand any more. She got up. 'I . . . I don't know what to think!'

'You're not going to go on believing him and protecting him! How can you?' Tessa cried passionately.

Ginny rushed from the room in floods of tears. He'd been in trouble before and they'd known but hadn't said a word, and now . . . Oh, she didn't know what to believe any more.

* * *

The following morning, as they were getting ready to go to Dale Street, Johnny came to the back door.

'I've just this minute got home, Tessa. Have you—'

'Heard? Yes. The police came yesterday.' She leaned against the sink. 'Oh, Johnny, how am I going to cope with all this? It will be in all the papers, everyone in the whole city will know!'

'I'm sorry, but people *will* understand. At least in this street they will. Everyone had him taped as a bit of a crook. Don't you remember that Christmas fiasco?'

She looked up at him, her eyes bright with unshed tears. 'Yes, of course, we knew he was a petty thief, a chancer – but bank robbery!'

'I know, and I'm the one who caught him.'

'You?'

He nodded and then told her. 'I don't know what he was going to do when he got there. He had no passport or anything.'

'Oh, he'd have lied his way out of that. Jumped ship, anything. Johnny, I feel so ashamed.'

'It's not your fault, Tessa.' He took her hand. 'You know we . . . I'll stand by you.'

'Will you? Truthfully?'

'Yes, truthfully. You're the best . . . the nicest girl I know and other people think that too. The fellers around here like your da, they won't blame him – well, not much. Nearly every family has its black sheep. Colin's yours.'

'But it will all come out.'

'Maybe it's best if it does. Clear the air, sort of. Then you can all start again.'

'Thanks. I really mean that.'

'How's Ginny?'

'In a terrible state. She's cried all night and the more we all try to reason with her, the worse she gets.'

'Surely to God she doesn't believe his story?'

'I don't know, but I think she does.'

'That fairy tale won't hold water! Won it all on the horses and the runner gave him the bags! God, you'd have to be an idiot to believe that.'

'I know, but where he's concerned she *is* an idiot. *And* he's using her.'

'How?'

'He's saying she was with him that Friday afternoon when everyone knows she was at work.'

'Can't her mam talk some sense into her?'

'She's tried. We all have.'

Johnny shook his head. Colin was worse than anyone he'd ever known. Fancy using someone like poor Ginny to try to clear himself.

'Will you . . . will you come with us?' Tessa asked.

'Yes. I've to go down there anyway. They want another statement from me, even though I told them all I knew when they came aboard as soon as we'd tied up. I'm not looking forward to it at all. I was even afraid we weren't going to make it home, not after the *Athenia*, but now we have, the last thing I want to do is this . . . *and* I've no job any more.'

'It couldn't have been a worse day and it's only just started.'

'Don't worry, we'll get through it.'

On the way into town they were all silent and preoccupied, none more so than Ginny. Over and over again the questions had flown round in her head, but at the bottom of her heart she just couldn't believe he'd do such a thing. May had told Tessa to stop trying to get her to see reason, she was in such a state already.

'She's so stupid,' said Tessa sadly.

'I know. She's bloody besotted with him,' May answered grimly.

The large room in Hatton Garden was full of people: police officers of all ranks, CID men, women who were obviously street walkers, and ordinary families like themselves.

Richie approached the counter where two desk sergeants and a constable were dealing with enquiries.

'Excuse me, I'm Mr O'Leary, I've come about my lad, Colin. You took him off the *Ascania* this morning.'

A well-dressed woman who was complaining that she'd lost her dog and no one was doing anything about it looked at him with interest, to the relief of the constable, who quite cheerfully could have strangled her.

'Right, take a seat over there, someone will be with you in a minute.'

May, Tessa and Ginny all found a seat on a long wooden bench that was half occupied by another family. Richie and Johnny stood beside them, leaning against the wall.

It wasn't long before the plainclothes police officer who'd come yesterday arrived.

'Is he . . .?' Richie asked.

'Aye, he is. Downstairs in the cells.'

'Can I see him?'

'No. He won't see anyone, except Miss Greely.' He shrugged. 'It's his right, just as it's his right not to say anything at all, apart from giving an alibi.'

Through all the confusion that filled her mind Ginny looked up. It was her he wanted to see. He didn't even want to see his da.

'He's up to something, Tessa,' Johnny whispered, while Richie and May remonstrated with the police officer.

'I know, and Ginny's in no state to be here at all.'

May sat down again, fuming. There was nothing anyone could do, apparently. The only person he'd see was Ginny.

Ginny didn't notice the dismal surroundings as she was led downstairs to the cells full of miscreants of one kind or another. Colin was in one by himself and as soon as it was opened Ginny threw herself at him, crying and flinging her arms wide.

When Colin caught her and pulled her close the feeling of relief was so intense that he started to shake. Thank God she still seemed not to remember their argument in the park before her accident. He'd been desperately worried she would have done. Then Ginny was prised from his embrace.

'Sit down there, miss, and *you*, sit the other side of the table.'

They did as they were told but Colin looked up at the man. 'Can't I even have a minute with her? You can see how upset she is.'

'No. It's not allowed. I'll stand by the door and there's to be no touching either!'

Ginny tried to pull herself together. 'They say . . . they say . . .'

'I know, Ginny, but it's not true!' he protested in a whisper. 'They wouldn't believe me. That bookie's runner set me up, giving me my winnings in those bags.'

'But you'd left! You'd taken all your things.'

'I know I did. I was going to America to get a better job, so we'd have a better life, both of us, Ginny. I was going to send for you when I got a good job and somewhere nice to live. I swear I was. I didn't tell you because . . . because I couldn't stand to see how upset you'd be. You'd think I was running out on you.' He was lying through his teeth but she was his only hope. 'No one would have known us there, Ginny. No one would have known we were related and it's not by blood anyway. We could have got married there, Ginny, and I'd have treated you like a princess, you know I would.'

Ginny smiled through her tears, forgetting all the days and nights she'd worried and wept for him.

'I didn't do that robbery, Ginny, I swear to God I didn't! I was unlucky and I'm sure that bloody Johnny Doyle had something to do with it. You know he doesn't like me. He's always tried to make me into a villain, just because I got caught up in a shop that was being robbed.'

'I . . . I believe you, Colin. I *knew* it wasn't you.'

'I had to say I was with you, Ginny. You were my only hope, and you still are. If you love me, then help me now, for God's sake.'

'How?' She would do anything, anything to help him. He'd done it all for her. He loved her and wanted to marry her and he knew he couldn't do that in this country. And he'd have given her everything she'd never had in her life before.

He glanced at the CID officer then back at her, dropping his voice to a whisper. 'Say you were with me on that Friday afternoon. Tell them you took time off from work to go out with me. We went to New Brighton, but you couldn't tell them that because they'd all have gone mad – and they *would*.

We went on the fair, had fish and chips, walked along to the fort and back, then we went home but not together, of course. You had your overall in a carrier bag. Please, please, Ginny, if you love me, tell them and don't let them scare you. They'll try, they'll *all* try, but if you don't stand firm I'll be in jail for years and years and we won't be able to get married, ever!' He leaned back in the chair. It was as much as he could do, now it was up to her.

When he'd said not to be scared she'd felt her heart turn over, but she'd do it. He was innocent. He wouldn't lie to her. How could she have doubted him? He loved her and she was the only one who could keep him out of jail. She nodded.

Colin let his breath out slowly. He just hoped to God she'd be strong enough to stick to her story because she was in for a right grilling, but at least now he had a chance. He stood up and so did Ginny.

'Miss Greely is ready to make a statement, aren't you, Ginny?'

'Yes.' Ginny jerked up her chin and squared her thin shoulders. She'd fight every step of the way for him.

The CID man returned to Richie and his family. He was fuming inside but he didn't let it show.

'Well, it seems as though *Miss* Greely is prepared to lie for him. She is saying she was with him that afternoon.'

'She can't have been, she was at work all day!' Tessa cried. Oh, she might have known he'd twist Ginny around his little finger.

'She says she went absent for the afternoon, didn't tell you, went off to New Brighton with meladdo down there. Can her employer throw any light on things?'

'No. On Friday afternoons he takes it easy. Most people have already bought the fish for teatime. He has a young delivery lad, but you couldn't believe the daylights out of him. He spends most of his time skiving, so he wouldn't know if she was there or not,' May answered. Jimmy Birrel spent his time in the Globe.

'What about customers? Would anyone have gone in and found the place empty?'

'You'd have to try and find someone and where you'd start I don't know.'

It lay unspoken between them that the police would get little or no information out of anyone in the area.

In the midst of all this, Tessa couldn't help but wish Johnny'd never let on to the police about Colin. If Colin had got to America he'd have been out of all their lives for ever. Yet deep down she knew Johnny'd done the right thing. Colin was utterly ruthless. He needed stopping. But look what he was doing to Ginny!

'Oh, Da, do something!' she cried. 'He's going to get Ginny into terrible trouble!'

'I know, but what can I do?' Richie replied.

'Well, if you can't do anything, I bloody well can and will. She's my daughter and she's not going to perjure herself for the likes of him. I want to see her,' May demanded.

'Follow me, missus. Maybe you can talk some sense into her. Tell her that perjury is a crime and she can go to jail as well as her boyfriend.'

'He's *not* her boyfriend! He's her stepbrother!' May snapped. She could *kill* him.

Ginny held out against them all. In vain did May plead and then shout at her and the police did the same. There were times when she broke down and sobbed under the tirade of shouted condemnation and threats heaped on her by the CID but she stuck to her story. At one stage they'd left her all alone in a cell for what seemed like hours and she'd been terrified but she hadn't broken. She hadn't let him down. They would have to cut out her tongue before she did.

When Tessa, Richie, May and Johnny were allowed to go home they were all exhausted. Despite Johnny's statement and the identification by both tellers, plus the fact that all the notes had matching serial numbers, they couldn't actually prove that it was Colin who took them. There was nothing anyone could do while Ginny stuck to her guns, giving Colin an alibi.

When they arrived home May closed the front door firmly. 'I've had enough, Richie, without having half the street in here wanting to know everything. I've a headache that's so bad I can hardly keep my eyes open. In God's name, what's the matter with her?'

'You go and lie down. I'll bring you up a cup of tea and some aspirins,' Tessa offered. If only they had let *her* talk to Ginny; she was sure she could have broken Ginny's resistance. Yelling at and threatening Ginny just didn't work. You got more by reasoning and coaxing.

Her da was soon asleep in the armchair and she wanted to go over and see Johnny, but she couldn't venture out of the house because *someone* was bound to collar her.

She had fallen into a light doze herself when she was awakened by the scullery door being opened. It was Elizabeth, still in her Hill's overall.

Tessa put a warning finger to her lips and gestured that she follow her into the room she shared with Ginny.

307

'What's up, Tessa? The whole street knows that your Colin's been arrested.'

'Oh, Elizabeth, it's terrible.' Tessa sank down on the bed. 'In fact it couldn't be worse.'

'All Mam could get out of Eileen and Mrs Doyle was that the police had called here last night and that Colin had been arrested on board Johnny's ship.'

'He was. He robbed that bank on County Road and got the first ship out. It was the *Ascania* and Johnny saw him and reported him and when they arrived this morning the police arrested him.'

Elizabeth's mouth formed an 'O'. She was momentarily bereft of speech.

'I told you it was terrible. And that's not all. He said he was with Ginny when the bank was robbed and she's lying for him. God knows what he's promised her or what she'll be going through now.'

Elizabeth gasped. 'Will she be able to stick to her story? Why does she want to lie for him anyway? I mean, robbing a bank is really serious, she must know that.'

'She does. He could get eight years or longer and they'll put her in jail too for perjury.'

'Oh, poor Ginny!'

'Poor Ginny's right. She . . . she's so besotted with him she'll believe anything he tells her. May's in bed with a headache and Da's worn out with it all and so am I. I wish they would throw him in jail and chuck away the key! Ginny would get over it. Oh, Elizabeth, I never thought she could be so stupid!'

'Does she know that she could go to jail as well?'

'She must do. The police must have told her that. We

haven't seen her. The last we saw of her was when she went with them to the cells – except her mam, of course.'

They both fell silent, thinking of Ginny's state of mind.

'What am I going to tell Mam?' Elizabeth asked.

Tessa gnawed her lip. Delia would have to be told something but at least she could keep her mouth shut.

'Tell her . . . Oh, you may as well tell her everything. She at least can keep things to herself.'

Elizabeth nodded slowly. 'When do you think Ginny'll be home?'

'I don't know, but I don't think they can keep her all night. She isn't the one who has done something wrong, it's *him*!'

Elizabeth squeezed her hand and left. Tessa's own head was thumping now and she lay down on the bed wearily.

It was half past six when both Ginny and Colin walked arm in arm down Naylor Street. They were fully aware of the curious gazes from behind the net curtains but Colin told Ginny to hold up her head. She had nothing to be ashamed of and neither did he. He grinned to himself as he thought of the expression on the CID man's face. He was livid but there had been nothing he could do. They had Ginny's sworn statement and his own. Put that beside the clerk from the bank's and it was stalemate. They didn't have enough evidence to charge him. The case was dismissed; they couldn't hold him any longer; he was a free man. He patted Ginny's hand, he really was grateful to her. However, he knew the police would be watching his every move from now on. He'd have to get out of Liverpool just the same.

There was only Richie in the kitchen when they arrived. 'Good God! You're out!'

'I told you I was innocent. I told you I didn't rob that bloody bank. No one believed me except Ginny.'

'Your mam's upstairs lying down,' Richie informed Ginny.

'I . . . I won't disturb her.' Ginny herself was exhausted. She felt as though every ounce of strength she had had been spent. It had been a nightmare and she didn't know how she'd held out for so long.

'Ginny's very tired too,' Colin said.

'Why don't you go and have a lie down? Our Tessa is,' Richie advised. Ginny nodded with relief.

Once they were alone in the kitchen Richie turned to his son. 'So? You got her to stick to her story then? Made her commit perjury?'

Colin didn't answer.

'Now what are you going to do?'

'Join the Army.'

Richie laughed. 'Oh, running away from Ginny again?'

'No, I'm not. She'll understand. Don't my King and Country need me? I'm eighteen. I'll go down to the recruiting office tonight. I've seen posters up everywhere.'

'And then you'll be far away from here by the weekend and you'll leave us to cope with all the gossip.'

Colin shrugged. It wouldn't be a bad life in the Army, in fact it would be a bit of excitement. He'd tell Ginny he was doing it for her, for everyone, for King and Country. She certainly couldn't argue with that. And he'd leave the money with her, he knew she'd keep it safe for him. She wouldn't touch a penny. He eased himself down on to the sofa and stretched out. He was bone weary himself – but he was free.

PART III

Chapter Twenty-One

1940

Life hadn't changed that much at all after a year of war, Elizabeth thought as she sat on the tram on her way home from work. She was still at Hill's but had progressed to being allowed to set, which she'd quickly mastered, the pin curls being the worst and the most time-consuming aspect.

The months following the Declaration had been called 'the Phoney War' for everyone had expected an invasion which had not come. There had been bombs. The first one had fallen in August on the other side of the Mersey, almost a year after the Declaration. Since then the sirens had wailed intermittently and in October some of the raids had caused damage and loss of life.

People had even got used to the blackout, but it had been a bit of a fiasco to start with. She'd walked straight into a lamppost that had been there for years and was fortunate not to break her nose. You just had to concentrate more, look where you were going and listen for cars and trams and buses. Bicycles were more of a problem, you didn't really hear them. She'd found a way around that though. As she walked she swung her shoulder bag by its strap backwards and forwards in an arc.

As she alighted from the tram, which had been painted grey and whose headlamps were masked with hoods, windows covered with wire mesh and bumpers painted white, she stopped and listened. She heard the footsteps growing fainter as the passengers dispersed, then she called out. 'Tessa? Tessa?'

'Is that you, Elizabeth?' Tessa called, crossing the road.

Elizabeth waited for her. It wasn't often these days that they met each other coming from work, with Tessa having to travel all the way to and from Kirkby to the munitions factory.

When they were near enough to see each other, Elizabeth peered at her friend closely. 'You look worn out.' Tessa's shoulders sloped with weariness and it was evident in her voice.

'So do you,' Tessa replied.

'I am but at least I don't have to work with all those terrible chemicals and gunpowder. Has anyone else's hair turned green this week?'

'I heard that Maggie Simpson from Athol Street's did.'

'Why in God's name don't they wear their turbans? It would protect their hair and they're not *that* bad. You always wear yours. Honestly, what with the chemicals and the peroxide they use to bleach their hair, and no turbans, it's a wonder they've any hair at all. Look at the state Alice Collins was in. I *told* her not to use full-strength peroxide, but no, she knew better and then who was it she came running to when it started to break off in chunks – me!'

'And she wasn't very pleased when you'd finished either.'

'I *had* to cut it that short or she'd have looked like a dog with a bad case of mange. She wears her turban now though.'

'I suppose I've been lucky really, I mean nothing awful has happened to my hair, my skin hasn't turned orange and I haven't had an accident, thank God. I'll never, ever forget Tilly Barton's screams when that detonator exploded in her hands and she lost two fingers. It was terrible, really terrible.'

Elizabeth shuddered and changed the subject. 'Did you see anything of Johnny today?'

Tessa shook her head. Both Mike and Johnny now worked in munitions. Not filling shells and assembling detonators but handling big bombs and engineering heavy weapons.

'Mike was talking about joining the Navy after Christmas. They'll be eighteen.'

'I know. Johnny said they'll go downtown together.'

'I wish they didn't have to go. I know I'm being selfish but . . .'

Tessa nodded, knowing what her friend meant. Over the last year her feelings for Johnny Doyle had grown and she knew Elizabeth felt the same way about Mike Flynn. Of course Elizabeth and Mike's meetings and outings had to be a closely guarded secret for Delia would be horrified and would most certainly have tried to put a stop to it. And Elizabeth, normally so forthright and defiant, was acutely sensitive about this, her first love. The last thing she wanted to do was announce it to her hostile mother.

'I wanted to talk to you,' Elizabeth said. 'I've made a decision.'

Some of Tessa's weariness disappeared. 'A decision about what?'

'About leaving Hill's and going to work with you.'

'With me? Out in Kirkby?'

'Yes. I've thought about it a lot. I know all the disadvantages. Having to trail all the way out there, having to get up at some ungodly hour and work till I drop with dangerous materials. But messing around with women's hair is too frivolous when I could be doing something really useful.

And all my clients are interested in is how their hair should be set or should they have it cut. You wouldn't think there's a war on at all, the conversations out of them.'

Tessa shook her head slowly. 'Your mam's going to go mad! She's still not forgiven you for leaving school and you know how she feels about factory work.'

'Well, there's a big difference between factory work in peacetime and wartime. She can't argue about that. Everyone's got to do their bit.' Elizabeth suddenly grinned. 'And I'll be earning pots of money. Now I only get money for "expenses". I have to rely on Mam for nearly everything and I'm seventeen.'

'Once your mam's finished with you, you won't get to be eighteen,' Tessa answered ominously.

'Oh, I know there'll be murder. I'm expecting it, but this time there won't be any letters full of excuses and apologies to Aunty Margaret. Even *she* can't complain about war work.'

'Why is everyone so terrified of Aunty Margaret? Have you met her?'

'No – well, yes, but I was a baby so I don't remember. It's just that Aunty Margaret's got money and had the guts and foresight to leave Liverpool. I'm not afraid of her and Mam isn't really, they *are* sisters.'

'So are you and Nessie!'

'That's different. I mean, Mam thinks she has to spend Aunty Margaret's money wisely.'

'Yes, I can see that, but surely not if it makes you or Nessie unhappy?'

Elizabeth shrugged. 'Oh, I don't know. She's never nasty or sarcastic in her letters. Will you come home with me?'

'You mean like I did before?'

'Yes.'

Tessa pursed her lips. This was going to be as bad as last time. 'I suppose so, but I can't leave them waiting for their tea. I'll have to go home first.'

'What's wrong with May doing the cooking?'

'She burns everything – and I mean *everything* – and she's always fussing about having to get ready for work.'

After the initial decision to close on the outbreak of war, the pubs, cinemas and theatres had reopened.

'OK, but will you come down straight afterwards?'

'I promise. This is getting to be a bit of a habit.' Tessa smiled at her friend as she disappeared inside the shop.

The kitchen was in the usual state of chaos when she arrived home. May had been in all day but the room was untidy and cluttered. There had been no attempt to do any of the ironing. The table was still littered with dishes and papers and bits of lipstick in old plastic tubes and she knew from experience what the scullery would look like. She sighed heavily. If the truth be told, she and Ginny ran this house. May contributed nothing except some of her wages. All she ever seemed to do was read newspapers and women's magazines, fuss over her appearance and drink tea.

'Isn't Ginny home yet?' Tessa asked.

'No, luv, she said she was going into town at the end of her shift to buy Christmas presents.'

Ginny was also in munitions though she worked a different shift to Tessa; like her, Ginny had far more money in her pocket than she'd ever had in her life before. So did Richie. He worked full time on the docks now – it was a Reserved Occupation, crucial to the war effort – and often there was plenty of overtime. Because of that they now had furniture in all the rooms as well as curtains and rugs. They even had a long runner of carpet in the lobby and up the stairs so when Jimmy and Harold Flynn went up or down it didn't sound like a herd of elephants. Her da had nailed it down; brass stair rods were still beyond their means. They had decent bedding though, warm blankets, heavy quilts, sheets and pillowcases and proper towels. They had many more clothes too.

Tessa took off her coat and pulled off the turban. She didn't mind it but it was loathed by many girls and women. She ran her hands through her short dark hair, and wondered just where to begin. Da would be in soon too, wanting a meal, and Jimmy was always hungry. When there wasn't overtime Richie was an ARP Warden, like Jack Harrison, Frank Flynn and Billy Keegan. Mick Collins was a volunteer fireman, something his wife never missed an opportunity to mention to the chagrin of her neighbours, especially Delia Harrison. 'Why him?' she had demanded of Jack. 'You can drive. In fact any fool can drive, what's so special about Mick Collins?'

'Delia, if I wanted to be a fireman I would be. I just think – hope – I'll be more use as a warden. I might volunteer for an anti-aircraft gunner, although I hope to God we don't need to use those guns very frequently.'

This had at least pacified her.

Jimmy and young Harold Flynn were messenger boys, not that they'd had any messages to carry yet, but they took great pride in the second-hand bicycles they'd been given. Had it not been wartime the bicycles would have been raced up and down the streets to everyone's peril, their riders included, but they were for 'official' use only and so great care was taken with them. They were washed and polished and oiled and kept under tarpaulins in bad weather.

Tessa decided she'd start with the meal and then when Ginny was home and the ordeal with Elizabeth and Delia was over, she and Ginny would roll up their sleeves and get stuck in. She wasn't seeing Johnny tonight; he and Mike were in the Royal Naval Reserve and went for training. May and the rest of them didn't mind living in a house that resembled a tip, but she did, and her Mam would turn in her grave to see what her family had come to.

It was almost half past seven when Tessa arrived at the shop.

'You look worn out, Tessa,' Delia commented. Elizabeth had said Tessa was going to drop in after tea.

'I am and I've still not finished. Ginny's gone to town for Christmas presents and the place, well . . .'

Delia nodded her understanding. It wasn't a bit fair on the girl, she thought. The others should pull their weight.

'Mam, there's something I want to tell you,' Elizabeth blurted out before Tessa had even taken her coat off.

Delia stared at her. 'Oh, now I see it all. You've dragged Tessa down here for support. I seem to remember that the last bombshell was preceded by the words "Mam, there's something I want to tell you". Now what?' she demanded.

'I'm going to leave Hill's and go to work in munitions. I can't spend all day with stupid, pathetic, wealthy old women who care more about their flaming hair than the state of the country. I've got to do my bit for the war effort—'

'I've heard that it won't be long before all girls and women will be sort of conscripted into munitions, working on the land or in the Army, Navy and Air Force,' Tessa interrupted.

'Then she can wait until they do and go and work for the Navy or Air Force.' Delia was fuming. Just what influence

Tessa had on Elizabeth's judgement she didn't know. But Tessa had been a thorn in her side ever since she'd come to Naylor Street. Somehow all the plans she'd had so nicely worked out for Elizabeth, Tessa had managed to thwart. She *had* felt sorry for the girl. She *did* like her – in her place. Both Elizabeth and Tessa knew that. But oh, she really should have put a stop to this friendship long ago. Well, she'd remedy that right now.

She turned to Tessa. 'And you, milady, can keep your nose out of other people's business! You've interfered once too often.'

Tessa shied away, tears instantly springing to her eyes.

Elizabeth was on her feet. 'Mam! How can you say such things to Tessa? She's had nothing to do with it. *I* decided on my own. She's said nothing. In fact when she's described what it's like working down there it's almost put me off.'

'And she's right about that! You are sliding further and further down the ladder, you'll amount to nothing, absolutely nothing in the end! A factory girl. A common little factory girl! Oh, that's very nice, isn't it? Won't everyone in the street be delighted! And how do you think I'll feel? And how will your aunt feel when you go surrounding yourself with girls and women just like Tessa?'

'Mam, don't you talk about my friend that way! I won't have it! I *won't*! When this war is over, if it ever gets started that is, I'll go back and finish my apprenticeship. I want to *do* something for the war effort and it doesn't require me to leave home and work on some farm or get a job where I'd be at the beck and call of some toffee-nosed soldier, sailor or airman who's just wearing a uniform so people will think how great they are when all they're doing is sitting at a desk!'

Delia got to her feet, her face scarlet with rage. 'How dare you speak like that, Elizabeth! How *dare* you! I forbid you to have anything more to do with Tessa O'Leary! You have had all the advantages that money can provide and now you're quite happy to sink to the level of a factory girl, like her. She came here with nothing! Not a coat on her back, running from the creditors, with a brother who had already been to Borstal twice, a useless wastrel of a father and a dying mother. God rest Mary O'Leary's soul. She was the only one in the entire family who had any pride and sense of decency.' She pointed a finger at Tessa. 'I *won't* have her undermining my authority and my plans in that sneaking manner!'

Elizabeth couldn't believe what she was hearing. Oh, she'd expected her mam to be angry, but she'd never expected this vicious attack on Tessa. What had got into Mam?

'I'm going into munitions, Mam, and Tessa will always be my friend, and I don't care what you say about it! Your opinion doesn't matter! You wait until Da hears this. You're a snob, Mam, that's what you are. You think you shouldn't live around here and have to mix with *these* people. Oh, no, you should be off somewhere in Breck Road or Walton where you wouldn't have to speak to them. You could walk around with your nose in the air as much as you liked!'

The sound of Delia's hand as it caught Elizabeth fully across the cheek was like a rifle crack. Just at that moment Jack walked into the kitchen.

'Delia! Delia! What the hell is going on?' he demanded, taking in Nessie's horrified gaze, his wife's almost puce complexion, Elizabeth's obvious fury, the red marks of Delia's fingers on his daughter's face and the tears that streamed unheeded down Tessa's cheeks.

'She's a snob, Da, that's what she is! I told her I'm going to work in munitions and she blamed Tessa. Then she started saying terrible, terrible things about Tessa,' Elizabeth cried.

'Do you hear her, Jack? She wants to be a common factory girl. She wants to work with *her*.'

Before Jack could do or say anything, Tessa jumped up and ran out of the back door, ignoring Elizabeth's cries that she come back. She'd never felt so awful or so humiliated in her life. She'd always thought Delia Harrison liked her. In times of crisis in the past she'd always helped and supported her. Now . . . now . . . she just didn't know what to think.

She collided with Ginny in the back yard.

'Tessa! Tessa, what's the matter?'

Tessa couldn't speak. She could only shake her head.

'Come on in and tell me all about it. Who's upset you now? I've never seen you like this.'

Tessa let herself be led into the kitchen where she sat down at the table. There was a letter on it addressed to Ginny, which immediately made her forget Tessa's problems.

Ginny picked it up and clasped it to her, unable to hold back the renewed flood of joy that filled her. She'd written dozens of letters to Colin but this was the first one he'd sent her. 'It's from Colin! Oh, at last! I haven't opened it yet but I'm so thrilled!'

It was too much for Tessa. She got to her feet and snatched the letter from Ginny's hand. 'For God's sake, Ginny! I don't want to hear about a stupid letter! I *hate* him and you're the biggest fool I've ever met! He's no bloody good, can't you understand that? Because of him and Da we finished up here broke and now . . . now . . .' She couldn't go on. What was the use? She threw the letter back at Ginny and fled into the front room where she collapsed on the bed and sobbed into the pillow.

* * *

Nessie had quietly closed her books and gone upstairs. She had no wish to be any part of the row that raged around her. Elizabeth was yelling that just because they had a shop that didn't make them any better than anyone else in the street. Da was shouting back, telling her not to be so hardfaced and how dare she upset her mother. Elizabeth took no notice, saying she would go and move in with Tessa and Ginny if her mam didn't stop being such a snob. Both she and Delia were crying. Nessie had never heard anything like it before – and the neighbours were bound to hear every word.

Elizabeth was ordered to bed but refused to go; Nessie heard the back door slam. Then, after a couple of seconds of complete silence, she heard her father's voice raised again and her mam starting to scream back. In the end Nessie stuffed her fingers in her ears and pulled the pillow over her head.

Ginny, her eyes red from weeping, her cheeks streaked with tears, opened the door of number twelve to Elizabeth.

'What's the matter with you?' Elizabeth demanded.

'Tessa . . . Tessa . . . called me names. It was over Colin. He's written to me—'

'Don't you know how upset Tessa is? Bloody hell, Ginny, don't you care about *anyone* else but *him*? Where is she?'

'In the front room.' Ginny sniffed. Why was everyone being so nasty to her? They'd spoiled her happiness at Colin's letter and she'd wanted to tell them he was coming home on leave after Christmas. But she knew her mam wouldn't be overjoyed.

Tessa was still sobbing quietly and Elizabeth's heart went out to her. Oh, she regretted nothing she'd said to her mam. Tessa was her friend. She put her arm around Tessa's shoulder and drew her to her.

'You take no notice of her, Tess! Da's giving her a right ear-bashing. I just don't know how she could say such things! She *is* a snob! I said I was going to move in here unless she changes her tune.'

Tessa raised a blotched and tear-stained face. 'You . . . you'd do that?'

'You should know me better than that, Tessa O'Leary. Didn't I threaten to face an Institution for Girls the last time there was a row? They both know I meant it.'

Tessa managed a weak smile. 'You always do. You always get your way.'

'No, I don't. Not all the time. But with something like this . . .'

'I can't understand why she . . . she said those things.'

'She's furious that I'm not just doing what she would like me to do. She didn't want me to leave school but I did. She doesn't want me to work in munitions but I *will* – and what's more I'm going to write to Aunty Margaret myself and tell her why. Come on, dry your eyes and go and wash your face. I bet our Nessie will be sent down for me later.'

'I don't think I can face Ginny yet. She's—'

'Got a flaming letter from *him*, I know. She told me. Can't the stupid little madam get it into her thick head that he doesn't love her and won't ever marry her?'

'I was awful to her, but I was so upset! I called her a fool.'

'I wonder what he's written to her about?' Elizabeth's mind strayed momentarily from their predicament.

'He'll want something, that you can be sure of,' Tessa said bitterly. She had never hated her brother so much as she did now.

'Should I ask her?'

'Oh, if you want to.'

'I don't want to, I just feel we should have some warning of what he intends to do or what he wants.'

They both went into the kitchen where Ginny was sitting by the fire, the letter in her lap.

'I'm sorry, Ginny. I shouldn't have yelled at you, but there's been a terrible row at home and everyone's upset.'

'That's all right,' Ginny replied, still with a note of injured pride in her voice.

Tessa went into the scullery to wash her face.

'What does he say or is that private?'

Ginny smiled and Elizabeth sighed.

'Some of it's private, but he's coming home on leave, just after Christmas. Oh, I'm so excited!'

'Well, that's good news for you, isn't it? But does he say anything about going abroad?'

'No, but he's bound to be sent somewhere soon. Do you think that's why he's coming home?'

'I don't really know.' Elizabeth wasn't in the least bit interested in what Colin O'Leary was doing. She hoped the Army would send him to the other end of the world and keep him there. He was trouble and that was something they had enough of right now.

It was late when Jack Harrison himself called at the O'Learys'. May had just come in and been informed of the situation. Her eyes had darkened with anger. Delia Harrison had gone too far this time and she'd tell her so when she saw her. Just because her bloody sister had had the nous to marry a successful businessman who had conveniently died two years later, leaving her enough to send money regularly, didn't give Delia the right to look down on her neighbours who were also her bloody customers, for God's sake.

'I've come to take Elizabeth home,' Jack stated.

'Then I hope you've made your wife see sense, Jack,' snapped May. 'She's no right at all to carry on like that. She lives in a slum like we do. If she wants to carry on with her airs and graces, then let her do it in Walton or Aintree, but then of course she'd have to rely on their bloody Margaret who, if my memory serves me right, worked in a factory herself before she up and went off to America. She wouldn't like that and neither would you, Jack, being dependent on your sister-in-law to keep you all.'

Jack nodded firmly. May's appraisal of the situation was very similar to the argument he had used with Delia.

'Get your coat on, Elizabeth.'

'If she carries on about Tessa any more, Da, I meant what I said, I'll move in here – as long as they'll have me.'

'I think we've heard enough on this subject, Elizabeth. Get your coat on. You're coming home. Your mother will say no more about it and Tessa will be welcome in *my* house at any time. There's enough fighting going on in the world without having to contend with it at home too. Get your coat and say goodnight to Tessa and Richie and May.'

Elizabeth knew her mam would give her the cold shoulder treatment from now on but she didn't care. She'd got her own way again.

Chapter Twenty-Two

Elizabeth had only been working in the munitions factory at Kirkby for a week before she began to wonder if all the trouble she'd caused was really worth it. The atmosphere at home was terrible, far worse than after she'd left school. Her mam hardly spoke to her. Most of her questions were greeted with a silent nod or shake of Mam's head. And she couldn't bear to tell Delia about Mike. Her father was also annoyed with her for being so awkward, even though for once he had actually supported her. But Jack's backing her had created a rift with Delia and it upset Elizabeth to know she was the cause. Nessie's silence also added to the burden. Nessie was different now, Elizabeth thought. Her sister's silence wasn't due to the fact that they'd quarrelled, they'd always done that, but it was the silence of disapproval, disappointment and a certain amount of sadness, which made Elizabeth feel strange and uncomfortable. Nessie too was upset by the all-too-noticeable coldness between her parents and sister.

Tessa hadn't been near the shop despite what Jack had said about it being *his* house. She was still very upset and no matter what Elizabeth said or how much she tried to put it to the back of her mind, Delia's cruel words kept coming back to her.

Elizabeth had accompanied Tessa that Monday morning and she'd found Kirkby to be a small, pretty village. There was the church with its big square tower, some cottages, a few shops and a pub called The Railway, which was very apt, it being situated almost beside the station. It was a pity that such a place should have its peace shattered by the huge single-storeyed munitions factories and the clanking of railway wagons that transported the ammunition.

'OK, luv, you go to the office, they'll sort you out,' the man on the gate had told her.

'I'll walk part of the way with you, but I can't be late,' Tessa had offered.

Tessa had left her at the office where she was given her official papers to sign, her identity pass, her hours of work and the Rules and Regulations. She'd also had a medical, of sorts. The doctor had rattled off a list of illnesses and conditions from a printed card and she'd answered 'No' to everything. He sounded her chest, looked down her throat, her ears and into her eyes and that was it. Then she'd been issued with her working clothes, which consisted of a navy blue boiler suit, a white turban and flat shoes. Everything was strange to her and that's when the first niggling doubts beset her.

'It's all so . . . sort of "military",' she said hesitantly to Tessa at the end of their twelve-hour shift when they boarded the special bus that would take them back into the city.

'Of course it is. What did you expect? We're making ammunition, for God's sake.'

Elizabeth shrugged.

'You haven't changed your mind, have you? Not after going all through that carry-on? It must be awful at home.'

'It is, but no, I haven't changed my mind. I just thought it would be different,' she'd replied, and as the week went on she found it indeed very different from anything she'd ever done in her life before.

She worked with three other girls in a room graded number eight. Every job was graded from one to ten. Group One was the most dangerous, the girls who worked there fitted detonators. She filled anti-tank mines with TNT which had a strong, obnoxious smell and needed stirring to stop it clouding. Her nose and mouth were protected by a mask, her hands with white gloves. She also filled 3.8 shells which then went to Group One where there seemed to be an accident nearly every day and she, like Tessa, cringed at the awful screams of injured girls and women.

'It's all the palaver we have to go through,' she complained to Tessa at the end of the week. They were both very tired. Elizabeth had never worked so hard in her life.

'I know, but I suppose it's necessary.'

'All that "Dirty Room" and "Clean Room" nonsense.'

They both fell silent thinking about the tedious but necessary procedure. First they were ushered like sheep into the 'Dirty Room' where shoes, clothes, hair clips and jewellery were removed and placed into lockers. Wedding rings were taped over. 'It only needs one spark and you won't live to see another day and neither will anyone else in your room,' they'd been told seriously. Then in the 'Clean Room' they were issued with the boiler suits, turbans and shoes rather like plimsolls. The buildings were set out with two rows of small rooms running down each side, with a wide blast-proof corridor between them.

'I don't mind the money though,' Elizabeth added with a grin.

She was irrepressible, Tessa thought. She'd never known anyone like her before.

'I thought you'd like that bit. What are the other girls like?'

'Not bad. At first they were a bit wary of me. They'd all worked in factories before and maybe I sounded a bit posh, my accent's not as broad as theirs. But once I said I'd been training to be a hairdresser things improved and news is spreading. I've even been asked to go to Emily's house to give her mam a home perm, but I don't know how to use them. I hadn't got as far as perming and dyeing and bleaching and doing roots. She said she'd pay me but I still don't want to run the risk of ruining her hair. I said I'd cut and set it and show them both how to pin wave it and brush it out.'

'Have you never thought of charging for advice?'

Elizabeth looked thoughtful. 'No. I really haven't learned much at all.'

'But you are quick to learn. Look how you cut Ginny's hair and mine and transformed Alice Collins—'

'Until the episode of the peroxide,' Elizabeth interrupted. 'No, I don't think I could charge.'

'Why not? You could build up a little business. Travel around and set people's hair or show them how to do it.'

Elizabeth looked aghast. 'How on earth will I get time for that?'

'Christmas isn't that far off, people always want to look their best for the parties and dances.'

'Do you really think there'll *be* parties and dances?'

'There were last year.'

'I know, but it's sort of different this year, more serious.'

'It'll be Mike and Johnny's last Christmas at home for

God knows how long,' Tessa reminded Elizabeth.

They sat in silence for the rest of the journey, their thoughts turning to the buildings that had already been bombed and lay in ruins. The Customs House, Wallasey Town Hall, Central Station and even the huge but as yet unfinished cathedral had been damaged.

Elizabeth knew for certain that the affection she'd always had for Mike Flynn had turned to love. She wasn't a kid now and neither was he. Whenever they went out together they had to be certain no one saw them until they got into town and inside the cinema. Mike didn't need an explanation for the 'cloak and dagger' stuff, as he called it. Delia would have had a fit.

'Why is Mam so awful to people like Tessa and you and your family?' she'd asked the night after the huge row. They'd gone to the pictures; they always did but they seldom watched the film. The Pathe News and Forthcoming Attractions was as far as they got.

'She's always had some funny ways of going on.'

'She thinks because of the shop and the money from America that we're all better than everyone else and we're not.'

Mike had sighed and put his arms around her, drawing her close and kissing her and that had been the end of the discussion. Soon he'd be going away to face not only the perils of the sea, but the dangers that lurked beneath it in the form of the U-boat packs that lay in wait just beyond the safety of the Western Approaches. She would write to him, of course, and she knew all his replies would have to be sent via his mam. But Eileen Flynn wasn't known for her ability to keep a secret; they'd have to go to Tessa's house, she decided. May wasn't quite as bad as Eileen and Ginny, poor deluded Ginny, was too wrapped up in dreams of Colin even to notice.

Tessa's thoughts were running on similar lines. After Christmas things were going to be miserable with Johnny away and *him* at home being fussed over by Ginny who was getting so excited that she was unbearable. Tessa was thankful they worked on different shifts and so didn't really see each other for long periods of time. She had her own little piece of news which she hadn't told anyone about yet – not even Elizabeth. Johnny had asked her if she'd get engaged after his first trip or first leave from Chatham whichever was the soonest. She'd thrown her arms around his neck and had clung to him; she'd felt like laughing and crying at the same time and she'd only been able to nod her acceptance. She knew no one would object, except perhaps Johnny's da. But she was a good worker and she'd make a good housewife, so she couldn't really see what his da could object to. They were going to announce it formally on Christmas Day. She had no ring but then how many women in this area did?

They alighted at their stop and had begun to walk down Scotland Road when the now familiar wail of the siren sounded its warning.

'Oh, God! Come on, Tessa, we'll have to make a dash for the shelter!'

'No! I hate that place. It's cold, damp, dirty and we're all squashed like sardines,' Tessa protested as she ran.

'Then where are we going to go?'

'Home. Under our stairs.'

'Under the *stairs*? Have you gone mad?'

'No, all the Flynns did it during the last raid and Mr

Flynn said it was as good a place as any. Didn't Mike tell you? Public shelters have taken direct hits too.'

The droning in the sky could be clearly heard now and the searchlights swept the dark heavens with wide silvery beams.

People were running past them, mainly in the opposite direction, and when they fell into the lobby of number twelve Tessa screamed for Jimmy, her da and May.

'Tessa, for God's sake why haven't you gone to the shelter?' Richie yelled. He was wearing his tin hat and his warden's coat. Already they could hear the explosions as bombs and incendiaries found their targets.

'I'm not going there!'

All three of them froze in terror as they heard the unmistakable whistling of a bomb growing louder and louder.

Richie got a grip on himself and shoved them all towards the space under the stairs.

'Da, where are you going?' Tessa cried.

'To see what I can do. It's my duty, remember.'

'Oh, sweet Jesus have mercy on us all,' May cried, blessing herself but thanking God she hadn't left for work otherwise she'd have been caught out there. She was thankful too that Ginny was on nights.

For three hours they sat, cramped, frightened and cold, listening to the droning and shrill whistling of falling bombs. Intermittently they heard the furious clanging of fire engines and ambulances and the dull, earth-trembling rumble as buildings collapsed. They also heard the sound of the anti-aircraft guns that were sending thousands of rounds of tracer upwards at the raiders caught in the dazzle of the search-lights.

'It's never gone on for as long as this.' Tessa tried not to let the fear show in her voice. They were all close to hysteria.

'I just hope to God Richie is safe.'

Elizabeth thought fearfully of her da. He too would be out there, somewhere in that hell of flames, explosions and tottering buildings, heedless of his own safety.

At ten o'clock, when the 'All Clear' sounded, Elizabeth crawled on her hands and knees from under the stairs. She was still trembling with fear but she had to go and see if her mam and Nessie and Da were safe. What would greet her when she opened the front door?

'Do you want me to come with you, luv?' May offered.

'No, no thanks, I . . . I'll be fine.'

'Well, if you're sure . . . If anything's . . . wrong you just come back down here.'

A dark sky broken with patches of red and orange shooting flames greeted her. Broken water mains flooded the street and gas from fractured pipes could clearly be smelled. The stench from broken sewage pipes was terrible and all around her were piles of rubble that until three hours ago had been homes and businesses. The docks had been hit again and the noise of fire engines and ambulances was constant.

She stumbled into the shop, her feet crunching on the glass-strewn floor. A blast had blown the window in despite the tape Delia had criss-crossed it with after the night the Customs House had been bombed.

'Mam! Nessie!' she yelled. Had they gone to the shelter? She knew her mam hated it almost as much as Tessa did.

Nessie, her cheeks streaked with tears, appeared from beneath the stairwell.

'Oh, where've you been? We've been worried sick.'

'I've been at Tessa's. We'd just got off the bus when the siren went. Where's Da?'

'Out with the others, I can't see him being home until morning,' Delia answered as she emerged white-faced and shaken. 'Why didn't you go to the shelter?'

'Mam, you know how awful it is and besides, there wasn't time. I thought ... I thought it was never going to end. Nearly all the houses in Paul Street have been flattened.'

Delia shook her head. God help them, most of them didn't have much to start with, now they had nothing.

'Mam, the shop window's in. There's glass all over the floor.'

Delia had expected far worse. 'We'll have a cup of tea and then we'll clean up. We'll save what we can for tomorrow, it'll be business as usual.'

'The water mains, the gas pipes and the sewage pipes are all broken. The tram lines and electricity lines are down.'

'Then we'll just have to make do until they get them fixed. Was there any damage in this street? A few of them sounded very close. Once or twice I'm certain this place moved.'

'Not that I could see, but the docks have been hit. There's fires everywhere.'

Nessie began to cry.

'It's all right, Nessie, honestly it is.' Elizabeth for the first time in her life comforted her sister. She was very shaken herself.

'Nessie, pull yourself together. We've got everything intact: the shop, the stock, the roof over our heads, and unless we hear different, you'll go to school as usual in the morning. It's important that we all carry on as best we can. That's the main thing now.'

They worked on late into the night and it was the first time since she'd had the row with her mother that there was some semblance of normality between them. Delia had sent Nessie to bed at midnight and she and Elizabeth wiped the dust and dirt from tins and packets that thankfully hadn't been too damaged. Food was too precious now to be discarded if the tin was dented or the packet torn.

It was four o'clock in the morning when Jack, his face covered in grime, his eyes red-rimmed, walked into the kitchen. Elizabeth and Delia were sitting at the table in the candlelight and firelight with cups of tea in their hands.

'Oh, thank God you're all right, Jack! I've been worried to death about you, luv.' Delia threw her arms around him and kissed him, despite the fact that his clothes were filthy.

'At least we've got the fire in the range and there was some water in the kettle.' Elizabeth got to her feet to make her father a drink.

'Was it very bad?' Delia asked

Jack nodded. 'It was the worst so far. There's fires burning all over the city. All the telegraph and phone wires are down, so are the tram wires. The water mains and gas mains are fractured, but you know that. They've already started to clear away the rubble and people are searching for relatives or whatever they can salvage from the debris. I saw an old lady, bent double with age and arthritis, poking with a long piece of wood at what was left of her home and calling for her cat! It was heartbreaking. Someone eventually came and led her away. I think it was a granddaughter.' He passed his hand over his stinging eyes, eyes that had seen so many horrific sights that night.

'None of us went to the shelter,' said Delia as she fussed

over him. 'You're safer under the stairs, I reckon. Those shelters are disgusting. There's nowhere to sit, wash, make a drink or even go to the toilet. They stink. I'm sure the Sanitary Inspector would close them.'

'Delia, luv, these days the Sanitary Inspectors won't be bothered about that. They've got their work cut out with the broken sewage pipes and the threat of disease. Thank God it's not summer, it would be unbearable.'

'I sent Nessie to bed, she can go to school later, and we've cleaned up the mess in there as best we can. It'll be business as usual.'

Jack nodded. He was worn out but they'd open at seven just the same and Elizabeth would report for work at seven o'clock too.

Tessa was still up, peering from the window at the glowing sky and wondering if it was worth going to bed as she'd have to start out for work even earlier than usual, what with the bomb craters and the unsafe and still burning buildings *en route*. Ginny would find her journey home a long and hazardous one. Suddenly she caught sight of someone wandering aimlessly up the street. The streetlights were out and all the blackout curtains were drawn but in the eerie orange light from the blazing warehouses by the docks she saw it was Johnny Doyle. Dragging on a coat she went out into the street.

'Johnny! Johnny? What's the matter? Where are you going?' She caught his sleeve.

He turned to her, his eyes filled with shock and grief. 'It's . . . it's . . . Mam.'

'What happened? Where is she?'

Johnny fought to control himself. 'She'd been to church – don't ask me why, Tessa. She was coming home along Scottie Road . . .'

A feeling of dread crept over Tessa. 'Didn't she go to the shelter?'

He shook his head.

'Then . . .?'

'A building collapsed on her. Oh, Tessa! Tessa! She's . . . dead! My da went to look for her after the "All Clear" and someone had pulled her out. He . . . Da could only recognise her by that little cross and chain he'd bought her.'

Tessa reached up and drew him closer. 'Oh, I'm so sorry, Johnny, I'm so sorry. I know what it's like to have your mam die.'

He looked down at her, his eyes filled with tears. 'You do. I'd almost forgotten. You *really* know.'

'Yes, I do, but at least it would have been . . . quick. All over with in a couple of seconds, not like my mam dragging herself around in agony for months.' She took his face in her hands and kissed away the tears. Her heart was aching for him. 'Go home now, you've got work later on. We can't give up, it's just what they want us to do. Think of your mam and go to work.'

Johnny held her tightly for a few minutes before he drew away. She was right. He'd go to work, thinking of Mam, and soon he'd be able to join up and do something really worthwhile. That's surely what his mother would have wanted.

When Eileen Flynn emerged with her brood from under the stairs she'd sent young Harold out to see what the damage was like and if anyone's house had been hit. Mike had wanted to go and see if Elizabeth was all right but Eileen told him firmly that her need was greater. Harold returned with his face and hands filthy and with his father, in the same condition, right behind him.

'I've brought 'im home. I caught 'im climbin' over a pile of rubble. 'Ave yer no sense, woman, lettin' 'im out? He could 'ave been killed.' Frank's nerves were shattered too although he'd never admit to it.

'I didn't send 'im out ter go climbin' and messin' about. Come 'ere, yer little get! 'Aven't I got enough ter worry about?'

'Well, no one's been bombed out in this street, thank God, but I'll 'ave ter get back, there's people buried under bricks and mortar in Paul Street. The whole flaming lot 'as gone over there. God 'ave mercy on their souls. They'll need a fleet of bloody ambulances. 'Ave yer time ter make us a quick brew, girl? I'm spittin' feathers, it's all the soot and dust.'

'It'll be half cold. It'll take all flaming night for the kettle to boil on that fire. Maureen, go an' see if Tessa's gorrany water.'

'Ah, Mam, it's freezin' out there!'

'I know and so does yer poor da! Now shift yerself before I give yer a goalong, yer selfish little madam!' Eileen took a swipe at her daughter. 'That's lovely, isn't it? A nice way to treat yer father, there's none of yer any good, what with meladdo there only interested in Elizabeth Harrison, that young hooligan out "*playing*" while the whole place is burnin' around him and now you!'

Maureen fled and before she returned the door was opened and Brenda appeared.

'Brenda! Luv! What's up with yer, comin' all the way down 'ere?'

Brenda burst into tears. 'Oh, Mam, I *had* to come. I was worried sick about you. All of you. I knew Da was out there, just like Thomas was, but I couldn't settle, I could see the fires and hear the bombs . . . I just wanted to see . . .'

'Come here to me, girl, and stop upsetting yerself, it's bad for yer and the baby. We're all fine, yer can see that for yerself. Our Maureen's gone to see if Tessa's gorrany water, then we can all 'ave a cup of tea before yer da 'as ter go out again.'

Brenda eased herself down on to the sofa. She'd had to walk all the way because the tram lines were just twisted spirals of metal; she'd passed three trams all of which had been abandoned and were badly damaged. One of them lay on its side like a beached whale.

'Oh, Mam, I've got terrible pains in my back! I walked all the way.'

Eileen threw up her hands in horror. 'Oh, Jesus, Mary and Joseph! Get your feet up on that sofa. Frank, make yerself useful an' find something to roll up as a cushion for her back. I hope ter God she's not started. What a time ter 'ave a baby.'

Eileen was seriously worried. If the baby came now it would stand no chance at all of surviving: it would be little more than a miscarriage. She called the Luftwaffe all the names she could think of and cursed them to hell and back, not knowing that this was only the beginning of Liverpool's ordeal by fire. It would be an ordeal that, before it was over, would bring them all to their knees.

Chapter Twenty-Three

Brenda didn't lose her baby. Eileen had insisted she stay in Naylor Street and she'd sent Mike along to the house in Breck Road to inform Thomas Kinsella that his wife would remain where she was until her mother felt she was well enough to go home.

'I'm prayin' ter St Anne, every day, that she'll not have a miscarriage. What possessed her ter walk all the way 'ere I don't know! Well, she's on the sofa and she's stoppin' there so I can keep me eye on 'er. Our Maureen an' 'Arold can just do more to 'elp,' she'd informed Delia in the shop later that week. Then she launched forth to the other customers about the state of affairs in Paul Street, which had taken not two but three direct hits. Twenty people had been killed or died from their injuries. There was nothing left but piles of rubble and a few gaps where the bricks had been carted away. 'It's shockin' 'ow they treated them women, so I 'eard. They sent them trailing to offices all over the city ter get new ration books and identity cards and food and clothing vouchers. Lots of them 'ad kids with them and they'd lost everything and with their 'usbands and sons away, too. It's just shockin'.'

'Shockin'!' Maisie Keegan echoed.

'Well, it certainly got my idle, useless feller off his backside. He's never worked so hard in his life. Got a bad back now or so he says. Bad back my flaming foot! It's "idleitis" he's got,' Katie Collins said cuttingly.

341

'A nice Christmas this is going ter be. Do yer think you'll 'ave trouble gettin' stuff, like?' Eileen asked Delia.

'It shouldn't be too hard, and I've got some "emergency" supplies if it gets really bad.'

'She would have,' Katie Collins said *sotto voce* to Maisie Keegan.

'Our Mike's goin' off to the Navy, the proper Navy, after Christmas, so maybe when 'e gets 'ome 'e'll 'ave got some stuff. It could be dead useful that, 'im bein' on convoy duty. They 'ave all kinds of fancy stuff over there in America.'

'Well, if it's "fancy stuff" you want, maybe you should go to Cooper's,' Delia said acidly.

'Don't go gettin' all airyated with me, girl,' retorted Eileen. 'All I said was they 'ad fancy stuff over there. 'E's got ter get there and back in one piece and 'e might not be on convoy duty. I'm only guessin'.'

Katie Collins shook her head. 'I don't envy them if they are. We're losing too many ships an' some of them cargo boats are so old they were sailing up the Mersey when Noah built 'is Ark!'

'Yer can always be relied on, Katie, for a bit of cheerfulness,' Eileen remarked sarcastically. 'Do yer think Eddie Doyle 'as got over the shock of Dora's death yet? Our Frank says 'e's even more miserable now than he was before.'

'Well, he would be, wouldn't he? Poor Dora getting caught like that in a raid,' Delia stated.

'Why was she going to church anyway? There's no special novenas on,' Maisie asked.

'God knows,' Eileen replied.

'Well, I think *He's* just the one who would know,' Delia

answered. 'Now, is anyone going to give me something for the Christmas Club?'

The Christmas Club was a fund Delia started immediately after Christmas each year and everyone paid a set amount each week, although sometimes they had to miss a week or two when things were bad moneywise. That way it ensured that there was some money for groceries for the festive season. Some of the women belonged to 'Tontines', which were run along the same lines.

'Well, this'll be the last until we start again after Christmas,' Maisie Keegan said, handing a sixpence to Delia. 'How much 'ave I got?'

Delia bent and picked up an exercise book from the shelf under the counter and flicked through the pages. 'You've got three pounds, four shillings and ten pence.'

'God, I've never 'ad that much before.'

'It's the war. The fellers have to do some work for a change, and there's all the "ovies" they've worked. How much have I got, Delia, luv?' Eileen asked.

Delia turned a page. 'You've done well this year, Eileen. Five pounds and fourpence.'

'Jesus, Mary and Joseph! Me dream's out! It must be with not havin' our Brenda at home and our Mike and Frank's wages an' our Maureen's few bob. It's more than I've ever had in me life and now there's hardly anythin' ter spend it on!' Eileen complained. For once everyone in the shop agreed with her, including Delia.

'We've got to do something *special* this Christmas,' Mike said to Johnny as they stood on the platform of the crowded tram.

'Too right we have.' Johnny was thinking of his mam and of Tessa. He'd bought a silver cross and chain from Cooke's pawnshop to be a Christmas and engagement present. He'd really wanted to ask his da for his mam's gold one but he wasn't sure what Eddie's reaction would be to the request. After all, Mam had only been dead three weeks.

The shock had affected them all in different ways. Most of the time all he felt was anger. Anger at the Luftwaffe. Anger at his da for letting her go out, for treating her like a doormat, and anger at God for allowing her to be caught in a raid. His da had become even more silent and morose and now went to mass every day. His younger brothers seemed lost and he often heard them crying at night.

The funeral had been terrible. Everyone had been great, they always rallied at such times, but without Tessa's support and comfort and the knowledge that she too had stood crying at the graveside of her mam it would have been unbearable.

'We'll treat the girls to a show,' Mike suggested.

'Where?'

'The Empire. I'll see if I can get tickets for the twenty-first. It'll be a proper treat. We all deserve one, I reckon.'

The nearer Christmas got the more excited Tessa became until she just couldn't keep her secret any more.

They were walking down the road after alighting from the bus when Tessa caught Elizabeth's arm and turned to her, her eyes shining. 'I've *got* to tell you! I just *can't* keep it to myself any longer.'

'What? You look as though you've won the Football Pools!'

'On Christmas Day Johnny is going to tell everyone that . . .' She suddenly felt shy.

'Tell everyone *what*? Oh, come on, Tessa, tell me, I'll burst with curiosity in a minute!'

'We're getting engaged.'

Elizabeth let out a shriek that could have competed with an air-raid siren and flung her arms around her friend. 'When? When did he ask you?'

'Last month.'

'Last *month*! Tessa O'Leary, you . . . you . . . spoil-sport!'

'I couldn't tell you! I promised. Don't you dare tell anyone – and I mean *anyone* – else. It was to be a surprise—'

'Oh, it's that all right!' Elizabeth interrupted, laughing. 'Have you got a ring?'

'No. I'm not having one, not yet anyway. Maybe after he's been in the Navy for a month or so, when he's got enough money.'

'Did . . . did his mam know?'

Tessa's expression changed. 'No, that's the awful part of it. She never knew and I really did like her.'

'I wouldn't fancy old misery-guts as a father-in-law.'

'He's got a reason to be miserable these days.'

'I suppose he has but he never treated her very well, did he? She was terrified to look sideways at him. You'd have been great company for her, Tessa. So, when is the big day going to be then?'

'I don't know for certain yet, but we were talking about May. Next May.'

'Isn't there some daft superstition about it being bad luck to get married in May?'

Tessa shrugged. 'I haven't heard of that one, and anyway it is a *daft* superstition.'

'You're right. It was probably dreamed up by the clergy so they could go on holiday or something,' Elizabeth replied with her usual lack of respect for priests and nuns when she was out of earshot of her mother. She was beginning to have what Sister Francis would have called a 'crisis of faith'. She'd looked around her on the night of the last raid and wondered if there was a God at all.

Tessa looked at her askance. 'You say some terrible things, Elizabeth Harrison. I'm sure that's counted as blasphemy.'

'Oh, shut up, don't we get enough of that at home and at mass, Mrs Doyle-to-be!'

Tessa grinned. It sounded very odd to hear herself described as Mrs Doyle. Odd – but very nice.

Mike and Johnny had managed to get four tickets for the Empire's Christmas Revue in the four and sixpenny seats.

'That's sheer extravagance!' Elizabeth remonstrated. 'Especially as you're—' Just in time she remembered that she'd been sworn to secrecy.

'It's not a waste. We're both off to Chatham soon.'

'And it's Christmas,' Johnny added, winking at Tessa who smiled back. She'd be miserable when he went away but she tried not to think of that.

'You two sound like a double act,' Elizabeth laughed. She delved into her bag, bringing out a white paper bag. 'I've pinched some barley sugar twists. Mam's been hoarding them, but she won't mind.' In fact she would mind and Elizabeth knew it but she was determined to make this the best Christmas yet for Tessa.

'Don't tell everyone in the queue, we'll be mobbed!' Johnny joked as the people ahead of them began to move forward.

They were very good seats, Elizabeth had to admit: the front stalls, but not right at the front where you'd get a crick in your neck from having to look upwards all night.

The theatre was full and there was an atmosphere of excited anticipation. They all settled back into their seats as the lights dimmed.

The conductor, resplendent in evening dress, raised his baton and there was a slightly discordant fanfare from the orchestra pit. Then above it, drowning out the instruments, rose the banshee-like wail of the siren.

Elizabeth grabbed Mike's arm but Tessa just froze in her seat.

'Oh, go to hell, Fritz! Gizza break, don't yer know it's bloody Christmas!' someone bawled from the back. Everyone cheered.

Both girls managed a weak smile, but inside they were quaking with fear. Mike and Johnny looked grim as they tried to concentrate on the show. The music could hardly be heard at times, the spotlights flickered and the huge chandeliers suspended from the ceiling swayed dangerously, but no one moved. The defiant audience cheered and clapped every song performed by the artists, who themselves were afraid.

Elizabeth, clinging tightly to Mike's arm, half rose from her seat at the sound of every explosion. 'How long is it going to go on for?' she begged of him.

He squeezed her hand. 'I don't know, but hold on to me,' he answered with a confidence he didn't really feel.

They had no idea of the time but it seemed the raid was lasting for an eternity, when a massive explosion rocked the building. Plaster flaked from the ceiling, the stage lights dimmed and silence descended. Then the rumour ran quickly through the theatre that St George's Hall, on the opposite side of Lime Street, had been hit and was on fire.

There was no panic as everyone filed out and huddled under the canopy that ran across the front of the building.

'Oh, Mary Mother of God!' Elizabeth cried, crossing herself. Tessa's face drained of all colour and she began to shake. Mike and Johnny gazed upward with impotent fury. The beams of the searchlights picked out the sinister outlines of the enemy bombers still overhead. They looked like giant bats and seemed just as evil.

'They're so bloody near you could almost reach up and snatch them out of the sky!' Mike said.

'And I know what I'd do if I caught one!' Johnny replied.

Everyone was stunned. As far down as William Brown Street the sky was bright as daylight and the heat was intense. The museum, the art gallery and the library had all been hit.

'There's nothing short of a bloody miracle that can save the Hall now,' someone close by said with a catch in their throat.

Flames were rushing and roaring from the long roof of the beautiful colonnaded building. The two huge bronze lions that stood guard over the plateau where the Punch and Judy show took place every Sunday appeared to be glaring their defiance. The flickering flames made their faces almost animate.

Many of the crowd were in tears, including Tessa and Elizabeth, as they watched Liverpool's greatest architectural

treasure burn before their horrified gaze. The Assize Courts
were burning out of control and thousands of legal documents
fuelled the flames. The noise was so tremendous that the
yells of rescue workers and the frantic clanging of fire
engines that were converging on the whole area could barely
be heard.

'I've come ter see the show, I've paid me money an' 'Itler
an' 'is bloody firework display ain't goin' ter ruin me night!'
came the shout from the back of the crowd.

'Good on yer, lad, I've paid an' all!' someone else shouted
and to both girls' astonishment, everyone began to move
back inside.

'Shouldn't we . . .' Tessa said tentatively.

Johnny put his arm firmly around her shoulders. 'No,
Tess, we're all going to stick together.'

They stayed in the theatre, their community singing, led
by the conductor of the orchestra, sometimes being drowned
out by the droning of the planes overhead and the ferocity of
the anti-aircraft batteries as they tried to shoot down the
raiders. It was three-thirty a.m. before the 'All Clear' sounded
and everyone cheered with what little voice and strength
they had left. For all of them it had been a nerve-racking
experience and they were exhausted. It was like something
out of a nightmare, Elizabeth thought, having to sit there for
hours, never knowing if you'd live to see tomorrow.

'It's going to take us ages to walk home and we've still
got to get up early for work,' Tessa complained.

The two boys exchanged fearful glances. Would their
homes still be standing? It looked as though the whole city
was on fire. As a harassed, grim-faced policeman remarked,
'What a fine bloody Christmas present!'

* * *

It was gone half past four when, after an horrendous journey, they finally reached Naylor Street. Both girls were trembling as the boys guided them around huge craters, buildings that were in danger of collapsing and others where firemen were fighting a losing battle. There were no streetlights and they had to pick their way over fire hoses, electricity and phone wires, broken gas and water pipes and tram lines that glowed red hot in some places and rose up in weird, unnatural shapes.

Tessa found Jimmy sitting with the Flynns on their doorstep. Not a window in any of the houses had escaped and the pavement and cobbles were covered with a carpet of crushed glass.

'Mam, are you all right?' Mike asked.

Eileen shook her head dazedly.

'Where's Da?' Tessa begged.

'He and Frank are out . . . out . . . there.' Eileen pointed a trembling finger towards the dock estate.

'Are my da and Mr Harrison out too?' Johnny asked.

Eileen could only nod. Her nerves were strung out like piano wires. She, like so many in the city, had been certain that she was not going to survive the night.

They learned next morning that St George's Hall had survived but the Gaiety Theatre, St Anthony's School, Crescent Church and St Alphonsus's Church hadn't, nor had many of the streets that bordered the dock estate.

After a brief doze, the girls set off for work again. Buildings were still smouldering and the emergency services continued digging in the piles of rubble. WVS women were handing out cups of tea and rounds of toast from a canteen lorry. Engineers from the gas, electricity, phone and sanita-tion companies were working frantically and shopkeepers were clearing up. They passed many signs bearing the words 'Business As Usual' and one that read 'Closed for Refurbish-ment and Decoration'. It brought a hint of a smile to both their faces. They weren't beaten yet.

At work there were familiar faces missing. The faces of those there were lined with worry and lack of sleep; their eyes were filled with mute misery and shock. Then, as they got back to a shattered city, after another exhausting day, the siren wailed and the raiders came again.

This time they all did run for the shelter, although Eileen took some persuading.

'If me name's on it then I want ter go in me own 'ome.'

'For God's sake, Mam, yer not stayin' 'ere and yer name won't be on any bloody bomb!' Maureen had yelled, which had snapped her mother out of her stubborn mood suffici-ently to make a swipe at her for swearing.

Again, it went on for hours. They were cramped, cold, hungry and thirsty and unable even to sit down, while outside and above them the sky was bright with the flames of burning buildings which acted as beacons for the enemy planes. More than once the whole shelter shook, its concrete base cracking. There were very few able-bodied men inside, they were all out doing whatever they could to help. No one cried aloud, except for the young children and babies, although every girl and woman was verging on hysteria. Delia decided at one stage that if things didn't get better they'd all start screaming and wouldn't be able to stop, so she suggested that they either sing or pray or both and she started them all off with 'Eternal Father Strong to Save'. Their voices were weak to start with, and quivered noticeably whenever there was an explosion, but they kept on. Catholic and Protestant alike, differences forgotten, they were all in it together.

When the 'All Clear' sounded Eileen Flynn looked at her daughter with annoyance. 'Didn't I tell yer ter take that pan offen the cooker before we come 'ere? The bloody bottom will be burned out!'

'Jesus, Eileen, is that all you've got to think about?' Maisie said.

At that their composure broke; they all fell about laughing, but it was laughter with more than a hint of hysteria in it.

Chapter Twenty-Four

'It'll be a "make do and mend" Christmas,' Eileen said to Delia with a look of resignation in her eyes. It was a feeling that every woman in the city had now. For the first time they'd experienced just what heavy and continuous bombing could do and they were all appalled, afraid and some of them were grieving too.

'I'll agree with you on that, Eileen. Thank God they packed it in after those two terrible nights,' Delia replied. It was Christmas Eve and she was giving out the Christmas Club money. It had all been checked against the book, counted out and put into brown envelopes marked with the recipient's name.

'I'll never forget that night as long as I live, an' if they start up again that won't be long. I'm tellin' yer, Delia, I've 'ad shockin' palpitations ever since.'

'Haven't we all. We're all damned lucky we've still got roofs over our heads.'

'Our Rita 'asn't, not any more,' Maisie said grimly. 'I tell yer, I'm wore out with 'er. 'Er nerves is destroyed and them flamin' kids of 'ers, I'll swing for the lot of them before long! I know me own aren't angels, not by a long chalk, but *that* lot! Runnin' wild they are. Up an' down the flamin' stairs by the minutes, yellin' and screamin' and fightin'. Some days I've gorra 'ead like Birkenhead what with the row out of them.'

'Well, what do yer expect, Maisie? They was never

allowed ter do anything in their 'ouse. Not with 'er feller acting like a tinpot soldier,' Eileen said, silently thanking God that her own sister, who had eight kids, had not been bombed out.

There was no stopping Maisie now. 'An' that's another thing, Delia. I'll have him 'ome soon and when 'e lands on me doorstep I'm goin' ter tell 'im that if he doesn't like the way I keep *my* 'ouse, then 'e can take the lot of them somewhere else! There'll be no crusts cut offen the bloody bread in our 'ouse!'

'That's not a very charitable thing to say, Maisie, especially at Christmas,' Delia said, still sorting out the envelopes.

'*You* don't have ter put up with them all. I'm tellin' yer, they'd drive the Archangel Gabriel mad!'

'Didn't she manage to save anything?' Eileen asked Maisie. Doubling, even trebling up was not infrequent now, so many families had been bombed out.

'Just some clothes an' blankets that were in an old seaman's trunk. They built those things ter last, I'll tell yer. Black as the hobs of hell on the outside, inside just a few scorched edges and the stink of smoke.'

'That's something we're all living with. It gets everywhere and nothing seems to shift it. I've got two of them Airwick bottles on the mantelshelf but you can still smell it,' Delia informed them.

'Do you mind if I have my Club money now, Delia? I'm sorry if I'm jumping the queue,' May asked.

'What's the rush?' Maisie queried.

'Same as usual, work. We're still cleaning up from the other night and I've been asked to get something a bit special for Christmas – just what I don't know.'

'Who asked for that?' Maisie demanded.

'Tessa, and our Ginny backed her up.'

'Just what are those two up to?' Delia asked, handing May her envelope.

'Well, our Ginny's getting so excited about *that* feller coming home she'll make herself sick. He's not home until after the holiday, thank God, so it can't be that.'

'Tessa's been courting Johnny Doyle for ages now, do yer think they might be planning something, what with him going away an' all?' Eileen asked.

'Well, she has been more cheerful of late, if any of us could be called "cheerful".'

'I'm sure our Elizabeth would know if there was an announcement in the offing,' Delia said speculatively.

'Aye, she would. They're like Siamese twins those two. When you see one, the other's not far behind.'

'So, what "special" something do you want, May?'

Maisie and Eileen looked on, very interested, while young Bertie Collins, who had been sent down on a message, started to trace his name in the dry soil from the potato bin. He'd be hours at this rate, he thought. Why did they always have to take so long with their shopping?

'How much boiled ham can I have, Delia, and have you got any tins of fruit?'

'No fruit, May. Jelly and a tin of evap. Pass me your ration book.'

May looked thoughtful. Everyone bought their fowl and vegetables in the market last thing on Christmas Eve, you got good bargains then. 'I wonder, should I get some flour and eggs and make a cake?'

Maisie and Eileen exchanged glances. May Greely

355

baking! May Greely making a cake! It was unheard of.

'Not that I'm turning away trade, May, but you might be better seeing what Skillicorn's or Lunt's have on offer. When do you get time for cake-making?' Delia suggested diplomatically.

'I think you're right, Delia. I won't get much of a break, we're open on Christmas Day and Bernie Daley will only give me an hour off! Talk about "goodwill to all men", that feller's never heard of it. Our Ginny and Tessa will have to cook the dinner.'

It was on Eileen's lips to say wasn't that what they always did so Christmas Day would be no different, until she caught a warning look from Delia.

'Will you put them to one side for me? One of the girls will pick them up later.'

Delia took the money May handed her and nodded. She certainly played on those two girls, she thought.

'I wonder what Tessa's up to?' Eileen speculated when May had gone.

'Well, no doubt we'll all find out soon enough.' Delia answered. She hoped it had nothing to do with Elizabeth and she hadn't been too pleased about May's remarks about Tessa. Although her relationship with Elizabeth was now less fraught, she hadn't forgiven Tessa for, as she saw it, enticing Elizabeth to the munitions factory. Siamese twins, indeed!

It made the street look like something from the front of a Christmas card, Elizabeth thought. As well as being Christmas Day, today was the day Tessa was going to announce her engagement. She wrapped her warm red dressing gown around her and stood looking out of the window at the fairytale scene of the snow glistening in the pale winter sunlight, covering the craters and disguising the bomb sites. It was going to be a perfect day for Tessa and it would help to relieve the strain and sorrow for Johnny. It would be the first Christmas without his mam. Without anyone to have decorated the house, done the shopping and cooked the traditional meal, Eddie and his two younger sons were going to his brother's house for dinner. Johnny was having his with Tessa and the rest of her family.

After mass they all wished each other the Season's Greetings which Father Walsh thought more apt than Happy Christmas or a Peaceful Christmas. There was not much for anyone to be happy about and definitely no peace. Tessa asked Eddie Doyle and his two young sons to come back with herself and the rest of the family just for an hour.

'Well, our Billy is expecting us and we don't want to be late and ruin the dinner.'

'You won't be late, Da, I promise,' Johnny urged.

'Don't look at me, Eddie, it's a mystery to us as well,' Richie added.

So they all agreed and began to walk home, hanging on to each other to prevent themselves from slipping and falling, as it was still freezing hard.

'It's dead good! We'll get the oven shelf after dinner and go out and slide down the street on it!' Jimmy said to Vincent Doyle, the youngest of Johnny's brothers, and Harold Flynn who was tagging on behind.

Eileen had overheard him. 'Oh no yer won't, meladdo! Them streets are dangerous enough without youse lot making them worse.'

'Ah, Mam, it's Christmas!' Harold protested but his protest

was ignored by his mother, which he took to be a good sign. He'd be all right, his da always went to the pub and Mam always fell asleep after dinner and he never took any notice of their Maureen. She'd got a gift box from Woolies that had perfume and stuff in it and had been made up with it. Their Brenda was coming over though, and with *him* too. He bet Thomas Kinsella had never made a slide in the street or used the oven shelf or a tray as a sledge, he was too miserable. And he was still afraid of his mam. Mind you, even if Mam did forbid him the oven shelf, he'd got a football for Christmas and you couldn't have everything. The casey would give them all hours of fun, long after the snow and ice had gone. In fact, some of his pleasure in making slides and snowmen and snowball fights dimmed as he realised he wouldn't be able to play footie until the snow cleared.

When they reached the shop Elizabeth turned to her mother. 'Mam, will it be all right for me to go to Tessa's for half an hour?'

'What for? You've only just left her and I'll need help with the dinner, you know that.'

'Yes, but . . . but, well, today is special.'

'It is, it's Christ's birthday,' Delia answered.

'And mustn't He be pleased at the way the world is celebrating it? By killing and maiming each other and blasting innocent women and kids to kingdom come!' Jack answered grimly.

'Mam, please?' Elizabeth begged.

Delia pursed her lips.

'What's so special?' Jack asked. The last thing he wanted today was another row between his wife and daughter.

Elizabeth became impatient. 'Oh, if you must know, she

and Johnny are going to announce their engagement.'

Delia looked taken aback. 'When was all this planned?'

'Weeks ago, but I was sworn to secrecy. His poor mam didn't even know about it before she was killed.'

'Go on then, just half an hour. Your mam hasn't slaved away to have the dinner ruined,' Jack said but he was smiling, unlike Delia.

'Well, that's a turn-up for the book, but I've got to say they are suited and he's away next week.'

'I just hope Elizabeth doesn't take it into her head to do anything stupid.'

Jack shook his head, glancing at Nessie, and Delia said no more.

It was all a bit of a squeeze, Tessa thought, but they managed it, and when everyone had perched themselves on something, she looked up at Johnny, her eyes shining, her heart full of love.

Johnny cleared his throat nervously. 'Da, Mr and Mrs O'Leary, we . . . we've got something to tell you.'

'Well, get on with it, lad, we're all waiting for that goose that's in the oven,' Richie urged.

'Tessa and . . . well, *we* have decided to get engaged. I know we're both under the age of consent and we really need your permission, but I'll be away soon and I reckon if I'm old enough to fight, then I'm old enough to get engaged.'

May clapped her hands to her cheeks: she'd thought it was something like this. 'Oh, isn't that great, Richie! Tessa, come here to me while I hug you, and you too, Johnny!'

'Will you . . . will you have a ring?' Ginny was utterly devastated but then remembered that Colin was due home soon.

'Not yet, but . . . here, Tessa, this is to make it sort of official.'

Tessa took the little box and unwrapped the paper, then she cried with delight and threw her arms around her new fiancé. It was the signal for Richie to shake Eddie's hand vigorously and May, Ginny and Elizabeth to dissolve into floods of tears while Johnny fastened the chain around Tessa's neck.

'I'll never take it off! Never. Not as long as I live!' Tessa said, quietly.

'Your mam would have been pleased. She liked Tessa a lot. She's a good girl, son,' Eddie said with a tinge of regret and sadness in his voice. He missed Dora far more than he thought he ever would. He'd never noticed or even mentioned how hard she'd worked to keep a good home, and now that home had started to look neglected and shabby. They all missed her.

'When . . . when will you get married?' Ginny asked.

'In May, and before anyone starts on the bad luck thing, we don't care!' Tessa said.

'It's just a load of superstitious nonsense anyway,' Elizabeth added. She was so happy for Tessa and she knew Mike was too, but it set her own thoughts on the same question. The announcement of her engagement certainly wouldn't be met with such joy and enthusiasm. It would mean yet another huge row and probably the permanent alienation of all her family, although she would be welcomed by Eileen and Frank.

After lunch Elizabeth and Nessie washed and dried the dishes while her mam and da dozed before the fire. It was still

bitterly cold and reminded Elizabeth of the first Christmas
Tessa had spent in Naylor Street. Everything had been so
different then. Who would have thought that they would be
in the middle of a war now? That May and not Mary would
be Mrs O'Leary? They had all certainly grown up: even
Nessie wasn't so bad these days.

'What are you thinking about?' Nessie asked as she wiped
her hands on the roller towel Delia kept in the scullery.

'Oh, how things have changed. You, me, Tessa . . .'

'And Mike Flynn?' Nessie queried.

'Yes, and Mike too.'

'Do you think you'll end up marrying him?'

Elizabeth shrugged. 'I don't know. Anything could happen
in the future, especially . . . especially when he's away.'

Nessie looked at her solemnly. 'But you do *hope* you
will?'

'Oh, God, Nessie, please don't start with the Grand
Inquisition, I thought you'd changed.'

Nessie looked hurt. 'I wasn't going to say anything to
Mam.'

'Then don't even mention it, please? I do . . . like Mike,
but . . .' She shrugged.

Nessie nodded and went through to the kitchen, leaving
her sister thoughtful and uneasy.

Saturday January 4 1941 had arrived and still the snow lay
heavily on the ground and each night the temperature
dropped, making the roads and streets hazardous. Jack said
to Frank Flynn that he'd never known so many horses that
had had to be put down because they'd fallen on the icy
cobbles. It was a pitiful sight to see them thrashing about,

screaming with the agony of broken legs. It was pitiful too to see the carters, with tears in their eyes, take the guns they all carried and put them out of their misery. Their horses were like old friends, some of the carters thought more of their horses than they did of their wives, Jack had said, and Frank had nodded his agreement, thinking that a loyal, dumb animal would be preferable to Eileen at times. A horse would wait patiently outside a pub, quite happy with a nosebag of oats, and wouldn't rant and rave about 'wasting time and money'. Everyone now threw the ashes from their fires on to the pavements and roads to help give a better grip for both people and animals.

Both Elizabeth and Tessa had been granted a half-day's leave to see Mike and Johnny off from Lime Street station.

They looked so different now, Elizabeth thought. The uniforms made them look older than eighteen. They were boys no longer, she mused sadly, they were young men and they were going off to war. She squeezed Mike's hand and he looked down at her and smiled into eyes that were unnaturally bright.

'Elizabeth, you promised, no waterworks!'

'I know I did, but . . . but look around, everyone is crying.'

The station was filled with couples embracing; mothers and sweethearts and wives clinging tearfully to their menfolk. Fathers were shaking the men's hands or were slapping them on the back.

'You will write to me?' she begged.

'I've promised a hundred times. They'll go to Tessa's address.'

'Oh, I wish we didn't have to be so . . . so secretive about it.'

'So do I, but for the time being it's best to say nothing of our plans.'

She nodded, her heart beating in an odd jerky fashion, her throat dry. On Christmas Night they'd gone for a walk, despite the bitter cold, and it had been then that he'd asked her to wait for him. To marry him when the war was over. She'd clung to him, pure joy flowing like wine through her veins. And when he'd kissed her she hadn't wanted him to stop – ever.

'I'll get you something, Elizabeth, something as a token.'

'Not a cross and chain, Mam will be certain to start asking questions.'

'What then?'

She'd thought for a minute. 'A brooch.'

He'd looked amused. 'What kind of brooch?'

'I don't know. Something . . . something unusual.'

'I've never been much of a one for looking at women's jewellery,' he'd laughed, 'but I saw a brooch once – well, it was more like a badge. An officer, a naval officer, was wearing it. It was made up of two gold fishes – strange fishes they were too, with long sort of snouts. The noses, or whatever they were, were holding up a silver anchor and above it was a gold crown with bits of it painted in red. It was so unusual, that's why I can remember it so clearly. Would you like something like that?'

Elizabeth deliberated. It did sound unusual. 'Yes, I think I would. I'd wear it all the time and no one could object to that. If Mam asks I'll say it's a military badge – well, a naval badge.'

'I wonder what it represents, or *who* it represents,' Mike pondered.

'Maybe Da will know. But I won't ask him until you give it to me,' she'd added hastily.

'I wish now I'd asked him what it represented and where I could get one, but I'll find out and when I'm home next, you'll have your brooch.'

The Tannoy system crackled into life and a disembodied voice informed everyone – not very clearly – that all naval personnel were to board the special trains immediately.

Tessa flung her arms around Johnny's neck. 'Oh, take care! Please take care of yourself, I love you so much!'

He held her closely. 'Don't worry, Tessa, I'll be back. It'll soon be May. We've got that to look forward to.'

Eileen and Brenda and Maureen were in tears. Frank was keeping a wary eye on young Harold who had a fascination with steam engines, and who was all too likely to take this rare opportunity of a closer look and get lost in this crowd – and then Eileen would be livid and blame him.

'Goodbye, Mam, Da, and you two, don't go misbehaving yourselves. Brenda, you see you take care of my niece or nephew and yourself too.' Mike embraced his family in turn and then caught Elizabeth to him.

'I love you, Mike. I'll always love you. Come back for me. I'll wait for ever for you!'

'Oh, Elizabeth! Elizabeth!' He hid his face in her hair so none of them could see the tears in his eyes. He was scared; they all were. God alone knew what faced them. 'I love you, Elizabeth. Take care of yourself.'

He finally disentangled himself from her embrace and with Johnny and four other lads from Naylor and Oriel Streets walked through the barrier that separated them from their loved ones. For some it was to be the last sight they'd ever have of those dear, familiar faces.

Chapter Twenty-Five

On a freezing cold night almost a month to the day later, it was Ginny's turn to stand on Lime Street Station, under the clock, waiting for Colin's train to arrive. She'd been counting the hours and the minutes but she hadn't told Tessa or her Mam because she knew they would ridicule her.

She could hardly contain herself, she was so excited. She hadn't slept properly for the past two nights either. She'd spent hours in front of the mirror examining her face for spots that might suddenly appear and fiddling with her hair until she'd made such a mess of it that Elizabeth had been called in.

'I just can't do *anything* with it! And I don't know what to wear,' Ginny had wailed.

Tessa, who was writing to Johnny via the Naval Dockyard at Chatham, raised her eyes to the ceiling. She certainly didn't view her brother's homecoming as anything to be overjoyed about. In fact Ginny was the only one who showed any enthusiasm at all and she was really taking it too far. Her da hadn't even mentioned it. All May had said was, 'Another mouth to feed,' and Jimmy was disappointed to learn that his elder brother hadn't actually done any fighting yet. Two of the lads in his class had fathers who had been rescued from the beach at Dunkirk when all the ships – even the Mersey ferries – had sailed to France to evacuate the French and British soldiers caught between the sea and the German Army. Now *that* had been exciting. Something to boast about.

All Colin had done was train at Aldershot.

'What in God's name have you been doing to it? Have you been cutting it? It's all lengths,' Elizabeth said disparagingly.

'Just my fringe. I only cut the tiniest bit off!' Ginny wriggled on the chair and looked apprehensive.

'Obviously your idea of "tiny" and mine is different. You look as if you've taken a pair of garden shears to it. I'll have to even it all off now and once I've set it I don't want any more fiddling with it, so stop fidgeting. What are you going to wear? It's as cold as the North Pole out there.'

'My best blouse, navy skirt and my good coat.'

'You'll freeze in that blouse, it's only got short sleeves,' Tessa remarked.

Ginny didn't reply. She'd put up with the cold.

'Presumably you'll be wearing a hat?' Elizabeth asked as she snipped away.

'The one I bought last year – I've got some new ribbon to put around it. There's nothing in the shops now. Nothing decent.'

'Well, there is a war on. I'll wave your hair – that'll look better under a hat and it won't be all flattened when you take it off.'

'Oh, I'm so thrilled!'

'You won't be if you don't sit still and my scissors slip and cut your ear!' And you're the only one who seems to be delighted at the return of the Prodigal. Even your Jimmy isn't over the moon,' Elizabeth answered.

'Oh, he's just a kid. All he wants is something to boast about to his mates. Even the Christmas raids didn't stop them all hankering after a hero to worship.'

* * *

The train was late. Ginny and every other woman on the station concourse kept checking the time by the big clock whose fingers seemed to move with infinite slowness. Ginny stamped her feet, turned up the collar of her coat and thrust her hands deeper into her pockets. Trains these days were always late.

There was an indistinct announcement over the Tannoy and everyone surged forward towards the barrier as, with a shrill whistle and a grinding of iron wheels on the track, the train pulled in, wreathed in clouds of steam.

There was total chaos as the soldiers, airmen and civilian passengers started to reach the barrier and it wasn't until a policeman and a railway official cleared the immediate area around the barrier that some semblance of order was restored.

In the crush Ginny's hat had been knocked sideways but she didn't care. In seconds he'd be here with her.

Colin saw her before she caught sight of him. His searching gaze had swept the faces of the crowd, to find that she was the only one of them who'd come. He was hurt and angry – everyone else seemed to have huge numbers of relatives fussing and crying over them. He was certain that had she been alive Mam would have been here. It was probably May's fault that his da and Jimmy hadn't come, and probably Tessa too. Then he remembered that Tessa wouldn't have come even if he'd been abroad and was coming home covered in medals. But he'd expected his da to be there, at least, and maybe Jimmy.

Ginny flung herself into his arms with such force that he almost overbalanced.

'Hey! Hang on a minute, Ginny, or you'll have us both

over! I've heard of "fond greetings" but this is a bit over the top!' He laughed, making no attempt to kiss her except on the cheek. He'd grown up a lot since he'd been away and she looked even more of a kid than ever. A silly, soppy, doe-eyed kid. He was used to women now. Proper women, and not all of them had wanted paying for their favours.

'Oh, I'm so glad to see you! I've missed you so much! It's been awful. Why didn't you write more often? I sent you hundreds of letters!' Ginny babbled.

He disentangled himself. 'Because I've not had much time, Ginny. I've been training, remember? There's a war on.'

'Oh, everyone is saying that all the time now,' she replied petulantly.

'Well, it's true. Right, hang on to me while I get us through this crowd.'

With shining eyes she clung to his arm while he, with his kit bag over his other shoulder, pushed his way forcefully towards the exit and on out to Lime Street.

'Will we go . . . somewhere first, like?' she asked shyly. She wanted time alone with him before they got home to their crowded kitchen.

'Where?'

'Well, I don't know. A pub?'

Colin looked at her with irritation. 'Ginny, you don't even look seventeen, let alone twenty-one, and I'm not being told to leave because you're under age, not in front of all the customers.'

'I'm nearly eighteen,' she protested.

She'd managed to change her shift so she'd be home in the evenings, like Tessa and Elizabeth, and could spend time with him while he was on leave. She was very tired when she got in, they all were, but that wouldn't matter. She could catch up on her sleep when he'd gone back. Although she didn't want to think about that.

'So, you're back then. How's it going?' Richie greeted his son from over the top of the newspaper he was reading. He hoped the Army would have knocked Colin into shape. He certainly looked well in his uniform, so maybe things were getting better.

'Bloody hard work, it is.'

'Hard work never killed anyone,' May said.

'We've had air raids, in case it's escaped your notice,' Tessa remarked.

'I did notice. London was pretty battered-looking.'

'And so are we,' May cut in with an edge of impatience in her voice.

'Well, this is a nice homecoming I must say! I don't know why I bothered, I've not had a civil word from anyone except Ginny.'

Ginny gazed at him adoringly. 'I'll get you something to eat and make a whole pot of tea, just how you like it.'

Colin smiled. 'That's my girl.'

He was sorry he'd come home now. You could cut the atmosphere with a knife. They were all obviously still annoyed about that bank raid. He'd been fool enough to turn down the chance to stay with one of his new mates in London for this.

'Just you remember, Ginny, that that tea has got to last,' May called to her daughter, who totally ignored her and put three heaped teaspoons in the pot.

'I suppose Ginny wrote and told you that Johnny and I are engaged?' Tessa asked.

'I suppose she did but I don't remember. That's a bit quick off the mark, isn't it?'

'It is not. We've been courting for ages.'

'I mean he's only a bit of a kid.'

'He's man enough for the Navy and so is Mike Flynn,' May shot back at him.

'I didn't mean it like that. I just meant he's a bit . . . well . . . young.'

'Oh, would you just listen to Old Father Time there! All of nineteen, he is,' May remarked sarcastically.

'I don't think it's young. Well, not in wartime,' Ginny said, bringing the teapot and mugs in, plus two rounds of bread spread with Marmite.

'Young or not, we're getting married in May, but I expect you'll be away.' Tessa hadn't expected him to be enthusiastic. After what had happened on the *Ascania*, Colin must hate Johnny. The feeling was mutual.

'I will be. Where will you live, at the pub?'

'Most probably. We really didn't have much time to discuss it.'

'They'll have you for a skivvy, what with Mrs Doyle getting killed.'

Tessa glared at him. Obviously some of the things in Ginny's letters he read and remembered.

'They won't,' she snapped.

'I bet his da is all for it, though. I don't suppose any of them know one end of a brush from the other or how to boil an egg. She waited on them hand and foot and she got no thanks for it, and neither will you.'

May's patience snapped. 'If you haven't got anything better to say than that, the sooner you get back to your flaming Regiment the better!'

Colin got to his feet, took the pot, a mug and the plate

from a dumbfounded Ginny and left the room.

'Well, you can't say he didn't ask for it, Ginny,' May said firmly. 'Not a "Congratulations" or "Good Luck", nothing but snide remarks.'

'Oh, Mam, that's a nice way to welcome anyone home! He's only got a week and then he'll be going abroad to fight and I . . . I . . .' Ginny broke down in tears and fled to the semi-privacy of the room she shared with Tessa.

'Ginny! Come back!' May called, but Ginny ignored her. 'For God's sake, what am I going to do with her, Richie? Did you see the look on her face when he said "That's my girl"? He can still twist her around his little finger. I get so worried about her.'

'She'll be all right, he's only home for five days. He'll be travelling back for his last day and after that, well, she said herself he'll be going abroad. And about time too.'

May sighed. 'Let's just hope he behaves himself for the next five days because I know I can't do a single thing with her.'

Tessa nodded her agreement and returned to her letter.

The following day Colin slept late. After he'd washed, shaved and dressed he decided to go for a bit of a walk to think about how he could keep Ginny quiet and content with the minimum of time and effort. She was a real pain in the neck, but she had his money so he couldn't upset her. He knew though that he'd made the right choice in giving the money to her to mind. He knew that wild horses wouldn't have dragged the knowledge or hiding place from her. Not after he'd trusted her completely, not after all she'd been through when she lied to the police.

He caught a bus and went down to the Pier Head.

It was viciously cold and a few snowflakes were borne on the east wind. There were other men in uniform just walking, like himself, taking in the familiar sights and sounds, or waiting to board trams and buses. He walked down the floating roadway and on to the George's Landing Stage where, leaning against a wooden post, he looked out over the grey waters of the Mersey. Today was the first of his five days and nights, and he certainly didn't intend to spend them all in *that* house with *them* and Ginny mooning around, hanging on to his every word. It would drive him mad. But she had the money. He could have a bloody good time on that much money but he wanted to save most of it. Still, he could ask her for a few pounds. He had no idea where she kept it and turning the rooms inside out looking for it would certainly make someone ask why. Oh, when this war was over he was going to America or Australia and he wouldn't be sorry to leave any of them. Especially not Ginny.

His attention was caught by four warships moving slowly up river against the ebbing tide, the vanguard of a convoy. He wondered just how many ships had set out and how many had managed to make it back. The speed of the naval vessels was dead slow, about ten knots probably. They were useless for protection. What was needed were big, fast ships that could home in on the U-boats, release their depth charges and make a kill. By the time the naval escorts got to a ship in danger it was too late, the U-boat had done its job and was away. He knew that having lost the battle for the air, the Germans were engaged in another: a battle for the Atlantic and the safety of the shipping lanes. He shook his head as four battered, rusting merchant ships came into view. They and two more on the horizon were all damaged in some way. Rigging and funnels gone, holes above the waterline. They looked like tired, grey old warhorses; six of them in total. Just six. How many had set out? How many men had been drowned or been killed? It was vital that the port be kept working otherwise Hitler could starve them into submission. He'd gathered as much from a conversation he'd overheard on the train – and *that* hadn't been wise. There were posters everywhere warning 'Careless Talk Costs Lives'.

'Well, I never expected to see you again, Colin O'Leary.'

He turned at the familiar voice. 'Vera!' She looked very smart, he thought, and wondered where she'd got the money for the cherry-red military-styled suit she was wearing under a thick black coat, the collar and cuffs of which were trimmed with black fur.

'You look . . . great! Have you got yourself a rich feller?'

Vera arched her neck and cast him a seductive glance from beneath her lashes.

'What if I have?'

Colin shrugged. 'It doesn't matter to me.'

'My feller *is* rich but he's old as well and he's away a lot so I'm on my own, if you know what I mean.'

Colin smiled at her. He certainly did know what she meant.

'What are you doing down here? I'd have thought you'd be working in munitions like everyone else.'

'I do, you can't get away with not bloody working there, but I've got some time off. I've come to meet him.' She indicated with her head the first of the cargo ships which was now almost alongside.

'He's in the Merchant Navy?'

'Yes, he's a Chief Sparks. He'd have been retired if there hadn't been this bloody war. I've got a dead nice house now. Two bedrooms, kitchen, scullery and a proper parlour. The third bedroom he's had made into a bathroom, would you believe? A bath and an inside flush toilet. Mam and our Nelly are dead jealous, that's when they bother to think of me. His wife died ages ago and they had no kids.'

'That's great, Vera, you certainly landed on your feet there.' Privately, Colin wondered how someone with Vera's reputation and humble background could have caught herself a Chief Electrical Officer.

'After tonight, he won't want to go out again. We go for a drink and something to eat and he's worn out by midnight. He goes into a deep sleep. He says they never sleep properly when they're at sea. Always waiting for the alarm to go.'

Colin smiled again. 'So, does he let you out on your own at all while he's on leave?'

'Of course. He doesn't keep me on a collar and lead. He knows I've got me mates from work, and if he thinks I'm off with a feller he doesn't say so. He doesn't get all narked like some fellers do. He just likes someone to meet him when he comes home and then a bit of company. I try not to go out very much when he's home, but for some fellers . . .' She shrugged.

'So, would you like to go out with me, say tomorrow night?'

Vera arched her plucked and pencilled eyebrows. 'Well, that's a bit too soon.'

'What about the night after?'

He was like an eager drooling puppy, she thought. The

Army had certainly done wonders for him, though. He looked smart and far more confident. He'd always been good-looking.

'OK. Where will you take me?' She wasn't going out to be stuck in some poky dirty pub. She'd had enough of that. She was used to better things now.

'The State on Lime Street.'

'Great.'

'I'll meet you at the tram stop at the top of Freemasons Row at half past seven.'

Vera smiled. 'Fine. I'd better go. See you then.'

The gangway was down and the crew of the cargo ship were starting to come ashore so Colin turned away. Things were looking up, but he'd need some cash if he was going to squire Vera around all week. She certainly wouldn't be content sitting in a park and he'd have to buy her little gifts. He'd have to ask Ginny for the money.

'Ginny, can I have a bit of a word, in private, like?' he asked, almost as soon as she'd set foot in the door.

Her eyes lit up and the weariness fell away. What was he going to say?

'Is Tessa in yet?'

'No.'

'Then come into the front room.'

'What is it?' she asked as she closed the door behind them.

'You've still got *our* money, haven't you?'

'Of course I have.' Oh, this was it! He was going to ask for some to spend on her, she *knew* it!

'Well, I'll need a bit for . . . certain things.' He could see by her expression that she was hoping it was to buy her something. Well, hell would freeze over before he bought her anything expensive.

'How much? How much will you need?'

Colin looked thoughtful. Too much and she would suspect it wasn't for a ring, too little and he'd never be able to keep Vera happy.

'About ten pounds. If there's anything left over I'll give it you back. I've got my Army pay.'

'I'll get it for you now.'

She opened a drawer of her clothes chest under the window. Delving in, she fumbled beneath the garments, took out two white five-pound notes and handed them to him.

'That's great, Ginny.'

She automatically assumed he'd be taking her out. 'Where are we going tonight?'

'We're not going anywhere. I'm still tired out. Later in the week.'

She nodded, trying to understand.

'Much later, I mean. I've made arrangements to meet some of my Army mates for a few bevvies on Saturday.'

Ginny's heart dropped like a stone. 'Saturday! But everyone goes out on a Saturday! Oh, Colin, can't you put them off?' she begged.

'No. We all made a sort of pact,' he lied. 'Every time we're all home together, and it won't be often, we'll meet up and have a drink. Don't look so upset, Ginny, luv, I've . . . we've got plenty of time. I don't leave until next Tuesday.' He had to keep her happy.

Ginny smiled. He'd actually called her 'luv' and last night he'd said, 'That's my girl'. She *was* his girl and she was being selfish. Who knew what Colin and all his mates faced? Maybe they wouldn't have a chance to get together again for years.

'Yes, we've got the rest of your week. I was just being selfish and stupid.'

He bent and kissed her cheek. 'No, you're not. You're being really thoughtful and understanding.' The lies tripped easily off his tongue and Ginny was pacified.

On Saturday night she watched him get spruced up with something akin to adoration. He was so handsome, especially in his uniform now it had been pressed and all the buttons and badges burnished so they shone.

'You're taking your time getting dressed up, who are you meeting tonight?' Tessa asked.

'He's going for a drink with some of his mates from the Regiment,' Ginny answered.

Colin smiled at her through the mirror.

'Really? The time he's spent polishing those buttons and cap badge, I'd have thought he was going out on a date.'

Colin glared at his sister. Why the hell couldn't she just mind her own business? He saw the look on Ginny's face change. 'Well, I'm not. We always have to do this "spit and polish" bit. We can't let the Regiment down,' he snapped.

Tessa shrugged but she could see Ginny was perturbed about something.

He kissed Ginny on the cheek again and went out, whistling.

'Why are you always so nasty to him?' Ginny demanded of Tessa.

'Because he's always so nasty to me ... us. Have you forgotten that he's brought nothing but trouble to us? He even got you to lie for him, and if you think he's going off to meet his mates then you're more of a fool than I thought.'

'What do you mean by that?' Ginny demanded angrily.

'He's not going to see the blokes he sees every day, for God's sake! He's going to meet someone. A girl. Oh, Ginny, for heaven's sake, can't you see him for what he is? And why did he need all that money? I saw him put two five-pound notes in his wallet when he thought I wasn't looking. I know him. That money was to pay for a night out, obviously a very expensive one, and maybe a present of some sort. He must get well paid!'

Ginny leaped to her feet. 'No! No, I won't listen to you, Tessa! You hate him, you've always hated him. He's not like that. I believe him. I love him and he loves me.'

'Oh, I give up!' Tessa cried. 'I'm going to Elizabeth's.' But before she could move Ginny had grabbed her coat, shrugged it on and pushed past a startled Richie who had come in through the scullery.

'Where's she going? What's up with her?' he demanded.

'My dear brother is obviously taking some girl out tonight but he's told her he's meeting some mates. When I told her not to be such a fool as to believe him she up and stormed off.'

'He's not home five minutes before he's causing trouble,' Richie said angrily.

'Well, I'm going to Elizabeth's. I don't want to be here when she comes back, nor do I want to be the one who has to say "I told you so".'

'Neither do I. I'm going up to the pub.'

Chapter Twenty-Six

Ginny didn't know where she was running to. She'd just *had* to get out of that house. They'd all back Tessa up, and she couldn't stand it. It was as if they all actually hated him. How could Tessa be so nasty and malicious when he was her brother? Poor Colin had only just got home and everyone was treating him like a criminal, an outcast. He *had* gone out to meet his mates. He *had*! Why didn't Tessa believe him? He'd kissed her, wasn't that proof enough?

She didn't feel the freezing cold. Most of the streets had been cleared of snow but it was still icy and she almost fell a couple of times. By the time she reached Scotland Road she was out of breath and trembling. She clung to a lamppost; it was so dark the only light came from the moon, around which there was a milky-white rim which foretold another heavy frost. It was the worst winter she could ever remember. Well, she wasn't going to let them carry on being so awful to him. She'd catch him up and tell him what Tessa had said; he'd reassure her and tell her that Tessa was lying; then she'd kiss him and send him on his way to enjoy himself.

She crossed the road with care, seeing in the distance the small crosses of light that came from the hooded headlights of a tram and the white flash of paint on its bumper. He'd be at the stop at the top of Freemasons Row but she'd have to hurry. She tried to run but it was too dangerous. She slipped a few times, only just recovering her balance. If she fell and hurt herself she'd miss him. She clutched at anything that would give her support. Lampposts, bollards, shop window-sills, and all the time the tram was getting nearer and nearer.

Finally she was within earshot of the stop and she could see a couple of figures standing waiting. She wasn't too late.

She took a few steps forward and then stopped. She just managed to stop herself from calling out to him. He definitely wasn't alone. Before her horrified gaze Vera Morley, dressed to the nines, linked her arm through Colin's and reached up and kissed him on the cheek. Ginny continued to watch, frozen like a rabbit caught in the glare of headlights. She was unable to run away, paralysed by what she was seeing: Colin laughing, then bending down to kiss Vera and say something that made her throw her head back and laugh too.

Ginny felt sick. She leaned back against the window of a shop and closed her eyes. No! *No!* She refused to believe it. She *wouldn't* think about it. She had imagined it. It was a dream; she'd wake up soon. But she didn't. She opened her eyes; it wasn't an apparition. You couldn't miss Vera with her bleached hair. She watched wide-eyed with disbelief as Colin took Vera's arm and helped her on to the platform as though she were a delicate piece of china. They disappeared from view, the conductor rang the bell and the tram trundled away, the noise growing fainter and fainter until there was nothing but silence and emptiness. Emptiness that filled her and turned her heart to ice. She couldn't move. She just stood there, looking in the direction the tram had gone, taking Vera Morley and . . . him into town to enjoy themselves.

Her feet and hands were numb, but she still wasn't aware of the cold.

'Are you all right, luv? Are you lost?'

She looked up to see a policeman, clad in his thick heavy cape, the hands in which he held his torch encased in cream woollen gloves.

'No. No . . . I'm not lost.'

'You're frozen, girl. Where do you live and what's the matter?'

Ginny tried to pull herself out of the trance that gripped her. 'There's . . . nothing the matter. I'm . . . I'm just off home now.' She pointed along the road. 'I live along there. In . . . in Naylor Street.'

'Do you want me to walk with you?'

She shook her head. 'No, no thanks. I'm . . . fine. Thank you, thanks.' She began to walk in the direction of Naylor Street and he shrugged and turned away. She was obviously upset, but then so were an awful lot of girls these days.

Ginny didn't turn into Naylor Street.

She wandered around the Dock Road and its adjoining side streets for hours. She ignored the shouts, cat calls and openly coarse remarks that were yelled at her from the doors of the pubs she passed. A couple of times she'd been forced out of her reverie by the presence of seamen and dockers who'd blocked her path. They'd turned away and left her alone after taking in the wax-like skin and wide, staring eyes, thinking she was a wandering lunatic.

Tessa had been right. They'd all been right. She was the one who was stupid. She was the only fool who'd believed him. He didn't love her at all. He only wanted . . . Vera Morley. How could she have believed in him so implicitly? She adored him, he knew that. He'd always known she loved him and wouldn't even look at another lad. Tremors of shock ran through her. Vera Morley: that painted, over-dressed tart! He preferred *her*. He'd looked proud to be seen with her hanging on to his arm. He'd treated *her* like a princess. Surely Vera Morley had tricked him into taking her out? But her heart told her that this time putting the blame on someone else wouldn't work. She'd seen him with her own eyes; she'd listened to his lies with her own ears. It was over. He didn't want her.

When she at last returned home May was sitting beside the range, waiting.

'Oh, Ginny, luv. I was so worried about you. Richie said you'd had a row with Tessa over Colin and had just run off.'

'Mam . . . Mam . . . I don't want to talk about it. Not now, please?'

May got to her feet. Her heart bled for her daughter but at long last she looked as if she might just be coming to her senses over him. She wouldn't press her.

'You're frozen. Let me make you a drink and then I'll wrap the oven shelf in a bit of towel and you can take that to bed with you. Tessa's already asleep so try not to wake her. You've both got work in the morning and so have I.'

'Mam, I don't want a drink or anything. I just want to sit here . . . get warm . . . think . . .'

May nodded; she thought she understood. Somehow Ginny must have found out the truth about Colin. That was the only thing which could have affected her so deeply. All they could do now was support her, give her time and comfort. And not even mention it, never mind torment her with the words 'I told you so'. May just wished *he* didn't have a few more days at home. She'd have a word with Richie about it. Maybe he could think of some way of getting that cheating, conniving little sod to go back before his leave was up.

The house was so silent, Ginny thought as she huddled in the chair by the fire, still with her coat on. Only the ticking of the clock on the mantel broke it and seemed to get louder and louder until it filled her aching head. She sat gazing into the flames and suddenly snatches of conversation and fragmented images began to come back to her. Images of Colin with Vera Morley in his arms once before. Only this time they were in the park and it wasn't cold or frosty. He had his arm around her and was kissing her. She clenched the arms of the chair so hard that her knuckles became white. *No! No!*

She didn't want to remember, but she couldn't stop the images. They were so vivid and real that she could smell the scents of that warm summer evening. The roses and the flowering beds were a riot of glorious colour. She saw Vera's mocking smile, heard her call her an ugly, stupid kid. Then Colin's face loomed up at her and he was saying the same thing and telling her to go away and leave him alone. He'd called her a bloody nuisance and told her to go home, and he'd called her mam a floosie. She remembered running away, her eyes full of tears, then the screech of brakes and the sound of a frightened horse. She clapped her hands to her cheeks. There was no escaping the memories now. When she'd come to and found him beside her looking pale and concerned she'd believed his explanation, but he hadn't been worried about her at all. He'd only been worried for himself if she'd been killed or injured. And now . . . now he was out with *her* again. Holding her, kissing her, and . . . other things. And he'd taken the money to spend on Vera Morley. The money! Oh, God! She'd lied for him. Barefaced lies that blackened her soul. Just to keep him out of prison. She'd believed him then too. She'd believed he was innocent. That he'd been set up. Oh, they'd all known he was guilty – except her. How could she have been so stupid? She'd suffered hours of torment at the hands of the CID and for what? He'd stolen that money! He'd had no intention of sending for her once he reached America. He was running as far away from her and everyone else as he could get!

She heard the scullery door open and then she watched him come into the kitchen. The only light came from the fire and the flames made his shadow loom large on the wall. She couldn't see his face properly so she stood up.

'Ginny! What are you doing still up?'

'I . . . I saw you, with . . . her.'

'Jesus! You've been up to your old tricks, following me. I can't even have a bloody minute to myself without you being there, all the time.'

She gripped the edge of the table to steady herself. His words brought back the memories again and she felt faint. 'You lied to me. You've always lied to me. Lied about everything. The money, America, wanting money to go out tonight. I . . . I've been sitting here and I've finally remembered everything. The park where I found you with *her*. What she said to me. What you said to me. What you called my mam. The way I lied to keep you out of jail. I *believed* you!'

Colin panicked. 'Ginny! Ginny, you've got to listen to me.'

'No! I've listened to your lies for long enough.'

He caught her wrist. If she started to yell she'd have the

whole house up and she'd tell everyone about everything. He would be arrested by the police – or would it be the Military Police? Either way, he couldn't let that happen. He had to talk her round. He'd done it before; he could do it again.

'Ginny, let me explain. I love you, you know that—'

Inside she was screaming: Lies! Lies! Lies! She hated him! She hated *herself*! She couldn't stand him touching her now and she tried to pull away from his grip.

'Stop struggling! Ginny, for God's sake, listen to me.'

She couldn't stand it any longer. Words and pictures flooded her head until she felt it would burst. Her fingers closed around the handle of the bread knife and she snatched it up and thrust it into him. She saw the horror and disbelief in his eyes, watched the colour drain from his face, and then he slid slowly to the floor, sprawling at her feet.

She was shaking all over. She couldn't think clearly. The pictures just wouldn't go away. Why was he lying there? She couldn't see his face. She looked at the bloody knife and the blood on her hands. Oh, God! What had she done! No! No!

She hadn't meant to hurt him. She hadn't meant to . . . kill him. He wasn't moving. She *had* killed him. She hadn't meant to, the pictures had driven her to strike out at him, to punish him for the hurt she was feeling. She bent down and shook him.

'Colin! Colin, wake up! I didn't mean it! Oh, God, I didn't mean it!'

He didn't move, not a single muscle.

She was frantic. He was dead. They'd come for her soon. They'd take her away and then . . . She began to fight for her breath, it was as if the noose was already around her neck. Oh, God, this is what it must feel like! she thought in panic.

She couldn't let that happen. She couldn't fight and gasp out her life at the end of a rope. Without really knowing or understanding she turned the knife around, gazed at it blindly then plunged it into her chest.

It was Tessa who found them both. She'd been restless all night. Ginny had been in such a state that May had said she'd wait up for her. In the darkness she felt around the bed but Ginny wasn't there. She shook her head, trying to dispel the drowsiness. It must be the middle of the night, so where was Ginny?

She got up and wrapped the quilt around her. The bedroom was freezing. She made her way into the kitchen. The fire was almost out so she reached up and lit the gas jet, then she froze in horror before she began to scream hysterically.

May was the first to run into the kitchen and when she saw both Colin and Ginny on the floor, and that floor covered in blood, she clutched the back of the sofa as a wave of dizziness and nausea washed over her.

'Oh, Christ Almighty!' Richie cried, pulling Tessa towards him.

'Da! Da! Is she . . .?' Tessa sobbed.

'I don't know, luv. Here, May, luv, keep hold of her.'

Tessa and May clung to each other for support, both on the brink of hysteria.

Richie bent down and gently turned Ginny on her side but he could see that she was dead. He closed her wide-staring eyes and then turned to his son. Colin was dead too. Rigor mortis hadn't yet set in. Both Ginny and Colin's skins were still faintly warm to the touch. He got to his feet, very shaken.

'I'll have to go for the police.'

'Oh, Mary Mother of God!' May reached out for his arm. 'How . . .? Is she— Is he—?'

'They're both dead, luv. I think maybe she killed . . . him and then . . . herself. She's still got the knife . . .' He choked. He couldn't go on.

'Oh, it's my fault!' Tessa sobbed. 'If I hadn't gone on about him going out to meet someone, she wouldn't have—'

'Stop that, Tessa!' Richie said sharply.

'She . . . she'd seen him with someone, I'm . . . sure of it. She was frozen and dazed and she'd been crying. I should have stayed with her! If I'd stayed up or made sure she went to bed then this . . .' May's knees began to buckle.

'Da! Da! She's going to faint!' Tessa cried and Richie caught his wife before she fell.

'Go and make sure Jimmy isn't up or awake, Tessa, I'll see to May.'

Tessa fled from the room. It was a nightmare! A terrible nightmare and Johnny wasn't here to hold her and comfort her.

Her brother was still asleep and she came back downstairs and stood at the door of the kitchen, clinging to the door-frame.

'Da, can I go for Elizabeth?' she begged.

Richie was so shocked and confused that he nodded. 'Get . . . ask Jack if he'll come too? I don't know what to . . . do.'

Jack, Elizabeth and Delia came back with Tessa. They were all white-faced and shocked. Elizabeth was comforting her friend, unable to believe what had happened.

'What a bloody mess, Richie!' Jack said seriously. Delia had gone into the front room to look for something to cover Ginny and Colin.

'I just don't know what to do. I can't believe it!' Richie shook his head.

'Well, it's real enough, Richie.'

Delia came in with a blanket which she draped over the two prostrate forms. 'Elizabeth, luv, put the kettle on. Everyone's in shock. Oh, May, come here, my heart bleeds for you!' Delia took a sobbing May in her arms and held her close, wondering how she would feel if it were Elizabeth lying there instead of Ginny. Jack had made Richie sit down and now turned to his daughter.

'Elizabeth, do you think you could wake young Jimmy and take him next door? The police will be in and out all night.'

'Jack! Eileen will have the entire street up, you know what she's like!' Delia protested vehemently.

'It'll be up anyway. We can't keep something like . . . this . . . quiet and the lad shouldn't have to see . . . them.'

Delia nodded. 'You're right. Elizabeth, go and get him.'

Tessa got to her feet. 'No, I'll go. He'll be terrified.'

'Are you sure, Tessa?' Elizabeth asked with concern. Tessa looked terrible.

Tessa nodded.

'Take him out the front way,' Delia advised, filling the kettle to make a pot of very strong tea. It was going to be a long night and she suspected that the worst part of it lay ahead, if anything could be worse than the scene in this kitchen.

Delia need not have worried about Eileen. This was too serious a matter for just idle gossiping. Eileen had wept for May, thinking of her own two girls. Yet the news still swept through the whole street like wildfire as first the police and then a doctor came. Finally an ambulance arrived and both Colin and Ginny were placed on stretchers, their faces covered by blankets, and put inside to be taken to the City Mortuary. Statements had been taken from everyone and the CID inspector had informed Richie that as far as they could see it was a murder and a suicide. There would be an inquest but that would be much later. The man was as tactful as he could be, feeling sorry for the devastated family.

'Oh, dear Lord! Why? Why? Suicide! My poor Ginny won't even be buried in consecrated ground! You know as well as I do, Delia, suicide's a mortal sin!'

And a crime – as was murder, Delia thought silently. Her heart went out to May. For Ginny there would be no requiem mass, no church service of any kind. She would be buried heaven knows where, while Colin would have a mass, and a grave. It didn't seem fair.

Mick Collins had seen Vera Morley with Colin and when he'd heard about the tragedy at number twelve he'd gone straight round to the police station at Rose Hill. Vera had been questioned, and everyone reckoned that May was right, Ginny must have seen the two of them together.

Tessa was still in a terrible state but Elizabeth had persuaded her to return to work on Monday. 'It will take your mind off . . . things, I promise you.'

'I don't think *anything* can take my mind off it!' Tessa exclaimed. 'I should have kept quiet! If I hadn't said all those things she'd be alive now.'

'Stop it! *Stop* it! You can't blame yourself. How were you to know what would happen? You aren't a mindreader or some sort of clairvoyant. It's *not* your fault! The police, Dr

Duncan and Father Walsh have all told you that and it's true!'

'Oh, Elizabeth, I wish Johnny were home!'

'So do I, but they've only just gone and neither Johnny or Mike is related so they can't get compassionate leave.' Elizabeth wished with all her heart that Mike could come home. She needed him so much, just as Tessa needed Johnny. 'Tessa, I know it's terrible, really terrible, but there's still a war on. Our lads need weapons and ammunition and it *will* distract you. I'll write to Mike if you don't feel you can write to Johnny. Mike will tell him.'

'I . . . I . . . couldn't write it all down, Elizabeth.'

'I know. Leave it to me.'

'How . . . how can I get married . . . now?'

'Stop that! Life has to go on. The best possible thing for everyone will be your wedding. Ginny would have hated it if you'd cancelled everything because of her. You know she would.'

'Yes. You know, it's a terrible, terrible thing to say, but I don't really care much about . . . him.'

'It's not that terrible, Tessa. No one liked him at all and the way he treated poor Ginny, well, in my view he got what he deserved. Leading Ginny on, getting her to lie for him about that money – because no one will ever make me believe he didn't rob that bank. What are we going to do about the money?'

They'd found the wad of folded notes when they'd been going through Ginny's clothes.

'I don't know. We'll leave that for Da and May to sort out. I just don't want to hear anything more about it.'

Elizabeth nodded. She could understand.

Tessa suddenly looked stricken. 'What will I tell them at work?'

'The truth. Ginny was on the opposite shift to us until lately so they don't know her well and no one knew him at all.'

Eventually Tessa had agreed and gone back to work.

A few of the neighbours turned up for Colin's requiem mass, mainly out of respect for Richie and Tessa and Jimmy, who had been told as little as possible and was utterly confused by all the conflicting stories. His mates' version of what had happened and his da and sister's were so completely different. Vincent Keegan had said that according to the *Echo* Ginny had murdered their Colin and had then killed herself. He didn't know what or who to believe.

However, they all turned out for Ginny's journey to her final resting place, a small plot of land on the opposite side of the wall that bounded Ford Cemetery. Even Father Walsh was perturbed by the situation. Ginny had committed two crimes, two heinous sins, but surely she'd been driven to them. They certainly weren't premeditated. He'd known her all her life. She'd always been quiet, dutiful, devout. The girl must have been completely out of her mind, for there wasn't ever the smallest bit of violence in her character. He'd heard all about Vera Morley too. But his hands were tied. He was the parish priest and the Church had decreed that things like this were absolutely beyond the pale. His young curate had different ideas though, so he'd agreed to let Father Sharpe follow the procession but without his clerical garb. 'As a private mourner, Father, and as long as the Archbishop doesn't hear of it,' he had said.

May was inconsolable as she followed the coffin,

supported by Richie, Tessa and Jimmy.

'Ah, God luv 'er. Me heart bleeds for her. It's bad enough 'er being dead at seventeen, but to 'ave no service, no . . . nothing,' Eileen sniffed to Maisie Keegan as they gathered at the graveside.

'She must have been, what's them words they say, Eileen? Official-soundin', like?'

' "While the balance of the mind was disturbed",' Delia answered.

'Aye, that's it. She must 'ave been demented and while it's wrong to speak ill of the dead, God forgive me,' Maisie crossed herself, ''e must have driven her to do it, the swine! Poor little Ginny Greely, all she ever did wrong was to love that flamin' no-mark who's no loss to anyone. Thank God Mary isn't here to see all this.'

'What do they do at things like . . . this?' Eileen asked.

'Jack's going to say a few words – Richie is so upset he can't do it. And our Elizabeth is going to read a bit out of the Missal and then we'll all say the Our Father, Hail Mary and Gloria. We . . . we thought that would be best. We don't know how . . . anything like this is done.'

'We never 'ad to know. But God will understand and He'll forgive, so Father Sharpe said. He's gorra lovely way with 'im for such a young priest,' Eileen finished, dabbing her eyes.

It was awful, Elizabeth thought as the ceremony commenced. Worse than anything she'd ever experienced. But she'd sworn she'd get Tessa through this poor little excuse of a funeral, and that's what she'd do.

When her father finished speaking she took a step forward,

keeping her eyes fixed on her prayer book and not the yawning mouth of the freshly dug grave where Ginny's coffin, covered with flowers, had been lowered. She was determined to keep her composure.

She glanced quickly at her mother who nodded her encouragement and then, with slightly shaking fingers, turned to the page she'd marked, cleared her throat and began. 'Enter not into judgement with Thy Servant, O Lord, for in Thy sight no man may be justified, unless through Thee. Remission of all her sins be granted unto her. Let not, therefore, we beseech Thee, the sentence of Thy judgement weigh heavily upon her whom the true supplication of Christian Faith doth commend unto Thee: but, by the succour of Thy grace may she be found worthy to escape the judgement of vengeance who, while she lived, was sealed with the seal of the Holy Trinity. Who livest and reignest, world without end. Amen.'

'Amen,' the little group added as she stepped back and grasped Tessa's hand. 'It's all over now, Tessa,' she whispered, 'and I'm sure she's happy. I don't believe God is so awful as to abandon her.'

Tessa nodded her agreement, but was too choked to reply.

'It won't be long until May now, and Johnny'll be home,' Elizabeth consoled her.

'I . . . I . . . want him now.'

'I know you do, but he'll be home soon, they'll both be home. We'll never forget her, poor little Ginny. Come on, Tessa, let's go home.'

Chapter Twenty-Seven

The snow and ice gradually gave way to the cold blustery winds of March: the branches of the trees in the parks swayed and bent before them as daffodils began to push their way upwards in the ground beneath. They were in full bloom in April when much warmer weather moved across the country.

None of them had really got over the shock of Ginny's death or the terrible circumstances·in which she and Colin had died. The whole street was still stunned; there wasn't a single house where, when Ginny's name was mentioned, someone didn't break down and cry.

For weeks Tessa, May and Richie went through the everyday tasks as if they were in a half-trance. At work, at home, in the shop, it was as if Ginny were still there. They just couldn't fully accept it.

The inquest that had taken place in March had only dredged up memories and opened wounds that were just beginning to heal. As expected the verdict on Ginny was 'Suicide' and on Colin, 'Murder'.

During those long and terrible months both Tessa and Elizabeth took comfort from the letters they received from Johnny and Mike, but Elizabeth did not have the joy of being able to read them over and over as Tessa did. Her letters remained with Tessa and she had to make special visits to be able to read them. But now on the very last day of the month the waiting was over. The boys were due back home and both

Tessa and Elizabeth had begged time off work to go and meet them. Not at Lime Street Station, but down at the Pier Head where the frigate *Hercules* – Johnny's ship – would tie up and the cruiser *Juno* – Mike's ship – would come alongside too.

It was a glorious day, mild and sunny. The breeze coming from the river smelled of salt but it was also balmy. The buildings of the waterfront were bathed in bright light; even the river itself wasn't the usual turgid grey but reflected the blue of the sky, and sunlight turned the crests of the waves to gold.

'Oh, it's such a beautiful day – don't the ships look sort of out of place?' Tessa said as they walked down to the Landing Stage.

'Yes. Those dull and rusted grey hulls look morbid,' Elizabeth replied.

It seemed to take for ever to get the ropes ashore and secured to the bollards, then the gangways finally manoeuvred into place.

'Where will I meet you?' Tessa asked. They would have to separate.

'By the main door of the Liver Building,' Elizabeth called as she pushed her way towards where *Juno* was berthed.

She shielded her eyes with her hand to try to pick out Mike, and when she saw him she started to wave and shout. Her heart was beating so fast that she felt breathless.

Mike pushed his way through the crowd of relatives and friends waiting for their nearest and dearest. Elizabeth flung her arms around him. 'Oh, I've missed you! I've missed you so much!'

'I've missed you too, Elizabeth. It wasn't so bad in the

day, they kept us busy, but it was the nights. I'd lie in my hammock and just think about you and what you had gone through . . . I just couldn't believe it when your letter arrived. Johnny wanted to come home – we both did, but we couldn't get leave on compassionate grounds.'

'It was terrible. It still is. No one can help remembering . . . her . . . and Tessa's blaming herself still.'

'Well, let's try and put all that behind us now,' he urged. She'd had a bad time of it, but Tessa had had the worst time of them all.

'How long are you home for?'

'Until May the eighth, only we're not supposed to tell anyone.'

She smiled up at him. 'Don't you know, "Careless Talk Costs Lives",' she quoted.

She held his hand tightly as they walked towards the Liver Building.

Suddenly he stopped.

'What's the matter?'

'Nothing. I got you your brooch.' He delved into his pocket and brought out a small box, which he handed to her.

She opened it. 'Oh, it's beautiful! It *is* a badge but it's so pretty it looks like a brooch.'

'And now do we consider ourselves to be engaged?'

'Oh, yes! You're mine now – for always.'

He bent down and kissed her, ignoring the amused and wistful looks cast at them. These days it wasn't such an unusual sight.

Tessa and Johnny had got there before them.

Elizabeth hugged Johnny and Mike hugged Tessa.

'You don't know how happy we are now.' Tessa's eyes

were shining and Elizabeth looked at her friend with relief.

'We do. It's good to be home. It's dirty, scruffy and a bit battered but it's home and it always will be,' Mike said.

'Coming up river and seeing the buildings at the Pier Head gave me a lump in my throat. I can understand now why so many sailors say it's the most wonderful sight in the world. A couple of the lads had tears in their eyes but wouldn't admit it.'

'Will we go and have something to eat?' Elizabeth suggested.

'Why not? Let's celebrate. I think we all need a bit of cheering up,' Johnny agreed.

They walked to Castle Street where there was a small Lyon's Teashop on the corner of Castle Street and Cook Street.

Mike ordered tea and homemade teacakes, limited to one per person.

Elizabeth took the brooch out of the box. 'Look. It's not just a brooch, it's a bit like your cross and chain.'

Tessa reached across the table and took her hand. 'So you've made it "official",' she smiled.

'But only between us. I ... I can't tell Mam or anyone else. Oh, I hate it, not being able to tell people. She doesn't know I'm here and not at work. I couldn't even wear my best things and I really wanted to. I look a mess.'

'You never look a mess,' Mike told her.

'I know you can't bear to start another argument with your mam, but the right moment will come. I know it will,' Tessa tried to cheer her up.

Elizabeth pinned the badge to the lapel of her coat and smiled at Mike.

'So, what's it like being in the Navy?' Tessa asked. She

didn't want to talk about Ginny. That would come later when she and Johnny were alone.

'It's not bad. The food's nothing to write home about but then Mam's cooking was always a bit hit and miss too,' Mike answered.

'It takes a bit of time to get used to sleeping in a hammock, but they're comfortable and they're necessary. You wouldn't believe just how cramped everything is. There's pipes and cables all over the place and you keep banging your head on the bulkheads if you forget to duck climbing from section to section. And the ladders are vertical, you slide down just using your hands.'

'Aye, I've nearly knocked myself unconscious many a time,' Mike laughed. He was over six foot and had had great difficulty in remembering to duck.

Both the girls were staying on in town. Elizabeth couldn't go home until much much later as her parents thought she was at work, and even then she'd have to say she'd been feeling ill. She'd blame it on the smell from the TNT. Tessa was going to make the most of her time off to look for something for her wedding.

'You'll have to remember to take that brooch off before you get in,' she said as they walked towards Lord Street and the boys had both boarded a tram at the bottom of Castle Street. Elizabeth had been loath to let Mike out of her sight. She wasn't as lucky as Tessa. She couldn't take Mike into the shop and say, 'We're engaged.' She couldn't even steal a kiss or hold his hand or look up at him and believe he was *really* home. At least now that he was away, she didn't need to tell so many lies as to where she was going and with whom. She did however keep thinking of what she'd said. 'Now we belong to each other.' She knew that was true and the thought cheered her up.

They stopped and looked in the window of Frisby Dyke's.

'That's quite nice.' Elizabeth pointed to a pale blue linen costume, the jacket of which was fastened with very pretty blue and gold buttons.

'I'd get a lot of wear out of it too. More than I would a proper wedding dress.' Tessa had decided that it wouldn't be very fitting to have the dress, veil and all the trimmings because it was so soon after Ginny's death.

'What colour would you wear with it?'

'White or cream. I think I'd settle for cream myself. Or perhaps navy blue.'

'I think I'd prefer navy. It's more serviceable and things are getting harder to buy now. I wonder how many coupons I'll need. I mean, I'll have to buy a blouse and a hat and shoes and bag.'

'You can have mine. I told you that ages ago.'

The suit looked very smart, especially with the navy rayon blouse the assistant had brought.

'Now doesn't that just finish it off,' the woman said, tying the folds of material at the neck into a loose bow.

'It's not going to look fussy? I mean, with the hat and all.'

'Oh, no, madam,' the woman protested then disappeared to find a hat.

'What do you think, really? They'd tell you anything just to get a sale.'

'No, she's right. It's great and for once in your life you *should* dress up, it's a really special day,' Elizabeth said wistfully.

The hat, shoes and bag completed the ensemble and

Elizabeth clapped her hands with pleasure. 'Oh, Tessa, you look . . . wonderful. Elegant but not too overdressed.'

'Are you sure?'

'Of course I'm sure,' both Elizabeth and the sales assistant said together and they all started to laugh.

She'd gone down to Eileen's later that night to welcome Mike home 'officially'. 'They'll both be going away again soon,' she'd replied to her mother's question as to where she was going at this time of night.

'Aye, and God knows when they'll be back,' Jack added, much to Elizabeth's relief.

She returned with the news that Johnny was in fine form and that Mike was also happy to be home and had brought her a little 'keepsake' – the brooch.

'See what he got for me. Isn't it pretty?' She opened the box and held it out for her mother to see.

Delia looked at it closely. 'Well, it's unusual. I've never seen fish like that before—'

'It *is* unusual and they're called dolphins. I've seen one before,' Jack interrupted, examining it.

'Where?' Elizabeth asked, as her father pinned it once more to her lapel.

'Old Len Williams, you know, from the market, his son's been in the Navy for years. He had one. It's a naval badge.'

'What kind of naval badge?' Elizabeth asked, genuinely interested and thankful her mother hadn't asked just why Mike Flynn had bought her anything at all.

'Submarines. It's the official badge of all submariners.'

Elizabeth's heart sank. Her da's words were ominous. Mike had bought her the badge of a branch of the Navy whose job it was to lurk beneath the sea and sink surface vessels, just as the U-boats were doing so successfully now. She hoped it *wasn't* an omen.

She hadn't arranged to see Mike that night. It wasn't fair, she'd told him. His mam was always worrying about him and, besides, her mam would get suspicious. They'd go out tomorrow. Tessa was seeing Johnny of course. She was cooking him a meal.

Everyone had welcomed Johnny home with hugs and smiles and words of welcome although Johnny sensed the sorrow in the air. Tessa had told him that if housing hadn't been so scarce they'd have moved. Every time she went into the kitchen she said she could see them both lying on the floor. She'd only just stopped having nightmares about it.

'You've got a fair bit of leave,' Richie said while Tessa and May were setting the table and cooking the bit of liver May had managed to get.

'Well, I won't be getting much from now on, I suppose.'

'Oh, hell and damnation!' May cried as the now familiar sound of the siren started.

'Leave it, luv, we'll have it later,' Richie said, pulling on his coat and taking his tin helmet from the hook where it was always kept.

'I'll come with you,' Johnny offered as May covered the frying pan with a lid and took it off the fire in the range, then shoved Jimmy and Tessa towards the lobby and the stairs.

'No, you stay here, lad. It's your first night at home, don't let the buggers ruin it. If I need help I'll come for you.'

'How often does it happen now? I know London's been

hit pretty badly,' Johnny asked Tessa as they all sat squashed in the space beneath the stairs.

'We've had a couple of raids, but nothing as bad as before Christmas,' she replied.

He put his arm around her and felt her trembling. 'Don't get upset, Tessa.'

'I'm trying not to,' she answered. 'At least you're here with me.'

The raid was a light one and as they crawled out then went back into the kitchen May put the half-cooked meat back on the range. 'Well, it's not totally ruined,' she remarked with grim satisfaction.

The following evening Elizabeth had to cancel her date with Mike for as soon as she and Tessa got off the tram, just after seven o'clock, the siren sounded and they'd both run as fast as they could along Scotland Road and down Naylor Street.

'I'll have to go home!' Elizabeth cried as Tessa reached number twelve and Johnny opened the door to her.

'Go on, Mike won't mind,' Johnny yelled at her. Already they could hear the droning in the sky getting closer and louder.

Elizabeth ran through the shop and into the kitchen. There was no panic now. Delia was organised. She'd managed to get an Anderson shelter put up in the back yard because theirs was much bigger than those of the neighbouring houses. And she'd sworn never to go to a public shelter ever again. She picked up the items that were always to hand in the scullery: blankets, matches, candles, a biscuit tin with whatever was available, usually only plain Marie biscuits, and a Thermos flask.

In the shelter there were two bunk-type beds which they sat or lay on. She'd covered the floor with rush matting and had a small paraffin stove that was used to boil water and give some warmth.

'I hope everyone else will be all right,' Elizabeth said worriedly, thinking of Mike. He was so near and yet so far; she'd feel far better, far safer, if she were with him.

'Don't go saying things like that. It's not good for anyone's morale,' Delia chided.

They played 'I Spy', Ludo and tiddlywinks, and Delia had her knitting. Elizabeth was supposed to be learning how to knit too, as was Nessie, but as the hours dragged on nerves were beginning to get frayed. Elizabeth threw down the needles and the ball of wool. 'Oh, how much longer? How much longer, Mam? Why don't they just go back and leave us alone?'

'Elizabeth, stop that this very minute! Pull yourself together.' Delia herself was worried sick about Jack for all around them they could hear the whistling and then the explosions. The area was taking a heavy battering tonight and he was out there. But she had to appear in control of herself for the sake of her daughters.

'Pass me that Thermos, we'll have a cup of tea.'

Elizabeth reached over for the flask and it began to shake in her hand although she knew her hands were steady. The shrill whistling increased until its piercing stridency forced them to press their hands over their ears. Naked terror was in all their eyes.

The whole shelter vibrated. The ground under their feet moved and cracks appeared in the concrete base. The blast threw Elizabeth to the floor and sent Nessie sprawling across the bunk, the candle falling on her arm. She screamed in pain and terror.

Delia was the first to recover, scrabbling on the floor for the matches, it was so much worse being in the dark. She relit the candle.

'Oh, my God, that was close!'

Elizabeth pulled at her arm. 'Mam! Da's out there and it sounds like *everywhere* is being hit!'

'Well, you're not going looking for him and neither am I. He'd have ten fits if he thought we were out there too. All we can do is wait and pray.'

'What time is it, Mam?' Nessie whispered, terrified. Would this moment be her last?

Delia looked at the wristwatch Jack had bought her for their twentieth wedding anniversary. 'It's just after nine o'clock. Calm down, Nessie, luv, it'll be over soon.'

But it wasn't. At midnight, with no sign of an end to the bombs, Jack appeared like a ghostly visitation in the doorway. He was covered from head to foot in dust.

'I can't stop! I just came to see that you're all right.'

'Jack, stay and have a cup of tea, please?' Delia begged him, filled with relief and reaching for the flask.

'Just a few seconds then, luv. It's bad out there.'

'How bad?' Elizabeth asked, praying that Mike and Tessa and Johnny were safe.

'There're fires everywhere. They've hit the docks heavily again. Maisie's house is just rubble and so is Katie's. They've gone to the public shelter but I don't envy them when they come out!'

'Oh, Holy Mother of God! What will poor Maisie do now? She already had their Rita and her kids staying with them.'

'Da, what about next door – Mrs Flynn?'

'Thank God her house is still standing, so far, but all the windows are in again and I think the front door has been blown into the street with the force of the blast of the one that hit the Keegans'.' Jack gulped back the tea. 'They'll all have to find somewhere else, God help them,' he added grimly before kissing his wife and daughters and going out once more into the night.

An hour later when they too emerged from the shelter they were shocked into silence at the sight that greeted them. Fires raged everywhere, silhouetting half-demolished buildings. Debris was strewn across the road and further down four houses were now just piles of rubble.

People were beginning to return to their homes, picking their way through the bricks, broken glass and ruptured pipes. When Delia caught sight of Maisie she quickly went across to her while Elizabeth hammered on the Flynns' door.

'It's me, Mrs Flynn! It's Elizabeth!'

Eileen emerged from the lobby with Mike behind her and Elizabeth flung herself at him, laughing and crying.

'Oh, Elizabeth, 'e's 'ad me demented over yer!' Eileen sniffed, wiping the dust from her face with her apron.

'Thank God you're safe!' he exclaimed. 'It was only because Mam was screaming at me that I didn't come and see you.'

'Oh, Mike, it's terrible out there. Far worse than anything we've had before and it went on for so long.'

'I know. Look, I'm going to find my da, they'll need all the help they can get.'

'If you see Da tell him we're all safe.'

Delia had her arm around a weeping Maisie. The devastation was terrible.

'Oh, God, me 'ouse! Me lovely little 'ouse!' Maisie sobbed.

Delia thought about the 'lovely little house'. It should have been pulled down years ago, but she could understand Maisie's feelings at the loss of every stick of furniture she'd struggled to accumulate over the years.

'Come on into the shop, all of you. We'll have a cup of tea to calm our nerves and then see what we can do to help. Come on, Katie. Eileen, that means you too.'

They followed her through the shop and crammed into her kitchen. There was broken glass everywhere and the furniture had been blown across the room and was piled in a heap against the far wall. Elizabeth helped Nessie to tidy up a bit so everyone could sit down.

Katie Collins turned on her daughter Alice who was loudly bemoaning the loss of her jewellery.

'Oh, shurrup, Alice, fer God's sake! We 'aven't even gorra clean pair of drawers an' all yer can think about is that tatty stuff yer used ter drape yerself in. Yer'd think they was the Crown Jewels! Gorrup like a flamin' Christmas tree sometimes, she was. I told 'er it was dead common ter wear all that stuff at once.'

'Eh, Mam, that cost thousands!' Alice retorted, exaggerating as usual.

'Cost thousands! Yer gorrit all from Woolies an' yer looked like a tart sometimes! I'm glad it's all flamin' well gone! Maybe I'll gerra bit o' peace from yer now.'

'Here, Katie, have this tea,' Delia intervened. 'I think I can make the Marie biscuits stretch out. We'll just have to wait for the men to come in and tell us how bad things are, then we can get going and see what we can rescue from this terrible mess.'

Chapter Twenty-Eight

Johnny and Mike made their way down to the docks early next day to see if their ships had been damaged. The sights that met their eyes were appalling and stunned them both into silence.

As they walked – half of the tram lines in the area being broken and twisted – they often stopped to help people salvage their belongings or tear with their bare hands at rubble underneath which people were trapped. Relatives were standing in groups or sitting on the kerbside with whatever they'd managed to collect, numb with shock or weeping. Men too were unashamedly in tears as they searched for their wives, children or parents.

'God Almighty! I hope the bastards that did this will be in the same state themselves one day!' Johnny cursed as the broken little body of a child, still clutching a rag doll, was lifted gently by a fireman and passed to her distraught father.

'What goes around comes around. They'll pay – in the end,' Mike answered grimly.

It took them all morning and part of the afternoon to reach the docks where firemen and dockers and stevedores were still working to keep the fires under control and pull out what cargoes could be salvaged. Their ships, thankfully, were miraculously untouched, but a corvette and another cruiser had been badly damaged; the corvette was lying on her side. Obviously the amount of water that had been pumped into her to extinguish the fires had made her list and then roll over.

'Sometimes the water does more harm than the bloody fire.'

'I know, but they had to douse the fires: she was still carrying depth charges and ammunition for her guns which could have gone off. Anyway, those things are like toy boats, they're so flimsy,' Mike answered.

They split up to report to their Commanding Officers. Because the loss of men and ships had been so heavy, when he'd completed his training, Mike had been promoted to an Engine Room Artificer and Johnny to Petty Officer. These days it didn't take very long to rise through the ranks. It was only because he wasn't twenty-one that he'd not been made a C.P.O.

There was plenty of work for them to do. All the debris that had been hurled across the dock from the other stricken ships and the dock sheds had to be cleared and the dockside itself brushed. Cargo had to be restacked and sorted through. Decks had to be scrubbed – just because there'd been an air-raid it didn't mean sloppiness was the order of the day. Soot and dust had to be wiped off superstructures, gun emplacements, ventilators and funnels – in fact everywhere it had settled.

When the May sunlight began to fade and the evening sky turned to duck-egg blue shot through with bursts of rosy light, Mike suddenly realised he'd had nothing to eat since his breakfast.

'Any chance of a spello, sir?' he asked his superior, a dour Scotsman named Macintosh.

'The cook's no here. What do ye think this is, laddie, a bloody restaurant?'

'No, sir. It's just that I haven't had even a cup of tea since this morning. You remember me telling you how come we were so late getting down here.'

'Aye, I do. Go over to yon woman an' see if she's anything t'gie ye.'

Mike proffered his thanks and went ashore, over to the mobile canteen manned by ladies of the WVS. He was exhausted, they'd had hardly any sleep last night. Even it they'd been able to sleep through the noise of the bombing, their terror and his mam's screaming every time there was an explosion ensured no one got a wink. While he could understand her reaction, it had still grated on his nerves.

'You look done in,' Johnny greeted him cheerfully.

'So they let you off too.'

'Aye. The Chief said seeing as I was officially on leave I could come over here then go home for a bit. I've worked my fingers to the bloody bone.'

'Home! You lucky bugger. I'll be here until after I drop or Mac drops or we both do. Will you get Tessa to tell Elizabeth where I am? We were supposed to be going out tonight. Fat chance of that now.'

'She'll still be at work. They both will.'

'Well, when she gets home.'

'She'll probably be home by the time I get back, if it takes me as long to get back as it did to get here,' Johnny said morosely.

'God, but where do you start out there? There's buildings still smouldering.'

'I know. I'd best get going. See you later.'

'Just how much later I don't bloody know!'

'Why did he have to stay?' Elizabeth demanded of Johnny when she went up to Tessa's after her tea.

'I don't know. His Chief's a bit of a stickler. Been a Navy man all his life and doesn't think any of us lot are up to the mark. He'll have that ship looking brand new before he's satisfied.'

'But Mike's on leave. We were going out.' She was very disappointed. It would have been the first few hours they'd spent alone together.

'All I know is that he'll get home as soon as he can. It's a mess out there. It'll take a week to clear the worst of it and get services running again.'

'Do you think they'll come back?' Tessa asked fearfully.

'No. They'll have got fed up by now. We've never had raids for longer than two nights in succession, but if Mike's not back by ten I'll go and see why. I promise.'

Elizabeth managed a smile. They'd had a terrible day themselves. Of course the further into the suburbs you got the less damage there was, but there had been enough around Kirkdale and Everton for her to think herself lucky she still had a home to come back to.

By ten there was still no sign of Mike and so Johnny set out again for the docks. He thought Mike's Chief was taking things too far. After all, they *were* on leave and they had worked damned hard! It didn't take him quite so long this time as some of the tram lines had been cleared and buses were running, skirting craters in the road and being directed away from buildings that were unsafe. He was amazed at just how quickly demolition was being carried out and telephone engineers, gas and electricity workers had been able to restore some of the most necessary services.

It was turned eleven though, he thought, glancing up at the clock tower of the Liver Building. You could just see the fingers of the clock by the light of the moon. He cursed the moonlight. It was perfect flying weather.

Two minutes later the siren sounded and, cursing, he began to run. The bloody thing hadn't given them much warning, he thought, you could already hear and see the planes and then the first incendiaries found their target, sending a shower of sparks into the air. He increased his pace, oblivious to the explosions around him. He had to get to the precious cargoes on the dockside. It had cost hundreds of men their lives and God knows how many ships had been lost to bring them in and now they were in danger of being destroyed.

He reached number two, Husskisson Dock barely able to speak. He stopped and leaned against the wall of a shed to catch his breath. Already fires were raging and fire engines were hurtling in from all directions.

The bastards! The bastards! he cursed to himself. Women, children and old people were back there, totally defenceless except for the anti-aircraft batteries. Ahead of him, outlined by the glare, was the S.S. *Malakand*. Men working frantically at the pumps were successfully dousing the flames over her No. 1 hatch. He jerked into action. 'Jesus Christ!' he cried aloud. The *Malakand* was loaded with one thousand tons of high-explosive bombs!

He ran the remaining distance and up the gangway as a shower of incendiaries burst around them. Explosions rocked the entire dock and soon the cargo sheds were alight as well as the ship. The fire engines continued to arrive, disgorging firemen to ply their hoses on the sheds on the east and south sides, dim shapes that became lost in the dense smoke. As he raced along the deck he could feel the heat through the soles of his boots. Sweat poured down his face from the searing heat, but he set to work with the crew.

The blaze had reached the contents of the cargo shed on the south side and the building erupted into a solid wall of flames.

'It's no use! It's spreading!' someone yelled.

He turned. The flames from the dock had reached the *Malakand*.

'She'll go up! Get the hell out of it,' the officer in charge yelled.

The fire was a blazing beacon and the raiders homed in on it. The heat and smoke were suffocating as more incendiaries fell and the bombers flew lower, so low at times that their black shapes seemed only a few feet above them.

Johnny began to cough and his eyes were smarting and streaming. The deck was red-hot. Above the cacophony he heard Captain Kinley give the order to 'Abandon ship' and he followed the others down the gangway and to a point where the shed was least affected by the fire. The *Malakand* was ablaze from bow to stern.

The Fire Officer in charge, Mr Lapin, shouted for them to help his men and Johnny grappled with a hose alongside two firemen, his arms and shoulders aching with the renewed effort. The enemy aircraft droned overhead, unheeded. It was useless, the blazing wall of cargo sheds made it impossible to get near enough to try to train the hoses on the ship.

Even worse, he could see the roof of the nearest shed was about to collapse.

Across his line of vision he saw a blurred figure running alongside the shed, trying to reach the line of firefighters. Whoever it was was taking a terrible risk, he was too close to the shed and the blazing ship. He rubbed his eyes with the back of his hand. In this hell of heat, smoke and flames it was impossible to recognise any individual, but as the figure ran towards them there was something about it that was familiar. A face flashed into his mind. Mike! He heard the others curse him as he began to run. The roaring and rushing of the flames drowned out his warning cries. He looked up and then launched himself bodily across the few feet that separated them. They collided, falling on the wet cobbles, rolling over and over with the momentum of the impact. There was a groaning, splintering sound as the roof of the shed collapsed just feet behind them.

They were both soaking wet, the cold water drenching them as a fire hose was played on them, extinguishing their burning uniforms.

Johnny dragged himself to his knees. Mike was lying sprawled on the floor.

'Get up! For God's sake, Mike, get up!' he yelled, dragging Mike to his feet.

Mike shook the water from his eyes. 'Johnny!'

'For Christ's sake, run! Come on, run! Run for your bloody life!'

Mike raced along beside him, his breath laboured, his legs moving like pistons until a blinding flash of white light and a roaring in his ears, so loud that he thought his brain would burst, sent him sprawling again. The *Malakand* had exploded.

The raid went on but Mike was so frantic that he refused to go to the nearest shelter, so they both half ran, diving for any sort of cover when the bombs exploded near them, and half walked until an hour later they reached Naylor Street.

'Oh, God Almighty, would you look at it! Would you just look at the state of it!' Johnny cried in impotent fury as Mike dragged him towards number ten. There was no need for lamplight, it was as bright as day. The whole city was on fire. 'At this rate there won't be a bloody building left standing!'

'Get in to Mam, they'll be under the stairs!' Mike urged his friend but Johnny refused.

'No, I'll go and see if Tessa's all right, then go down to see Da.'

Tessa, May and Jimmy had been huddled together for hours under the stairs and they were all sobbing. It seemed as though the end of the world had come. Many explosions had come close enough to rock the house; plaster had flaked all over them, and the dust filled their lungs. May had managed to tack up a blanket as some protection from flying splinters of glass.

'Oh, sweet Jesus! We'll never come through this, Tessa!' May had screamed once. Tessa had bitten her lip hard and held Jimmy even tighter. He'd wanted to go out on his bike, they'd need messengers, he'd pleaded in vain.

When they heard Johnny's voice, Tessa burst into tears: she'd been terrified that he'd been killed.

'Oh, thank God! Thank God! I . . . I . . .'

'Are you all all right?' he rasped, his throat dry from the smoke and the dust.

'Yes. Oh, how much longer will it go on?' May sobbed.

'I don't know and that's the truth. Is your da out there?'

Tessa nodded, tears streaming down her cheeks. 'And Jimmy wanted to go too. On his bike.'

Johnny looked at the lad. He was scared stiff but he was trying not to show it. 'Do you think you can do it, Jimmy? I won't tell you any lies, it's like . . . like hell out there but they will need messenger boys.'

'No! No!' Tessa cried, clutching the boy to her.

'Tessa, luv, you don't understand. I can't stay here with you. I've got to go and see if Da and the boys are unhurt, then I'll have to go out and help – they need every pair of hands. Go on, Jimmy, get your coat, your tin hat and your bike and call for Harold Flynn too.'

'Is Mike—?' Tessa queried, half afraid of the answer.

'Mike's fine. I'll call and see Elizabeth. They've got their own shelter, haven't they?'

Tessa nodded.

Johnny bent and kissed her and then he was gone, gently pushing young Jimmy before him.

'Oh, God help us! God help us all!' May sobbed in fervent prayer.

As Johnny went into the shop that had neither door nor window he saw Jimmy and young Harold start to cycle along the pavement. Their faces were white with fear but they pedalled furiously. They knew where to go for their instructions.

Above him the raiders still droned like a swarm of

angry bees, there must be at least three hundred of them, he thought with fury. He found Delia with her arms around her daughters. Nessie was crying hysterically.

'Johnny! What . . . what are you doing here?' Delia cried. She'd been praying hard for hours now and there was still no end in sight.

'I've just come to tell you that Tessa and May are fine.'

'Thank God!' Delia said with genuine relief. These days there was more to worry about than silly snobbery.

'Young Jimmy and Harold Flynn have gone up to the air-raid post and I'm on my way to see if everything is all right at the pub.'

'Mike? What about Mike?' Elizabeth cried.

'Don't worry. He's OK too. He's with his mam now but he'll be back out with me for the rest of the night.'

'How much longer? Oh, Blessed Virgin, why don't they leave us alone! Haven't we suffered enough for one night!' Delia was just holding on to her sanity.

'It can't be for much longer, they must have run out of bombs by now!'

'Did you see Jack or Richie or Frank?'

'No, but I'm sure I will before the night's over. I'll tell them everyone's OK and that we've still got roofs over our heads – for now,' he muttered.

A terrific explosion shook the whole shelter and both Elizabeth and Nessie screamed, Nessie holding her hands over her ears.

'Hush! Hush! It's all right. It's the *Malakand*. She's full of bombs and she's on fire. There'll be more explosions until she's blown sky high, then she'll probably take the whole dock with her. Hang on for just a while longer!'

When he got to the pub, to his horror he found it was on fire. Catching the arm of the nearest fireman he yelled at him, 'Was there anyone inside? My da runs it. Are my two brothers inside?'

'Not as far as we know. A woman further up said Eddie Doyle was out with the ARP and the two lads were with her. Is that your family?'

Johnny nodded thankfully. The kids were safe and so, as far as he knew, was his da, but everything he had owned, even down to a change of clothes, had gone up in the inferno that had been his home. For once he was glad his mam wasn't alive. He satisfied himself that his brothers were indeed with a kindly neighbour, then he turned and began to run back towards Scotland Road. Nearly every house and business had been hit. There'd be plenty to do before the night was over.

The bravery of the men and boys that night became legend-ary. As Liverpool burned they fought back with everything they had. The young messenger lads, trembling with horror at the sights they saw, kept going; communication was imperative between the police, the fire service, ambulances and the ARP volunteers. Firemen battled for hours with bombs and land mines exploding all around them. Volunteers helped lead people to safety, ambulance crews drove at top speed trying to save time lost by having to skirt fires and falling buildings. And still there was no let-up.

Johnny finally caught up with Mike in Banastre Street where, until earlier that night, an ARP post had stood. Now it was nothing more than rubble. He was clambering over a pile of bricks and dodging half a dozen stampeding terrified horses, some with their manes and tails on fire.

'Get something, Johnny! Anything that we can use as a lever!' Mike yelled. Sweat was pouring down his blackened face. His scorched uniform was covered in soot and dust and his hands were cut and bleeding.

'Will this do?' Johnny yanked at a long spar that had once been part of a doorframe.

'That warden over there said a wall collapsed and he's sure there are people underneath it. Did you find your da?'

'No, he's out, but the lads are with Mrs Weston. The pub's gone – well, it was burning like hell when I left. Tessa's OK and so is Elizabeth. They're all bloody terrified but who can blame them?'

'Push down on that end, I think I can prise one of these blocks up. Jesus! They made these buildings to last. These blocks weigh a ton!'

Johnny pushed down with his entire weight as Mike, the veins in his temples standing out with the effort, prised the corner of a square slab up. Johnny hung on to the lever and two other men scrambled across to give him a hand.

With a crack and a shower of dust the slab moved upwards sufficiently for Mike to see two bodies.

'Can you shine a torch down here?' he yelled up as he eased himself down into the space.

Johnny clambered down to give him a hand.

'Is that bloody slab safely out of the way?' Mike asked.

'Yes. Those two have moved it aside. Come on with the bloody light!' he called.

Bright torchlight swept the darkness, falling first on a split and jagged roof beam which had to a small degree protected the blackened, bloody faces of two men, and Mike felt himself sway. One was his father, the other Jack Harrison.

Chapter Twenty-Nine

He couldn't speak. He just stared in disbelief at the two half-buried bodies, arms flung above their heads as if they'd known and had tried to protect themselves. But there had been no protection, not even their tin hats, that could withstand the weight of the slabs of stone and the tons of bricks that had come crashing down. Johnny had to help Mike out of the crevice and he sat on the concrete slab, put his head in his hands and cried.

Johnny sat down beside him. He couldn't believe the ill luck that had led Mike to the very spot where his father had died. Suddenly he remembered how he'd felt the night his mam had been killed. It all came flooding back. The shock, the disbelief, the sorrow. He looked around him. How many more? he thought. How many more would die tonight? There was nothing anyone could do. He felt so helpless. He was surrounded by fiercely blazing buildings and still the planes droned overhead, clearly visible in the light from the buildings that incendiaries had set on fire. They couldn't take much more of this. The city and its people couldn't stand much more of this continuous bombardment.

He helped Mike gently to his feet. Together they would lift Frank and Jack over to a place of level ground, close their eyes, fold their hands across their chests and wait for an ambulance to take them to a church or church hall until they could be buried.

They did everything together, careless of their own safety, ignoring the inferno that surrounded them. Like a pair of mechanical figures they went through the motions, Mike barely aware of what he was doing. They sat on the kerb, bone-weary, eyes smarting, the slight burns on their hands beginning to sting.

'What . . . what am I going to tell Mam?' Mike asked brokenly of the lad who only hours earlier had saved his life.

'The truth. I . . . I only hope it was quick, and even if it wasn't, tell . . . tell her it was.'

Mike felt as though he himself had been crushed. 'And Elizabeth? Elizabeth . . .?'

'Oh, God!' Johnny realised the burden was doubly heavy for Mike. His father and Elizabeth's father too.

'I'll go to Elizabeth first. She'll have her mam and Nessie, and Delia's always been . . . stronger than my mam. Oh, God Almighty! Mam was in a terrible state when I left, how she's going to take . . . this, I don't know.'

'She'll cope, Mike, they all will. We're not beaten! We'll never be beaten!'

Mike looked at him. 'What about your da?'

Johnny shook his head. 'I can only hope and pray. Come on, get up, there's an ambulance coming now.

'Where will you take them to?' Johnny asked the driver, who looked as if he'd had no sleep for a week.

'The Royal. Mill Road's taken a direct hit, Walton's had a near miss, the Nurses' Home took the brunt of it, so has Broadgreen. They can't take any more casualties at Stanley Hospital and neither can the Northern. I wish to Christ I could get my hands on just one of those bastards! Pregnant women and babies! Bloody babies at Mill Road!'

Mike just nodded as he lifted the limp form of his father inside. A proper funeral would come later, if anyone survived to bury the dead.

It was with leaden feet and heavy hearts that both lads walked down Naylor Street, still ignoring every danger that surrounded them. They'd seen the worst.

'Do you want me to come too?'

Mike shook his head. He felt a bit more in control of himself now.

'You go and see Tessa. Tell her—'

'I will,' Johnny cut in firmly. Nevertheless he escorted Mike past his own house, still standing but soon to be wreathed in sorrow, up to the Harrisons' shop, through the kitchen, the floor of which was covered with broken glass and wrecked furniture and crockery, and to the door of the shelter in the yard. Then he just gripped Mike's shoulder in a gesture of support and turned away.

Mike stood there for a few seconds. There was no easy way to put this when he was feeling so broken himself.

As soon as she saw him Elizabeth tore herself from her mother's arms. 'Mike! Mike! Oh, thank God you're safe.'

For a second he held her close and then shook his head.

Delia gazed at him in bewilderment, and her heart began to beat faster. There was something wrong. She knew it.

Slowly Mike disentangled Elizabeth's arms and held her away from him.

'Elizabeth ... Mrs Harrison ... I've just come from Banastre Street.'

Delia was on her feet, pushing young Nessie aside. 'No! Oh, please God, no!'

Elizabeth's eyes were wide and full of fear.

'It's ... it's Mr Harrison and ... and my da. They're dead,' he choked.

'Da! My da ... and ... and yours ... dead?' Elizabeth couldn't take it in.

'Yes. A building fell. It would have been ... quick!' He couldn't hold back the tears. Reaching out for Elizabeth, he drew her to him and broke down.

Delia sat as though carved from stone, holding a sobbing Nessie. Mike felt similar racking sobs tear through Elizabeth as he clung to her. Well, their love was in the open now but he didn't care. Death was a great leveller.

Gradually Elizabeth's sobs diminished and he released her, gently propelling her to her mother who reached out and took her hand.

'I'll have to go now, Mrs Harrison. Mam doesn't know ... yet.'

'Oh, Lord have pity on us tonight, we ... we've all lost so ... so much.' Delia managed to keep her voice steady. Inside she was screaming for Jack but she had to try and stay calm for the sake of her children.

Mike stumbled back out into the street, knowing that the hardest part was yet to come.

When dawn came the raiders finally turned for home, the anti-aircraft batteries fell silent and the first rays of the sun pierced the cloud of smoke that hung over a city in ruins. In the middle of what was left of Derby Square the solitary statue of Queen Victoria stood untouched surveying the destruction.

For a radius of three-quarters of a mile surrounding

her there was hardly a building left standing. Along the waterfront and in the docks ships had been damaged and sunk; sheds, warehouses and their contents destroyed; dock communications interrupted; gates, basins and quaysides struck; cranes left as mangled, twisted lumps of metal – and still the *Malakand* burned.

The Head Post Office, the Central and Bank Exchange, the Mersey Dock buildings, Oceanic Buildings, India Buildings, George's Dock buildings and the Central Library had been badly hit. St Luke's Church at the top of a devastated Bold Street and the parish church of St Nicholas at the Pier Head were only two of dozens of churches that lay in ruins.

Never had the city suffered so much. And it was destined to go on suffering until that week was over and the last of the raiders dipped its wings over the waters of the Mersey on May 8. They never returned.

Eileen had taken it very badly. Neither Brenda, whose baby was nearly due, nor Maureen, now a quieter, more serious Maureen, could console her. She sobbed for hours on end until Brenda, at her wits' end, went to Delia for help. It seemed insensitive to worry Delia, but there was no one else. The rest of the neighbours, bombed out and homeless, were scattered all over the city.

'I'm so sorry to bother you at a time like this, Mrs Harrison, but you *know* what it's like. I don't. I . . . I . . . loved my da, we all did. Oh, he had his faults and there were always rows, but we loved him. But Mam . . . Mam's going to make herself really ill if she carries on like this. She'll lose her mind.'

Delia nodded. She'd spent long hours in tears herself as the raids had continued night after night. She couldn't believe that Jack had gone for ever. Oh, people thought she was strong but that strength had come from Jack. From his love for her and the two girls, from his guidance in business matters, from the security of his always being there, caring for them all in his quiet, unassuming way. Theirs had been a good marriage, but from now on she'd have to cope alone with . . . everything. She prayed that God would give her the strength.

Both men had been buried in St Anthony's churchyard, surrounded by the smouldering ruins that had cost them their lives. It had been a terrible day for them all. Mike, his own heart breaking, had supported Eileen's sagging figure throughout the mass. She was in such a state that Dr Duncan had been called and had given her a mild sedative.

'Just enough to get her through the day,' he'd said to Brenda as she had shown him out.

Delia had held both her daughters' hands, but Elizabeth, unable to stop the tears, looked frequently at Mike, trying to draw comfort from him.

Nessie and Maureen Flynn found it barely comprehensible. They were already in a state of constant terror because of the bombing; now they were heart-broken too. For Maureen it was worse. Her mother wasn't as strong as Delia appeared to be.

Father Walsh was worn out. He and Father Sharpe had had virtually no sleep for days. They did what they could to console their parishioners and had spent hours during the air raids helping the rescuers, giving Extreme Unction to the victims who were Catholic and praying just as earnestly over those who were not. And, witnessing so much suffering, Father Walsh had had a few doubts about the God he'd always believed in so fervently.

Remembering the old priest's strength, Delia knew she had to help her neighbour. 'I'll come up to her, Brenda. You should go home, luv, all this isn't good for you, not now. Your da wouldn't have wanted anything to happen to the baby.'

'How can I leave her like this, especially as our Mike's leave is nearly over?'

'You'll have to, Brenda. She'll come round eventually. It might be the best thing for her. There's still your Maureen to keep an eye on her.'

'That one hasn't got the sense of a two-year-old!' Brenda had declared vehemently.

Delia steeled herself for the visit. She might not be much of a housewife, but Eileen had always been a kind, caring mother and a loyal, loving wife, despite the frequent rows with Frank. Well, there'd be no more rows between them in this house, she thought wearily as she pushed open the front door.

Eileen was sitting in a chair by the range, her head in her hands, still sobbing.

Delia went over and took her hands. 'Eileen, luv, this has got to stop.'

'I . . . I . . . can't 'elp it.'

Delia reached out and held her. 'I know what you're going through, Eileen. God help me, I *know*. But for the sake of Brenda and the baby, for Maureen and young Harold, who's been so brave, you've *got* to pull yourself together. I've had to. Grieve alone, that's what I do. When the girls are in bed or when Elizabeth's at work and Nessie is at school.'

Eileen looked at her mystified. 'Work? School?'

'Yes. Everyone's even more determined now to keep things going. The troops still need ammunition and Elizabeth says each shell she fills, each anti-tank mine makes her feel she is doing something her da would be proud of. They got a bomb in the gardens of the Convent but Mother Superior said it will take more than that for her to close her doors. They all say a special prayer every day that soon the Anti-Christ, as she calls Hitler, will be defeated. Eileen, luv, would Frank want to see you like this? Would he want you to just give up? Be beaten down and defeated?'

Eileen shook her head.

'No and neither would . . . Jack.' It was so painful just to say his name aloud. 'You've got to think of Brenda now. She's due in a couple of weeks.'

'It's a mercy she 'asn't gone into labour already, what with . . . with . . . everything.' Eileen wiped her eyes and sniffed.

'Come on, I'll put the kettle on, there's something I want to talk to you about.'

For the first time since Frank's death there was a glimmer of interest in Eileen's red, puffy eyes. 'What?'

'Your Mike and our Elizabeth.'

'What . . . what about them?'

'I think they've been holding out on us.'

Eileen was very confused. ''Olding out?'

'Yes. I'd say they were more than just good friends.'

''As she said anything?'

'No, the little madam hasn't.' Delia managed a smile. 'But I'm going to get the truth out of her before he sails.'

Fresh tears sprang to Eileen's eyes. 'I don't want 'im to go. I couldn't stand to lose 'im too! Oh, 'e'll 'ave to stay at home. I can't manage.'

Delia sighed. 'He'll *have* to go. No one wants them to go, but it's their duty and they won't shirk it. They're all good lads. Now, why don't you start by tidying up a bit? Make a fuss of Brenda, Maureen and young Harold. Those young lads have really gone up in my estimation. Out in the thick of it, cycling all over the city with urgent messages. They all deserve medals.'

'Aye, but who'll give medals to the likes of us, Delia?'

'No one, so we'll just have to give ourselves a pat on the back, keep the home fires burning, like the song says, and make do with that.' Delia didn't notice the irony in her referring to the old World War One song when many of her neighbour's homes were now little more than ashes.

When Elizabeth returned from work Delia had made a huge effort and was cooking the evening meal on the fire in the range. Her gas cooker was useless, of course, as the gas supply was cut off.

'Right, I want some straight answers from you, miss.'

Elizabeth sat down. She was so weary now, but she wasn't alone in her troubles. Nearly everyone at work had suffered in some way. Mary Clarke who worked in her room had lost her father and grandfather and her home as well, but her mam had made her come to work. 'Fill as many of those shells as you can, girl,' Mrs Clarke had said.

'What kind of answers, Mam?'

'How long have you been seeing Mike?'

Elizabeth looked up at her mother and was surprised to see she wasn't annoyed. 'Seeing?'

'Courting, then?'

Elizabeth was too tired and heartsore for any more lies. 'Over a year. I . . . I love him, Mam. I won't give him up.'

Delia sat down at the table facing her. 'Did I say anything about giving him up?'

Elizabeth's eyes widened. 'You don't mind? You're not upset?'

'No. A couple of weeks ago I would have been very annoyed. I'd have been livid. But not any more. Losing your da has changed . . . everything. Who knows what tomorrow will bring? I don't, not any longer.' Delia couldn't stop her tears and Elizabeth got up and put her arms around her mother, incipient tears sparkling on her own lashes.

'Oh, Mam! Mam! Why did it have to be Da and Mr Flynn? Why couldn't they have bombed the flaming prison? Da was so good and kind and—'

'Elizabeth, don't go on! I can't stand it.'

'I'm sorry, Mam, truly I am. And . . . and Mike's due to leave in two days' time.'

'I know that too. I sat with Eileen this afternoon. Go and bring him down here.'

'Now?'

'Yes, now. I want to give you both my blessing and . . . this.' Delia slowly pulled off the small ruby and diamond ring from the third finger of her left hand. It was her own engagement ring. 'Hold out your hand.'

'Oh, Mam!'

'Go and get him, Elizabeth.'

Elizabeth smiled through the tears which had begun to flow in earnest. This was something she'd never expected, but after these last few days so many things seemed to have changed, her mother amongst them.

There was something that Tessa wanted to change too. The date of her wedding.

'How can I go ahead now?' she said to May.

'I know how you feel, luv, but, well, everything was planned, you've got your outfit and he'll be sailing very soon, I'm certain. They won't be left to kick their heels around here, not after the nights we've had.'

'But Elizabeth and Mike, it's terrible! I can't ask them to come to my wedding when they've both only just buried their fathers. I just can't. Mrs Flynn's in a terrible state and so is Elizabeth's mam.'

'Delia's always been able to cope and Eileen's a lot better. She's made their Brenda go home.'

'But it's all too soon, far too soon. I can't do it.'

'Tessa, do you want to marry Johnny?'

'Of course!'

'Then, for God's sake, marry him before he sails, like you planned. You've seen what can happen, without warning . . . People have had to face disaster. I know no one will mind, but if you're worried I'll go myself and ask Delia and Eileen. It was always going to be a very quiet "do".'

So Tessa had agreed. Both Delia and Eileen had admitted that it was the best thing to do. Even they would welcome the chance to put aside their grief and the harrowing sights for a couple of hours.

'At least you've got a church to be married in,' Elizabeth said when Tessa told her of their decision.

'I'm . . . I'm going to put my flowers on your da's grave. He was always good to me.'

Elizabeth nodded slowly, her heart heavy.

'I never thought your mam would have agreed to you and Mike getting engaged, let alone given you her ring!'

'No, neither did I, but she's changed. We've all changed.'

'It would be a miracle if we hadn't, with what we've gone through. When do you think you'll get married?'

'I don't know. We haven't really talked about it. We both felt it was too soon.'

'But you'll still be my bridesmaid and Mike will be best man?'

'Yes, if you don't mind your bridesmaid wearing black.'

'Of course not. I wouldn't have expected otherwise. Johnny's had to buy a suit. When the pub went up he lost everything. There's still some confusion over his uniform, getting a new one, I mean, to replace the one he lost. The one he was wearing is scorched and filthy dirty.'

'There's confusion everywhere you turn, but we'll get through it. If we broke down now we'd be letting everyone like . . . Da down. That's what Mam keeps telling us. I don't know how she keeps going. I hear her crying in bed at night and it's terrible. I cry myself and so does our Nessie, but poor Mam's been left to do everything.'

'Elizabeth, it's only natural,' Tessa consoled her friend. She'd long ago forgiven Delia her harsh words during the big row.

The church looked bare and cheerless. There were no flowers, except the few blooms Tessa carried and the flower in Johnny's buttonhole. Elizabeth was dressed in black, as were Delia, Eileen, Maureen and Nessie. Young Harold wore a black armband on the sleeve of his jacket, as did Eddie Doyle and his two young sons. Mike wore his uniform, the one he hadn't been wearing the night the *Malakand* had exploded. There was only immediate family present.

Father Walsh smiled tiredly at the young couple standing before him. A wedding was a nice change, even though there was sorrow and suffering on the faces of the wedding party. Tessa and Johnny, both of whom he'd baptised, looked tired too.

Tessa looked shyly up at Johnny. If only Mr Flynn and Mr Harrison were alive – and Ginny. But this was not a time for 'if only'. She concentrated on the priest's prayers and on the promises she was making to Johnny. She wished her mother could have been with her today.

It was over so suddenly, Elizabeth thought, as she took Mike's arm and followed the new Mrs Doyle and her husband down the aisle and out into the sunlight, trying to ignore the blackened wreckage that seemed to be everywhere they turned. She and Mike had consoled each other. Each knew what the other was going through. When they were alone together, after Delia and Nessie had gone to bed, they'd talked and cried and clung to each other. Mike had proved to be a comfort to Delia too. She especially appreciated that he'd been the person who had found Jack and had treated the older man's body with dignity and respect, which obviously Jack had been unaware of, but was important to Delia.

* * *

Tessa and Johnny had no honeymoon, just one night, Johnny's last before sailing, spent at Tessa's house. May and Richie had given them their bedroom. The joy they discovered in each other that night would have to console them through the long separation to come.

The following day Tessa, Elizabeth, Delia, Eileen and Eddie Doyle had gone to see the boys off. Eileen was happier than she'd been for a long time. Brenda now had a baby son and was going to call him Francis Joseph after his two grandfathers, now both deceased.

'We won't ever forget Da now, Mam, not when we've got little Frank.' Brenda had smiled through her tears as she placed the tiny bundle in her mother's arms.

At the dockside Tessa clung to her new husband. 'Promise me you'll take care! Don't go doing anything stupid. I don't want a dead hero.'

'I'll do my duty, Tess, but I promise I won't do anything daft. I'll be back before you know it.' He tried to sound cheerful. God knew *when* they would get back.

Mike had hugged and kissed his mother and sister and then turned to Elizabeth. 'You take care of yourself.'

She clung to him. 'Oh, Mike, I don't want you to go! What if they come again?'

'You'll come through it. You're a born survivor, Elizabeth Harrison. And when I get back I'm going to remedy that.'

'What?'

'Your name. Harrison. There's going to be a new Mrs Flynn before the summer's over. If your mam will give her permission.'

'Nothing would please me more,' Delia said, overhearing him.

The loud *whoop-whoop* sound, the signal for every man to get aboard, startled them all. It was a sound made only by naval vessels, merchant ships still held to the three long blasts on their steam whistles.

With a last kiss on Tessa's cheek Johnny followed Mike down to the Landing Stage and they both turned to wave before separating to board their respective ships. Soon the naval escort would depart to meet up with the convoy assembling somewhere beyond the Mersey Bar.

Elizabeth linked her arm through Tessa's. Her emotions were in turmoil. This was her happiest moment since her da had been killed, for Mike had publicly declared his intention of marrying her, but of course it was tinged with sadness. She knew she'd never stop praying for either of them. Her da's soul and Mike's safety.

The further behind they left the boys the more their spirits plummeted. They all felt dispirited as they walked from the tram stop and around the corner into Naylor Street, where one of the neighbours was keeping an eye on the shop.

'What's that?' Nessie cried, pointing to a big black shiny car.

'It's a car,' Maureen Flynn answered.

'I know that, silly, but it's outside the shop, Mam! No one's ever seen a car like that around here before. Oh, I hope it's not more bad news.'

'We'd better find out who it belongs to, then,' Delia answered, quickening her steps. But as she drew nearer to the shop a figure emerged from inside and she stopped dead.

'Mam! Mam, what's the matter?' Elizabeth cried, tugging at her mother's sleeve.

'I don't believe it! I don't believe it!'

437

They all looked mystified and then Delia ran forward and into the arms of the plump, smiling, well-dressed woman.

'It's yer Aunty Margaret. It *is*!' Eileen cried. 'She's hardly changed at all!'

The two women were laughing and crying at the same time until Eileen interrupted them.

'I never ferget a face. It's little Maggie Sullivan as was.'

'Eileen Flynn!' Margaret cried, still with a faint trace of her Liverpudlian accent. 'I'd have known you anywhere.' She kissed Eileen on the cheek and hugged her. Eileen wrinkled her nose appreciatively at the smell of expensive perfume that wafted around the other woman.

'Oh, this really does call for a bit of a celebration. I think I can manage some biscuits and tea,' Delia cried, still unable to take in the fact that her sister, who had gone to America twenty years ago, was now standing beside her.

'Delia, keep them. I've got cookies – sorry, biscuits, cakes, candies and the Lord alone knows what else in my luggage. I thought you'd need them.'

Elizabeth and Nessie were struck dumb. They'd never expected to see 'Aunty Margaret' in the flesh, never mind here in their street and now in their home.

Everyone stared at her as she seated herself in the chair by the range, taking in her expensive clothes and hair-do, the make-up, the manicured nails and the two rings she wore, both of which sparkled brightly. She wore nylons too, Elizabeth noted, and she had a big leather handbag that she called a 'purse'.

Delia kept touching her as if to reassure herself that this wasn't an apparition, it really *was* her sister.

'How in the name of God did you get here?' she demanded when everyone was settled with a cup of tea.

'By ship,' Margaret answered, taking a sip of tea. It seemed to have a sort of 'smoky' taste to it, but she'd been away for so long she couldn't really remember what 'the great British cuppa' was like.

'I thought no one was carrying passengers now.'

'Oh, they will for a consideration, but they won't take any responsibility for your safety. "There'll be no compensation for the family," they told me, quite firmly. "What family?" I told them back.'

Delia was astounded. 'You came over with a convoy?'

'Sure did. It was pretty scary at times, too. They were a grand bunch of guys though. They nicknamed me "the unsinkable Molly Brown".' Margaret laughed.

'Why?' Elizabeth asked.

'Oh, after that American woman who was on board the *Titanic*. She made it. She was quite a character, so I hear tell.'

'But why did you come? I don't mean I'm not overjoyed to see you.'

Margaret's expression changed and she took another sip of tea. 'Well, I read in the papers and saw on the newsreels what's been going on over here and I thought, Maggie Van Holste, this is not the place to be right now. Your place is over there with what family you've got. But, Holy Mary, was I ever surprised ... No, that's not what I mean: *shocked* at what they've done to the place.'

Delia nodded. She wished Margaret had let her know of her imminent arrival in some way. 'It's been ... unimaginable. You must have missed Elizabeth's letter. Jack and Eileen's Frank are ... dead. They were out there during the bombing and a wall . . . fell on them.' Delia fought to control herself and she heard Eileen sniff.

'Oh, no! If I'd only known, Delia!' Although very shocked Margaret pulled herself together. There'd be time later to talk about Jack and she could see Eileen was upset.

'We've just come back from seeing Eileen's lad Mike, our Elizabeth's fiancé, and Johnny Doyle from the Globe go to sea, to pick up another convoy.'

'So, congratulations are in order, Elizabeth.'

Elizabeth smiled at her aunt. 'It's been a very bad time.'

'I can see that for myself. It looked like something from an H. G. Wells novel as we came up river. I just couldn't believe it.' Margaret put the thoughts from her mind – for now. Later she would tell Delia how unprepared she'd been for the reality and what she intended to do about it.

She addressed herself to young Harold. 'Now, young man, go out to the car and tell the driver to bring in my trunks and we'll have a real treat of a tea. Do you still call it tea? I've gotten used to calling it dinner.'

'We have that in the middle of the day,' Harold ventured. He'd never met anyone like this woman who spoke with a strange accent and had sailed across the Atlantic on a cargo ship and who seemed to have plenty of money and food.

'I remember now. Dinner is at lunchtime and tea is at dinnertime. I've forgotten how long I've been away.'

'How long do you intend to stay?' Delia asked, thinking her sister was well named by the crew of that ship. This 'Molly' was pretty unsinkable too.

Margaret settled back in the chair. 'For ever if needs be. I've put the house up for rent. I can sell it if I need to and get a good deal.'

'You mean you've left that beautiful house and all those luxuries to come to . . . this?' Delia was astounded.

'I told you, family comes first, and by the look of things you need all the help you can get.'

Delia broke down and her sister went to comfort her. Margaret had been right. She was needed here, and so was her money.

Chapter Thirty

There were no more raids and people started to pick up the threads of their lives again. Margaret van Holste made such a difference. She had a way of cutting through red tape and demolishing the petty officials who crossed her path. She had brought with her food and clothing, all of which was swooped upon with cries of delight by both her sister's family and the Flynns, for she had taken pity on them and now included Eileen, Maureen and Harold as extensions of her own family. They were still all 'getting by' though, as she put it. There were things that even she couldn't put right or obtain.

She'd had a serious talk with her niece and had been surprised that Elizabeth was so mature for her age.

'I suppose it's the war,' Elizabeth said.

'I always thought that girls back home were precocious, but half of them would think themselves hard done by if they couldn't have a bath or shower, never mind having to resort to gravy browning and the like instead of nylons, and being allowed only four inches of water in the tub and having to go into the yard to "go to the bathroom" as they call it. What's wrong with "lavatory" I don't know.'

'But they haven't gone through what we have.'

'I know, child. But one day it will be over and what will you do then?'

'I don't know. I haven't thought about it. We take each day, each week as it comes.'

443

'Of course you'll marry Mike, and in the best wedding gown that money can buy, but what then?'

'I . . . I . . . suppose I'll go back to hairdressing, if there're any salons still open.'

'You do well at it, I've watched you.'

'I never finished my apprenticeship.'

'Does that matter so much?'

'I don't suppose so now.'

'Well then, start thinking about having your own salon.'

'Me! I'm not even trained!' Elizabeth had cried.

'You can employ someone who is and learn from them.'

Elizabeth had shaken her head. She couldn't seem to get her aunt to understand that things were different here; she just couldn't snap her fingers and get everything taken care of. They were fighting for their very lives. America wasn't at war with anyone, although they supplied money and arms. And what would Mike think about her having her own business? What kind of a job would he get when it was over? He'd had no chance to start evening classes before they were suspended for the duration. She'd told her aunt she would think about it.

Margaret then turned her attention to her sister and younger niece.

'Will you keep the shop going?' she asked.

'What else can I do? We had a bit put by for emergencies, but I . . . I used it for Jack's funeral. I've no other source of income, apart from what Elizabeth earns in that factory.'

'What about Nessie?'

'What about her?'

'What does she intend to do when she leaves the Convent? She's a bright girl.'

Delia smiled. 'She's had a very expensive education, thanks to you.'

'When all this is finally over – and please God we'll all live to see the day – would you both consider coming back home with me? Nessie could finish her training there and teach.'

'And what would I do?'

Margaret stared at her with mild surprise. 'Why, live with me. There's plenty to keep you occupied. I'm on the committees of several societies and charities. You'd enjoy it, Delia.'

'I couldn't live off you.'

'Holy smoke, Delia, why not? You're my sister and Lars left me a lot of money. And I don't have anyone to share things with, simple things like taking tea and reminiscing. I miss the company of my own family. Will you think about it? We'd have a good life.'

'What about Elizabeth?'

'I've already spoken to her. She won't leave and neither will Mike, not when Eileen's on her own without a man to sort things out for her. So I'll buy her a hairdressing salon.'

'Margaret, you just seem to be able to . . .'

'To what?'

'To wave a magic wand and make things right. But it's not as easy as that. Liverpool, battered though it is, will always be home. I don't know if Nessie or me could settle anywhere else.'

'Well, we'll see. Will I put it to Nessie?'

'No, let me do it. It'll be the best way.'

Nessie, to everyone's surprise, thought it the best idea she'd ever heard of. America! America, where everything

445

was so new and modern and up to date, like you saw in the pictures. Maybe she'd qualify for one of their colleges and all the social events that she heard went with it. Girls and boys went to the same schools over there and mixed freely and there were marvellous clothes and no war! Oh, yes, she'd love to go, even if Elizabeth and her mam didn't.

'It will be to live, Nessie, not just for a holiday.'

'I know that, Mam, but I think it'll be the best thing for both of us. Apart from Elizabeth, what is there to stay here for?'

For your da's grave and all the memories, Delia thought. But it was so early yet. This war could still go on for years and years.

Mike was on watch. He stood with Macintosh on the bridge, scanning the horizon and the sea with binoculars. The weather was bad for the time of the year, but then the great Western Ocean was always unpredictable, which made it the most dangerous of them all. A cold drizzle was falling. The sea was heavy, breaking over *Juno*'s bows, and the wind from the south-south-west was threatening to develop into a full gale. They were well into the danger zone, some sixty miles north of the coast of Ireland. Ahead of them, strung out, was the convoy. They must be close to where the *Empress of Britain* had gone down and a shiver ran through him, but he dismissed it as superstition. Macintosh had already informed him as they'd sailed into Liverpool Bay where the wreck of the *Ellan Vannin* – the Isle of Man mail ship – lay, a watery tomb, for all on board had perished. He'd also said he would point out where the *Titanic* had sunk.

'Christ, Chief! I'll be taking to the boats and rowing back!'

he'd retorted and Macintosh had grinned sardonically.

'We're in for a wild night, laddie,' the older man said ominously. He delighted in trying to upset the enlisted men. The ship was indeed beginning to plunge and strain as the strength of the wind increased.

'Any sign of the convoy? Darkness will be on us soon.'

'Faintly, sir.'

'Bloody fool merchantmen! Can they no' follow instructions! They'll be scattered by dawn in this weather and have nae protection at all.'

A huge wave broke over *Juno*'s plunging bows.

'Look! Look, far over to port!' Mike yelled, pointing to where a huge column of water rose in the air, followed by a terrific explosion.

'God ha' mercy on them! It's a tanker, she'll go down by her bow, she isnae full. She's top heavy.'

Mike watched in silence, peering through the binoculars and the curtain of drizzle. It was the first time he'd ever seen a ship sink. There had been no warning. Not a sight nor a glimpse of the U-boat.

'Is there anything we can do, sir? Anything?'

'No. They'll no' survive for long in this water and those that do, well, maybe the U-boat will pick them up. Some of the time they do. I'll gie their Navy their due, they're no' as evil as their Army.'

'Or Air Force,' Mike added. Nothing was now visible except a few bits of wreckage. It sobered him considerably.

The weather got worse as what passed for daylight began to fade until, scanning the sea, Mike yelled and cast the binoculars aside. 'It's *Hercules*! *Hercules* has been hit, sir!'

'Gie me those things!' Macintosh demanded and Mike

passed him the binoculars. His heart was pounding. Johnny! Johnny was on that ship!

'Can't we turn back, sir? For God's sake can't we turn and do something? I've a mate, more like a brother he is, that's on *Hercules*.'

'There's nae turning back, lad, ye know that. Only the old man can gie that order and he willnae give it.'

Mike grabbed the binoculars and began to peer at the frigate. Smoke and flames were coming from her stern and she was listing badly to port. His cry was like that of a wounded and maddened animal as he watched another torpedo find its mark and *Hercules* sank further down by the bow. She was almost vertical now and he could just about see figures jumping into the sea from her disappearing Boat Deck. It must have been impossible to lower any boats. Those that weren't on fire were plunging down with her – as was Johnny! Johnny who had saved his life the night the *Malakand* had been hit. His best mate, and there wasn't a single thing he could do about it. He was fighting for his self-control, knowing the senior man would put him on a charge if he broke down.

There was a dull thud, but he took no notice, his gaze fixed on the foundering *Hercules*. Then *Juno* shuddered and another huge column of water erupted high into the air. The cruiser listed to starboard, sending him and Macintosh sprawling.

'Torpedo! We've been hit!' Macintosh yelled.

Everyone looked tired, Elizabeth thought when she went into the kitchen. Mam was out in the shop, trying to tidy things in the darkness. Nessie was diligently poring over her books and her aunt was writing a letter.

'Sit down at the table and I'll give you your tea. It's in the oven.' Margaret got up and bent over the cooker.

'I can't see why Mam has to try and keep that place tidy, there's not much in it and it's dark, she can't see what she's doing.'

'I've told her the same myself, Elizabeth, but I think keeping busy takes her mind off . . . things.'

Elizabeth nodded and looked without enthusiasm at the meal of Woolton pie and a meagre portion of mashed potato. The pie took its name from the Minister of Food; it was made entirely from vegetables and tasted terrible. But food was so scarce now that no one ever complained. As she ate she thought of Mike. She really shouldn't complain, everything they had was brought in by convoy and he was out there somewhere, risking his life to make sure the food and arms and fuel *did* get through.

After tea she helped to wash up and then sat, worn out, on the sofa as Margaret switched on the wireless set she'd bought. Sat on the top of the food press, it cheered up the long evenings.

'Oh, good, *ITMA*. Delia, come in and listen, luv. I love this. It cheers me up no end,' Margaret said, fiddling with the knobs. Both Delia and Elizabeth nodded and Nessie closed her books. The programme brought smiles to their faces and for a short time they forgot their troubles, until it finished and the cynical, upper-class voice of William Joyce, known as Lord Haw Haw, came clearly over the airwaves.

'Germany calling! Germany calling!'

'Oh, I hate that man!' Delia said with venom.

'Everybody does, he's a traitor. Sitting somewhere in

Germany and broadcasting lies and German propaganda!' Margaret replied. 'I wonder what it'll be tonight? More cities flattened? The people of London all waving white flags? The man's a fool as well as a traitor.'

Elizabeth wasn't taking much notice, she always tried to ignore it.

'Soon you will be getting telegrams. Telegrams from the Admiralty. You all know the type I mean. "The Admiralty regrets . . ." ' The voice was full of malice and contempt but they couldn't help beginning to pay more attention to him. Elizabeth looked worriedly at her mother.

'Take no notice, the man's a liar.' Margaret tried to calm her sister and her niece.

'Unfortunately for you poor deluded fools, the Admiralty *does* regret to announce the loss of three of your ships from one of your pathetic little convoys. The *City of Glasgow*, a cargo ship, and two of the escorting warships: the *Hercules* and the *Juno*. So be prepared. You have been warned. Why don't you all give in or capitulate . . .' The rest of the sneering abuse was cut short as Margaret got up and switched the wireless off. Elizabeth was staring at the set with horror.

'No! No!' she cried. She jumped up, tore her coat from the hook and, after a struggle, pulled off the brooch and threw it into the fire. 'It *was* an omen! It *was* unlucky!' she cried before she ran out.

She found Tessa in tears, being comforted by May and Richie.

'Tessa! Oh, Tessa, have you heard? Did you listen to *that* man? Both . . . both of them . . . gone!' She burst into tears and both May and Tessa put their arms around her; all three of them clung together in shock and desolation.

'Don't believe the daylights out of that bloody traitor!' Richie tried to console them.

'But he always knows the names of the ships, Richie,' May said shakily.

'I'll give you that, luv, but they could be just picked at random.'

'But they *were* on convoy duty and he must get the information from somewhere. From their U-boats, probably,' May replied.

'All we can do is to wait. We'll know one way or another when the telegrams do arrive,' was all Richie could say.

When Elizabeth went home, red-eyed and exhausted, Delia got up and put her arms around her.

'Elizabeth, luv, don't give up hope!'

'Oh, Mam! First Da and now . . .'

'I know. I know,' Delia soothed her. 'But you mustn't believe everything you hear.'

'Mr O'Leary said that, but most of the time it's . . . true.'

Margaret shook her head at her sister. The time she had spent here had given her an inkling of what they'd all been through and this latest blow made her more determined than ever to take Delia and Nessie – and now it looked like Elizabeth too – back to New Jersey. And she'd go soon. It would be dangerous, but she'd done it before and she'd do it again, just to get them out of this terrible predicament they were in, where grief and suffering were always present.

'Get to your boat station, Flynn, we're going down!' Macintosh had shouted but without any panic in his voice.

Every light had been extinguished and from the angle of the deck Mike had realised they were beginning to settle by

451

the stern. Bloody U-boats! Just how many of them were there? He had fished in his pocket for his electric torch. Other small flickers of light could now be seen in the darkness. He knew the drill, but he'd hoped he'd never have to go through it.

Four boats had been lowered, the others had been smashed by the column of water. In pitch darkness they had managed to unhook the huge blocks. He heard someone yell, 'Mind the blocks!' and then they were plunging downwards, frighteningly close to the dark shape of the sinking cruiser. They hit the head of a breaker then plunged down into the trough, taking in water. They all knew the danger they faced and strained to pull away, otherwise they'd be dragged into the maelstrom as *Juno* went down.

He saw glimpses of the lights from the other boats but the great combers roaring down from windward were too steep to enable them to stay together. The sole thought in all their minds was survival.

The only officer in the boat was Macintosh and as the wind rose to gale force and the spray flew over them in sheets, he decided the only thing they could do was ride to a sea anchor and hope for a break in the weather.

The heavy seas filled the boat and they had to bale continuously. Everyone was cold and saturated, many of them were sea-sick, but there was no time to feel terror at the sight of the mountainous walls of water that bore down on them. Unless they continued to bale they would be swamped.

'Mr Macintosh, sir, the sea anchor's gone!' someone yelled.

'Lash three oars together, laddie, they'll have tae do!' Macintosh yelled back.

To Mike it seemed as though there were hours and hours of baling. Time had no meaning and there was no sense of place either. His brain was sending only one message to his leaden limbs: Bale! Bale! Bale! It was with a feeling of detached surprise that he realised that the light he had thought he had seen in the distance was the breaking of a wan dawn, struggling through the tattered clouds.

The wind and the sea had abated a little and he slumped back against the boat's gunwale. The indomitable instinct to stay alive had brought him through so far. They were up to their knees in water. The faces of the men were grey and haggard. Four of the crew were dead from their injuries and exposure and Mr Macintosh recited the Burial Service then committed their bodies to the sea.

'There's nae use trying to sail, we'll ride tae that improvised sea anchor and hope. The best advice I can gie ye is to pray!'

Mike dropped his head and tried to remember the formal decades of the Rosary but couldn't. All he could remember of the Lord's Prayer, learned when he was four years old, were the words 'Our Father which art in heaven'.

These he repeated over and over to himself until he heard the faint cry and looked up.

'There's something out there, sir,' a young rating shouted.

'Where? I canna see anythin'.'

'Just to starboard, sir.'

'It's wreckage, just a spar of wood.'

Mike stared hard at the object. 'No, sir, it's not! There's someone clinging to it.'

'All right then, pull toward it. Come on wi' ye, lads, pull together!' Macintosh shouted.

It was heavy going. The boat hardly seemed to be moving, Mike thought as he strained at the oars, but eventually the jagged piece of wood was clearly visible and so was the face of the man clinging to it, eyes closed, skin waxy and lips blue. He didn't seem to be alive. Frantically Mike lunged out as far as he could and caught the splintered keel and pulled it towards them. They might not survive – any of them – but at least they'd go together. For, against all the odds, the man he heaved into their own boat was Johnny Doyle.

Neither Tessa nor Elizabeth slept that night and in the morning they got up, weary, grief-stricken and sick with worry.

'I won't believe it until I get a telegram, I just *won't*,' Tessa said firmly as they made their way home after their twelve-hour shift.

'Then neither will I. But . . . but at least the telegram will come to you, I'll have to go to Mrs Flynn's.'

'How is she taking it?'

'The same as we are. Mam went in last night to tell her and she just broke down again. Like we did. Like we've been fighting all day to keep from breaking down.'

'Did anyone else at work, the other three in your room, know any more?'

Elizabeth shook her head. 'No. I asked but no one has any relatives on either ship. Oh, Tessa, I don't know what I'll do if . . .'

'I don't either,' said Tessa quietly. 'But it's worse for you, you've already lost your da. And Johnny and I did at least spend one night together.'

Tears sprang into Elizabeth's eyes. Yes, Tessa had had one

wonderful night; by comparison, she'd had nothing.

They agreed to inform each other immediately there was any news and both went into their respective homes bowed down with worry.

Elizabeth ate the meal put in front of her, and answered all questions briefly; her mother and aunt looked at each other with concern. They were both helpless. Everyone was. All they could do was wait and that was the hardest part of all. Not knowing.

They had all decided to go to bed early.

'We're all worn out, we might as well go to bed and try and snatch a few hours' sleep, especially you, Elizabeth,' Margaret urged.

'I'll stay down here for a bit longer, if you don't mind?'

'Of course we don't mind, but I think you'd be better coming up, you have to get up so early.'

'Oh, please, Mam? Just a bit longer?' Elizabeth begged.

Delia nodded. She couldn't force Elizabeth to do anything.

When they'd all gone Elizabeth just sat, staring into the fire. If *Juno* had really been sunk, it didn't necessarily mean he had ... drowned. And the same went for Johnny. She wondered if Tessa had thought of that. They had lifeboats; they drilled for such eventualities.

Then that moment of hope had gone. Suppose he had not been able to get into a boat? How long could he survive in the waters of the North Atlantic? They were bitterly cold at any time of year. Even if they had launched the lifeboats, what if no one spotted them? She pushed the thought from her mind. She *had* to hope. She *couldn't* give up on him.

She'd fallen into a light doze when the sound of the doorknocker woke her with a start. It took her a few minutes to gather her wits. Who in God's name was it? It was almost eleven o'clock.

Tessa was standing on the step. Over her nightdress she clutched a shawl and in her hand was the dreaded telegram.

'Oh, Tessa! Tessa! No!'

Tessa smiled. 'It's all right, Elizabeth. They're both safe. I called next door to see if Mrs Flynn had heard anything.'

'They're safe! Both of them?'

Tessa nodded. 'It was true, both ships were sunk, but they got away somehow and were picked up by an American cargo ship. Look.' She shoved the telegram into Elizabeth's hand.

Elizabeth switched on the light, scanned the few lines. She leaned against the doorframe, suddenly feeling weak, and then they clung to each other. They were weeping again, but this time it was for joy.

Epilogue

1944

Tessa and Elizabeth sat on the step of number twelve, Naylor Street. They'd both continued to suffer agonies of worry when Mike and Johnny were away, but it seemed that Captain Johnny Walker with his 'hunter-killer' warships was winning his battle with the U-boats. Things were still hard. Everything was on ration but they'd all got used to that and to the blackout, although there had been no further raids on Liverpool.

Elizabeth and Mike had been married when Mike had eventually got home. It had been a much grander wedding than Tessa's. Margaret had paid for everything and they were all astounded when she managed to procure food and drink that hadn't been seen for years. She'd also paid for the two-day honeymoon in Llandudno's most exclusive hotel.

Now they all knew that something was going on, something big. It was rumoured that a huge invasion force was being assembled, ready to cross the Channel to liberate France. Bombing raids on Germany itself had increased and now many of their towns and cities were in ruins. America had finally come into the war when the Japanese had bombed the naval base at Pearl Harbor, totally unprovoked and without any warning. Now, at last, in May of 1944, after nearly five years of war, the end seemed to be in sight. At least they prayed it was.

Tessa and Elizabeth were making the most of the long light evenings. They both loved these minutes at the end of the day. In the warmth of late spring they could relax after the long hours they still worked.

'Who would ever have thought things could have changed so much from the day you moved in here?' Elizabeth mused.

'I know. It's so difficult to believe. It all seems to belong to another age.'

'It was. Thank God we didn't know what was in store for us. Do you ever think of him? Your Colin?'

'Occasionally. Usually when I think of Mam.'

'Sometimes, when I catch a glimpse of someone who looks like Ginny, I have to stop myself calling after her. Yet it's so long ago now.'

'I know May still thinks about her and grieves. I suppose she always will. Sometimes she takes flowers to that little bit of land.'

'I wouldn't have wanted her to have gone through everything we've faced. She was so quiet and timid,' said Elizabeth.

They both fell silent for a few minutes, memories of Ginny filling their minds.

'So, when are your Mam and Nessie going then?'

'Next month. Mam's given notice to the landlord. I can hardly believe I'll be on my own then!'

'Do you think you've really made the right decision?'

'Yes. One day Mike will come home for good. He'll probably get a decent job, being an officer now.'

'I hope Johnny will too and I hope we'll be able to find

somewhere to rent, even if it is just one room to start with. I
... I ... wouldn't feel easy here. You know how thin the
walls are.'

Elizabeth smiled. She knew what Tessa meant.

Suddenly Tessa looked stricken.

'What's the matter?'

'Mam. I promised her I'd make something better of
myself. Be a stewardess.'

'You can keep part of your promise. You could get an
office job.'

'Me?'

'Yes, you. It's not *that* hard. Sometimes it can be really
boring. It would help if you learned to type.'

'Where in the name of God would I do that?'

'There's that Commercial School in Slater Street. Machin
and Harper's. I know you have to pay but you could save up.
Then you're bound to get a job. It's their policy – if I
remember rightly – to find you one. One of the customers
told me when I worked at Hill's.'

'Will you go back there?'

'No. Bold Street's in ruins, especially at the top end by St
Luke's. I'm to have my own salon, so Aunty Margaret says.
She'll leave me the money.'

'You'll miss them terribly.'

'I know I will, but maybe one day we could go over
and visit them. It will be better for Mam. She can leave
behind all the bad memories. And our Nessie can't wait to
go.'

'And talking of Nessie . . .' Tessa pointed down the road.

When she reached them, Nessie grinned. 'You can't sit on
that bloody wall now, it's gone. Along with the tannery. So

the two of you sit on the step instead.' Tessa and Elizabeth both laughed.

'I've always envied you – I never had a best friend. And now my life's going to be so different.'

'You're still going, though?' Tessa asked.

'Yes.'

'Well then, you'll make lots of friends.'

'Maybe I will when I get to New Jersey.'

Elizabeth gazed past her sister and into the far distance as if trying to remember everything.

'Tessa and I have always been close. We've come through poverty, hardship, death and destruction, terror, despair and relief and happiness. War has made no difference to us.'

Tessa smiled and took Elizabeth's hand. 'No, the ties will never be severed.'

Headline hopes you have enjoyed reading THE TIES THAT BIND and invites you to sample the beginning of Lyn Andrews' heart-warming new saga, TAKE THESE BROKEN WINGS, available now in Headline paperback . . .

Prologue

June, 1916

'Will it die, Da?'

George Peckham squatted down so he was on the same level as his little daughter and picked up the injured and frightened blackbird fluttering feebly in Hannah's cupped hands.

'I've never told you a lie, Hannah, have I?'

The child shook her head while slowly stroking the soft, dark feathers.

'I reckon you're old enough for the truth and sometimes the truth can hurt, luv. I'm afraid it *will* die. Look, its wing is broken and if it can't fly then it can't look for food or be with its friends. The ground isn't a safe place for birds.'

'But couldn't we feed it, Da?' There was a catch in her voice and she gazed at him pleadingly.

George sighed and passed the bird back to her. Hannah was so like her mam. At the age of six she was a beauty, just as Jane had been. She had Jane's pale complexion that looked like alabaster in some lights. Her hair was very dark brown, as were her eyes that were fringed with long thick lashes which cast a half moon shadow on her cheeks when she was asleep. Fine-boned and petite, you could always tell what kind of a mood Hannah was in by her eyes. Sometimes they were full of mischief and laughter, at others hard with determination and stubbornness, but now her eyes were luminous with incipient tears that threatened to brim over and trickle down her cheeks.

'There'd be no point, luv. Even I can't mend broken wings. Best leave it by the wall, we've a long way to go.' He didn't say it would be kinder to wring the tiny neck and put an end to its misery. Things were bad enough for her without adding to her confusion and unhappiness.

He stood up, brushed the dust from his uniform and looked down Victoria Terrace. It would be the last he'd see of it for a long time, and his spirits plummeted further.

Once the three-storied houses had been the very comfortable homes of the well-off. They were smaller than those in Upper Husskinson Street, Upper Frederick Street, Rodney Street or Faulkner Square, but had been well maintained in earlier years. They were a sorry sight now though. The decorative iron railings up to the once-impressive front doors were unsteady, twisted and rusting. The glass fanlights above the doors were broken and fly-speckled. The paint was peeling from the front doors, the steps were worn and broken and now families crowded every room: the cellar, the attic, the bedrooms and the downstairs reception rooms. But number ten had until today been home for himself and Hannah, and just eighteen months ago it had been home for Jane too. Jane, the pretty, shy, quiet little Welsh girl he'd fallen head over heels in love with. The girl he'd married and who had carried and lost two babies before Hannah had been born and had thrived.

Hannah was still clutching the blackbird. He could see there was *no* way the determined little girl would simply leave it to its fate. 'Oh well, take it if you must,' he capitulated. 'But hold it gently but firmly.' He slung his kit bag over one shoulder and pulled the cap bearing the badge of the 20th King's Liverpool Regiment – the Liverpool 'Pals' – slightly forward to shade his eyes. Then he took her hand. The utter dejection and trepidation he felt at having to leave her weighed heavily on him, as did the fear of what faced him now.

Hannah stared up at her father who was dressed in clothes she'd never seen him wear before. They were stiff and scratchy things too.

'Why do I have to go and live with Cousin Gwyneth, Da? Why can't I stay with Mrs Sweeney? Why do you have to go?' He had already tried to explain these things to her but she didn't really understand. She knew her Mam was in heaven. She remembered her Mam and had cried for her to come back, for Mam had never shouted or smacked her. Mam had always seemed to be smiling and she'd sung too, in a language Hannah didn't understand. Until she got sick and the angels had come to take her to heaven.

Da had told her he had to go to a place far away from Liverpool, across the sea, to help with the war but she didn't understand about war and battles.

'Hannah, luv, I've told you why. I have to go away and Mrs Sweeney's got her hands full with all her kids and there's no room.'

'But Cousin Gwyneth only has a tiny cottage, you said so.'

George sighed. 'I know, but it's not crowded out like Mrs Sweeney's. It's family you're going to. Your mam's family.' He squeezed her hand trying to reassure her but he himself needed reassuring that he *would* come back for her. The war was going badly.

Hannah liked Mrs Sweeney and the young Sweeneys; there were half a dozen of them but the six-year-old twins Harry and Lily were her friends, though often they would only play with each other. Hannah held the bird to her and felt its little heart fluttering with fear.

'I'm going to look after it, Da,' she said firmly. 'I'm going to feed it and keep it warm and make it better, then it'll be *my* friend.'

George nodded. If that's what she wanted then he wasn't going to argue. It would die anyway in a couple of days.

When he'd been conscripted he'd folded the papers up, placed them on the overmantle and then despair had overwhelmed him. How could he leave her? She was just six and her mam had only been dead a year and a half. Of course the neighbours had been great, as they always were in times of trouble. Between them they'd nursed Jane and kept the home going when he wasn't there. When he was out at work they'd taken it in turns to look after Hannah. His wage from the small iron foundry down at the docks had been just enough to keep them; now his Army pay would all be sent to Cousin Gwyneth for Hannah's keep, apart from a few shillings for his tobacco and Rizla cigarette papers.

Just who to leave Hannah with had been a hard decision to make. Everyone in the street was short of money and space, even though all the lads and most of the men were away fighting. Some of the girls and women were now taking the jobs the men had left and there was a bit more money in some pockets, but there were many people who were still living in dire poverty, families with as many as fourteen children to feed and clothe. So he'd sat for hours deciding who would be able to care for Hannah and then he'd written to Jane's relations.

He knew Hannah's choice would be to stay with the Sweeneys and he knew Ada and Tom and their brood would welcome her, but Ada's idea of cleanliness was far from his, and there were always rows and fights going on, mainly due to the fact that Tom was fond of his ale, though there was never any violence. Anyway, Tom would be following him to France in a few weeks.

When he'd told Ada of his plans for Hannah's future she'd folded her arms across her bosom and looked concerned. 'What in God's name do yer want to send 'er there for?' she'd asked.

'They're family, Ada, and you've got your hands more than full with this lot.' He'd gestured around the room with his hand. The twins were under the table, a favourite refuge, while their elder brother Arthur was tormenting them, trying to get them to come out. Sam and Gerald were arguing over who should have the cricket ball they'd had the stroke of fortune to find and Kate was chanting a poem she had to learn at the top of her voice, totally oblivious to everything.

'Will youse lot shurrup? I can't 'ear me own voice!' Tom roared.

'Gerrout from under that table the pair of youse or you'll go ter bed,' Ada commanded the two youngest of her brood.

George had looked around the room. It was untidy. It always was. There were old ashes and cinders in the hearth. The range was rusty in parts and hadn't seen a blackleading brush for many a month. The top of the table was covered with old, stained newspapers and dirty dishes. There was no curtain of any kind on the back kitchen window and the panes of glass, some of them with cracks across them, were dirty.

'I know you mean well and I know how much you thought of Jane,' George went on.

Ada nodded. 'I loved the bones of that girl, yer know that, George. God 'elp her, dead an' buried at thirty,' she sniffed. Then her attention had been diverted by young Harry.

''Arry Sweeney, gerroff that chair before yer fall an' break yer neck!' she'd yelled at her youngest son who was balancing in a rickety chair and leaning across the top of the range, trying to extricate something from the clutter on the overmantle.

'I know, Ada,' George replied dejectedly.

'While 'Annah is alive, poor Jane won't ever be forgot. 'Annah's the dead spit of 'er.'

'I know but she gets her stubbornness from me.'

'Oh, aye, she's as cute as a bag of monkeys too. No one will get the better of 'er without a fight,' had been Ada's reply. He prayed his daughter's toughness would stand her in good stead.

It was a long journey, he'd explained that to her. First there was the tram to the Pier Head, then the ferry boat and then an omnibus to Denbigh which her da had told her would take a long, long time. Finally Cousin Gwyneth would be waiting for them with a pony and trap to take her to the little cottage she shared with her mother a mile from the village of Henllan. But it would be just the place for her blackbird. It was quiet now, covered by the folds of her heavy knitted shawl.

All the way there George tried to keep her spirits up by pointing things out to her. New Brighton, with its old Fort and lighthouse, as they'd crossed the choppy waters of the Mersey on the ferry. Then all the fields and woods and animals she'd never seen in their natural state before. These were things he too had never seen and he doubted he ever would again. Finally she'd fallen asleep and he'd lifted her gently on to his lap, her shawl still covering the bird, encircling her in his arms, wishing he could hold her like this for ever.

It was dark as the omnibus came slowly down the hill to Lenten Pool to stop at The Hand pub that stood at the intersection of the roads out to Henllan and to Groes. He was stiff as he got off and looked around, still carrying a sleeping Hannah and his kit bag. With relief he spotted the pony and trap on the other side of the road outside the church.

'Have you been waiting long, Gwyneth?' he asked Jane's second cousin. Already he was feeling apprehensive. Gwyneth Jones' thin face looked as though it had never been creased in a smile. She was dressed plainly but warmly, for the night air was chilly. Her back was ramrod straight and she looked decidedly annoyed.

'I suppose it was the fault of that contraption,' she said, jerking her head in the direction of the bus.

'I suppose it was, but it's a very long journey.'

Gwyneth tutted. 'I had to wait here. No decent respectable woman would wait outside there.'

She made the pub sound like hell. The whole family had been very religious, he remembered. They'd come to the wedding and had looked thoroughly shocked for the entire day.

'I agree it's not the best place,' he said. Hannah had woken up and was looking around in confusion as George set her down.

'She's slept for the last bit of the way.'

'Then I hope she'll not be awake all night. Mam needs *her* sleep.'

George passed the small carpet bag that contained Hannah's clothes and the rag doll Jane had made, up to the woman. His heart was heavy. He was beginning to feel that he'd made the wrong decision.

'Well, then, lift her in. I've to have the trap back by ten. It belongs to Mr Parry, see.'

Hannah looked up at her father. She was wide awake now and she didn't like the look of Cousin Gwyneth at all. Everything was suddenly strange.

'The money is to come regularly?' the woman asked.

'It will. I've sorted everything out and I know she'll be in good hands. You're family.' He crouched down and drew Hannah into the circle of his arms. He'd do anything not to have to leave her. He just prayed the war would be over soon as he pushed her fringe out of her eyes.

'You'll have to go now with Cousin Gwyneth. I have to wait here until I can get a lift from someone going back to Mold. I'll catch another bus there. You be a good girl, work hard at your lessons and help in the house. I'll write to you and you can write back to me.'

Gwyneth sniffed disapprovingly.

George kissed his daughter on the forehead and stroked her cheek. 'Bye, Hannah, remember your da loves you and always will and your mam is looking down on you from heaven.' He choked but fought to keep his voice steady. 'I'll come back for you one day, if I can.'

As Hannah gazed at him mute misery filled her large brown eyes. Then she put her arms around his neck and buried her face in his tunic. 'Bye, Da. I'll say my prayers every night and I'll be good,' she promised, her voice muffled.

George buried his own face in her hair. Having to leave her was tearing him apart inside. He felt as desolate and heartbroken as the day Jane had died. He'd promised then he'd take the best care he could of their daughter, but neither of them had known that the war would separate him from Hannah. Slowly he disentangled himself from her embrace, stood up and lifted her into the trap.

'Thank you, I really do appreciate this. I know Jane would prefer her to be here than in a crowded city while I'm . . . I'm away.'

The hint of a smile lifted the corners of Gwyneth's mouth. 'It's no bother, there's more than enough to keep her occupied.'

Hannah turned around in her seat, her eyes fixed on her da's face as Gwyneth flicked the reins and whip and the pony moved forward. She still held the bird in the folds of her shawl but with her other hand she waved to him.

George's gaze never left the tiny forlorn figure until the trap was swallowed up in the darkness, then he turned and walked towards the pub. He had a long night ahead of him.

Liverpool Songbird

For Ruth Gladwin of Stephens Innocent and Mark le Fanu of the Society of Authors, without whose support and advice this book would never have been published. And for Anne Williams, my editor, whose faith in me has never wavered.

AUTHOR'S NOTE

My sincere thanks go to Eric Sauder, co-author of *R.M.S. Lusitania*, for allowing me to use descriptions from his excellent and informative book, which for dedicated nautical readers is a 'must'.

I would like to point out that although *Lusitania* and *Aquitania* were built only seven years apart, there were few similarities between them. *Lusitania* being by far the most luxurious and opulent of the two, I thought it would add to the enjoyment of my readers to use the interior descriptions of the *Lucy*, as she was fondly known on Merseyside.

All the songs I have used are in the public domain.

Lyn Andrews
Southport 1995

PART ONE

Chapter One

1925

'I don't want to go, Mam! I'm tired, I want something to eat and then I just want to go to sleep.'

'Alice, luv, if you don't go, there won't *be* anything to eat. Please, luv, go for yer mam.'

Seventeen-year-old Alice O'Connor looked pleadingly at her mother. 'Can't our Lizzie go instead of me?'

'Our Lizzie can't sing, you know that. You can, so they'll cough up a few more pennies.'

Alice sighed heavily. That was true at least, but she was so tired. She was bone weary from working from morning till night in Tate and Lyle's sugar refinery at the bottom of Burlington Street. It wasn't much of a job; all she did all day was brush up, but the floor space was enormous. It was tiring, she was on the go all day and the foreman never seemed to take his eyes off her. She knew he regarded her as the dregs of society which his superiors, with misguided benevolence, saw fit to employ in the most menial capacity and pay accordingly.

Every time she looked up she caught him glaring at her.

'Use some elbow grease, Alice O'Connor, you idle little slut! Put your back into it, girl!' was what he'd bawled at her this afternoon. She wasn't idle, she was just tired. All she'd had to eat all day was a dry bun and a cup of very weak and watery tea. And she wasn't a slut either. She

3

couldn't help the way she looked because her family had nothing. The O'Connors were the poorest of the poor in Benledi Street and existed permanently in the terrifying shadow of the workhouse. It was only because of the few shillings she and her elder sister Lizzie brought home, and the generosity of the neighbours, that they still had a roof over their heads at all.

Da sometimes found work as a casual labourer down at the docks but he didn't try very hard and what he did earn was spent in one of the seventy pubs in the area, usually The Widows on Scotland Road. Sometimes Mam met him at the dock gate and tried to cajole him into parting with a shilling or two, but the price she paid was high. A black eye, cuts and bruises, or worse. Sometimes she sent Mary, who at seven was the youngest, into the pub after him. Then he was shamed into parting with some money but Mam still didn't come off lightly. He'd belt her when he got home for showing him up in front of his mates.

'Isn't there anything to eat, Mam? I'm starving.'

Nelly O'Connor shook her head. 'No, luv. I managed to cadge a couple of stale loaves from Skillicorns but the kids 'ad them when they got in from school. I've 'ad nothin' meself, Alice.'

Alice looked around the dismal kitchen despairingly. Her sisters Agnes and Mary and her brothers Eddy and Jimmy were huddled silently around the pathetic little fire that burned in the dirty, rusted cast-iron range. Their faces were pinched and white and they all wore stiff, ugly, bottle-green corduroy clothes, stamped with the letters L.C.P. so they couldn't be pawned. At least they were warm and serviceable, she thought, even though to have to wear them was in itself a stigma. They were provided by the Liverpool City Police – the scuffers, as they were known.

'Where's me da?'

'Where do yer think, Alice?' Nelly said sharply. It was a stupid question to ask on a Friday night when Tip had had an afternoon's work down at the Princes Half Tide dock. He would now be drinking his wages away in the pub.

Every penny he got his hands on was soon spent – on the drink. That was the cause of all their problems. Nelly didn't tell him exactly how much Lizzie or Alice earned because something had to be kept for the rent, but there was never much left for other things – the basics like food and clothes, light and heat. Every day was a struggle just to exist, to keep body and soul together. Ever since Lizzie and Alice had been babies he'd been like this. He'd become disillusioned with life and the grinding poverty they all lived in and strived hard to overcome. But there was no escape from worry and misery for Nelly. Oh, she too could have drowned her multitude of sorrows in a bottle of cheap gin, but then what would happen to her kids? Sometimes people asked her why she put up with him. Why didn't she leave? Well, where could she go with six kids? she'd answer. The workhouse, that's where.

Alice had deliberately walked along Vauxhall Road on her way home from the refinery to avoid passing the pub in case Tip saw her and demanded her wages. She knew from experience that it wasn't much use trying to hang onto them, he'd just knock her flying and take them.

'Where's our Lizzie?' she asked.

'Still on her way home, as far as I know. She said she was going to hang around Holden's shop to see if she could beg a few bits.'

'And if she does she'll eat them,' Alice said bitterly although she really didn't blame Lizzie, her sister had been working all day too. It was everyone for themselves in this family and had been for as long as she could remember, except for Mam. Mam often went without to give them whatever food there was.

The front door banged shut and then Lizzie appeared in the doorway, clutching a brown paper bag. Like Alice, she was thin and pasty-looking. Her faded flannel dress hung loosely on her and was covered by a voluminous old black shawl. Even though she was a good bit older than Alice, her stunted frame and gaunt features made her look younger.

'What did yer get, Lizzie?'

'Not much. A bit of tea, a twist of sugar an' a small tin of condensed milk.'

Nelly relieved her of the small parcel. 'Well, it's better than nowt. We can have a cup of tea at least.'

Alice looked questioningly at her mother. 'How? There's not enough fire to boil the kettle up.'

'I'll go an' get those few bits of wood from the stairs. Where's that old iron bar? Eddy, I saw you with it last.'

'I left it in the yard, Mam, yisterday.'

'Mam, if we pull any more boards off the stairs they'll fall in,' Alice added.

Nelly ignored her and went out to the yard. Downstairs all the floorboards and doors had long since been used for firewood. A fire not only gave them some warmth, it was also necessary for cooking. The younger kids scoured the streets after school, picking up rubbish from the gutters, begging old boxes, newspapers, bits of wood, rags, anything that would burn.

Lizzie sat down wearily in the old bentwood chair. 'I'm worn out an' I'm hungry an' I'm cold.'

Alice had little sympathy. 'So am I but I've got to go out again.'

'Where to?'

'Well, I'm not going far. I'll go up to the Rotunda, there's usually a good crowd on a Friday night. I wish I had some stockings and a good warm coat though.' She regarded the battered pair of men's boots she wore with thankful resignation. At least she had boots; often in the past she'd gone barefoot in the depths of winter. They all had. As for a good warm coat, that was a luxury she'd never had.

Tears had misted Lizzie's grey eyes. 'I did once. Remember all those things Tommy bought me?'

Alice nodded. Once Lizzie had been 'walking out' with Tommy MacNamara from William Moult Street. The whole family were villains of the first order but he'd bought Lizzie some decent clothes and shoes and stockings. He'd also sworn to break Da's neck if he tried to pawn them and Da had been afraid of him. Lizzie had looked like a real lady then, walking arm in arm down the street with Tommy. So grown up, so smartly dressed. Lizzie had been quite attractive too. After an outing with Tommy, she would sit and tell Alice all about the places Tommy had taken her to and the people they'd met. Alice had promised Lizzie that when she was old enough to 'walk out' she'd tell her sister all the great things she'd done and seen too. But poor Tommy had been killed in the Great War and everything had gone to Solly Indigo's pawnshop in Burlington Street. A smile played around the corners of Alice's mouth. Lizzie had let her wear some of those clothes and it had felt great being warm and decently dressed.

Nelly came back with an armful of splintered stair boards which she carefully fed, piece by piece, into the range where they burned and crackled with a cheerful glow. It wouldn't last long and it did nothing to improve the room, Alice thought, looking around dejectedly. The walls were stained with brown patches of damp, as was the ceiling. The window panes were so dirty it was impossible to see out of them, not that there was anything pleasant to see other than the back yard. A piece of cotton lace curtain, grey with age and smuts from the fire, was tacked across it and two of the panes were broken, the holes stuffed with rags.

7

There was a gas jet on the wall beside the door but there was no money for a luxury such as gas light. They made do with bits of candles. There wasn't much furniture either. A table with a broken leg had been inexpertly mended with a bit of thin hemp rope twisted round and round the broken joint. A battered old armchair, from which the stuffing was protruding in several places, was pushed into the corner by the range, beside an old scarred chest of drawers. The bentwood chair, now occupied by Lizzie, four old paint tins that served as seats for the kids, and two misshapen cushions from a sofa constituted the rest of the furnishings. There were no ornaments, pictures or bric-a-brac such as other people had and they'd never owned a tablecloth or rugs for the floor.

Upstairs there were two bedrooms and neither had any furniture, just some straw-stuffed mattresses covered with stained and grubby ticking. There were no sheets, no blankets and no quilts, just a pile of old clothes, little more than rags. They all slept head to tail, Nelly in with the girls in one room, the lads in the other and they fared better because there were only two of them. Tip usually never made it upstairs but sprawled in the armchair in the kitchen.

Nelly put the kettle on the fire and when it was nearing boiling point she emptied the tea and the sugar into it. Alice went into the small, dark, airless scullery and came back with three chipped mugs. Nelly used a large iron nail to pierce the tin that contained the condensed milk, and when the soupy liquid had been transferred from the kettle to the mugs, she handed one to Alice, one to Lizzie and cupped her cold, chapped hands round the third.

'There now, get that down yer, luv, an' then get going,' she urged.

The tea was making Alice feel a bit better. 'I'm going to the chippy on the way home, Mam, but I'm going to eat my portion. I'm not havin' him pinch it off me.'

8

'Oh, he'll be too drunk. He'll probably have passed out long before you get back, Alice. See what you can get, luv, we're all starving and perished and that fire's dying back already.'

As she pulled the front door closed behind her, Alice shivered. It was freezing cold. The wind was from the east and it was bitter. It seemed to come down Benledi Street straight from the river as though there were no warehouses or factories in between. There was sleet mixed with it too. She pulled her shawl closely round her body, wishing again that she had a pair of thick woollen stockings and mitts for her rapidly numbing fingers.

She walked up the street and onto Scotland Road, avoiding as many of the pubs as she could, just in case one of the figures that came stumbling out was her father. It wasn't far to the Rotunda Theatre at the junction of Scotland Road and Stanley Road, but it seemed like miles when you were half starved, half frozen, and tired out. Still, if she didn't manage to get a few coppers she'd be going to bed even hungrier than she was now.

She passed a few people she knew; some spoke to her, some didn't. No one in this neighbourhood was well off but at least they all seemed to have more than she did. She was looked on with either scorn or pity at work, mainly because of her appearance. They didn't have money for coal to heat up water for such luxuries as a bath. It was hard enough for Nelly to try to keep their clothes clean, using water boiled in the kettle and carbolic soap. Once a week they did have their hair washed but the rest of the time they had to make do with cold water, a bit of rag and half a bar of Fairy soap which Nelly usually managed to buy or beg from either Mrs Holden's shop in Silvester Street or Burgess's in Burlington Street.

Alice passed Daly's Tobacconists, Stanley's Pawnshop, the Maypole Grocery, W. Costain Provision Merchants, Bentley's Cabinet Makers, and Reiglers. The smell issuing from the Pork Shop brought tears to her eyes but she trudged on until she reached Stanley Road and crossed over, threading her way between the traffic. She hoped there were no scuffers around or she'd be chased away for begging. You could actually be arrested, it depended on the mood the scuffer was in, but most of them turned a blind eye. No one would willingly go begging if they had a choice and the police seemed to understand that.

The theatre was an impressive building, built on and round the corner. It belonged to Bent's Brewery. It was four storeys high with ornate windows and stonework and topped with a dome that bore its name in large letters. On both sides were awnings over small shops, giving it the appearance of an arcade. It was brightly lit and crowds were milling around the main entrance at the front. There were Mary Ellens selling fruit and nuts and she knew she would have to compete with their bellicose cries. There were also two lads juggling with coloured balls and an old man playing a mouth organ. She sighed. It wasn't going to be easy.

She folded her shawl back from her head and ran her fingers through the mass of tangled, tawny coloured curls, unaware that despite her drab clothes, the pallor of malnutrition and exhaustion, she was a pretty girl. Her large, soft brown eyes, fringed with thick lashes, were her most attractive and appealing feature. The mass of unruly curls framed an oval face with a slightly upturned nose, high cheekbones and well-defined eyebrows.

'Well, this ain't earning money, Alice O'Connor,' she said firmly to herself, so she took a deep breath and began to sing.

> Just a song at twilight,
> When the lights are low
> Where the flickering shadows,
> Softly come and go.

Her clear, strong, soprano voice rose above the discordant notes of the harmonica and people began to take notice of her.

She progressed slowly along the arcade on the right of the building to the arcade on the left and back again, her hand held out appealingly. She was truly grateful for the pennies and halfpennies that were pressed into it but she realised she should have got here earlier. She'd noticed the time on a clock in Stanley's window. It was after seven and the show started at half past. People wanted to be in their seats by then. She began 'Beautiful Dreamer' but the crowd was thinning and the doorman was eyeing her menacingly. The jugglers and the old man had gone but she put her heart and soul into the last verse, knowing that in a few minutes everyone would have gone inside and further effort would be a waste of breath.

As the last notes died away, a well-dressed lady dropped a silver threepenny bit into her hand.

'You have a lovely voice, child. Such a pity it will be wasted. With training and grooming you could be inside on the stage, instead of out here begging.' She smiled kindly before turning and hurrying inside.

Alice stood alone on the pavement. The commissionaire had closed the doors, shutting out the biting wind, but he continued to regard her with hostility through the glass panels. For a few seconds she stared malevolently back, then turned away. The lady had said she could be in there singing, if she had the right training and grooming, whatever that meant. It was something that had never occurred to her. People did earn their living singing, and a good living it was too. You only had to see the number of punters who crowded into the 'Roundy' to realise that. She'd only ever sung in the streets of Liverpool and she'd done that from the time Mam had realised she had a voice people would listen to and had taught her a couple of songs. They were old-fashioned now but no one seemed

11

to mind. It was a form of begging but they'd all been very glad of the coppers she'd managed to earn.

What was it like in there? she wondered. Where did they all sit, or did they stand, and what kind of people performed? She peered closely at a large, brightly coloured poster pasted to the sooty bricks of the wall. There was Leo Barnes, the world-famous ventriloquist, whatever that was. Sidney Romano, a virtuoso on no less than five instruments, and Miss Letty Lewis, the Cockney Songbird. She read the words slowly, hesitating over the unfamiliar ones. She had gone to school, spasmodically, and could read and write and add up in her head. What exactly was a Cockney Songbird, though? Maybe it was a stuffed bird in a cage that sang when you turned the handle. She'd seen one of those in Solly's shop once. Did this Letty Lewis have one of those?

Hunger put a stop to her deliberations and she walked quickly back to Reigler's shop.

'A whole meat and tattie pie, please, mister.'

'Have you got the money, girl?' Fred Reigler asked suspiciously. He'd been caught out like that before. There were so many hungry kids in this area, aye, and they were crafty too.

'Yes, I have. Here.' Alice indignantly handed over the coins.

A hot pie the size of a man's fist, with a thick pastry crust, was passed over to her. She walked out, breaking pieces off and stuffing them into her mouth. Oh, nothing had ever tasted so good and she still had sixpence left for Mam.

She finished the pie and found herself standing at the top of the entry, or jigger, that ran behind the theatre and out into Boundary Street. Now that her belly was reasonably full her curiosity was aroused. She decided to see if there was another way into the building, a back door maybe.

There was, but there was also an old man, reading a newspaper, sitting in a little box-like room. Flattening herself against the wall she sneaked past and walked cautiously down the dark, narrow passageway. The sound of people clapping became louder, which intensified her curiosity. She wanted to see what it was like inside and who everyone was applauding.

Halfway along the jigger there was a trap door, like the doors leading into the cellars many of the houses in the surrounding streets had. It opened quite easily and she realised that it must be the entrance for deliveries. She slid neatly down the slight incline and found herself in a gloomy, narrow corridor lit by a single gas jet. The clapping was louder now and nearer. Two doors faced her. She bit her lip wondering what was on the other side of them. Tentatively she reached out and pushed the larger of the two gently. It opened a crack and she peered through, her eyes widening in amazement. The theatre was huge and there were hundreds of seats. Like armchairs, they were, and covered in a soft red material. The stage was brilliantly lit and heavy red curtains edged with gold fringe were looped back across it, revealing a backcloth depicting a sunny flower garden. She'd never seen anything like it in her life. It was like something from a dream.

Her eyes grew wider and her astonishment increased as she heard the orchestra play the opening bars of 'Beautiful Dreamer'. Her gaze fell on the tall, slender figure of Letty Lewis. She had masses of golden curls piled high on her head, held up with a silver ribbon. She wore an evening gown of pale pink satin that sparkled with beads and silver fringe. But what fascinated Alice was the song she was singing. She could sing *that* song just as well as Letty Lewis, if not better. Hadn't the lady who'd given her the threepenny bit told her so? She watched, totally enthralled, until Miss Lewis had finished, taken two bows and

13

left the stage, then she closed the door on that enchanted world.

She looked down at her creased and grubby skirt, black shawl and heavy boots, at her red, work-roughened hands with their broken, dirty nails. No one would ever pay a lot of money to listen to her sing, like they had for Miss Letty Lewis, the Cockney Songbird.

The few coins she'd earned were clutched tightly in her hand and she remembered that Mam would be waiting for them. No, there would be no stage in a fancy theatre for little Alice O'Connor, just the cold, harsh streets of Liverpool.

Chapter Two

Alice trudged home with as much energy as she could muster. It was easy to pick out their house, she thought; it was the only one in Benledi Street that was in darkness. The bits of candle stubs didn't give out much light. She peeped enviously in through the windows of those houses where the curtains hadn't been drawn. Inside them there was light and warmth and people she was sure had easier, more comfortable lives than her own.

Only Mam and Lizzie were in the kitchen. Lizzie was curled up in the armchair with her feet tucked under her, her shawl swathed tightly round her. It was the best way to try to keep warm. Mam was sitting in the bentwood chair, her eyes screwed up in concentration as she poked pieces of cardboard into the boots of Eddy, Jimmy and Mary who were all obviously in bed.

'I got sixpence, Mam, and I've had a pie so there's no need to fetch me anything else. I was a bit late getting started but a lady gave me a threepenny bit.'

Nelly got to her feet. 'Here, Lizzie, you finish this. I'm going up to Daly's for chips and I'll stop off on the way and see what I can get from Burgess's.'

Lizzie reluctantly uncurled herself and picked up Jimmy's boots while Alice sat in the chair her mother had vacated.

'Don't be too long, Mam, or *he'll* be in.'

Nelly didn't need Lizzie to remind her of that, and worn

out though she was, she managed to hurry down the hall.

'Give me a pair, Lizzie, I'll help you,' Alice offered, picking up Mary's boots. They were at least two sizes too big for their younger sister and had to be kept on with bits of rope passed under the instep and tied across the top. They rubbed, and Mary always had blisters.

Lizzie handed Alice a piece of thick cardboard and Alice sighed. It wasn't an easy task because they had no scissors or even a sharp knife. In the dim light she began to tear off a piece.

'Do you think we'll ever have decent boots or be able to pay to have them cobbled when they get holes in them?'

Lizzie shrugged carelessly. 'I suppose the kids will all grow up and get jobs an' maybe our Agnes and Mary will get married.'

Alice paused. 'Wouldn't it be great if we could get married, Lizzie? Just think, to get away from here and *him*!'

Lizzie was scornful. 'What feller would want you or me? Look at the pair of us. Walkin' rag bags, we are, and with not a pick on us.'

'Tommy Mac wanted you, Lizzie.'

'Aye, that's when I was a bit of a kid. Besides, there's not many around here like Tommy. He understood. He was brought up – dragged up – like us, Alice.'

'We've not been dragged up. Mam takes care of us the best way she can. How many hidings has she had so we can eat? Ma Mac never gave a hoot for any of her kids.'

Alice poked her fingers into the body of the boot, squashing the cardboard down as flat as she could, knowing from experience how lumpy cardboard chafed. 'I went and had a look inside the Roundy. I went down the back jigger. Oh, Lizzie, you should have seen it! It was dead posh! And there was a lady singing, Miss Letty Lewis, the Cockney Songbird. I'll always remember that name. She looked like an angel, Lizzie, I swear to God she did.'

16

Lizzie knew what the inside of the theatre was like. Tommy had taken her, a lifetime ago. When she thought about it, it brought tears to her eyes. 'It's a waste of time lookin' in places like that, Alice. It only makes you more miserable in the end.'

'It doesn't. Do you know what she was singing, Lizzie? One of *my* songs. I could have sung it better too. The lady who gave me the threepenny joey told me I could.'

'Oh, stop tellin' fibs, Alice!'

'I'm not! She did say it. Training and grooming she said I needed, and then I could sing on the stage.'

Any further argument was curtailed as the front door was thrown inward with a crash that made the window panes rattle. The two girls looked at each other with dread.

'It's Da!' Lizzie whispered fearfully.

'An' before Mam's back! Get a move on, Lizzie! Go out the back way an' warn her. He'll scoff her chips and poor Mam must be faint with hunger by now.'

Lizzie sprang to her feet, panic giving her strength, and darted into the scullery just as Tip O'Connor staggered into the kitchen from the hall.

Alice forced herself to smile and be pleasant.

'Hello, Da. Sit down here.'

Tip ignored her, glaring through small bloodshot eyes at the dreary, dimly lit room. 'Where's your mam?'

'Out, lookin' for firewood. She won't be long,' Alice lied stoutly, praying that Lizzie would be able to waylay Nelly at the top of the street. 'Why don't yer go up to bed? I'll give yer a hand. There's a few holes in the stairs.' She wished malevolently that he'd fall through the stairs from top to bottom.

Again he ignored her but lurched over to the chest of drawers and wrenched open the top one where Nelly kept what few bits of spare clothing they had.

'Where's she hid it?' he bellowed.

17

'Hid what, Da?'

'Me dinner! Where's me bloody dinner?'

'Da, you know there's nothing in there but bits an' bobs of clothes.'

He rounded on her. 'Then where's she put me bloody dinner?'

'There ain't none. We've had nothin' either, Da. Mam was waiting for you, for your wages, like.' She didn't dare look at him. She fixed her eyes on the floor.

'Bloody leeches, the lot of yer! Always wantin' money. Where can I get money? Who's going ter give me any bleedin' money?'

'I know, Da,' Alice coaxed, 'times is bad. Sit down an' get a bit of sleep.' If she could get him off to sleep, not even the house falling down around him would wake him, but he was being belligerent and obstinate. He staggered into the scullery and she heard the three mugs and two plates being smashed and thanked God that the kettle and the stew pan were made of stronger stuff, although they were acquiring a few more dents by the sounds of it.

'Alice O'Connor, were you born in a barn? Leavin' the door open like that!'

Alice froze as she heard Nelly's voice. Lizzie hadn't managed to warn her. She darted to the doorway waving her arms and mouthing the words 'Me da! Me da!' but she was too late. Nelly walked into the room, a greasy parcel and a paper bag hugged against her, just as Tip emerged from the scullery.

Nelly's eyes narrowed and she pursed her lips. She wasn't going to part with the chips readily. She was no match for him, she never had been, but as she thought of the kids shivering upstairs, Lizzie out God knows where and seeing Alice with fear in her eyes, a hard glitter came into Nelly O'Connor's tired eyes.

'Giz me dinner!' Tip demanded.

'Our Alice went out tramping the streets – singing –

18

for the money for this, an' we're all hungry. You could have bought your own dinner, you had wages.' She knew what the result of this defiance would be and braced herself.

The blow sent her reeling against the wall but she hung grimly onto the parcel of food even though her ears were ringing and lights danced sickeningly before her eyes.

He lunged towards her again but Alice stepped in front of him. 'Leave me mam alone!' she yelled.

'Shut yer bleedin' gob!' Tip yelled back, catching her by her hair, shaking her as though she was a rag doll and then throwing her in the direction of Nelly's cowed form.

Alice bit back the tears of pain. He must have pulled out a handful of her hair.

'Get to bed, luv! Get up the stairs and leave him ter me,' Nelly hissed.

Tip's attention was caught and held for a second by the figure of Lizzie standing transfixed with terror in the doorway.

'Get hold of our Lizzie an' the pair of you get to bed!' Nelly urged.

Lizzie needed no telling. She ran. But Alice didn't follow her. Stubbornly she stood in front of her mother although Nelly tried to push her away.

Tip made another attempt to grab the food, brushing Alice to one side. Nelly turned her back on him and then with a groan fell to her knees as his clenched fist hit her squarely in the middle of the back.

'Mam! Mam!' Alice screamed although all this was nothing new. She'd been brought up with his drunken violence. 'Give him the flaming chips, Mam!'

Nelly didn't answer and Tip sent her sprawling with a kick.

It was too much for Alice. The unfairness, the injustice, the sheer brutality shot through her like a flame. Looking round she seized the wooden chair and with all the strength she could muster lifted it above her head and smashed it down hard across her father's head and shoulders. It broke into pieces and uttering a roar like a wounded bull, Tip turned on her.

She managed to shield herself with her arms from the first couple of blows, but then he kicked out at her knees and her legs buckled. She lay on the floor curled up in a ball trying to protect her head and her stomach. Each burst of pain was worse than the last and faintly she could hear both her mam and Lizzie screaming. Then there were other voices, the pain became unbearable, and she felt herself sinking into a black abyss.

When she came to, Alice was lying on the mattress in the bedroom. Her whole body felt as though it was on fire and as she tried to move, a groan of agony escaped her.

'Lie still, Alice, luv. He's probably cracked your ribs.'

'Mam? Mam, are you all right? Where is . . . he?'

Nelly smoothed the straggling wisps of hair from her daughter's face. 'He's downstairs, out cold, Alice. Lizzie ran up the road for Alf an' Bernie Maguire. She said he was killing you. Bernie laid into him with his docker's hook. I thought he'd killed him, but he's just unconscious.'

Tears of pain, relief and exhaustion slid down Alice's thin cheeks. 'Oh, Mam. I'm hurtin'.'

'Hush, luv. It's all right, yer mam's here. Get some sleep now, you'll feel better in the morning.' Nelly doubted she would but there was no money for doctors and she wouldn't let them take Alice to hospital. No one ever came out alive from hospitals.

Alice closed her eyes. She felt that bad she wished she was dead. She wished Da had killed her, then she'd be out of her misery and the scuffers would come for him and he'd hang at the end of a rope in Walton Jail. It would have been better for everyone. Tomorrow, well, tomorrow she'd have to try and drag herself to work, or failing that she'd have to go singing in the streets, they *had* to have money. And it would all go on and on, forever. Her sobs increased although it hurt her to cry. She couldn't face any more, she just couldn't. She'd run away. She'd manage on her own and it would be one less mouth to feed, one less for Mam to worry about. But what about Mam? Oh, she was too tired, too shaken up and sore to think any more. But she had to get away. If Da started again, she'd kill him. She didn't know how, but she would, and then she'd be the one they would hang.

She couldn't move the next morning. Waves of pain washed over her and every joint ached. Nelly brought her a cup of weak tea and a slice of bread and dripping, but she couldn't eat it. She begged her mam to have it but Nelly shook her head firmly and said she'd give it to Lizzie. She also said that Bernie Maguire had been back. He'd come up and looked at her and then gone downstairs, hauled her da into the back yard and belted him hard, swearing it would be nothing compared to what he'd do if he ever laid a hand on Alice again.

'So, that should keep him quiet for a bit, any road,' Nelly finished with grim satisfaction.

Alice turned her head away. For how long though? Her da had a short memory. Bernie had belted Da before when he'd thrown little Mary bodily out of the front door into the street. It hadn't stopped him starting on them when his bruises had gone down, and the Maguires would only step in when they felt like it. No one would dream of sending for the scuffers if they thought things could be sorted out among themselves.

Alice drifted in and out of sleep all day and all night, and when she woke again properly she knew what she was going to do. She wasn't going to stay here. She'd find herself a room – just a cubbyhole would do – and she'd work all day and sing all night. She'd bring money home to Mam but she wasn't going to live in Benledi Street any

21

longer. She couldn't. She just couldn't stand the sight of Da any more, whether drunk or sober. She didn't trust herself. She'd be gripped by that terrible rage again and she'd kill him, even if she had to wait until he was asleep to do it. She *had* to get out.

Three days later she left the house. She'd told no one of her intentions – Lizzie would have tried to stop her and then would have told Mam. It hurt her to think about the worry she would cause her mother but she knew Nelly would have begged and pleaded with her and she couldn't have stood that.

As she walked slowly and still painfully up the street, she didn't turn round. When she reached Scotland Road she noticed the shops being decorated and realised it must be nearly Christmas time. That meant that a Cooper's van would come round and a parcel would soon be delivered to number ten Benledi Street, from the Goodfellows Society. It meant food, exotic and luxurious food like oranges, apples, fruitcake and capon. Food they never saw at any other time of the year. Da would lay claim to most of it but it comforted her a little to think that her share would go to Lizzie, the kids or Mam.

She had no money so it was useless to try to find a room yet. Instead she made her way down Burlington Street, across the bridge over the canal and to the gates of the sugar refinery. They were locked and she called to the keeper who came out of his little hut and glared at her.

'What do yer want?'

'I work here. I'm the brusher-up.'

'Not any more, you ain't. Mr Roscoe said he ain't seen hide nor hair of yer since Monday, so they've got someone else. Now, clear off an' stop wastin' me time.'

She turned away, stunned. It was something she hadn't thought about. She had been too preoccupied with other

22

things, but she should have known. Jobs weren't kept open, there were always a dozen people waiting to fill your shoes if you didn't turn up. She sat down on the step of the Golden Fleece, near to tears. Now what could she do? She hadn't reckoned on losing her job. She watched a couple of barefoot urchins poking at something in the gutter, something that moved. They squealed with laughter and jabbed at it again with a sharp piece of wood. She caught the faint distressed mewing and picking up a stone she hurled it at them.

'Gerroff! Leave the poor thing alone, you cruel little sods!'

One of them rubbed his arm where the stone had caught it and they both thumbed their noses at her before running off across the road. She got up and went over to the edge of the kerb. A tiny, scrawny black and white kitten was lying on its side. She bent down and scooped it up, tucking it into the crook of her arm and covering it tenderly with her shawl. The poor little thing was half dead but she couldn't leave it here. It looked too young to have been taken from its mother; how it had escaped being drowned in the canal she didn't know.

'We're a bit alike, you and me, cat. Half starved, beaten up, an' with nowhere to go,' she said aloud. Well, standing in the middle of Burlington Street feeling miserable wasn't solving anything for herself or this poor scrap. It was a long walk into town so she'd better get going.

Church Street and Lord Street were her best bets. There were always plenty of shoppers around. She'd stop and have a rest and a drink of water from the Steble Fountain at the top of William Brown Street, then maybe she'd head to Castle Street and Water Street where all the offices were. People would come streaming out onto the street at lunch time. After that, if her voice and her strength held out, she'd go to the Pier Head; that, too, was always crowded. If she was lucky, by the end of the day she might well have earned enough to pay for a bed for the night, a hot meal at the Sally Army place and some milk for the poor creature who lay shivering under her shawl. Tomorrow she'd really try and get herself sorted out.

Just the thought of not having to go back to Benledi Street made her feel much better, much brighter and more optimistic, so she quickened her steps as she headed for Byrom Street.

Chapter Three

She hadn't done too badly, she thought, as she sat on the steps of the Trafalgar Memorial in the middle of Exchange Flags, the open space at the back of the Town Hall. It was surrounded by fine buildings, including the Cotton Exchange, the centre of trade in the commodity on which the wealth of the city had been founded. These days the business was done inside and not out on the Flags, but there were always people hurrying about, mainly messenger boys.

The kitten was still lying in the crook of her arm. She'd earned a shilling and she'd reckoned the kitten had helped. People had caught sight of it and their expression had softened. Maybe it was a lucky charm, or maybe it was because people felt more generous, it being nearly Christmas.

The afternoon was bleak. Grey clouds went scudding across the sky, driven by a strong north-easterly wind. It would be colder and more blustery down at the Pier Head where the wind gusted in from the Mersey estuary, but it couldn't be helped. If she was to be able to afford a hot meal and a bed, she'd have to earn at least another sixpence.

She got to her feet and walked towards the back of the Town Hall and out into Castle Street where the wind cut through her thin clothes, making her shiver. A lazy wind, Mam called it. It went through you instead of round you.

She turned right down Water Street which led to the George's Dock Gate, the Pier Head and the landing stage. She'd start at the entrance to the Riverside Station, keeping out of the way of the scuffer. Posh folk arrived there on the boat trains, to board the big liners that went all over the world. She wished she knew more than two songs. She was getting sick to death of her small repertoire.

She took up her position on the corner of Prince's Parade at the head of the line of waiting cabs, both horse-drawn and motorised. The kitten was now lying on her breast with its head poking out from the folds of her shawl and the first passengers from the Euston to Liverpool boat train were emerging. There was the usual cluster of porters and half a dozen or so street urchins darted in and out between them, pleading to be allowed to carry bags and cases for a penny. They continued to tout for business until they were chased off by the porters, for they often ran off with the luggage. She was heartened to see a good many well-dressed people emerging into the cold winter's afternoon, pulling fur collars closer round their ears. Gloved hands held small, smart hats more securely against the gusts of wind. She took a rather painful breath, attempted to square her shoulders and began.

> Beautiful dreamer
> Wake unto me,
> Starlight and moonlight
> Are waiting for thee . . .

A couple of coins were dropped into her hand but then she caught sight of the burly figure of a policeman, accompanied by a railway official, bearing down on her and she quickly turned and melted into the crowd, following the throng along the Prince's Landing Stage, out of sight of the officers of the law and the London and North-Western Railway Company.

On the landing stage itself there were carriages and horse-drawn wagons and a good many people going about their business. The mountainous black hull of the biggest liner in the world, Cunard's *Aquitania*, towered above everything. Its four red and black funnels disgorged black smoke, a sign of its imminent departure.

Well, this was as good a place as any, she thought, taking up her stance by the small wooden Post Office. It was noisy, very noisy and she knew she would have to put more effort into her performance just to be heard above the shouts of news vendors, carters and the repeated blasts of the steam whistle of the *Duchess of York*, the signal warning those crew members still inside the Style House that it was time to drink up and get aboard.

With a lot of difficulty she had started into the second verse of 'Just A Song At Twilight' when a motorcar coming along tooted its horn loudly and repeatedly and the kitten leaped from her arms.

She uttered a shriek, her song forgotten, as the little animal tottered over the cobbles and beneath the hooves of a shire horse that had also been startled by the din.

'No! No, Mog, come back!' she screamed, darting out after it.

'Hey! Hey, you! Look out! *Look out!*'

She heard the cry and turned her head in time to see the gleaming metal of the car's radiator at close range. She opened her mouth to scream but the breath was knocked out of her as the bonnet of the car caught her squarely and tossed her onto the road.

She was oblivious of the commotion around her as the two young men in the car jumped out.

'Oh, God, she's not dead, is she?' the younger of the two cried, looking down anxiously.

David Williamson bent over her, holding her wrist, feeling for the pulse. 'No, she's breathing but how badly she's hurt I can't tell. I don't think we should move her.'

Charles Williamson gnawed his bottom lip. 'She just ran out in front of me! She never even looked!'

'No one's blaming you, Charlie,' David said curtly. 'But what the hell are we going to do?' He looked around. The small crowd was dispersing, losing interest once they'd seen it was only a slum girl who'd been knocked down, no one of any importance.

'Isn't there a policeman anywhere?' Charlie asked.

His brother looked up at the *Aquitania*, his expression harassed. 'I haven't got time for questions, statements or form filling. I'm supposed to be aboard now.'

'Well, I can't hang about either. I promised I'd be back with the car and Father will be furious if I'm late. You know how keen he is to be off early to Southport, to this reception at the Prince of Wales.'

David Williamson made a decision. He'd told Charlie to get a move on, hence their unusual speed. Then he'd seen something leap from the girl's arms and she'd screamed and run after it. So, in his opinion he was partly to blame for what had happened. 'We can't just leave her here,' he said. 'I'll have to take her aboard. I'll carry her, you bring my case.'

His brother was appalled. 'You can't do that! They'll have a fit! Just look at the state of her.'

'I don't intend to keep her for the voyage, Charlie. There's a doctor on board. I'll get him to have a look at her then give her some money and fetch a cab to take her to hospital if she needs to go.'

'Mister! 'Ere, mister, this is 'er cat.'

David Williamson's attention was diverted by a small and very scruffy boy who with one hand tugged at his uniform jacket and with the other held out a tiny, mud-spattered kitten, dangling it by the scruff of its neck.

'It's that damned cat! The one that caused all this!' Charlie glared at the animal.

'It's 'ers, honest it is, sir.' The lad looked hopefully up

28

at David. As soon as he'd seen the men jump from the car and the crowd start to gather he'd darted over to where the carter was hanging on hard to the bridle of the horse, pushed quickly and fearlessly between the huge, iron-shod hooves and yanked the tiny bundle of fur up from the cobbles and out of danger.

'Charlie, give him a couple of pence and bring the cat too.'

Charlie Williamson cast his eyes towards the grey sky before handing over the money and relieving the lad of the kitten. With his thumb and forefinger he held it up and looked at it with disdain. It was a sorry creature.

As David picked Alice up gently, she moaned; her eyelids flickered open and then closed again. He explained the position briefly to the Third Electrical Officer who was stationed at the crew gangway.

The man looked askance at Alice's limp form and the kitten that Charlie was holding. 'I'm not taking responsibility for anything. Not her or the livestock!' he grunted.

'Oh, for God's sake, Robinson, I'm not asking you to! She'll be off the ship before we sail and so will the cat.'

'On your own head be it then. If the old man hears about it there'll be hell to pay.'

'If no one tells him, he won't know about it, will he?' David snapped. 'Come on, Charlie, bring the flaming cat, and then go for Dr Kendrick. Anyone will direct you to the surgery.'

As he carried Alice for'ard to the officers' quarters, along the narrow companionways that hummed with the vibration of the huge engines that would turn the four massive screws when she sailed out of the Mersey in an hour's time, the few crew members he encountered just stared or raised their eyes to the ceiling and passed on their way to perform their allotted duties. That all junior officers were mad was the general consensus of the lower ranks.

The junior engineers' quarters were far from spacious or luxurious. A small cabin, seven foot by seven foot, was fitted out with a bunk, a small washbasin and stand, and a set of drawers and wardrobe combined. There was hardly room for one person, let alone more. David laid Alice down on the bunk and removed her dirty, battered boots.

Beneath his brusque exterior, David Williamson was a compassionate young man. He had two younger sisters and he had been brought up to show sympathy for the plight of the poor. Admittedly, living as he did in Crosby, he didn't come into contact with many of the sad wretches, but he'd seen enough of their lives in the squalid dock areas that seemed to characterise all the ports he'd ever visited to realise how desperate their existences must be.

Taking a towel from the washbasin he soaked it with cold water, wrung it out and wiped some of the dust and grime away from the girl's face, and suddenly realised that she was quite lovely. Thin, too thin, but with some flesh on her bones and decent clothes on her back she would be quite a beauty. He looked anxiously at his watch. He had to report for duty in ten minutes, they were sailing in an hour's time.

Charlie and the doctor arrived simultaneously and crowded into the tiny cabin.

'What's all this about, Williamson? Oh, I see.' Kendrick nodded his understanding as he caught sight of Alice on the bunk. She was beginning to show signs of movement but his attention was diverted by the kitten which, deposited by Charlie, had curled up beside Alice and gone to sleep. 'What the hell is that?'

'It's hers. She ran after it, straight out in front of the car. There wasn't anything we could do,' David informed him.

'Then why the hell didn't you take her and it to the Royal Infirmary or the Northern Hospital?'

'Er, no time, really. Got to get back with the car, you see,' Charlie explained hurriedly.

'Well, it was a bloody stupid decision to bring her on board, that's all I can say. I should report you.' He scowled. 'Well, let's have a look at her then.'

Alice was still stunned. The small, crowded unfamiliar room kept closing in on her and then retreating and there was a strange humming noise and a warm, oily sort of smell. She struggled to get up.

'Hold on, young lady. Lie still for a few more minutes.'

She stared up at him apprehensively; no one had ever called her young lady. 'Who are you?'

'I'm a doctor who should be checking his drugs, dressings, surgical appliances and nursing staff, that's who.'

Alice lay still, barely taking in his words, but reassured by the quiet authority in his voice. The humming noise was soothing and she relaxed as gentle hands examined her.

'A bit bruised. Maybe a cracked rib or two, I can't really tell, and probably concussed. We can't keep her but she really should go to hospital for observation.'

The word 'hospital' galvanised Alice and she struggled to sit up. 'I'm not going to no hospital! It's . . . it's like the workhouse. You never come out of no hospital alive, me mam says so!'

'Don't be ridiculous, girl, this is nineteen twenty-five! You need rest and nourishing food and,' he added under his breath, 'a bath.' He turned to David. 'There's no serious damage. Nothing that a few days' rest won't cure.' Squeezing past Charlie, he opened the door with some difficulty.

'Thanks.'

'No trouble, but get her and it ashore before you ruin your career entirely.'

Alice stared around her timidly. 'Where . . . where is this?'

31

David smiled reassuringly. 'A cabin on board the *Aquitania*.'

Her eyes widened. 'What?'

'Don't get alarmed. You ran out after your kitten in front of the car and I brought you here. And the kitten's not hurt. That was the ship's doctor. How do you feel now?'

'Sore. It hurts when I breathe and if I can't breathe properly, I can't sing.'

'Sing?'

'That's how I earn me living . . . now. Street singing.'

'Don't you have a family?'

'Yes, but . . . but I don't live with them any more. Me da . . . well, it was him that cracked me ribs, not your car. So I left.'

He looked at her pityingly. 'What's your name?'

'Alice. Alice O'Connor.'

'Well, Alice O'Connor, I'm sorry but you can't stay here, we sail soon.'

'Where to?'

'New York. America,' he added in case she didn't know where the city of New York was.

She looked up at him wistfully. He was really handsome. He had thick, dark, curly hair, his face was tanned and his brown eyes were full of concern. He'd been kind to her and it was warm and comfortable in here. She wished she could stay. She was sure she'd like America.

'Are you sure you feel all right?'

She nodded but the movement caused her to close her eyes and clasp her head.

'No, you're not!'

'I'm just hungry. I haven't had nothing to eat all day.'

'Nothing? Nothing at all?'

'No.'

He glanced at Charlie appalled. 'Good God Almighty! Why didn't you say so?' It had never occurred to him that she might be starving.

She didn't reply.

He dug into his pocket and handed her a coin. 'Here, my brother will take you ashore. Go and get something to eat and then take a hackney cab up to the hospital. Tell them what happened and what Kendrick said about concussion.'

She stared in utter disbelief at the coin in the grubby palm of her hand. It was a guinea, a golden guinea! She'd never even seen one before but she had heard about them. 'All this . . . is for me?'

'It won't go far,' he said, thinking that he spent more on a suit than she had probably seen in her entire life. As the eldest son of a solicitor he'd never known hardship. Quite the opposite. He experienced a strong pang of guilt. Time was pressing and Charlie was fidgeting. 'Here, seeing as we've managed to deprive you of your livelihood for a while, you'd better have this too.' A ten-shilling note was thrust at her and she snatched it from him before he changed his mind. This was certainly worth getting knocked over for. She picked up the kitten and gently folded her shawl round it. It mewed weakly at being disturbed. It *had* brought her luck, she thought. She'd been right to keep it.

Gently David helped her off the bunk, gave her her boots and guided her to the door. 'You will go to the hospital when you've eaten?' he asked firmly.

She smiled up at him. 'Yes.'

The smile was one of pure joy and it completely trans-formed her face. She was truly beautiful when she smiled, despite the dirt, he thought. 'Promise me?'

'I said I'll go, didn't I?' she answered him. But not when, she added to herself.

'Goodbye then, Alice O'Connor, and good luck with your singing.'

'Who knows, one day we might be paying to come and listen to you,' Charlie interrupted heartily, attempting to

33

cover his embarrassment and his eagerness to get away and be rid of her. She looked a fright.

David saw the look of wonderment that filled her eyes. He frowned at his brother and shook his head. Trust Charlie! Why the hell had he said such a fatuous thing? Why go putting fantastic and utterly unattainable notions in her head?

When they'd gone he looked down at the bunk and sighed. He'd have to get it stripped – the cat would have had fleas and she was probably alive with bugs. Poor girl, a verminous state was something she obviously couldn't help, part and parcel no doubt, of being poor.

He dismissed her from his mind as, reaching for his cap and glancing at his watch, he turned his thoughts to his duties and the impending dressing-down that was almost certainly waiting for him.

Chapter Four

Robinson acknowledged Charlie and Alice with a nod as they went ashore but Alice was too preoccupied to notice. Get a meal, her rescuer had said, but that in itself presented a serious problem. Who would believe that she had been given a sovereign and a ten-shilling note? She'd get arrested for stealing, sure as eggs were eggs. She clutched Charlie's arm.

'What's the matter now?' he asked apprehensively, hoping she wasn't going to faint or cause him to lose more precious time. He should have been on his way back now. Nor was he very happy about leaving his father's brand new Minerva down on the waterfront. It was locked but there would be a tremendous row if the paintwork was marked. He sighed, thinking of the sporty little Jowett two-seater he'd set his heart on. He didn't want to get into his parents' bad books.

'Will you come with me, like?'

'Where to?'

'Over there. That eating house.'

'I haven't got time to be escorting you into eating houses.'

Alice stared at him hard. He'd been driving the car so it was his fault and he wasn't going to deprive her of a slap-up meal.

'Well, I'll get arrested if you don't. No one's going to believe that someone like me, in this state, has come by all this money honestly, like, now are they?'

She had a point, he admitted to himself reluctantly. He was embarrassed by the odd glances they were attracting, the fresh-faced, well-dressed young man and this dirty, scruffy, undernourished ragamuffin. He just hoped people weren't thinking he'd picked her up. Paid for her 'services'.

'An' if I get nicked then what will you tell him?' She jerked her head in the direction of the landing stage and the *Aquitania*.

'Oh, all right. I'll come with you and tell them you didn't steal it, but that's all. I'm late. Very late.'

Alice nodded with satisfaction. It was getting dark and as soon as she'd eaten she'd have to think things over. She'd have to make new plans, for she'd never imagined she'd have such wealth. 'Where do you live?' she asked conversationally.

'Crosby.'

She'd heard of it. 'Is that far?'

He shrugged. 'It depends on how you look at it. It's not far by car or train, but it is if you have to walk.'

They had reached their objective and Charlie pushed open the half-glazed door for her then followed her in.

It was warm and fuggy inside, thick with odours of food, stale fat and unwashed bodies. Alice sat down at a bare wooden table in the window and he went to the counter to explain the situation to the burly harridan who appeared to be in charge of things.

'That . . . that girl over there,' he pointed to Alice who nodded. 'She's got money but it's not stolen. My brother gave it to her.'

The woman stared at him unblinkingly.

'Yes, well, I . . . I just wanted you to know that she didn't steal it.'

The woman looked him up and down and Charlie began to blush.

36

'Right. Fine,' he muttered, turning away. He needed a drink but he wasn't going to get one until he got home. If they hadn't stopped at the George on the way to the ship, all this would never have happened. He went back to Alice.

'Right, that's settled,' he announced with relief. 'Goodbye and good luck.'

She smiled at him and he turned and walked to the door.

'Hey!' she called.

Charlie turned. 'Now what?' His tone was sharp.

'You never told me your name, or his.'

'Mine's Charlie Williamson and my brother's name is David. Now goodbye, Alice O'Connor.'

She watched him disappear into the winter gloom, and then turned her mind to important things. Like food and a saucer of bread and milk for Mog.

She ordered soup, mutton chops with peas and boiled potatoes, jam sponge pudding with custard and extra bread and butter and a pot of tea.

''Ave everything that's on offer, why don't yer! Save time an' me bloody legs!' the blowsy waitress remarked sarcastically.

'I might just do that an' all,' Alice shot back. 'An' anyway, it's yer job.' It must be last Christmas since she'd had as much food to eat and the whole lot only came to two shillings! She could more than afford it. There were still eight whole shillings left from the ten-bob note. The guinea was pushed inside the pocket of her skirt and she'd tied a knot in the pocket to keep it safe. She clasped the thought of her riches to her in astonished delight.

When the edge had been taken off her hunger her headache started to recede and she began to take more notice of what was going on around her and beyond the window. She jumped nervously as the *Aquitania*'s steam whistle blasted out repeatedly, using the same signal as that of the *Duchess of York* to summon lingering crew members from the pub. She'd be leaving soon and then he'd be gone too. He'd been so good to her and she would really have liked to stay. It had been a warm, cosy little room. She wouldn't have taken up much extra space.

She'd heard tales about America. Dinny Kavanagh from up the street went to sea and he always seemed to have plenty of money. She'd heard him say you could make a fortune in America without even breaking your back. It was known as a place where the poor got on in life. New York, David Williamson had said they were sailing to. Would it be like Liverpool? she wondered. Would it be bigger or smaller? Oh, he had been so nice, so kind, even bringing the doctor to see her. She'd never met anyone like him before. He was obviously well off, his clothes were good and she'd noticed the watch on his wrist and the gold signet ring on his finger. And yet he'd bothered with the likes of her and he'd laid her on his bed, taken off her boots, wiped her face with that cool towel. He'd really seemed to care about her, he'd even saved Mog. Lots of people she knew had been knocked down, sometimes by cars but mainly by runaway horses. No one made a fuss about them, except maybe the scuffers – if they died.

As she finished the last slice of bread, she felt drowsy. She didn't need to go singing tonight. She'd go to the Sally Army hostel and get a bed and then sleep. Oh, wouldn't it be great to have a bed to herself, a clean bed. She looked down at her clothes and then turned her hands over. The bed might be clean but she certainly wasn't. She'd have a bath, that's what she would do. Now that was a real luxury. She'd never had a bath in her life. When they'd been little her mother used to stand them in the sink in the scullery and wash them. Nelly would be getting worried about her now and she had enough on her plate. Alice really didn't want to upset her. She'd just have to think of a way of getting word to her that she was doing just fine. But she didn't want to think of her Mam.

Reluctantly she left the warmth of the eating house and went into the sharp, frosty dusk, but instead of turning towards the city she made again for the Prince's Landing Stage, quite why she didn't know. When she reached it, the *Aquitania*'s gangways were being hauled up and the tugs had taken up the hawsers. High above her on the boat deck, so high she got a crick in her neck looking up, people were waving down to friends and relatives. The whole ship was ablaze with lights. By, it was a magnificent sight and he was on there – somewhere.

She stood watching as the ship moved slowly away from the stage and out into the river escorted by the tugs. The customary three long blasts on the steam whistle echoed around the waterfront and were answered by some of the many ships out in the river, including the ferries. It was their way of saying 'God speed' and 'Safe journey'. Soon she had passed the New Brighton lighthouse and was just a blur of light fading into the cold winter darkness.

Alice sighed and turned away. David. David Williamson, she said to herself. She'd remember that, the way she would remember Letty Lewis, the Cockney Songbird. That called to mind the night she'd stood outside the Rotunda. Training and grooming, the lady had said. Would she ever be able to get them both? Would she find them in America? The thought held her spellbound for a few seconds. Well, why not? Now she had money. That Charlie had said maybe one day they'd be paying to hear her sing and if she was singing on the stage, in a dress like Letty Lewis had worn, he'd certainly sit up and take notice of her. Suddenly it became of paramount importance that she see David Williamson again and not dressed as she had been this time, in tatty, dirty rags.

Other people had gone to America – thousands of them. She'd seen them waiting for the ships and they'd been hard up too. There had been no pennies to give to her for entertaining them. Even the biggest ships took poor people, if they could pay. Her fingers closed round the coin in her pocket. Surely a golden guinea would be enough for her fare. And she had eight shillings. When she got there she could sing, in the streets to start with, while she sorted out the training and grooming and maybe . . . maybe she'd see him again.

These astonishing new ideas hurtled through her mind, making her head spin. Oh, what she wouldn't give to get away from here. Away from everything and everyone – except Mam. She'd write to Mam. A proper letter explaining that she wasn't to worry. She'd be all right. Alice resolved to take it to the house later on. No sense in wasting money on stamps. You could buy a single sheet of paper and an envelope in a newsagents. She'd shove the letter through the letter box. She knew Nelly wouldn't mind her going to America, not if she was to have a chance in life, a better life. That's all Mam had ever wanted for them all and she wanted to make Mam proud of her. It would make all the hardships and beatings worthwhile – well, in a small way, but there was just a chance that if she went in, Mam might try and talk her out of it.

Alice walked up James Street not noticing anything that was going on around her, too absorbed in her thoughts. Only when she got to the bottom of Lord Street did she realise where she was. Bunny's department store was on the corner, its windows lit up, but she passed it without a glance and walked along Church Street, still deliberating what to do.

She at last stopped outside Marks and Spencer. In the window they had stockings marked 6d. a pair. Good, thick, warm black ones. She darted inside and found her way to the appropriate counter and when she emerged sixpence lighter, it was with a pair nicely wrapped up. There was no point in wasting money on new clothes when there were plenty of second-hand shops around. She could probably rig herself out for three or four shillings and that would include boots. But she hadn't been able to resist a pair of stockings.

Her new-found wealth amazed her when she thought of all the luxuries it afforded. She could get a tram to anywhere in the city for twopence. She could go across the river on the ferry for the same price. She could buy more food, lots of food. She could have a bath, complete with soap and towel, for sixpence, at Burrough's Gardens Baths. Yes, that's what she'd do. She'd buy some clothes and get the tram from Byrom Street. She didn't want to walk along Scotland Road in case she bumped into Lizzie or the kids or, worst of all, Da. She'd write the letter, sneak down the jiggers, shove it through the door and then get a tram back into town. Then she'd get a bed and in the morning – well, who knew what the morning would bring? She had had so many novel experiences today that she felt as though hundreds of mice were darting around in her stomach. She liked being rich, she decided, it suited her very well indeed.

Had David Williamson or his brother Charlie seen her when she emerged from the public baths in Burrough's Gardens they would hardly have recognised her. She'd been very apprehensive at first about the big cast-iron bath into which the hot water had gushed, filling the small cubicle with clouds of steam. She'd paid her money and had been handed a towel, a piece of soap and a long-handled scrubbing brush stamped with the words 'Liverpool Corporation'. The attendant, a thickset woman swathed in a white cotton overall, had shown her into the cubicle and with a sort of spanner thing had turned on the taps. When the bath was three-quarters full, she turned off the water.

41

'Bring the towel an' brush back ter me when you're done. The soap yer can keep, what's left of it,' she said flatly, shutting the door and leaving Alice alone.

She gingerly put her right foot into the water. It felt wonderful but she'd make sure she hung on tightly to the side of the bath just the same. She lost no time in stripping off her clothes and wrapping the kitten in her shawl. Then she lowered herself in. As the warm water covered her body, she relaxed so much that she nearly dozed off, but pushing aside her lethargy she worked up a lather with the soap and began to scrub away the dirt and grime.

At a second-hand shop at the bottom of Great Crosshall Street she'd bought a heavy flannel skirt, a paisley print blouse, a new shawl, a petticoat, a pair of drawers and boots. The shopkeeper had thrown in a bit of velvet ribbon to tie up her hair. She looked with distaste at her old clothes lying in a pile on the floor. She wasn't even going to take them away with her, she was going to ask the attendant to get rid of them. That was what having money meant, she thought with satisfaction.

There was a tiny mirror on the wall and when she'd finished she was amazed at the image of the girl who stared back. It was a new Alice O'Connor. Her skin glowed pink from the brisk rubbing and she'd towelled her hair vigorously and tied it up with the ribbon. Was this what the lady had meant by grooming? If it was, then all she needed now was the training.

She tucked the kitten into her new shawl. 'Right, Mog, all I've got to do is get a letter to Mam and then it's a new life for you and me. You'll grow into a big fat cat, you see if you don't.'

She got a single piece of writing paper and an envelope from Daly's on the corner of the street. Josie Daly had been in her class at school but Alice didn't like her. Now she'd have to be nice and ask her to lend her a pencil.

'Who're you writing to, Alice O'Connor? I didn't think

you knew anyone important enough to write to.'

Alice just stared at Josie who was eyeing her up and down. The retort 'Mind your own business' sprang to her lips but she couldn't afford to alienate Josie who was holding the pencil.

'It's to me mam, if you must know, Josie.'

Josie rolled her eyes expressively. 'Oh, aye, an' I came over on the last boat with a cargo of Irish confetti! It's a feller! It's got to be, you're all dressed up. Where did you get those things?'

Alice decided it would be easier to play along. 'I bought them. Me feller gave me the money, but don't let on,' she hissed, jerking her head in Mr Daly's direction.

Josie smirked and tapped the side of her nose before handing over the pencil and turning away to serve someone else.

Alice sucked the pencil, trying to formulate words and sentences in her head. It took her a while but at last she was satisfied with her efforts.

In a short while, Alice was picking her way through the pitch-dark maze of back entries that she knew like the back of her hand. Soon she emerged into Benledi Street. Keeping in the shadows, away from the circles of yellow light cast by the street lamps, she reached number eight but then she gasped, shrinking into the doorway as Nelly emerged from number ten.

'Alice? Alice, is that you, luv?' Nelly peered into the darkness. 'I've been out of me mind, girl! Are yer all right?'

Alice knew it was useless to remain silent. She stepped forward and pushed the letter into Nelly's hand. 'I'm fine, Mam, honest.'

'What's this? Where did you get this letter from?'

'It's for you, Mam, from me. I . . . I'm going away.'

'Going away? Going where, Alice?' Nelly noticed her daughter's changed appearance. 'Where did you get those clothes? You look . . . different.'

'Oh, never mind the clothes, Mam. I *am* different. It . . . it's all in the letter. Everything. I wrote it all down. I'm going to America, it's my big chance. You always said we should have a fair chance. Well, I've got it.'

Nelly stood shaking her head in disbelief, unable to comprehend what Alice was saying. 'Alice, in the name of God, what have you done?'

'Nothing, Mam! I got knocked over but I'm fine, it was the best thing that ever happened to me.'

'Come on in, luv,' her mother coaxed.

'No! I . . . I can't. I won't. I hate him! If I come in he'll take all me things to Solly Indigo and then he'll get drunk and start belting me again. I'm going, Mam. It's my only chance!' She couldn't bear to see the look that was creeping into her mother's eyes.

'You can't, Alice! Come on inside, yer da's out.'

'No, Mam. It's all in the letter. You're not to worry. I'll send you money and I'll . . . I'll come back when I'm famous from singing in the theatre. I promise I will, Mam. I swear to God I will!' Before Nelly could say a word, Alice hugged her quickly and then turned and ran up the street, the tears coursing down her cheeks.

Nelly leaned against the door of the house, her hand to her mouth, her eyes fixed on the disappearing figure of her daughter. 'Oh, Holy Mother of God, look after her!' she prayed, then she looked down at the now crumpled envelope. Would she ever see Alice again? A great weariness came over her and she brushed away her tears. She couldn't blame Alice. What was there here in Benledi Street to stay for?

For the first time in her entire life Alice O'Connor slept in a bed that was clean, comfortable and not shared with anyone else apart from her good luck charm, the cat. There were no sheets but she hadn't expected any. There were plenty of blankets though and a pillow, and the room was warm, heated by a stove in the centre. She lay staring drowsily at the regimented line of beds. Oh, this was sheer luxury and with no drunken arguments or fights to interrupt her sleep and tomorrow . . . tomorrow was going to be even better than today, she just knew it was. It had upset her to leave Mam but at least she had been able to talk to her, to give her a quick hug. She hadn't left Mam to fret, not knowing where she was at all.

She left the hostel at eight o'clock the next morning, after having had a wash and tidied her hair in the communal and very basic bathroom. Today she felt a different person entirely, as if she'd washed the old Alice away last night in the bath.

She made her way again to the eating house at Mann Island and her appearance was so changed that the waitress didn't recognise her at first. She ordered a bacon butty, a mug of tea and a bowl of bread and milk for Mog.

When they arrived, the woman looked at her suspiciously. 'You done all right fer yerself, girl. Why did that feller give yer all that money yisterday?'

'Mind yer own business!' Alice shot back at her knowing what she was implying.

'We don't have tarts in 'ere. This is a respectable caf.'

Alice got to her feet. 'I'm not a flaming tart! An' I'm not coming in here again to be insulted.' She gulped down the tea and clutching the sandwich and her cat, stormed out. She'd eat her breakfast on her way to the shipping offices. 'Never mind, Mog,' she said when they got outside, 'I'll give yer some of me bacon. And we've still got half a crown left and the guinea. That's twenty-three shillings and sixpence altogether. I don't suppose they'll charge for you, but in case they do you'd better keep still and quiet under me shawl.'

There was a line of people waiting outside the Cunard Building, all dressed much as she was, so she joined them and waited patiently until the doors were opened and the crowd moved forward. It seemed an age before it was her turn.

'Yes, miss?' The clerk behind the polished wood counter eyed her with a look of resigned boredom.

'I want to go to America. To New York, on one of those.' She pointed to a large poster pinned to the wall above the counter. It depicted the three black hulls and seven red and black funnels of the *Mauretania, Berengaria* and *Aquitania* against a dark, smoky sky and was topped with the words 'CUNARD – THE FASTEST OCEAN SERVICE IN THE WORLD'.

'Well, you've missed the *Aquitania*, she sailed yesterday. The *Mauretania* is due in today, she'll sail again in two days – to New York,' he added.

'Then I'll go on that one.'

'Right. I assume it's a single ticket? You won't be coming back?'

Put into words, someone else's words, it sounded very final, rather frightening and yet exciting. She nodded.

'Name?'

'Alice O'Connor. Miss.'

'Five guineas, please, miss.'

Her mouth fell open and her eyes widened with shock. '*Five guineas!*'

'That's the price of a single ticket steerage class. For that you get bed and board, simple food but wholesome, on a fast, safe ship. You'll be there in less than five days.'

'But . . . but I've only got one guinea. It's a golden one though,' she added hopefully.

'You'll need another four, miss.'

'Another four? Isn't there a cheaper ticket?'

'No, and you'll find that prices are pretty much the same at other shipping lines and they all take far longer to get there.'

'They all charge the same?'

The clerk tapped his pen impatiently on the edge of the inkwell. It was a situation he often came up against. Couldn't any of them read? The prices were displayed prominently enough on the walls. 'Well, you might get a tramp that's going across the Atlantic, that would be cheaper, but how long it would take I don't know.'

The people behind were getting impatient. He dismissed Alice with a nod and called, 'Next!'

She turned away, devastated. To acquire one golden guinea had been a miracle; four more were an impossibility.

She wandered disconsolately along the Strand towards the Albert Dock, then along Wapping to the Salthouse and finally the King's Dock. He'd said a tramp and she knew he meant one of those small, creaking, rusty ships you often saw in the docks or chugging out to the Mersey – slowly. They didn't look very safe. Well, beggars can't be choosers, Alice O'Connor, she told herself, trying to revive her drooping spirits and banish her disappointment. It was vitally important that she get to America. Over the last two days it had become her sole ambition. It was her destiny – she just knew her luck would change when she got there. Maybe she'd better take his advice.

It was past lunch time when she finally found the captain of a tramp steamer who would even listen to her. Everywhere else she'd met with cold, firm rebuttal or open disdain and hostility.

The *Castlemaine* wasn't very big. It only had one funnel. A dirty tattered flag hung limply from its short mast, from which the paint was peeling, and there was a lot of rust on the hull. In fact, there were more red patches than black ones.

'What do you want, girl?' the tall man standing on the deck beneath the bridge barked as she walked gingerly across the plank of wood that spanned the dirty, oily strip of water between the ship and the dock wall.

'I want to go to New York. I can pay.'

'Oh, aye. Why haven't you gone to the big companies?'

'I tried. They're too expensive. Oh, please, mister, are you going to America?'

He looked her up and down. A fine looking girl and no mistake. 'I am and it's Captain Burrows to you, not mister.'

'Then will you take me, Captain? Please?' trying desperately to look appealing. She didn't like the look of him much, he reminded her of her da, but he had said he was going to America.

'How much have you got?'

'A guinea. A golden one.'

He laughed. 'Gold or not makes no difference, it's not enough. I charge at least two. You've got to be fed.'

She was becoming desperate. 'I won't eat anything, I'm used to going hungry. Will that help?'

'No, it won't. You'd be taking up a berth that I could get maybe three guineas for.'

The tears started in her eyes. Her money wouldn't last long and she just couldn't go back. She never wanted to go back to that life. If she didn't get to New York she'd never ever see David Williamson again and that now mattered a great deal to her.

'We could come to some arrangement though. You're not a bad looking judy.'

Alice's cheeks flushed as his meaning dawned on her and she shuddered. 'I'm not a girl . . . like . . . that.'

He shrugged. 'Suit yourself. If you change your mind, come back tonight. We're leaving on the midnight tide.'

She walked slowly back along Wapping and sank down on the top step of a bonded tea warehouse, her gaze wandering to the river and the ships that were plying to and fro, and those that were far out along the Crosby Channel heading towards the Bar Light and the open sea.

Ever since she'd made her decision to leave Benledi Street she'd had good luck. She'd earned a few shillings, she'd met David Williamson and been on board the *Aquitania*. She'd had good food, a bed, a bath and new clothes. Surely luck wasn't going to desert her now. Oh, she knew that a better life awaited her across the ocean, it *did*. She'd never been so certain of anything before. But what would David Williamson think of her, if she ever saw him again, if she'd made a whore of herself just to pay her fare? If she stayed though, her money would be spent and she'd be back where she started, dressed in dirty rags, singing in the street to keep food in her belly and a roof over her head. She might even be forced in the end to go back to Benledi Street.

'It looks like we've run out of your bit of luck, Mog,' she said despondently to the ball of fur in the crook of her arm. Mog gazed up at her, as if she understood, and Alice stared blankly into the distance.

How long she sat there she didn't know. All the memories of a deprived, cruel and violent childhood pressed in on her. There had been nothing good in her past, except her ability to sing, and she'd ever done that to earn money, never really for pleasure.

When she finally got to her feet, she was cold and stiff. Her mind was made up and although she didn't know it, some of the softness had gone from her eyes. She was going. She didn't care what it cost. It might not be so bad, she told herself. After all, Mam had put up with it at least six times as she, Lizzie, her brothers and Agnes and Mary proved. But what would Mam think of her? Her heart plummeted but she pushed the thought of Nelly firmly to the back of her mind. Mam would never know and life was cruel and hard. She had no intention of... of... well, carrying on with *it* once she got to New York. She squared her shoulders, settled the kitten, wrapped her shawl tightly round her and raised her chin determinedly.

I'm not really being a whore. I'm just paying me way, she told herself firmly as she retraced her steps back along Wapping towards the King's Dock.

Chapter Five

The cabin she was given, which was to become her home, her refuge, and her prison for the next three weeks, was dark, cramped and dirty. She wrinkled her nose as the odours of bilge water, coal dust and stale food assailed her nostrils.

'It's worse than our flaming scullery!' she exclaimed acidly. She thought of the only other cabin she'd ever seen and wondered what kind of room she'd have got on the *Mauretania*, had she been able to afford the fare.

'What do you expect for the pittance you're paying?' James Burrows snapped back. He was already regretting his decision. To take the *Castlemaine* across the Atlantic in the depths of winter was no easy task, without burdening himself with a passenger. One that looked like trouble, too.

He'd left her with the promise that he'd be back later when they'd cleared the Bar Lightship, and she sat down on the edge of the narrow bunk, feeling desolate.

'We've got nothing to unpack, have we, Mog?' she said flatly. She hung her shawl on a hook behind the door. At least the room was warm, she thought. Like a coal hole but warm. There was that faint oily smell she'd noticed on the *Aquitania*. Perhaps all ships smelled the same.

She'd given Captain Burrows the sovereign and now she looked for somewhere to hide the half-crown which was all the money she had in the world. The bulkheads were bare, there was no porthole. A small hurricane lamp hanging from a hook was the only source of light. Lifting up the thin flock mattress she managed to prise up one of the boards that formed the base of the bunk. She ignored the scattering of insect life this caused, for she'd lived with bugs for too long to be concerned or squeamish about them.

With her money hidden and her eyes accustomed to the gloom, she pondered James Burrows' departing words and a feeling of dread replaced the desolation. The worst was yet to come. She wondered how long it would be before they were clear of the estuary and the Bar Light. An hour, two, hopefully much longer. They didn't appear to be moving very quickly.

After half an hour she had managed to allay some of her fear, but sitting down here with nothing to see or do to distract her wasn't helping. There was also the stench, the noise and the vibrations to contend with. Everything creaked and rattled and it was disconcerting. She could also hear the sea and it alarmed her to think that only a thin wall of rusty old metal separated her from it. She decided to go up on deck.

At the end of the narrow passageway was a steep ladder. It was pitch dark. She climbed up on deck and stared around, holding tightly to the rail. It was cold. A stiff wind had sprung up and it whipped her hair across her face. The smell of the river was strong but she took deep breaths of comparatively fresh air. She could see the lights strung out along the coastline like a necklace. Turning back, she could see in the distance the lights of the trio of buildings at the Pier Head and it suddenly hit her that she was leaving Liverpool. She was leaving behind everything she had known, everything that was familiar, and a sob rose and caught in her throat. 'Oh, Mam! Will I ever see you again?' she whispered.

'He says you're to get below. You're not supposed to be up on deck.'

She turned sharply at the sound of the voice. A tall thin lad of about her own age, with a shock of unkempt dark hair that fell into his eyes, was regarding her with open curiosity.

'Who are you?'

'Georgie Tate. I'm the cabin boy.'

'Well, it's not much of a flaming cabin!'

He shrugged. 'That's nothing to do with me. Cabin boy's only a name, a bloody stupid one an' all.'

'What do you do then if you don't see to cabins?'

'General dogsbody, that's what I am. I do everything, everything that's rotten. Swab the decks. Clean the heads, help in the galley, give the donkey man a hand.'

Most of the list she didn't understand. 'What's a donkey man?'

'The feller who looks after the donkey boiler. How much is he charging you?'

'A guinea and . . .'

He suddenly grinned. 'And what?'

She turned away. 'Never you mind what!'

'Well, yer luck's in.'

She still couldn't look at him. Was this a regular thing? she wondered. Besides the cargo, did the *Castlemaine* always carry a whore? 'I'm not a whore!' she snapped. 'I . . . I've got reasons why I *had* to come on this floating rust bucket.'

'All right, don't get airyated with me, girl! What's yer name, anyway?'

'Alice. Alice O'Connor.' She looked at him more carefully. He wasn't laughing at her, his dark eyes were regarding her with concern. 'What did you mean, me luck's in?' she asked cautiously.

'He won't be down for hours yet. There's a storm brewing up out there.'

'How do you know?' Relief was mingled with alarm.

'I just do an' I heard Timms, the mate, saying so. Have you ever been to sea before?'

'No.'

'Not even on the ferry?'

She shook her head, thinking she was seventeen years old and she'd never even crossed the river in her life.

'Then I hope yer a good sailor. But,' he finished cheerfully, 'it doesn't last.'

'What doesn't?'

'Seasickness.'

'Oh.'

'Don't worry, I'll look after yer, Alice.'

He seemed pleasant enough and she was grateful for his concern. 'How long have you worked here, on this . . . lump of scrap?'

'Two years. I ran away from home.'

'What for?'

'Me mam died and the owld feller married again. A real bitch, she was. I hated her an' she hated me, so I ran away to sea.' He paused. 'Why are *you* running away, Alice?'

'Because of me da and . . . other things.'

Before he could question her further, James Burrows bellowed at him from the bridge. 'Get that bloody woman below!'

Georgie hastily pushed her towards the stairway. 'I'll come and see yer when I can. I promise.'

'Thanks,' she replied, descending again into that suffocating darkness, but feeling that she'd at least met someone she could talk to.

She had no idea of the time but she was tired. She stripped down to her petticoat and drawers and pulled the blanket up over her and, clutching Mog to her, tried to sleep. Exhausted, for a moment she sank into oblivion but what seemed like minutes later, started awake. Everything was creaking and groaning and she wondered fear-fully if the ship would spring a leak. The movement seemed to increase and the engines thudded and the single screw vibrated noisily. She clung tightly to the edge of the bunk. She had no idea where the kitten was. Her alarm increased as she watched the hurricane lamp swing to and fro like the pendulum of a clock and the sound of the waves hitting the hull became frighteningly loud. She felt queasy, claustrophobic and . . . trapped.

As the hours passed, it got worse. The ship pitched and rolled and she was flung bodily from the bunk onto the floor where she lay whimpering in terror until nausea swamped her. Oh, she wished she was dead. In fact she knew she must be dying for she'd never felt so bad in all her life. She felt so ill that all the terror receded. Even if the ship was torn apart by the waves or swamped and sent plunging to the bottom of the Irish Sea, she couldn't have cared less.

Some time during the night she heard Georgie Tate's voice and felt someone lift her and put her back on the bunk. A damp cloth was passed over her face.

'Oh, I want me mam! I want to go home! I'm dying,' she moaned.

'You'll be all right, Alice. It'll get better, honest it will.'

'It won't. I want to die! Oh, let me die, please!'

'I'll come back and see you later,' he promised.

She was past caring.

He did come back, three times, and so did James Bur-rows. He glared at Alice's prostrate form and that of the black and white kitten which was clinging to her skirt with its claws.

'Get that bloody stinking mess cleaned up, Tate, and get rid of that bloody cat!'

'It's doin' no 'arm, Captain. It'll keep the vermin down.'

James Burrows nodded his agreement. 'Bloody women, more trouble than they're worth! I'm too soft-hearted, that's my trouble,' he muttered as he slammed out.

Ten hours passed but Alice didn't know or care. Georgie had cleaned her up and had tried to get some thin gruel down her but it had come straight back up again. The cat had greedily lapped up the rest of the gruel from the chipped enamel dish Georgie had put on the floor.

'It's dying down now, Alice. You'll feel better soon, honest you will.'

He hadn't lied; by midday the sea was calmer, the swell only moderate and the wind had dropped, but they'd lost time. If they met more bad weather, and at this time of year it was almost guaranteed, then it would be a long time before the voyage was over, Georgie knew. But he'd look after her. Once she'd got over this she'd be all right. She'd have her sea legs. He'd decided he liked her. She wasn't a whore, she was just running away but it was different for girls. If they had no money and no job then it was usually what they turned to. But he wondered just what the circumstances were that had driven her to make such a bargain with Captain Burrows.

It was two days later when Alice woke from a deep sleep and looked around her, amazed that she was still alive. She certainly hadn't died, unless heaven was a dark, poky, smelly room. She sat up, pulling the stained blanket up to cover her nakedness. She blushed, wondering just who had seen her in this state. She vaguely remembered hearing voices, men's voices. Then she heard someone singing, not very tunefully, and realised she was hungry. She found her skirt and blouse, her stockings and her boots, put them on and opened the cabin door cautiously.

Georgie Tate was in the companionway, sloshing a wet and dirty mop up and down it.

He grinned as he caught sight of her. 'I told yer you'd be all right, didn't I?'

She blushed. 'Was it you who . . . well, I remember

hearing someone talking to me.'

'It was me, oh, an' the skipper came down once to look at yer. Are yer hungry?'

'I'm starving. I never thought I'd ever say that again.'

'It doesn't last – well, not usually. Come on, I'll get you something.'

'Where's me cat?'

He grinned. 'It's around somewhere, probably earning its keep.'

'It's too little!'

'Oh, stop goin' on about the bloody cat! They 'as nine lives and they like ships. Nearly every ship 'as a cat to keep the mice an' rats down. Our last one died of old age an' I give it a proper burial an' all. At sea. Its name was Salty. 'As yours got a name?'

'I just call it Mog.'

She followed him to the galley, yet another small, cramped space and another that was not very clean either.

'Yer can have bacon or bacon an' bread.'

'I'll have a bacon butty, please.' She suddenly remembered that that was the last thing she'd had to eat before she'd left Liverpool. 'How . . . how long was I sick?'

'Best part of three days.'

'Three days! Where are we now?'

'In the Atlantic. We've just passed the old Head of Kinsale. Where the *Lucy* went down,' he teased.

She'd heard of the sinking of the *Lusitania* and her eyes grew wide with fear. If a ship like that could sink, what chance had something as small as this?

'I was only teasing yer. She was sunk by a torpedo, in the war.'

'Then just stop it, Georgie Tate! I'm not used to boats an' you know it.'

'Ships,' he corrected her. 'Anything bigger than the ferries is a ship.'

'This isn't much bigger than the ferries,' she replied with spirit.

She ate the thick sandwich and washed it down with the mug of tea he gave her. 'Was that you singing?' she asked when she'd finished.

'Yeah.'

'What were you singing?'

' "Show Me The Way To Go Home".'

She'd thought she'd heard it. 'I sing. Do you know any more songs?'

'Oh, aye, plenty. "Always", "It Had To Be You", "Lime-house Blues".'

She'd never heard of any of them. 'That's what I do, for a job, like. Sing.'

He regarded her with incredulity. 'Honest? On the stage, like?'

'No. I ... I was a street singer.'

He looked disappointed but she was the first girl who'd taken any interest in him and she was pretty.

For the first time in three days she remembered that she hadn't 'paid' her full fare and a shadow crossed her face. 'What's he like?' She jerked her head in the direction of the deck above.

'Better than some. He's hard, but when yer make yer living tramping around the world in an owld tub like this, yer got to be hard.'

'Is he ... is he married? He looks old.'

'I think he was, once, an' he's not that old. He's not bad, Alice, really. He's fair, I'll say that for him. He pays up on time, too.'

She pursed her lips. She'd made a bargain with him and he'd expect to be paid up on time too. That time would probably be soon. 'Is there anywhere I can get a wash?'

He nodded, suddenly uncommunicative, seeming to sense what was in her mind.

'Where?'

'I'll fetch yer some water an' yer can borrow me comb.'

She nodded her thanks and made her way back to her cabin.

He didn't speak when he brought her a metal bowl half full of water, a bit of lye soap and an old towel. He handed her a cheap comb and she smiled nervously at him, disconcerted by his silence, sensing his disapproval.

She felt better when she'd washed herself all over. There was no mirror but she combed out the tangled curls, tied them up and hoped they looked tidy. The piece of ribbon now bore more resemblance to a piece of string. She wondered how long it was going to take to get to New York and if there was any chance of washing her clothes. She also began to wonder what she would do with herself all day. The waiting for Captain Burrows was almost more than she could bear.

She'd straightened the bunk, after checking that her precious half-crown was still under the boards, and she was wondering whether to ask Georgie Tate for some more water to scrub the place out when the door opened and she looked up, her heart sinking. The moment she'd been dreading had arrived. The tall angular figure of Captain Burrows filled the doorway.

'You've recovered then?'

She nodded, looking down at her boots.

'So when we hit the next squall or storm I don't want to see Georgie Tate running round after you like a wet-nurse and neglecting his duties.'

'The next one?'

'It's New Year's Day and we're heading across the Atlantic Ocean, girl! It's not a bloody day trip to New Brighton or Llandudno.'

'I missed Christmas?'

'We all did. So what?'

'Is it really New Year's Day?' she pressed, stalling for time.

'Aye, the first of January, nineteen twenty-six.'

In other circumstances she would have been glad, wondering what this year would bring. Instead she sat on the edge of the bunk, biting her lip.

Captain Burrows gazed at her. She was still pale, there were dark shadows under her eyes and he wondered how old she was. Sixteen? Seventeen? Eighteen at most.

'Haven't you got any family, girl?'

'Yes, but me da is always drunk. He was always belting . . . me.' She was going to say Mam, but she didn't want to think of Nelly now. 'We never had nothing,' she finished. She took a deep breath. She'd better get this over with. 'Ain't you . . . don't you want to . . . be paid, like?' she stammered.

He didn't answer but she couldn't look at him. She was too ashamed, too afraid.

'I don't know.'

'Why?'

'Because I haven't made my mind up yet. There's plenty of time.'

She stood up. All she wanted to do now was get it over and done with. She certainly didn't want to have to go on day after day, night after night, sick with apprehension. 'I always pay me way.'

He looked down at her, at the determined jut of her chin, the pursed lips, the huge soft brown eyes that challenged him, yet in whose depths fear lurked. She wasn't a whore, he'd known that as soon as he'd spoken to her. Probably no man had ever had her, and she looked so like Maggie that his heart turned over. Maggie when she'd been young. When she'd loved him, when she'd been uncomplaining, waiting eagerly for her husband to come home from sea. Then she'd grown peevish, sullen and unresponsive and finally had run off with a bloody soldier. It was Maggie he was seeing now, not Alice. 'Oh, what the hell,' he muttered to himself.

'All right, girl, it's pay day!' He snapped, starting to unbutton his shirt.

Alice turned away from him, fiddling with the buttons of her blouse. Oh, God, let it be over soon! she prayed. And please don't let me think of Mam or . . . David. David Williamson.

Chapter Six

She lay staring up at the bulkhead, the tears slowly sliding
down her cheeks. It had been terrible. It had hurt her and
she'd bitten right through her lip, drawing blood, to stop
herself from screaming. She felt bruised and battered
and . . . dirty. It was no use asking Georgie Tate for more
water and soap. This dirt couldn't be washed away, it was
inside her. She never wanted to have to go through it
again and when he'd finished, he hadn't spoken to her.
He seemed angry. He'd dressed and left, slamming the
door shut behind him. Maybe he wouldn't bother her
again. Maybe she'd paid in full now, but she couldn't be
sure.

At last she fell asleep, a fretful, dream-filled sleep where
she saw Mam standing pointing accusingly at her, Lizzie
calling her a whore, Da picking little Mary up and throwing her out through the door. And then she saw David
and Charlie Williamson driving that big shiny car, laughing
together, but they didn't see her and she had to run and
keep running so they wouldn't catch up and knock her
down.

She woke, shaking, sweating and sobbing, and realised
that Georgie Tate was sitting on the end of the bunk,
staring at her. She didn't care what he thought. He was a
friend, the only friend she had in the world, and she had
to talk to someone.

'Oh, Georgie! It was awful! It was awful!' she sobbed.

He patted her arm ineffectually. 'Never mind, Alice, it's over now.'

'No, it's not! What if—'

'He won't,' he interrupted. 'He's not like that. Oh, 'e goes to the whorehouses, like everyone else, but he's . . . he's never brought one on board.'

James Burrows was a baffling enigma to his crew. A man who got drunk and visited the brothels the way they all did when they reached port. But a man who read books and listened to good music on the gramophone he had in his cabin. 'He's in a terrible temper,' Georgie added.

'Is that . . . bad?'

He shrugged. 'He never usually gets that mad over something . . . like . . . that.' He didn't say that there had been speculation among the crew that he'd finally gone insane.

'It's all them books, an' all that howling music,' had been Georgie's contribution to the debate. He'd got a clip round the ear from Tibbs for his pains.

She began to relax. If Georgie said he wouldn't come to her again, she could face the rest of the voyage. After all, Georgie knew him better than she did.

'Will I get you something to eat or a mug of tea?'

'Tea, please. I . . . I'll feel better then.'

'Will I teach you them songs now?'

She managed a smile and nodded.

She was stunned by the sheer vastness of the heaving grey-green ocean. As the days passed, there was nothing for miles and miles, as far as the eye could see, but that mass of water. Not a ship, not a bird, not even a fish. Whenever he had a spare few minutes, Georgie would sit with her on deck. Gradually, day by day, they exchanged confidences and life stories. He became increasingly fond of her but knew nothing could ever come of it, this love, this admiration. He never reached out for her, he avoided all physical contact. He knew what she looked like semi-naked and she was beautiful. He could never think of her ... like that, nor of what Captain Burrows had done to her, without feeling ashamed. Ashamed of his own masculinity.

'And that's all you know about this David Williamson?' he asked when she'd finished relating the events that had led up to her leaving Liverpool.

'Yes, but it made me want more, a better life, and I know I can have it in America. I know I can earn my living on the stage. So, will you teach me all the songs you know?'

'I said I would.'

'How do you know so many?'

He grinned. 'It's a secret.'

'Stop teasing me, Georgie Tate.'

'I go to the theatre, well, vaudeville, but I don't tell this lot. They'd think I was cracked, like the skipper. That's where I hear them, an' I remember them. Not all the words but most of them. You should go, Alice. Times Square is the place for it. It's great.'

'I will. That's where I'll go to sing.'

So they sat on deck in the shelter of the squat funnel and they sang. He began by teaching her a song that had been his mam's favourite, 'If You Were The Only Girl In The World'.

He was truly amazed when she first sang 'Beautiful Dreamer'.

'Alice, that was great! I know yer said you could sing but I never realised yer 'ad a voice like that! Yer really should be on the stage!'

She grinned ruefully. 'Aye, the landing stage.'

It became a ritual. Every evening as the half-light that passed for afternoon gave way to enveloping darkness, her clear sweet voice would ring out across the *Castlemaine*'s deck and over the cold grey waters of the great

Western Ocean. The rest of the crew, a surly, taciturn and mainly ignorant collection of misfits, grew to look forward to evening, to hear her increasing repertoire. When she sang 'Just A Song At Twilight', strong, hard men felt stirrings of gentler emotions few knew they even possessed.

On the bridge, James Burrows would sigh heavily, wondering if it was merely the effect of the immensity of the ocean or the isolation of his command that made the sweetness and clarity of that voice tear at his heart and stir up an aching loneliness. At times he would seethe with a rage he didn't understand and curse himself for a fool for ever having agreed to take her on this trip. Sometimes he thought her voice was like that of an angel, sometimes like that of a siren that would surely lure them to their doom.

The storm put an end to the singing. Burrows had noted the signs. The rising wind that drove the ragged clouds across the face of the moon. The broken white tops of the waves and the ominous increase in the force of the swell. The barometer was falling fast; a storm of quite violent proportions was imminent. Burrows ordered Tibbs to lash everything down.

When the storm caught them, Alice was frightened, but not sick. She spent most of her time in her cabin, lying on the floor, praying, gabbling the same words over and over again as she was thrown from bulkhead to bulkhead. 'Oh, please, God, don't let us sink! Don't let us drown!'

The ship shuddered and groaned as it struggled to rise from each trough, metal plates straining and timbers protesting as hundreds of gallons of water streamed from its decks. Sometimes it seemed to James Burrows as he saw the next mountainous wall of water bearing down on them that they'd be breached, completely swamped. He was freezing cold, soaking wet and at times mortally afraid.

'Come on, old girl, you can't let it beat you now! You can't give up!' he coaxed, no thought in his mind other than just surviving the next wave.

As though in response to his urging, the *Castlemaine* would rise steeply and then hang suspended for a couple of seconds, everything calm and deathly still, and then with a shudder she'd plunge down again into the depths.

Water seeped in everywhere and added to Alice's terror. She saw no one, for the entire crew worked ceaselessly just to keep the ship afloat. This isolation had more than once induced her to struggle to the door and scream for Georgie Tate or Captain Burrows, but no one had even heard her cries. After two nights and two days she was exhausted.

The following night she slept heavily and the next morning she struggled up on deck and was shocked to see the havoc the sea had caused. The mast and rigging were reduced to little more than broken, splintered spars. The lifeboat had been torn from its davits, its remains – a pile of matchwood – lay in the apex of the funnel. Hatch and ventilation covers had been ripped away and the weight of water had crushed and twisted the wheelhouse. Georgie and two other men, eyes dark-rimmed, faces haggard with lack of sleep, were clearing up and lashing planks of wood over open hatches.

'Are yer hurt, Alice?' Georgie called.

'No. Just a bit bruised. I was . . . I was terrified though,' she shouted.

He managed a grin. 'So was I,' he yelled.

'Any man who wasn't is a bloody fool! You learn to respect the sea but never to trust it.'

She looked up to the bridge from where James Burrows was watching the crew and Georgie went back to work.

Burrows saw the fleeting look of fear in Alice's eyes. 'You needn't worry your head any more, girl. I've enough to do without wasting time on you.'

Her shoulders slumped with relief. 'Will it get like that again?'

'I damned well hope not, we've lost enough time. These storms can be a thousand miles wide so there's no skirting them.'

She shuddered and he turned away.

'Will yer give us a song ternight, Alice?' Georgie called. 'We could do with a bit of cheerin' up.'

' "Show Me The Way To Go Home" would be bloody appropriate,' Tibbs growled. His shoulder hurt like hell. He'd been thrown from top to bottom of the stairway.

She nodded. Things were beginning to look brighter. The weather wasn't too bad now but best of all Burrows had said he wasn't going to be bothering her again.

'I'll sing like . . . like a Cockney Songbird.'

'You're not a Cockney. You have to be born in London, in the sound of Bow Bells, to lay claim to that title, Alice,' Tibbs informed her.

'Well, a Liverpool Songbird then.' She liked the sound of it so she said it again. If Letty Lewis could be the Cockney Songbird, why couldn't Alice O'Connor be the Liverpool Songbird? She laughed. 'I'll sing to you all the way to New York if you like. I'll take requests.'

No one answered. Surprised and furtive looks were exchanged and they all seemed to move together in a conspiratorial group.

'What's the matter? What did I say?'

Tibbs looked at Georgie. 'You'd better tell her, lad. I thought she knew.'

'Tell me what?' Alice demanded.

'We're not going to New York.'

'What! Why?'

'We're going to Charleston, that's why.'

'South Carolina,' Tibbs added.

Alice looked from one to the other, shaking her head. 'But . . . but he said he was going to America!'

'We are. Just a different part of it, that's all.'

Alice turned and stared up at the bridge, then before anyone could stop her she was up the ladder like a flash. She flung the door open and it crashed back on its twisted hinges.

James Burrows glared at her. 'No one comes up here unless I ask them to! Get off my bridge!'

She was too furious to care. She'd been through hell. The loss of her virginity, sickness, stark terror and for what? 'You lied to me! You cheated me! You said you were going to New York! You know I would never have come if you hadn't said that!' she screamed.

'I said I was going to America. You never mentioned New York. You never mentioned a specific place. America, you said. That's where you wanted to go!' he shouted back.

'I didn't! I want to go to New York and you cheated me! You took ... everything! I want me money back!'

'I'll give you your bloody money; it'll be worth a guinea to be rid of you! We're going to Charleston, now get off my bridge before I throw you off!' he roared. He caught her by the shoulders and thrust her out into the arms of Georgie Tate who had followed her up. 'Get her out of my sight!' he bellowed, seething with anger and guilt – she had looked so like his wife on the day she had stood screaming abuse at him, the day she'd left, fifteen years ago.

Georgie helped her down.

Alice's fury drowned in the welter of emotions that now swamped her. Hate, disappointment, disgust and bitter shame. 'I hate him! I hate him! The dirty ... lying ... cheat!' she sobbed.

Georgie helped her to her cabin, scooped up her cat and dumped it in her lap, trying to console her. 'It's still America, Alice.'

'But it's not New York and I have to get to New York, you know that!'

'Alice, he won't be there, not now, an' it's just a dream! You're just chasing after a dream. You can sing anywhere.'

'I want to sing in New York. I want to be rich and famous so he'll come and see me. Is it far, Georgie? Is this place, Charleston, far from New York?'

He nodded. 'It's a long way. A very long way. America is a big country.'

She lay down on the bunk, her face turned away from him. She'd finally put her dreams into words. She *did want* to be rich and famous so Mam would be proud of her and David Williamson would come and listen to her. Then she could forget everything that had happened on this ship – when she *was* the Liverpool Songbird.

'Will yer still sing for us, Alice?' Georgie asked timidly.

'No! I'll never sing on this ship again! Oh, go to hell, Georgie Tate!' she cried unfairly.

'It's not my fault, Alice,' he said miserably, closing the door and leaving her with her shattered hopes.

Chapter Seven

It was three days before she would speak to Georgie again. She didn't stir outside her cabin and she left most of the meals he brought her untouched or half eaten.

It upset him to see her so miserable. He had persuaded Tibbs to retrieve her fare from Burrows, the monetary part of it. She'd just nodded her thanks when he'd handed it to her.

'Alice, yer going ter have ter eat! Yer going ter get sick,' he pleaded.

'I am sick. I'm sick to death of this flaming ship and *him* and . . . everything! What am I going to do now? You tell me that, Georgie Tate?'

'You could go back to Liverpool. We're picking up cotton an' going back,' he suggested timorously, fully aware how this suggestion would be received.

'No! I'm never going back! I told you that, not until . . .'

'Oh, Alice, use yer sense! It's a dream. The likes of us never get what we want.'

'I will! I'll do it! I'll be rich and famous!'

'Yer can sing, Alice, but yer can't talk properly. You . . . we don't know about manners an' things like that.'

She stared at him sullenly. He was right. 'I can learn,' she said stubbornly.

He gave up. 'So, what will yer do when we get there?'

'I don't know. I've got my guinea, I'll get somewhere to stay.'

'I could let you have a pound, when I get paid off, like.'

She softened. 'I couldn't take your money. You work too flaming hard for it. They've got you for a flaming skivvy.'

'I want yer to have it, Alice,' he urged, desperate to let her have the only tangible proof of his affection he could give her.

'We'll see.' She kicked her heels idly against the side of the bunk. The only place she'd ever known was Liverpool. She had no idea what any other city or town was like. She'd gone over and over things in her mind, cursing James Burrows, Tibbs, the entire crew, but most of all herself. Basically she was an optimist and finally she'd become pragmatic about her position. She was heading for a strange country where everything and everyone would be alien, but it had to be better than Liverpool. And now her curiosity had been stirred. 'What's it like, this place?' she asked finally.

'It's all right, I suppose. I've only ever been once before. It's hot, there's lots of strange plants and things and lots of blacks too. They all used to be slaves, so Tibbs said. He knows heaps of things about the places we go to.'

She'd seen black people before; being a cosmopolitan port, Liverpool had its share of all nationalities.

'Do you think I'll be able to earn anything, Georgie, street singing? Enough to live on until I get on the stage?'

He shrugged. 'Last time I was there I saw a lot of blacks singing. They were good, too.'

'Oh, well, I've got a bit of money to tide me over.'

'They have different money, Alice. Dollars.'

She looked confused. 'So?'

'You'll have to get your money changed.'

'How do I do that?'

'Captain Burrows will change it for you.' Instantly he knew he'd said the wrong thing.

'I'm never going to speak to him again. I'll starve first!'

72

'Well, maybe if I asked Mr Tibbs, he'd do it. He might know where there's some cheap rooms too. Will I ask him?'

'If you like,' she said ungraciously.

'Won't you come up on deck ternight? It's gettin' warmer now. You don't have ter sing,' he added, seeing the look of chagrin that crossed her face.

'No! I hate that lot!'

'Well, we all miss yer.'

She turned away, her lips set in a tight line, and he left her, filled with determination to help her in any way he could.

Next day she was surprised when Tibbs came to see her.

'Georgie Tate said you'll need your money changed and you'll be wanting somewhere to stay.'

She nodded.

'Don't be so bloody bad-tempered, girl. It doesn't suit you. You should have made sure of our destination before you sailed with us. How much money have you got?' he asked before she had time to snap at him.

'Twenty-three shillings and sixpence.'

'It's not much.'

'I know but it will have to do until I can earn some more.'

'You could earn some here. We'd have a bit of a whip round if you came up and sang us a few songs.'

'No! I'm not singing for you, for anyone on here again!'

'Suit yourself. Well, give me the money and I'll bring you the dollars, at the going rate.'

'How do I know you won't rob me?'

'God damn and blast you for a suspicious little tart!'

She was about to yell back at him but bit back the words. It was true. She'd acted like a tart and she was suspicious. She unearthed her money and handed it to him.

'When we dock I'll come and fetch you and I'll take

you to a rooming house I know. It's nothing fancy, but it's cheap, clean and decent.'

She nodded her thanks.

'I'd wipe that look off your face if you want to get a job. No one will want to employ you if you keep scowling and glowering like that.'

She pulled a face at his retreating back and thought about what Georgie had said about manners and the way she spoke. She'd have to try to improve herself.

The following day when Georgie brought her meal he handed her some small, green coloured banknotes.

'What's this?'

'Your dollars. Mr Tibbs sent them.'

'They don't look worth much.' She thought they looked very insignificant and insubstantial compared to the gold sovereign and silver half-crown.

'Well, they buy just as much. Why don't you come up top? It's like an oven down 'ere.'

'I might, later,' she replied, but she'd already decided she'd sulked down here long enough. It *was* like an oven and her thick clothes were uncomfortably hot. 'How long will it be now, before we get there?'

'Another two days.'

'How long is it since we left?'

'Nearly three weeks. We lost time with the weather.'

She seemed to have been cooped up for a lifetime, she thought, and even though she would hardly admit it to herself, she was becoming more interested in the place they were heading for.

When she finally went up on deck she was amazed by the change in the weather. The sky was a clear azure blue and the sunlight danced on the calm blue-green water. The tops of the waves sparkled with silver spangles and the wind was warm. It even smelled different. She unbuttoned the front of her blouse as far as was decent and rolled up her sleeves.

'So, you've emerged then?'

She managed a smile at Tibbs. 'It's hot.'

'When you get to Charleston, buy some lighter clothes. Cotton is best and it's cheap.'

She looked down at her stained, creased clothes and wrinkled her nose. 'I need a bath. I had one before I left.'

'This isn't a fancy passenger liner, but ask Georgie Tate for some water and he might wash your clothes – if you ask him nicely.'

'I can wash me own things! My own things,' she amended. 'Anyway, I haven't got any others to change into.'

'Wrap a blanket round you, they'll dry quickly.'

She regarded him thoughtfully. 'Will you really find me a place to stay?'

'I said I would.' He had two daughters of his own, one the same age as her. He didn't like the thought of Alice being left to fend for herself on the streets of a strange city in a foreign country. She looked so young, so vulnerable, although he knew she was a sharp little minx and she had guts. Many women would have died – literally – of fright during that storm. 'You'll have to look fairly presentable or they won't give you a room, so get yourself cleaned up.'

Georgie brought her soap, a towel, a bowl and two buckets of sea water. She washed herself all over, then washed her hair. She spent a happy half-hour rubbing and rinsing her clothes. Georgie took them away while, wrapped in her bunk blanket, Alice sat and waited for him to bring them back. They were a bit stiff and retained a slight smell of salt but they were clean and she felt and looked much better when she was dressed again. It was dusk, a warm, heavy, purple-coloured dusk when she went up on deck.

'That's an improvement,' Tibbs, who was standing watch, commented.

'Will we be there soon?'

'The day after tomorrow, early in the morning. The best part of the day.'

'Georgie said it's not too bad a place.'

'It's a damned sight better than New York. A dirty, stinking, violent place that is. God knows why you were so set on going there. Charleston's a beautiful city, once you get away from the docks. There's a fort in the harbour, Fort Sumpter, where the war between the states started.'

'The Great War?'

'No, you little ignoramus, long before that. In eighteen sixty-one it started. The war that freed the slaves, although to listen to a lot of people in Charleston it might have been yesterday. One song you'd better not learn is "Dixie".'

'Why?'

'Because you'll be lynched, although there's some who would applaud you!'

'I don't know that one anyway.'

'I'll teach you a song, if you like.'

'What song?'

'One you might come to look on as your own one day, if you stay in America.'

'Mine?'

'Not literally. It's called the "Star Spangled Banner".'

'What's that?'

'A flag. The American flag. The Stars and Stripes. "Old Glory" as it's sometimes called.'

'Why would I want to sing about flags?'

'Alice O'Connor, you're impossible, do you know that?'

She grinned up at him. 'Go on then, teach me it. I might want to sing it one day.'

He had quite a fine baritone, so he'd been told. 'Right, listen closely.' He began the first lines of the American national anthem.

He was cut short by a shout from the bridge. 'Mr Tibbs, this is a British ship! If you want to sing a national anthem, sing your own!' James Burrows yelled.

'I hate him!' Alice said venomously as the mate fell silent. 'Mr Tibbs, can you learn me to speak properly?'

He was surprised. 'Why?'

'Because I'm sick of being . . . common an' ignorant.'

'It's teach, not learn.'

'Will you teach me?'

'I can't teach you everything.'

'I've got two days and I'll try to learn as much as I possibly can.'

He grinned at her. Somehow she'd managed to worm her way into everyone's affections. 'You're the strangest little minx I've ever known, Alice O'Connor.'

He was right, Charleston was a beautiful city, Alice thought as two days later the *Castlemaine* nosed her way into the harbour, past the fort that Tibbs had told her about. Fancy such a little place like that starting a war, she thought.

She was fascinated by the colour of the sea. It was a sun-spangled ultramarine. The funnels, masts and rigging of the ships in the harbour presented a familiar sight and as they drew closer she could see more of the city and eagerness began to bubble up inside her. The buildings were white or pale grey and they gleamed in the morning sunlight. Palm trees and tropical plants grew in profusion between them and carts, lorries, cars and carriages lined the waterfront. The whole atmosphere seemed different from that of Liverpool, she thought. Despite the hustle and bustle on the waterfront, the city beyond seemed tranquil, as though sleeping in the sun.

When the engines were shut down and she heard the clanking of the anchor chain, she went back down to her cabin to collect her shawl. She wouldn't need it but she was loath to leave it behind; it had cost her money. Georgie had persuaded her to leave Mog behind. She was a bit bigger now and had the run of the ship. Georgie saw that she was fed and soon she would be able to catch her own meals.

'Cats aren't like dogs, Alice. They don't *need* us, not really. They're ... independent. Mr Tibbs taught me that word,' he finished proudly. 'Besides, we need a cat more than you do.' So she'd agreed in the end. After all, she'd have enough trouble looking out for her-self in this new country.

She looked around the little room that had become so familiar and felt a tremor of apprehension. She'd come all this way, to the other side of the world. What lay ahead?

Georgie appeared in the doorway.

'Are yer ready, Alice?'

'Will you be coming with me and Mr Tibbs?'

'No.'

She was a little disappointed. 'Oh, I thought you would be. Well, thanks, Georgie, for everything. You've been a real friend. I wish ... I wish I had something to give you.'

Georgie looked embarrassed. 'I've got this for you, Alice. Go on, take it. I ... I want you to 'ave it.' He held out a dollar bill.

'But you'll need it. You earned it.'

'I'd only waste it on drink.'

'You could use it to go to a vaudeville show.'

'No. It's yours.'

She added it to the others. 'Thanks, Georgie, I ... I'll always remember you.'

'Alice, when yer get famous, will yer ... will yer sing the song I taught yer?'

She smiled at him. A dazzling, confident smile. 'I will, I promise. You believe in me, don't you, Georgie?'

He could only nod. His throat seemed to have closed over.

She put her arms round him and kissed him on the

cheek. 'You've been good to me and I'll always remember you, Georgie Tate.'

Tibbs was waiting for her at the gangway and as she left she turned and waved to Georgie who was standing gazing after her, a look of mute misery on his face.

'Where are we going now?' she asked, unable to believe that she was once again on land, that there was solid unmoving ground beneath her feet. She had arrived. She was in America. Not in the place she really wanted to be – she was as far away from David Williamson as she'd ever been – but it was a start.

'Away from the docks,' Tibbs answered. 'Stay by my side and don't dawdle.'

At close quarters there was nothing tranquil about this part of the city, she thought. Bales of cotton were piled mountainously high on the dockside. The streets thronged with people and traffic, and were lined with telegraph poles and warehouses. 'The Lloyd Shirt Manufactury and Laundry. Established 1887' she read over one building they passed.

'Where are we now?'

'On Meeting Street. We're heading towards the Old Market end.'

She twisted her head from side to side, exclaiming at the new sights, sounds and smells. 'Are all those places banks?'

'No, the banks and insurance offices are on King Street.'

'What's that?' She pointed to a three-storey building which sported striped awnings over its windows and an imposing entrance, above which fluttered a large red, white and blue flag.

'The post office and court house, and that's the Star Spangled Banner.'

Her gaze alighted on a large white house that stood behind tall iron railings. 'Oh, look at that! It's so beautiful!' she cried, her eyes going rapidly over the gardens, where flowers the like of which she'd never seen bloomed in myriad profusion, to the tall, white, pillared balconies linked with open verandas.

'There are some fine houses here. Some of them are over a hundred years old and have been in the same families for as long, too. There are more on the East Battery and Rutledge Street and there's the Grove – a mansion – built just before the War of Independence. A very long time ago,' he added, forestalling the question he could see forming.

She was warm, sticky and thirsty when they finally arrived at the Old Charleston Market and he led the way to a small, faded pink stucco building.

'Is this it?'

'It is. The Park Rooming House it's called.'

'Where's the park?'

'Do you have to take things so literally? Just shut up, let me do the talking and mind your manners.'

She followed him inside. The hall was dark and cool, the floor tiled and devoid of any carpet or rugs. Beside the small old-fashioned desk stood a large plant in a ceramic pot, covered with brilliant pink flowers. She'd never seen anything like it before and reached out gingerly to touch it.

'It's called a bougainvillaea.'

'You don't half know a lot of things.'

'I read. If you want to improve yourself, you should find time to read. Can you read?'

'Of course I can! I went to St Anthony's.'

Any further conversation was curtailed as a small woman, dressed entirely in black, appeared.

'Good morning, Miss Shelton, ma'am. Do you remember me? Mr Tibbs, Mate of the *Castlemaine*.'

'Why indeed I do, sir.'

'Do you have a room for this young person? She came over with us from Liverpool.'

80

The woman eyed Alice up and down. 'For how long?'

'I don't know. How much is it, please, ma'am?' Alice replied carefully.

'A dollar a week. Fresh linen and towels are provided, but no meals. There's a bathroom down the hall.'

'Well, for two weeks then, please.' She handed over two of her precious dollars and gave her name which was entered in a large book.

'Right then, you'll be fine here. Miss Shelton will be able to answer all your questions.'

Alice smiled at Tibbs. 'Thanks for helping me.'

'Well, we can't have you saying we all let you down, can we? Goodbye and good luck, Alice O'Connor.'

When he'd gone, Alice followed Miss Shelton down the hallway to the room she'd been allocated. It was quite small but after the cabin it seemed spacious. The walls were painted white and slatted wooden shutters were closed over the open windows. The sunlight that filtered in fell across the tiled floor in a pattern of oblique lines. There was a narrow bed covered with a clean blue and white cotton counterpane and drapes of muslin were looped back against the wall. A chest of drawers, a cane chair, a bleached oak towel rail over which was draped a pristine towel completed the furnishings.

Alice pointed to the muslin drapes. 'What's that for, please?'

'It's mosquito netting. They're insects, a sort of fly that bites. There's no need to use it now, not at this time of year.'

Alice suddenly remembered it was January. 'Is it winter here?'

Miss Shelton smiled. 'It is. It can be chilly and wet but we never get snow or frost. Now we do have regulations, you'll find them on that card, and you must abide by them otherwise you'll have to vacate the room.' She indicated a small printed piece of cardboard tacked to the back of the door. 'There are numerous places to eat in the vicinity but decent girls don't go near Beresford Alley, or Myzack and Princess Streets. You *are* a decent girl?'

'Oh, yes, Miss Shelton, I am!'

'Will you be looking for work, Miss O'Connor?'

'Yes.'

'Doing what?'

Although pleasant enough, Miss Shelton didn't look like the kind of woman you could say street singing to. 'Er, waiting on or cleaning, a maid, I suppose.'

'You'll find that jobs like that are done by the blacks,' Miss Shelton said sternly.

'Oh, well, maybe shop work.'

'Then you will need to go to the authorities first, since you're an immigrant.'

Alice had a deep mistrust of anything to do with authority. 'Do I have to?'

'Yes.'

'When?'

'As soon as possible. How long have you been travelling?'

'Three weeks and it was awful. There was a terrible storm, it went on for days. I was sick.'

Cecile Shelton softened. Her new lodger was a very pretty girl and she'd obviously had a long and terrifying voyage.

'Well, maybe tomorrow then. I can take you myself, I have to go downtown.'

'Oh, would you, ma'am? I'd be really grateful. I don't know anyone. It was New York I really wanted to go to, but ... here I am.'

'Well then, I'll leave you to freshen up. Is your luggage still on the ship? Is someone going to bring it down?'

'No. I ... I haven't got any. It ... it got lost ... in the storm,' she lied, seeing Cecile Shelton's eyebrows rise. 'Is there anywhere I can buy some things – cheaply?'

LIVERPOOL SONGBIRD

'Oh, yes. There are some thrift stores. I'll give you directions. When you're ready, just ring the bell on the desk in the hall.'

When she'd gone, Alice looked around. This was real luxury, she thought, fingering the bedspread and towel and looking more closely at the muslin netting. Fancy them even going to all that trouble so as not to have people getting bitten by flies, and there were certainly no bugs here either. She'd find the bathroom, have a bath and then she'd go out and do some exploring. She'd get something to eat, go to one of those thrift stores and then find the areas where she could earn money singing – she knew a lot of songs now. She'd start outside the theatres, like she'd done in Liverpool.

She sat down on the bed and stroked the crisp cotton counterpane. Her spirits rose. She had a roof over her head, some money for food and a couple of second-hand dresses. It never really got cold and Miss Shelton seemed kind and friendly in a stiff sort of way. From her experiences so far she decided she liked America. It was certainly better than Liverpool and Benledi Street. She'd got this far and was confident that all she needed was her voice and her looks to rise to fame and fortune. Little did she realise that youth, beauty and a golden voice were attributes that were plentiful in Charleston.

Chapter Eight

The thrift stores Miss Shelton directed her to were not second-hand shops as she'd imagined they would be. Everything was new. The clothing was of an inferior quality and badly finished off but though it was cheap and didn't compare with the garments sold in the stores in the prosperous parts of town, it was beyond Alice's slender means. In the end she asked a store assistant if there were any second-hand shops. The answer was negative but the girl told her that market stalls by the harbour sold cheaper goods. Alice thanked her and walked back down Meeting Street.

She bought two cotton dresses, some cotton underwear, a pair of stockings and a new straw hat from a black woman who had set up her stall in the shadow of a mountain of cotton bales.

'Can you tell me where I can get shoes?'

'Lige has the boots an' shoes. Keep on walking down there.' She pointed with a stubby finger towards the Harbour Master's offices.

Alice threaded her way between the dockside traffic and bought a pair of flat leather shoes that looked as though they hadn't had much wear.

The following day she set out looking clean and neat in the striped green and white dress and the wide-brimmed hat. She asked directions to the theatres and noted the time of the performances and the street names. She wandered from the harbour front and then through Beresford Alley, Princess and Myzack Streets where the brothels abounded. Then she retraced her steps up Meeting Street and out to the East Battery and Rutledge Street, where the houses were magnificent mansions set in gardens shaded by palms and filled with flowers.

On her wanderings she became acutely aware that what Georgie Tate had told her was true. She saw many black singers and musicians. Competition was going to be tough.

In the days that followed she tried all the theatres and moving picture palaces. She sang her heart out outside stores and hotels until she was moved on by irate doormen and managers. She earned a very small amount. Only coins were handed to her, dimes, quarters and cents, never a dollar bill, and she encountered open hostility from both black and white Charlestonians.

Now she was beginning to cut down on her meals to save her precious dollars. At first she'd found the food in the many small food shops and cafes in the less salubrious parts of town very different to what she was used to. There were vegetables and fruit she'd never seen before so she sampled them all – and put on weight. Her shoulder blades no longer stuck out, nor did her collar bone protrude and emphasise the hollow at the base of her throat; her breasts became fuller, her cheeks plumper and her appearance provoked many an admiring glance and comments and invitations of the baser kind. These she was used to and she dealt with them with scathing sarcasm. But now she was eating less she realised how quickly she'd become used to regular meals, as well as clean lodgings and clothes, and the opportunity to wash properly. She was also acutely aware how fast her money was running out.

By the end of her second week, after she'd reluctantly handed over another dollar, she was becoming more and more worried. She had to find a job. She'd gone to all the theatres and asked for work but had been told that there was nothing, nor were they holding auditions in the foreseeable future. She hadn't even known what the word meant, until they'd explained it to her.

After her third week, her bright dream of success was growing increasingly dim and she decided she'd have to try for something else, anything at all, but again she had no luck. The stores had no vacancies and when she finally took her courage in both hands and started to call at private houses, asking for a job as a cleaner or maid or laundry girl, she found Cecile Shelton's prediction to be true. There were very few white menials in this town.

In desperation she stopped outside a house in the East Battery and gazed at it longingly. It was a mixture of square columns and oval verandahs. A gleaming motorcar stood outside the door. What must it be like to live in a house like that, to have all the comforts and security that money brought, she wondered. It was obviously no' use going to ask for work – there was a black gardener carefully trimming the profusion of bougainvillaea and jasmine that cascaded over the perimeter wall and a black maid was shaking a duster from one of the large open windows upstairs. She'd have to try singing. She'd give them Georgie Tate's favourite; it might bring her luck.

She began 'If You Were The Only Girl In The World'. She had hardly got into her stride when the front door opened and a woman emerged dressed in a pale grey crepe dress that seemed to float around her shapely calves. Her hat was a small silver-grey confection with a white satin rosette on the side, her shoes were a soft dove-grey leather, as were her gloves, and she carried a white clutch purse. She was preceded by a dignified elderly black man dressed in a formal suit, who opened the car door for her.

Alice carried on singing as the woman handed something to the butler, but the notes faltered and died away as the car moved off. The butler crossed over and held out fifty cents.

'Mrs Phillips would be glad if you'd go away, girl, and don't come bothering folk again and lowerin' the tone of the neighbourhood.'

Alice took the money and began to walk slowly away. There couldn't have been more contrast between herself and Mrs Phillips. She had everything, Alice thought bitterly, while she herself had nothing. The gracious old houses depressed her; they were a reminder that so far she'd got nowhere in this land of opportunity. She was hungry but all she had was a dollar and fifty cents. It was enough for lodgings for another week but it left just fifty cents for food and that would only last two days. Miserably she turned her steps towards the Park Rooming House.

She'd hoped Miss Shelton wouldn't be in the hall, but her hopes were dashed.

'Quite a pleasant afternoon, isn't it, Miss O'Connor?'

'I suppose so,' she replied listlessly.

'Is there something wrong? Haven't you been able to find employment?'

'No. I've tried everywhere.'

Cecile Shelton tidied the papers on the desk into a neat pile. 'I see.'

'I'm not trained for anything, you see. I've only got a dollar fifty to last me all week. I . . . I was wondering if you'd let me stay on, give me a week's credit just until I get some work.'

'But you've been here three weeks and have found nothing.'

'I know, but I'm bound to get *something* soon!'

The older woman sighed heavily. 'I'm very sorry, Miss O'Connor, but I can't do that. I can let that room three times over. Cheap, clean, decent rooming places are hard to come by and this isn't a charitable institution.'

Alice hung her head and her shoulders slumped. By the weekend she'd be on the street. She felt she couldn't go to her room now, it wouldn't be hers for much longer. Instead she left the building and made her way to White Point Gardens.

It was late afternoon and she stood staring out over the expanse of blue water, feeling utterly desolate. All her hopes and dreams had turned to dust. She'd made a mistake, a terrible mistake in coming here, trusting in tales of wealth and unlimited opportunities. Oh, why had she let herself become infatuated with stupid dreams? She'd never sing on a stage in a theatre. She'd never be rich and famous and she'd never see David Williamson again. She was bitterly aware that that brief meeting with him had fanned the flame of her ambition. He was a stranger who had picked her up from the gutter and shown her kindness, and because of that she'd travelled three thousand miles across the world, and for what? To end up homeless, that's what. She was homesick. She missed Mam terribly and Lizzie and all the kids. She'd never see them ever again. She was stranded high and dry in a foreign land, with no money, no job and no prospects of one either. She really should have written to Mam, at least to let her know she had got there safely, but letters cost money.

She noticed that the sun was sinking, long shadows were creeping over the flower beds, dulling their riotous colours. The trees looked ghostly with their long trailing fingers of grey moss and the figure on top of the Jasper Monument was deep in shadow. Twilight descended rapidly here.

She left the confines of the gardens and walked quickly back down the East Battery, trying to ignore the beautiful houses with their brightly lit windows. There were a few cars and carriages on the streets but she ignored them until one stopped beside her. She quickened her steps in alarm.

'Miss! Miss, don't be frightened, Miss India only wants to know can she give you a ride home?'

Alice stopped, turned and looked up at the black driver of an old-fashioned closed carriage. She couldn't see the occupant.

'What do you think I am, flaming stupid? How do I know who's in there?'

'Miss, I'm just carrying out instructions.'

'Then let me talk to whoever's in there.'

He got down and opened the carriage door.

'Where are you going? It's not safe for a young girl to be out alone at night.'

It was a woman's voice but Alice was still wary. 'Is there just you in there?'

A woman's head and shoulders appeared from the gloom. 'Of course there is.' She alighted with the help of the driver and Alice could see she was small, plump and middle-aged. Her clothes were ostentatious but expensive and her large flower-bedecked hat partially hid her face.

'I'm Miss India Osbourne. You're very wise to be so suspicious. Caution is a good quality. Now where are you going?'

'The Park Rooming House off Meeting Street.'

'You see, you have to cross town and there's white trash and black trash hanging around on street corners. Get in, I'll drop you off.'

Alice got in. She was curious. 'Don't you live along here, ma'am?' she asked as with a jolt the carriage moved off.

'No, I live on West Street. You're not American, are you?'

The carriage lurched and Alice caught hold of the leather strap that hung by the door. 'No, I come from Liverpool, England.'

'Have you been in Charleston long?'

'Three weeks.'

'You've no family here then?'

'No, ma'am.'

'No friends or acquaintances?'

Alice shook her head. 'The only person I know is Miss Shelton at the Park.'

'What's your name?'

'Alice. Alice O'Connor.'

'And do you have a job, Alice?'

'No, ma'am. I've tried. I've tried hard but there's nothing and I'm not trained for anything.'

'Then what have you been doing for money?' India Osbourne had quickly taken in Alice's cheap clothes.

'I've been singing in the street. I used to do it in Liverpool, but there's too many other people here doing the same thing. I'd hoped I could get a job singing on the stage.'

'Your voice is that good?'

'Well, so people have told me, but no one will even listen to me. I couldn't even get an ... audition.'

India Osbourne sighed. 'I'm sorry things are so bad, Alice. If you get very lonely perhaps you would come to visit me or maybe we could meet next Sunday. I often drive along the Battery; sometimes I like to take the air in the gardens.'

Alice felt so miserable and homesick that she warmed to the older woman. 'That's very kind of you, ma'am. I'll come to the gardens, if you don't mind.'

They had reached the Park and Alice prepared to get out.

'Well, I'll see you next Sunday, Alice.'

'I'm dead grateful ... very glad. I'll look forward to it.'

'I hope you have some luck this week.'

'So do I or I don't know what I'll do.'

By Friday, she'd managed to earn a dollar. A dollar for the entire week, she thought. There'd been days when she was so hungry that she'd felt faint. You should be used to it, she told herself, but she hardly had the strength to walk the streets. She'd made up her mind that if Miss Osbourne turned up on Sunday, she would ask her if she could help. Well, she was rich and she must know plenty of people – rich people; maybe one of them would give her a job. She didn't mind how menial it was. If she could just earn enough to pay her lodgings and have one meal a day she'd manage until something better turned up. But that's what she'd told herself before, that some lucky chance would present itself, and it hadn't. Very probably Miss India Osbourne wouldn't present herself either next Sunday.

White Point Gardens were almost deserted when Alice arrived, just as dusk was falling. Only a few people strolled along the pathways or were seated on the benches. She sat down beneath a live oak from which the trailing fingers of grey moss drifted gently in the evening breeze. This will be a waste of time, a flaming wild goose chase, she thought, but only minutes had passed when she saw the small, ample figure of India Osbourne threading her way between the trees and shrubs. She was wearing a dress and jacket of a particularly bright peacock blue. It was trimmed round the neck and on the jacket facings with pale lemon crepe. The colour matched the large hat trimmed with blue ribbon. She looked like a small fat parrot, Alice thought.

'Ah, you're already here, Alice.' She was puffing and wheezing as she sat down and eased her feet slightly out of the elegant shoes that were a size too small. 'Ah, vanity, vanity! How do we suffer for it,' she sighed as the pressure was relieved. 'How have things been this week?'

'Oh, I'm so glad you turned up ... er ... came. Things are terrible. I've had no luck. I've no money for another week's lodgings – well, I do if I don't eat. I can't get a job and I just don't know where to turn, honestly I don't.' Her voice cracked with emotion. It was all true.

India Osbourne looked at her in concern. 'Alice, why did you come to Charleston?'

'Because I couldn't stand my da belting Mam and me. We had nothing and it was the middle of winter and it was freezing cold. I lost my job because Da battered me so badly I had to stay off. I'd heard tales about America, how you could get on, get good jobs. I really wanted to go to New York.'

'New York? Whatever for?'

She felt so miserable that she didn't care how stupid and feeble her motives for coming sounded. 'I was singing at the Pier Head in Liverpool where all the big ships leave from and I got knocked down by a car. He . . . the man . . . he was so good and kind to me. He took me on board the *Aquitania*, got the doctor to see me and gave me money, more money than I'd ever seen in my whole life. I . . . I'd never met anyone like him before.'

India clasped her plump hands together and shook her head. 'So, you fell in love with a stranger?'

Alice was startled. She hadn't looked at it like that. But she did love him, she must do, to have come all this way. 'I suppose I did. I told him I sang and his brother said something about one day they might pay to hear me and . . . and I . . . that's what I want most in the world. For him to see me, dressed like a real lady, singing on the stage.'

India impatiently brushed away a tiny silver-coloured moth. 'Does he live in New York?'

'No, he lives near Liverpool.'

'But how will he hear you sing? Even if you'd gone to New York, if he doesn't live there what is the point?'

'I don't know. Oh, I don't suppose I really thought about it properly. I wanted to follow him. I thought that with him being in and out of New York with the ship, I might see him again. I had to get away. I had to have a chance in life and I'd never have got it in Liverpool – you don't know what it's like there if you're poor.'

'So you used the money he gave you for your fare?'

'Yes, only . . . only it wasn't enough.'

India shot her a knowing glance from beneath her lashes. She didn't need to be told how the girl had made up the difference.

'They . . . they cheated me. I thought they were going to New York.'

'I see, and now you're stuck here with no money, no job and no fare to go home, even if you wanted to go?'

Alice nodded miserably.

India sat up and smoothed out an imaginary crease in her skirt. 'Alice, let me hear you sing.'

'Sing?'

'Yes, sing. I might be able to help you.'

Hope surged through Alice. 'Really?'

'I said might. Let me hear you sing first.'

Alice thought of her repertoire. It would be better to sing something modern. 'I'll sing "Always".'

India Osbourne nodded and settled herself more comfortably on the bench. As Alice's voice broke the twilight stillness with sweet clarity, she nodded to herself. Yes, she'd do well. Very well indeed. She did have a good voice. In fact, an exceptionally fine voice. She was young, talented, beautiful and still innocent. A rare combination. A very rare combination.

Chapter Nine

All the way to West Street, Alice couldn't believe her luck. She'd been at her wits' end. She'd given up her dreams but she must have a guardian angel somewhere who was looking after her.

'I've a big house on West Street,' India had informed her. 'Part of it I use as a club. I have girls who sing to entertain my customers and they stay with me. I give them a home, a very good home with all the comforts, and in return they give me whatever tips – gifts of money – people pass to them as an extra thank you for their performance. I charge an entrance fee, quite a substantial one. It keeps all the undesirables out and my girls are all well worth it, they're very professional singers. Because of the Prohibition Law, no alcoholic beverages are supposed to be served but people come to enjoy themselves and we're all very discreet.'

'And you'll take me? You'll give me a home and I can sing in your club?'

India nodded, smiling. 'But I had to hear you sing first, Alice. You'd be no use to me as just a pretty face.'

'Oh, Miss Osbourne, it's . . . it's like a fairy story come true! I'll go and get my things from the Park now.' She felt like throwing her arms round India Osbourne's plump shoulders and hugging her.

'How much stuff have you got there?'

'Only another dress and the clothes I came over in and

they're all a bit tatty looking now. They weren't new when I bought them.'

'Well, leave them there. I can't have you looking like the rag picker's child. You'll need some elegant clothes for my establishment.'

'You mean you'll buy me clothes as well?'

India nodded and suspicion began to creep into Alice's mind.

'What for? Where's the catch?'

'There isn't a catch. I run a nightclub, a select one. My girls are all singers and wear evening gowns. You haven't got any decent clothes, let alone an evening gown, so I'll buy them and take the money from your tips. Is that fair?'

Alice nodded. It sounded all above board.

The house was a large one on the corner of West Street. It was of red brick and was built in the Colonial style with long sash windows. Plush blinds were now lowered over these windows but a soft light filtered through.

'We don't open on Sundays. It's not at all the thing to do. I do have standards,' India said sanctimoniously as Alice followed her up the steps.

Inside the hall, Alice's eyes widened and her mouth dropped open at the sheer opulence of the place. The walls were covered with a deep cyclamen-coloured paper that sported an ivy leaf design in an even deeper pink. The light was electric and the shades were of frosted glass. There were potted plants and gold-framed pictures in profusion and the rich plum carpet was so thick her feet sank into it.

'This part of the house is where we live; through that door there is the club.' India's manner was brisk and businesslike.

'Can I see the club, please? I've never even heard of one before.'

India opened the door with a theatrical flourish and Alice gasped. The room was decorated in shades of blue, from dark navy through sapphire to pale aquamarine. There was a sort of small low stage at one end with midnight-blue velvet curtains fringed with silver draped tastefully behind it. Numerous small delicate tables were dotted around the room, as were chairs, their seats upholstered in blue velvet. But it was the stage that held Alice's rapturous gaze. A stage! A real stage! She was going to sing here, in a nightclub with an audience who would pay to listen and might even give her money, tips as India had called them. Oh, why had she ever doubted herself? Many times over the last weeks she'd regretted leaving Mog on the ship. She had been a lucky mascot but now it seemed that luck hadn't deserted her after all; in fact it was smiling on her. This was far more than she'd ever hoped for.

India took her arm firmly and drew her back into the hall.

'Like I said, we don't open on Sundays and you must be hungry and thirsty and would probably like a bath. There are three bathrooms, one on each landing.'

Alice followed her up the staircase still in a state of bemused incredulity. Her mind couldn't take in all the palatial rooms or the fact that this was to be her home. The room India now showed her was beyond her wildest dreams and quite the most magnificent bedroom she'd ever seen. The carpet was cream but covered with a design of roses in brilliant hues. The curtains were crocus yellow and heavily fringed, as was the bedspread. The headboard and footboard, the dressing table, wardrobe and writing desk were of polished mahogany. There was a white porcelain washbasin with gilt taps and cakes of scented pink soap. Large thick white towels hung from the rail on the adjacent wall. A long low rosewood table stood at the foot of the bed and held a bowl of fresh flowers, a bowl of fruit and an array of ornaments. A low, buttoned-back chair covered in gold damask was set by the window which was open slightly, the breeze lifting the net curtain gently.

'I . . . I must have died and gone to heaven! This . . . this is for . . . me?' Alice at last managed to stammer.

India laughed, an affected, brittle laugh. 'Well, what on earth is the point of having money if you can't spend it on beautiful things? Why keep it in a bank? There are no pockets in shrouds, I always say. Everything you will need you'll find in the dressing-table drawers. I'll send some food up and then you can have a good night's sleep and we'll talk about your job in the morning.'

'What do I call you, to thank you, like?'

Again there was that affected little laugh. 'Miss India. Everyone else does.'

Alice was sitting on the bed still dazed when a young mulatto girl brought up a tray laden with food. She didn't speak so Alice just smiled her thanks. She was glad she was alone for she knew as she attacked the bowl of thick soup that her manners left a lot to be desired, but she was starving. There was a plate of ham and sweet potatoes. There was corn, dripping with butter, crusty bread, a large slice of sticky chocolate cake and there was wine too. She'd never tasted wine so she sipped it cautiously. It was light and dry and full of bubbles. Oh, this was heaven!

When she'd eaten everything, she stripped off her clothes and filled the basin with water. She felt too nervous to go along to the bathroom. She might come back and find all this gone, find that it had all been a dream after all. She'd leave exploring the wonders of the bathroom until tomorrow; she'd had more than enough luxury for one day.

The soap was perfumed and the towels were soft. She took the tortoiseshell-backed hairbrush and brushed out her long mass of tawny curls, then she opened the dressing-table drawer and gasped as she drew out a nightdress and robe of alabaster silk, so flimsy it was as light as thistledown. She held it against her and looked at the reflection in the long cheval mirror. Then she rubbed it gently against her cheek, savouring its cool, perfumed fragility. She pulled it over her head and then turned slowly to observe the effect in the mirror. This was to sleep in? It was far too good for that; it was like a stage dress and a better one than Letty Lewis had worn at the Rotunda. It billowed around her like rippling waves, the layers of snowy lace like the foaming tops of the Atlantic waves.

She turned down the bed covers and stroked the soft, lavender-scented sheets and pillowcases. She'd thought that luxury was the bed in the hostel, then she'd been overwhelmed by the bed at the Park, but they were nothing compared to this. This was fit for royalty.

She was still marvelling at her good fortune when the door opened and a small, pretty girl appeared. She had large, lustrous dark eyes fringed with luxuriant lashes and a cloud of short blue-black curly hair. She wore a robe of pale blue satin edged with rows and rows of matching lace.

'Hi, I'm Marietta.' The tone was friendly, the voice low and soft, the vowels drawn out.

'I'm Alice. Alice O'Connor. I . . . I can't believe this place.'

'Not many people can!' came the amused reply. 'Isn't it awful? Her taste's terrible. Still, I suppose it's apt.'

'I think it's like a palace.' Alice defended her benefactress in a curt tone. Besides, she thought it was very tasteful.

Marietta sat down in the chair. 'Where did she find you? You're from England, aren't you?'

'In White Point Gardens. I was starving, broke, not a hope of a job and about to be chucked out of my lodgings. And now I've got all this and I'm going to sing on a stage, a real stage, and for a proper audience.'

Marietta raised her dark eyebrows. 'Is that what she told you?'

'I saw it. I saw the nightclub. Oh, it's been my dream! It's all I ever wanted to do, sing on a stage. I just can't believe this.'

Marietta studied her fingernails. 'Neither can the Charleston Sheriff's Department or the South Carolina State Police. She's as sly as a fox, is Miss India Osbourne. They never find any liquor on the premises and they can't charge her with anything else either. No evidence.'

Some of Alice's euphoria disappeared and was replaced by suspicion. 'She said it was against the law to serve drink.'

'It is. It's a crazy law, but . . .' Marietta shrugged her plump white shoulders.

'But what?' Alice demanded.

'Honey, the place is a speakeasy.'

'A what?'

'A club where illegal booze is sold, amongst other things.'

'What other things?' Alice's suspicion was rapidly deepening.

'Alice, just what did she tell you, for Christ's sake?'

'That she'd give me a home and that I'd sing for the paying customers and any money, tips, she called them, I'm to give to her, for my keep, I suppose. That's fair, isn't it? I've never seen a house like this. I've never been anywhere so grand.'

'Jesus! I didn't think there were any innocents left in the world. You think that's *fair*? You think she's a soft, kind-hearted woman who has picked you up off the streets and given you a home?'

'Yes.'

Marietta laughed pityingly.

'Don't we sing?' Alice was feeling very uneasy.

'Oh, sure, honey, we sing but it's not all we do.'

Understanding was dawning on Alice. How could she have been so blind, so stupid? She'd been desperate but she should have known. She'd been too trusting, too dazzled by India's 'kindness', all this luxury, the promise of ambition fulfilled. It all had a price. 'What is this place?'

Marietta got to her feet. 'This place is The Star of India. It's a speakeasy and a whorehouse. We sing and she sells cola, fruit juice and lemonade as a legitimate cover. She charges an entrance fee. A big fat one. That pays for us, for *all* our talents. We have some high an' mighty customers, all solid respectable "gentlemen". That's how come no liquor's ever found. She gets ample warning of a raid and it's all gone by the time the police arrive. She runs this place well; it's all very discreet, she has rules.' Marietta laughed cuttingly. 'The biggest bloody hypocrite in town, that's Miss India Osbourne!'

Alice sagged as though she'd been punched in the stomach. She felt sick and winded with the shock. 'A wh- whore . . .' she stammered.

'A whorehouse,' Marietta said flatly. 'I suppose she made sure you've no kin and no friends?'

Alice nodded. The feeling of nausea was being replaced with a fury akin to that which had overtaken her when she'd smashed the chair on her father's head.

'And you didn't go back to wherever you were staying for your things?'

Alice jumped to her feet. Her eyes were blazing in a face drained of all its colour.

'Where are you going?' Marietta asked.

'To find her! To find Miss India flaming Osbourne!'

Before Marietta could stop her, Alice had run down the stairs. Her bare feet and the thick carpet made her descent silent. There was a slight noise coming from a door on her left, the one opposite the club, and she flung it open.

'Alice!' India cried in surprise.

'You sly old bitch! You bloody liar! This is a flaming whorehouse! It's a speak . . . speak . . . something! I'm not staying here! I'm not a whore!' she yelled.

India's smile vanished and her eyes became hard. 'Oh, don't come that Miss Prissy Purity with me! How else did you pay your passage? Did you expect me to believe those lies about a stranger giving you money? You have to pay for everything in this life, one way or another, and you sure as hell know that's the truth!'

Alice did know but she plunged on, 'I won't stay here! I won't and you can't make me! You can go to hell, *Miss* Osbourne!'

India shut the door but not before she'd glimpsed Marietta standing at the bottom of the staircase. 'It's not me who'll go to hell, Alice O'Connor, it's you if you quit! You've got a choice. Stay here with me and have the comforts of life or go out on the streets and starve. You'll be forced to sell yourself in the end, so why not get well paid for it and live in luxury? Go back out there and you'll be raped sooner or later, maybe even killed. It's your choice. You said you wanted to sing on the stage and that's what I'm offering you. A chance. It's only right that I get some remuneration for my pains. I'm a businesswoman. I had nothing when I started out, not even a good voice! There was no one to look out for India Osbourne!'

The door opened and Marietta came into the room.

'Oh, take her back upstairs, Marietta. Talk some damned sense into her.'

Alice was still shaking but she let the other girl lead her back upstairs. She sat down heavily in the dainty chair. 'I don't care what she says. I'm not a whore. I won't do it. I won't!'

'You mean you've never . . . you're still a virgin?'

'No. I had to do it to pay my fare, but only once! I won't do it again. I won't be turned into a whore. I won't!

I can't let Mam down by doing . . . that.'

Marietta sat down on the bed. 'I said that once myself, honey, and so did all the others. I came here from Louisiana. I ran away from home, if you can call a stinking shack in a bayou home. I was full of plans and dreams, like you. Plans but no money and no training, just a singing voice. Not a bad one but nothing startling. I was singing outside a place down near the harbour. I'd been raped, beaten up, and I was starving when she found me. Some men just take without paying up. It's easy being here, honey, believe me. We've all got hard-luck stories to tell and no one damned well cares whether we live or die. Not even the police.'

'Oh, leave me alone!' Alice yelled at her.

'Sure, but I just wanted you to know that what she said is true. Go back out there and you may well end up in the harbour – dead.'

Alice covered her face with her hands. Oh, God, now what? She knew from bitter experience that she would starve back on the streets, and she didn't think India or Marietta were just trying to scare her. Marietta wouldn't lie about being raped and beaten up.

Oh, it had been different at home in Liverpool. Mam was there, she'd watched over her. The house in Benledi Street hadn't been much but it had been a roof over her head. A home of sorts. Here, if she left India's house there was nothing. No place to call home, no future and no hope of one. And no Mam. The anger left her and the tears welled up in her eyes. She couldn't even go back to Liverpool, she had no money. She'd let herself be hypnotised by dreams and ambitions. By the hope of a dazzling future. Georgie Tate had been right. She was chasing an impossible dream and it had suddenly turned into a nightmare.

She caught sight of herself in the long mirror. A beautiful girl with a wild tangled mane of hair and the eyes and expression of a hunted animal. She couldn't bear to look at herself. With a malicious swipe she swept the ornaments from the top of the dressing table and her fingers closed over the handle of the hairbrush. One hefty throw shattered the glass in the mirror and the image disappeared but it didn't help. She knew she was trapped. There was no way out.

Marietta uttered a scream when the mirror smashed but Alice didn't even notice. Her gaze alighted now on the bowl of flowers on the low table. She picked it up and with all her strength she hurled it at the window. The sound of breaking glass was deafening; the whole lower half of the window shattered and the floor was strewn with glass.

Marietta grabbed hold of her. 'For Christ's sake, Alice, are you crazy? She'll kill you!'

'I don't care! I don't care!' Alice screamed.

'You will. You'll have to pay for this.'

The door was flung open and India was confronted by the devastation and a seething, unrepentant Alice.

'You goddamn little slut! Look at the mess! You ungrateful, vicious . . .' India struggled for words and breath. Her stout body, encased in a tight corset, wasn't used to moving quickly up flights of stairs.

'You trapped me, you sly, evil old bag!' Alice yelled back.

'If you speak to me like that again, Alice O'Connor, you'll be out of here so fast it will make your head spin!'

Angry, vituperative words bubbled up in Alice's head but before she could speak, Marietta caught her arm.

'For God's sake, Alice, that's enough. Keep your mouth shut or she'll kick you out,' she hissed.

India was quivering with rage. 'You just listen to Marietta and be thankful I'm a charitable woman.'

Alice laughed, a harsh, derisive sound, but Marietta squeezed her arm warningly.

'I'll send Chrissie to clean up and Amos will fix the window but don't you think that's the end of it. Oh, no! You'll pay for all of this. You'll forfeit all tips and pin money until every single thing has been paid for.' India shot both girls a malevolent glare before turning and leaving, slamming the door behind her.

Alice's anger was spent and she flung herself face down on the bed. 'She's turned me into a whore,' she sobbed. 'What else can I do? Get raped or murdered.'

Marietta stroked her hair. 'You must have quite a voice for her to keep you after that outburst.'

'I wish I couldn't sing a note. I hate her!'

'It's not just her, Alice, it's goddamn fate! It's being born poor. But it's better than being a whore out there, honey, I really mean that. You ask the others and they'll tell you it's true.'

Alice raised a tear-streaked face. 'I'll save every cent until I've enough to get out of here and go home.'

Marietta looked at her with pity. 'She provides everything, Alice. All she lets us keep is three dollars a week.'

'I don't care. I don't care if it takes me years to save it up. I'm going home – one day.'

Chapter Ten

The window was reglazed and the mirror and ornaments replaced but Alice's acceptance of her situation was far from complete. She met the other girls. They came to see her, to introduce themselves in ones and twos, and they all had heartrending stories to tell and backgrounds like her own. And they all said that life in this house in West Street wasn't really bad.

'Miss India has rules and the clientele are at least gentlemen compared to the houses on Beresford and Myzack,' Laura, a pretty blonde from Atlanta, Georgia, assured her.

'Sure, but at least they don't pretend to be anything other than brothels.' Marietta was sarcastic. She was the most outspoken but Alice learned that Marietta had been with India the shortest time, apart from herself.

'Is it every night? Do we have to sing and . . . well . . . you know?' She wasn't able to say it. She swallowed hard, trying not to think about it.

Laura laughed. 'Oh, Lordy no! We have quiet nights and we have a "rest" on Sundays. We have to be available but it's not party time every night. Sometimes I don't have any clients and I get so bored I count the flowers on the wallpaper, but some of us have our regulars.'

It all depressed Alice terribly. She'd lived all her life cheek by jowl with poverty and there had been times when she'd been desperately ashamed of being dirty and dressed in rags, but it wasn't like this shame. This was so seedy. Everything was false. It was all a great pretence.

At first she was determined to take no interest at all in the clothes that were brought and hung up in the wardrobe and placed in the drawers of the dresser. She fought hard to suppress her natural curiosity, but when Marietta took the dresses out, one by one, and laid them across the bed, she just wasn't able to help herself. She'd glimpsed clothes like these in the posh shops in Liverpool's Bold Street but she'd never stood with her nose pressed against the window of Cripps or De Jong et Cie and longed for such gorgeous creations. There hadn't been any point. All she'd longed for then had been one good meal a day.

Almost reverently she smoothed out the folds of the evening dresses. The pale lilac georgette with its floating panelled skirt. The turquoise satin, the bodice of which was covered with tiny silver bugle beads and pearls. The shell-pink crepe de Chine, cut in the new short fashion with a huge bow of pink and silver ribbon at the hip. There were underclothes of pure silk. Low-heeled leather pumps and silk stockings. Day dresses of printed cotton and muslin and a smart suit of pale blue linen. There was a hat, a clutch bag and gloves to match.

Marietta smiled sardonically, holding out the cloche hat of fine white straw edged with blue ribbon. 'For Sundays. She insists we all look smart and ladylike on Sundays, the hypocritical old cow! Oh, and she's arranged for someone to come in and see to your hair.'

'What's wrong with my hair?'

'It's too long. Too old-fashioned. You're to have it cut.'

Instinctively Alice's hand went to her thick sun-streaked curls. 'No!'

'Honey, why do you keep arguing? It's easier in the end just to fall in. Besides, it will suit you short. There'll be no need for you to have it marcel-waved or have to suffer agonies wearing curling pins.'

The hairdresser was a small dapper man with black hair that was oiled and smoothly plastered down. He sported a small moustache and spoke with a slight accent.

'This will be a joy to cut!' he exclaimed as he began to brush out Alice's mane of hair.

As she watched the last of her long thick curls fall to the floor, the tears sprang to her eyes and brimmed over. The transformation was complete. Mam wouldn't recognise her now. In fact, no one would. She even had a new name, for India had decided that Alice was too plain, too ordinary. She was now to be called Alicia. Alicia O'Connor. Gone was the dirty, skinny little slummy. The girl who looked back at her from the mirror had a softly waving bob that ended just beneath her ears, making her look older than seventeen. Next week she would be eighteen but birthdays had always been irrelevant. She'd never had a birthday present or any kind of celebration, so why worry about it now? The collar of the raspberry-pink cotton day dress, trimmed with navy piping and a large floppy bow, added to the illusion of maturity. Only the large brown eyes, misty with tears, remained the same.

'Alicia, you look good. Real good.'

'Oh, I hate that name, Marietta. I really *hate* it!' She pointed to her reflection. 'That's not me. Not the *real* me. It's someone different, the real me has gone.' She was glad Mam couldn't see her. Yes, she looked very elegant, some would say even beautiful, but she knew Nelly would have preferred the daughter she knew, the girl dressed in rags with the mass of tangled hair. The girl who had been ignorant and half-starved but who had earned every penny decently. Even the way she'd begged in the street had been honest. She'd given something in return for the coins she'd received. A song. A bit of entertainment to relieve the boredom of waiting for the theatre to open.

'What will you wear tonight? It's your debut.'

Alice shrugged. 'I don't care.' At any other time she'd have been as excited as a child with the array of finery that hung in the wardrobe. She'd have fingered each outfit and agonised over her final choice.

'Honey, try and look on the bright side of it,' Marietta pleaded.

'What for? There is no bright side.'

'Yes, there is. You'll get to sing on a stage before a real audience. Isn't that what you've always wanted to do?'

'That doesn't matter now. I don't care if I never sing again. I don't want to sing in this place.'

'You wait until you hear the applause, it's marvellous! It's like a drug. You'll want more and more, you'll get hooked.'

'I don't want any applause. My singing's not what they want me for. It's not,' she struggled to find the right word, 'it's not real, not genuine.'

'You'll change your mind.'

'I won't.'

But she did.

Her final, reluctant choice as to what to wear settled on the turquoise beaded satin, the skirt of which only came to mid-calf, showing the white silk stockings and white leather pumps with a Louis heel and a strap over the instep. The camiknickers she wore beneath the dress were of cream silk edged with imported lace. Marietta fastened a band that sparkled with beads round her short hair and clipped long diamanté earrings to the lobes of her ears. 'Have you decided to go ahead with Miss India's choice of song?' she asked.

Alice had been thinking about that all the time Marietta had been fussing with her hair. She hadn't wanted to sing the old familiar songs, she doubted she'd ever sing them again. Nor would she sing 'If You Were The Only Girl In

The World,' poor Georgie Tate's favourite, or 'Always'. She remembered how she'd sung that for India Osborne only a few days ago. How she wished she'd never opened her mouth.

'Yes. It's different.'

'Oh, it's that all right! It's like a dirge. Not the type of song for this place.'

Alice didn't have any sense of what fitted any more. Everything looked and felt alien. She was shaking with nervous apprehension as she went downstairs to the night-club, and beads of perspiration sprang out on her brow.

Resplendent in a crimson and black evening gown, India stepped onto the small stage and made shushing gestures with her plump hands.

'That dress makes her look like a goddamn slice of watermelon,' Marietta whispered spitefully.

'Oh, Marietta, I'm scared! I'm scared stiff and I'll forget the words, it's all new!' Alice gripped the other girl's arm tightly as India announced her as 'a young lady from England with the voice of a nightingale'.

The group of three black musicians played the opening bars of 'The Londonderry Air', a traditional Irish piece, and Marietta pushed her gently forward to face her first audience comprised entirely of men in evening dress.

Alice swallowed hard and took a deep breath. Her opening notes were faltering but as her voice filled the room, she found her nervousness slipping away. If she could forget everything that had happened to her just these few minutes she'd be happy. Now, she told herself, she was the equal of Letty Lewis, the Cockney Songbird, but she knew she sounded far, far better. The Liverpool Songbird's voice was stronger, clearer, sweeter and the thunderous applause that broke out as the last notes died away confirmed the knowledge. No one was applauding dutifully. This *was* genuine. She couldn't help herself. A dazzling smile transformed her face and seemed to lighten the entire room. Her eyes sparkled and she tapped her foot as she began the popular, lively "Bye 'Bye Blackbird'. She forgot everything and everyone. The drunken violence of her da. The *Castlemaine*, Georgie Tate, Mr Tibbs and Captain Burrows. She forgot Mam and Lizzie and India and Marietta. She was singing for just herself, because she really enjoyed it. She was singing on a stage. A real stage, not the streets of Liverpool or Charleston.

Again the applause was deafening and she stepped from the podium as though she was walking on a cloud.

'Oh, Alicia, you were fantastic!'

Marietta's praise was sincere. Alice smiled back but the feeling of elation began to evaporate and her heart sank as she saw India approaching. To Alice's horror she was accompanied by a tall, well-built man she judged to be in his thirties. The euphoria was replaced by a cold, hollow feeling in the pit of her stomach; the beat of her heart slowed and the palms of her hands were clammy.

India was all smiles. 'Alicia, dear, that was wonderful. A truly wonderful performance. Mr O'Farrell is absolutely delighted with you and so eager to meet you.'

Alice looked up at the man. He was old, though not as old as most of the clientele, and he was quite handsome. His thick, dark brown hair was cut short. He was clean-shaven, his skin lightly tanned. His eyes were a startling blue and admiration and curiosity were discernible in them.

'Miss Alicia, I'm charmed to meet you.'

He took her hand and his skin felt warm and dry. She was surprised by the lilt in his voice. 'You're Irish.'

'It's not a sin. I can't help it.' There was amusement in the blue eyes and in his voice.

She looked away, confused and apprehensive.

'Alicia, this is Mr Michael Eugene O'Farrell, President of O'Farrell Enterprises.'

She couldn't look at him. She felt sick.

112

'Would you like a drink?' he asked quietly. She was very young, little more than a child, he mused. Yet she was truly beautiful and her voice as she'd sung the plaintive words of a song he'd always loved had been so sweet and pure that it would tear the heart out of you, as his mother would say. 'I don't mean the moonshine India sells at inflated prices.'

Alice shook her head, and looked up. Thankfully India had gone. 'I . . . No, thank you.' She swallowed hard. Oh, best to get it over and done with. 'Shall we?' She made a half-hearted gesture towards the doorway in the hall. He nodded so she turned away from him and made for the door and the staircase beyond.

As she showed him into her room, he strode in as if he knew the place well. She closed the door behind him, momentarily leaning her forehead against the cool wood, desperation rising up in a great tide within her.

Faster than she'd thought he would, he spun round and, reaching out, gently turned her towards him. Her eyes tight shut, she tilted her face obediently up toward his. Gently he kissed her cheek then her lips and he felt her flinch.

'I won't hurt you, Alicia.'

She opened her eyes and he saw the naked fear and revulsion in their depths.

She couldn't help herself. 'My name's not Alicia, it's Alice. Alice O'Connor and I . . . I'm not a whore.'

He drew away from her. 'You mean you've never . . .?'

She shook her head. 'Only once and I was really, really desperate. I couldn't afford my fare.'

He took her hand and drew her towards the chair, indicating that she should sit down. He took a cigarette case from his pocket and proffered it to her. She shook her head, so he lit one for himself and sat on the edge of the bed. He had no intention of forcing himself on her. He didn't frequent places like this very often. He'd been restless tonight, bored and unable to put his mind to anything serious, so he'd come out looking for a diversion.

'You're a long way from home, Alice O'Connor. You're from Liverpool, aren't you?'

His actions had surprised her. She hadn't expected him to consider her feelings, let alone be aware of her origins. 'How did you know?'

'The accent. It's one you don't forget. I was born in Dublin and I sailed from Liverpool.'

She shrugged. She'd thought she'd lost her Liverpudlian twang.

'So, how did you end up here? You've a voice like an angel and "The Derry Air" is one I've always liked. It's not exactly a modern song nor one you'd expect to hear in a place like this. Is it another of India's attempts to be cultural?'

Again she shrugged but she looked up into his face. She didn't want to talk, to explain, she just wanted to get it over and done with.

He saw the flash of fear. 'Alice, I'm not going to rape you. I've never forced myself on a woman and I don't intend to start now.'

Her chin jerked up and she looked at him with relief and some amazement. 'But you've paid!'

'So, I paid my entrance fee. Sure, it won't break the bank.'

'Then . . . what?' she stammered, still unsure of him.

'Tell me about yourself. How you got here. Where you learned to sing.'

She eyed him warily. 'Why? Why do you want to be bothered with me?'

'I like to study human nature. I'm interested to know how a little bit of a girl like you ended up here, over three thousand miles away from home.'

Simply and often haltingly she told him her story, sometimes wiping away a tear.

His expression changed. A frown creased his forehead and the blue eyes became cold and hard as she spoke of her da and then Captain Burrows. She didn't tell him about her feelings for David Williamson. She'd told India and somehow it had seemed to increase the hold the woman had on her, and when she'd put it into words it sounded so vain, so stupid.

When she'd finished, there was a silence between them and she wondered what he was thinking.

To Mike O'Farrell it was an all too familiar story. He'd seen many girls like her in Dublin in the area he'd lived in. He'd known girls whose fathers had beaten them black and blue week after week, some in the street where he'd lived. But for the fact that she had the face of an angel and a voice to match, God alone knew what would have happened to her.

'Do you think we . . . we should go down soon?' She wanted to remind him of his promise.

'Do you have to sing again?'

'No, but . . .'

'But there may be other customers?' He stood up. 'Get your coat.'

'What?'

'I said get your coat or wrap or whatever you wear to go out in.'

'I don't understand. Are you going to take me out?'

'I am. There will be no other customers tonight. I'm going to take you to a place I know where you'll enjoy yourself and, Holy Mother of God, don't you deserve a bit of pleasure out of life?'

She was incredulous but then her eyes narrowed. 'Why are you doing all this for me? Is there a catch in it?'

'No, there bloody isn't! Let's just say you sang a song that reminded me of home and I want to show you a bit of gratitude for that, nothing else. Nothing sinister in it at all.'

Suddenly all Alice's fears fell away and she grinned at him. 'You're mad!'

Mike threw back his head and laughed. 'All Irishmen are mad, didn't you know that, Alice O'Connor?'

She laughed with him but suddenly the laughter died in his eyes and he became serious.

'Of course we're mad. Why the hell do you think we take the emigrant ship in droves and leave behind the most beautiful country on God's good earth? Oh, we've a free state now, all the years of fighting are over, but there's still no work, very few opportunities.' Then, quick as it had gone, the gaiety reappeared. 'Ah, go on and get your coat, you bewitching little rossi!' he laughed, shooing her across the room.

'India won't like it.'

Mike crossed his arms over his chest and his brow furrowed in a frown. 'India can go to hell and if she complains, I'll blow her little business wide open.'

Alice laughed and snatched up a short velvet jacket from the wardrobe. India would be furious but she didn't care. Mike O'Farrell wasn't going to force himself on her and he was making sure no one else did either, at least not tonight. She refused to think about tomorrow. He was taking her out to enjoy herself and she trusted him and that's all that mattered for now.

India did protest, strongly, but Mike silenced her with a few well-chosen questions.

The plump little woman was seething. 'I've spent a fortune on her and you've no idea of the damage she's done. Smashed up her room in a fit of temper!'

'Is that so? She's a girl of rare spirit then. Ah, you'll be suitably recompensed – in time.'

India tried a different tack. She looked up at him coyly. 'Then we'll be seeing you more frequently?'

Mike wanted to hit her. 'Oh, very definitely, Miss Osbourne. Probably every night.'

'Did you mean that?' Alice asked as he hailed a cab.

'I never say things I don't mean,' he replied as he handed her into it.

She'd never been in a motorcar. She would have bubbled over with excitement if it hadn't reminded her of David Williamson and the car that had knocked her down. She wondered where he was now. Halfway across the Atlantic, or at home in Liverpool? If she closed her eyes she could see his face. It was something she often did. She could remember the way he'd looked down at her, his eyes full of concern.

'Don't you want to know where we're going?' Mike O'Farrell's question put an end to her musings.

'Where?'

'The Plantation Club. Oh, it's nothing like The Star of India,' he added reassuringly, seeing the fear return to her brown eyes.

'Then what's it like?'

'It's small and dark and smoky. I want you to hear a different kind of music. I want you to enjoy yourself.'

'Where is it?'

'In Beresford Street.'

'But . . .'

'I know. It's not a very refined area but you'll be safe with me.'

She wished she understood him. He *must* have some kind of motive. Was all this concern just to calm her suspicions? But he'd paid for her. He could have taken her at India's. No one she'd ever known had really considered her feelings except Mam and David Williamson, and she didn't want to think of either of them now. She tried to focus on the present and keep her wits about her. Who knew what she'd let herself in for with this strange Irishman. . .

Chapter Eleven

Mike O'Farrell was right. The club *was* dark, small and so fuggy with cigar and cigarette smoke that it caught the back of her throat. When they'd alighted from the cab she'd followed him down some steps to the basement of a warehouse but she hadn't felt at all uneasy. The atmosphere in the club was something she'd never experienced before. As her eyes became accustomed to the gloom, she could see that most of the patrons of the Plantation were black. The few other white people were, like themselves, in evening dress. The music was being provided by a group of five black musicians. But what music! It made her tingle all over.

'It's great! I've never heard anything like this. What is it and what are all those people doing?' Already her feet were tapping and she watched the couples on the dance floor with amazement.

'They're dancing, believe it or not. The dance is called after this city – Charleston. The music is jazz, ragtime, and it's going to sweep the world.' He ushered her to a small table on the fringe of the dance floor but she didn't take her eyes off the exuberant dancers until two tall glasses filled with a light amber-coloured liquid were placed in front of them. She looked at the drinks suspiciously.

'Take that look off your face, sure it's only tea. Iced tea. That's all they serve here. The city fathers have

119

already tried to close them down for playing this "Devil" music and corrupting people's morals, so no risks are taken with liquor.'

Alice tasted hers. It was tea.

He laughed at her expression. 'You don't have to drink it.'

'It doesn't taste right like this. Cold and with no milk.' She sipped it again, pulled a face and then turned her attention back to the dance floor.

Mike watched her. Her eyes were sparkling; her body, even seated, was moving in time with the rhythm and her fingers tapped the table top. The music had obviously captivated her. Joy and vivacity radiated from her like the rays of the sun. He'd never before experienced any of the emotions that were now coursing through him. He smiled to himself sardonically. Was he falling in love, and at first sight, with this chit of a girl? It was the only explanation for how he felt. He hadn't even had a drink, she was intoxication enough. He wanted her, any man would, she was young and beautiful, but he also wanted to protect her, cherish her, keep her away from anything and anyone rough, demanding or cruel. Such beauty and talent should be nurtured not crushed by lust and greed. But he was almost old enough to be her father. Was it possible to love someone you'd only known for an hour? Would she tell him that? Would she laugh cruelly and reject his love, if it was love?

'Oh, I wish I could dance.' Alice's wistful cry cut through his thoughts.

'I'll get someone to teach you. I'm too old to be throwing myself all over the place like that,' he laughed. He enjoyed dancing, the old-fashioned kind of dancing, but he liked to listen to the music, watch other people doing the Charleston and the Black Bottom. Privately he thought that anyone over twenty-five executing those abandoned frenetic steps looked a fool, and Michael

Eugene O'Farrell had no intention of making himself a laughing stock.

Alice's reply was cut short as a tall, slim black man approached the table.

Mike got to his feet and stretched out his hand. 'King! How are you in yourself? I've brought a friend. Alice O'Connor. Alice, meet "King" Oliver. This is his place.'

Alice smiled and shook his hand.

'We haven't seen you much lately, Mike.'

'Import and export. Business and travel. You know how it is.'

'Travel to Europe?'

Mike nodded. 'I caught Paul Whiteman's show at the Grafton Galleries in London. It sure was really something to hear.'

'I'll bet. Don't you dance, Miss O'Connor?' Oliver asked, seeing Alice's gaze fixed once more on the dancers.

'No. I never had any time, before I came here, to America.'

'But she can sing.'

'Really?' There was a genuine interest in Oliver's voice.

'Oh, I can't sing anything like this,' Alice said hastily, looking from her host to Mike.

'Ah, go on. Don't keep putting yourself down. You sang "'Bye 'Bye Blackbird" tonight and it was great altogether.'

'But that was different.' Alice was becoming nervous under the intense but friendly gaze of King Oliver.

'I thought it was your ambition in life to be able to sing on stage and become famous?' Mike chided. 'Isn't that what you told me not an hour ago?'

'It is! But . . .'

'Will you sing for me, Alice?' Oliver asked.

'Now? Here?'

He nodded.

Before she could protest, Mike pulled her to her feet. 'Sure she will. She's got a voice that with training wouldn't disgrace the Charleston Grand Opera House.'

'But I haven't got any training! I only know a few old-fashioned songs,' Alice protested as both men propelled her gently but firmly towards the stage.

'OK, boys, '"'Bye 'Bye Blackbird'', follow her,' Oliver instructed the band while Alice turned to face her audience. It had all happened so fast she didn't feel nervous. There wasn't time. She smiled down and over what looked like a sea of eager, expectant faces and her heart began to beat faster. This was a real audience, a proper audience. Men and women, black and white, who wanted nothing more than to enjoy themselves. To be entertained by her, Alice O'Connor.

She'd never enjoyed herself so much! She felt glowing, tingling, alive! Oh, it had been wonderful. If she never sang another note publicly it wouldn't matter now. She'd had this magical, glorious night. She'd completely lost track of the time and she'd forgotten about India Osbourne but eventually Mike had led her back to the table and placed her jacket round her shoulders.

'Time to go.'

'Oh, I don't want to. I want to stay here for ever.'

He took her hand. 'Out of the question.'

'Mike, I don't want to go back to India.'

King Oliver had appeared beside them. 'Is that where you found her?'

'Tonight was my first night. I had no money, no job. I had no choice.'

'I'll offer you a job, Alice. Here, but I can't pay you much.'

She was astounded. So astounded she couldn't reply.

Mike grinned. 'So? Answer the man.'

Alice found her voice. 'Oh, please! Yes, yes, please!' Tears of joy and pure relief filled her eyes and she grasped Mike's arm to steady herself. She felt dizzy.

'Then see you tomorrow, Alice. About eight o'clock?'

'Pinch me! Pinch my arm so I'll know I'm awake.'

Mike laughed and gently nipped the soft skin above her elbow but she was still in a daze as he led her up the steps and out into the street. She looked up at the sky. A soft, heavy, midnight-blue sky with thousands of stars all looking brighter than she'd ever seen them look before. 'Oh, I can't believe it! I've got a job! I just can't believe that someone's going to pay me money to sing! I won't have to sweep floors, beg or . . . do anything else for it.'

Mike refused the offer of a cab. They'd walk towards town and the Battery. He wanted time to work things out. To think, to try to get his thoughts and ideas into some kind of order. Alice almost skipped along beside him like a child, humming to herself and singing aloud snatches of the songs she'd rapidly picked up from Andy, the pianist, who'd told her she had a good ear for music, that she was a 'natural'. She hadn't really understood what he meant but she was thrilled just the same. This was what she'd come to America for. It was for this that she'd endured seasickness, the storms and the attention of James Burrows. It was coming true, all of it. It really was happening.

As he looked down into her face, glowing with sheer happiness, Mike made up his mind. She wasn't going back to the house on West Street. It might not work out, he had no idea how she would behave or even react to his suggestion, but he was willing to try.

Alice suddenly stopped, realising they had turned into Rutledge Street. 'Where are we going now?'

'We're nearly there.'

'Where?'

'Home.'

Her jaw dropped and she stared at him. 'You *live* here on Rutledge?'

He nodded. 'And from now on, so do you.'

'Me?' she gasped.

'You're not going back to India. You've got a job now. You need somewhere to live, I've got plenty of room.'

The suspicions swooped back into her mind. Was this what he'd been planning all night? Were he and King Oliver in cahoots, as Americans said?

'No. I ... I can't. You'll want a big rent and ... and what will people say?'

'Goddamn you, Alice O'Connor! You're the most suspicious woman I've ever met! I'm offering you a decent home, a more than decent home. A life of bloody luxury compared to what you're used to, and you think it's some plot to sell you into white slavery or something else as desperate!'

Instantly she was contrite. 'I'm sorry. It's just that no one's ever been good to me, not without a price.'

He opened the ornate gate set in the white stuccoed wall and led her into a garden bathed in moonlight. A garden filled with palmettoes, magnolias, jasmine, bougainvillaea and tropical plants Alice had never seen before. The moonlight seemed to make the stuccoed walls of the house shimmer against the midnight-blue sky. She caught her breath in disbelief. Her gaze wandered to the shuttered windows on the upper storey, then down to the windows on the ground floor, which were open and blazed with light. A balcony ran along the entire front of the house, supported by four white pillars with latticework in a strange Eastern design connecting each column.

'This is your house?' she breathed in awe.

'All mine. Legally left to me by my father.'

His voice was bitter, Alice thought, as he led her up the wide front steps and onto the porch. Gently he pushed her down onto a swinging, white-painted rattan seat covered with soft, upholstered cushions.

She'd passed houses like this many times on her wanderings around the city. She suddenly remembered the lady in grey, Mrs Phillips, who had given her fifty cents

124

to go away and not lower the tone of the neighbourhood. This neighbourhood.

'Why are you doing all this for me? You only met me tonight and you thought . . . you thought I was a whore. You even paid for me. You know what I am and where I come from.'

He looked out over his well-tended gardens and it was as if the years had rolled back and he was seeing them for the first time, as he'd done nearly twenty years ago. A lad of seventeen he'd been then, filled with anger and the raging fire for revenge.

'Because I know what it's like to be poor. To be cold and hungry. Ragged and despised. I know what it's like to have to beg.'

She was astounded. 'You?'

'Yes, me. Michael Eugene O'Farrell from the Coombe in Dublin.'

She looked at him in silent mystification.

'Where did you live in Liverpool, Alice? The exact area.'

'Benledi Street, off Scotland Road.'

'A slum? Rotten, falling down, bug-infested houses? Streets of them. Back to back with a filthy alleyway between them?'

She nodded.

'Just like the street where I was born and where I lived until I was seventeen. The houses were beautiful Georgian buildings originally, but when they dissolved Grattan's Parliament, the high and mighty up and left. Now they're just derelict, with a family in every room, including the cellar. There were eight families in our house and things were desperate for everyone. Oh, Dublin's changing but there's still terrible poverty. The treaty and the civil war have changed some things but before that even if you were rich you had no rights. Catholics couldn't vote. Oh no. No Catholic was even allowed to go to Trinity College

– the university.' He took out his cigarette case, lit one and drew deeply on it as old memories stirred in him. 'There were three of us – that lived. Me, Kitty and Deidre, and Da and Mammy. When I was eight, didn't Da leave us. He emigrated. Took the ferry from Kingstown to Liverpool and then the ship to America. Oh, the plan was all worked out. He promised faithfully he'd send for us. There was only enough for one fare, you see, and Mammy had begged, borrowed and starved to get that together!' He ground the cigarette out viciously beneath his heel. His face was in shadow so Alice couldn't see the hatred in his eyes but she could hear it in his voice.

'He didn't send for you.'

'No, he bloody well didn't! Not a word. Not a letter or a bloody note.'

'How did she manage?' Alice's thoughts were of Nelly and how she'd begged and borrowed, and she'd had some wages to help, occasionally, after she'd prised them out of Da.

'She begged in the streets, like you. I got what bit of work I could. I'd turn my hand to anything and when I didn't get anything I stole. She always said God didn't put a mouth on this earth that He doesn't feed but that's a bloody lie! Typical, empty, useless platitudes the Father used to spout on Sundays at Mass. Well, my father turned me into a thief but I swore that one day I'd find him and make him pay for every goddamn lie I had to tell my mother. Aye, and for every single one of her tears!'

'And did you?'

'I did so. I worked my passage from Liverpool. I knew he'd come south, to Charleston. The only bit of information Father Maguire managed to get for us. So I followed him, riding freight trains, cadging lifts where I could until I got here. It wasn't hard to find him then. He'd had the luck of the Irish all right, he'd made a bloody fortune. Mainly by gambling and then by buying up property.

Renting it for a while then selling it on. Houses that were falling down like the one he'd left us all in, but could still be rented to two or even three families. Mainly poor black families.'

He paused to light another cigarette.

'What did he say?' she asked.

Mike laughed and there was a lifetime of bitterness in the sound. 'When I arrived here at this house? When I saw all the magnificent rooms and furniture? I was seventeen and all I could think about was my mammy and my sisters going barefoot in the snow along the quays or up Sackville Street, as it was then, begging, while he had been living like a bloody king. I beat him half to death.' Feeling her shrink back, he smiled. 'There's no need to be afraid of me, Alice. I've never raised a hand to any man since that day. I never needed to.'

'And then?'

'Then I went back to Dublin. I took his conscience money and bought a house. A grand, well-appointed house in Donnybrook and moved them all in there. He had a stroke while I was home, so I came back to oversee his "investments" and make some of my own. He died a year later. He couldn't stand being crippled. He couldn't stand seeing me taking over.'

'Didn't you ... didn't you ...'

'Feel guilty? No. Not once. What kind of a man is it that lives in the lap of luxury, knowing his family are starving in a hovel?'

'Is your Mam ...'

'Alive?' He laughed but this time there was no bitterness or pain in the sound. 'Yes, she'll live to be a hundred. Both Kitty and Dee are married with families of their own. She won't live with either of them nor will she come to live here. She still insists it's *his* house. The one he denied her. The girls keep an eye on her, she wants for nothing. She has a woman who comes in to do the housework and don't they have a fight every week over something, then she sacks poor Molly but takes her back on the next day. Oh, she's a desperate stubborn woman, but she values her independence.'

'Will you ever leave here? Go back to Dublin for good?'

He shrugged. 'I might. One day. Maybe when they repeal this bloody stupid prohibition law and there's no more money to be made selling bootleg whiskey.'

'Is that what you do?'

'Among other things. Import and export. Oh, I'm very careful and I'm not greedy. He left me a rich man, my father. I don't want to make a vast fortune like some do and I don't tread on anyone's toes either. I intend to die in my bed of old age, not with a bullet in my back.' He got to his feet and held out his hand. 'So, that's why I'm offering you a home, Alice O'Connor. Lodgings, nothing else, no strings attached.'

'Then I'll pay my way.'

'There's no need.'

'I won't be a kept woman!' she flashed at him.

He threw up his hands in mock horror. 'All right! All right! You can pay me a token rent which I will bank in your name. Come and I'll show you inside and you can meet Alexander.'

'Who's he?'

'My butler. He'll put some manners on you, Alice O'Connor, and between us we'll make a lady of you.'

He led her from room to room and her eyes grew wider and wider. When he'd said his father had lived like a king, he'd meant it. The reception rooms were large and airy and filled with expensive furniture, most of it imported, which had been lovingly cared for over many years. The dining room was decorated in pale yellow and green silk, the rosewood table and chairs and buffet gleaming in dark contrast. The electric lights were covered with shades shaped like Oriental lanterns. Prints of Chinese and

Japanese rural scenes decorated the walls. A magnificent Chinese carpet covered most of the floor but the exposed boards had a mirror-like polish on them. In contrast, his study was a sombre room, dark woods, dark green carpet and drapes. Then he led her up the wide staircase and she gripped the delicate wrought-iron scrolls of the banister, feeling once more that everything was a dream.

There were numerous bedrooms and bathrooms decorated in pale pastel shades, but the room he led her into and informed Alice was hers made her gasp aloud. The walls and ceiling were covered in silk which, when viewed in one light looked pale lilac and in another, pale blue. The material was draped and pleated across the ceiling and gathered into a rosette in the centre, from which hung a crystal chandelier. The carpet was pale blue, like the walls, and the ivory damask curtains at the deep sash windows matched the bedspread. The headboard and footboard of the bed were ornate, inlaid with mother-of-pearl in an intricate Oriental pattern, the mosquito netting elegantly tied back with pale blue cord. The tables beside the bed and beneath the window were small, carved and gilded. In the name of God, how much money did he have? He must be as rich as the King of England! She stared up at him, her thoughts quite clear in her eyes.

He smiled. 'I'd give it all away if I could have spared my poor mother one minute of hardship, one hour of heartache and worry over that bastard!'

She sat down on the edge of a chair. 'I don't know what to say, or do. How can I pay you back?'

'Write to your mother, Alice. Tell her you're safe and well, that you've got a job and a home and send her this.' He placed a fifty-dollar bill on the table beside her.

She gazed at him. 'I'll pay you back,' she said stoutly. 'If you won't take any rent, then the money you put in the bank can go towards paying you for this. Please. I'd feel better about it all.'

He nodded. 'And tomorrow Alexander will take you shopping.'

'But what will people think about me moving in here? I mean your friends, like?'

'I don't care. I don't move in the exalted circles of Charleston society. I'm "new" money, not quite respectable. If your relations haven't been here for over a hundred years or fought in the War of Independence, all the best homes are closed to you.' He could see she didn't understand him, so he smiled. 'Ah, don't worry your head about it. Good night, Alice O'Connor.'

She smiled at him, a smile of such radiance that his heart lurched. He turned away. He must be the biggest eejit in the entire bloody world, he thought. But he was sure now of his feelings. He loved her.

When Alexander brought him his usual nightcap of bourbon, Mike could see the man had something on his mind.

'Come on, out with it now. You've a face like thunder.'

Alexander drew himself up. 'Who is the young person upstairs? Is she staying the night? Will she require Ruth's services?'

'She's my good deed for the day. I rescued her from The Star of India. She's far too young and naive to be in a place like that and she's only been in Charleston a few weeks.'

Alexander's eyebrows rose and he inhaled deeply. He'd only caught sight of her for a few minutes, but long enough for him to see she was a pretty girl and as his employer had just said, young and naive. The look of innocent wonderment on her face had been clear for all to see and he'd warmed to her, though of course he'd make it clear to Mr O'Farrell that he didn't appreciate her being introduced into the house without his being fully informed. But now it appeared she was a prostitute. He struggled for words and with his composure. 'You've brought a . . .

130

whore home, here, to this house?'

The amusement died in Mike's eyes. 'She is *not* a whore! Hard up, uneducated, living by her wits but not a whore. She's going to live here and work, sing at the Plantation.'

The light of battle flooded into Alexander's dark eyes. 'And how's that going to look in this part of town? Folk will talk and the Hendersons' butler is sure to ask me straight out and then gloat 'cos we've a . . . a nightclub singer living here.'

Mike stared at Alexander. He liked the man. He was efficient, honest and tactful. He was also a snob but Mike didn't hold that against him. All the butlers he knew were the same. He certainly didn't want to lose him. 'I don't care what anyone thinks but obviously you do. So, what do you suggest? Apart from throwing her out which I won't do.'

Alexander began to ponder the matter, his dignity restored, his feelings and opinion considered. What he wanted to say was that he considered it high time Mike O'Farrell was married. He'd dropped enough hints over the past two years about there never being any 'company' calling. No ladies brought home for dinner or escorted to the opera, balls or soirees. Lately the hints had not been very subtle. All to no avail. But maybe, just maybe, this one could be the one. Not one he'd have chosen, of course, but she was young and she could learn.

'We could say she's your niece. Your dead sister's child?'

'Jaysus! Alexander, can't you do better than that? Besides, both my sisters are alive and well, thank God and God bless the mark!' Mike spoke part in seriousness, for although he denied it, he was superstitious.

'Well, the daughter of some old friend in Dublin who's died then.'

'She's from Liverpool but I grasp your meaning. He begged and pleaded with me, in his will of course, that she should become my ward. I'd be her legal guardian.'

Alexander nodded but there was no relaxation of the disapproval in his stance. 'What about her singing at that place?'

Mike refilled his glass. 'It's a perfectly respectable club, unlike most, and I won't stop her singing. You can tell people she sang on the stage in England or Ireland or anywhere you choose. Tell them what you bloody well like, but I'm not going to stop her. Anyway, I can't. I've no claim on her at all and she's been kicked in the teeth by fate often enough already. Most of all by her own father. She's come from the slums of Liverpool, the way I came from the slums of Dublin.' Years ago he'd told Alexander his life story one night when he'd been very drunk, morbid and moribund. In return Alexander had told him that his grandfather had been a slave on a plantation in Georgia, and not a house servant but a field hand, before Mr Lincoln and the war had freed them all.

Alexander nodded slowly. 'You're her legal guardian until she's twenty-one and she had a very promising stage career until her pa died.'

'And stated, in his will of course, that I had promised to be her guardian and further her career over here,' Mike added.

Alexander still didn't look totally convinced.

'What's the matter with that story?'

Alexander looked down at his highly polished shoes. 'If, well, if she were to be your fiancée . . .' That was as far as he got.

Mike flung open the door. 'Out! Don't push your luck any further!'

Chapter Twelve

Lizzie walked wearily down Titchfield Street having managed to beg a few potatoes from Burgess's on the corner of Burlington Street. It was a long walk to Silvester Street and Holden's shop. She'd have to walk the length of Titchfield Street and then turn into Blenheim Street. She had sixpence, the last of her wages, and it would have to last until next week. She had to try and see what she could get from Ivy Holden and still have change over.

The wind was fierce and blustery. It lifted the straw and bits of paper from the road and blew them into a swirling, eddying sort of dance. The smell of horse manure was strong; although motor lorries were becoming increasingly numerous, many commodities were still transported by horse and cart. A few spots of rain touched her face but she was too tired, hungry and dispirited to notice. Christmas was approaching but it only made her feel more miserable. You didn't automatically get a Goodfellows parcel. You had to be recommended, but then nearly every family in Benledi Street deserved strong recommendations. The fact that her family were the poorest of the poor and needed a parcel most didn't count for much. A few families, like the Garrettys and the O'Hanlons, did share a bit of their parcels, but the rest didn't. She had no interest in the red and yellow crepe paper streamers or the holly and tinsel that were being put up in most shops. She didn't even notice the words 'Happy Christmas' that were painted in whitewash on the shop windows nor that the more adventurous and artistic proprietors added sprigs of holly too. Christmas was the same as any other time of the year for them. It could be worse, in fact, if Da had no money for drink to celebrate with his mates.

She walked slowly; exhaustion made it hard to find any energy at all. Morosely she thought about other Christmases. Last year had been the second without Alice. Mam had surreptitiously wiped away her silent tears all that day and Lizzie had heard her crying when she thought everyone was finally asleep.

Lizzie often wondered what kind of a Christmas Alice had had last year. In fact she often wondered what kind of a life Alice had now. She had a job singing and a place to stay, that much they knew, but they didn't know anything else. Da collected the letters from the main post office. Mam had tried, and she had tried, to sneak off to the post office, telling them that Da couldn't come down himself because he wasn't well enough, and were there any more letter from America? They'd both been turned away by officious clerks demanding proof of identity and letters of permission from Da. They'd only ever seen that first one but Lizzie knew Alice sent money. She didn't know the exact amount and they never saw a penny of it. Da could barely read so he probably just threw the letters away. But at least Mam could console herself that Alice was safe and well and happy.

There had been a couple of good Christmases, or what passed for good in their house, Lizzie reflected, but they'd been during the war years. She held the paper bag tightly to her under her shawl. Those four years had been terrible years for everyone they knew. She knew Mam had felt guilty that she had no son old enough to go and fight for King and Country. Many's the night she had prayed they'd come and take Da off to go and fight, but being a docker was a reserved occupation. He'd had plenty of work, about which he had complained constantly, and money too, but they saw very little of that.

'How can I go and sit with Mary O'Hanlon and Jinny Thomas and all the rest when I don't know what they're going through?' Nelly had said time and again. But it had broken her heart to see the telegrams arrive, day after day, week after week, month after month. The neighbourhood had been decimated. Nearly all the lads she'd grown up with were dead or crippled. Tommy had been killed too. Lizzie's eyes misted with tears. Poor big-hearted, loud-mouthed, generous Tommy MacNamara. People had said he was daft but he wasn't. A bit slow, that's all, and that was because he'd had to bring himself up. All Ma Mac cared about was her gin and stout, certainly not her kids. She was in the pub morning, noon and night and Tommy's da was inside Walton Jail more often than he was out of it.

Tommy had volunteered, unlike his older brothers. She'd heard Ivy Holden telling Mam that Ma Mac had enough white feathers to stuff a pillow. Tommy's brothers had been carted off by the military police in the end. Big Kevin Mac had been killed too and as for the rest of them, as far as she knew they'd just disappeared off the face of the earth. People said the army was still looking for them.

The whole family were villains of the worst kind. Even Tommy fenced stolen goods and was in on almost every crime they'd committed. Except for anything violent. He had no stomach for beating people up, he'd said. Of course war was different, he'd explained.

He'd been kind and gentle and loving to her. He'd bought her lovely clothes and shoes and even underwear. Mam had gone mad about that. Fellers only bought you things like that after they'd married you. She'd retorted that Tommy was going to marry her, he'd told her so. He'd bought her perfume and little trinkets and bits of cheap jewellery. He'd taken her to music halls and they'd gone on day trips to New Brighton and even Llandudno. And best of all, Da had been terrified of the whole Mac-Namara family so she'd been able to give Mam all her wages. Even after Tommy had gone off to war she'd been able to earn a good wage in munitions and they'd also managed to hang onto it by threatening Da with the terrible things Tommy or his brothers would do if they found out he'd taken it off them. Even though they were in Flanders they had mates at home who would do them favours, like giving Da a good hiding. Lizzie had never been sure about that threat but it worked. Da had believed it. Things had been better then, they had had money for coal and a bit more food and some second-hand clothes for the kids. And then on the terrible day they heard that Tommy and Big Kev had been killed, Da had taken all her clothes and shoes, the cheap trinkets and bits of jewellery to the pawnshop. He'd not let her keep a single thing. Now she had nothing tangible to remember Tommy MacNamara by, only memories and images.

She was unaware that tears were mingling with the raindrops on her cheeks. Now she was old and drab. Any chance, any small claim to attractiveness had gone. She'd be a 'spinster of this parish' for the rest of her life. Or until Da went too far and killed one of them. He was becoming more and more violent. Poor Mam hadn't been able to get up for days after he'd found out that Alice had gone. He'd blamed that on Mam, but she'd been given a hefty clout too.

The rain had become heavier and Lizzie tried to hasten her steps. It was dark, one of the street lamps had gone out, and as she turned into Blenheim Street she collided with someone. She slipped on the wet cobbles and fell awkwardly, sprawling in the road. The potatoes escaped from the bag and rolled into the gutter, followed by the silver sixpence. She wasn't really hurt, physically, but as she saw the sixpence roll down a grid, she just sat in the road and burst into tears.

'Come on, girl, up you get. Are you hurt? I didn't see you, the lamp's out. Have you broken anything, do you think?'

She looked up and through her tears she saw the concerned face of a policeman. His helmet was pulled well down and the collar of his cape was turned up against the weather. Instinctively she shied away from him. Scuffers meant trouble.

'Come on now, luv. I'm not going to hurt you. I promise.' He held out a large hand encased in thick cream-coloured woollen gloves.

Tentatively Lizzie took it and was drawn gently to her feet. He towered over her. All the scuffers were tall but he was one of the biggest she'd ever seen.

'No damage done.' He was still looking concerned.

'No, but I've lost me spuds an' me sixpence. It rolled down the grid. It's all I . . . we had.'

Jack Phillips looked at her closely. He was a kind man and he considered himself to be fair in his dealings with the people on his beat. Every working day of his life he was confronted with the wretched poverty they lived in. He knew all the real hard cases, the villains, the drunkards.

'You're Tip O'Connor's girl, aren't you?'

Lizzie shrank away from him, terrified now that she might be tarred with the same brush as her da.

'Then I know you've a lot to put up with, luv. He's not the best father in the world, is he?'

She slowly shook her head.

'Pull your shawl over your head, you're getting soaked. I'll rescue the spuds but the sixpenny joey will have gone into the main drain by now, especially with all this rain.'

Lizzie did as she was told and stood in silence watching as he poked around in the gutter with his truncheon for the potatoes. One by one he put them in the large pocket inside his cape.

'Come on, I'll see you home.'

'No!' The word was uttered in a terrified voice.

He sighed deeply. He understood. He was respected in this area but he certainly wasn't liked, but then it wasn't his job to be liked. He wasn't paid to be popular. 'What if you slip again? There's that much soggy litter around here it's a fair bet you will.'

Lizzie knew what Mam's reaction would be but she was too weary, too shaken and too distressed to argue. The rain had become torrential. It was swept almost horizontally along the streets by the increasing gale. She bent her head against the force but was completely taken aback when the scuffer put his cape round her thin shoulders. It reached down to her feet.

'It's not too far to walk and besides, this tunic is good thick worsted,' Jack said, seeing the astonishment in her eyes.

No one had ever done anything like this for her before – well, not since Tommy had been killed. The tears welled up again.

'What number is it?' he enquired.

'Ten, but I'll be all right when we get round the corner.'

'I said I'll see you safely home, luv, and I never break a promise.' His smile was wry. God help her, she looked as though she was about to drop of starvation and exhaustion any minute and she must be soaked through. God alone knew how long she'd been out in this weather.

'Have you got a job?' he asked in an attempt to lessen her fear of him.

She nodded. 'It's not much an' Mam or me don't see much of the money. He takes it.'

He didn't need to be told that. He'd arrested Tip O'Connor for drunken brawling too many times to remember. His name was at the top of the list of habitual drunkards in the station house.

'How do you manage then?'

She shrugged. 'Mam always manages to pay the rent, she's only ever got behind once. People are good, too. You . . . well . . . the police help with clothes an' boots for the kids.'

'Where does your sister work now? The one who I used to see singing outside the Rotunda?' He'd seen and listened to the girl many times, turning a blind eye to this form of begging. She had a wonderful voice and one of the pleasures in his austere life was music. He was a bachelor and lived with his mother in Media Street, off Kirkdale Road. She refused to move to a better area, even though her husband had been dead for over ten years. 'This is my home and I've good neighbours. I'm too old to be pulling up my roots and moving to God knows where' was the answer he always got when the subject was broached.

'Our Alice went to America, nearly a year ago. Just before Christmas. We had a letter from,' Lizzie thought hard, 'a place called Charleston. She's got a job and a decent place to live. I wish . . . I wish I could have gone with her.' She'd never said those words aloud before. She missed Alice terribly and so did Mam. But if she, too, had gone, then there would be no one to go out and earn a wage. The rest of the kids were too young although Jimmy did sell newspapers and bootlaces, whenever he could. But he was like Da. It was like trying to get blood out of a stone getting money out of Jimmy.

They had arrived at her front door which despite the weather was slightly ajar. Jack could see the flaking plaster, the patches of rising damp, the missing floorboards. The whole damned street needed demolishing and the houses rebuilt, but that was too much to ask of the landlords. They'd never put their hands in their well-lined pockets so people like the O'Connors could at least have a decent roof over their heads, not one that leaked like a sieve.

Awkwardly Lizzie took off his cape and handed it back to him. It was so heavy, the rain soaking into the wool, that she struggled with it.

He took it from her and removed the potatoes from the pocket. 'Here, wrap them in your shawl or you'll go dropping them again.'

She did as she was bid then looked up at him again. 'Thanks for seeing me home.'

'What's your name? You never told me.'

'Lizzie.'

'Short for Elizabeth? It's my mam's name too, but she gets called Bessie.'

Nelly had heard their voices and had come to the door. Her eyes widened in fear when she saw Lizzie with a policeman.

'Oh, Holy Mother of God! What's she done?' she cried. 'She's a good girl, honest she is, sir. I won't believe anything you tell me she's done!'

'She hasn't done anything wrong, Mrs O'Connor. There's a lamp out in Blenheim Street and in the dark I bumped into her. Sent her flying would be more truthful. She's not hurt and we salvaged the spuds, but I'm afraid the sixpenny joey's gone. Straight down the drain, it went. She's soaked, so I'd advise you to get a hot cup of tea down her and a few blankets round her before she gets pneumonia.' At the sight of Nelly's face he could have bitten his tongue. How bloody stupid! How bloody tactless! There would be no fire and therefore no hot water and probably no tea either. Just a few potatoes and maybe a bit of stale bread.

'Would you mind if I just stepped in for a second, Mrs O'Connor? Just while I get this cape on again?'

Nelly nodded silently. What else could she do?

It was colder and damper inside than it was out in the street, he thought as he shrugged the heavy garment over his broad shoulders and fastened the metal clasp, stamped with the Liver bird. He earned four pounds and ten shillings a week, with two shillings and sixpence extra for boot allowance. This entire family had only sixpence and that had now gone. He looked at the pinched, pallid faces of the two women and silently cursed a society that did very little for its poor, its sick, its elderly, its war heroes. Most of them were decent people. These women battled daily to overcome dirt, disease and hunger while their priests urged them to go on having kids they couldn't feed, for the glory of God and their reward in the next life. He wasn't a deeply religious man but the plight of the O'Connors stirred a flame of anger in him. He dug into his trouser pocket and brought out a ten-shilling note. Charity such as this was deeply frowned upon by his superiors and he had to admit they did have a point when it was argued that any money would only end up in the pubs in the area.

'Mrs O'Connor, is there any way you can hide this from him – your husband?'

Nelly's eyes were riveted on the note. It would keep them for weeks if she was careful. 'I'll find a way, so help me God I will, sir.'

He thrust the note into her hand, confident she wouldn't go up and down the street announcing the fact that a scuffer had given her ten shillings.

Suddenly Lizzie smiled up at him and he realised that she was younger than she looked.

'Thanks for everything,' she said, feeling suddenly shy.

'Well, it's nearly Christmas. I'll be off now but you get a fire going and take those wet things off you, Lizzie.'

They stood in the doorway and watched him walk back up the street, shoulders straight, head unbent before the rain driving into his face. 'Well, I've never known a scuffer do that before, but God bless him just the same,' Nelly said as he turned the corner out of their sight.

As he walked down the road Jack Phillips couldn't get the image of Lizzie O'Connor sitting sobbing in the road out of his mind. He'd put them forward for a Christmas parcel and also for police issue clothes and a small donation from the Police Benevolent Fund, and what's more he'd keep his eye on them all, particularly Tip O'Connor. Maybe they'd get lucky. Maybe Tip would become involved in another drunken fight. He'd have no money for a fine, so a couple of days in jail would give the family a better Christmas . . .

'I'll go out and get some coal and some chips,' Nelly said as she shut the door.

'But Mam, he'll know we've got money then.' Lizzie stared at her mother anxiously.

'I won't light the fire until he's gone to sleep – passed out more like. I'll put the chips in the scullery under the sink so he won't smell them. Later you can go over to Mrs O'Hanlon and ask to warm them up in her range. It'll be late but at least we'll eat. I'll wake the kids up for it.'

Lizzie smiled. 'Mam, you're dead crafty.'

'I have to be and I've had plenty of practice,' Nelly replied, grimly snatching her shawl from a nail on the wall.

'He was dead kind to me, Mam. He took his cape off and put it round me and it was so thick and warm.'

'If only they were all like that. Half of them think that it's our own fault we're poor, the other half – well, at least they're fair-minded and charitable. If it wasn't for them, half the kids along Scottie Road would be barefoot and naked. Oh, I know they get poked fun at wearing that horrible green stuff with its stamp, but I'm not too proud to take what's given.'

'You'd best go, Mam, or you won't get back before me

da comes home and then it will be like the time he battered our Alice.'

Nelly's expression changed. 'I'll never forgive him for driving her away. Never!'

'Go on, Mam,' Lizzie urged.

As she closed the door behind her mother, Lizzie leaned against it and pushed the wet strands of hair away from her face. He'd been good to them, that scuffer. He'd treated her gently and with respect, as if she was really someone worthy of note. And she didn't even know his name.

PART TWO

Chapter Thirteen

1927

Alice straightened her hat as Ruth turned down the bed and picked Alice's discarded nightdress and wrap from the floor.

It was Tuesday and on Tuesdays Alice went down to West Street, the opposite end from India's house, where a modicum of respectability remained. She went to the home of Alfredo Bransini, the Italian tenor, now retired, for what he called 'voice training' and she called a singing lesson. She'd been going for a year now, ever since the Plantation had been closed down. Mike always swore that the illicit liquor that had caused its demise had been deliberately planted and the police informed. There had never been any kind of trouble there before.

When the police rushed in, there had been pandemonium but Mike had managed to get Alice out the back way and home, so she wasn't carted off downtown. Still, she missed the place terribly. In the end, King Oliver had moved north with his musicians but she'd had to stay behind. The singing lessons had been by way of a consolation but it wasn't the same as singing to an audience where you didn't have to worry about things like breathing properly or whether the whole lesson would degenerate into a shouting match. Signor Bransini lost his temper at the drop of a hat and yelled at her, usually gesticulating wildly with his arms. After a while she'd learned that the best way to deal with this was to shout back and gesticulate just as wildly. It was all very wearying.

'Alexander says Mr Mike is waiting,' the black girl announced after having gone to the door of the room in response to the butler's summons.

'I'm ready.' Alice glanced around her, making sure she'd forgotten nothing and sighed. She'd been here for two years now and she'd become accustomed to the splendid rooms and the luxuries of life. She didn't need to tidy away or wash her own clothes, Ruth saw to that. Alexander supervised the small staff that comprised Ella the cook, Jimmy who did the garden and any small jobs around the place, Ruth who doubled as parlour maid and ladies' maid, and Florence who was a maid of all work. Alice had been very wary of them all for the first few weeks. But she'd been even more wary of Mike O'Farrell. And although her suspicions had gradually faded, she still found his treatment of her puzzling. He was an enigma. He didn't seem to want anything from her. Oh, he kissed her, usually on the cheek or forehead, but it was a brotherly kiss. Officially she had been his ward, and then three months ago a sudden mad, crazy notion had made her ask him if he loved her.

Mike had been completely taken aback but soon recovered. 'I'm very fond of you, Alice, but God help the man who falls for you,' he answered.

She was stung. 'Why?'

'Because you are a hard-hearted, crafty little madam.'

'I'm not!' she cried. 'Have I ever been stubborn or conniving?' Once she wouldn't have known what a word like 'conniving' meant. 'How can you say that?'

He laughed. 'You must be to have got this far. We're alike, Alice. Maybe that's why we get on so well.'

'We do get on, don't we? But ...'

'But what?'

'Well, it doesn't *look* right.'

148

He sighed. He'd thought she was happy with the explanation he'd concocted for her living beneath his roof. She had recently been included in the occasional dinner parties that he'd given for his business associates – all men. Alexander had taught her how things were done and not done, and she'd struggled to suppress her accent. She'd done well but she'd been quick to note the glances of curiosity and speculation shown – and just as rapidly hidden – by these men, all of them 'new' money like Mike himself.

Understanding dawned on Mike. 'I can see Alexander's hand in this. If it's announced that we're married it will look better, be more socially acceptable, more respectable.'

'I've always been respectable! Mam brought us up decent. Decently,' she corrected herself.

He leaned back in his chair and scrutinised her face. 'Setting aside Alexander's meddling, just what *do* you want, Alice?'

She shrugged. 'I don't know. Alexander says guardians often marry their wards.'

'In fairy stories and usually to get their hands on the poor girls' money.'

'Mike, be serious. Maybe if people thought I was your wife we'd get invited to places.'

The laughter left his eyes. 'I'm a Catholic Irishman, Alice. Marriage will be for ever for me, even if divorce is becoming easier in this rip-roaring age. It's " 'til death do us part" for me and when I say those words I'll mean them.'

'You're a bloody hypocrite, Mike O'Farrell! You've never set foot in a church for years. If you did, it would probably fall down around you and the priest would keel over with the shock. I didn't say I *wanted* to be your wife, just . . . just . . .'

'Now who's the hypocrite? You want me to present you as my wife?'

'Well, why not? We could say it was a very quiet wedding, no fuss. Just a small announcement in the newspaper.'

'You've got it all worked out pat, the pair of you. You see, I was right. You *are* a conniving little madam.' He got up and walked to the mirror over the mantel shelf and adjusted his tie.

'There won't be any . . . any sharing the same bedroom or anything like that.'

He looked at her in the mirror. She was asking a great deal. To everyone they would be man and wife and yet they must sleep apart. Kisses would be without passion. Embraces, except those in public, would be nonexistent.

'And what about the rest of the staff?' he asked. 'It will seem to them to be a very odd marriage.'

'Alexander has told them all that they shouldn't tell *anyone* at all. This arrangement, as he calls it, will increase their status, but I don't think they care about that. It's only Alexander who's a snob. Besides, if anyone says a word, he's promised to have them dismissed and with no reference.'

'That man has too much bloody power in this house,' Mike muttered to himself.

'But if they keep quiet they'll get a bonus.'

'He's very generous with *my* money,' Mike sniffed, gazing thoughtfully at his highly polished shoes. 'All right I'll humour you,' he pronounced finally. 'Have it your way. I don't want a domestic war to start over it. I value my peace and sanity.' If only she *did* love him, he thought. He'd willingly marry her now, this minute. But there was always his pride standing between them. She'd never accept him and he wasn't prepared to make a fool of himself. This 'arrangement' would probably be the nearest he'd ever come to actually marrying her. It also meant that in public he could show affection for her and that was better than nothing at all. Perhaps in time she'd learn to love him. Or was that just wishful thinking or something you read in books?

She hadn't replied. She was stunned by his acceptance of what was in fact Alexander's idea.

And so to the outside world she was now Mrs Alice O'Farrell. At least it had pleased Alexander who wore a smug expression for days. Now all the innuendos would cease; the fact that the story was a sham didn't seem to bother him at all. The 'proprieties' were being seen to be observed and his own dignity therefore was protected.

It was Alexander who interrupted her thoughts. 'Mr O'Farrell says Signor Bransini will be angry if you're late again. If you don't go down now he's going without you. Ma'am,' he added, almost as an afterthought.

Alice frowned. This sardonic tacking on of her formal but fictitious title was Alexander's way of reminding her of her real place in the household. But it also told her there was to be no more chatting idly with Ruth and certainly no more giggling with young Florrie.

'Oh, all right, I'm coming,' she called. Mike watched her trip lightly down the stairs and his heart beat faster as it always did when he looked at her. In the two bitter-sweet years she had been with him, there had been many times when he'd physically ached to hold her, kiss her, love her, and it had taken superhuman strength and a bottle of bourbon to keep his desires in check. There had been other times when he'd wanted to pour out his feelings like a moonstruck boy. His fear of rejection and ridicule increased after one night when she'd had too much wine at dinner and talked in greater detail of the incident that had led her to be taken aboard the *Aquitania*. She'd mentioned a man's name, the name she hadn't revealed when she'd first told him her story that night in India's. He should have known there was a man in her life somewhere, the root of her ambition.

He'd felt a jealous rage sweep over him but he'd fought

it down. He had no right to be jealous, he had no claim on her. She wasn't his wife. Maybe in time she'd forget this man. It seemed to have been a very brief encounter. What could she really know about this David Williamson? She'd not even spent a full hour in his company.

He handed her down the last few stairs. 'Mrs O'Farrell, have you any idea of the time at all? I've bought you two watches, or is it three?'

It was true. He'd bought her quite a lot of jewellery, expensive jewellery. He'd often told her, when she forgot all decorum and shrieked like a delighted fishwife when he presented her with another magnificent bauble, that if she was going to be his wife, albeit in name only, then she had to look the part.

'I'm not late. My mantel clock said it was only two minutes to ten.'

'And Signor Bransini is expecting you at ten fifteen and the traffic down there will be all snarled up.'

She didn't reply as Alexander opened the front door. Mike handed her into the car and closed the door. She smoothed down the pleats in the skirt of her peach-coloured crepe dress and patted the matching cloche hat. No vestige remained now of the girl who had arrived in Charleston on the *Castlemaine*, at least not outwardly. She always told herself that she'd never change, not inside where it mattered. She'd always be little Alice O'Connor from Benledi Street, no matter where she went, what she did or how she was dressed. She wrote regularly to Nelly, always enclosing money, but she'd only ever had one letter in reply. More of a note it had been, written on cheap paper in a spidery hand and with poor spelling. Nelly had said how glad she was that Alice now had a great life, but there was no mention of the money. Still, maybe Nelly had asked someone to write it for her, she was virtually illiterate. If she had, then she certainly wouldn't want half the street knowing her business. The letter was the only tangible thing she had from her life in Liverpool, the only thing to remind her where she'd come from. The gutter.

As they pulled away down the street she turned and looked at Mike at the wheel beside her. She was fond of him and very, very grateful to him for taking her away from The Star of India and giving her a chance in life, but lately she'd become bored. She wanted to sing on a stage, and since the Plantation had closed down, she hadn't been able to do that. All the other clubs were so seedy and often violent that Mike had flatly refused to take her anywhere near them.

'I've been to rough places before,' she'd countered.

'Not as Mrs Michael Eugene O'Farrell,' he'd replied in a tone that told her the subject was closed.

'What *is* going on in that devious mind now, Alice?' he enquired, breaking into her thoughts.

'I want to sing again.'

Mike sighed. 'We've been through all this before, Alice. You're not going to sing in those desperate places downtown. Alexander would take a meat axe to the pair of us!'

'No, not in those.'

'Then where?'

She bit her lip. She couldn't tell him she was bored stiff. Not after he'd given her so much and asked nothing in return. 'Here. At home. Couldn't we have a soirée? Ruth told me the Hendersons next door often have them.'

He turned and looked at her in astonishment, narrowly missing hitting an omnibus. 'In the name of all that's holy! Who the hell would we invite?'

'You must know some refined people. Let's ask the Hendersons.'

'They'd sooner walk barefoot to Savannah and back than cross our doorstep. They're "old" money and Episcopalian too.'

'Oh, please, Mike. You must know someone. All those

friends of yours must have wives and daughters.'

He looked thoughtful. She had a point. His associates couldn't care less about respectability or social position, but their wives did. Nearly all of them were trying to claw their way onto the fringe of society, new money trying to become old money in a single generation, but with little success. They kept on trying, though, and gave their own dinners and parties and soirées, or so he gathered from the complaints he heard from their spouses. He'd been invited of course, but so far he'd been spared having to attend, never mind host, these 'entertainments', by keeping Alice in ignorance of their invitations; he knew Alexander had been meddling again. 'I'll think about it. Ask around, test the water, so to speak.'

Her eyes danced with excitement and she leaned over and kissed his cheek. 'Oh, you're really good to me. I honestly believe in guardian angels! Someone's been looking out for me ever since I left Liverpool.'

'Would a guardian angel come in the guise of a scruffy cat, do you think?' he laughed.

She laughed with him. 'It wasn't a scruffy cat!'

'Maybe cats have guardian angels too. That cat's life certainly changed for the better when you found it, Alice.'

'Sometimes I wish I'd kept her. I know being a ship's cat is all right, but sometimes . . .'

'Oh, Jaysus! I couldn't have stuck the cat as well!'

She laughed again and then turned her mind to planning her soirée.

The increasingly elaborate plans formulated mainly by a self-satisfied Alexander had to be shelved as, before she could write out invitations, Alice received one herself. It was printed on stiff white card and was accompanied by a letter, both delivered to her on a silver tray by Alexander. Mrs Maura O'Hare, wife of Gerry whose great-grandfather had been hanged in Cork for stealing and butchering a calf to feed his family, had had the same idea. She had also heard that Mrs O'Farrell had a wonderful voice and begged Alice to agree to sing for her guests.

'Did it come in the post, Alexander?'

'No, by hand, ma'am.'

'Do I use a card to reply?'

'A single sheet of notepaper will do. It's not the St Cecilia Society Ball.'

'What shall I sing? She won't want any of the ragtime numbers, will she?'

'Indeed not. I hear Mrs O'Hare is becoming quite well known for her "improving" entertainments.' There was a faintly sarcastic emphasis on the word 'improving'.

Alice panicked. 'Oh, God, she won't want me to sing anything from an opera, will she?'

'Maybe an operetta.'

'But I don't know anything like that!'

'There's a lovely song called "Lorena". It's an old one but still a favourite for soirées. I heard it was sung next door recently.'

'Can you teach it to me?'

Alexander nodded; he'd known the mention of the Hendersons next door would settle the matter. 'Another old favourite in this town is "Jeannie With The Light Brown Hair". I heard tell Confederate soldiers used to sing it.' There was a note of cold resentment in his voice but she didn't notice it.

'It's that old? Well, that's two. Will they be enough?'

'Are you the sole artiste, ma'am?'

'No. She says Miss Euganie Walton will play two sonatas, whatever they are.'

'Miss Walton?' Alexander's eyebrows rose a fraction as he wondered how someone as nouveau riche as Mrs Maura O'Hare had managed to get the niece of a senator even to cross her threshold let alone play the piano. 'Then two will be enough.'

'What do I wear? Full evening dress? Long gloves, short gloves, no gloves?'

'Full evening dress and long gloves,' Alexander replied. 'And not too much jewellery. It's not done to flaunt money,' he added patronisingly.

'I haven't got any money, it's Mr Mike's and well you know it!' Alice shot back with spirit. 'And he pays you good wages, so get off your high horse!'

Alexander ignored her. Beneath the aloof exterior was a kind heart and he liked Alice. She'd learned quickly and eagerly but despite all the clothes and jewels, she'd never be a lady. It was a true saying that you can't make a silk purse from a sow's ear, but she did have her own pert charm.

Alice spent hours learning the words of 'Lorena' and just as many hours choosing what to wear. In the end she settled for the jade-coloured chiffon that shaded to a deeper green at the hemline. Tiny pearls and silvery beads were sewn across the loose bodice in a sunburst pattern and edged the hem of the hip-hugging sash.

'You look like an angel, Miss Alice,' Ruth enthused, after helping Alice with her toilette.

Alice smiled back and then a wide grin split her face as she caught sight of Mike standing in the doorway. 'Do I really look all right? I mean I've worn everything Alexander told me to wear, but not too much jewellery.'

'Alice, you look grand. You'll have the men and boys for miles around thinking up excuses to beat their way to the door after tonight.'

'Oh, I don't want anything like that. I just want to sing again. For people, an audience.'

He took the black velvet cape that lay across the bed and draped it over her shoulders. 'I have a feeling that after tonight you will be doing just that. I think you'll be in great demand and that I will have to attend God knows how many of these polite but deathly boring evenings.

156

And before you attack me, I'm not saying *you* are boring. But give me a good old-fashioned hooley any day of the week.'

The O'Hares lived in a large house on the East Battery and as they arrived, in the midst of cars that were disgorging people Alice had never seen before, Maura O'Hare came forward to greet her. She was rather a plain woman, Alice thought, in her early thirties, and the magenta evening dress with its black fringe did absolutely nothing to enhance her looks.

'Mrs O'Farrell! I'm so glad you could come. I thought he kept you locked up. We see so little of you in town.'

Alice smiled.

'Alice is rather shy, Maura. Not really used to high society yet.'

Maura O'Hare shot Mike a penetrating glance to see if he was mocking her with his reference to high society. It didn't appear so.

'Then I'm even more pleased that you've agreed to sing for us.' She'd heard rumours that Alice O'Farrell had sung nearly every night in Oliver's club until it had been raided and shut down. Nor did she look at all shy, Maura thought as she led Alice into the salon.

The dove-grey walls, drapes and carpet of the room could have made it appear cold, flat and uninteresting, but cushions and huge flower arrangements of deep pink cyclamen, tearoses and the fragrant pink and cream Stargazer lilies lifted it, making it very elegant. Obviously Maura O'Hare had had a designer in, Alice thought, because judging by the clashing colours of her dress and hair she had very little taste.

She recognised some of the men but none of their wives, who in the main were over-dressed, obviously vying with each other in the size of the precious stones they wore. 'Like flaming Christmas trees,' she muttered to herself. Aye, and you'd have looked like one too, Alice O'Connor, left to your own devices, she chided herself.

Mike had said the soirée was for a charity. Mrs O'Hare had charged an entrance fee. The fact that the proceeds from the evening would go to a good cause was the only reason Miss Euganie Walton had agreed to attend. Miss Walton stood apart, literally and metaphorically. It was obvious that she was a lady in the true sense of the word.

Mike jerked his head in Miss Walton's direction. 'She comes from one of Charleston's best known families.'

'She looks – oh, what's that saying of Alexander's?'

'A pearl amongst swine?' Mike suggested, grinning. 'Ah, maybe that's a bit too strong. Come on, let's introduce ourselves. I don't care whether it's etiquette or not. Besides, most of this crowd wouldn't know etiquette if it jumped up and hit them in the face.' He took Alice's elbow and steered her across the room. 'Miss Walton, may I present your fellow artiste and my wife, Mrs Alicia O'Farrell.'

Alice shot him a malevolent look before smiling at the girl, the only woman in the room close to her own age. 'It's not Alicia, it's Alice. He's teasing me.' She looked round the room. 'What a lot of people and I don't know anyone.'

'Neither do I, Mrs O'Farrell. I believe I'm to accompany you. It's "Lorena" and . . .'

' "Jeannie",' Alice supplied. 'The one with the light brown hair. It's a bit old.'

'It's so old it should be given a decent burial,' Euganie Walton replied, her eyes full of laughter.

Alice smiled back conspiratorially. 'Shall we bury it tonight?'

'What would you really like to sing?'

Alice thought. ' "Alexander's Ragtime Band" would be a bit too racy, I suppose.' She laughed then grimaced, thinking of Alexander's reaction and the wrath she'd bring down on her head for spoiling the 'improving' and charitable evening. She'd probably never be let out again.

'I'm afraid it would shock these, er, ladies to the core.'

Alice raised her eyes to the ceiling. 'I know and I'd be banned from most of the parlours in town. What about "Whispering"?'

'Fine. "Whispering" it is.'

'Now just what are you two ladies whispering about?' Maura O'Hare joined them, totally at a loss to understand why both her young artistes went into fits of laughter. It was very unsettling.

'Just what the hell are you up to?' Mike asked, leading Alice to her seat as the O'Hares' butler repeatedly struck a small gong to indicate that his mistress wished to make an announcement. Alice's eyes were full of mischief.

'Nothing.'

'Don't be lying to me, Alice. I can see the divilment in your eyes.'

'Just a bit of a change in the programme.'

Mike looked stern. 'Alice, don't wreck the party. Remember, people have paid. It's for charity and Maura O'Hare has gone to a lot of trouble over it all. Besides, any ragtime and you'll never be asked to sing again.'

'It's nothing like that. It's just a bit more modern than that owld dirge.'

'Be careful, your accent is slipping,' Mike grinned.

'Oh, shut up. Euganie is going to start,' she hissed back.

She watched Euganie Walton closely and realised that she was a talented pianist. The applause for her showed genuine appreciation, she thought, when Euganie finished her pieces and stood up, though quite a few men had to be nudged into awareness and even wakefulness by their wives. Well, no one was going to sleep through *her* performance, even if she had to say so straight out.

Alice's smile for Euganie Walton was warm and sincere as she approached the piano. 'I've a mind to sing "Alexander's Ragtime Band",' she hissed indignantly. 'That would keep them awake all right. Some people are *so* rude.'

'It's very warm in here and you know that saying about music and the savage breast,' Euganie smiled, as the applause died down.

'You're too polite and kind. I tell you the savage in here will be me if I see one pair of closed eyes or hear a single snore.'

She felt a little nervous, she always did at first, but she knew it wouldn't last.

'Are you ready, Mrs O'Farrell?' Euganie asked in a louder tone and nodded to the butler who again beat a tattoo on the gong.

Alice nodded. Her voice was clear and filled with emotion as she sang the opening lines, 'The years creep slowly by, Lorena, the snow is on the grass again . . .'

Mike watched Alice with increasing pride. When she sang, whether it was around the house or in public, be it ragtime or traditional ballads and love songs, she never failed to charm him. He glanced around and saw that everyone was awake and taking notice. His lovely Alice was possessed of great beauty and talent and all these women thought she belonged to him, one way or another.

He supposed that from Alice's point of view their 'marriage' was working well. At home she treated him with a sort of offhand affection. Not quite as a father figure but as an older brother. At least that's what he told himself, and maybe time would change things for the better. There were instances of affection. The little gifts, inexpensive trinkets she'd found for him on her wanderings around the city. The small and very battered book of *Moore's Melodies*. The way she'd sit on a footstool at his feet, reading. Often she'd look up at him and ask him the meaning of a word, and how he'd longed to stroke the shining, softly waving hair. He had done so, once. She'd been struggling with *Morte d'Arthur* and he'd explained the love of Arthur for his Queen Guinevere and her love for the young knight Lancelot.

'Oh, Mike, wasn't that sad?' she'd said when he'd finished, and her eyes had misted with tears.

'It's just a story, Alice,' he'd replied and had let his fingers caress the fine, tawny-coloured hair.

He didn't know what Alexander had bribed, coaxed or threatened the staff with, apart from the 'monthly bonus' he paid, but they were very discreet. No word of the unusual nature of their 'marriage' was heard outside the house – he'd have been one of the first to hear it. As for the circle they moved in, to outsiders they appeared to be the perfect couple.

It was so ironic that he'd never laid a finger on her. He wished with all his heart that she did belong to him. Would it be such a great mistake to tell her so? Was he deluding himself, thinking she'd spurn him? Would she? Would she use his love as a weapon against him, if he ever failed to grant her wishes? Or was he needlessly depriving himself of her love? He wasn't getting any younger. Nearly every other man in the room was married. Properly married. Maybe he'd give it some more thought.

Chapter Fourteen

The week before Christmas, after dinner, Alice was sitting on a footstool at Mike's feet, staring into the fire. 'I love Christmas now. I used to hate it. We—'

'I know. No presents, no happy family sitting round a table full of food in a kitchen that was warm, with the fire roaring away up the chimney.'

He understood. He knew what it felt like.

'And creeping in at the back of the church for Mass, hoping no one would notice that you hadn't a decent rag to your back. And then, on the way home, having the other lads making a mock and a jeer of you. Lads who had good tweed jackets and fine strong boots. Lads and girls who had toys.'

'Sometimes we were lucky, we had a parcel of food.' She told him about the charitable Goodfellows organisation.

'With us it was the Quakers. If you ignored the Father giving out about them from the high altar. "Blessed are the poor." He almost used to shout the bloody words. What the hell would he know about being poor? Him with the belly on him from three square meals a day and a housekeeper to see to him. Even a drop of Jameson's or Powers to keep out the cold. I had seventeen Christmases like that, Alice.'

'So did I,' she replied quietly.

'Well, all that's in the past now. There'll always be food and a fire and gifts.'

She nodded thankfully.

'Will we go out and get the greenery?' He smiled, trying to banish the memories and lift the mood.

Holly, ivy and the fir tree filled the house, all brought down from the northern states where these evergreens flourished in the colder climate. Like the previous year, Alice had been on countless shopping sprees, taking Ruth with her and, once, Alexander. Mike knew that that occasion was to choose a present for him. He'd sighed heavily as he'd watched her go. The only perfect gift she could give him would be herself. For a man who made snap decisions in business he was unable to come easily to this one. He'd found himself looking at rings when he'd gone to purchase a necklace for her.

For Alice, though, life regained some of its old spark. She threw herself wholeheartedly into the preparations for the festivities. She'd had three more invitations, three more requests to sing, all from friends of Maura O'Hare. But her own soirée caused an argument.

'Why don't you want me to have it on Christmas Eve?' she demanded when Mike vetoed the date. 'You said Christmas will always be something special from now on and Christmas Eve is just the right time.'

He regarded her thoughtfully as he lit a cigar. 'Because I like a bit of peace and quiet then. Christmas is a family time and, strange as it may seem, we *are* a sort of family. You, me, Ruth, Alexander, Jimmy, Ella and young Florence. I thought you'd understand, Alice. All those other Christmases, remember? And I don't want my house full of drunks and women screeching with laughter like demented banshees.'

Alice bit her lip. 'They're not *proper* family.'

'Well, they're as near to one as either of us is likely to get. My mother, Kitty and Dee won't make the Atlantic crossing and neither will your mother.'

'Mam couldn't. She's got the kids to see to and anyway,

what's wrong with the people I'm inviting? They're your friends.'

'They're not friends, they're business associates. It's different entirely.'

She lost her temper. 'You're a flaming hypocrite! You really are! You have them here to dinner, you go laughing and joking with their wives at parties but you won't call them friends and you won't let them come here to my party!'

'*Our* party, and I can choose who I want or don't want to entertain in my home.'

'You keep telling me it's *our* home! Now all of a sudden it's *yours*. You promised me I could have a party.'

He sighed. He'd caught the tremor, the pleading note in her voice. 'I'm not going back on that, Alice. I just don't want you to have it on Christmas Eve.'

'Well, the day before then?'

'The day before it is,' he replied resignedly.

She flung her arms round him and kissed him but sadly he realised that she was like a spoilt child; she was using endearments and gestures of affection as weapons to get her own way. The kiss was exactly that – a gesture.

Alice was very disappointed that Euganie Walton was unable to come to her party. She received a note saying Euganie was really sorry but she had another invitation which she'd already accepted. But all her other guests turned up and she judged it to be a success even though she knew Alexander was looking down his nose at the behaviour of some of the guests and only looked happy when the last of them had departed, unsteadily. He was a terrible snob sometimes, she thought.

They had their quiet family Christmas, like the previous year. She'd bought gifts for everyone. Mike gave the staff money, knowing it was always appreciated more than trinkets. The two of them had lunch in the dining room but later they went and had tea in the kitchen which was the only room in the house where she felt really comfortable. She *was* still the same person, inside, she often told herself.

She wore the gold collar set with seed pearls that Mike had given her and he sported the gold cufflinks, small replicas of the Tara Brooch, set with emeralds, that she had had specially made. She'd seen a picture of the brooch in one of his many books about Ireland. He ignored the fact that they'd been paid for with his money, touched that she'd gone to so much effort, put so much thought into the choice.

That evening they sat in the drawing room as darkness was falling, neither of them making any move to switch on the lights.

She sighed deeply. 'It's been the best Christmas ever. I mean that. Better even than last year. You spoil me.'

'You just ate too much last year,' he laughed. Then he smiled at her more seriously. 'It's been one of the best Christmases for me too, Alice, and you deserve to be spoilt – just a bit.'

She grinned. 'Just a bit, mind. You spoil me something rotten all the time and I don't deserve it. I don't give you anything back in return.'

He smiled again. 'Ah, but you do, Alice. You give me company, friendship, amusement, laughter and the joy, the sheer joy of listening to you sing.' It was all true. Oh, he supposed that what she gave him couldn't be assessed in monetary terms. It was all beyond price, in a different league from just dollars and cents.

Alice sat down on the rug at his feet and began to pluck at the lace edge of her handkerchief. She was suddenly shy.

'You . . . you know, if I could have chosen from all the men in the world to have as a da, I'd have picked you.'

His smile vanished and he managed to suppress the groan. The light in his eyes died. So, at last. This was really how she viewed him, what she really thought of him. It hurt. It hurt like hell but he was so glad, so relieved now that he'd said nothing about his love for her. It didn't make the pain of rejection any easier to bear though. His expression was bland. The mask was back in place. The one he wore whenever he didn't want to disclose his true feelings, the mask of the slightly amused, benign Irishman at ease with the world.

'Will you indulge me? Sing for me. Sing the Christmas carols. It wouldn't be Christmas without carols and then we'll have a drink for the day that's in it.'

Perched on the arm of the long sofa she started with 'O Little Town of Bethlehem' but when she began 'Silent Night' she noticed the little group standing by the door, just in the hallway. Ruth, Jimmy, Florrie, Ella and Alexander gazed back at her. She smiled to herself. She supposed they were her family now. Maybe one day she'd go back to Liverpool, like she'd promised Mam she would. She'd sung on a stage, of sorts, and of course at the soirées, but she wasn't famous. She probably wouldn't ever be but she'd got far more from life than she'd ever dreamed of. To ask for more would seem like a sin.

As her silvery, dulcet voice filled the room, Alexander thought he saw tears on his master's cheek, caught for a brief second in the light of the tiny candles that adorned the Christmas tree.

After the Christmas and New Year celebrations were fully over, Charleston began to prepare for the great balls and events held by the Cotillion and the St Cecilia Societies, a social whirl that would go on until Lent. Alice read the notices for them in the *News and Chronicle* with hungry interest, knowing she wouldn't be invited. She was 'new' money and this was a circle of society quite different from the one she'd got used to.

'Oh well, I suppose Euganie Walton will be in demand,'

she said wistfully when she'd finished. Mike didn't reply. He'd been very quiet, she mused, sort of distant, since Christmas. He'd been out a lot and even when he was in he secluded himself in his study. The Cotillion Society Ball was on Saturday, to be held at the South Carolina Society's Hall, she read once again, and there would be a musical interlude when Miss Sofia Scarlatti, the highly acclaimed diva from New York, would sing two arias, one from *Tosca* and one from *La Bohème*.

'What's a diva?' she asked Mike.

'I've no idea.' He was busy reading the business section of the newspaper. 'Go and look it up in that dictionary I bought you.'

'It's not that important.'

'Every new word should be important, Alice. That's the way you learn.'

'You sound like a school teacher and an old dragon of a father,' she grumbled.

'Well, isn't that the way you see me?' he questioned with a dry, brittle laugh.

She went for the dictionary. ' "A prima donna. A great woman singer. From the Latin goddess",' she read aloud. 'She must be very grand.'

The following day Alexander brought in a calling card from Euganie Walton.

'She's here?'

'In the small salon, ma'am.'

'Why didn't you bring her in here?'

'It's not done,' he answered flatly.

'Oh, well, bring her in now.'

As soon as she walked through the door, Alice could tell Euganie was bothered about something. She looked agitated and uneasy.

'Mrs O'Farrell. Forgive me for calling at such short notice.' Euganie belonged to a generation that clung tenaciously to correct etiquette.

'Oh, call me Alice. Mrs O'Farrell makes me feel a hundred.'

'Then you must call me Euganie.'

'Sit down, please, Euganie. Did you have a nice Christmas?'

'Yes. I was really sorry I couldn't come to your soirée.'

'Well, it's nice of you to come and see me now. You must be very busy; I was reading about all the balls and parties in the paper.'

Euganie looked uncomfortable. 'Well, that's really why I'm here. Oh, I hate to ask! It looks . . . so bad, as though we're using you.'

'What for? I don't understand.' Alice was confused.

'Miss Scarlatti has gone down with a head cold and a sore throat. There's not enough time to . . . to, well, get anyone else of importance. Oh, this is really embarrassing, Alice. I begged my mother not to send me.' Euganie twisted her hands in her lap and looked at the floor.

'What? What's so embarrassing, Euganie?'

'Could you possibly stand in for her?'

'*Me?*' She almost shrieked the word.

Euganie nodded.

'I can't sing opera! I don't know anything about it! You've heard me, Euganie, I can only sing popular ballads or jazz.'

'I've heard you and with a voice like that you can sing anything. I know you go for voice training. Oh, Alice, please, it would make such a difference to the evening.'

Alice pressed her hands against her flushed cheeks. To sing at one of Charleston's most prestigious events, in front of everyone who was anyone in this town. To replace Miss Scarlatti! It was too much.

Euganie was watching her closely. 'Please, Alice. They won't expect you to sing grand opera, really they won't.'

They both looked towards the hall from where they

could hear Mike talking to Alexander. Alice called to him
to come and join them.

He was surprised to see Euganie Walton. 'Miss Walton.
Now isn't this a pleasure. How are you in yourself?' He
bowed slightly.

'Mike, Euganie says Miss Scarlatti can't sing for them.
She's got a cold or influenza or something. They want me.'

'We want her very much, Mr O'Farrell. I know it looks
awful, just asking on the spur of the moment, but—'

'I can't do it, Mike!' Alice interrupted.

Euganie looked at him pleadingly. 'I'm sure she'll be a
great success.'

'Of course you can do it, Alice. You can do anything
you put your mind to. You've a great gift.' Although
outwardly agreeing with Euganie, privately he was
annoyed. They were all so damned high and mighty with
their society balls, their opera singers. They would cut
Alice dead in the street and himself too, given the chance.
Just like the snotty bloody Hendersons who lived next
door. But he wanted Alice to have her moment of glory.
To show them all that this slip of a 'slummy' had a voice
to equal all their prima donnas. To show them that a
voice like Alice's was a gift, a talent, not something that
could be made or bought with any kind of money, 'new'
or 'old'.

Euganie sensed Alice's resolve weakening and she
looked gratefully at Mike. 'You do have a great gift, Alice.
I'll help you as much as I can. We'll sort out pieces, I'll
teach you them. Signor Bransini will be only too glad to
help, too, I'm sure.'

'No, he won't. He'll just yell at me and wave his arms
like a windmill and make me worse!' Alice wailed.

'But you'll do it, won't you?' Euganie again looked to
Mike for support.

'Of course she will. It's what she was born to do – sing.'

Alice looked at them both and then nodded slowly,

wondering just what she had let herself in for now.

Euganie returned home with the good news and then came back with an armful of sheet music.

Alice asked Alexander for coffee and instructed that the coffee pot be kept filled.

She sang 'The Londonderry Air' but Euganie said it wasn't really a 'strong' enough piece. The 'Rose of Tralee', Mike's favourite, was definitely out of the question.

Eventually she agreed to 'The Last Rose of Summer', quite a difficult piece to execute really well, according to Euganie. She also agreed to the Brahms 'Cradle Song' and finally she passed Alice the score of the Easter Hymn from *Cavalleria Rusticana*. 'It's beautiful, Alice. So moving.'

Alice was aghast. 'I can't do this, it's all in a foreign language.' The notes and words of Mascagni's Intermezzo danced before her eyes. 'Euganie, I can't even read it!'

'I'll teach you. I'll translate and you can learn.'

'Oh, God Almighty, I'll make a terrible fool of myself. I will.'

'You won't!'

Alice paused. 'Euganie, you really don't know about me.'

'I know you have a voice that is the equal of any prima donna I've ever heard.'

Alice twisted her hands together. 'I . . . I was born in Liverpool. We were poor. Very poor. I used to sing to people waiting to go into the theatres. How can I stand up in the South Carolina Society's Hall and sing to all those people? I'm nothing.' She was on the point of saying she wasn't even Mrs O'Farrell, but decided against it.

Euganie dismissed her fears. 'Oh, Alice. None of that matters. No one knows or needs to know. You have something special. Something no one else in this town, maybe even this state, has. And you have such potential. Do you want to go on just singing at soirées for ever?'

'No, but I don't know if I can sing classical stuff.'

'Just try, Alice, please?' Euganie begged.

It was a long day and by mid-afternoon Mike swore he could stand no more. He said he knew that by Saturday she would sing like an angel – like the cherubim and seraphim put together – but right now his head couldn't take any more of what sounded like the banshee on a bad night. Alice threw a cushion at his departing back. Her own head was aching and in her heart she agreed with him. It *did* sound awful and she'd never, ever learn these words. All three pieces were new to her and she *had* to get them all perfect. Word, note and pitch perfect. Otherwise she'd die of embarrassment.

'Oh, he's right, Euganie. I sound terrible. I keep missing those very high notes.'

'It's just the C, Alice, and it will get easier with practice.' But it was to get worse. When Euganie finally left, Alice was exhausted. Her head ached and her throat felt dry.

Next morning Alice agreed with Euganie's suggestion that Signor Bransini must be called in. Mike hastily left the house muttering excuses and Alexander, with Ruth and Ella in tow, decided it was time to go on a household shopping expedition, leaving young Florrie to provide coffee and sandwiches and suffer the sounds coming from the small salon.

On Friday afternoon everyone was utterly exhausted and Euganie said the best thing would be for everyone to have a rest now. Both she and Signor Bransini would call, briefly, on Saturday afternoon for a final rehearsal.

But there wasn't much rest for Alice. Now she had to turn her attention to what she would wear. There was no time to go shopping or to have something made. By the time she had been through her entire wardrobe, most of which had ended up on the floor, she was nearly in tears. There was nothing suitable. Nothing. But what in God's name *would* be suitable? How was she to know? She buried her face in the folds of the skirt of her favourite duchess satin dress when Alexander arrived back with a large box.

She looked up at him. 'What's that?'

'Mr Mike asked me to go into town and choose something for you, ma'am.' From the layers of tissue paper he drew out the most beautiful dress she'd ever seen. It was white chiffon over white silk and was floor length. Around the hipline was a wide sash finished on the left side with a bow. The entire thing was encrusted with silver bugle beads, as was the bodice. Its back was cut very low with floating panels of chiffon coming from the shoulder. There were white satin pumps decorated with diamanté stones, long white gloves and a headband of white satin adorned with two ostrich plumes.

'Oh, Alexander! It's perfect!'

'Well, this one had to be special.'

She held it against her. 'You don't have to tell me that! Oh, what would I do without you, Alexander?'

What passed for a smile crossed his face and for the first time Alice felt he approved of her. 'I won't let you down,' she said.

'Just don't you let Mr Mike down, never mind about me. Why don't you go out for some air? You've been cooped up in the house too long. It will clear your head. I'll send Ruth up here to hang this up – and everything else!' he added.

She nodded; it was a good idea. If she stayed in she'd drive herself mad with worry. She'd go to White Point Gardens. Despite the association with India Osbourne, it was one of her favourite places.

It was almost half past four by the time she got there. The wintry sun was sinking low in the sky, its rays shining over the blue waters of the harbour. The trailing grey strands of tree moss wafted gently in the breeze. She had so much to be grateful for, she mused. When she'd arrived on the *Castlemaine*, down there at the harbour wall, she'd had no idea how much her life would change and in so short a time. She'd been full of hopes and dreams but she'd been so ignorant, so naive. She hadn't even known a word like 'naive'! She hadn't known how to dress, how to hold a conversation. She'd been poor little Alice O'Connor from Benledi Street and now, now she was someone of note. Tomorrow night she would be feted as Mrs Alice O'Farrell, Charleston's own diva.

'I *can* do it. I *can*. Euganie says I can!' She spoke the words aloud. She had a voice every bit as good as that Miss Scarlatti. She'd look every inch a lady, too, in the white chiffon dress, wearing the jewels Mike had bought her, She felt far more relaxed now, she told herself as she wandered between the beds of formal flowers and short avenues lined with shrubs. She was confident that she would look just as beautiful as any society woman listening to her. Mike had taught her that if you had guts and determination you could do anything, go anywhere. That's what this country was all about.

She had reached the last grove of palmettoes, their fronds rustling in the freshening wind. At the end of the pathway stood the tall white column surmounted by its statue that faced out across the bay. She looked up at it without curiosity. The face of Sergeant William Jasper beneath the martial helmet bore a determined, defiant look. One hand was pointed seaward, the other held a large flag. From portraits she'd seen she knew that the flag was blue and the small crescent in one corner was silver. Mike had told her it had been erected in memory of the Second South Carolina Regiment, which under Colonel Moultrie had defended Fort Sullivan in the War of Independence against the British in June 1776. The inscription bore Jasper's rallying cry: 'Let us not fight without a flag.'

She turned away from it. It was getting chilly. She'd go

home now, have some tea and a rest. She glanced carelessly towards the harbour then her eyes widened, her hands flew to her cheeks and she gasped. Tied up down there was a ship she would never forget. A ship whose black hull and four red and black funnels she'd never thought to see again. A ship she'd often dreamed about. The *Aquitania*! The *Aquitania* was here in Charleston and he . . . he'd be here too! She forgot about everyone and everything. Mike, Euganie, Alexander, the Cotillion Ball and her debut into society and semi-classical music. Clutching her hat she began to run, along the pathway, through the gates and down the road that led to the harbour, the ship and a very special member of her crew.

Chapter Fifteen

She was flushed and out of breath by the time she reached the gangway and the ship's officer who was standing at the bottom of it looking bored. Her heart was thumping against her ribs.

'Oh, can you help me, please?'

He grinned. 'I hope so, miss.'

What a difference clothes made, Alice thought as she smiled back at him. 'Could you get a message to someone on board?'

'Most of the passengers are ashore, doing a tour of the city, but they'll all be back for dinner at about eight.'

'No, it's not a passenger. He's crew, David Williamson, but I don't know exactly what he does. What his job or his rank are.' She gazed earnestly up at the man.

'He's an engineering officer, miss.'

'Could you tell him Alice O'Connor from Liverpool is here and wants ... would like to see him, please? If it's possible.'

He looked up the gangway and caught sight of a steward who had come on deck for a smoke. 'Morrison, come here, I've a job for you,' he called.

Reluctantly the man came down to them. 'I was just 'avin' a spello, like, sir. A quick fag while the bloods are ashore.'

'Take this young lady up to the First-Class Smoking Room and then go and find Mr Williamson and tell him he's got a visitor. If he's not on duty he'll be in the Pig.'

Morrison nodded. He wished he could find time to spend in the Pig and Whistle, as the crew bars on all ships were called. He hadn't even finished his cigarette and in half an hour or so the passengers would start arriving back, asking for tea or something stronger as they dressed for dinner. There was no time for poor bloody stewards to be knocking back drinks in the Pig.

Alice followed him, her heart beating now in an odd jerky way, her stomach churning with apprehension. There was that faint oily smell she remembered so well, and the humming noise emitted by the ship's generators. She was really here, on board the *Aquitania* again! In a few minutes she would see him again too.

'Here yer are, miss, rest yer feet while I go and dig 'im out.'

Oh, it was so good to hear that familiar accent again. 'Thanks. Look, I'm really sorry you've had to go without your smoke.'

Morrison gaped at her. 'You're a Scouser! A posh one though.'

She laughed. 'I'm not posh but I'm proud of coming from Liverpool.'

His face split in a wide grin. 'Oh, yeah, the 'Pool is great. Put yer feet up an' 'ave a blow,' he urged before he went to find David Williamson.

Alice looked around, thinking that last time she was on this ship she would have been astounded by the elegance of it all. Now she was used to luxury. Even so she had to admit the room was very elegant. All the chairs and sofas were covered in deep crimson brocade and were anchored to the floor. The small tables with their crystal ashtrays were mahogany. At either end of the room were magnificent marble fireplaces with gilt-framed mirrors above them. Above her the deckhead was adorned with intricate plaster work. In fact it really didn't look like a room on a ship at all.

She stood up and went to check her appearance in one of the mirrors. She was still standing there, wishing she had worn her new outfit, when she heard him come in. She turned, her eyes dancing with excitement, her face alight with joy. He was just as she'd remembered him. No, he looked even more handsome in the white tropical uniform, the high, brass-buttoned collar contrasting with his tanned face.

'My God! It *is* you! I'm afraid I was . . . well, I couldn't recall you. I asked Morrison to describe you and I was still mystified.' He smiled a little lopsidedly. 'I don't know any "real lookers", to use Morrison's expression. Well, not here in Charleston.' He took her outstretched hand. It was only Morrison's description of her that had made him come up here, for he was tired, having only just finished his watch. Now he couldn't believe his eyes. This stunningly beautiful girl dressed in the height of fashion, whose eyes were full of laughter and zest for life, was the same dirty, scruffy bag of bones he'd carried on board two years ago. 'I remember your eyes, but not this.' He spread his hands palm upwards in a gesture that enveloped her appearance.

'I look a bit different to the last time, don't I? I couldn't even speak properly then.' He still held her hand and the physical contact made her blood sing.

He smiled to put her at ease. 'I don't seem to remember that there was anything wrong with the way you spoke. You'd just had an accident, remember?'

She remembered very well and withdrew her hand. God, but she'd been crawling with bugs that day. Her cheeks began to redden.

'What happened? How did you get here? What happened to the cat? Sit down and tell me, please,' he laughed. Alice laughed with him, nervously, overcome with the momentousness of her impetuous action.

'Would you like a drink? Soda, tea, coffee, something stronger?'

She sat down a little unsteadily. 'No. No thanks.'

'Maybe later.'

She smiled but strange feelings were welling up inside her and she was glad she'd sat down. 'I live here now. I've been here two years.' She smiled again before embarking on an edited version of the events that had led to this day and this meeting.

By a quarter to seven Mike was getting worried. The heavy dusk was deepening into darkness. She'd only gone out for an hour, a breath of fresh air, so Alexander had informed him.

'Do you think she's really panicked over this performance tomorrow night?' he asked.

'She didn't seem too jumpy. Well, no more than she's been for the last couple of days.' Alexander pursed his lips. 'She liked the dress and seemed in lighter spirits when she went out.'

'Then where the hell is she?'

'Maybe she's gone over to Miss Euganie's house.'

'Without a calling card?'

Alexander shrugged. 'You know Miss Alice.'

'Maybe I should telephone.'

'Or she might be with that Mr Bransini.' Alexander always refused to call him Signor.

'I'll phone him as well.'

'He doesn't have a telephone.'

'Then I'll send Jimmy down or maybe even you.'

Alexander looked affronted. 'I'll send Ruth. She's got more sense than Jimmy or little Florrie.'

Alice wasn't at the Waltons' house and fifteen minutes later Ruth arrived back from West Street with the same information.

Mike wasn't too worried – yet. Alice knew how to take care of herself and she knew the city. She would more than likely have had money in her purse too. Enough for a cab home. She'd probably had some hare-brained idea, met someone, forgotten the time. Punctuality was not her strong point. 'I'll give her another half-hour and then I'll go out looking for her. We'll all go out looking for her.'

At half past seven Alice walked up the front steps and into the hall. She still felt as though she was walking in a dream. Oh, he was so nice. He'd been genuinely interested in her story. He'd laughed at the amusing parts, looked sympathetic at the intense and upsetting ones, and she'd finally taken her courage in both hands and invited him to the ball – Mrs Walton had been so relieved that she had agreed to sing that she'd told Euganie to tell her she could bring anyone she liked as guests.

The minute she walked into the drawing room Mike flung down the *News and Chronicle*. 'Jesus, Mary and Joseph! Where the hell have you been?' he demanded. 'You've had everyone worried about you. Why didn't you telephone? Now I'll have to let the Waltons and Bransini know you've arrived home safe and sound. And hasn't the worthy Mrs Augusta Walton been having ten blue fits thinking you'd run out on her!'

She looked contrite. 'I'm sorry. I really am sorry. I didn't even think about the time. Oh, Mike, the *Aquitania*'s in! Here, in Charleston! She's on a cruise. It's a new idea they're trying out and there's some sort of union trouble at home. She's here until early Sunday morning and I . . .' She faltered. She'd have to tell him she'd seen David. 'I met someone I know. A friend. He . . . he helped me once. I asked him to the ball tomorrow night – Euganie said I could ask anyone.' Her cheeks were flushed and her eyes danced with happiness. Her dream had come true. It was fate. The union trouble, the *Aquitania*'s cruise, Sofia Scarlatti's indisposition, the Cotillion Ball. He'd hear her sing at the most elegant of all Charleston's social functions and she'd be dressed like a princess.

Mike felt a pool of ice form in the pit of his stomach. His eyes lacklustre, he picked up the newspaper. He couldn't look at her. 'I see. Does he have a name, this friend?'

'David. David Williamson.'

He drew in his breath. She'd confirmed his fear. By some malign chance she'd found *him* again. For a single mad moment he'd prayed it wouldn't be him. He could tell by her eyes and the joy she positively radiated that she was besotted by this man. 'And what does he do? I hope to God he's not a stoker.' He managed a twisted, sardonic smile. 'Wouldn't that upset the high and mighty of the land tomorrow night.'

'He's an officer. An engineering officer. You have to sort of work your way up. Take things called "tickets", so he told me. He wants to be a captain one day. He . . . he's very nice. He comes from a good home. His father is a lawyer or something like that.' She'd only just found all this out.

'At least he won't disgrace you tomorrow night then. And tell me, Alice, just how did you describe yourself and all this?' He threw out his arm in a wide sweeping gesture.

'I . . . I told him you were my guardian.'

'Oh, that was really clever of you, Alice!' He was openly sarcastic now. 'Sometimes you are a complete eejit! What happens when you're announced tomorrow as Mrs Alice O'Farrell?'

'I had to think of something quickly! I'll ask Euganie to announce me as just Alice O'Farrell. I told him . . . I told him I've changed my surname to yours, to make things easier, less complicated, like. Because you're my guardian.'

He shrugged. 'O'Connor, O'Farrell, I don't suppose he's really too interested. Or is he?'

'Mike, why are you being like this? Why are you being so flaming horrible? I'm sorry I was late, that I had you worried. I really am, but how could I tell him the truth? That I'd lived here with you for two years and then decided I wanted to be known as Mrs O'Farrell? What would he have thought of me?'

'Does he mean that much to you, Alice? Why didn't you tell me?'

She shrugged and made to turn away. 'I . . . I suppose . . .'

He caught her wrist. 'The truth, Alice!'

'I suppose because I never thought I'd see him again. That if I did he wouldn't remember the dirty ragged slummy with the scruffy half-dead kitten that he'd knocked over with his car at the Pier Head. The girl he'd given a guinea and a ten-shilling note to. More money than I'd ever had in my life. Money I used to come here. He . . . he was part of the dream.'

He released her. 'I see.'

'He's a friend, Mike.'

'And a friend your own age, Alice. Much younger than your . . . guardian – was that what you said?'

She nodded. 'I'm tired, Mike.'

With an effort he pulled himself together and managed a smile. 'We all are, Alice. Worn out with this Cotillion Ball nonsense. Oh, I know it's partly my fault for encouraging you. I'll tell Alexander to take your supper up to you, I'm going out.'

'Where are you going?' She was concerned. He looked upset although she knew he was trying to hide it.

'Out with some friends. If I'm going to have to put up with all those old bores tomorrow night, then I'm damned well going to enjoy myself tonight.' What he really meant was that he was going out to get drunk, to drown all his anger, jealousy, hurt and disappointment in a bottle of good Jameson's. This was no night for bourbon.

She heard all the noise and the shouting in the early hours when he finally got home and Alexander was trying to get him up the stairs to bed. She got up and looked sleepily over the banister rail.

'I wouldn't bother, Alexander. The pair of you will end up falling down the stairs. He won't hurt himself – drunks never do – but you might, so leave him.'

Alexander nodded and steered Mike in the direction of his study. She went back to her room, back to her hopes and dreams. She knew she'd have trouble trying to get back to sleep.

She slept late but it was lunch time when Mike finally emerged.

'I hope you're not going to get in that state tonight,' she snapped.

'Jesus, Mary and Joseph, don't start giving out! No one is going to show you up, Alice. You'll have your night of glory, your triumph and with *himself* watching you.' God, he felt awful. He was getting too old for wild drunken sprees. Where the hell was Alexander with that 'hair of the dog'? He turned towards his room, his head pounding. Alice stared at him as he stomped upstairs, puzzled by his behaviour. He seldom got so drunk and he seemed to have already taken an irrational dislike to David Williamson. Why? He wasn't in love with her himself. He'd said he wasn't. In fact, he'd said he would pity any man who *did* fall in love with her. No, he was just like, well, like the guardian she'd told David he was. She sighed heavily. Euganie would be here soon for the final rehearsal.

Mike was his usual affable, courteous self, thank God, Alice thought, when David Williamson arrived at seven o'clock. Her heart turned over at the sight of him, resplendent in the dress uniform of the merchant marine. She couldn't speak as he shook Mike's hand and then turned and took her own.

184

'I hardly know what to say, Alice! I can't find the words. You look—'

'Divine. Stunning. Magnificent, ' Mike interrupted smoothly. 'But then I'm an Irishman and we're renowned for the blarney.'

Alice looked up quickly and caught the sardonic look in Mike's eyes.

'You're right, sir. Any single one of them – no, all of them describe just how she looks.'

Before Alice could say a word, Mike handed her wrap to the younger man and called to Alexander to tell Jimmy to bring the car round to the front of the house.

'He's going to drive us there and come back later to fetch us. It'll be like a three-ringed circus down there. The road will be blocked, I shouldn't wonder.'

'I've never been to anything like this before. I asked around and found that it's a great honour to be invited to attend,' David said conversationally. He was still trying to equate this radiantly beautiful young woman with the girl on the dockside in Liverpool. She'd clearly had a great piece of luck, to be transported from dire poverty to what could only be described as opulent luxury.

'I'll tell you something,' Mike said affably. 'We don't usually move in such grand circles as a rule. We're "new" money, you see.'

'Really? I didn't think the class system existed here.'

'Ah, don't you believe it. It does here in this city at least. I'd say Charlestonians were worse in some ways. Weren't all their ancestors British? Isn't the place named after one of your kings? No, we're only invited because their star turn let them down.'

Alice was annoyed. It sounded awful put like that. As though her new friend Euganie Walton was a terrible snob and she herself was second best – which of course she was.

'Euganie's not like that!' she said coldly.

'No, but she's probably the only one who isn't. You won't find the likes of Mrs O'Hare and her friends where we're going. Ah, but you'll be all right, David. You're British and an officer and a gentleman.'

David looked mystified. He could sense the tension in the air. Maybe O'Farrell really resented the fact that his ward was being used as a sort of stopgap. Maybe he'd been snubbed at some time. He was Irish 'new' money: to a crowd of snooty colonials that probably meant he was viewed very much as an upstart.

It seemed as though everyone in Charleston was on Meeting Street tonight, Alice thought as excited anticipation mounted in her. The sidewalks were crowded and chauffeurs and carriage drivers cursed and swore as they tried to manoeuvre their vehicles along the street.

Outside the Charleston Club with its double circular staircase leading from the street to the Colonial doorway, and to the massive, dome-topped columns of the Scottish Presbyterian Church on the corner of Tradd Street, everything was at a complete standstill and chaos reigned. After five minutes of leaning forward and shouting questions and instructions to Jimmy, Mike had had enough.

'God Almighty, what a bloody mess! It's only across the street in the middle of the next block. We'll walk the rest of the way or we'll be stuck here until midnight. Jimmy, if you can get yourself out of this mess, go off home and don't bother coming back. We'll get a cab; it's bound to be as desperate as this later on. That's if it's cleared at all!'

The two stairways leading to the doors of the South Carolina Society's Hall were thronged with people. Slowly they ascended the flights of steps until they reached the second floor. Despite the crush, Alice could see that the huge room was pure Colonial in style.

She gasped. 'Oh, it's . . . it's . . .'

'Grand,' Mike finished for her. 'And stop looking like

a tinker's brat at a picnic,' he hissed. 'Haven't you as fine a home as any of this lot?'

Alice wasn't listening. She was overawed by her surroundings. One complete wall contained long windows and fireplaces sporting high mantels so that the whole room was filled with light and colour. Between the windows, placed on tables, were massive floral decorations, great banks of colour, mauve, lilac, blue, purple, indigo. There was trailing wisteria, with the contrasting dark green foliage of laurel and vine leaves, vibrant oranges, reds and the aureate splashes of yellow jasmine. As she drew closer she spotted intricate arrangements of flowers, ferns and twisted pieces of bleached white driftwood, worked into collages of ships and anchors, shells and fish, backed by spiky palm fronds symbolising Charleston, 'City of the Sea'.

At the far end of the room was a semicircular platform over which was a raised balcony supported by Colonial pillars festooned with ivy, vines and smilax. The balcony was also ablaze with colour, coleus, geraniums, oleander and roses of every hue. The centrepiece was a huge cornucopia – the horn of plenty – woven from bleached palmetto fronds, its mouth spilling forth a profusion of flowers.

'Oh, this is spectacular!' David Williamson, too, was overawed. He'd been to many beautiful places, sailed on the floating palaces that were the Cunard transatlantic liners, but this was magnificent.

Through the crowd Alice saw Euganie Walton with an older very severe-looking woman who was obviously her mother. Euganie wore a dress of silk organdie in a delicate shade of blue and her hair was held back by two diamond-studded clips. She caught sight of Mike and with some difficulty made her way over to the little group.

'Oh, Alice, you look gorgeous!'

'So do you.'

Introductions were made.

'Is it always such a crush?' Mike asked.

Euganie laughed. 'Yes, but it will soon sort itself out.'

'Where will I have to go to sing?'

'There.' Euganie pointed to a small stage flanked by potted palms which screened the black musicians. 'But not until the intermission. You can enjoy yourself first, Alice.' Euganie turned to David. 'One of my friends was telling me she had a tour of your ship, Mr Williamson. She said it's quite magnificent.'

'Maybe Mr Williamson will give you a conducted tour before they sail, Euganie,' Mike said smoothly.

'We sail in the morning, very early, I'm afraid.'

'Ah, well, never mind. I'm sure Euganie will be only too pleased to put your name at the top of the list on her dance card. Doesn't he look grand in that uniform and,' Mike glanced around, 'he's the only one actually *in* uniform. They'll all be dying of curiosity and you'll cause a stir.'

'Oh, Mr O'Farrell, you're shameless!' Euganie laughed.

Alice smiled at Euganie and then turned to Mike.

'Did you remember mine? Alexander said he'd given it to you.'

Mike withdrew it from his pocket. 'I have so. Alexander said that by now you'd be in such a state of nerves you'd go and lose it.'

'I see you still have that custom here.' David was amused. 'It went out of fashion after the war at home.'

'You should see what kind of dances they think are fashionable here,' Mike chuckled.

David laughed with him. 'Oh, I know what you mean, sir. The Charleston.'

The orchestra burst into life and Mike held out his arm to Alice. 'The first dance is mine. A privilege of age, I think.'

David turned towards Euganie and extended his arm.

The evening was so hectic, Alice thought. It was going so fast and she really wanted to savour every minute. She had danced with Mike and David but other young men – strangers – had also sought her out. She just wanted it to go on and on for ever but all too soon the intermission was announced.

It was Euganie's formidable mother who came to conduct her to the stage.

'Go on, Alice,' Mike encouraged her. 'This is your moment of triumph. Go on up there now and show them all what you can do. Show them you're better than any diva from New York.' His smile and words of support were genuine.

'Good luck, Alice,' David called as the stately dowager led her through the press of people.

Mrs Walton announced her and thanked her for so kindly stepping in for Miss Scarlatti at such very short notice. Alice smiled but she wasn't listening. She was going over the short speech, the first she had ever made, that she and Euganie had rehearsed. She knew she looked elegant; the admiring glances of the men and the often envious ones of the women assured her of that.

The great hall fell silent. Only the gentle rustling of evening gowns and the swishing of fans was heard for a second or two and then those sounds died away too. Oh, let them all wonder and whisper about where she'd sprung from and who her family were, Alice thought. She didn't care. This *was* the dream. She was living and breathing it.

Her voice carried clearly. 'Ladies and gentlemen, I can't hope to emulate Miss Scarlatti and I won't try. The pieces I've chosen are all well known and are not grand opera but I hope you will enjoy them.'

She turned slightly and indicated to the half-hidden orchestra that she was ready. She smiled over the heads of the crowd and began the 'Cradle Song', the easiest piece, one that everyone knew; it would give her confidence, Euganie had advised. After the first few bars, all trace of nervousness disappeared. Her clear soprano gave the piece new life, new movement, new concord. Her face was transformed with an ethereal glow, a beauty that came from the sheer joy of the force that possessed her.

Chapter Sixteen

It would be spring and then summer soon, Lizzie thought despondently as she trudged home from work. Already there were buds on the trees in the public parks and there had been a few mild days. She didn't really mind spring or autumn but the long hot days of summer were often hard to bear. She didn't know which was worse, winter or summer. You either froze or sweated. In summer the heat hung heavily over the rows of narrow streets. In the small overcrowded houses it was sweltering. Sometimes at night she felt as though the heavy air was pressing down on her chest, making breathing hard and sleep almost impossible. The back jiggers with their rubbish and putrid remains of vegetables and the privies in the back yards stank to high heaven and attracted flies by the dozen.

Rich people lived in houses with large windows in their bedrooms and on the ground floor, ones that opened out onto gardens with trees that provided shade. She'd seen them in Prince's and Newsham Parks, sash windows pushed up and crisp white net curtains which gave an illusion of coolness, moving slightly in the breeze.

At least these days Da wasn't so much trouble. He had money which she was sure came from Alice, the occasional few days' casual work which suited him, and there had been one or two short spells in Walton Jail. In fact he'd spent the last two Christmases there, the best Christmases they'd had in many a long year. She was sure that Constable Phillips had organised it. They'd had two parcels of food and five shillings from the Police Benevolent Fund. They were quite friendly now, she mused. She often saw him on his beat and he'd walk all or part of the way home with her. At first she'd been embarrassed, her eyes down, her head bent, ignoring the looks of censure and curiosity from friends and neighbours alike. Even Mam had mentioned it.

'There's nothing wrong with him, Mam, we just have a chat,' she explained to Nelly.

'I'll give you that, Lizzie, but you know what folk around here are like with the scuffers.'

She hadn't replied. She enjoyed their talks. They lifted the gloom and weariness at the end of the day. It was just general talk, local gossip, the weather, the problems of living in a city like Liverpool. Their strollings had ceased to be a cause of gossip. They drew amused glances now, at the slight, mousy girl in her cheap and often grubby clothes and the six-foot-five, barrel-chested, dark-haired policeman. She never let him carry anything for her, no matter how heavy the burden; it would somehow demean him. She knew from what he'd told her that if it was reported that he was escorting a young woman and carrying her bundles on a regular basis, he would be disciplined. It *would* demean him and the uniform he wore. So sometimes she had to struggle home from the bag wash, the washing in a bundle clutched to her chest, her arms aching, for she had never mastered the art of carrying the bundle on her head, the way most of the older women and the shawlies did.

As she trudged along, Lizzie spotted his familiar figure on the corner of Westmoreland Street, ostensibly keeping his eye on the pub of the same name. You couldn't miss him, he was so tall. Her expression brightened.

'Hello, Lizzie. Another hard day?'

She smiled up at him. 'No, it wasn't bad and it's payday tomorrow.'

'Aye, for me too.'

She just nodded, wishing her wage compared with his. They got good pay, did the scuffers, since the riots in 1919, but then they had a lot to put up with, not only from the 'civvies', as he called ordinary people, but from the 'higher ups' too. She'd thought he'd been pulling her leg when he'd told her of all the rules and regulations and the fines.

'The weather's a bit better now. Soon be spring.'

'Aye,' he agreed. 'I don't know where the time goes to.'

They'd reached the corner of Benledi Street.

'Lizzie, would you consider coming for a sail with me to New Brighton on Sunday?' he asked quietly.

She was so astounded that she could only gape at him.

'I don't get a Sunday off very often,' he went on, to fill her awkward silence.

'Well ... I ... yes,' she stammered. 'But ... but ... I ain't got no Sunday clothes.' Her cheeks burned with the shame and embarrassment of having to admit this.

'That doesn't matter, Lizzie. It's you I want to take on an outing, not a dressed up doll.'

'Our Alice's the pretty one, she always has been.'

'You underestimate yourself, Lizzie. To me you're a great looking girl.'

The smile that spread across her face erased the lines of care and deprivation. 'Am I?'

'Indeed you are, Lizzie.'

They agreed to meet at the Pier Head at two o'clock but she didn't tell her mam until the Saturday night.

'Do you think Maggie O'Hanlon would lend me a coat, Mam, for tomorrow afternoon?'

Nelly looked surprised. 'What for?'

'Well, I'm going to New Brighton for the afternoon and I've nothing decent at all.'

'Who's taking you?'

Lizzie fiddled with the edge of her frayed cuff. 'A feller.'

'What feller?'

'Jack, his name is.'

Nelly looked shrewdly at her daughter for a few minutes. 'It's Jack Phillips, that scuffer, isn't it?'

Lizzie nodded but to her surprise there was no exclamation of disapproval. Nelly strongly suspected that Tip's spells in Walton and the fact that these days he was far less violent were all due in some part to Jack Phillips. It was almost a year now since she'd had so much as a belt from Tip and that was a bloody miracle.

'Don't get your hopes up, luv. He's a decent enough feller but we're not his class of person at all.'

'It's just a bit of an outing, Mam.'

Nelly looked at her fondly. Her poor Lizzie. She'd been so broken-hearted when that big, daft Tommy Mac had been killed. He'd been her one chance to escape from number ten Benledi Street. Since then, well, Lizzie looked far older than her years and had had nothing in life to look forward to.

'Then go over and ask Maggie,' she said kindly, 'but don't tell her where you're going and who with. Their Fred's had a few run-ins with Constable Phillips and he's got the bruises to prove it.'

As soon as she'd got in from work on the Saturday she'd washed her hair but no matter how many times she combed it, it had no life, no shine, just hung limply around her pallid face. On Sunday, in desperation, she twisted it into a knot at the back of her head. It made her look even older and plainer but there was no help for it.

The coat she'd borrowed from Maggie was navy blue which didn't do anything to lighten her appearance, but it was new, bought from Blackler's, no less, with a windfall her da had had on a horse. It covered the shabby skirt and blouse and came down to Lizzie's ankles and for that she was thankful, for she had no stockings or shoes, just boots, the old-fashioned kind women used to wear, laced up but with a small heel. She had no hat. She looked at herself in the window of the tobacconist's shop on Scotland Road as she waited for the tram – Mam had let her have tuppence and hopefully Jack would pay the return fare. The image of herself gazing back from the shop window was depressing. The coat really didn't suit her as Maggie was much bigger than she was. Oh, she was so plain, and as dull as ditchwater and swamped by the huge garment, the sleeves of which she'd had to turn up twice.

Jack was waiting for her at the top of one of the covered walkways that led down to the floating landing stage. He looked so different, she thought, out of uniform. He wore a tweed jacket with leather patches at the elbows and well-pressed grey trousers. A grey knitted pullover covered an open-necked shirt and in place of his helmet he wore a flat tweed cap. That surprised her. Somehow she'd thought he'd have worn a bowler or a trilby.

He walked to meet her. 'That's a nice warm coat, Lizzie. You'll be glad of it, there's a real bite to the wind.'

'It's not mine. I borrowed it,' she admitted.

'Well, what does that matter?' he said kindly. 'I thought we might go up the tower and then for a bit of a walk along the front, then have a cup of tea and something to eat before coming back. Would that suit you?'

She looked up at him, her eyes full of excitement. 'Up the tower? Really?'

'Really. And tea.'

'I've been to New Brighton but I . . . we . . . never went up the tower.'

A frown creased his forehead and then he remembered that when she'd been young she'd been 'walking out' with Tommy Mac. That was what she meant by 'we'.

'Well, it'll be something new and we'll have a great day even if the sun doesn't shine.'

He bought the tickets and they climbed the staircase that led up to the open deck.

'We can come down into the saloon, if you get cold.'

'No, I want to see everything from up here.'

He watched her intently and with mild amusement tinged with pity as she exclaimed over seeing all the buildings on the waterfront and all the ships. She clung onto the rail with one hand and pointed as New Brighton tower, the fort and the lighthouse at Perch Rock drew closer. The ferry wasn't too crowded as the weather was still cold and he was glad of it. In the summer and on Bank Holidays people were crammed like sardines on every ferry, and on the beach of the small holiday resort you were lucky to get a few feet of sand to yourself. There were always kids running around, kicking up sand and nagging their parents for a penny to see the one-legged diver or the Punch and Judy show.

The wind has loosened the knot of Lizzie's hair and it blew untidily around her face but she didn't care. Eventually they sat down on one of the long wooden benches that were in reality life rafts.

'I don't often get a Sunday off and when I do I don't do much or go anywhere. This makes a nice change.'

'It's like a holiday for me.'

She looked years younger, he thought, with her hair loose, her eyes full of excitement and her cheeks tinged with pink by the wind. He judged her to be in her late twenties. He was thirty-seven, so it wasn't much of a gap. Not so wide that people would think he was just an old fool out with a young girl. He'd grown fond of her and, as Nelly had suspected, he was responsible for the cessation of violence in the O'Connor house. A year ago, on the way to Rose Hill Station after he'd arrested Tip O'Connor, who was drunk and decidedly disorderly, he'd described at great length what he would do to him if Tip ever laid a finger on any of his family again – a description he'd repeated when Tip had sobered up a little. He knew the man was a bully and a coward but he made sure he saw Lizzie often enough to satisfy himself she hadn't been beaten, and enquired frequently after her mam.

There was still about twenty minutes before the ferry would tie up, so they sat and watched the shipping for a while, until he spoke.

'You know you could get a better job, Lizzie.'

'Who'd have me? I can read and write but I'm not clever. I've got no proper manners and I don't know how to . . . talk to people.'

'You could learn manners. You *are* clever and you talk to me. Your Alice had the nowse to get out and make a life for herself.'

'Our Alice was always different to me. It was something to do with her being able to sing, and besides she's younger.'

'There are other girls from Scotland Road who've done it, Lizzie,' he urged. She had no self-confidence. It had all been beaten out of her. 'Girls who've made a good life for themselves. Look at Maggie and Davie Higgins. They've got a whole building now for all the wedding dresses, veils and bridal things she sells. She doesn't sew them herself now, she just designs them and people come from all over, she's built such a fine reputation.'

'She used to live in Silvester Street, didn't she?'

He nodded. 'And there's Dee Chatterton who married Tommy Kerrigan and went off to Canada. They've got a fruit farm and I hear they're going great guns, expanding all the time. Abbie Kerrigan married Mike Burgess and he's a sergeant in the CID now and they live on Queen's Drive. They all came from Burlington Street. So you see you *can* change your life, Lizzie, if you have the determination. They were all hard up, the Kerrigans were as poor as church mice most of the time.'

'But they were never as badly off as us,' Lizzie pointed

out. 'At least their fathers had work or went looking for it and didn't spend their wages before they got home.'

'Sal Kerrigan could have told you something about that, Lizzie,' Jack insisted quietly. 'Her Pat couldn't pass a pub on the way home from work.'

Lizzie knew the Kerrigans vaguely. Sal was dead now and Pat was living in Ireland with Evvie and Keiran O'Brien. The two older lads had been killed in the war, along with Joan's husband. Monica had become a nun but then left the order. Lizzie didn't remember her very well.

'Your mam's not on her own for being beaten,' Jack went on. 'Do you remember that terrible business with Abe Harvey in Burlington Street? He didn't drink but he was a fanatical and a violent man.'

She remembered most of it, although it had been at the beginning of the war. His son Jerry, who was dying, had up and belted Abe with a poker and killed him. Jerry hadn't been hanged for it. He'd died just afterwards of consumption. A smile played around the corners of her mouth.

'What's the smile for?' He couldn't see anything in that particular case to amuse anyone.

'I was thinking of Hannah Harvey. They had more money than us but she was plain and quiet, like me.'

'Oh, aye. Hannah did best of all although she wouldn't look at it like that, not after having her husband shot and dying in her arms.'

It had been the talk of the entire neighbourhood, in fact most of the city, when she'd been wed. Timid little Hannah Harvey, the daughter of a labourer on the tugs, had become the Countess of Ashenden and lived in that huge house in the country with her little boy and dozens of servants. And apparently her husband had owned acres and acres of land and a famous and fabulous collection of jewels.

'Something like that only ever happens once in a blue

moon, Lizzie. It was just circumstances. She's stayed very quiet, never uses her title, never mixing with society, so I heard.'

Lizzie smiled again. 'They were all lucky, but can you see me in an office or a shop or running a big house? No, factory work's all I'm fit for, and I'm glad of it.'

'I don't believe that, Lizzie, but we'll agree to disagree, shall we?'

It was a wonderful day. You could see for miles from the tower and at the bottom of it was a huge ballroom. There were the amusements, a helter-skelter and a ferris wheel but she hadn't wanted to try them. They'd walked along the promenade and, because it was low tide, along the causeway that led to the old fort. Then they'd had fish and chips, bread and butter and tea and scones in a small but very nice cafe. It was the first time since Christmas that she'd had a full belly.

They didn't sit up on deck on the way home, it was too cold and almost dark. Downstairs the saloon was warm and smelled of engine oil. She fell asleep, her head resting on Jack's shoulder and he put his arm around her. Poor little lass, he thought tenderly, what kind of a future did she have? Maybe he'd been wrong to bring up all those other girls who'd done well for themselves. Maybe she'd remembered Tommy MacNamara. Maybe now she'd get depressed.

She still felt warm and sleepy on the tram but as they walked down Benledi Street the wind chased the drowsiness away, and Lizzie realised, with a touch of regret, that her cherished day out was coming to an end. Finally they reached number ten.

As she stood on the broken, uneven doorstep, Jack thought how small and vulnerable she looked. 'Next time I'm off on a Sunday, will we go on another outing, Lizzie? We could get a train to Chester.'

She was amazed. She'd thought no further than today. 'You want to take me on another outing?'

He nodded.

'Yes. Yes of course I'll come, Jack. It's been great today, it really has and I'm dead grateful.'

'I'm glad. You deserved a treat.' He raised his cap. 'Good night, Lizzie, I'll probably see you in the week, when I'm on my beat.'

She went inside and closed the door but Jack stood looking at the peeling paint and battered wood for a few minutes, deep in thought. He'd grown fond of her but if anything was to come of it, it would all have to be thought out and handled carefully. How would his mam take to Lizzie? How would Nelly manage without Lizzie's wage, and would Lizzie leave this hovel at all? He turned away. It was early days yet, he wasn't even sure of her feelings for him. She might not have any at all, except gratitude. But more and more he wanted to give her a good home; a safe, secure and comfortable life. One day.

Chapter Seventeen

Alice was silent all the way home in the car. She didn't listen to what Mike was saying and when he pressed her for an answer to a question she replied in monosyllables. Only now was it really beginning to dawn on her that she would probably never see David Williamson again.

The ball had been a great success. *She* had been a great success. When the last notes of the Easter Hymn had died away there had been a few seconds' total silence and then the applause had been deafening. To Alice's ears the sound seemed to shake the room. It was Mike who had stepped forward to hand her down from the platform. She'd positively glowed with radiance and pleasure, oblivious of the look of pride on his face.

After the intermission she was suddenly so popular that she had only had one dance with Mike and two dances with David – and how the minutes of those two dances had slipped by, minutes full of laughter, excitement and pure joy. She was like Cinderella in the fairy story. For this one night she was the toast of Charleston society and in those two dances she'd found her prince. But during the final dance he had spoken the words which now chilled her heart.

'You are certainly the belle of the ball tonight, Alice,' he'd stated, finding it more and more difficult to equate this girl with the one he'd seen, just once, in Liverpool.

She laughed, blushing with pleasure. 'I told you I could sing.'

'Yes, I seem to remember that you did, but never in a million years did I dream you had a voice like that. You should be at Covent Garden.'

'Where's that?'

'London. It's the home of opera. Or maybe Milan or Paris, Vienna – everywhere there's good music.'

'I'd be terrified. No, this is quite good enough for me. I've done enough travelling.'

He smiled down at her. 'I've never met anyone like you before, Alice. You are the most extraordinary person.'

Her eyes sparkled and exhilaration swept over her. Her heart felt as though it would burst and she wanted to sing once more. To sing all night and just for him.

'Who would ever have thought that the drab little sparrow could rise so high in the sky and sing like a lark.'

His words reminded her of India who, when she'd presented her for the first, and last, time had likened her to a bird, a nightingale.

'Have you been to all those places?' she asked.

'Not all, but I've been to quite a few countries. I'm an expert on the indigenous dock workers across the world!' He saw the puzzled look in her eyes. 'Take no notice of me, Alice, I was just trying to be funny. Now we stick to the Atlantic run, except of course when there are strikes at home.'

'Is there much trouble?' She hoped it wouldn't affect Mam and the kids. She'd go on sending the money; things were never as bad if you had a bit of money in your pocket.

He looked serious. 'Yes. The General Strike may have ended over a year ago but there's still a lot of unrest. People are resentful and there are still strikes.'

Alice seized on his words. 'So you might come here again?'

He looked at her a little wistfully. 'Alice, if there's another strike we'll be laid up, no more jaunting around these exotic tropical places. Then when it's over it'll be back on the Atlantic run again.'

She'd smiled, the dance had finished and she'd been whisked off by another young man she'd never met before that night. David's words hadn't really sunk in. Until now.

Jimmy had been waiting with the car. He'd been told by Alexander to ignore the earlier instruction. Have them come home in a common taxi cab when there was a fine motorcar, certainly not! They'd given David a lift back to the ship and Mike had shaken his hand and said if he was ever in this part of the world again he must come and visit them. There had been confidence in his smile. He read the newspapers. He knew what was going on back in Britain. He doubted they'd ever see David Williamson again.

David had taken Alice's hand. 'It's been a wonderful night. Maybe one day I'll see you on the stage of the Royal Opera House, Covent Garden, Alice. Do you remember what Charlie said?'

'Yes. He said one day you might pay to hear me sing.'

David had smiled at Mike. 'My younger brother. I thought he was being crass at the time but now I know he was being prophetic. Goodbye, Alice and thank you, both, for an evening I'll always remember.'

They'd watched him go. After he'd released her hand he'd walked swiftly up the gangway and then turned to give a quick wave before disappearing from sight.

'You're very quiet, Alice.' Mike's voice broke through her reverie. She'd hardly said a word and they were nearly home. He knew she was thinking of Williamson and he had to admit that the lad was pleasant, well-educated and well-mannered.

'I'm tired.'

'I expect you are. It's very tiring being the centre of attention.'

She turned and looked at him to see if he was teasing her. He wasn't.

'I mean it,' he said. 'It's exhausting. You've been in a state of nervous tension for days. But you were wonderful, Alice. You could see the looks of pure amazement slowly creeping over their faces. I wouldn't have missed it for the world. You weren't the paid entertainment as Sofia Scarlatti would have been. You were entertaining them because you wanted to and I think they realised that.'

He meant every word. He'd watched the faces of Charleston's society and the stunned looks had soon been replaced by genuine admiration. It had given him a glow of smug satisfaction, for they all thought that she was his wife and he'd almost burst with love and pride. It had taken a lot of guts for a virtually untrained girl to step into the shoes of Sofia Scarlatti, whose entire youth had apparently been spent at La Scala, Milan. Alice had been the star of the whole evening. Beautiful, confident, charming, talented. He'd been too busy with his own thoughts to turn and see how David Williamson was taking her performance, nor had he wanted to. He'd seen the expression in Alice's eyes whenever they alighted on the handsome young ship's officer. But it wasn't love. She was infatuated, that was all. She'd fallen in love with an image. She didn't know much about him at all and after tonight she'd probably not see him again and with any luck she'd forget him eventually.

As Alexander took their cloaks, Mike pulled a small box from his pocket and handed it to her.

'What's this for?'

'That's not very gracious, now, is it? Open it.'

She knew she should feel thankful, curious and excited, even exuberant but she felt empty and desolate. She opened the small red Morocco leather box. Inside was a gold pendant and chain. The pendant consisted of two letters. L and S entwined, and above them was a bird set with diamonds. She looked puzzled.

'Didn't you once tell me that you wanted to be known as the Liverpool Songbird?'

She smiled. 'I did. More than anything else in the world.'

'Now it's true. Well, almost. After tonight's performance, would you rather it was the Charleston Songbird? I could get the letters changed.'

She shook her head. 'No. This is beautiful. Thank you.' She closed the lid. 'I think I'll go up now. I really am tired.'

He nodded but his face was set in lines of disappointment. Every other gift he'd given her had been accepted with cries and shrieks of pleasure. 'I'll see you in the morning, Alice. Good night.' He turned away and headed for his study.

Alice went slowly up the stairs and when Ruth had helped her undress she sat down at her dressing table and began half-heartedly to brush her hair. The face of the girl who stared back at her was full of mute misery. Oh, she was sure he must love her. She'd not misread the look in his eyes. She'd not imagined the pressure of his arms round her waist, holding her closer than was deemed correct. She knew she'd been a great success but perversely it really didn't mean that much to her now. He was going away. In a few hours the *Aquitania*'s anchor would be raised. As she lay in her bed she would hear the three long blasts on the ship's whistle, the *Aquitania*'s farewell to Charleston and his, too, in a way. She couldn't let him go. She *had* to tell him how she felt. But how could she get to see him and to see him alone?

She looked down at the pendant Mike had just given her. No, she didn't want to be the Charleston Songbird. It was Liverpool or nothing. Liverpool! That's where he was going. They'd sail up to New York and then across the Atlantic to their home port. She felt a great surge of homesickness rush over her. Home for him probably meant a big house, his parents and Charlie. Home for her meant Benledi Street, Mam, Lizzie, Agnes, Mary, the boys Jimmy and Eddie. But, oh, how she longed to see them all again. She took the pendant from its box and fastened it round her neck. She gently fingered the letters. L and S. The Liverpool Songbird. Well, why not? The shadows of depression and despair melted away. She could easily get a job now. No one would turn her away or deny her audition and then . . . she would see David again. She'd see him as often as his ship came in. Their relationship would grow and he'd tell her he loved her and always would.

All other thoughts were banished from her mind as she stood up and began to rummage through her wardrobe, flinging clothes across the bed. From a cupboard she dragged out a trunk she'd noticed was stored there. It was full of clothes, men's clothes – Mike's father's, she assumed. She quickly emptied it. Her shoes went in first, then underwear, then dresses. She was so engrossed that she didn't hear the door open or notice Mike standing in the doorway.

'Alice, what are you doing?'

She got to her feet. 'Oh, Mike!' Her hand went to the pendant, almost defensively – 'I . . . I'm . . . packing. I . . . I want to go home.'

'This is all very sudden. You've never shown any inclination to go back. You know I would have paid for a visit.' Anger and bitterness filled his eyes. 'You have Charleston at your feet and you decide to go home! Jaysus, Alice! Don't lie to me. I'm not blind nor am I an eejit. You're going after him, David Williamson.'

'I'm not! I really do want to go home. I miss Mam so much.'

'Stop that bloody nonsense, Alice!'

She shrank back. She'd never seen him so furious before. In the depths of his dark eyes there were pinpoints of fire and the expression on his face frightened her. Now, for the first time, she saw him not as a benefactor or a friend she could laugh and joke with, but as a tall, strong, angry man. A man who could hurt her or who could force her to stay here. She hid her fear well.

'Oh, all right!' she said defiantly. 'Yes! Yes, I'm going after him. I. . .'

He could see the words forming on her lips but he didn't want to hear them. 'How do you know he wants you to follow him? Have you thought of that? How much do you really know about him? I'll tell you, Alice, not a bloody thing! He might well have a girl back there. He might even be married. You don't bloody know.'

'No! No, he's not married, there's no girl. I'm sure he would have said something.' For a moment her heart stopped. She felt sick. What if there *was* a girl?

'Why? We invited him out, to a rather grand evening as it turned out. He wasn't obliged to tell us his life story. All I got out of him was that he wanted to be a captain eventually.'

'Stop it! Stop it! I don't want to hear any more.' If she listened to Mike, she might begin to doubt herself and the rightness of her instincts. 'I want to go home!'

Mike felt as though his heart had been turned to stone. That ice water was running through his veins instead of blood. He wanted to take her in his arms and hold her tightly and keep her here. He wanted to kiss her and love her and erase all thoughts of Williamson from her mind. How could he let her go? How could he tell her that this house would be like a mausoleum without her? That his life would have little purpose or direction. And if he did tell her and beg her to stay, what answer would he get? That she didn't want him? That she could never love him? That maybe in time she'd even hate him if he tried to keep her here. But surely he had to try.

'Alice, are you absolutely determined? Are you sure?' He'd fought a hard battle to keep the jealousy from his voice.

'I am! I know . . . I just know . . .' She spread her hands helplessly.

He turned away. He wasn't going to beg. He wasn't going to act like a fool – an old fool. His pride wouldn't let him. He had to retain some self-respect.

Alice was on the verge of tears. She didn't want to admit that there was even a slight possibility that Mike was right. She *knew* David wasn't married, but a girl?

'All right, Alice. Go. I've no claim on you.' The words were spoken in a harsh, brittle tone. Mike couldn't bring himself to put a single note of warmth in his voice.

'Can . . . can I . . .'

'Can you what?' He'd turned to face her, completely in control of himself again.

Alice looked at him with child-like pleading. 'Can I take all my clothes?'

'Sure, though there won't be many of them suited to a cold spring in Liverpool.'

She just hung her head. 'Mike, I . . . I . . . I'm sorry. You've been so good to me. I don't know how I would have ended up but for you.' Her hand went to the pendant. 'Can I . . . keep this? I don't want anything else.'

He nodded curtly and left the room. Alice began to pick up her clothes and fold them. She had saved some money, enough at least to get her home to Liverpool. She still had a horror of being penniless and so she had what she called her 'emergency' money.

She looked up sharply as the door opened. She hadn't expected Mike to return and was surprised and anxious to see him standing there.

Mike stared back at her. He'd gone straight to the safe where her jewels were kept. He'd had a mad impulse to pick them up and throw them one by one out of the window, but common sense prevailed. He'd taken a small bundle of dollar notes, one of many, and put them in his pocket. He'd shut the safe and sighed heavily as he'd turned toward the staircase.

'Take this. You'll need it,' he said quietly.

She looked down at the small bundle of green bank-notes he'd thrown on the bed.

'It's the same amount that I paid India to release you. She drives a hard bargain. Take it.'

Her cheeks burned with shame remembering just how she'd paid her passage to Charleston and how and where she'd met Mike. And now she was walking out on him. There looked to be a couple of hundred dollars in that bundle on the bed. 'Oh, Mike, I really am grateful.' There was a catch in her voice.

'I'll get Alexander to organise your packing and see to the luggage. There's no rush, Alice. There won't be any trains leaving tonight.'

'I'd thought I could go . . .'

'On the ship?' he finished for her. 'It's full. Not a single berth left. I heard him tell Euganie that. So, you'll have to go by train to New York. Oh, don't worry, Alice. You won't miss the boat. The train is far quicker.'

'Will I see you in the morning?'

He didn't answer. He left the room, slamming the door so hard that the portraits on the landing walls shook. Let them all think what they liked. He didn't bloody care.

Alexander looked around the room in disbelief. She *was* going. He hadn't believed it when he'd been summoned and told that Alice was leaving, that she was going back to England. Was it for a visit? he'd asked, so stunned he'd forgotten that it was not his place to question his employer. No, it was not, had been the curt reply. He'd wanted to ask what had happened, what had been said.

They'd all waited up, wanting to know how Alice had fared. They were all dog-tired but they'd been overjoyed when Jimmy had told them she'd been a huge success. But then there'd been a row or a fight of some kind. They'd all heard the raised voices and then the door slam and Mike's heavy tread on the stairs. Both Mr Mike and Alice had tempers.

'The first train is at six o'clock tomorrow morning,' he said sadly.

Alice nodded. 'When I've finished, could Jimmy take me down to the station?'

'You can't wait at the station until tomorrow morning.'

'This morning.' Alice nodded towards the clock. It was ten minutes past one.

'Well, you still can't go hanging around that place. Jimmy will wait with you, in the car.'

'No. That's not fair, Alexander. There must be a ladies' waiting room.'

'Why are you going?' Alexander felt that he could ask this now.

'I'm . . . I'm homesick.'

'You never told anyone that.'

'I didn't think I should. I didn't think it was "done" to tell the entire household everything.'

'Will you come back?'

'I don't know. Maybe, one day. You see, I promised Mam I'd go home when I was famous.'

Alexander shrugged. He supposed it was as good an excuse as any but he'd be sorry to see her go.

Jimmy brought the luggage down and put it in the hall. There was a miserable, depressing air hanging over the house, Alexander thought as he came downstairs. Everyone was upset to see Alice go, particularly Ruth and himself. Mr Mike was in his study, even though everyone else had now gone to bed. He could see the sliver of light under the door. He looked at the trunk and the cases and then back to the strip of light. Oh, to hell with propriety now. Ruth, Ella and Florence had been in tears and he couldn't have his staff upset like this. It wasn't like the bad old days any more. He was paid a wage. He didn't have to keep his mouth shut. Mr Mike could sack him but he'd soon find another job and, anyway, the place wouldn't be the same without Alice. He did knock but there was no reply, so he opened the door and went in.

Mike was sitting slumped in the deeply buttoned leather armchair. The room was dark. Only the desk lamp was switched on. Alexander noticed that the cut-glass whisky decanter was half empty.

'Now what? Can't a man get a bit of peace in his own bloody house?'

Alexander decided that a coaxing approach wouldn't work. 'She's going and you're letting her go,' he said belligerently.

'So what? If she wants to go, let her.'

'We'll all be sorry.'

Mike's temper rose. He'd been drinking for an hour but he wasn't drunk. Far from it. Perversely, tonight it seemed that the more he drank the more sober he felt. 'I'm sure she'd like to know that. Now leave me alone. If she wants to make fool of herself—'

'She ain't just homesick then,' Alexander interrupted quickly.

'Don't you have eyes and ears all over the damned place? Don't you know as well as I do that she's going chasing after that bloody young Williamson?' Mike yelled. 'Young, that's the important word, Alexander. *Young*.'

Alexander gave up all pretence of ignorance. 'But I heard she only met him once before, back in Liverpool, and then just for a few minutes. She got hurt or something.'

'Of course she only met him once before! She doesn't bloody know him. She only thinks she does.'

'Then go and talk her out of it. Go and change her mind. She can't go chasing around the world.'

'She managed to find her way here – and anyway, it's none of your damned business.'

Alexander persisted. 'We're like a family. You said so yourself at Christmas.'

'I must have been drunk.'

'No, you weren't. Miss Alice is part of this house now. Part of the family. Go and talk to her.'

Mike wanted to yell that he would do no such thing. That he'd been humiliated enough for one night. Instead he shook his head firmly. 'No.'

'And that's definite?'

Mike lost his temper. 'Get out of here, Alexander!'

'Ruth, Ella and Florrie went back to bed crying their eyes out. I think—'

'Go to hell!' Mike shouted. He snatched up the decanter and hurled it at the marble fireplace.

It shattered into a thousand shards. 'Get out of here before I sack you! Before I sack the whole bloody lot of you!'

Alexander left sadly. His sadness was for Mike, for Alice and for all the staff, his family.

When the car was loaded Alice gave Alexander a quick hug before getting in. When she'd come downstairs she'd turned towards the study but Alexander had shaken his head warningly. So she walked out into the starlit night, looking sadly back at the house that had been her home for over two years. It had been more than a house, more than a home. It had been a new world. A new life.

She asked Jimmy to drive down to the harbour first, for reassurance. She got out and walked across the road and then breathed a sigh of relief. The ship was still there. Not quite so many lights blazed now, at least not from the portholes. People were asleep.

'Wait for me, I won't be long,' she told Jimmy before she hurriedly crossed the road and ran down towards the harbour. She'd just catch him. She'd tell him she would see him in New York. That she, too, was going back to Liverpool.

There was great activity on the dockside. The longshoremen were already getting ready to cast off the ropes that held the ship to its moorings. The anchor was almost up, she could hear the last clanking, grating sounds. No! She was too late. She scanned the boat deck, the only deck that seemed to be fully illuminated, apart from the bridge. She could see a few figures moving up there.

'David! David!' she yelled as loudly as she could and waved her arms frantically to attract attention.

There was no reply and everyone ignored her. They were all engrossed in their work. She jumped nervously when a voice from above bawled, 'Cast off aft!' a command echoed by the longshoremen. She watched with disappointment as the huge black hull moved slowly away from the harbour wall. She was just ten minutes too late. Even if they hadn't allowed her on board, she could have got a message to him. She went back to the car and told Jimmy to drive on.

She felt stiff, cold and emotionally drained by the time she boarded the Atlantic Coast Rail Company's train. The sun was just creeping up over the horizon. It would take thirty-six hours to get to New York, so she'd been told when she'd bought her ticket. There would be rest stops in Emporia, North Carolina, in Richmond, Virginia, Washington DC, Baltimore and Newark. But as the train pulled out, her weariness, her sadness at leaving left her. She was going home. Home to Liverpool and to Mam, and she was going in style too, but best of all she'd be going home with David Williamson. She'd have nearly five days of being close to him. He did get time off, he'd told her that. Oh, she couldn't wait to see the look on his face when he saw her. He'd also told her that fraternising with the passengers was definitely frowned on but she didn't care about that. Rules were meant to be broken. She could hardly wait.

Chapter Eighteen

'I've seen yer before, miss, haven't I?'

As Alice passed her hand luggage to the white-gloved steward she smiled at him. 'Yes. I came aboard in Charleston and you went and found Mr Williamson for me.'

He grinned. 'And here yer are again.'

'Here I am. But this time I'm going home to Liverpool.'

'For good or just for a visit, like?' He knew he wasn't supposed to ask such personal questions, but he also knew she wouldn't mind. She was different. She was a Scouser, but obviously a wealthy one.

As she followed him down the warm companionway with its deeppile carpets and light oak-panelled bulkheads, she was aware of two familiar things. The faint smell of oil and the hum of the generators that sounded like a large cat purring. She wondered briefly whether Mog was enjoying her life on the *Castlemaine*. This all felt so familiar. This ship that was returning to Liverpool's heart, the River Mersey, she could now look on as being part and parcel of home.

'Will Mr Williamson be working?' she asked when the steward finally opened the door of her cabin and placed her bags on the bunk.

'Oh, yeah. Everyone turns to on sailing day, from the old man down to the bell boys. Never a minute to call yer own. Sometimes there's murder with the passengers, like, if they've been double-booked. The Purser nearly 'as a fit when that 'appens.'

She gave a fifty cent piece and he grinned again. 'I could get word to him, if yer like, but it won't be until we're out of the Hudson.'

'Would you do that for me?'

'Course I will, miss. Why don't yer go up on deck when we leave. Yer won't be able to see everything at its best, like, 'cos it's dark but it's great. Ellis Island, the Statue of Liberty – that's lit up – and then under the Verazzano Narrows Bridge – that's got lights on it too.'

'Thanks, I might just do that but I am tired. It's taken me thirty-six hours to get here by train.'

'It'd take a damned sight longer if yer were at 'ome, if yer get me meaning. They're all out on strike again.'

Alice took off her coat and hat and looked around. The cabin, or stateroom as he'd called it, was on the promenade deck and had every imaginable luxury. There was a separate sitting room with a green brocade-covered sofa and a walnut table and writing desk. The sleeping area was painted cream with gold and pale green mouldings on the doors. It was lit by electric wall lights that looked like gold sconces with candles in them. There was a proper bed complete with brass bedstead, not a bunk. In one corner was a marble washbasin with gold taps and hot and cold running water. A large oval mirror was mounted on one wall, over a walnut dressing table. The carpet was deep forest green. In a curtained-off section was a marble toilet that flushed. Beside the bed, on a table under the bell for the stewardess, was a telephone. She touched everything, marvelling at it all.

This *was* a first-class luxury cabin, she reminded herself. She was paying for all this. Twenty dollars, to be exact. It was sheer extravagance but she was going home in great style. She thought of the *Castlemaine* and its dark, cramped and smelly cabin, the terrors of the storm, and of Georgie

Tate. She wondered idly what he would think if he could see her now and if he would ever come to hear her sing – should she be booked to appear in Liverpool, that is.

A stewardess, a middle-aged, rather severe looking woman, dressed in a starched white uniform dress and cap, appeared and asked her if there was anything else she desired before she started Alice's unpacking. A pot of tea, perhaps? Alice didn't want to send the woman away nor did she really want to sit and watch her clothes being hung up and placed in drawers. She wouldn't know what to talk to her about or if you were supposed to talk at all. She said tea would be lovely.

After that she went up onto the boat deck as she'd been advised to do and as the ship moved slowly and majestically down the Hudson River, the white wake of her bow wave visible against the dark water, a rush of excitement held Alice in its grip. Oh, how much her life had changed. It was miraculous, that's what it was. She could never have dreamed that such good fortune, such luxury, such wealth could be hers.

There had been no time to write to Mam but she'd sent a telegram saying she was coming home on the *Aquitania* which would tie up at the landing stage on Friday at about noon. She hoped the brown envelope that would be delivered by a boy on a bicycle wouldn't upset Mam. People still had a horror of telegrams, after the awful years of the Great War. They'd all come down to meet her, Mam, Lizzie, Jimmy, Agnes, Eddie and little Mary. Oh, she longed to see them, hug them. She wanted to see their faces when they saw her dressed to the nines and paying for porters to carry her luggage and then they'd all go home in a taxi cab or maybe they'd go somewhere for a bit of a celebration. A meal, somewhere nice. Perhaps Reece's Restaurant.

'It's such a pity it's so dark.'

Alice jumped and then her face lit up. David Williamson

stood behind her. 'Oh, you didn't half give me a fright!'

'I didn't mean to. I was amazed when Morrison told me you were on board. I had to come and see for myself. I thought he'd got mixed up, or he'd been drinking. I've only just managed to get away.'

'I . . . I . . . decided to go home.'

'For a visit?'

She shook her head. 'No.'

'Was Mr O'Farrell upset? It's very sudden, after all.'

'I've been homesick for quite a while. I kept thinking about people, family, and after meeting you and the ball and everything, I just couldn't stay. He was upset and I suppose he's got a right to be, after everything he's done for me.'

'So, what will you do when you get home?'

Her eyes danced with excitement. 'Sing.' She laughed. 'I've got the training and the grooming now. It was one of the reasons why I went to America. But just one. The main reason was . . . was . . .' Suddenly the words wouldn't come out. She swallowed and tried again. 'I . . . I . . . went because . . .' Again her voice faltered, the words deserted her.

He took her hand. 'I really have to go now, Alice, or I'll get fired. I just had to make sure it *was* you.'

The physical contact with him sent her blood racing and her heart pounding. 'But I will see you again, soon?'

'Of course. We could take a stroll on deck tomorrow afternoon, if the weather's not too bad.'

Alice had a sudden vision of the cabin of the *Castlemaine* and herself lying on the floor wishing she were dead. 'Will it be very rough?'

'Not for a day or so at least.' He noticed the apprehension in her eyes. 'Don't worry, Alice, this ship was built for the North Atlantic. "Speed and Safety" is Cunard's motto. What's your cabin number? I'll get a message to you, a time and place.'

'It's B78, on the promenade deck.'

He turned away but then, seeming to remember something, he turned back. 'Alice, would you consider giving a performance here on board?'

She was startled. 'Me? Sing here?'

'Yes. I know it will be a great success and our passengers will be delighted with the diversion.' He stopped and frowned. 'I need a better – more appropriate – word than "diversion".'

'Entertainment?'

He smiled and her heart lurched again and she longed to reach out and touch his face, very gently.

'Entertainment sounds much better. You were magnificent in Charleston; you shouldn't hide your light under a bushel, as the saying goes.'

She nodded her agreement. Why not? She couldn't be any more nervous than she'd been at the ball. She just prayed she wouldn't be seasick again.

They met in the First-Class Lounge, an enormous room with a glass-domed ceiling, its ornately plastered coving depicting garlands of flowers tied with ribbon bows. The bulkheads were covered with burnished mahogany panelling. The carpet and the upholstery on the chairs and sofas was a shade of carnelian red. Two huge marble fireplaces graced each end of the room and beside each was a buffet.

There could be no displays of affection in such a public place. Such things were most certainly frowned on and often remarked on, too. She was beautiful, there was no doubt about that and she was a delight to be with.

'So, what do you do on here?' she asked, hoping to be able to understand and learn more about him.

'I'll simplify it, Alice. It's far too boring and technical to go into in great detail.' Her large, soft eyes were wide with interest and he warmed to her. 'Basically, I help to see that the engines keep running to turn the screws –

propellors – to "drive" the ship at different speeds. It's all valves and pressure gauges, terribly boring.'

'Oh, I'm not bored!' she replied but he could see the slight crease between her brows that denoted wandering concentration.

'I am!' he laughed. She was so easy to talk to and he was drawn to her. 'Tell me about yourself, before Charleston?'

Panic gripped her but she kept on smiling. 'That's not fair! I don't know *anything* about you, except that Charlie is your brother and you work here on this ship.'

'Well, I've got two younger sisters, one seventeen and one nearly nineteen. I live in Crosby, my father is a lawyer and I joined the Merchant Navy when I left Merchant Taylor's school. I've seen many different . . . exotic places and now it's your turn!' He leaned towards her. 'Where do you come from, Miss Alice O'Connor?'

She drew back and pulled a face. 'A terrible place, really "desperate" as Mike would say, but I don't want to think about that. I just want to sing.'

Somehow she'd managed to tell him very little of her background but she shared her hopes of appearing on the stage of Liverpool's theatres.

'Would you come and see me? You'd have to pay this time, I'm afraid.'

'Of course I will – and I know Charlie will. He started all this. I thought he was quite mad at the time, but he was right. You know, Alice, you'll be wasting your time staying in Liverpool. You should go to London.'

She tried to hide the stricken look in her eyes. 'I think I might be a bit nervous about that.' She didn't want to go anywhere where she'd have no chance of seeing him.

'Nervous? You'll have travelled the Atlantic twice. You've been to Charleston, New York and all those other places you mentioned.'

'They were only train stops, we didn't stay for long.'

'Alice, you shouldn't be apprehensive about anything. You're young, you're beautiful and you're very, very talented.' There was no mistaking the sincerity in his voice or his eyes.

She blushed furiously. He *must* feel something for her. He couldn't say such things and not have some affection, some love. It was just so awkward for him; maybe when they arrived in Liverpool she'd see more of him and then he'd be able to show her exactly how he felt about her. He must surely realise that it wasn't just homesickness that had prompted her rapid departure from Charleston.

She agreed to sing on Wednesday night, after dinner, in the Music Room on the boat deck, weather permitting. She'd sing the pieces she'd sung for Charleston society and then a couple of the more modern, popular songs. She'd also wear the white dress she'd worn for the ball.

Fortunately the weather held. It was breezy and there was quite a heavy swell, but conditions were nowhere near anything that could be termed rough or stormy. Given that there were other entertainments on offer, she was amazed at the number of passengers who gathered in the sumptuous Georgian-style room, with its pale green and yellow furnishings, and inlaid mahogany and rosewood panelling. A glass skylight, adorned with plaster cherubs holding garlands, made the room brighter and the diffused lighting offset the darkness of the wood panelling. There wasn't a stage of any kind, so she stood next to the gleaming grand piano. The resident pianist smiled at her.

'A good turn-out, Miss O'Connor.'

She bit her lip anxiously. 'I hope I don't make a fool of myself. It's my one dread.'

'No one as lovely as you could do that, and anyway, I'm sure they'd all forgive any gaffe,' he replied gallantly. He could see she was very nervous.

It was the Cotillion Ball all over again. In fact, she thought the response was better because after her introductory pieces everyone, including herself, seemed to relax. The evening lengthened as she sang requests. Champagne was sent to her for refreshment and it was after eleven when she finally managed to get away.

She was thrilled to see David waiting for her when she emerged into the companionway.

'You see, Alice, you had nothing to worry about – you were fantastic! They all loved you. I saw a few eyes being dabbed when you finished "The Londonderry Air".'

'I didn't see you. I didn't know you were there.'

'I was at the back; I crept in. I couldn't miss it, now could I? I look on you as my sort of protégée.'

She didn't really know what he meant but she wasn't going to ask. Instead she smiled at him.

'Will anyone be meeting you in Liverpool?'

'Yes, they'll all be there on the landing stage. I sent a telegram. It cost three dollars but I didn't mind.'

'Isn't it amazing that messages can be sent like that across the world?'

They had reached the Purser's Bureau and she was about to reply when a middle-aged man approached them.

'Please forgive me for intruding, Miss O'Connor, but I had to speak to you.'

She smiled politely but wished he hadn't interrupted. She wanted to be with David. To her dismay, David nodded.

'There's no need for you to apologise, sir. If you'll excuse me for fifteen minutes, there are a few things I have to attend to. I'll see you later, Alice.'

'Where?' There was a distinct note of pleading in her voice.

'First-Class Reading and Writing Room?'

She turned to the man, annoyance and suspicion in her eyes. 'Yes?'

'Miss O'Connor, it's a long time since I met anyone remotely like you.'

She managed a wry smile. How long was she going to have to stand here and listen to this old fool? When would he get to the point? *Was* there a point? He looked very ordinary, a bit on the drab side, grey hair and grey eyes. Of course, his evening clothes were impeccable.

'Shall we walk?'

Inwardly she sighed. Thank God David had said fifteen minutes.

'I'm returning from New York where I've had some business to attend to, although it wasn't a terribly successful trip.'

'Everyone's going to Liverpool.'

'Actually I'm not. Well, I'm not staying in Liverpool. I'm going straight to London on the boat train. I'm an agent, Miss O'Connor. A theatrical agent.'

A year ago she wouldn't have known what he meant; now she stopped and looked at him with interest. 'You mean you book people to appear on the stage?'

'Yes. I prefer to call them artistes but as I said, it's a long time since I met anyone like you. You are quite remarkable, Miss O'Connor.'

'Could you get me an audition?' She was eager now.

'I could get you any number of them.'

She beamed at him, her eyes sparkling. 'In Liverpool?'

'In Liverpool or Manchester, Leeds or Birmingham, but what I had in mind was auditions for the London musicals. You'd be wonderful in *Showboat* or *No, No, Nanette*. Every bit as good as Gina O'Donnell.'

She'd heard of these musical plays. 'But won't I need to know how to act?'

'You could learn, there are schools and academies.'

'In Liverpool?'

'I was thinking of London.'

They had reached the Writing and Reading Room and Alice sat down on a grey silk brocade sofa. 'I don't even know your name.'

'It's Victor. Victor Hardman. My agency is one of the best.'

'What would be the right thing for me to do?'

'Get enrolled at a theatrical school, audition for parts. I presume you'll have to earn a wage and I could get you work in some of the better class music halls.'

'And what do you get in return?'

'Ten per cent of all your earnings. I'm not trying to fleece you, Miss O'Connor. That's the standard rate. You'll get work, plenty of it. I can almost guarantee it.'

It was utterly fantastic. No one had ever offered her anything like this. No one had had this much faith in her, except perhaps Euganie Walton. She could be the star of a London musical! Little Alice O'Connor from Benledi Street. That thought lessened the euphoria. She couldn't leave Mam and the kids so soon. She couldn't say she was off to London when she'd only just set foot in the door.

'I want to sing in Liverpool first,' she said. 'It's an ambition. At the Empire or the Rotunda. I have my reasons and I haven't seen my family for a long time.'

'That's all right by me. I know both the managers, I'll write to them, and when we dock I'll have a messenger boy deliver the letters. But you will have to move to London if you want to be a real star. You'll have to live there. I can find you a place to live, a drama coach or a place in a drama class, and advance bookings. Shall we say in a month's time?'

She couldn't speak so she just nodded.

'And my percentage?'

She bit her lip. It was all too much. It had happened so quickly. There had been no time to think, to ponder. It was fate and for the first time she really began to believe that she had a talent, an exceptional talent. After all, Victor Hardman must have heard hundreds of singers. It must be true, what he was saying, that she had something better than most, a truly wonderful talent that would make her rich and famous. All she'd wanted to do was sing on the stage like Letty Lewis. That had been her original dream ever since the night she'd sneaked into the Rotunda. It had changed slightly after she'd met David Williamson. Then she'd wanted to sing on a theatre stage for him, just for him. She shook her head to try to clear her mind a little. It was crammed full of thoughts and ideas all jumping and jostling with each other. She'd never see David if she was in London and he was plying the Atlantic. She could stay in Liverpool and see him when his ship was in or she could go to London and become a star.

'Well, Alice O'Connor, what do you say?' Victor Hardman pressed, eager to secure this young woman and start her on the road to international success. Having her on his books would increase his bank balance, his credibility and his standing; after a frustrating trip in New York he was anxious for all three.

Alice swallowed hard, for the sides of her throat seemed to have stuck together. She looked around helplessly. 'Can I . . . can I think about it?' she managed to get out at last.

'Of course, but don't take too long. I'm not a very patient man and I've an ulcer that's beginning to play up. Probably too much rich food and drink on this ship.' He smiled ruefully and patted his stomach. He reached into his jacket pocket, withdrawing a pen, notepad and a business card.

'Here's my card, now let me take down your address.'

'Well, we might have moved but I suppose number ten Benledi Street will do for now. It's off Scotland Road. If we do move, I'll let you know.'

The agent's smile returned as David Williamson appeared. 'Ah, there you are, sir. I've just been setting out a glittering future for Miss O'Connor's inspection and, I hope, her acceptance.'

'What kind of future?' His tone was a little suspicious.

'Mr Hardman is an agent. He can get me work.' Alice looked up at David. Oh, how was she going to decide?

'I've offered her a career on the London stage. Top parts. Almost guaranteed success in shows like *Showboat*. You only get one real star in every generation and this young lady's it.'

'There will be a contract?' David was still wary. Alice was very young and unfamiliar with business deals, of that much he was certain.

'Drawn up by my lawyer. Miss O'Connor can have it checked out. It's all above board. No nasty surprises in the small print. I'll have it in the post to her as soon as I possibly can. Two copies. One for myself and one for her to keep.'

David relaxed and smiled at her. 'Alice, this is absolutely wonderful! Wasn't it timely that I persuaded you to sing tonight? Do you understand what it all means?'

Her heart sank like a stone and the pit of her stomach felt horribly cold. Oh, she knew very well what it all meant and he was urging her to accept it. The tears pricked her eyes but she fought them back.

'Alice, you can't turn down an opportunity like this.' He looked mildly concerned.

'No. No, I can't,' she answered, knowing that once again she'd be miles away from him. Did he in fact care for her at all? He *did*, she told herself firmly. He cared so much that he wouldn't stand in the way of her career. That's what she *must* keep thinking.

Chapter Nineteen

They had sat and talked for what seemed like hours, although he'd done most of the talking. There was such an ache in her heart as she'd listened to him enthuse about the opportunity she was being offered. It *was* the chance of a lifetime. She *must* take it. She was so *very, very* fortunate. She knew all that but she had just wanted to crawl away to her cabin: the fact that being a star would mean being in London and away from him never seemed to enter his head. At last he'd escorted her back and before he'd left her he'd taken both her hands and kissed her gently on the forehead. Both were the gestures of affection that a brother would make to a sister and she had cried herself to sleep.

The following morning she confirmed all the arrangements with Victor Hardman. First of all the Rotunda, then the Empire and then London. He'd also told her that she might not have to work the Halls for very long, maybe not at all. He wasn't certain but he'd heard a rumour that Gina O'Donnell was not well and was thinking of leaving *Days of Grace*.

But now it was Friday morning and, in the dismal grey light of the early March morning, the *Aquitania* made her way up the Mersey, majestically weaving her way between all the other ships in the river, who sounded their whistles or foghorns in greeting.

Below decks a sort of organised chaos reigned. People

were getting ready to disembark. Most of the luggage had been removed from outside cabin doors last night but there were still small cases, Gladstone bags, and the odd forgotten trunk in the companionways. Stewards and stewardesses moved quickly and with experience to help the exodus, all waiting to be paid off and get home themselves. They were almost all Liverpudlians and knew that there would be gatherings of relations waiting for them among the crowds who had come in their lunch hours, just to see the great ship tie up.

Alice had not slept well and had got up early, so early it had still been pitch dark. She'd had breakfast as they slowed down off Port Linus, on the coast of Anglesey, where the pilot had come aboard to take the ship up safely through the treacherous channels of the Mersey estuary.

At last through the fine, drizzly rain the familiar buildings of the waterfront slowly became visible and her heart began to make odd jerky movements as she clung to the rail. She was home! She could see the twin towers of the Liver Buildings with their Liver birds, the domed roof of the Mersey Docks and Harbour Board building, and between them the third of the trio, the soot-blackened but imposing Cunard building. Behind them she could just make out the Church of St Nicholas, the sailor's church. The docks were full of ships from the Elder Dempster Line, Booth Line, Lamport and Holt, Canadian Pacific, Shaw, Saville and Albion, and a dozen more companies, their liveries and house flags all so familiar, bright dabs of colour on a drab, cold Mersey morning.

She'd said goodbye to David last night. He was working now – everyone was. She was still confused about his feelings for her. She loved him, that was a certainty, but he'd been adamant about her going to London. He was so certain that it was the right thing for her. Clearly he wanted the best for her and surely that must mean something. Yet she seemed to be no closer to him emotionally now than when she'd met him in Charleston.

Determinedly, she put all thoughts of David from her mind. Her family, her *real* family, would be waiting down there among the crowds of people and the wagons, lorries, carts and cabs. Mam would have got them all scrubbed and dressed in decent clothes. Would they even now be straining their eyes, trying to make out where she was standing? Oh, Mam would be in tears – they all would, herself included.

The luggage boat had already departed for the stage and the tugs had taken the huge 45,000–ton ship in tow and had begun to manoeuvre her towards the landing stage.

The crowd was nearer now, it was possible to see individual people. How far down they looked. It was an incredible sight. Now people beside her began to wave and call out and were receiving similar greetings from ashore. Oh, she just wanted to get home now. To get off this ship that had changed her life so much. She started to wave too, her gaze scanning the upturned faces.

The hawsers were taken up and the ship secured. The gangways were lowered and Alice was almost weeping with disappointment. She couldn't see them! Not one of them. No one had come to meet her. She'd left this city with tears in her eyes. Now she'd returned and tears were stinging her eyes yet again. She waited for as long as she could in case they were late, but she knew the crew were eager to be paid off. She had to pull herself together, to fight down this bitter dashing of her hopes, she told herself as she directed the porter with her luggage towards a waiting taxi cab.

'Where to, miss?'

'Benledi Street,' Alice replied flatly.

He looked at her in astonishment. 'Are yer sure?'

'I'm sure!'

The porter and the cab driver exchanged glances.

'It's dead rough down there, miss,' the porter ventured.

'I know. It's where I come from. I lived there all my life except for the last two years.'

The cab driver took in the smart oatmeal wool coat with the deep fur collar and cuffs that she'd bought in New York, the amber-coloured cloche hat and the matching leather pumps. The hands that held the cream clutch bag were encased in soft cream kid gloves. He shrugged. 'Right, Benledi Street it is, you're payin'.' His face split into a wide grin. ''Ave yer come into a fortune then?'

Alice couldn't help but smile back, despite her distress. 'I suppose you could say that. I sing, on the stage.' She prayed that wouldn't turn out to be a lie. 'And I sang on the ship too.'

'Oh, worked yer passage then?'

'No, I paid for it. I did a special performance. It helps to make the time go quicker. You get fed up of seeing nothing for days on end but the sea.'

The man nodded before turning his attention to the traffic chaos on Mann Island. He had a brother who was a waiter on the *Sythia*. Nearly every family in this city had someone who went away to sea.

Nothing had changed much, Alice thought as they drove down Byrom Street and along Scotland Road. All the shops, the pubs and the churches looked exactly the same. Except that now there wasn't even the bit of greenery and tinsel that had been in evidence when she'd left.

Something must be wrong, she told herself. Maybe they hadn't received the telegram. That *must* be it. Or maybe Mam and Lizzie were out at work. They couldn't just take a day off to go and meet someone off a ship, not even a daughter or a sister. They'd get the sack. There were so many rational excuses and reasons. Why hadn't she thought about them last night when she'd been unable to sleep? But she'd been full of hope last night. Hope that they'd come to meet her. She'd been so confident that they would.

'What number do yer want, miss?' The driver's question broke into her thoughts and she realised that the cab had attracted a crowd of small, scruffy boys who were running alongside it, pointing and whistling.

'Number ten, please.'

'I'll take yer bags in for yer if yer like. This lot will have them nicked before yer can turn around. They should all be in school! Should 'ave the School Board round 'ere. That'd sort them out. Gerroff, you little bugger!' he bawled at one lad who had reached out to touch the leather case he'd just placed on the top step.

Alice got out and looked around as she stood on the pavement. Nothing had changed here either and the house looked ominously quiet.

'Are yer sure they're in?'

She shrugged. 'The door will be open, it's never locked. None of them ever are.'

He rolled his eyes expressively. 'Oh, aye, I know what yer mean. There's nothin' to pinch.'

She ignored his remark and delved into her purse for the money to pay him as he pushed open the door and transferred her things from the step to the hall. The hall was still devoid of lino or rugs, let alone the luxury of a long 'runner' of carpet that people who were better off had down their halls. Oh, this was a great homecoming. A flaming empty house. Tears were not far away again as she walked slowly down the passage and pushed open the kitchen door.

Nelly looked up from the range where she was trying to coax a fire from the rubbish the lads had gleaned from the gutters, before they'd gone to school.

'Mother of God! Alice! Alice, is that you, girl?'

Careless of her pale beige coat and hat, Alice flung

herself into Nelly's arms and began to sob, all the pent-up emotions bursting out. 'Oh, Mam! Mam! I missed you so much! I wanted you to be there. You never came to meet me!'

'Oh, Alice, luv, you're home. You're home now with yer mam. It's all right, luv. Hush now, queen,' Nelly soothed and Alice's sobs gradually grew quieter.

'Oh, Mam, why didn't you come to meet me?' Alice asked after wiping her eyes and blowing her nose on her handkerchief, unearthed from her discarded bag.

'Alice, we didn't know you were coming home. How could we?'

'I sent a telegram from New York. It cost a fortune.'

A look of understanding mingled with regret crossed Nelly's face. 'Our Agnes said someone had come with a letter. I never even opened it. I thought it was from the landlord. I chucked it on the fire.' She gazed up at her daughter in wonderment. 'Oh, never mind that now. You're home.'

Alice looked around. Everything was exactly the same. There was no sign of any new or added comforts. It was freezing cold and Mam looked even more worn out and thinner.

'I sent money, Mam. I sent it regularly each month. Money for food and coal and clothes. Where's it gone?'

Nelly looked back with sadness in her tired eyes. 'Do yer really *have* to ask that question, Alice? You know what he's like. I couldn't manage to save even a bit. The first lot came when he was here and after that, well, he went down to Victoria Street and told them that any further foreign mail was to be held there until he collected it. He went every month, regular as clockwork.'

Alice passed a hand over her forehead. Her head was beginning to ache. She should have known but she would never have credited him with so much sense – or rather cunning. Even if Mam had gone to the main post office in Victoria Street, they wouldn't have given her the letters even though they were addressed to 'Mrs' O'Connor. If 'Mr' O'Connor demanded them, he'd get them.

'Where's everyone?'

'Lizzie's at work, the kids are at school.'

'And Da?'

'It's Friday afternoon, Alice. You should remember what that means, luv.'

The nightmarish feeling that had come over her began to fade before the surge of rage that made her tremble. 'Oh, I know where he is and by God have I got something to say to him!'

'Alice, don't get upset. It's a waste of time, luv. I know. Tell me how you've been. Tell me about all the things you've done and the people you met. What was America like? Look at the style of you! I wouldn't have recognised you, luv, if I met you walking up the street.'

Alice was unmoved. 'There'll be time for all that later, Mam.' She opened her bag, pulled out her purse and extracted a white five-pound note. 'Go round to Holden's or Burgess's and get something for tea, a slap-up tea, Mam. Call at Martingale's and get them to deliver two hundredweight of coal, best anthracite, no rubbishy slack. We're all going to eat well, in a warm kitchen, and then we're all going to Sturla's for clothes and furniture!'

Nelly was staring at her open-mouthed. 'Oh, God, Alice, where did you get all this money?'

'I did nothing wrong, nothing I'm ashamed of. I've committed no mortal sins. I was lucky and I'm going to go on being lucky. I've got work, and we're never going to be cold, hungry, dirty and crawling with bugs ever again.' She turned towards the door.

Nelly caught her arm. 'Alice, where are yer going?'

'To find me da and when I do, Mam, well . . .'

Nelly clapped a hand to her mouth and shook her head. Alice was no match for Tip, not when he had a belly full of ale, or whisky as it was now. That's what all the money Alice had sent had been spent on, she thought bitterly, that and gambling.

Alice was aware of all the curious and envious looks as she strode purposefully up Benledi Street. Well, let them all wonder and jangle as to where she had got the fine clothes. She didn't care. She was going to move her mother and the family out of the area as soon as possible. She'd find a nice house in a respectable area, but first she was going to sort out her da once and for all, and the fact that she was only five foot one didn't deter her. She knew how to use her brains now. Da's were addled with booze, not that he'd ever had that many in the first place.

As she walked along Scotland Road, ignoring the admiring glances and the whistles that came from pub doorways, she fumed. All this time she'd thought that the money she'd sent, Mike's money, was being used to give her family a decent standard of living. How could she have been so flaming stupid? Because she'd lived in luxury, because she'd lived with and moved among people who had scruples, she'd forgotten how bad things were at home. How devious, how cruel and unfeeling her da was.

As she approached The Widows she saw a policeman coming towards her. 'Officer!' she called.

It was Jack Phillips. 'Yes, miss?' His tone was respectful.

'Come with me, I want you to make an arrest.'

'An arrest? Who and for what?' He looked totally mystified.

'My father and for assault.'

Jack looked serious. 'Who has been assaulted?'

'Me. Well, not yet I haven't been, but I will be.'

'I don't understand, miss, and I'm not sure I can comply with your request.'

'Oh, to hell with all that! I'm going in there and I'm going to tell that old sod I want every penny of my money back. I sent money home from America, for my mam and the family and he . . . he drank it!' She was shaking with temper, her words tripping over each other.

'Now I know who you are. It's been puzzling me, I never forget a face. You're Lizzie's sister, Alice. Alice O'Connor who went to America!' He paused. 'But I can't arrest someone for something he hasn't done yet.'

'How do you know our Lizzie?' Alice demanded, aghast. 'What's she done? I've only just got home and Mam didn't say anything.'

He grinned. She had certainly done well for herself and by the sound of things the fortunes of the O'Connor family were going to look up. She didn't have that beaten, gaunt look that Lizzie had when he'd first picked her up from the wet cobbles. Alice was a real beauty. Even with smart clothes Lizzie would still look homely beside her sister. 'She hasn't done anything. We have a bit of a chat now and then, that's all.' He didn't want to go into any detail about his as yet unannounced affection for Lizzie or the money he sometimes gave her, though not regularly. That wouldn't have done at all.

'Will you just follow me and stand by the door of the pub?'

'I suppose I could just be passing, but not lingering too long.'

'Then for God's sake keep behind me. I'll need protection. He'll belt me. Isn't protecting people supposed to be part of your job?'

He grinned. This one was in no way like Lizzie. She had guts to march into a pub full of hard-bitten men. He'd enjoy being a witness to this, there'd be a good chance that Tip O'Connor would go down for quite a long stretch. He'd make sure he kept four or five paces behind her.

She flung open the door but the pub was so fuggy with cigarette smoke that she stood just inside the room rubbing her smarting eyes. Gradually every head was turned towards her. Women never entered the saloon bar of a pub. They used the snugs and parlours and this one looked as though she shouldn't be here at all, not the way she was dressed.

Bernie Maguire was the first to recognise her. 'Bloody 'ell, it's little Alice O'Connor! 'Ere, Tip, it's your Alice!'

Alice turned on him 'You've got a bloody short memory, Bernie Maguire. One minute you're laying him out cold because he'd half killed me, the next you're propping up the same bloody bar!'

Tip turned and glared at her from small, bloodshot eyes.

Alice took a step towards him. 'So, Da, this is where the money went. Buying bevvies for half of Scottie Road! It was *my* money, Da! I sent it for Mam and the kids, not for you!'

'Don't yer talk like that ter me, girl!' he growled. She might never have been away. There was no word of greeting or surprise, let alone regret or remorse.

'I want it back. I want every bloody penny of it back, Da. So you can start by having a whip round from all your mates here!'

'Yer 'ardfaced little bitch! Don't yer bloody shame me in front of me mates. In front of the whole bloody neighbourhood!' Tip yelled.

Alice held her ground. From the corner of her eye she could just see the sleeve of a dark blue uniform jacket in the open doorway.

'I don't need to shame you, Da! You're a bloody disgrace to yourself! You're a no good, idle, vicious drunk and you always have been!' she yelled back, her cheeks burning, her eyes full of rage.

Tip lunged at her, catching her a glancing blow on the shoulder.

She stepped back. 'Go on, Da! Belt me, like you've always done, I don't care. I want that money back and I want it now!'

This time Tip's aim was better and the blow caught her on the side of her head. She staggered back, falling against Bernie Maguire. Some of the men began to mutter their disapproval, others nodded grimly. A man couldn't let a bit of a girl like that carry on the way she was doing and get away with it.

None of them had noticed Jack Phillips in the shadows. But as he moved quickly forward the customers of The Widows fell back – the policeman was well over six feet tall and built like a barn.

'I want him arrested for assaulting me and for stealing my money!'

A howl of rage erupted from Tip but no one went to help him as his arm was twisted up his back and handcuffs were snapped on. 'Tobias O'Connor, I'm arresting you for common assault and the fraudulent misappropriation of money. You have the right to remain silent . . .'

The crowd drew in a collective breath and Alice smiled grimly. 'You'll get at least five years' hard labour in Walton for that, Da!' she yelled as he was led away.

'Yer shouldn't 'ave done that, girl,' Bernie Maguire muttered.

Alice turned on him. 'He's a thief! He as good as stole that money from me. It was for Mam, not him. When did he ever give me anything except black eyes, bruises and cracked ribs? We all starved, froze, and got beaten up for years and you know it. Mother of God! You've belted him yourself often enough.' She turned away from him, her gaze sweeping over the assembly of grim-faced men. 'You're all the bloody same! You're all in here enjoying yourselves and what are your wives and kids doing? Taking in washing? Trying to sell bootlaces or matches? Begging in the streets, the way I did? You make me sick, the lot of you!'

'Watch yer mouth, girl,' the landlord warned quietly.

'I'll have the whole bloody lot of you arrested if anyone

so much as raises a hand to me or any of mine!'

'Jesus, Alice, you're just askin' for trouble! Go home, girl,' Bernie Maguire urged.

'I wouldn't stay here if you paid me – and people do pay me, to sing in theatres and at posh balls. I mixed with the best. I entertained the high and bloody mighty on the *Aquitania* but I'll never forget that I sang barefoot and in rags in the streets of this city while he was in here, drinking!'

She took a deep breath once she was outside. She could hear the raised voices from inside and she smiled. Well, she'd certainly given them a piece of her mind and they'd stood and taken it, something they would never have done from their own wives and daughters. But then their wives and daughters didn't have money behind them, or the self-confidence it brought.

A police sergeant had joined Jack Phillips. 'Are you the person accusing him?' he asked Alice.

'I am, and your officer saw him belt ... hit me, and he took my money too.'

'You'll have to come to the station then, miss.'

'Look, I've just got home. I came in on the *Aquitania* and my mam needs some help. Can I come down later, please? He's not going to run off or complain, now is he?'

He pursed his lips but finally nodded. 'Don't be any longer than an hour.'

She flashed a smile at Jack and set off for Benledi Street. When she got home Nelly was still out so she decided to walk round to Holden's and meet her. Holden's was the nearest of the two corner shops whose proprietors had been good to them over the years. As she turned the corner, she nearly collided with her mother who was laden down with bags of shopping.

'You should have seen Ivy Holden's face when she saw the five-pound note! I told her that me dream's out, that you'd come home and you'd done well for yourself too.'

Nelly peered closely at her daughter. 'What's the matter with your face, Alice?'

'Da belted me in The Widows, so I had him arrested for assault. There was a policeman passing at the time, one who has chats with our Lizzie, so he told me.'

Nelly stared at her in horror. 'Oh, Jesus, Mary and Joseph! *You* had him arrested!'

Alice took her mother's arm. 'Mam, we'll all be better off with him in Walton. They'll make him work, and work flaming hard, and there won't be any whisky in there!'

'But Alice—'

'Mam, you've suffered for years. He's battered you, he's kept you short or, more often, given you no flaming money at all. He's no good. We're better off without him.'

'Oh, God, how long will he get? Will you have to go to court?'

'About five years, longer I hope, and yes, I'll have to go to Hatton Garden when they bring him up before the stipendiary magistrate. In fact I'll have to go down to Rose Hill in an hour. But stop worrying, Mam!'

'Alice, you shouldn't have done that. He *is* your da.'

'And I've rued it every single day of my life, except for these last two years. I just don't understand you, Mam. He had it coming to him and we're all going to have a better life. Especially you. We're going to move to a nice house with good furniture. We'll have proper beds with sheets and blankets and we'll have thick soft towels. You'll all have new clothes and you'll never have to worry about rent, or coal or anything else ever again. I've got work. I'm going to sing in the Empire and the Rotunda and then ... then I'm going to London and I'll be a big star, Mam. But I'll tell you all about it – Charleston, the *Aquitania* – every single thing, when we've got a fire going and had something decent to eat.'

Nelly shook her head as Alice took one of the hemp bags, lent by Ivy Holden, and led her towards Benledi

Street. She couldn't take it in, she couldn't understand it all. Alice had just got home and yet now she was talking about going to London and being famous and rich. And she had changed. This wasn't her skinny, ragged little Alice. This girl had just had her father arrested in a pub full of his mates and neighbours.

They reached the front door and Alice pushed it open and smiled.

'We're going to have a proper home, Mam. Something you've never had in all the years you've lived here.'

Nelly felt the tears well up in her eyes. She squeezed Alice's hand and a slow, uncertain smile spread over her face.

Chapter Twenty

By the time Eddy and Mary got home from school, there was a meal on the table and a fire roaring up the chimney.

They stared at their sister, open-mouthed.

'Is that our Alice?' Eddy asked incredulously.

'Yes, it's me, lad, all the way from America,' she laughed. He seemed to have grown taller but he still looked pale and undernourished. Then she hugged Mary and swung her round in delight.

'You're ten now! Ten!'

'Alice, where did you get them clothes? They must 'ave cost a fortune.' Eddy reverently stroked the fur cuffs of her coat that had been flung over the back of the armchair.

'Oh, don't you worry, you'll be dressed up to kill by this time tomorrow. All of you. There'll be no more police hand-outs. Now come on, get stuck in.'

They needed no second telling. Nelly tried to exercise some control and stop them cramming the food into their mouths with their hands, snatching pieces of bread and butter like wild animals. They'd never tasted butter before. She moved quickly round the table slapping hands and clipping ears.

'God, Mam, you'd need an army general to put some manners on this lot,' Alice sighed, 'but I suppose there's not been much on the table, has there?'

Nelly shook her head.

'Well, all that's over now and Mam, will you please sit down and eat.'

'I'll have a bit later on.' Nelly watched with satisfaction as the food disappeared.

'No you won't, Mam. That's what you've always done. You starved yourself to feed us. Now sit down and tuck in while there's still something left to tuck into.'

Her mother shook her head. 'Old habits die hard, Alice.'

'Is our Jimmy working, Mam?' she asked, when Nelly had finally sat down.

'Not really. Nothing steady, like. He gets a few days, now and then.'

'Where is he now?'

'Shovelling coal into sacks, down at the docks some-where. Lots of lads do it. It doesn't pay much, a few coppers, but it's better than nowt.'

While the children ate, quarrelling over such luxuries as cakes and biscuits, with Nelly constantly admonishing them, Alice was deep in thought. She'd forgotten what living in number ten Benledi Street was like – the total absence of the bare necessities, never mind anything approaching comfort, the fact that there were no cleaning materials of any kind, dishes, pans or utensils. You've got a short memory, girl, Alice thought to herself grimly. There were still no beds either. The house smelled of damp, unwashed bodies and half-dry old woollen jumpers that hung on a rack and pulley near the ceiling. She couldn't stay here. She would *not* sleep on a bug-infested mattress. She'd have to go to a hotel for a few days. The Stork in Queen Square wasn't bad. And she couldn't take them to Sturla's, the local department store, in their present condition. They were filthy, their clothes grubby, creased and torn. No, they'd have to have a bath and probably their hair needed delousing. God, how did I ever live like this? she asked herself. Coming home had suddenly turned into a humbling experience.

Nelly leaned back, replete, and surveyed the table. Not a crumb was left. It was a good job Alice had saved something for Lizzie, Agnes and Jimmy. She got to her feet.

'What are you going to do now, Mam?'

'Clear this lot away.'

'Oh no you're not! We're going to take all these chipped mugs, enamelled plates, the old stew pan and kettle and the other few bits in the scullery and chuck them out. In fact we're going to chuck everything out into the yard.' She turned to her brothers and sister. 'Right, you lot, down to Burrows Gardens Baths. Buy some paraffin and Durback soap on the way. Soak your hair with the paraffin then give it a good wash with the Durback. That should shift the nits. And then we're going to Great Homer Street and you're all getting rigged out. You too, Mam.' Alice took her purse from her bag and delved into it. She'd changed her money from dollars to pounds on the ship.

'What about Lizzie, Agnes and Jimmy?' Nelly asked.

'We'll be back by the time they get in. My clothes should fit the girls if there's no time to get them new ones tonight and we'll just have to guess Jimmy's size. Do they stay open late, Mam?'

'Until eight on Fridays.'

'Good. I'll buy beds and bedding too and a decent tea service and new pans. They can deliver them – I should think they'll be delighted to. It'll be a big order and all in cash!'

'Are you coming with us to the baths or will we come back here?' Nelly asked, still slightly dazed.

'I'll wait for the others. You come back here for me.'

Alice started to clear the kitchen. She kept three chipped enamel plates for Lizzie, Agnes and Jimmy's supper and also three badly discoloured mugs for their tea. The pitifully small and battered collection of things that Nelly had managed to acquire and keep she dumped in the back yard which was already full of rubbish. Then she went upstairs. Nothing had changed much. The damp patches were still on the walls, but they'd grown bigger. The black mould still surrounded the ill-fitting window frame that was so rotten it would be easy to push it out altogether. The old straw-stuffed mattresses, covered in their dirty ticking and piles of rags that served as bedclothes, were still on the floor. Tears pricked her eyes as she thought of the sheer luxury she'd lived in for the past two years. Well, she couldn't move this lot by herself, so she'd wait until they all came back from Sturla's and they'd chuck them into the yard too. She felt no qualms about having her da arrested. Not when she looked around these rooms.

She heard the front door open and turned to make her way down the stairs, which in itself was perilous, most of the boards having been used for firewood. Lizzie was talking to someone and the other voice was that of a man.

As she came into the hall, Lizzie stopped dead. 'Holy Mother of God! Is that you, Alice?'

Alice jumped down the last two steps and flung her arms round her sister. 'Oh, Lizzie! Lizzie! I've missed you so much, I really have.' She could feel every one of her sister's ribs, and the bones of her shoulders dug into her.

'Alice! Alice, it's . . . it's . . . great! God, look at you!' Lizzie stood back, still holding Alice's hands, while she surveyed her sister's outfit.

Over Lizzie's shoulder, Alice saw the huge figure of Jack Phillips. He was smiling.

'I'll come down to the station soon, I promise.'

'It'll wait for a while,' he answered.

'Why have you got to go to the police station?' Lizzie asked anxiously.

'Because this afternoon I had Da arrested. He belted me and he'd used all the money I sent for Mam. Constable Phillips here marched him down to the nick.'

Lizzie turned and looked at Jack for confirmation.

He nodded.

'I hope he rots in Walton for ever!' Alice declared. 'Come on and get your supper. Where's our Agnes? Is there any sign of Jimmy yet?'

'Oh, Agnes gets in a bit later, she's got further to walk. Our Jimmy's got a few days' coal shovelling.'

'I know, Mam told me.'

'He'll work until he drops and he'll be filthy when he does get in.'

As if to prove her point, the back door opened and Jimmy stood there covered from head to foot in coal dust, his shoulders sagging with weariness.

'Don't touch our Alice, the state of you!' Lizzie cried.

'God Almighty, Alice! Alice, it *is* you!'

'Just sit down and get that down you.' Alice ruffled the short, badly cut hair and instantly a small cloud of black dust wafted over her hand. 'Then you can go down to Burrows Gardens Baths like everyone else. When they get back we're going to Sturla's to buy half the shop. I've chucked everything out.' She grinned and then turned to Jack Phillips. 'Do you think you could give me a hand with the stuff upstairs? There's not much but it's bound to be alive with bugs. They'll all have proper beds and bedding tonight.'

'But won't the bugs get into all the new stuff too?' Lizzie enquired, tucking into a plate full of steak and kidney with mashed potatoes and gravy, all cooked in pans borrowed from Mary O'Hanlon and Jinny Thomas.

'No. We're not staying here, we're moving.' Alice looked up at Jack Phillips. 'Do you think you could find out if there are any houses, in a better street than this, to rent immediately?'

'There's a house at the bottom of our street, Media Street, that's empty and has been for two weeks.'

'Do you know the landlord?'

'Very well. I can ask him tonight, when I finish my shift.'

Lizzie looked at her sister, so confident and in control. 'Alice, Mam might not want to leave here,' she said carefully. 'She might not want to go away from all her friends, all the neighbours who've been so good to us. They've not had much themselves but they've kept us out of the workhouse for years.'

'Lizzie, it's not miles away!'

'It's not far, just off Kirkdale Road,' Jack agreed quietly.

Alice flashed him a grateful smile.

Lizzie, too, smiled at him. 'We'll be neighbours then.'

Alice noted the look on both their faces and felt pleased. It seemed as though Lizzie had found someone special at last and he didn't seem to mind the state of the house or Lizzie's old and faded clothes.

'Where did you get all the money from, Alice?' Lizzie asked.

'I worked for it, at first. Then the club was closed down. They have a stupid law over there, called Prohibition. No one's allowed to drink, at least not in clubs and bars. They don't have pubs.'

'It's not so flaming stupid, they could do with one like that here,' Lizzie said grimly.

The front door slammed and Alice took the second plate from the oven in the range.

Agnes stood in the doorway, silent, unable to believe her eyes.

'It's me, Agnes. I've come home. Haven't you grown up!'

'I'm sixteen now. Oh, Alice!'

There was yet another tearfully joyous reunion and while Agnes ate, Lizzie explained all Alice's plans. Jack and Alice were moving the mattresses into the yard and Jack said they should burn the lot, they were a health hazard.

'The whole house is a health hazard,' Alice agreed. 'They should burn the whole street to the ground.'

'I know, but they won't. Will you come with me to the station now that we've cleared upstairs?'

Alice sighed. 'I will and it'll be a pleasure. In fact it'll be pure joy to see him go down.' She remembered Mike telling her how he'd felt when he'd arrived on the doorstep of the house on Rutledge Street. Well, she couldn't belt the living daylights out of her da, it was physically impossible, but this was the next best thing. She turned to Lizzie. 'Look, while I go down to Rose Hill, you and Agnes get a wash and wait for Mam. Tell her I won't be long.'

Alice picked up her coat and followed Jack Phillips out. As they walked along Scotland Road, she questioned him. 'It's strange you being friends with our Lizzie,' she ventured.

'I knocked her over, one dark winter's night. I picked her up and took her home.' He shrugged. 'Ever since, we've been friends. I take her out on trips now and then. She deserves a bit of pleasure.'

Alice looked up at him. 'Just now and then?'

Jack grinned. 'Well, as often as I can. Incidentally, I had a bit of a word with your da about a year ago.'

Her eyes grew hard. 'I could kill him, I could, and with my own two hands!'

'No, you couldn't. Look what he did to you today. Your face will be black and blue tomorrow and anyway he's not worth it.'

'I don't care about my face. It's nothing to what Mam and the rest of us had to put up with. That's why I left. He half-killed me and he once threw our poor little Mary out into the street. Bernie Maguire belted hell out of him both times, but give Bernie a couple of glasses of the hard stuff and his memory goes. You saw that this afternoon. But Mam says Da's not laid a finger on anyone for a year now. Your "bit of a word" seems to have worked.'

247

Jack smiled. 'Maybe. Anyway, you look as though you've done well for yourself.'

'I have. I didn't at first. I was down to my last few cents. Then I got a job, singing in a nightclub – I think they might have them in London. And I got . . . er . . . lodgings in a house the like of which you'd never believe. I got lucky. There was a gentleman who helped me. He was very kind.' She looked up at him. 'He was older than me, very rich, but he came from the Dublin slums originally. He understood me and what I'd been through. Because I could sing we got asked to parties, soirées, and I sang in the intermission at one of the grandest balls in Charleston. I sang on the ship, too, on the way home, and now I've got an agent. When I get this lot sorted out I'm going to have to go and see the managers of both the Roundy and the Empire.'

Jack nodded. 'You always had a beautiful voice, Alice. All you needed was a chance and you got it.'

They'd arrived at the red-brick building and he held the door open for her.

'Oh, at last! The pair of you have decided to come in.' The desk sergeant was openly sarcastic and none too pleased.

Alice glared at him, not in the least intimidated. 'I had things to attend to. Things more important than my da.'

'Right then, let's get it all down on paper. Phillips, I'll take her statement, you do your own. Madam, do you want to see meladdo downstairs? He's swearing and yelling like a trooper.'

'I never want to see him again – except perhaps in court. I sent fifteen pounds a month home, for two years. It was expressly for my mother. I sent it in letters addressed to her, not him, but after the first one he went to Victoria Street and told them in future he'd collect them. He's managed to get through three hundred and sixty pounds. He misappropriated it. They never saw a penny of it.'

After the formalities, she went out and hailed a passing taxi. She knew it was extravagant, it wasn't far to walk, but she was running out of time.

They were all waiting, and Lizzie and Agnes had managed to give themselves a good wash down in the scullery with a bar of mild Fairy soap Nelly had bought.

It didn't take long to get to Great Homer Street. 'Right, we've got an hour. Mam, you see to the beds, bedding, towels and furniture. I'm going to find the floorwalker and explain everything. If necessary I'll speak to the manager himself.'

Nelly took her arm. 'Alice, luv, there's no need to go mad, we don't need too many things. There's the future to think of.'

'Mam, the future is taken care of. I've got money and I'll earn more, so stop worrying.'

Nelly was still cautious. 'It's just that . . .'

'I know, Mam, it's like being a kid let loose in a toy shop, that's the way I felt. Go on, pick what you want.'

The floorwalker respectfully accompanied Nelly as she selected her purchases while the manager himself accompanied Alice. She'd been living abroad, she was in the entertainment business, she told him confidently. When she'd arrived home this morning on the *Aquitania* – first class of course, she stressed – she'd found her family in dire straits due to the selfish malevolence of her father. She would be buying furniture, beds, linen, household goods and clothes for them all. She would be most grateful if he could store most of the furniture for her as in the next few days they would be moving house, but would it be at all possible to have some delivered tonight? She was dreadfully sorry it was so late. Of course, everything would be paid for in cash.

The manager, an avaricious gleam in his eye, said he'd

recall the driver from home, or drive the van himself if necessary. And they were not to rush choosing things, time meant nothing, nothing at all.

She flashed him a brilliant smile. 'That's very good of you, but we don't want to inconvenience you too much. I'm hoping to appear at both the Rotunda and the Empire before I go to London at the end of the month. If I do, there will be complimentary tickets for yourself and your wife.' Good God, she thought as her little speech came to an end, is this really *me* speaking like this? So confidently, even with a touch of arrogance and to a man who two years ago would have had her ejected if she'd set foot in the place.

The van driver came back and with the help of the manager and the floorwalker loaded most of the things into the van. Staggering underneath a pile of boxes, Nelly, Lizzie, Agnes and the kids waited for Alice to pay the manager and thank him again.

She counted out the large white banknotes then held out a gloved hand. It had cost her one hundred and fifty pounds, a small fortune, but it brought her close to tears when she saw all their faces glowing with pleasure and excitement.

The manager beamed. 'Miss O'Connor, it's been a pleasure, a real pleasure to have your patronage. I hope you'll come back if there's anything you've overlooked.'

'Of course, and I won't forget the tickets.'

Jack Phillips joined them in Benledi Street straight after work and helped them get the beds up. Nelly shook out the crisp white sheets and tucked them neatly round the new mattresses. Then she covered them with the soft blankets, fluffed up the pillows and finished off with the heavy cotton bedspreads patterned in different colours. Most of the clothes were left unpacked, as there were no wardrobes.

'How many bedrooms does this house in Media Street

have?' Alice asked, as she rummaged in a box full of straw for the new tea set.

'Three. There's a parlour, a kitchen, a scullery and—'

'A yard and a privy, like this, I suppose,' Alice cut in.

'Yes, but bigger and in far better condition. There's a coal bunker in the yard and a wash house.'

Nelly looked up. 'Oh, I never got a mangle or a dolly tub or a washboard!'

'Mam, for God's sake don't start worrying over the washing yet. The boys can have one room, Mary and Agnes can have another, and you and our Lizzie can have the third.'

'What about you?'

'I'll be staying at the Stork, Mam, at least to sleep. It's nearer for the Empire and . . . and at the end of the month I'm going to have to go to London.' She put on a falsely cheerful smile. 'But let's not think about that now. We all deserve a cup of tea, it's been a tiring night.'

When Jack had gone, promising to do what he could about the house, and the younger kids had gone to bed, wearing pyjamas and nightdresses for the first time in their lives, Alice urged Nelly to go to bed too.

'Mam, you're worn out. Go on up, please. Get a good night's sleep, you've no more worries.'

When Nelly had gone, Alice, Lizzie and Agnes sat in front of the range in the dismal kitchen, the glowing embers of the fire and the one gas jet on the wall giving a poor illusion of comfort.

'Will you really be going to London, Alice?' Agnes asked. She was pale and thin, her light brown hair making her look like a younger version of Lizzie.

'Yes. I'll have to sing in the music halls before I can get a part in a real show and I'll live in digs. Victor Hardman is going to arrange it all. What are you going to do, Agnes?'

Agnes shrugged her thin shoulders. 'Carry on working

in the match factory, I suppose, until I can find something a bit better. I've always wanted to do shop work but no one would even look at me the way I was dressed.'

'Jack told me you can do anything if you really want to,' Lizzie said. 'He reminded me about Abbie Kerrigan, Dee Chatterton, Maggie Higgins and Hannah Harvey.'

'I'll bet you've got as much money as Her Ladyship now,' Agnes said, awestruck. Alice thought of Hannah Harvey. You really couldn't get much higher in society than the Countess of Ashenden and Hannah was the only really rich person she knew much about; then she remembered Mike. She smiled and shook her head. 'No, but I know someone who has. Mike O'Farrell – he became my guardian, and then my husband.'

'Your husband!' Agnes almost shrieked the words.

'No. Not really my husband. It was just to stop any gossip and we got invited to more places being a "respectable couple".' She didn't want to dwell on her departure from the house on Rutledge Street so she changed the subject. 'What about you, Lizzie? That Jack Phillips seems fond of you.'

'I think he is but I don't know for sure. He's been so good to me – to all of us, Alice.'

'If he asked you, would you marry him?' Alice asked quietly.

'I don't know. He lives with his mam, and . . . she might not take to me.'

'So what? It's him you'd be marrying, not her. Besides, she might be glad of someone to look after her in her old age.'

'Oh, I don't know, Alice. It's been such a—'

'Long, tiring day,' Alice finished for her. 'For us all. Go on to bed, the pair of you. I'm going to get a taxi to the Stork.'

She hugged them both, clinging on to Lizzie. 'Oh, Lizzie,' she whispered, 'I'm so happy I came home. I got the chance of a new life when I went away and now I want you all to look on tomorrow as the beginning of your new lives.'

'It will be, Alice, and now, if Jack asks, I will marry him. You see, before, I couldn't leave Mam. Agnes and me were the only wage earners and Agnes doesn't get much. Mam did a bit of office cleaning, when she could get it, but she's worn out, Alice.'

'I know, Lizzie. I haven't forgotten what life was like in this house and I never will. But we're all going up in the world now and I'll be so happy if you do get married. You deserve to be happy, you've had a rotten life so far.'

'Go on and get to the hotel or they'll be shut,' Lizzie urged with tears of pleasure in her eyes.

Chapter Twenty-One

To Alice's frustration, the departure from Benledi Street was delayed as the landlord of the house in Media Street was away on business for a few days. Alice fretted but Lizzie told her to stop it.

'It's only a few days, Alice, for God's sake,' she scolded.

'But I wanted everyone out of here before I do my first show. Victor's arranged everything, every detail. Mr Gregson at the Rotunda is expecting me to call to see him soon.'

'Well, if you don't go and see those blokes soon, there'll be no show. At least not one with you in it.'

She was right, Alice mused as she walked along Scotland Road towards the Rotunda.

When she reached it, it was closed but she remembered the back entrance, the stage door.

The same old man was in his little box, reading the *Daily Post*.

'Is Mr Gregson in?' she asked.

He looked up annoyed, then his expression changed when he took in her appearance. 'Yes. Who wants 'im?'

'Miss Alice O'Connor. He'll be expecting me.'

She waited impatiently until he came back and then ushered her along the corridor and into a small office.

Gregson greeted her effusively. 'Miss O'Connor, Alice, I'm delighted to meet you. I was getting a little worried in case you'd changed your mind. Victor wrote and told me how talented you are. When I telephoned him in London he couldn't have been more enthusiastic or confident. Will you audition for me?'

'Of course.'

She followed him down the labyrinth of corridors until they finally arrived on the stage. The atmosphere was strange. Very quiet, very hushed, almost like a church, she thought.

'What kind of a repertoire do you have, Miss O'Connor? Victor and I didn't really discuss it in detail.'

'Everything from "Beautiful Dreamer", "'Bye, 'Bye Blackbird" to the Easter Hymn from Mascagni's *Cavalleria Rusticana*.'

'Well, we won't need that one. Have you a favourite piece?'

'I have,' she smiled, 'but I don't think you'd be interested. Shall we try "Whispering" and then "Always"?'

He nodded his agreement. They were popular songs.

From somewhere in the dark nether regions of the wings a man appeared and sat at the piano. Gregson disappeared down the steps that led to the seats in the front stalls.

She looked up. She could see nothing. There were no lights burning in the auditorium, just a couple on the stage itself. She went through the two numbers with ease, then, just to support her earlier statement and without the accompaniment of the piano, she sang 'The Last Rose of Summer'. In the silent theatre and without any instrumental backing it seemed almost celestial.

Gregson virtually ran up the steps. 'Vic said you were good, but I never thought you were *that* good. Can you start next weekend? One of our regulars has let us down. Friday, Saturday and Sunday?'

'For how many weeks?'

'That depends. Vic said you wanted to do the Empire

as well and then I believe you're off to London.'

'I'll do two weekends here and I have to go and meet the manager at the Empire. With luck I'll do two week-ends there, and then as I promised Victor Hardman I'll have to go to London.'

Gregson rubbed his hands together, thinking of the increase in profits from the box office. 'I'll get the posters done today and advertise in the *Echo*.'

'You may not need to advertise. I should think there'll be half the neighbourhood here once word gets round that one of their own's on. I was born and brought up off Scottie Road. In Benledi Street.'

He looked at her in amazement. She wore a fine wool crepe suit in forest green, trimmed with jade green. Her hat was jade green velour with a huge dark green bow on one side. She wore silk stockings and dark green leather pumps with a T bar across the instep. Her bag and gloves, both leather, both dark green, completed the outfit.

'Would it be possible to have some complimentary tick-ets for my family?' she asked.

'How many would you like?'

'Is sixteen too many? Best seats?'

'Just for Friday then.'

She smiled. 'Shall we work out a proper programme now or would you like me to do it and send it in to you?'

'We'll work it out now. Will you need to rehearse?'

'On Wednesday and Thursday, in the morning.'

As she followed him back to his office, her heart began to beat faster as she remembered the night she'd crept in and seen Letty Lewis.

It was as though he read her mind. 'How would you like to be introduced – billed?'

She smiled broadly. 'As the Liverpool Songbird.'

They moved house on Tuesday. Alice was relieved to have had Tip's trial over, and him safely in Walton Gaol, before the family started their new life in Media Street. She had ordered a van in good time to take all the new furnishings and clothes.

Mary O'Hanlon, Jinny Thomas and Ethel Maguire, Nelly's closest neighbours and friends over the years, came to see them off.

'God love yer, Nelly, but yer deserve all this.' Mary O'Hanlon took Nelly's hand and squeezed it.

'Yer do, girl,' Ethel sniffed, 'and we'll all miss yer. There's no good us sayin' we'll have happy memories of the good times, 'cos there bloody well weren't any.'

'Oh, give it a rest, Ethel, you'll 'ave *me* in tears next. I've lived here all me married life.' Mary's voice was full of emotion.

'Well, yer not going ter live over the water or out in the wilds, are yer? It's only down the road a bit an' I wish our Peggy would up an 'ave our Joe nicked. I've 'ad almost as many clouts as you 'ave, Nell.' Jinny smiled grimly, trying to lighten the atmosphere.

'Will I get our Lizzie's feller to give him a talking to, if you know what I mean, Jinny?'

'It wouldn't do no good, Nelly.' Small-boned, with rounded shoulders, Jinny had a slight hump on her back from being constantly hunched against the weather, and from hard work. 'God, I wish they'd take "obey" and "until death do us part" out of the bloody wedding vows. There's been no "better", it's all been flaming "worse". Is that scuffer really your Lizzie's feller?'

'I think so, although neither of them have said anything,' Nelly replied.

'And your Alice is on the Roundy Friday, Saturday and Sunday. God, I'd love ter see her, Nelly,' Mary sighed, folding her arms under her ample chest.

'Get the sixpence off your Maggie, she's working, and it's the chance of a lifetime. I'm going ter gerra loan off our Peggy,' Jinny announced.

'Wait until the news gets around, Nelly, the whole of Scottie Road will be there, up in the gods of course! Your Alice. God, everyone will beg, steal and borrow just to see her. The pawn shops will be bustin'! Your little Alice up there on the stage!' Mary shook her head in wonderment.

'I still can't get over it myself. These last days have been like . . . like a dream.'

'Then keep on dreamin', Nelly, girl. There's not many around here who even have dreams, never mind see them come true.'

'Mam, the taxi's waiting and our Eddy is actin' up!' Agnes called, resplendent in one of her new outfits. From her new cotton knickers edged with a bit of lace, to her smart blue cardigan suit, silk stockings and navy shoes and hat, she felt every inch a lady.

Mary nudged Ethel with her elbow. 'Don't those two girls look different with their hair cut short? Our Maggie's been wanting to get hers done and I've 'ad murder with 'er time an' again. Now I've seen those two and what's more she'll see them, I might as well save me breath. I 'ave ter say it takes years off your Lizzie, Nelly.'

'Mam! He's kicking the toes out of 'is new boots!'

Nelly sighed. 'Some things never change, do they?'

Before she could move, Alice came out of the house and slammed the door shut behind her.

'Well, that's it. Goodbye number ten Benledi Street – and good riddance!' She frowned as she saw the pushing and shoving that was going on between Eddy and Jimmy. She moved smartly and clipped her youngest brother over the ear.

'You behave yourself, Jimmy O'Connor! I'm having no messing about from you! Get in that taxi cab with Mary and Agnes and leave our Eddy alone or you'll get another belt around the ear and that's a promise!'

'Ah, eh! It was 'im that started it! It's not fair!'

259

'Well, she's not changed much either, 'as she, Nell?' Ethel chuckled. 'Always the one with the backchat, always the one ter stand up to 'er da. She's always had guts, 'as your Alice. She gets them from you. Well, good luck to 'er!'

'Come on, Mam, everyone's ready.' Alice hugged all three women briefly, heedless of their grubby, greasy pinafores. 'There's no amount of money can buy what you've done for us and given us over the years. Mam's not far away, you come and visit whenever you like. And if anyone starts knocking you about, tell our Lizzie and she'll get Jack Phillips to have a bit of a word. It worked wonders with my da.'

Nelly echoed Alice's sentiments as she hugged them in turn, wiping away a tear. Mary sniffed and both Jinny and Ethel were clearly fighting with their emotions.

'I'll have some tickets sent down for you – all of you!' Alice called as the cab pulled away from the kerb with the usual following of small, grubby, shouting kids.

The three women watched the cab turn the corner.

'Do yer think she'll be 'appy in Media Street, Ethel?'

Ethel raised her eyes skywards, pursing her lips and shaking her head. 'Jaysus, Mary, it's not the bloody moon she's gone to! I'd swap places any day of the week. All that furniture and more being kept in Sturla's. Every comfort, no worries except what yer going to 'ave fer tea an' should yer wash the antimacassars on the sofa in the parlour today or tomorrow. I've got young Vi and Vinny Murphy and the baby livin' in my parlour. Well, it's no use standing 'ere jangling while the front step's as black as the hobs of hell an' he's still snoring in 'is pit, the idle, useless git!'

Chaos still seemed to reign the next day in the new house as there was so much to unpack and arrange. Alice arrived at half past eight, to see the kids got to school and that everything was being sorted out before she went for rehearsal. She found Nelly sitting upright on the brown hide sofa in the parlour. In addition to the sofa there were two armchairs, a plant stand with its glossy-leaved aspidistra in a brass pot, a sideboard that Alice planned to adorn with a lovely set of crystal comprising a fruit bowl, a biscuit barrel and cheese dish, and a glass-fronted cabinet, as yet bare, as were the mantel shelf and the walls which were waiting for the pictures and bric-a-brac Nelly had chosen.

'Mam, what are you doing in here? Are you feeling all right?'

Nelly turned to her. 'A parlour, Alice! Me with a parlour and it full of furniture. It'll be too grand to use, Alice. I'd be frit to death of the kids smashing something.'

Alice took her hand. 'You'll get used to it all, Mam. Mrs O'Hanlon and Jinny Thomas and Ethel Maguire will be calling in to see you. You can have your cups of tea in here.'

Nelly was horrified. 'What! Use that good china that's going to go in that cabinet – when we find it.'

'Oh, Mam, it was bought to be used, not just admired.'

'They won't expect it, Alice. They'd be terrified of breaking it. No, I'll use the other stuff.'

Alice smiled at her. 'At least you've got a choice now, Mam. Will we have a cup of tea before I go to rehearsal?'

Nelly got up. 'You know half the neighbourhood will be there, luv, on the night.'

'I know, so I'd better do my best and wear my party frock!' Alice laughed.

They decided that she would sing an Irish medley, the area being predominantly Irish Catholic. She chose 'The Rose of Tralee', 'The Londonderry Air' and 'I'll Take You Home Again, Kathleen' for her first spot. Her second would be livelier, a selection of the songs she'd sung and heard in America. She'd thought long and hard about the

Irish selection; the first two had been such favourites of Mike's. She knew they'd go down well with the audience, but would she be all right? Would she break down? She'd been so busy that she'd hardly had time to think about either Mike or David. David was away, that much she knew, having scanned the shipping pages in the *Journal of Commerce*. But perhaps it would be best in a way. If he were to come to see her at all she'd prefer it to be at the Empire; that really was Liverpool's premier theatre.

She'd decided to wear the green chiffon dress she'd worn for Maura O'Hare's soirée, and was just fastening the band of green ribbon decorated with diamanté stones when Mrs Harris, the dresser, came in.

'It's not time yet, is it?'

'No, luv. But there's a lad out there asking for you. A bit scruffy, he is, but he said he sailed with you on the *Castlemaine* and he's got a present for you.'

She leaped to her feet. 'Georgie Tate! It's got to be Georgie Tate! Oh, bring him in, Mrs H, bring him in.'

He'd hardly changed but she could tell he'd tried to look his best for tonight. He stood awkwardly in the doorway, clutching a cardboard box.

'Georgie! Oh, come here and give me a hug! I never thought I'd ever see you again.'

He put the box on the floor as she threw her arms round him.

'You've made it, Alice. I told yer it'd be all right in America.'

'It nearly wasn't, but yes, it's all turned out great.' She smiled at his awed expression. 'Are you still sailing on the *Castlemaine*?'

He nodded. 'But I got a bit of promotion, like.'

'You're not the cabin boy now?'

'No. I learned how to fire the donkey boiler and when old 'Arry died, they gave me 'is job.'

'So you've got on yourself then?'

'But not as well as you 'ave, Alice.' He remembered the box and picking it up pushed it into her arms. 'It's for you.'

She opened the lid and a radiant smile lit up her face. 'Oh, Georgie! Isn't it beautiful!' Nestling in the box on some straw was a tiny black and white kitten.

'It's one of the last litter old Mog had.'

She stroked its downy little head. 'Had?'

'We found her dead one morning in the corner of the galley she always slept in. But she'd had a busy life, and she went peacefully.'

'Oh, Georgie, Mog was my lucky charm and I often thought of her.'

'I know, that's why I brought her son for yer.'

'Mrs Harris will look after him until the show's over. I'm going to call him Georgie to remind me of you.'

He went bright red from the tips of his ears to his forehead. 'Would you . . . would you sing me mam's song, Alice? Please?'

A slight crease appeared between her eyebrows. The programme was set; still, she couldn't disappoint him. She had promised. She smiled. 'Of course I will. I'll sing it first – just for you.'

They both heard her five-minute call and the sharp rap on the dressing-room door.

'You'd best get to your seat quickly, or we'll both be late. And thank you, Georgie.' She hugged him again.

She had a quick word with the stage manager, who nodded, and then went to consult the conductor of the orchestra.

She could only see the first two or three rows, the lights were so bright. The rest of the theatre seemed to be in total darkness, but she knew they were there – all of them. When she was announced, when Mr Gregson said, 'Ladies and gentlemen, it's my pleasure to introduce to you Miss Alice O'Connor, the Liverpool Songbird,' her heart leaped and she nervously fingered the gold pendant Mike had bought her.

Gregson's words drew a great response. She walked to the front of the stage where the microphone was placed.

'Ladies and gentlemen, there's an addition to the programme. A request. A promise I made two years ago to a Liverpool lad who befriended me.'

Nelly and Lizzie, in the front row of the dress circle, exchanged puzzled glances.

Alice carried on, 'It was his mother's favourite. So, for Georgie Tate who taught it to me, "If You Were The Only Girl In The World".'

She stepped back and nodded to the conductor.

As she sang, the memories came flooding back. The nights she'd sat with Georgie on the deck of the *Castlemaine* when he'd taught her this song and others. Then she'd been dirty, ignorant, but full of hope.

The applause was loud in her ears and she threw her arms wide with joy as the opening bars of 'The Rose of Tralee' were played.

She forced herself not to think of Mike, David, Nelly or any of her family as she went through the medley. At the end when she gave a little bow there was a tremendous roar from the upper circles, the gods. The noise was deafening as everyone stood and clapped and cheered and whistled. Her heart felt as though it was going to burst and tears of pure joy trickled down her cheeks. This wasn't the Plantation, or the Charleston Cotillion Ball, or even the *Aquitania*, it was the Roundy, and it was the best. The best ever because this was her home and these were 'her' people. She knew out there sat Mam, Lizzie, Jack and all the rest of the family. And there'd be the O'Hanlons, the Thomases, the Maguires. Now she was truly the Liverpool Songbird.

There were shouts of 'Encore!' from the better seats and 'More! More, Alice, girl! More!' from up in the gods.

She looked at Gregson in the wings and he nodded; the supporting acts weren't all that good; if she wanted to go on all night it was fine by him.

Only when the orchestra struck up did the applause die down and complete silence fall.

These are for you, Mam. For all the times you went without so I could eat. For every bruise and black eye and cut you took for our sake, she thought. She also knew she'd have to exert an iron control over her emotions.

She looked up at the dress circle. 'This is a very special song for me. It's old-fashioned but it was taught to me by someone I love very dearly, my mam.'

She took a very deep breath as Signor Bransini had taught her to do.

> Just a song at twilight,
> When the lights are low
> Where the flickering shadows
> Gently come and go . . .

Her voice soared through the theatre. Sweet, clear and full of emotion. Only once did she falter and her vision was blurred by tears, but it only seemed to add feeling and sincerity.

In the front circle Nelly's tears flowed freely. Lizzie dabbed her eyes with Jack's handkerchief and even Agnes was sniffing to hold back the tears. The three younger children were mesmerised and sat totally still.

They wouldn't let her go. Every time she bowed and ran towards the wings, Gregson led her out again. She sang every song she knew, including the three she'd sung at the ball in Charleston. The Easter Hymn she sang without accompaniment, for the orchestra had no score for it. The audience didn't understand the foreign words, but everyone sat enthralled. Without any conscious effort their spirits seemed to rise like Alice's voice.

It's like ... like something that should be sung in church, Nelly thought and said a quiet prayer to the Blessed Virgin for the great gift that had been bestowed on her Alice. Just to listen to her erased all the years of terrible hardship and shame. Everyone – and they were all hard up – had pitied the poor O'Connors, but no more. Not after tonight.

Alice was exhausted and emotionally drained when she finally got back to her dressing room. Gregson had had to bring down the curtain in the end.

Mrs Harris was waiting, her face aglow with pleasure and there was respect in her eyes. 'I've never heard anything like that, Alice. Never, in all the years I've been here. Talk about bringing the house down. You're too good for places like this. It's opera you were born for.'

Alice shook her head. 'No, I wouldn't like that. It would be much too grand for the likes of me. I'll be more than happy with stage musicals.' She struggled to control her overflowing emotions. 'He had to bring the curtain down. I couldn't do any more. I just couldn't, but it all means so much, so very much. You see, I used to sing outside here. I sang to the queue for pennies. Begging, in rags and often barefoot.' She brushed away a tear with the back of her white-gloved hand.

'These came for you.' The dresser handed her a huge bouquet of pink roses. There was a card attached to them.

'I only just heard and there's not a seat to be had all weekend, but good luck. I told you I'd pay to see you and I will. At the Empire. Sincerely, Charlie Williamson.'

She sat down, her face buried in the bouquet; more memories came flooding back. The dockside, the blaring of the car horn, the startled whinny of the horse, her scream as Mog jumped from her arms and cowered beneath the huge hooves, and then the shiny chrome radiator of the car. The smell of engine oil, the humming sound, the face, full of concern, bending over her as she regained consciousness. David's face. And then the doctor and Charlie and those words. Those words that had inspired her and taken her across the world following her dreams, her ambitions, impossible though they had seemed then. But the dream had come true and she knew, she just *knew* that David loved her. It was only fate, in the guise of timing, that kept them apart.

There wasn't time to dwell on her thoughts, the small room was quickly filled with her family and Mr Kay, the manager from Sturla's, and his wife. She felt as high as a kite and hugged them all, even Mr and Mrs Kay who were virtual strangers.

'Oh, Alice, Mam was so cut up when you sang just for her!' Lizzie's face was glowing with pride, her eyes moist. 'We all were. It's a good job I don't wear rouge and powder otherwise it'd look such a mess.'

'Oh, Lizzie, I didn't mean to make you cry, but I nearly broke down myself.'

'I know, we could tell, and then Mam began to sob, but quietly.'

Jack had elbowed his way in, towering over everyone, as usual. 'Alice, I've ordered two taxis. I think your mam's a bit over-wrought,' he added.

Nelly was sitting on a chair, very still, very quiet, as though detached from everything that was going on around her.

Alice was all concern. 'Mam? Mam, are you feeling faint?'

Nelly came out of her trance-like state. 'No. No, luv, I'm fine. It just got a bit hot and crowded.' She clutched Alice's hand tightly. 'It's a gift from God, Alice. I never realised it until tonight. I've never heard you sing like that before.'

'I had voice training, Mam. For over a year I had singing lessons.'

'But that last one, Alice, I couldn't understand it but it

sounded as though it should be sung in church. That's when I knew. That's when I thought, it's a gift from God.'

'I know, Mam, but I'll never forget who it was who first taught me to sing – you. Now come on, let's get everyone home, we're all worn out.'

She helped Nelly to her feet and Lizzie took her arm. Alice detached the note from the flowers and thrust them into Nelly's arms.

'Not the last roses of summer, Mam, the first. From now on you'll always have roses. Every week.'

Chapter Twenty-Two

The following Monday, the trio of Nelly's old friends called for a bit of a jangle and a good look round. Alice had gone to see Arthur Jackson, the manager at the Empire.

Nelly opened her door, wiping her wet hands on her all-enveloping pinafore.

'Mary! Ethel! Jinny! Come in. It's great to see you.' She ushered them into the hall with its cream paintwork and the runner of good Axminster down the hall and up the stairs, where it was secured by brass rods. On the wall was a picture of Our Lady, Queen of Peace.

'Glory be to God, Nelly! You've even got carpet on the stairs!'

'That was our Alice's idea. I told her lino is much easier, it just needs a quick mop over, but no, she wouldn't 'ave it. I make them all come in the back way.' Then, knowing her neighbours well, Nelly asked if they'd like to do the 'grand tour', as she put it.

Mary O'Hanlon made no show of refusing the offer. 'Well, that's what we've come for, an' ter see you of course.'

'Aye, only the fact that it was Sunday yisterday and all the kids were 'ome, we'd 'ave come sooner,' Ethel added.

'Well, I'll show you round and then we'll have a cuppa.' Nelly beamed as she flung open a door. 'Right, this is me parlour.'

They all gaped.

'It . . . it's like a palace, Nell! Cut glass, roses, and, oh, a china cabinet – I'd put our Maggie on Lime Street for one of them!' Mary inspected the cabinet closely while Nelly tutted at the very idea, although she knew Mary was not serious.

'Velveteen curtains! *Velveteen!* And a carpet, no rag rugs!' Jinny was just as impressed.

They exclaimed and marvelled at everything, especially the new gas cooker in the kitchen.

'No more ashes to rake out, no more blackleading or taking a chance on how hot the oven gets. Eh, many's the bit of meat I've ruined in that bloody oven of mine. An' yer know how often we 'ave meat. Once in a month of Sundays. Isn't it a bloody miracle. How does it work? Do yer just turn these knobs an' out comes the gas?'

'Well, to tell you the truth, Mary, I'm a bit wary of it still,' Nelly confided sheepishly. 'Our Lizzie and Agnes think it's great though, but I'm terrified we'll all get blown sky high or someone will leave the gas on and we'll be found dead in our beds.'

'Oh, you'll get used to it in time, Nelly. Would yer look at that, Jinny! Tiles all round the sink and draining board.'

They all trooped upstairs to marvel and exclaim over the furnished bedrooms, the bedside rugs, the quality of the linen. Then it was down into the kitchen for tea. None of them wanted to sit in the parlour so they settled themselves round the kitchen table.

'She's spent a fortune, Nelly.'

'Aye, over a hundred pounds, and she pays the bills. The rent, the coal, the gas, the electric, she's even talking about having a phone put in! A phone, I ask yer! I don't know anyone else who has one so what use would it be?'

They all nodded their agreement.

'Where is Alice?' Ethel asked.

'At the Empire, seeing about the weekend after next.'

'You've got to admit it, Nelly, she was really great. She brought the 'ouse down every single night, so I heard.'

'They wanted her to stay on, offered her extra money.'

'And they put the admission price up too,' Ethel added grimly.

'But she's promised this Victor person to go to London.'

Mary nodded her thanks as Nelly refilled her cup and passed her the sugar bowl. Mary put three heaped teaspoons in. Sugar was a luxury. 'What exactly does he do, this feller?'

'He's very important in London, so she said. He's going to get her into a stage show but she'll have to do a few of the music halls first, just to earn some money for her keep and get some stage experience. He'll find her decent "digs", as she calls them. You know, lodgings. He says she'll do even better in London.' Nelly shook her head sadly. 'I've only just got her home and she's off again.'

'An' what does this feller get out of all this? Blokes like that don't do things out of the goodness of their hearts.'

'He takes ten per cent of everything she earns. She says that's normal too, she's got a proper contract, all legal, like. It came by post. Well, the post feller knew we'd moved here so he brought it here special like. She sent one back an' kept the other one.'

'Do yer trust this Victor chap, Nelly?'

'I don't know. I've never met him. She does and so far she's had nothing but good luck.'

'Aye, well, I hope it keeps fine for her. I wouldn't fancy living in London meself. All that traffic an' all them people. Did yer know they 'ave trains that run under the ground? In tunnels! Wouldn't that put the fear of God up yer!'

'Well, we've got trains that run up in the air, the docker's umbrella. The *overhead* railway. Will you have a biscuit?' Nelly offered the plate around. 'Jesus, Mary and Joseph, listen to me. "Have a biscuit?" I've never been able to afford even the broken ones they sell off cheap.'

'Do yer think you'll like it 'ere? What are the neighbours like?' Jinny asked, dipping a gingernut into her tea.

'Well, her next door sort of smiled at me yesterday. And the one from number six said "Nice ter see yer, Mrs O'Connor. I went ter see your Alice." But I've seen no one else. Our Lizzie's feller lives just at the top of the street.'

'Wouldn't yer think his ma would come down an' introduce 'erself?'

'I don't think she's like that. Our Lizzie will have her hands full with that owld one, I can see it comin'.'

Suddenly Nelly remembered her washing, half done and out on the line that stretched across the back yard and half still in the copper in the wash house. 'Me washin'!' she said, struggling to her feet.

Jinny grinned broadly. 'Oh, to 'ell with the flamin' washing. I've left mine to steep in the dolly tub.'

'And I'll go down the bag wash this afternoon. We wanted to come and see yer, Nell. The flamin' washing can wait. Anyway, by the time it's dry it's covered in smuts. Makes yer wonder why yer even bother sometimes. All that rubbin' and scrubbin' when half the time it don't look any better.'

'You'll get talked about, not having it out on the line yard by dinner time,' Mary stated with a sniff.

'Oh, to 'ell with them all an' all that flamin' nonsense! 'Er at number twenty never does 'ers until Tuesday, sometimes Wednesday, the lazy mare! They'll all be just "droppin' in" ter see yer soon, you mark my words, Nelly O'Connor. Yer could charge a ha'penny a time.' Ethel laughed. 'You're already the talk of the neighbourhood, what with moving here and your Alice and your Lizzie an' her scuffer.'

It was nearly an hour later when they left and Nelly washed up the cups and went back to her washing. She hoped they would come again, she thought as she pegged out the clothes. Aye, and she wouldn't mind a few more callers too, for she felt lonely and isolated with the kids at school, Agnes and Lizzie at work and Alice out most of the day and going back to that hotel at night. She wouldn't have Alice home much longer either. A leaden feeling came over her and she felt a headache starting.

Alice's fame had spread through the city. Every seat in the house was booked for every performance and the management of the Empire, which faced the magnificent neoclassical façade of St George's Hall with its statues, lions and cenotaph, were delighted with her.

She was introduced to everyone. The stage hands, the conductor and members of the orchestra, and her dresser, Miss Fairchild, who was considerably younger than Mrs Harris but just as enthusiastic.

'It's great to have someone local be such a success,' she gushed as she arranged a row of bottles, small boxes and brushes on the dressing table.

'I'm not the only one. Half the stars on the stage and the wireless come from Liverpool,' Alice said, shaking out her stage dresses.

Miss Fairchild stopped her, ignoring Alice's sigh. 'I know, but they all went to London,' the dresser reminded her.

'And I'm afraid I'll be going too very soon.'

'More's the pity. Now what will you be wearing?'

'The white chiffon.' Alice paused. 'I don't want to upset you or anything, but I can see to myself.'

'No you can't. You'll need someone to do up buttons, see that your hair and make-up are right and that there are no visitors.'

Alice sighed again. If this was how it was then she'd just have to accept it. She hated anyone fiddling with her hair and she wasn't impressed by having her face painted like a doll. She loathed being ordered around by fussy women. But it was all part and parcel of her life now.

Friday night was a repeat of her success at the Rotunda. She was on stage for the first half of the performance and when she got back to her dressing room she was breathless, her eyes sparkling, her cheeks tinged pink with exuberance. The room was full of flowers.

'Where did all these come from?'

'Admirers.'

'Men?'

Miss Fairchild smiled wryly. 'Men, stage door Johnnies. Have you never heard of them?'

'No. What do they want?'

'To take you out to supper and . . .' She left the sentence unfinished but Alice knew what she meant. It was like The Star of India but the price here was only some flowers and a meal.

'Alf on the stage door said two of them are *very* persistent,' Miss Fairchild confided conspiratorially.

'Who are they? Did they give a name?'

'Apparently both the same name, brothers. Charlie and David Williamson.'

Alice was instantly on her feet and heading for the door.

'Where are you going?'

'It's David! David and Charlie! I've *got* to see them!'

'Well, you're not going rushing out there, it's not done. I'll go and tell Alf to let them in.'

It was only a few minutes but it seemed like an hour, as Alice paced the floor nervously. Three times she checked her appearance in the mirror and on the third occasion rubbed off her lipstick and some of the rouge. She hated stage make-up but it was necessary because of the brilliance of the lighting.

'Here we are, Alice, as promised, although we had to

fight our way through a mob.' David was laughing. Like everyone else in the theatre, he'd been thrilled with her performance, even though he'd heard her sing before.

He kissed her lightly on the cheek. 'Each time I hear you sing, you get better and better.'

'I wouldn't have recognised you,' Charlie grinned. 'Now if you'd looked like this two years ago, I'd have stayed with you in that grubby little cafe for ever.'

Charlie was just as charming as his brother, she thought. 'We've come to take you to supper, at the Adelphi.'

She stopped herself from shrieking out, 'At the Adelphi!' It was Liverpool's finest hotel where all the wealthy and titled people stayed.

Miss Fairchild was already holding her cape and evening bag, and it was Charlie who took them from her and put the rich velvet wrap round Alice's shoulders.

'We've already booked, so there's no rush,' he said as they left the theatre and walked the short distance along Lime Street to the hotel.

The sumptuous foyer and reception rooms didn't draw gasps and cries of admiration from Alice. She was used to luxury now. The house on Rutledge Street and the *Aquitania* had made opulence common place. She barely glanced at her surroundings as they were ushered into a fine grill restaurant to a table laid with a crisp white damask cloth, real silver cutlery and crystal glasses, and a small arrangement of flowers as a centrepiece.

David removed her cloak and passed it to a waiter. The maître d' was very respectful.

'Well, to start we'll have a couple of bottles of Bollinger, please. This is a celebration.' David smiled at Alice. 'And then we'll peruse the menu for a while.'

The man nodded and walked away, snapping his fingers to attract the attention of the wine waiter.

'You'll take London by storm, Alice,' Charlie enthused. She blushed slightly. 'Oh, I don't know. I've no real stage experience. I'll need to learn to act.'

'Oh, don't worry about that. When Gina O'Donnell first starred in *Showboat*, she had no acting experience, so I heard. I follow the stage careers of beautiful ladies. It's sort of a hobby. I go to London as often as I can.'

David looked at him pointedly. 'That's why we're not often home at the same time. It's something Mother gets upset about.'

'Well, you're away more often than I am,' Charlie shot back.

'Don't start becoming tedious, it's Alice's celebration. I've followed her career. I'm her biggest fan. Anyway, who is this Gina O'Donnell?'

Alice just sat watching David. He'd said he was her biggest fan, that he'd followed her career. She felt as though she was on a cloud.

'She's Irish, she came to Liverpool in nineteen twenty-two with her sisters. She's very beautiful, gorgeous red hair and so . . . so bubbly. She's got a temper to go with her hair, I believe.'

'Then she won't want me for competition, will she?' Alice pointed out.

'She's in *Days of Grace* now but I also heard she's not been well lately. There are rumours that she's going home to get married.' Charlie laughed as the cork from the first bottle of champagne popped.

'I don't know where you get all this gossip from but let's forget her, this is Alice's night,' David insisted.

They both raised their glasses to her. 'Here's to you, Alice, may you conquer the world!' Charlie said expansively.

'And I echo that. It's just a pity we sail again tomorrow, but I wouldn't have missed tonight for the world.'

As David casually imparted his news Alice felt the excitement of the evening evaporate and the wine suddenly had a bitter taste.

She went to see him off. She drove down to the landing stage and stood, as she'd done two years ago, and watched the *Aquitania* until she was just a dot in the distance. She'd gone on board and they'd had ten minutes together. With the ship due to sail, it was all he could spare.

'You were really wonderful last night, Alice,' he said warmly.

'Thanks, I enjoyed my supper too. Charlie's so funny sometimes.'

'And sometimes he goes too far.'

She laughed, unsure of herself. 'I . . . I'll be in London soon. Will you come and see me?'

'When I get some decent leave, I will, but you'll no doubt see Charlie before me. He does escape there as often as he can. He seems fascinated by the place – the theatre in particular – but don't let him monopolise you, Alice, he can be a bit overpowering at times.'

She protested. 'Oh, he's not.'

He took her hand. 'I'll have to go now, Alice, I'm sorry. I always seem to be rushing away from you, but the sea is my life, my career, you do understand?'

She'd managed a smile. 'Of course I do. I have to go to London for *my* career.' But the tone of her voice had had little conviction in it.

She did see Charlie. He called at the theatre on the Saturday night, took her to supper at the Adelphi again and asked if she would like to go to Southport for lunch on Sunday. There were some very good hotels and restaurants and the Marine Drive was quite beautiful. She agreed, for he was a link with David and he was fun to be with. 'It's being stuck in a gloomy, dismal office all day that makes me desperate to get out and about. An office full of old bores. Oh, they're all very polite and distinguished, but so boring!' He went on to tell her a bit more about his job as an accountant, which he obviously disliked. 'When I escape I tend to go mad – just a bit!'

'You don't look in the least like an accountant,' Alice said. 'I mean I've never met one but I imagine them to be old and dull and, well, boring.'

'I know, but Father wanted me to do something "professional". The law is unbelievably boring and medicine is so grisly and gruesome that I opted for accountancy. It pays well.' He now had the highly polished, maroon-coloured little Jowett sports car he'd coveted for so long.

'And will David be a captain one day?'

'The master of a ship, Alice,' he corrected her. 'One day, but it seems to take years to get there. It appears to be a matter of waiting for dead men's shoes and they all seem to live until they're about eighty.'

She shuddered. 'That's a horrible expression.'

'But true. Can we go out again this week?'

'I'm sorry, but I really must make arrangements to go to London.'

'But I will see you before then?'

'We'll see,' she laughed.

On Tuesday, to her surprise, Victor Hardman paid her a visit at Media Street. Alice introduced him to her mother and showed him into the parlour.

'Will I make some tea, Alice?' Nelly whispered.

'Yes please, Mam.'

He sat in an armchair, while she sat on the sofa facing him. In the centre of the sideboard was a vase full of pale pink roses and their perfume hung heavily on the air.

'I was getting myself organised,' she said defensively before he could ask why she hadn't been in touch, apart from to return the contracts.

'No doubt you were. If you hadn't turned up at the Empire or the Rotunda on the nights I booked they would have been on the phone to me, so I knew nothing had gone wrong there.'

'I played the six nights at the Rotunda and six nights at the Empire and I had to get the family sorted out.'

He glanced around and she uttered a prayer of thanks that he'd not had to come knocking on the door of Benledi Street. 'And they both wanted me to stay. They both offered me more money. Even a percentage of the box office takings, a very small one. I did the whole first half of the show each night and to packed houses.'

'It's no more than I would have expected. This is your city. Your home town. But down to business. I've arranged for digs in a house in Bloomsbury. The lady is a widow and needs the money but she'll only take decent people. Mrs Winters, her name is. I've also arranged for you to appear at the Falstaff, the Queens, the Bedford in Camden Town and Collin's in Islington. That should cover your expenses. You'll have to get some stage dresses made or bought.'

Alice looked worried. She had dug deeply into the money Mike had given her. 'How much will I have to spend on them?'

'About five or six guineas. No need to have anything very expensive.'

'They're expensive enough!' Mike had bought all her clothes and she now wondered just how much they had cost, especially the evening gowns.

'And I've managed, with a lot of greasing of palms, to get you the lead in *Days of Grace*, starting in four weeks' time.'

'*Days of Grace*? But . . . but what about acting? What about . . . Miss O'Donnell?' she asked, her heart racing.

'Gina never had much in the way of drama lessons; she was a natural, like you.'

'But won't she be annoyed, upset?'

'Gina's going home to Ireland. She's marrying her agent, Edward Vinetti. At the moment her understudy is playing the lead.'

'Why is she giving it all up? She's only young. I did hear she wasn't well, but—'

Victor stood up. 'She's going home because she's dying, Alice. She's got consumption.'

Alice was stunned. How terrible. Oh, how unfair life was. She'd never even seen a picture of Gina O'Donnell, but she'd heard she was young, beautiful and talented. Then she shivered, remembering Charlie's words about 'dead men's shoes'.

'How often will I be able to come home?'

'What do you want to come home for? I'm offering you a fantastic career on a gold plate and all you can do is ask about coming home.'

'I'm not being ungrateful. I have my reasons.'

He saw, or he thought he did. 'You want to see the family from time to time.'

She nodded. 'And someone else, too.'

He studied her face. Her eyes had become misty as though she was reliving a beautiful dream. Then it dawned on him. 'Ah, the young man on the ship?'

She nodded again. It had been wonderful that night at the Adelphi, but now it looked as if it would be months before she saw him again and he'd stressed that the sea was his life. Nor had he declared himself. The little gestures he made, just holding her hand or kissing her cheek or forehead, couldn't be called passionate by any stretch of the imagination.

'Are you in love with him, Alice?'

The question, asked so directly, took her by surprise but eventually she nodded.

'And does he love you?'

'I . . . I don't know. He's never said.'

'Alice, you have to be a special kind of girl to marry a sailor, no matter what his rank is. You'd spend half your married life on your own. You'd have to bring up any children on your own and I just can't see you doing that.

And even if you married him, you'd have to choose between him and your career, and I don't want you to have to make that choice. Nor is it money I'm thinking of. You have a great gift, Alice, and you're very young. It would be nothing short of criminal to give up such a career. Don't waste what you have, don't deprive hundreds – thousands of people of the opportunity to see and hear you. To bring a little pleasure into their lives, even if it is only for a few hours.'

Nelly came in with the tea and Alice thanked her. Seeing the look on both their faces, Nelly decided not to linger. She closed the door quietly behind her.

'Fame doesn't last for ever,' Alice countered.

'No, it doesn't. There are always younger girls coming along. What kind of a family does he come from?'

'Posh. His father's a barrister. His brother's an accountant. I don't know what his sisters do, if they do anything at all, that is.'

'In that case you'd have to give up your career if you married him. Married middle-class women just don't go out to work. Especially not to appear on the stage in public. At private, select events, yes.'

Maura O'Hare's soirées and the like, she thought.

He finished his tea and got up. 'I'll meet you off the train at Euston Station on Sunday morning. I believe the sleeper gets in about seven o'clock.'

She nodded. She knew she should feel thrilled. Over the moon, or 'me dream's out', as Mam always said, but she felt miserable and confused as she closed the front door after him.

Nelly came into the hall. 'He's gone then?'

'He's gone, Mam, and I've got to get the overnight sleeper train to London on Saturday night. He's got it all arranged. A place to live, some work and then I'm to have the main part in *Days of Grace*. Mr Hardman's managed to swing it for me.'

'Then why are you looking so unhappy, luv?'

'Because I don't know when I'll be able to come home again to see . . . everyone.'

'Alice, you can't waste your life, your gift.'

'I know, Mam, but it's going to be so hard to go away again, and this time I feel I have even less choice than I did the first time I left.'

Chapter Twenty-Three

Alice was miserable and apprehensive as she walked up the platform towards the barrier in Euston Station. Everyone had cried when they'd seen her off. She'd been near to tears herself. Four weeks she'd had at home, that was all, and it might be months before she got home again. She hadn't felt like this when she'd gone to America. So much had happened now; she'd changed so much.

Victor Hardman was there to meet her and to drive her to her digs in the quiet, respectable road in Bloomsbury. She glanced despondently out of the window, knowing she must pull herself together and soon.

Mrs Winters, her landlady, was a small plump woman, dressed in dark clothes, obviously still mourning her husband. Alice wondered how long he'd been dead, but she didn't want to ask. She showed her up to quite a big room with a bay window. The curtains, carpet and bedspread were of good quality and the furniture, although old, had been well cared for.

'It's lovely, thank you,' she replied to the woman's enquiry as to the suitability of the room.

'Then I'll expect to see you in my office in Islington tomorrow, Alice,' Victor Hardman said. 'We've a busy few days ahead.'

She nodded and after they'd both gone she sat on the bed and kicked off her shoes. She'd never felt so lonely in her entire life before. She lay down on the bed and gave in to the depression she'd been fighting all day. 'Oh, David! David! I'll never see you again, I just know it!' she sobbed into the pillow.

She didn't have much time to think after that miserable afternoon and night. There were people to meet, theatres to visit and shopping to do for stage dresses. The two outfits she bought were promptly taken back to the shop as they were totally unsuitable, Victor told her. He went with her on the next trip and she bought two of the flashiest, over-trimmed dresses she'd ever seen. Once she'd have thought them gorgeous, but not now. She hated them. Nor was she very impressed with the theatres. They were shabby compared to those in Liverpool.

'What kind of people come to these shows?' she asked. Although many poorer and modestly paid people went to the Rotunda, so too did richer people who arrived in cars and taxis, wearing evening dress.

'If you mean are they similar to the first-class passengers on the *Aquitania*, then no. They're working-class people who want to have a good night out. They only get one day off a week, most of them.'

She nodded. 'Then they'll get it.'

'I was beginning to think you were becoming a snob.'

'A snob? Me? I come from the slums of Liverpool. I've only just moved the family into that house in Media Street. It cost me a small fortune too. I need the money.'

'You'll get it when you start in *Days of Grace*.'

Her first performance was at the Bedford in Camden Town. It had been agreed that she would sing mainly the rather old-fashioned songs, and she was told that the audience would join in, in fact she should encourage them to do so. They loved a good sing-song. Then she would do a couple of her jazzy numbers.

She had to use a communal dressing room; she'd had one to herself at both the Rotunda and the Empire and she couldn't help feeling she was going down in the world, not up. There were no dressers either, so she did her own hair, applied her own make-up and fastened her own dress, the bright red one with all the red and black fringing. She loathed it. The room was noisy and hot, for there were other girls and women in various stages of undress. Suddenly she caught sight of a woman with blonde hair piled in curls on top of her head, in what was now a very old-fashioned style. Her dress was old-fashioned too and looked slightly faded and worn. With a tremor of shock she recognised the woman. It was Letty Lewis. She made her way across the room and as she drew nearer she could see how heavy the singer's make-up was. It only served to emphasise the lines at the corners of her eyes and mouth.

'Miss Lewis?'

'I'm Letty Lewis, luv. Do I know you? I ain't seen you around before. New to the game?'

'No, not new, but this is my first time in London.'

'What's your name?'

'Alice. Alice O'Connor. I'm from Liverpool.'

The woman smiled and the lines on her face deepened. 'Oh, I had some really good times up there. They're really appreciative, not like the crowd you get in some parts. They're not bad in here.'

Alice ignored the churning of her stomach. 'I saw you once. I wasn't in the audience. I crept round the back. I couldn't afford the price of a ticket. You sang "Beautiful Dreamer".'

'Did I? Lord luv a duck, I can't remember what I sang last week, let alone all those years ago.'

'Two and a half years ago it was, that's all.'

'Then you've come up in the world and fast.'

Alice smiled. 'I was lucky, but you were my inspiration. I was singing in the street outside and a lady was good enough to give me a threepenny bit. She said all I needed was some training and grooming. I didn't even know what she meant. Then I saw you and I knew I wanted to be like you. That's how it all started. That and something a man once said to me.'

'Never believe a thing a feller tells you, Alice. Then you won't get hurt. But was I really your inspiration?' The smile and interest were genuine.

'You were. I went to America. I did well, very well. Then I came home to Liverpool and did well there too.'

'You need luck in this game, and plenty of it. You should have stayed in America, that's where the big money is.'

Alice shook her head sadly. 'I couldn't. There were reasons.'

Letty shrugged. 'Isn't that your name they're calling?'

'Oh, God, yes!' Alice pushed her way through to the door and then ran along the corridor.

Letty Lewis followed her. There was a juggling act on after Alice, then a magician, then herself. She'd go and listen to the girl, Letty decided, see how good she was.

They were a noisy audience, Alice thought, but she finally got the silence she needed after the first verse of 'Always'.

Watching from the wings, Letty Lewis turned to Tommy Clarke, the stage manager. 'She's too damned good for this place. That's *real* talent.'

'I know. She's in line for *Days of Grace*, the lead, too.'

'Well, good luck to her. I hope she makes the most of it because it doesn't last long. An' it's bloody hard on the way down.'

'If she's got any sense she'll marry a feller who can keep her in luxury.'

'Do they ever have any sense?' the older woman cackled. 'I didn't at her age.' And with that she turned her wise, experienced gaze to the sparkling young girl in front of her.

She'd done her spots at the other theatres and her spirits

felt lighter. At the end of every performance the applause had been deafening. Every manager wanted her to stay – they knew that with the stage musicals and the cinemas, the days of the music halls were numbered and they were desperate to make as much money as they could while the audiences were there. But the day finally came when Alice went with Victor to do her first rehearsal of her first stage show, the long-awaited *Days of Grace*. The cast seemed friendly enough, particularly Lucy Venables who had been understudying.

'Am I relieved you've come to take over. I know I can never live up to Miss O'Donnell's standard and so do the audiences. Bookings have been falling off and that's no good for anyone! The first thing they do is drop our wages and they're not much to start with,' she grinned.

'I would have come sooner,' said Alice, almost apologetically, 'but Mr Hardman had made firm, longstanding bookings for me and he says he never cancels because it's not good for his reputation. It's not good for business or my career either.'

Lucy nodded, and started to explain some of the intricacies of Alice's part.

It was a hard, exhausting day. Not only did Alice have to sing, she had to speak and act as well, something she'd never done before. Her movements were jerky, her lines stilted even though she'd learned them over the past weeks until she was word perfect.

'Oh, God. I was awful!' she said to Lucy when she came off.

'Not with the songs though, you've a great voice and, don't worry, the rest will come. Just wait until you have to wear that bloody awful costume and the even worse wig! I've tripped over that damned frock more times than I can remember.'

Alice found out at the end of the week, when there was a dress rehearsal in the morning, specially for her, that what Lucy had said about the dress and wig was true.

There was no one she knew in the audience to see her debut, except Victor Hardman, but that didn't bother her now. She would have hated David to see her in this awful get-up and with her face painted like a doll. To her surprise she got a standing ovation as she took her final bow.

She received rave reviews and bookings picked up. Every night there were bouquets and cards and invitations. She wished she could send all the roses home to Nelly but she made sure they all went to hospitals and churches. She had opened an account with Cunningham's the florists on Scotland Road and a bouquet of roses was to be delivered to Nelly each week. She wrote once a week too, telling of all her good fortune and sheer awe at being called a 'star' in the newspapers and sending Nelly the clippings. She knew that this was what her mam would want to hear, not the fact that there was still something missing in her life, that it really wasn't all glamour and fun.

'Don't you ever go out with any of these men?' Lucy asked, flicking through the invitations. 'Some of them are very well off and there's one here who's got a title.'

'No. I go with Victor for a quiet supper then back to Bloomsbury. If he can't make it, I go on my own. They know me now and give me a nice secluded booth in a corner, so I can have my meal in peace.'

'I don't understand you, Alice. Did you have to leave someone in Liverpool?'

'Not really, he left me.' She paused then said quickly, 'But not in the way you think. He's an officer on the *Aquitania*.'

'Not much of a romance then, is it? You down here, him trailing back and forth across the Atlantic.'

'No, it's not. But I had to choose.' Her voice was filled with longing, but deep down she realised what she'd just said wasn't true. She hadn't had anything to choose between. She didn't even know if he loved her. She'd seen more of Charlie than of him.

'Why don't you come on out with us?' Lucy invited her. 'Me and a couple of the girls are going for a bit of supper and a drink to a place round the corner.'

She agreed but it didn't do much to lift the depression that was beginning to plague her. She kept telling herself how lucky she was. There were girls in the chorus who would kill to live the life they thought she lived, but it didn't work. She was miserable and homesick, something she'd never been in Charleston. She'd written to Mike once, just to let him know she'd arrived home safely and that her career looked very promising. She'd had one letter back. Brief but to the point. He'd thanked her for her letter and wished her success and he'd signed it, 'Sincerely'. Sometimes she looked back on those days with Mike as the happiest she'd known. Had she treated him fairly? She felt a twinge of guilt. Oh, but Mike was a man of the world. And once he got used to it, his world wouldn't be all that different without her in it, of that she was sure . . .

A week later she was wakened by Mrs Winters knocking on her bedroom door. Alice dragged on a robe and opened the door, rubbing the sleep from her eyes.

'It's a telegram for you, Alice.' Mrs Winters held out the small, buff-coloured envelope but her eyes were on the girl's face. No one liked telegrams, they were usually harbingers of bad news.

Alice opened it, her eyes wide now, scanning the lines. It was very short, but to the point.

'ALICE. MAM VERY ILL. COME HOME. LIZZIE.'

'Oh, Mam!' She threw the paper on the floor and ran her fingers through her hair.

'What is it, Alice?'

'It's Mam, she's very ill. I've got to go home. Now! Right now, this very minute.'

Mrs Winters was instantly efficient. 'I'll bring you up some tea and toast. Get dressed, pack a small case and I'll let Victor know. Lucy will stand in for you. Then I'll call you a taxi. Come on, Alice. By the time you get home she may have rallied. It might be something like influenza that she'll get over. Your sister didn't say what was actually wrong, now did she?'

The rest of the day passed in a blur of being pushed into cabs and onto trains. As she waited at Crewe for her connection, she walked up and down the platform ceaselessly, her mind in turmoil. She exhausted herself and fell asleep on the last leg of the journey, waking only when the train stopped with a jolt in Lime Street.

She ran down the platform, threw her case into the first taxi she saw, gave the driver the address and then fell back against the seat. She begged the cab driver to hurry.

'If I go any faster, luv, we'll overturn going round one of these corners. It's not a bloody race track – there's still a lot of horse-drawn wagons and there's no shiftin' them.'

It was dark and she seemed to have been travelling all day. When she arrived she thrust a ten-shilling note into the driver's hand and didn't wait for her change.

Agnes opened the door to her insistent knocking. Alice caught her and hugged her briefly. 'Oh, Holy Mother of God, what's the matter? What's she got? Why didn't someone tell me she was ill?'

'Because we didn't know. She'd been down to see Mrs O'Hanlon and when she got back she said she didn't feel well. "I'm just tired. It's old age creeping on," she said. Then she collapsed. Alice, it's pneumonia and it's bad.'

'Pneumonia! She's never had a bad chest! Not ever, not even in Benledi Street with all the cold and dampness and never having enough to eat.'

'The doctor said it wasn't anything to do with getting

cold or living in a damp place. He said it was vi . . .' Agnes struggled with the unfamiliar word, 'viral pneumonia.'

'Is that better or worse than the other kind?'

'I don't know. He said she should go to hospital, but you know Mam. She's terrified of hospitals, just the way she was about the workhouse.'

Alice ran upstairs and opened the door of the bedroom Nelly shared with Lizzie. Before she could cry out, Lizzie placed a finger on her lips and moved towards her.

'Don't start crying or carrying on, Alice. You'll only upset her,' Lizzie whispered.

Alice fought to control herself. 'How long has she been . . . like this?'

'She collapsed yesterday. We thought she'd just been doing too much. Mrs O'Hanlon's got rid of her lodgers and Mam went down to help her clean up after them. She said the lodger's room was like a pigsty and that Mrs O'Hanlon couldn't offer it to anyone else in that state. Our Agnes and me got her to bed but then she began to gasp and fight for her breath, so I sent for the doctor. She won't go to hospital, so he's left her some medicine but he said . . . he said she was exhausted. That she didn't have a strong constitution, so she had no strength to fight it.'

Alice swallowed hard and went and knelt on the floor beside the bed. Nelly was propped up with pillows but she looked small and suddenly frail and her breathing was very laboured.

'I'm here, Mam, it's Alice. I've come home.'

Nelly's eyes opened slowly and she tried to smile.

Alice took a thin hand, roughened by years and years of work. 'They've given me a few days to come home and see you. I'll go back when you're better.' She was trying hard to keep her voice steady.

Nelly became agitated and Alice got up and smoothed the prematurely greying hair away from her forehead.

'Hush now, Mam. Don't get upset.'

Nelly's words were slow. 'Alice, don't stay too ... too long.'

'Mam, in a few days you'll be up and about, then I'll go back.' She was fighting to control the tears and trying to keep her voice from cracking with anguish.

'No. Don't ... don't waste ... the gift.' Nelly was struggling hard now.

'You know I won't, Mam.'

Nelly closed her eyes. 'The ... Lord giveth ... and He taketh away, Alice.'

Alice could barely make out the words. She bit her lip and laid her cheek next to Nelly's, the tears pouring down her face and wetting the pillowcase.

Lizzie gently put her arm round Alice's shoulders and drew her away.

'Let her rest. I've sent for Father Mulcahey.'

Alike seized on this slim hope. 'Sometimes the sacrament makes them better. You know it does, Lizzie. Ma Wentworth from Athol Street had it three times. Oh, Lizzie, she can't go! She can't! She hasn't even had a year's comfort and security in this house. Surely God won't take her now, not yet, not until ...' She dissolved into quiet sobs and Lizzie clung to her.

'God is good, but if her time's come ...' Lizzie murmured. She had little faith that the sacrament of extreme unction would cure her mam. She'd sat here all day, watching Nelly getting worse.

She took Alice's hand and they both knelt beside the bed and Lizzie produced her rosary beads. She had already covered a small table with a clean cloth. Two candles, blessed, stood in small china holders. There was a bowl of Holy Water, a cupful of clean water in another bowl. A clean white handkerchief was also laid out, as was a saucer containing bread crumbs.

The parish priest arrived just as a taxi drew up outside

the house. He nodded to the man who got out and silently paid the driver: Father Mulcahey was carrying the Eucharist and could therefore converse with no one.

Again it was Agnes who opened the door. She beckoned the priest inside and stared up at the stranger.

'Yes?'

'Does Alice O'Connor live here?'

'Yes, but you can't see her now. Me mam's dead poorly.'

'I thought someone was, seeing the priest, but may I come in? I've travelled a long way and I'd like to see Alice before . . . before I go back to America.'

Agnes gnawed her lip, torn by indecision. America *was* a long way.

'All right, come on in. You can wait in the parlour and I'll tell her you're here, but if she won't see you, you'll 'ave to go.'

He nodded. 'That's fair enough. It's O'Farrell. Michael O'Farrell.'

Chapter Twenty-Four

As he looked around the room he realised what she'd spent his money on. That was just like her. She loved her mother dearly, he knew that. Just as he'd loved his own whom he'd seen lowered into the earth at Glasnevin Cemetery only a few days ago. That was why he'd come back. He hadn't come because of Alice, but once in Liverpool the urge to see her had been too strong for him to overcome. He'd got a cab and gone to Benledi Street only to be told she'd moved to this house. Benledi Street, and in particular number ten, had reminded him forcefully of his own childhood and youth. He'd looked at the peeling paint, the rotten wood, the cracked and broken steps and the dirty, fly-blown windows. The house was empty but it wouldn't be for much longer, there was a family moving in the day after, a family of eight who had been living in a cellar, so the woman next door had informed him.

His passage was booked on the *Berengaria* sailing to New York. He was going back to America tomorrow. But would he go? Now it looked as though Alice was about to lose her mother too. The priest hadn't been called for a simple ailment.

There was a knock on the front door, and since Mike was the nearest, he answered it.

A small, rotund man with glasses, well dressed and carrying a black bag, stood on the step. 'How is she now?' the doctor asked.

'I'm sorry, sir, I've only just arrived. I've no idea.'

Agnes appeared from the kitchen and ushered the doctor upstairs and Mike went back to his solitary musings in the parlour. He sat on the sofa and dropped his head in his hands. He knew how Alice must be feeling. He understood.

His mother's body had been taken to the church where it had remained until the funeral Mass the following day. It was an Irish custom. He'd sat in the chill, silent church all night with her. Just the four candles, one at each corner of the bier, and the flickering red light from the sanctuary lamp pierced the darkness. During those long dark hours he'd found it impossible to pray. If God was so good, as they were constantly being told by the clergy, then why did He allow such poverty and hardship to flourish? Oh, the Church came up with half-baked answers. No mere man should challenge God's reasons. All would be revealed on the Last Day. In the meantime one should believe blindly and without questioning.

That didn't wash with him and hadn't done for a long time. Who actually decided which person, which family, should suffer? Maybe he shouldn't be blaming God at all. Maybe it was all the fault of society. Of greedy, callous, cheating men. The survival of the fittest.

He remembered his boyhood in the Coombe. The biting, stinging cold rain and sleet driving in from the sea, sweeping up the Liffey. His threadbare clothes, his often bare feet numb with cold. The gnawing pains of hunger. The humiliation when he'd had to beg. The desperation when he'd turned to stealing. And the lies he'd told his mother about where he'd got the money or the bits of food.

He remembered standing at the foot of the statue of Daniel O'Connell at the bottom of the street that now bore the name of the man who had won Catholic emancipation for Ireland. He'd taken Kitty and Dee, young as they were, their little faces pinched and white, in the hope that people would take pity on them and be generous. It had been Christmas, although exactly which Christmas he couldn't remember. Only that the people rushing to do the last of their shopping had no time or money to give to the three ragged urchins, three out of a whole army of starving men, women and children that wandered the cold streets of Dublin.

He heard footsteps on the stairs and looked up hopefully. The front door was opened, then shut, and he heard a car pull away from the kerb. The doctor had gone. Obviously there was nothing else he could do. He hesitated to smoke, they might not like it. Instead he leaned his head against the back of the sofa and closed his eyes. He remembered the first time he'd come to Liverpool, all those years ago, following his father to America. He could almost feel the dust and the heat and the long miles he'd travelled on the American freight trains. His da's face when he'd confronted him. And his face when he'd died, twisted into a sneer by the stroke. Did he still hate him? There was only one answer to that question. Yes, and he always would. There seemed to be no sign of Alice's father. Maybe he, too, was dead. And Alice? Oh, how he missed her.

After she'd gone, there had seemed no point in anything. The house was like a morgue. He'd been bad-tempered, sullen and had been drinking heavily until Alexander had threatened that the entire staff would leave if he didn't pull himself together. In a highly indignant and irate manner his butler had told of the barefaced lies he'd had to tell people that there had been a very private domestic occurrence in Dublin that had upset his employer, hence the heavy drinking and sullen attitude and depressed moods. Mike smiled wryly to himself. Only Alexander could get away with that. So he'd made an effort. Thrown himself into his work, increased his fortune and, when people asked about '*Mrs O'Farrell*', he'd told them that – like the angel from heaven that Alice surely was – she'd gone to Dublin to help nurse and comfort his poor mother who was not in the best of health. He himself was very distraught about the 'drastic domestic occurrence' that had upset him too, and about which he couldn't utter a single word, on his mother's life, it was so private. And, as to how long his mother would need Alice, sure it was almost impossible to know, wasn't it? And with that he would change the subject. But there was little pleasure in life. He had no time to enjoy his money, he wouldn't allow himself the time. Over the months the pain had begun to ease.

He had no idea if she and David Williamson were engaged. Or even worse, married. He had asked the cab driver if he'd heard of her. The man had. He'd been effusive in his praise. He'd been to see her and she was the best. She was one of their own, too. The Liverpool Songbird, she was called, and they were dead proud of her. Mike had smiled at that, remembering the pendant he'd given her. He'd sold all the other jewels after she'd gone and Ruth had removed every trace of her from that bedroom. It was now virtually sealed, the furniture covered with dustsheets, the shutters always tightly closed.

He got up and walked into the hall and knocked gently on the kitchen door.

Agnes opened it, clutching Georgie the cat for comfort, her eyes red and puffy. 'Go on upstairs to your mammy, girl, I'll watch the others.'

She passed the cat to Mary and then fled past him and he looked at the solemn, frightened faces of the three children in the room.

'Who're you?' Jimmy asked belligerently.

Obviously he took after his father, Mike thought ruefully. The other two were very quiet and still. 'I'm Mr O'Farrell, a friend of Alice's.'

'You're Irish,' the lad said.

'I am so, but I live in America. That's how I met Alice. Will I tell you about how I got there on the ship and then riding the freight trains and the desperate things I did?' He saw the first spark of interest in their eyes. At least he could be of some help, keep them interested, keep their thoughts away from upstairs where their mammy lay dying.

When he heard the ponderous footsteps coming down the stairs, he knew they belonged to the priest and that Nelly O'Connor had breathed her last. He went into the hall as a sobbing Agnes fled past him into the kitchen.

'She's gone then, Father?'

The priest nodded.

'God have mercy on her soul.'

'She'd had a hard life. It had weakened her, but God was good, she had every comfort in her last days.'

Mike felt his temper rising. Again the bloody pathetic empty platitudes. 'If she'd had them earlier, Father, she might not have died. If someone had done something about the beatings and the deprivation, the constant worry of just keeping alive and keeping her children alive, the shame of not having even a ha'penny to put on the collection plate. Just think of all those pennies, sixpences, shillings and maybe the odd florin or two that could have kept her, her family and many other families supplied with a loaf of bread and maybe a few fishes.' Mike's voice was harsh, the sarcasm heavy and intentional.

The priest was not used to being spoken to like this. 'You're an Irishman? A Catholic or . . .?' The voice had a sharp edge to it.

'I'm not an Orangeman if that's what you can't bring yourself to say. I'm a Dubliner and I was brought up a Catholic. I've just buried my own mother, God rest her and God bless her memory. She, too, had a hard life when I was young. Our parish priest always used to remind us of the Beatitudes, particularly "Blessed are the poor". I never did see any reason, understanding or compassion in that, Father. Especially as our particular fellow lived in comfort and had a full belly. I wonder, when Christ said those words, did He mean that the clergy were to be exempt?'

The other man looked horrified. 'That's blasphemy!'

'Is it, or is it just a question?'

'You've lost your faith. You've fallen from a state of grace.'

'I fell a long time ago, Father. Will I show you the scars? Or just the door?' He was in no mood to have moral issues, blasphemy or lack of faith heaped down on his head. By his accent the priest was a Mayo man. Maybe that explained everything. They were dour and devout to the point of martyrdom in the west.

As he closed the door he turned and saw Alice standing at the top of the staircase. 'Oh, Alice, I'm sorry.' He held out his arms and she flew down the stairs. There was no cry of recognition, no question as to why he was here. It was as if she'd been expecting him.

'Oh, Mike! Mike, she's dead! I can't believe she's gone! At the ... the end she just opened her eyes and tried to smile at me. She ... she couldn't speak. Oh, Mam! Mam!'

He held her tightly as she sobbed, the pain of his own loss twisting the knife in the wound.

Lizzie came slowly down. 'You're Mr O'Farrell?'

He nodded.

'I'm going down the street for my ... friend. I won't be long.'

Mike nodded and drew Alice into the parlour and sat her down on the sofa, his arms still round her.

'I was in London. They never told me! Our Lizzie should have sent for me sooner,' she sobbed.

'Don't put the blame on her, Alice. She doesn't deserve it.'

She looked up at him, realising for the first time that it *was* actually him. 'What ... how ...?'

'I came home for a funeral too. My mother was buried three days ago. I had a few days with her and I'll always be thankful for that. You had a few hours, Alice. You didn't arrive too late. Take comfort from that.'

She was a little calmer now. 'I'm sorry. How ... what did your mother die of?'

'A massive heart attack. She'd had a couple of strokes, the last one two weeks ago. That's why Kitty wired me.'

'I ... I *am* sorry.'

'She had twenty years of good, comfortable living, Alice. Loved by her daughters and grandchildren, respected by her neighbours, and her faith never deserted her. She went to Mass every day, and I know she made charitable donations to her old neighbours. I comfort myself with that.'

'Mam ... Mam only had a few months and I was so selfish. I could have stayed in Liverpool, everyone begged me to, but no, I had to go to London to become a bloody "star".'

'Don't blame yourself. A talent like yours should never be suppressed.' He smiled. 'Are you a star?'

She nodded. 'I suppose so. I met an agent on the ship coming home. I'm the lead in *Days of Grace*.'

He didn't want to mention David Williamson but he couldn't stop himself. 'And what happened to your young engineering officer? Do you still see him?'

'No. I did when I first came home, but not since I've been in London.'

The knowledge should have cheered him but it didn't. He hated to see her so smitten with grief and his own grief was still raw. He'd taken a photograph of his mother and her rosary beads as simple tokens to remind him, although both his sisters had urged him to take more.

The door opened and a giant of a man entered, immediately making the room seem smaller.

'I'm Jack Phillips, Lizzie's friend. I'm also a police constable.'

Mike nodded. He should have guessed by the man's size and bearing. 'Mike O'Farrell, a friend of Alice's from Charleston.'

'I've told Lizzie to put the kettle on and to get the younger kids to bed. I've also sent for the two women who do the laying out. Tomorrow I'll get in touch with the Co-op Funeral Directors.'

Alice managed to smile gratefully at Jack. She couldn't think about arrangements. 'Will you stay?' she said, turning to Mike.

'My passage is booked on the *Berengaria* to sail tomorrow, but to hell with it. I'll not leave you in this state, Alice.'

'I'll sleep here tonight. I'll share with Mary and Lizzie. They . . . they'll want Mam's room to lay her out.'

'Then I'll go to a hotel. Jack, can you recommend one, a decent one?'

'There's no need for that, Mike. We've got a spare room.'

'Thanks. I'll give you a hand to arrange things,' Mike offered.

Jack nodded. Neither Alice nor Lizzie were in any fit state to cope with the formalities and he'd be glad of some help. He couldn't take time off. It wasn't his mother or a very close relative who had died.

Mike found it strange at first. Two old women came and laid out the mortal remains of Nelly O'Connor. Then white sheets were hung round the walls. A candle was placed at each corner of the bed and a crucifix hung on the wall behind it. A small, cheap Holy Water font was hung on the wall near the door. All this was done by a trio of silent, grieving women who, he was told, were Nelly's friends from the old street. How customs varied, he thought. How much easier for her to be taken to the church, but that would have been inconvenient for the worshippers as obviously the funeral wouldn't be for a couple of days.

It was late when he and Jack left the house and walked down the road to Jack's home. Jack introduced Mike to his mother who went upstairs to make up the bed in the spare room. Jack indicated that Mike should sit down. He glanced around at the comfortable, homely living room. There was no real luxury but everything was clean and well cared for.

'Will you take a drink with me, Jack, for your hospitality?'

'I will,' Jack said, smiling gratefully. 'I have to say this, Mike, she had a terrible life did poor Nelly O'Connor. God alone knows what she ever saw in Tip in the first place, but she stuck it out. At least her last days were spent in comfort – thanks to Alice – and not in dirt and poverty and with only a pauper's grave.'

'I'll pay the funeral expenses. I told Alice she'd have the best. My mother had a hard life too. We had nothing but she always said that she wanted to go out with some style, God willing. Well, Mrs O'Connor will go in style, too.'

'That's very generous of you.'

'Will there be a wake? Is it the custom here?'

'For some, but I don't think they'd want one. They're too upset and I don't hold with them myself. They usually end up in a drunken brawl. Grief, guilt, overwrought nerves and drink don't mix very well. Old scores and slights are mentioned and then one thing leads to another and we get called in. It's not very dignified.'

'With that bit I'd agree. It's our custom in Ireland to take the body to the church to lie overnight.'

'On its own?'

'Usually, yes. Sometimes a nun will keep a vigil, but I

stayed with my mother. I felt I owed her that much, I'd been away so long.'

'Will you be able to get another sailing?'

'That's no problem. Cunard run a very fast, efficient and regular service.' He paused and looked straight at Jack. 'Maybe I'll get the *Aquitania*.'

'I know about him,' Jack said quietly. 'Lizzie told me.'

Mike nodded.

'He's pleasant enough, I suppose,' Jack went on. 'Never met him, of course, but I've seen his father, in the Crown Court. He's a big noise barrister.'

Mike nodded again and they let the matter drop. 'And what of himself? Has he been warned off or did he just disappear?'

'He's in jail. Walton. He got six years for assault and fraudulent misappropriation of money. Alice put him there.'

'Alice?'

'Aye. The day she arrived home and saw the state the family were still living in, she marched into the saloon bar of The Widows, packed with hardbitten men, and cursed him up hill and down dale. And she didn't mince her words to the others either. Of course Tip belted her, so I arrested him. She's got guts, has Alice. She got up in the dock and told everyone how he'd beaten her and the entire family for years. That he'd spent every penny of the money she'd sent specifically for her mam and addressed to her mam. He denied it. He yelled across the court that she was a liar. She yelled back that she'd call the post office clerk as a witness and where did everyone think he got so much money from when he never did a stroke of work?'

'Jaysus! I know she's got a temper but she must have been breathing fire. So, that's where all my money went. To finance a drunken wife beater.'

'Your money?'

Mike nodded. 'She insisted on working – singing – until the place was closed and after that . . .' he shrugged. He looked squarely at Jack Phillips. Jack was about his own age and he liked the fellow. He was obviously a man of principle. Mike felt so alone now, despite his sisters and their families. He'd loved his mother and now he ached for Alice's love and what was he going back to? Nothing. A big silent house and a few business acquaintances. He wanted to talk of his love and his grief; maybe it would help. He sighed and decided that Jack Phillips was a man to be trusted with those two emotions which were tearing him apart.

The glasses were refilled time and again as Mike told Jack his life story and of his love for Alice. Jack, in return, confessed his love for Lizzie, and the fact that he'd told Tip O'Connor that he'd break every bone in his body if he laid a finger on any of them. They were in similar positions, they told each other. They were both in love with younger women although Jack had no competition.

'You'll be able to marry her, Jack, after a suitable period of mourning.'

'Who'll see to the rest of the family? Agnes is only sixteen.'

'You think Alice will go back to London?'

'Yes. She's got some kind of a contract. If she breaks it she could be sued in court.'

Mike nodded. He'd be willing to pay any amount to free her and take her home with him. But where was home? Oh, he'd inherited the house, made his own money to add to his father's and made his mark in Charleston but there was no one there at all who mattered. And what about Dublin? The homeland was always close to an Irishman's heart, his own included, but Dublin was a changed city and with his mother dead he hadn't the heart for it.

* * *

There was a brief shopping expedition for mourning clothes. Lizzie and Alice made the purchases between them, while Jack and Mike made all the arrangements and completed the formalities. Nelly would go to St Anthony's, her old parish, where she'd worshipped until her death. It was the one thing she'd insisted on after she'd moved house. Every Sunday they'd all gone to nine o'clock Mass in the church beside a pub called the Throstle's Nest. On this, her last visit, there would be a full Requiem Mass and the hearse would be drawn by two black horses, with black plumes on their bridles. The rest of the family would go in two open carriages, the weather still being fine, and the whole procession would be led by the official mourners employed by the Co-op Funeral Directors. Normally, except for very grand funerals, the bereaved walked behind the hearse and there were no official mourners. But this was to be a very grand affair, Mike had spared no expense. Nelly O'Connor and his mother had one thing in common: the most expensive funerals that both Liverpool and Dublin had seen in a long time.

Alice, supported by Mike, went in the first carriage with Jack and Lizzie; Agnes and the others followed in the second one. They were all surprised and touched to see a line of people the whole length of Scotland Road. Men doffed their caps and hats, women crossed themselves, a few of the old shawlies dipped a bit of a curtsy, as though the cortège was that of royalty. Oh, Mam would have loved this, Alice thought, glad that the heavy black veil that covered her hat and extended to her shoulders hid her face and her red, swollen eyes.

'She never 'ad much in this life, God 'elp 'er, but she's going out like a queen,' Mary O'Hanlon sniffed as she and Ethel and Jinny sat in their pew watching the mourners file into the church.

Ethel wiped her eyes. 'God forgive me for saying this,

an' in His holy house too, but I hope that swine rots in prison!'

'Amen to that, Ethel,' Jinny said grimly. 'An' God forgive us both for cursing a man in His holy church.'

'She's got money now, has Alice. Did you see the fine gentleman, Mr O'Farrell, from America?'

Jinny nodded. 'He's only just buried his own ma, God rest her an' God bless the mark afterwards.'

'And that Jack Phillips will sort that old devil when he gets out of clink.'

'She'll marry 'im, yer know, Ethel,' Mary said.

'Lizzie will?'

Mary O'Hanlon nodded and wiped her eyes again as Father Mulcahey began the *De Profundus*.

'Out of the depths I have cried to thee, O Lord,

'Lord hear my voice.

'Let Thy ears be attentive of the voice of my Supplication. If Thou, O Lord, shalt observe iniquities; Lord who shall endure it?'

Most of the congregation didn't fully understand all of the words, or too much of their sentiment, but they made the responses at the end of the prayer.

'And let perpetual light shine upon her. Amen.'

Alice tried to keep back the tears but her body shook with her sobs. She'd never see her mam again. She knew, she believed, that Mam would be in heaven. She'd had her hell and her purgatory, too, here on earth, all the years she'd put up with Da, because long ago she'd made vows to 'love and to cherish, for better or for worse'. Alice hadn't informed the Governor of Walton of Nellie's death; she hadn't even thought about her father. There was a great ache, an emptiness in her heart, in her whole body.

She and Lizzie held each other's hands tightly when they went up for Communion. They had to pass the coffin, covered with roses and white Madonna lilies, and they both stopped, and laid a hand on it.

'Goodbye, Mam,' Lizzie said softly while Alice choked with emotion.

Only the closest neighbours and Jack's mam went back to the house for the buffet Mike had ordered from Reece's. There were bottles of a good Madeira wine and a couple of bottles of Jameson's too, but no one lingered too long. Lizzie urged Mary, Ethel and Jinny to take all the remaining food and wine home with them.

'Oh, God luv yer, Lizzie, but we couldn't. It'd be like taking from the dead,' Mary said.

'It'll be no such thing. I'll get it packed into baskets and you take it home, ladies, otherwise it'll be out and into the bin with it,' Mike retorted.

'Ah, you're a good, generous man, Mr O'Farrell.'

Alice managed a smile before the tears again threatened to overwhelm her.

Chapter Twenty-Five

It *was* the *Aquitania* that Mike was due to sail home on, and he was hoping that Alice would want to come and see him off. He'd thought that Williamson might have called at least to express his condolences to Alice. There had been enough obituaries in the papers and surely he read the newspapers, but there had been no sign of him. There hadn't even been a card. So much for his affection for Alice.

They said their farewells in the house in Media Street and Mike felt the same longing, the same desire, the same frustration... yet his pride wouldn't allow him to declare his love for fear of ridicule, like the night she'd left Charleston.

'So, you'll go back to London, Alice?' He tried to make his voice light.

'I've got a contract and besides, I have to work, otherwise I won't be able to stop thinking of ... Mam.'

'I could buy you out of the contract, if you want out.'

'And what would I do then, Mike? Mope around here?'

'You could come back to Charleston.' He held his breath, every nerve in his body on edge, every muscle tensed.

'No, but thanks, for everything. I really mean that. I couldn't have coped without you, but I can't go back to Charleston.'

He hid his bitter disappointment well. 'You know you

only need to send a cable, Alice, if you need help.'

She nodded and then there was a pause before she spoke again.

'Mike if . . . if ever you come back to see your sisters, will you come and see me?'

'I will, that's a promise, but it might be a long time. You might be married to a duke or someone like that, by then.' He attempted a smile but it died before it reached his eyes.

She smiled. 'No. Though a girl from round the corner did marry an earl, but he was crippled in the war and she was widowed in a horrible way. He died in her arms. No, I don't want to be like Hannah Harvey, or the Countess of Ashenden as she is now.'

He hugged her and kissed her on the cheek, while his whole being longed to hold on to her for ever, to carry her off in his arms to Charleston or Dublin or anywhere where she'd forget David Williamson.

When he left Liverpool, the weather was fair but he knew it probably wouldn't last. They picked up passengers in Cobh in County Cork and passed the old Head of Kinsale and were out into the Atlantic Ocean before he encountered David Williamson passing through the First-Class Smoking Room.

'Ah, Mr Williamson. Haven't I had my eyes peeled since we sailed just looking for you.'

'Mr O'Farrell! I had no idea you were aboard. How are you? Have you been home on business or was it pleasure?' His attitude was polite and pleasant.

'I came home to bury my mother,' Mike said flatly.

'I'm so sorry. Please accept my condolences.' Williamson's manner had now changed to one of grave respect and Mike wondered if he'd been trained to handle such a variety of situations. Was there some sort of course they all went on to enable them to cope, to use the right words for every occasion?

'Condolences accepted. Have you seen Alice?'

'No, she's in London. She's doing very well, from what Charlie tells me and from what I read in the papers. Charlie's going down to see her next month, I believe.'

Mike's expression changed. 'If you read the papers and hear so much from your brother then you'll know that Alice is in Liverpool and has been for the past four days! Her mother died.' Suddenly all Mike's anger erupted. 'You're a self-centred, thoughtless bastard, Williamson! All the politeness and concern is only skin deep. You know how she feels about you.'

David was shocked both by Mike's news and the personal attack on his character. 'I don't understand, sir. How *does* Alice feel or think?'

'If you made the effort to see her you'd find out, wouldn't you? She followed you to America, although why she bothered I don't bloody well know,' Mike snapped and walked away before he lost his temper entirely and punched that sanctimonious, patronising little upstart in the face.

David stared after him, astounded by his words and attitude. Alice had told him she'd gone to America fired by ambition and he could see no reason to disbelieve her. Maybe O'Farrell was jealous. Maybe he'd fallen in love with his ward and asked Alice to marry him. Had Alice turned him down? Perhaps that's why she had left Charleston so hurriedly, and why O'Farrell was behaving so oddly. David Williamson shrugged his shoulders and went on to see to his next task.

It wasn't a good crossing, it being the end of September, although the Atlantic was the most treacherous of oceans and storms were frequent even in summer. There were very few people in the dining rooms for meals, and the sounds of breaking china and glass accompanied their eating.

Mike had never suffered from seasickness and as he stood in the First-Class Writing Room watching, through the long floor-length windows, the heaving grey mass of water that seemed to match his mood, his thoughts were on the future. His future.

What was there to keep him in Charleston? Why hadn't he gone home years ago? Why shouldn't he sell up and go back to Dublin? Dublin *was* home and he knew every inch of it and each inch had its memories. He'd buy a house, maybe not in the city itself. Maybe in Dalkey or Sandycove or even Dunlaoghaire. He'd find things to occupy himself with. His sisters had friends and his nieces and nephews were growing up. Why live out a solitary existence in Charleston where he had few friends and no family? That patronising, ambitious little snot of a junior officer didn't love Alice at all and when she finally found out, as she surely would in time, she'd need someone to help pick up the pieces. Why not himself? Maybe she'd even come to love him – just a little.

As the bow of the ship plunged down into another trough and thousands of gallons of foaming water crashed down on her, Mike hung onto the bar across the window and came to his decision. He'd go back to Charleston and sell up. Wind up the business or find a buyer for it. That wouldn't be hard and he'd get a good price. Then he'd come home to the most beautiful country on God's good earth, as he'd described it to Alice the first time he'd met her. He would wait. With age came patience, and only a narrow strip of water would separate them then, a channel it took only eight hours to cross instead of an ocean that took nearly five days, and that on a fast ship like this one.

At the beginning of October Alice went back to London.

'I don't care what you say, Lizzie, I'm having a phone put in. If there had been one earlier . . .'

'Alice, stop blaming yourself. It was all so quick.' Lizzie

changed the subject. 'Where will I be able to phone you?'

'At Victor's office or at the theatre. Mrs Winters doesn't have a phone. I'll write the numbers down.'

They all went to see her off at Lime Street and she hugged every one of them in turn.

'Agnes, you'll have to help Lizzie, it's not going to be easy for her.'

Agnes had already realised this but gave her assent anyway.

'Now you three, particularly you, Jimmy, no nonsense. Mam will be watching you.'

'From up there?' Mary pointed to the glass-domed roof of the station.

'From up there, luv. She'll be watching over you. If you work hard at school then when you're fourteen, maybe we'll send you to a school to learn to use a typewriter.' Mary was bright and showed all the signs of becoming a beauty. Alice's eyes met those of Lizzie; they were thinking along the same lines. No more dirty, badly paid, monotonous factory jobs. Agnes was now employed in Bunny's on the corner of Church Street and Whitechapel. Jimmy was apprenticed to a plumber, so he'd have a trade in his fingers and would always find work. Eddy and Mary were still at school.

There was no one to meet Alice at Euston, so she got a taxi to Bloomsbury.

Mrs Winters welcomed her warmly. 'The show must go on, Alice, and time is a great healer. I missed Mr Winters terribly for years.'

'How long has he been gone?' It was the question she'd always wanted to ask but never had.

'Almost eight years now. But not a day goes by without my thinking of him. But life must go on – like the show.'

When Alice arrived back at the theatre, everyone was glad to see her, especially Lucy.

'It'll be great to get back in the chorus. I just don't

have, well, that special something. I've no confidence in myself and none in the role and it shows.'

'It'll be good in some ways to get back to work.'

'It'll take your mind off things, Alice, and you should go out more, you really should.'

'Maybe I will, soon.'

It wasn't long before Charlie Williamson turned up in her dressing room with a huge bouquet.

'I told you I'd see you soon.'

She smiled at him. He obviously didn't know about Nelly. 'I've been home, Mam died. I've only been back here a week.'

He looked concerned and guilty. 'Oh, Alice, I'm so sorry, I really am. So, you'll need cheering up a bit. I've booked supper at the Savoy.'

'Will you give me fifteen minutes to change?'

'I'll wait outside. I parked the car nearby as there's a nip in the air already.'

She'd never been to the Savoy Grill before. It was very impressive, far more opulent than the Adelphi, but it didn't compare with the First-Class Dining Room of the *Aquitania*.

'Mike O'Farrell came to see me,' she said by way of conversation after their orders had been taken.

'He travelled all the way from Charleston?' Charlie asked, amazed.

'Not especially to see me. He, too, had just buried his mother and he said he couldn't be in Liverpool and not call to see me. I don't know what I would have done without him. He took care of everything, from all the formalities to the buffet, and he insisted on paying for it all too.'

'Well, he is your guardian, after all.'

She didn't reply. She thought she detected a note of petulance in his voice.

'Is David home? He did promise to come and see me when he got some decent leave.'

'I can't keep up with all his comings and goings. He has Maisie demented with the washing. Mother told her to send it out to the laundry with everything else, but she won't. It won't be back in time, is the stock reply.'

So, they had a maid, Alice thought but without much surprise.

'He did have a week's leave, but he spent nearly all of it studying for yet another ticket.'

She felt disappointed and it must have shown in her face, for Charlie leaned towards her. 'It's his career, Alice. He enjoys it and he's ambitious.'

'I know,' she answered in a small voice as the hors d'oeuvres were served and the wine poured.

'But *I'm* not in the least ambitious. I'll be happy to toddle along contentedly earning my salary in obscurity for years. I *could* become ambitious though, given the right incentive.'

Alice looked at him in surprise. She sipped her wine slowly. She'd had nothing to eat since lunchtime and she didn't want to make a fool of herself or say things she would later regret.

'All I ever wanted, Charlie, was to sing on the stage. After the day you knocked me down and took me aboard the ship, my great ambition was for David to hear me sing on stage. I suppose in my stupid naive way that's why I followed him to America.'

'Did you? You never told me that before. I thought Mr O'Farrell had sent for you.'

She shook her head. 'No, it was all part of a dream, Charlie. I wanted to go to New York but I didn't have the fare for a decent ship. I got a tramp and ended up in Charleston. It was quite by accident that I met Mike O'Farrell.' She thought it prudent not to disclose the fact that Mike wasn't her guardian. There would have to be

315

endless explanations and she didn't want that. 'He's been very good to me.'

'Yes, David said he was very protective of you.'

'What else did David say?' She just wanted to talk about David.

'That you were stunning. That you had them all at your feet. That it was a great honour to be invited to that very, very exclusive ball.' He paused. 'Alice, I wouldn't expect to see David very often if I were you.'

She looked up, puzzled, the fork halfway to her mouth. 'Why not?'

Charlie shrugged carelessly, not wanting to make trouble. 'As I said, the sea is his career and it takes years to reach the top.'

She could understand that. She'd had ambitions too. Fate had been kind to her and she'd got the breaks early, but it wasn't like that for everyone.

'Does he ever write home when he's away?' she asked, pushing the petits pois round her plate. She really wasn't very hungry.

Charlie laughed. 'Now that's a huge bone of contention at home. Mother says he should. Father says it's a waste of time and energy because by the time he posted the letter in New York and it was processed, it would come back on the *Mauretania* or the *Berengaria* – they're the Royal Mail ships – and he'd already be home. And he's not very good with letters. Oh, he'll send a cable if it's someone's birthday, or there's been a change of port or a long delay, but that's all.'

As Alice listened, she wondered why Charlie seemed to be putting his brother down. He did it jokingly, but the jibes were there just the same.

On the way home, wrapped in her satin quilted evening coat with a long, floating chiffon scarf swathed round her head and shoulders, she wondered whether Charlie was trying to warn her about something. Was he telling her, in a roundabout way, something Victor had stressed, that it was a special type of girl who married a seafarer? David had told her himself that the sea was his life, so she shouldn't expect him to be running around after her and driving to London and back when he had important examinations to study for. But surely he could find time to write or phone when he was at home. He had said he was her biggest fan.

It was when they reached her digs that it suddenly dawned on her. Maybe Charlie didn't want her to see David because he was falling for her himself. After all, he drove frequently to London. There were always flowers, champagne and supper in the best places for her.

He got out of the car and held the door open for her.

'Thanks for the meal, Charlie, it was really something special. It's very good of you to drive all this way to see me. It *is* a long way.'

He smiled. 'I'll come down every week, if you would like me to, Alice.'

'No. No, really, Charlie. I do get very tired and I'm ... I'm not over Mam yet.'

Instantly he became solicitous. 'Oh, I'd forgotten. Forgive me for being so crass, Alice, but I will come down again soon.'

'At the end of next month maybe?' She tried not to sound off-putting or dismissive. She did like him, he was good company, but she certainly didn't love him and never would. He was just a friend.

Chapter Twenty-Six

Alice stood in Victor Hardman's office and looked out of the window at the traffic in the street below. November was a miserable month. Gloomy and often foggy. Fog so thick you could hardly see a hand in front of you. Fog that made breathing hard for many people. She remembered the long, bitter winters in Benledi Street. Now she had good clothes to keep out the cold, a warm home, nourishing food, and she travelled in comfort.

It seemed a lifetime since she'd dragged herself home from a day's work to a cold damp house where there was no food and no fire and she had been forced to go out and sing in the streets. She wondered if, as they grew up, Jimmy, Eddy, and Mary would remember those days of terrible hardship. She and Lizzie and Agnes would always remember. A smile played around her mouth as she thought of her sister. She was glad that Lizzie had found Jack Phillips. It was an odd match. But he had a good steady job, a nice home and he'd treat her well.

For the first time in months she thought of her father. He still had a long time to serve in jail and it was a harsh routine in Walton. If he survived, when he came out he'd go looking for them all. Well, Mam had gone, she herself had gone, and Lizzie would be gone soon, if she had read the signs right. Jimmy would be nineteen, Eddy sixteen and Mary fifteen, and all Agnes had to do was send for Jack Phillips if Da landed on the doorstep one day.

Victor finished his conversation and replaced the receiver sharply. He wasn't having a good morning and his ulcer was playing up. He leaned back in his chair. 'So, what's the matter with you, miss? Not happy with the idea of the new part? *No, No, Nanette* has been running for over two years, and it's a very successful show, Alice.'

'I know, I went to see it – Charlie took me. I wanted to see what it was like and I didn't want to go on my own.'

'You don't need to make excuses, Alice. You can go where you like and with who, or is it whom, you like.' A thought suddenly occurred to him. She seemed quite taken with this Charlie. Was she going to tell him she was getting married? 'Isn't he the brother of your young mariner?'

'Yes, but Charlie is just a friend. He cheers me up, that's all.'

'So, what's the matter with you now?'

She turned again towards the window, not wanting to face him. 'I don't want to star in *No, No, Nanette* or in any other show.'

He sat up abruptly. 'Why the hell not? Do you want more money? Is that it?' he snapped. It all came down to this in the end, usually. Oh, they pouted and sulked and used every trick and excuse in the book, but money was always the root of the problem.

'No, I don't want any more money. I'm not greedy, you know how I live.'

'Yes, very modestly for someone in your position and at your age. You're one of the thriftiest stars I know. You hardly spend a penny on yourself, except for your clothes, and you don't have trunks full of them either, considering the public image you have to live up to.'

'I can remember what living in poverty was like. Real poverty. It's something that stays with you.' She saved hard. Quite what she was saving for she didn't know yet. But the fear of being reduced again to the way she'd lived in Benledi Street never really left her.

She turned to face him. 'I want to go home. Well, go back north, away from London.'

He stared at her, unable to speak for a few seconds. 'What the hell for? You told me yourself you've come from the gutter, from singing in the streets, to become one of the highest paid entertainers in this part of the business and with a regiment of fawning supporters. It's a dream come true and now you want to throw it all away? Jesus, Alice!' He thumped the desk, making the inkstand and the phone rattle.

'I don't want supporters – fans. It *is* a dream come true, or it was. It was all for Mam, and now she's gone, so what's the point?'

He stood up and walked to the window to face her, gripping her wrist and searching her face for some inkling of an explanation. 'It's that bloody seafaring fool, isn't it?'

She snatched her hand away. 'He's not a fool!'

'He is, because he doesn't appreciate just what you've achieved. Or maybe he does and he's jealous. He never comes down here to see you or take you to supper, does he?'

She couldn't argue with that. 'If I go back north, there'll be more chance of seeing him, I don't deny that, but . . .'

'But what? Has it ever occurred to you that he really has no romantic interest in you?'

She turned on him furiously. 'He has! He told me he'd followed my career! If you remember, it was him who asked me to sing on the ship.'

'Thinking, no doubt, about his own prospects. It would be seen by his superiors as showing initiative. A feather in his cap.'

'He said he was my biggest fan!'

'Then why does he never come to London? Or is this "romance" being conducted by proxy, via his brother Charlie?'

She was smarting with the humiliation. 'There isn't time for him to be traipsing up and down to London. They dock one day, disembark the passengers, clean the ship up, bunker up, load up with fresh stores and are away again in two days.'

'Oh, for God's sake Alice, don't take me for a fool. He must get leave. No company expects its employees to work like that month after month without a break, especially its officers. And from what I remember they employ an army of cleaners and tradesmen to clean up and repair any damage, and another army of dockers to do the bunkering.'

'He's studying!' she snapped back. 'Anyway, I'm sick of London. Sick of all the "fawning" as you call it.'

He sat down again at his desk. 'So, what will you do up north?'

'They still have plenty of good theatres. When I first met you, you said you could get me jobs in Manchester, Birmingham, Leeds.'

'Alice, have you thought of how it's going to look? People will say you're sliding, coming down in the world, a has-been.'

'I don't care what they think or say, I—'

'Then you should, Alice, because without them you've no bloody job at all!' he yelled at her, finally losing his temper.

'I want to go home!' she yelled back.

He threw his hands in the air in a gesture of resignation. 'All right! All right! Pack your bags and go home. I'll get you what jobs I can, but touring is no life, Alice. No life at all and you still won't see much of lover boy.'

'I'll manage.'

'It's your life, your career, Alice, but you're wasting it.'

They were an echo of Nelly's words and she shivered, but she'd had enough. She felt miserable and lonely. She'd made no real friends. Occasionally she'd go out with Lucy and the others, but not very often. She also knew that because of this they thought she was a snob.

'Can I ask a favour?'

He'd gone back to his paperwork as though he'd forgotten about her. 'Now what?'

'Can I use your telephone?'

He gathered up a sheaf of papers and stood up. 'Help yourself. I'm going out for some fresh air.'

She felt better as she dialled the number. Now at least the confrontation was over, along with the shouting.

It was Mary who answered.

'What are you doing off school?'

'I'm sick. I've got a bad cough and our Lizzie said I was to stay in bed today. Mrs O'Hanlon's coming up later with me dinner.'

Alice caught her breath and immediately thought the worst. A bad cough. Oh, God, not consumption, she prayed. 'Isn't Lizzie coming home at dinner time?'

'No, she's meeting her Jack.'

Alice sighed. 'Well, when she gets in, will you tell her I'm coming home. Tomorrow. Tell her there's nothing wrong. I'll explain it all tomorrow.'

Down the wire she could hear Mary coughing and spluttering until she finally got over the spasm.

'Mary, don't you get out of that bed again. If the phone rings, ignore it!'

As she replaced the receiver she bit her lip. Maybe it was just as well that she was going home. She hadn't liked the sound of that cough at all.

She packed her belongings and gave Mrs Winters a message for Charlie, should he come calling for her.

'I'm sorry to see you go, Alice,' Mrs Winters said as they waited for the taxi, 'and leave such a good career, but it's your business. It's your life.'

On impulse Alice hugged her briefly. 'Thank you for everything.'

That evening, when the train finally arrived at Lime Street Station, Lizzie and Jack were waiting at the barrier. Lizzie looked worried.

'Alice! What's wrong?'

'Nothing.'

Jack took her case. 'Is this all?'

'The rest is being sent on. Come on, we'll get a taxi.'

'We'll get the tram and like it,' Lizzie said firmly and Jack led them across the road to wait at the tram stop.

'Is Mary any better today? I've been worried sick about her since yesterday.'

'I had the doctor out to her and it's just a chest cold. He left some linctus – which is murder to get down her – but she's better today. She can stay off school the rest of the week.'

'Oh, thank God. I had visions of, well . . .'

'She hasn't got *consumption*.' Lizzie whispered the word for it carried a social stigma and there were quite a few people waiting in the queue.

'Where were you yesterday dinner time anyway?' Alice queried once they had settled themselves on the tram for the short journey.

'I met Jack. I'll tell you when we get home.' Lizzie looked over her shoulder and smiled at Jack who was standing on the platform chatting to the conductor. He knew a lot of them and the drivers too.

They got off at Kirkdale Road and walked the short distance to Media Street.

'Our Agnes will have given them their tea and cleared up by now,' Lizzie stated as they knocked on the front door.

Jimmy opened it, scrubbed clean and in his Sunday clothes.

'Where are you going, meladdo, all done up like a dog's dinner?' Lizzie demanded.

'I'm going to Frankie's, then we're going to the Astoria.'

324

'Well, don't you be late in and don't go getting into trouble. I don't like that Frankie Kennedy, he's a bad influence on you.'

Eddy and Mary were sitting at the kitchen table, with Georgie stretched out in front of the fire, his fur sleek, purring softly. Eddy was engrossed in a book and Mary was learning, by rote from an atlas, the capital cities of the countries of the Empire. It surprised Alice to see them so quiet and industrious.

'Did you bribe them or threaten to murder them?' she asked.

'Jack had a long talk with them all about what to do with their lives and how if you worked hard at school, you'd get a good job and therefore have a better life.' Lizzie smiled again at Jack. He took a real interest in all of them and could explain and coax far better than she could. He should have been a teacher, she'd told him, he had infinite patience and yet that air of authority needed to keep a class of unruly hooligans in order. He'd replied that there just hadn't been the money for anything like that and besides, he'd fought in the Great War and needed to earn a living when he left the army.

Lizzie made a pot of tea and beckoned Alice into the parlour. Jack followed.

'All right, our Alice, what's up? Why have you come home?'

'Because I'm fed up with London. It's just bed to work. It's not what I expected. I've no real friends and everyone I care about is up here.'

Lizzie looked appalled. 'You mean you've given up your career? You've given up singing?'

'No. I'm going to sing up here, in the north. Victor will find me work. There are plenty of good theatres here, better than some down there.'

Lizzie digested this in silence. Maybe it was just as well. 'Will you live here?'

'No, there's no room. I'm going to ask Charlie Williamson to find me a house, on the Wirral or near Chester. I thought about it on the train.'

'Oh,' was all Lizzie said.

'You don't sound very interested.'

'I am, it's just that, well, I've been dying to tell you *my* news. Jack and me are getting married after Christmas, that's where we were yesterday, buying the ring.' Lizzie stretched out her left hand, on the third finger of which was a small diamond solitaire.

All Alice's irritability left her and she jumped up and hugged Lizzie. 'Oh, Lizzie! Lizzie! I'm so happy for you! And you, Jack! Oh, bend down, I can't reach up to give you a kiss!'

Laughingly Jack obliged and Alice congratulated them again.

'You'll be going to live up the road then?' she asked when they'd settled themselves down again.

'Yes. Jack's mam wasn't too sure at first, but now we get on just fine.'

Alice wondered at this. Mam had always said two women in one kitchen didn't go. Not for very long, anyway.

'Our Agnes is nearly seventeen and the kids are all much better behaved now and I'm just down the road, if they need me.'

'Have you set an actual date yet?'

'Saturday, the first of February, at St Anthony's. Jack's got to get a dispensation from Father Godfrey because it's not his parish.'

'Will Father Mulcahey marry you?'

'No. He's retiring. It's a Father Rimmer. You will be my bridesmaid, Alice?'

'Of course,' she answered, but she suddenly and inexplicably felt sad.

* * *

The following day she phoned Charlie and made arrangements to see him at the weekend. In the meantime, he said he would make enquiries with estate agents.

They all had their evening meal together. Jack was on duty but he'd be calling in later, Lizzie said.

Alice had been thinking about things. She'd mulled the idea over and over in her head all day.

'Lizzie, I've been thinking.'

'What about?' Lizzie asked, pouring the gravy over Jimmy's meal. If he did it himself there wouldn't be enough to go round and she'd have to make more. He had an appetite like a horse.

'Well, you're getting married and going to live with Mrs Phillips.' She thought she saw Agnes raise her eyes to the ceiling and then pull a face, but she wasn't sure. 'This house is only rented so I'm going to buy a house. I've saved every penny since I went to London.'

'You! Buy a house? God Almighty, Alice!'

'What's wrong with that?'

'Nothing, it's just that, well, people like us don't *buy* houses.'

'People like us have come up in the world.'

'You might have, Alice, but I'll be happy enough with Jack in a rented house. I don't want anything grand.'

Alice ignored the note of censure in her sister's voice.

'It won't be "grand". I'm not thinking of a flaming palace like Hannah Harvey lives in, but there will be more rooms than this house so what I was thinking was that you and Jack can live here and the rest of you can come and live with me, in a nice house in the country.'

There was total silence as they all looked at her across the kitchen table. A silence filled with shock. It was Jimmy who broke it.

'In the country! I don't want to be stuck in the country, there's nothing to do! Frankie Kennedy said they went to Ireland once to a place in the country and it was awful.

There was nothing to do except go to church. That was the big event of the day.'

'And how am I going to get to work? I'll never see any of my friends!' Agnes was equally indignant.

'We'd have miles and miles to go to school,' Eddy complained.

'And you won't be there all the time, Alice,' Mary added.

Alice had been unprepared for this wall of opposition and complaint. She'd been sure they would all jump at the chance.

'But it'll be much better for you. Away from all the muck and the fog and the germs. Clean fresh air, good country food.'

Jimmy was openly mutinous. 'Well, I'm not going, Alice.'

'And neither am I,' Agnes stated flatly. 'We've been happy here, Alice, and besides, Mam ... well, Mam died here. It would be like ... sort of like leaving her on her own.'

Alice got up. 'Oh, suit yourselves! I was only thinking of you! This isn't exactly what you'd call a world away from Scottie Road, is it?' She stormed out and ran up the stairs to the bedroom she was sharing with Lizzie. The one Mam had shared with Lizzie.

She sat down on the bed. Oh, they were so ungrateful! They all had short memories. It was to put food in their mouths that she'd walked the streets of this city, singing. And since she'd left Liverpool she'd worked so hard, saved when she could have easily spent all her money on clothes and jewels or running around London nightclubs. All she'd wanted to do was give them a better, healthier life. Lizzie obviously wouldn't leave, she'd be happy here, but the others could have so much more, if they wanted it.

She looked across the room and caught sight of herself in the mirror on the wall. She wasn't a girl any longer, she was a woman, but had she become too grand for them? Were her expectations of them too high? And what was that Agnes had said? It would be like leaving Mam on her own. It was ridiculous but she too seemed to feel her mother's presence in the room. She dropped her eyes, afraid that over her shoulder in the mirror she would see Nelly's face. She'd changed, but surely for the better. But was she now too sophisticated for them? Had she grown too far away from them and their simple expectations of life? She suddenly remembered how she'd always sworn that whatever she did, however far she rose in her profession, she would still be the same inside. But she wasn't. She looked up and across at the mirror. A woman stared back. An attractive woman with large brown eyes and softly waving tawny-coloured hair. What had happened to little Alice O'Connor from Benledi Street? Had that girl gone altogether? Had she climbed so high that she'd grown too far away from her family and her humble roots, of which she'd always been so proud?

When Lizzie came into the room, there were tears on Alice's cheeks.

Lizzie took her hand. 'I know you meant well and I told them that, but they're city kids, we all are. You'll probably enjoy it, I suppose it will be a sort of escape for you, but they'd hate it, Alice.'

'I know, Lizzie, and I'm sorry. I seem to have lost sight of what I really want, what I really am.' She pressed a hand to her heart. 'Here. Go and tell them I'm sorry and that I'm not upset or annoyed with them.'

'But you're still going to go ahead with the house? You won't stay here?'

Alice shook her head. 'No, I'll be in and out like a fiddler's elbow. I'll just disrupt things, and besides . . .'

'What?'

'I can feel Mam here, Lizzie, and I . . . I don't think she approves of me any longer.'

Lizzie was scornful. 'Oh, that's just plain daft, Alice! Mam would never, ever haunt you, if that's what you're trying to say. She loved us, she couldn't have been a better mother, not married to the likes of Da and taking all those beatings. For God's sake, Alice, don't be so flaming morbid!'

Alice managed a smile. 'You were always the one with plain common sense, Lizzie.'

'And wouldn't I need it with a sister like you!' The words were accompanied by a smile and a laugh.

Chapter Twenty-Seven

Christmas was a very busy time for Alice. She was booked to appear for a week in Manchester, then a week in Leeds and then, after the holidays, a week at the Empire.

She seemed to find herself most of the time on trains and in taxis, and some of the digs left much to be desired. Sometimes Charlie drove her to the theatre. He had been very good about helping her to find a new home, and they'd looked at houses near Chester and on the Wirral. She had almost made up her mind about a picture post-card cottage with a thatched roof, low beamed ceilings and a lovely front garden in Saltney Ferry, near Chester. It certainly wasn't a palace but there was plenty of room should any of her brothers and sisters decide to change their minds, or come to stay for a bit of a break.

Charlie had arranged for a man from the village to do the garden and any odd jobs, and his wife would come in and clean while Alice was away. She'd also see that there was plenty of food in the pantry for Alice's return.

Lizzie and Jack had gone to see the cottage and after admiring everything, tried again to point out the disadvantages of Alice buying it, not least of which was the fact that she would be running two households.

'You'll need furniture and carpets and curtains and all the other things like pots and pans and sheets and towels, like when we moved to Media Street, and you know how much all that cost.'

Alice knew she had a point, but she was determined to get away from the small rows of closely packed terraced house and dank, dirty courts. At least her new home had a bathroom, for one of the bedrooms had been converted. A proper bathroom was something the house in Media Street didn't have. But she did go home for Christmas itself, loaded down with presents and food, the cottage still being only partly furnished.

She, Lizzie and Agnes sat up late on Christmas Eve, reminiscing about other, less happier, Christmases.

'Oh, we're just making ourselves miserable, let's talk about something else,' Alice said after Lizzie had related the events of the Christmas after Alice had gone to America.

'The wedding plans?' Agnes suggested.

'Yes, it's not too far away now, Lizzie,' Alice replied and they all talked on into the early hours of Christmas morning, all hoping the new decade would prove to be better than the last.

Two days after New Year, Alice opened at the Empire. Her 'spot' was for the last half-hour of the show which gave her plenty of time to dress.

Miss Fairchild was delighted to see her back. 'I'm so glad you decided to come home,' she beamed as she buttoned up Alice's dress.

'London seemed to have lost its excitement, its glamour for me. It's just too big. I used to do the show, perhaps have supper with Victor, then go back to Bloomsbury. In the mornings or sometimes in the afternoon, if there wasn't a matinée, I'd rehearse.'

'Not much of a life.'

'No.'

As Miss Fairchild brushed Alice's hair and then covered it with one of the new fashionable, silver mesh, close-fitting caps, there was a knock on the dressing-room door.

'It's not time yet. We've fifteen minutes,' Miss Fairchild called out.

'I know. But there's someone here to see Miss O'Connor,' Alf shouted back from the corridor outside.

Alice sighed. 'Charlie again.'

'Don't you want to see him?'

'He's been so good to me, so helpful, that I just can't send him away.'

'Of course you can. It's just before your performance. We could say you've a bad headache, or an upset stomach caused by nerves.'

'No. Let him in.'

Miss Fairchild shouted Alice's instructions and the door opened.

Alice gave a cry of delight, her heart leapt and she jumped up from the stool in front of the dressing table and its mirror surrounded with lights. 'David! David! I never expected to see you!' Her eyes were shining with happiness.

'Well, I've got a week's leave and plenty of studying to do but I thought, to hell with it.'

Charlie appeared behind him. 'You mean I twisted your arm until you said "Oh, to hell with it!"'

'You look wonderful, Alice. You seem different, so . . . sophisticated now.'

She smiled wryly.

'What made you come back?' he asked.

'Oh, I was homesick and fed up with London.'

'The homesickness I can understand, but why throw away your career?'

'I haven't. I've just moved it up north. They'll be having the stage musicals at theatres here soon. It's not the other side of the moon.'

'Supper again?' Charlie asked and she nodded, delightedly.

Miss Fairchild interrupted. 'I'm going to have to ask

333

you two gentlemen to leave now, we've only got five minutes.'

They left but when Alice went on stage her heart too was singing. Oh, he was still the same. He hadn't changed one bit. She'd made the right decision to come back, to buy a house in Saltney Ferry. His visit was proof of it. He'd come to see her, even though he was still studying so hard. She'd dismissed Charlie's remark about twisting David's arm from her mind. She put everything into her performance, for she was singing for him and in some songs directly to him. She couldn't see either of them, but when she sang 'Always' her voice was full of emotion.

This time supper was in a small but very smart restaurant in Bold Street. 'I thought it might be a bit quieter than the Adelphi,' Charlie said. 'It's got a secluded, exclusive atmosphere.'

All through the meal Alice's eyes never left David's face and she looked as though someone had switched on a light inside her.

Charlie and David did most of the talking, keeping up a laughing banter, but Alice felt uncomfortable with the thought that on Charlie's part some of the remarks might be serious. She and David didn't have a minute alone together, Charlie saw to that, she thought with some annoyance, except when he excused himself for five minutes. 'Call of nature, I'm afraid,' he'd whispered. It wasn't strictly true, but it would give David time to tell Alice about his plans.

'Have you settled into your new home now, Alice?' David asked, as Charlie left.

'Well, not really, I've been so busy, but by February I should have some time to get everything sorted out properly. Things tend to go a bit flat in February and March, as people don't want to leave their firesides.'

'I know it's very belated, but I was sorry to hear about your mother.'

She nodded. 'I still miss her.'

A silence hung between them.

'Alice—'

'I'm—' They both spoke at once.

'You tell me what you were going to say,' she urged.

He fiddled with his wine glass. 'Company policy has changed. Bookings tail off in January and February. The weather most of the time is atrocious and fewer people make the Atlantic crossing, so they can manage with just the *Berengaria* and the *Mauretania*, so we're off cruising again. To the islands of the West Indies.'

Her heart dropped like a lump of lead and she felt sick with disappointment. He was going away again for two months.

'We'll be calling at Charleston again. I had a wonderful time there, thanks to you, Alice, and Mr O'Farrell.'

She thought his tone changed when he spoke of Mike.

'Alice, you know that the sea is my life,' he said earnestly.

She gazed across the table at him. 'I know. Just like singing is mine. Not totally my life though.'

He nodded but didn't seem able to respond.

'So?' Alice questioned when the silence became unbearable. 'You were talking about your life.'

'I . . . well, I was just, er, remarking on what the sea meant to me.' He turned as he saw his brother re-enter the room.

Charlie returned to the table. At least, he thought, she didn't seem too upset at David's news.

'Yes.' She didn't want to think about it now so she changed the subject. 'My sister's getting married on the first of February.'

'Lizzie?' Charlie asked with interest.

She nodded. 'She's marrying her policeman, they'll live with his mother.'

335

David smiled at her. 'So, you'll be a bridesmaid then.'

'Yes, me and Agnes and Mary. The lads are complaining already about the suits and stiff collars they'll have to wear. She doesn't want a great fuss, but she's waited a long time for her happiness and I think she does deserve a grand do.'

'You don't look very pleased about it, Alice,' Charlie remarked.

'It's just that I don't want to upstage Lizzie. I don't want to spoil her day. So many people know me now, I don't want them to turn up just to see me.'

David refilled her glass. 'That's very considerate and kind of you, Alice. And who is the best man?'

'I don't know, they haven't said. Probably one of Jack's mates from work.' She smiled at him. 'Will you come and see me again before your leave is up?'

He looked uncomfortable, even a little awkward, Alice thought.

'I'll try, but there's so much to do and I do have some prior engagements.'

She was disappointed, wondering what the 'prior engagements' were.

'But you'll have Charlie to squire you around all the northern cities.'

'If she'll let me, that is.' Charlie sounded petulant.

David laughed. 'You know I rely on you to tell me how Alice's career is going.'

Charlie said nothing and Alice sensed a certain coolness between them.

'I'll go for the car,' Charlie said. They'd borrowed Mr Williamson's Minerva for the evening as there were only two seats in Charlie's Jowett sports car.

Two days later Alice went back to Media Street, at Lizzie's request.

'Honestly, Alice, it's bad enough trying to organise this

wedding without having my chief bridesmaid always missing.'

'Lizzie, you know what it's been like for me.'

'Oh, I'm not going to argue, Alice. Now about your dress and headdress.'

'Haven't you sorted that out yet? What would you like me to wear? It's *your* day, Lizzie, not mine or Agnes's or Mary's. We all take second place to you.'

'I was going to have you in that pretty shade of green, *eau de nil*, until Jack's mam and Mary O'Hanlon had a fit and said it was unlucky.'

'That's just superstitious nonsense.'

'Well, I'm not taking any chances. I thought pink. A deep pink or maybe magenta. That would brighten up a grey February day.'

It was not one of Alice's favourite colours but she said nothing.

'With circlets of pink and white wax flowers. Maggie Higgins sells them at her Gowns by Margo.'

Even worse, Alice thought, but then checked herself. Lizzie just had different taste, she liked different things, that was all. If everyone had the same taste, life would be very boring.

'And what about your dress, have you got it yet?'

Lizzie blushed. 'Yes. I got that and the veil and head-dress from Maggie's too.'

'From Gowns by Margo?'

Lizzie nodded. 'I can never think of her as anything other than Maggie Higgins from Silvester Street. But she has a good price range and she designs them all herself. And she's honest. I know if I chose a dress that cost pots of money but made me look like a May horse, she'd tell me.'

'She would too, that one. She always had a tongue so sharp it's a wonder she's not cut herself with it!'

'It's white taffeta, cut very plain with just a bit of lace

set into the bodice and two tiny bows of blue ribbon at the wrist. That's her trademark. I'm having a headband, or "bandeaux" as she calls it, with just a few small white wax roses at the front and a long veil.'

'It sounds gorgeous, Lizzie, and you'll look like a dream.' Alice meant what she said. Sometimes, she reflected, things turned out for the best. If Tommy Mac had survived there would have been no dress from Gowns by Margo.

'I wish I could get the same enthusiasm out of our Jimmy and Eddy. All they do is moan and complain, saying their mates will skit them.'

'Oh, take no notice, Lizzie. All men hate weddings and dressing up.'

'Jack has ordered carriages. Won't that be something?'

'Is he wearing his uniform?'

'Yes, so I suppose he'll at least be warmer than me. Maggie advised me to wear a flannel petticoat underneath. She said it won't show.'

'Who's going to give you away?'

Lizzie's mouth was set in a hard line. 'Well, it certainly won't be Da, thank God. No, Mr O'Hanlon is giving me away. He's going to borrow a suit from his brother.'

'I hope he behaves, Lizzie. He's almost as bad as Da with a few drinks down him. He'd cause an argument in an empty house!'

'Mary's threatened him. She told me she said if he puts one foot wrong, he'll be carted off to Rose Hill 'cos half the police force will be there as guests. They won't, but he's not to know that.'

Alice laughed. 'And who's the best man?'

'I don't know yet.'

'God, Lizzie, it's only four weeks away! Surely he can find one of his mates?'

'Oh, it will all be sorted out, Alice,' Lizzie said, refusing to meet her sister's eyes. Jack had kept in touch with Mike

O'Farrell and had written asking if it was at all possible, if Mike was over in Dublin buying a house, would he stand for him? He didn't want Mike to come especially, just if he was in this part of the world. If he wasn't, then Tom Burns, his sergeant, would be his best man.

Jack and Lizzie had discussed it often, before Jack finally wrote to Mike.

'It's a way of bringing them together, Lizzie,' he'd argued.

'So was Mam's death and his ma's death. I would have thought that with all the sadness and shock it would have brought them closer, but it didn't.'

'Everyone was upset, Lizzie. No one was thinking about love and happiness.'

'But now because we're getting married you think she'll be more receptive?'

'You never know, they did part friends.'

'Our Alice has a temper, Jack, and she can be so contrary at times. I don't think she'll take kindly to our meddling.'

'Let's just wait and see,' he'd replied and so the letter had been written. So far there had been no reply from Mike, and Lizzie knew they were running out of time.

A telegram arrived the following week in the form of a cable from the *Mauretania*.

'DELIGHTED TO OBLIGE. WAS ON MY WAY HOME ANYWAY. MIKE.'

'We're going to have to tell her,' Lizzie said.

'I know.'

Lizzie put her arms round him – she barely came up to his chest. 'You're matchmaking, Jack Phillips!'

He grinned down at her. 'So? He loves her and I thought that if they got together, especially for a wedding . . .'

'Oh, I hope she doesn't realise what you're up to and throw a tantrum and refuse to be chief bridesmaid.'

'She won't, and anyway, even if she does, there's Agnes and Mary.' Like Alice, Jack didn't want Lizzie's day over-shadowed by her sister's fame.

'When is the *Mauretania* due in?'

'I don't know but I'll find out. He may want to go to Dublin for a few days first, take the overnight ferry on the same day the *Maurie* docks, which might be a better plan all round.'

Mike had been surprised and touched when Jack's letter had arrived. He had been in the process of packing up. He'd sold his business for a fat profit and also the house and most of its contents. He had no intention of buying a house the size of this one, so what furniture he'd decided to keep would be shipped over later. He'd finalised the details, by letter, with a solicitor in Dublin and was now the owner of a detached, Victorian villa in Dunlaoghaire whose two long piers reached out like arms to encircle the harbour where the mail boat arrived and departed each day.

Both Kitty and Dee had urged him to move into their mother's house, which was standing empty and would be nearer for visiting, but he'd refused. It was his mother's house. He wanted somewhere new, outside the city, but still in County Dublin and near enough for a drive into town.

He read Jack's letter again. Of course Alice would be a bridesmaid. How would he cope with that? He'd heard from Jack that she'd come home but that she still didn't see much of Williamson. Charlie, yes, but the other one seemed to be away all the time. Alice had told them he'd be sailing around the warm waters of the West Indies for two months. Mike had taken hope from that piece of information. Maybe there was still a chance, especially at a wedding. 'You're a crafty sod, Jack Phillips, that you are,' he'd said to himself, smiling.

340

'I can't see much to smile about,' Alexander had remarked acidly. He'd stayed on to supervise the packing. The rest of the staff had gone, with tears and a good bonus in their pay packets.

Alexander had impeccable, glowing references and had been offered three places already. Mike had given him a gold hunter watch and chain with a tiger's eye fob, plus a gold cigarette case, inscribed, and six months' wages. Alexander had been more than just a butler, and leaving him was like leaving a friend.

Jack met Mike at the landing stage on a bitterly cold Tuesday morning. They'd had to anchor in the Sloyne until a large enough place on the landing stage had become available. The *Berengaria* had saluted her sister ship as she'd passed, en route to New York, with the three traditional blasts on her steam whistle. 'And God be with the lot of you,' Mike had muttered.

He shook Jack's hand warmly. 'Jesus, Mary and Joseph, I hope it's not going to be like this on Saturday.'

'A bad crossing, was it?'

Mike hailed a taxi. 'It was bloody desperate. We went through three blizzards in a day. I think there were only half a dozen of us in the dining room each day, but never mind all that, how are you in yourself, Jack?'

'Fine. Everything is under control. What about you?'

'Great altogether, although those two rossies beyond in Dublin are not too happy that I won't live on their doorsteps. Kitty is moving into the old house, she's got six kids. Dee had more sense, she's only got three. I think she puts bromide in Fergal's tea and I'll bet she doesn't own up to that in confession,' Mike laughed. 'How's Alice?'

'She's fine. She's promised Lizzie she'll sing. Do a solo piece, probably "Ave Maria".'

'When's she coming up to Liverpool?' He sounded nonchalant, or hoped he did. But he was longing to see her. To laugh and smile with her, to take her hand, to kiss her cheek – as a friend would in greeting, except that he wanted to kiss her lips and hold her like a lover.

'She's supposed to be coming home on Wednesday night,' Jack informed him.

'Tomorrow.' He would see her again tomorrow. He felt his pulse quicken. Maybe at a wedding she might just soften towards him. Maybe.

Alice arrived home on Wednesday night, just after the evening meal had been cleared away. She wore a dark blue velour coat with a thick silver fox fur collar which was turned up round her ears, while her navy hat was pulled well down.

'You picked a wonderful time of year to get married, Lizzie, it's freezing! We'll all catch our deaths! Is it tomorrow we've to go to Maggie Higgins's for the final fitting?'

Lizzie nodded.

'Where's Jack tonight, on duty?'

'No, it's been a rest day today.'

'I wish I had rest days.'

'I thought you had plenty of time to yourself. I thought you enjoyed the peace of the country.'

'I do, it's just that I'm never there much. I seem to spend my life on trains.'

'You travel first class.'

'It's still a train though, isn't it?'

Lizzie took a deep breath. She'd have to tell her soon, otherwise Jack would land on the doorstep with his best man in tow. 'Alice, I've got to tell you something.' Lizzie looked down to hide her excitement and plucked at the edges of her cuffs, as though removing bits of imaginary fluff.

'Holy Mother of God. You're not expecting, are you?' Alice cried.

'No, I'm not! Would I have a white dress and veil and a Nuptial Mass if I was? It . . . it's about Jack's best man.'

'What about him? I thought you'd sorted all that out. Who has he asked?'

Lizzie grinned. 'It's Mike O'Farrell. He's sold up and bought a house in Ireland. They . . . they should be here any minute now.'

Alice jumped up. 'Mike? Mike has come over to be best man?'

Lizzie nodded. 'They've kept in touch since Mam died.'

Alice wasn't sure how she felt. Glad, sorry, surprised. 'Why didn't you tell me, Lizzie?'

'Because . . . well, I wanted it to be a surprise.'

Alice pressed her hands to her cheeks. 'Well, it's certainly a surprise.'

'And we didn't know for certain that he could make it until three days ago. He sent a cable from the ship.'

Before Alice could reply she heard the front door open and then voices, Jack's and the one with the gentle lilt that she remembered so well, and then he was there in the room beside her and she smiled at him. A warm, genuine smile.

'They've told you, I see,' he laughed.

Alice stretched out her hands in greeting. 'About two minutes ago.'

Mike took them in his. 'You get lovelier with time, Alice. I was trying to work out how old you are now.'

'That's not very gallant of you, is it? At least you're honest. I'm twenty-two.'

'Ah, then you're still only a babe in arms,' he joked, still holding her hands. He fought down the urge to take her in his arms and kiss her.

'And you're still full of the blarney, Mike, but it's good to see you. I'm still a bit dazed, they could have told me sooner but it was *supposed* to be a surprise.'

'They're a pair of eejits – made for each other!' he

laughed, searching her face for something, some sign of affection, but although she was still smiling at him there was no special light, no special glow of love in her brown eyes.

Lizzie and Jack exchanged glances and both men sat down.

'Lizzie tells me you've bought a house in Dublin. That you sold up.'

'I did, so. Ah, what was the point of it all, Alice? I'd never particularly liked that Charleston house, however magnificent it was. It was *his* and when he died it was convenient for me to stay on. But then I decided to come home. I've got a house in County Dublin, not the city itself. It's out at Dunlaoghaire, by the sea.'

'What will you do?' Alice asked.

They'd slipped easily back into their old ways. Just like a couple, Lizzie thought, watching them closely.

'You mean apart from being persecuted by my sisters? Oh, there's so much to do and see. It's a changed city in many ways. The beautiful Georgian buildings may have been built by Englishmen, but it's *our* city now. There are museums, libraries, art galleries and statues by the dozen. I can stand all day on the quays. There's always someone who'll talk to you, tell you their life history if you've the time and inclination to listen. And all Irishmen like a good chat about the horses. I heard two of them on the Ha'penny Bridge last time I was home. "Did you get anything on that horse you had in Leopardstown?" says one. "Ah, no, aren't they still out looking for the contrary animal with flash lamps!" It was great altogether,' he laughed. Then he became serious. 'Maybe I'll set up some sort of trust, for the poor, particularly kids, but not one administered by the clergy, there are too many penalty clauses attached. If you've not behaved, missed Mass, been a troublemaker, then there's nothing down for you.'

'Surely not.' Alice was frowning.

'It happened in nineteen eleven in the lock-outs. If you were in Larkin's union, then you starved. The union ran out of money and support from the Liverpool branch. There was no strike pay. But I'd rather trust the union with my money than the clergy, any day.'

The look that passed between Mike and Alice was one of understanding. Of bitter memories recalled and shared.

'So, you see, I'll barely have a minute to myself.'

'You'll not stand for election as a TD for Dail Eireann?' Jack asked.

'No, Jack, I've no interest in politics. I've no strong views either way about the Taoiseach's policies.'

Lizzie suggested that the men went into the parlour and she'd bring them some tea; she and Alice had some details to discuss.

'Are you pleased to see him, Alice?' Lizzie asked when she returned to the kitchen.

'Yes, I am, but I . . . I feel guilty, Lizzie. He was so good to me and I just ran out on him.'

'Well, you're older and wiser now. He thinks a lot of you.'

'I know, he always made sure I was all right.' She misconstrued Lizzie's words.

'Maybe a lot more than you think.'

'No, Lizzie, he's always been a friend, a very good and generous friend.'

Lizzie stood up. 'The way David and Charlie Williamson are?'

'No. Charlie, maybe. But David . . .' Alice's expression softened.

'Oh, for God's sake, Alice, grow up! Face it. You never see him – a few meetings here and there. You don't even know him very well. He's all part of your dream, an impossible dream. Forget him!'

Alice also got to her feet, surprised and annoyed by

Lizzie's vehemence. 'Well, all the rest of the dream has come true, Lizzie, hasn't it?'

'Yes, and you're still not happy, are you? When the dream becomes reality it's not a dream any more; it dies, Alice. Oh, I'm going to say good night to Jack, I'm worn out.'

Alice sat for a long time after Lizzie had gone to bed. She could hear the two men talking in the parlour but she couldn't make out the words, nor did she want to. Lizzie was trying to make her face the reality about David and most of what her sister had said was true. She seldom saw him, but that didn't mean she didn't love him or that he didn't care for her. If they were married she would still see little of him; it was something she'd have to accept – gracefully. Then she remembered Victor's words about the women of middle-class families. She sighed heavily. She was no longer an ignorant, dirty, scruffy waif, but even if she married David, she'd never be middle-class, she'd always be a working-class girl from Benledi Street.

Chapter Twenty-Eight

Saturday dawned cold but clear. There had been a heavy frost overnight and all the windowpanes were covered by delicate traceries of ice that looked like lacework. Alice had the boys light fires in all the rooms, even the bedrooms.

'At least we'll be warm when we leave the house,' she commented. 'And, thank God, it's not snowing, raining or blowing a force-ten gale,' she added as she helped Lizzie with her veil and bandeaux.

'How is Agnes managing?' Lizzie asked.

'Fine. She's got those two hooligans well under control and our Mary's no trouble. Our Jimmy was complaining about his collar being too stiff and too tight, but she told him he was lucky you didn't have him in top hat and tails, that you'd seriously thought about it. You should have seen the look on his face! All three of them are moaning about not being able to have any breakfast.'

'Well, I'm not having everyone in church nudging each other and wondering why they're not going to Communion.'

'Our Agnes told them that too. She said they should be thankful you're so considerate. The wedding could have been at eleven o'clock or even later instead of at ten and they'd all be famished and near to fainting by then. Mind you, I'm a bit hungry myself.'

'Holy Mother, I couldn't eat a thing, I'm so nervous!'

Alice was already dressed in the magenta taffeta dress that had a sash round the hips, which ended in a large stiff bow. The circlet of wax flowers was already fixed firmly onto her head. She thought she looked awful but at least people wouldn't spend too much time gaping at her. Until she sang, that was. She'd decided on Schubert's arrangement of 'Ave Maria'. She stood back to admire her handiwork and smiled. 'Oh, Lizzie, you look a dream! Mam would have loved to see you.'

'She can, Alice. I believe she *can*.'

Alice nodded. Lizzie had always been plain, but in her wedding finery, her face lit up with love and excitement, she was transformed. Alice helped her downstairs.

Mr O'Hanlon stood awkwardly in front of the fire in the kitchen. He knew Mary would make his life a misery if he spoiled Lizzie's day and made a show of her before the entire congregation and the fine gentleman from America. Especially as she'd be dressed up to the nines for once in her life, mainly in clothes borrowed from neighbours. He'd made a show of her for most of their married life, she'd said acidly, but today was different. Let no one have any complaint about Ignatius – known to all as Iggy – O'Hanlon's behaviour.

The two boys looked bored already, Alice noticed.

'Eddy, go out into the scullery and get the flowers. Did they send pins for the buttonholes?' she asked her sister.

Agnes nodded. She was worn out already from trying to keep her siblings under control and clean. Like Alice, she wasn't very impressed with her dress.

'And don't you dare open your mouth about these awful frocks, Agnes, or I'll kill you! It's *her* day.'

Agnes nodded and fervently hoped that Tommy Healy from further down the street wouldn't come to the same conclusion she and Alice had reached.

Eddie brought in the flowers and placed them on the table.

'Now go and stand at the front door and let us know when the carriages arrive.' Alice was pinning on Mr O'Hanlon's buttonhole.

'They left Jack's house ages ago so they should be here soon,' Agnes informed them.

She was right, for no sooner had Eddy got to the door than he came pounding back down the hall. 'They're here! They're here!'

Jimmy muttered something about what his mates would think of them in their daft outfits, a sentiment fully agreed with by Iggy O'Hanlon who ushered him, Eddy, Mary, Agnes and Alice to the door.

'It's going ter be a birrof a crush,' he remarked.

'Not if everyone keeps still.' Alice's gaze was fixed firmly on her brothers.

Jimmy mumbled something under his breath and Eddy looked sullen as they climbed in. Half the street had come out to see Lizzie, and the women stood in groups, arms folded, chatting, admiring or criticising, while their children ran up and down, shouting and yelling with the excitement of the occasion.

Lizzie had a bit of trouble with her long veil but was finally installed. She beamed with happiness at her neighbours, and didn't feel the least bit cold. What she did feel was nervous. Very nervous.

The aisle of St Anthony's had never looked so long, she thought as she tucked her arm into Iggy O'Hanlon's while Alice and Agnes arranged the train of her dress and the veil. The two boys, to their great relief, had been sent on up to the front pews where Mary, Ethel and Jinny (all in borrowed finery) had pride of place.

The church was full. There were even people standing at the back and up the side aisles. It wasn't often there was a wedding of such grand proportions. Three brides-maids, two open carriages of the type you saw royalty using, and the flowers in the church must have cost a fortune. They'd also heard that the best man had come all the way from America. Imagine that. And the bride's sister was Alice O'Connor, a big star in the theatres in London. The information was whispered around the church.

The organ burst into life and Alice kept her eyes down, not looking left or right. She wanted people to look at Lizzie, not her.

Mike looked very handsome in morning dress – pinstriped trousers, white shirt, pale grey tie and black jacket without tails. Jack, too, looked fine, resplendent in his dress uniform, the buttons and badges highly polished, his helmet placed on the seat of the pew.

Throughout the Mass, Alice tried to concentrate. Lizzie was happy, she was radiant with joy. But she herself felt strangely out of place although this was her church, she'd been baptised here, and these were her people. As she stepped out and walked to the altar rail, turning to face the congregation, she caught Mike's gaze. He smiled at her, a smile of encouragement and pride that reminded her of Maura O'Hare's soirée and the Cotillion Ball.

Her voice rose clearly and sweetly and the congregation was reverently hushed. There was not a single cough, sniff or shuffling of feet.

Mike bent his head and closed his eyes, giving the appearance of being deep in prayer. In fact his heart was being torn in two. She looked so beautiful, despite the unfortunate dress, and it was so long since he'd heard her sing. He must have been mad to have come, but he'd been drawn inexorably, like a moth to the flame and he was burning up with desire and despair. He prayed to God, something he seldom did, to give him the strength to overcome his pride, or at least be able to hide the emotions that were tearing him apart. Surely, surely she must feel moved by the ceremony. Could she not see, or at least have some inkling of the love he felt for her?

Jack had pressed him to speak of his love. How could she know how he felt if he didn't tell her? he'd reasoned. But the demon pride still wouldn't allow him to expose his feelings to her. Besides, what if by some miracle she agreed and they got married, what about her career? He couldn't take that away from her. It was what drove her on, it was what had made her pull herself up from the gutter to become the star she was born to be.

But as the last silvery notes died in the silent church, he was remembering what Jack had urged on him.

The rest of the day went well, the photographs, the meal laid on at the Stork Hotel and the happy couple duly dispatched for three days' honeymoon at the small but very select Cleveland Guest House in Southport.

Mike had ordered cabs to take the family and Mary, Ethel and Jinny home. After a day with only one glass of champagne that he thought tasted worse than lemonade, and Mary giving him looks like daggers that would kill you stone dead, Iggy O'Hanlon headed for the nearest pub.

'Just you remember your Vinny wants that suit back termorrer!' Mary called after him from the window of the cab.

'Well, at least he looked the gear an' behaved 'imself,' Ethel remarked.

'Aye, 'e can stop out all night now for all I care.' Mary leaned back against the leather seat. 'God, but I'll be glad to get these shoes offen me. They're our Maggie's an' they're too flamin' small!'

'Lizzie looked very well, I thought,' Mike said.

Alice wore her navy coat with the fur trim over her dress, for the winter afternoon was already fading and the temperature was dropping. 'She looked beautiful. Not like our old Lizzie at all.'

'Does it not make you think of other weddings?'

'What other weddings? Don't tell me our Agnes is going

to elope with that Tommy Healy. What bit of gossip have you heard that I haven't?' she laughed.

'Nothing, I swear to God.'

She looked up at him, her eyes questioning. 'Then what weddings?'

He managed a smile. 'Ah, take no notice of me, I have this terrible habit of rameishing on. I suppose it's back to work for you now?'

She nodded. 'Manchester, the opera house, although it's not opera I'll be performing. And what about you?'

'Oh, I'll get the ten o'clock boat to Dublin tomorrow. I've got so many things to do. I've hardly unpacked and I'll have those two sisters of mine in on top of me wanting to arrange things and organise me.' He tried to sound offhand. He was glad he hadn't taken Jack's advice. She had obviously not had a single thought all day about a wedding of her own, unless it was to David Williamson and that didn't bear thinking about.

March was wild and wet and Alice had begun to feel the strain of her hectic lifestyle, so she asked Victor to find her an understudy for her three days in Blackpool.

'I'm worn out, I feel awful and I know I'm not giving my best performances.'

He agreed. He reminded her that he'd warned her that touring was hell.

Things had settled down well in Media Street, she thought, staring out of her lounge window at the sodden fields beyond her garden fence, fields that were becoming dark and obscure as evening approached. Georgie, who had grown from a kitten into a sleek, well-fed cat, was stretched out in front of the fire. So far Lizzie hadn't had a row with her mother-in-law and Agnes seemed to be coping very well at home, far better than anyone had thought possible. Lizzie had told her that they'd had a couple of letters from Mike and when the weather got better he was going off to do a tour of the country – his country, most of which he'd never seen.

She felt miserable and lonely. Everyone seemed to have busy, interesting lives, except herself. The rain dripped persistently down the windows. What was it that Lizzie had said to her? 'When the dream becomes reality it dies.' Lately she'd begun to think there was a lot of truth in that statement.

Already it was nearly time for dinner, but she couldn't be bothered to cook something. She didn't feel hungry. She'd begun to wonder why she had bought this cottage in the middle of nowhere. She knew no one and she hardly ever saw the Laidlaws, the couple Charlie had hired as gardener and cleaner and who looked after Georgie when she was away. She didn't want to spend any more time alone. She'd ring Charlie.

At last someone answered the phone and went off to find him. As she waited she could hear laughter and music in the background. There was obviously something going on there too.

'Alice. How are you?' Charlie asked and she could tell from his voice that he'd been drinking.

'As miserable as sin. I was wondering if you could come down and see me, but obviously you've got company.'

'Well, there is a bit of a do going on but they won't miss me.'

'No. No, Charlie, I can tell you're enjoying yourself and it's a horrible night to have to drive so far and then back home again. I'm all right, really I am, just at a bit of a loose end.' She forced some cheerfulness into her voice.

'I'll come down tomorrow, early. We'll have the day together. Go for lunch and maybe a stroll around Chester, then get some dinner. How does that sound?'

'Great. I'll see you tomorrow then. Enjoy the rest of the evening.' She replaced the receiver before he had a chance to start apologising.

She looked at the clock on the mantelpiece. It was much too early to go to bed; she'd listen to the wireless then have an early night. She scooped up the cat and sat in an armchair and closed her eyes. Georgie settled himself and began to purr. It was a miserable night and she was just feeling sorry for herself. Depressed because she was tired. She'd be fine in the morning.

It was still wild and windy the following morning, but the rain had stopped, there were a few breaks in the cloud and the sun struggled to shine through. She dressed with care. A close-fitting knitted suit in pale beige under her new chocolate-brown coat. Her hat was beige, trimmed with brown satin ribbon, and as a last touch of elegance she wound a long cream silk scarf round her neck, letting the ends fall over her shoulders and down her back.

Charlie arrived at ten o'clock, looking none the worse for wear.

'Alice! As gorgeous as ever!' He kissed her on the cheek, feeling more confident than he'd felt for a long time. *She'd* phoned *him*; usually it was the other way round. She did look smashing and they were going to spend the whole day together.

They laughed and joked all the way to Chester and Alice felt so much better. The sun was shining now, the clouds had disappeared, but the wind was still strong and she had to hang on to her hat.

He parked the car outside the Grosvenor Hotel and ushered her inside, guiding her into the grill restaurant.

'Just to make up for my tardiness last night, we'll have champagne.'

'At lunchtime?'

'Why not? Some people have it for breakfast.'

She wrinkled her nose with distaste. 'I think I'd sooner have tea. What was going on anyway last night when I phoned?'

'Oh, Captain Walmsley and his family were over for dinner. He and Father have been friends for years, they went to school together. Mother and Mrs Walmsley are great friends too. They've got a son in the Royal Navy, he's away, but Cecelia, Eunice and Victoria were all there, and David, of course.'

Her eyes lit up. 'David's home?'

'Well, he'd have to be, wouldn't he? I mean, the dinner was for him and Cecelia.'

She stared at him and a sickening feeling washed over her. 'Why?'

'Their engagement, of course.'

The room began to rotate slowly. No! He couldn't do this to her! She loved him. She'd loved him for years, since the day he'd picked her up in his arms and carried her aboard the *Aquitania*. There was a rushing noise in her ears. 'I . . . I . . .'

Charlie thought she was going to faint, all the colour had drained from her face. 'Alice, you didn't realise?'

'How . . . how could I?' The room was still rotating and all sound seemed to be blocked out, all but the strange rushing noise.

'I thought he'd told you. It's been on the cards for years. She's the ideal wife for him. She's been used to having her father away so much. She'll cope admirably, she has her own interests and circle of friends. Her father is the captain of the *Samaria*, so he'll help David all he can with his career. At the rate he's going he could be one of the youngest masters in the entire line.'

'I . . . I . . . thought . . . he . . .' She couldn't go on, the words were choking her.

'He's fond of you, Alice, and he really does admire you tremendously because you've done so well. He's always saying he's your biggest fan.'

The tears were blinding her now and she hung her head. 'I thought he loved me.'

'Oh, Alice, I'm sorry, so sorry! But you've still got me. You know I worship you.' He reached across the table and tried to take her hand but she snatched it away.

'It was just a dream. A mad, impossible dream. And . . . and everyone warned me.' She wasn't aware that she'd spoken the words aloud. 'I've been chasing a dream. All these years I've been fooling myself!'

'No, Alice. You've got the best part of the dream. Your career.'

She stared at him blankly. 'But . . . but it was all for . . . him. Don't you see, it was all for him.'

'He does admire you, Alice.'

Admire. Admire. Admire. The word beat inside her head and she felt so small, so humiliated, so ashamed. 'Because I came from the gutter? He picked me up, remember? I'm not good enough, that's the real reason. I came from the slums, my da's in jail and I put him there!'

She got up, looking around wildly and knocking a glass of champagne over but she didn't notice. 'I want to go home! I . . . I . . . can't stay here!' She ran from the dining room, unaware of the shocked and surprised looks of the other diners.

Charlie grabbed her bag, threw a five-pound note on the table, almost snatched her coat from the waiter who had approached, and ran after her.

By the time he reached the street she was already sitting in the car, huddled down in the seat, sobbing. He felt such a heel. He'd really thought she knew or had guessed, that it was himself she was really interested in.

'I want to go home,' she sobbed.

'Oh, Alice, darling, I'm so sorry. Please, sweetheart, put your coat on. You've had a terrible shock and it's freezing cold.' He tried to tuck it round her but she pulled away from him.

The commissionaire came over and asked if he needed

any assistance. Was the young lady ill? Charlie thanked him but refused the offer, thinking he'd better get out of here fast before they became the centre of an incident.

He swung the crank handle once and the engine turned over. He threw the handle into the back, leaped in beside Alice and put his foot down on the accelerator.

He heard her scream, then choke, and turned to look at her.

He was horrified. 'Oh, Christ Almighty!' he cried, slamming his foot down hard on the brake. One of the long flowing ends of her scarf had become caught up in the spokes of the wheel and she was being strangled! He began to yell for help and to tear the scarf loose. The commissionaire, who was an ex-army man, rushed to his aid. Within seconds and by sheer brute force they had wrenched the scarf clear and loosened it from round her throat but her face was a pale mauve colour, her eyes were closed and she was fighting for breath.

'For God's sake, get a doctor!' Charlie yelled at the man.

'A doctor will be no good, sir, it's hospital she needs and quick. Take her to the Countess of Chester's Hospital. You can't miss it!' the man yelled after the rapidly disappearing car. It had only taken a few seconds, one turn of the wheel, but it had almost cost the poor woman her life, he thought as he dispersed the small group of people who had gathered and went back to his post.

Chapter Twenty-Nine

Charlie sat in the waiting room with his head in his hands. He was close to despair and wanted no one to see the tears in his eyes. He'd nearly killed her. Why the hell hadn't he checked that that damned scarf wasn't trailing? It was all his fault. He should have driven down last night. She'd have been at home. Safely at home. He could have explained properly, calmed her down, reassured her.

There had been a time when he'd thought David *had* fallen for her, but when he'd deliberately picked an argument with him to find out, David had told him that what he felt for Alice was admiration. He did feel a certain amount of affection for her, nostalgic affection for the waif who, against all odds, had become a star, but she wasn't going to form any part of his life, that belonged to the sea. Cecelia knew that, so he'd assumed that Alice knew it too. But she hadn't.

'Mr Williamson?'

Charlie looked up at the grim-faced woman dressed in dark blue with the stiffly starched apron and cuffs, a starched and intricately pleated cap covering her hair.

He stood up. 'Can I see her, please? How . . . how is she?'

'She's comfortable.' The tone was crisp.

Charlie's taut nerves snapped. 'What the hell is that supposed to mean?'

'Mr Williamson! Control yourself. I will *not* stand for such language!'

'I'm sorry, Sister, please forgive me, but I'm so worried.'

'She is just that. Comfortable. She's been very lucky indeed. She won't see you, I'm afraid. Has she relatives? Mother, father?'

'No, neither. Her sister and brother-in-law are her closest relatives. He's a policeman,' he added, thinking it might be useful.

'Right then, and how do we contact them?'

Charlie tried hard to concentrate, to collect his thoughts, to remember. There was a phone at the house in Media Street but they'd all be out, Agnes and Jimmy at work and Eddy and Mary at school. There was no phone at Jack's house. 'I think the local police station is Rose Hill, Liverpool. If Constable Phillips isn't there, then maybe someone could go to his home. It's in Media Street, Liverpool, but I don't know what number.'

'Thank you. And now I think the best thing for you to do is go home.' Sister's eyes were steely; she had no time at all for this irresponsible generation who tore around the country in their flashy motorcars.

Charlie nodded miserably. If Alice wouldn't see him, there was no use in staying. 'But she *is* all right?' He looked pleadingly for confirmation.

Sister nodded.

'I'll phone later on, or perhaps tomorrow.'

In reply he got a curt nod before the woman turned and walked away.

Alice lay in the hospital bed dazed, slightly dizzy and weak. When she'd arrived they'd put a mask over her face which had made breathing easier, but her throat felt as though scalding hot water had been poured down it and her neck hurt. They'd been very good to her, although she didn't remember being driven here, she must have passed out. After the doctor had gone, Sister had asked her if she wanted to see the young man who was waiting outside. She'd shaken her head vehemently.

They'd given her some medicine and she drifted in and out of sleep for the rest of the day. Then when she'd woken properly it was dark, the lights had been switched on and Lizzie and Jack were there. A sob made her catch her breath but she reached out and Lizzie took her hand and held it tightly.

'Oh, Alice! Alice! You gave us a terrible fright! It's taken hours to get here and all the way I've been in such a state.'

Tears welled up in Alice's eyes.

'I'm going to go through every bloody book I can lay my hands on to see if there's anything I can charge that bloody lunatic with!' Jack's expression was grim.

Alice shook her head. It really wasn't Charlie's fault. She'd been so upset, she'd rushed out – but she didn't want to think about that now. She didn't want to think about either Charlie or David Williamson.

Lizzie stayed holding her hand tightly while Jack went in search of the doctor and the ward sister.

The fact that he was in uniform seemed, to a certain degree, to impress them both.

'I'd like to know exactly how my sister-in-law is, sir, if you don't mind.'

The doctor frowned. 'She's very, very lucky, that's how she is. She could have broken her neck. She has a very badly bruised larynx, in fact the whole throat is bruised and swollen and there's a slight strain. That's due to the force with which the head was jerked suddenly and violently backwards.'

Jack looked concerned. 'When can she come home?'

'Tomorrow, I think. She's had a sedative for the shock and should sleep tonight. There's nothing more we can do, it's just a matter of time. Time will reduce the swelling and the bruising but she mustn't even try to speak for at least five days.'

'Thank you, sir.'

The doctor turned away and Jack addressed Sister. 'I'll arrange transport, ma'am.'

'I'd telephone first, but I'd say she should be discharged at about noon.'

Jack thanked her and went back to relay the information to Lizzie and Alice.

After Lizzie and Jack had gone, Alice lay awake staring blankly at the blind that covered the window on the far side of the ward. Tomorrow she could go home, but where was home? Her cottage in Saltney Ferry or the house in Media Street?

If she went to Media Street, would she get any rest with everyone in and out at all times of the day and night and with Mary, Ethel and Jinny calling in too? On the other hand she'd have company, she wouldn't have much time to brood. If she went to the cottage she'd have all the time in the world to rest, but she would spend all day thinking, thinking about things she wanted to forget. Eventually she fell asleep, the dilemma unresolved.

She felt better the following day. Less dazed, less shocked, although her throat still felt as though it was on fire. She was instructed to drink as much as possible, although nothing that contained citrus like orange juice, and tea was only to be drunk when it was tepid. She must eat only soup, blancmange, semolina pudding and the like, but she didn't feel like eating anything. She just wanted to go home.

Jack and Lizzie arrived at noon. Jack had managed to persuade the inspector at Seel Street, the police garage, to lend them a car for a few hours. It was an emergency, he'd explained. Once he'd mentioned Alice's name there was no problem. The inspector's wife was a great fan.

'Alice, luv, do you want to go to the cottage? I'll stay

with you for as long as you need me. Or do you want to come home, to Liverpool, to Media Street? I'll only be up the road and our Agnes is very capable. They're all out of the house for most of the day and I'll keep any visitors away until you feel up to seeing them. The cottage?'

Alice shook her head. No, it wasn't really home. It had never had that special feeling; she hadn't really spent much time there at all and now she never wanted to go back. Someone could go and pick up her things and Georgie and then she'd sell it. Home was where her family were.

Lizzie looked relieved. She had talked to Jack about it all and they'd agreed that Lizzie would stay with Alice at the cottage but she hadn't really relished spending all her time stuck out in the country.

Jack was given a list of instructions by Sister while Lizzie helped Alice dress, then he guided them outside to the parked car.

'Where did you get the car, Jack?'

He helped both Alice and Lizzie in. 'I borrowed it from the police garage. Oh, it's all right, it's on loan for a few hours. I'll drive you home and then take it back.'

After she had sipped the concoction the hospital had given her, Alice went straight to bed.

'Our Agnes has warned them she'll murder them all if they come in banging doors and clattering up and down the stairs, so you try and sleep,' Lizzie told her. 'And I've told Mary O'Hanlon, Ethel Maguire and Jinny Thomas that you are not to have any visitors for a week. Those were the hospital's instructions. I've also told Agnes and the others that if that Charlie Williamson phones, to tell him to clear off – politely.'

By the end of the week Alice felt better. At least, she was over the shock, the pain in her neck had eased and her throat was not so sore. She'd said a few words to

Lizzie, telling her briefly what had happened. It had been awfully hard to stop herself speaking. Even more so because she wanted to pour out to Lizzie all the pain and heartache. How hurt and miserable she was.

Their old neighbours came, en masse, after church on Sunday and expressed their concern and sympathy.

'We've all said an extra decade of the rosary every night for yer, Alice, luv,' Mary informed her. 'An' they've said prayers in the school too.'

'An' I went to Benediction yesterday an' all,' Ethel announced. 'I told my lot they could all fend for themselves for an hour. "Get yer idle, useless da ter make yer tea," I said. Well, yer should 'ave seen the gob on 'im! Off down the pub like a shot he was!' Ethel shrugged. 'But yer comin' on great now, Alice. So your Lizzie tells us.'

'You were dead lucky, Alice. I reckon it was yer mam watchin' over yer,' Jinny said sagely and with deep conviction.

Alice thanked them but when they'd gone she burst into tears.

'Alice! Alice, stop it! You're not supposed to get upset!' Lizzie put her arms round her sister and held her close. 'Why the hell did Jinny Thomas have to go and say something like that?'

Alice leaned her cheek against Lizzie's shoulder. 'Oh, Lizzie, I miss her so much.'

'I know, we all do. I'll tell you one thing though, if she'd been here, this wouldn't have happened. She'd have given that Charlie a right tongue-lashing and told him to clear off at the start.'

'It wasn't his fault, Lizzie.'

'Of course it was!'

Alice was quieter now. 'No, I ran out of the Grosvenor without my coat, hat or anything. I . . . I was too upset, I didn't know what I was doing.'

'Alice, hush, you mustn't talk too much yet. Not until you've seen the specialist next week.'

'He told me that ... that ... David has got engaged. He's going to ... to ... marry someone else. Her father's a captain.'

Lizzie didn't reply. She wanted to say that it really didn't come as a surprise to her. David Williamson had shown no romantic interest in Alice at all and she'd told Alice so. It was all a fantasy Alice had built up in her mind.

'Oh, Lizzie, I hate them! I hate them all. The whole bloody family!'

Lizzie smiled at her. 'That's better. That's more like the Alice I know. And I agree. They wouldn't let you over their doorstep, Alice, no matter how well-dressed or how famous you were. That Charlie never took you home, did he? You'll get over it. I did. It was awful after poor Tommy was killed, I had nothing to live for, but life had to go on. Mam needed me.'

Alice managed a weak smile. Lizzie was right. She had been walking out with Tommy Mac and she'd known he loved her. It must have been much harder for Lizzie.

As she walked back up the street towards home, Lizzie was relieved. Alice seemed to be over the worst. She'd survive, and without the bloody Williamsons. This was her home and she was surrounded by people of her own class who really cared about her.

Alice's appointment with Mr West at Rodney Street, the Harley Street of Liverpool, was at ten o'clock the following Friday and Lizzie went with her.

They were shown into a magnificent Georgian house and into a room with deep sash windows, highly polished floor, Arabian rugs, antique furniture and deep, comfortable chairs. The receptionist was very pleasant, explaining that Mr West was running a little late but that they wouldn't have long to wait.

Alice felt quite calm now. Her throat was still a little sore if she talked too much but she'd had enough time to think over what Lizzie had said. The affection she'd thought David Williamson had for her *had* been a fantasy. He'd been bound up in her dreams for years. The pathetic, idiotic idea that she loved him had been born the day he'd carried her aboard the ship and had stirred her emotions, emotions that had grown and become deep-rooted in her mind. It still hurt her terribly to think about him and she seemed to see his face everywhere, but Lizzie told her firmly to put him out of her mind. Now she must concentrate on her career. Hadn't there been some talk of her making a gramophone record?

'Miss O'Connor, would you follow me, please?' The receptionist's voice broke her reverie.

Lizzie gave her a smile and a nod of encouragement and settled down to wait.

Mr West was a tall, thin, distinguished-looking man with silver-grey hair, a goatee beard and gold-rimmed spectacles. He was studying notes in a brown folder when she was ushered in.

He smiled. 'Please sit down, Miss O'Connor.'

Alice sat while he referred to the notes again and then gently felt her throat. He asked her to swallow hard several times, then to repeat a rhyme and read a paragraph from a book.

He nodded. 'Good. You're progressing, Miss O'Connor. The swelling and the bruising have almost gone.'

'When will I be able to sing again, Mr West?'

He looked at her with mild astonishment. 'Sing?'

'Yes. It's my career. I . . . I . . . was quite well known in London. I starred in musical stage shows.'

He looked at the notes in the folder again and then looked directly into her eyes. 'Miss O'Connor, it would be very cruel and unprofessional of me to lie to you, but you will never sing again. The vocal cords have been too badly damaged. You do realise that you were being strangled and could have died? You were very lucky.'

She stared at him, stunned, not fully understanding the importance of his words. 'I'll ... I'll ... never ...'

He shook his head and then pressed a button on the wall.

The receptionist appeared.

'Would you bring Miss O'Connor's sister in, please?'

The colour drained from Lizzie's face when she saw Alice. Alice was sitting like a statue, so still, so pale and in what appeared to be a state of deep shock.

'I'm Mrs Phillips, sir. Her sister.'

'I'm terribly sorry but I have had to give your sister some very bad news. I had no idea that she was on the stage.'

'What is it?' Lizzie asked in a hoarse whisper, her eyes never leaving Alice's face.

'She'll never be able to sing professionally again. Maybe in years to come a verse or two at a family get-together, but not on the stage. Her voice would go completely and the damage would be irreparable.'

Lizzie's hand went to her mouth to stifle the cry. Oh, Holy Mother of God! She'd thought that Alice was going to be fine, that she'd be given the all-clear to return in a month or so to her profession and she'd forget David and Charlie Williamson.

Mr West suggested that when they got home Lizzie should call their local doctor who would administer a sedative for the shock. He was extremely sorry to have had to impart such bad news, but it had been necessary, unfortunately.

Lizzie thanked him and led Alice out and hailed a taxi. All the way home Alice didn't say a word and her hands were as cold as ice.

Lizzie stoked up the fire in the parlour and was about to phone their doctor when Alice stopped her.

'No, Lizzie. I don't want to be drugged. I don't want to live in a half-dazed world.'

Lizzie immediately went to her side and held her closely. 'Alice, it'll be for the best.'

'No it won't! Oh, Lizzie, I promised Mam I wouldn't waste my gift, and now I have!' The tears were spilling down her cheeks. 'She ... she said to me just before she died, "The Lord giveth and the Lord taketh away." I ... I ... had everything I'd ever wanted, Lizzie, except for *him* and that wouldn't have worked out. I know that now. But I wasn't satisfied. I wasted it. I threw it all away because I'd forgotten who I was and where I came from.'

'Alice, stop that, it's nonsense! I won't have you talking like that. Mam was proud of you and she'd have understood.'

'No, Lizzie, she wouldn't. She knew me too well, she was warning me. It was pride, and vanity, and wanting something I couldn't have, and now ... now there's nothing.'

Lizzie drew away and gently pushed Alice down onto the sofa and took her hands. 'You *do* have someone, something, left out of all this mess, Alice.'

'What? Who?'

'Mike. Mike O'Farrell, and he loves you, Alice. He always has done. He told Jack.'

Alice shook her head. 'No, Lizzie, he was just fond of me.'

'It was – is – more than just fondness, Alice! For God's sake, don't be so blind and stupid again! Why do you think he left America and came back to Ireland? It was to be nearer to you if you ever needed him.'

Alice stared at her uncomprehendingly.

'It's the truth, Alice. You can ask Jack. Mike's loved you since the day he first met you.'

'Then why ...?'

'Because he's a proud man, Alice. He's older than you

and you once told him if you'd had a choice of fathers, you'd have picked him. How do you think he felt then and would feel later on if he told you he loved you? And not like a father loves a daughter. Or should do,' she added grimly, thinking of their own father in Walton Gaol. 'He's afraid of rejection, of you thinking him an old fool. He'd marry you tomorrow, Alice. For God's sake don't throw away your hopes, your life, the way I did before I met Jack! Don't just give up, Alice!'

'I didn't know, Lizzie. I just didn't know. I walked out on him. I . . . I . . . can't go to him now, like this, with nothing.'

'Alice, you can't sing but that won't matter to him. You're alive, you're young, you're beautiful. He loves you. He won't want anything more.'

Alice dropped her head. 'No, Lizzie, I can't. I just can't expect him to pick up the pieces. To take . . . second best.'

Lizzie stood up and, shaking her head, left Alice on her own. She knew what she was going to do.

Alice sat rigidly still. She couldn't take it in. She was still reeling from the shock of her visit to Mr West and now Lizzie was telling her that Mike loved her. That he'd always loved her.

She thought back to her years in Charleston. He'd taken her away from India's. He'd saved her from becoming a whore. He'd given her everything because he'd loved her and he'd asked nothing in return. She remembered his smiles of encouragement and pride but behind those smiles had been love. A love that had endured everything. He'd stood back and watched her at the ball with David Williamson. He'd smiled and been polite when all the time his heart must have been torn with jealousy. And that night she'd left him. Then at Lizzie's wedding he'd asked her if it made her think of other marriages and she'd been flippant. Oh, he'd hidden his feelings well, very well.

As she laid her head on her arms and began to sob,

deep inside were the first stirrings of realisation and love. An awareness of the fool she'd been. She'd had to lose everything before she could realise what really mattered. That Mike loved her and she loved him. Not a wild fantasy love but a quiet enduring love, and now it was too late, she could never go to Mike like this, when that great gift, her talent, had gone.

As the days passed, Alice became listless and depressed. She was tired of being brutally honest with herself, looking deep inside herself, searching for the girl she used to be and longing for the time, those few short weeks, when with Mam they'd moved here to this house. She'd been happy then, really happy, but she'd also been happy in Charleston. Confident and glad to be known as Mrs O'Farrell, the young, beautiful and talented wife of the wealthy Mike O'Farrell. She knew she'd been envied by so many of the people they'd mixed with. But all that had happened before the *Aquitania* had docked on that fateful day.

Her heart was aching with misery and loneliness, despite being surrounded by family. Most mornings it was hard to get up but soon she would really have to make an effort to pull herself together, but she was so weary, so very weary.

'Are you going to stay in that dressing gown all day, Alice? It's ten o'clock.' Lizzie's voice was sharp.

Alice had her head in her hands and didn't look up or answer.

'There's a package arrived for you.'

'A package?'

At last Lizzie saw some interest, some animation in her sister's eyes as she handed over the small brown paper parcel. 'It came by registered post to our house.'

Alice stared at it. There were foreign stamps on it. Irish stamps.

'Well, open it. I'm dying to see what's in it.'

Alice tore off the paper to reveal a velvet-covered box and a folded piece of notepaper. She opened the box slowly. Inside was a brooch. A very beautiful brooch in the form of a peacock. Its tail was spread wide like a fan and was studded with diamonds, emeralds, rubies and sapphires; its body was gold and blue enamel.

'Oh, Alice, it's gorgeous! It's a peacock! Jack and I saw them in the botanic gardens on our honeymoon. They were beautiful.'

'They are, but ... but they can't sing, Lizzie. They can only make a horrible screeching noise.' She laid the box down on the table and turned the folded piece of paper over in her shaking hands. Had Mike heard? Was he being cruel? Was this his way of trying to hurt her? If it was, it was all she deserved for the years of pain and anguish she'd caused him.

'You read it, Lizzie. I ... I can't.'

Lizzie opened the note.

'What does he say?'

'It's not a letter, Alice. It's a song, or a few lines of one.'

'Read it!' Alice's voice was strident. She wanted to know how he felt; she wanted to know the worst.

But come ye back, when summer's in the meadow,
Or when the valley's hushed and white with snow,
For I'll be here, in sunshine or in shadow ...

Lizzie fell silent; there were no more words, there was nothing else to read. She gently lifted Alice's chin and looked into the brown eyes that were swimming with tears. 'For God's sake go to him, Alice. Forget your pride, go to him!'

Epilogue

The pale sunlight of that early spring morning sparkled on the grey-green water of the bay and washed over the harbour at Dunlaoghaire and the mail boat that had just docked.

As the passengers began to disembark, he scrutinised their faces, but it was the sunlight sparkling on the stones of the brooch she wore on the lapel of her coat that finally caught his eye. Then it fell on the tears on her cheeks as she ran to him and he caught her and held her in his arms.

'Oh, Mike, I've been so stupid! I . . . I . . . never realised. I never realised that it was you I loved.'

He held her away from him and smiled into her eyes. A smile full of love and happiness. 'That doesn't matter. You're home now, alanna. We're both home.'

He kissed her gently on the lips and she clung to him.

'For better or for worse, in sickness and in health, till death do us part, Alice. Mrs Alice O'Farrell. And this time it will be legal and sanctioned by God and man.'

Headline hopes you have enjoyed reading LIVERPOOL SONGBIRD and invites you to sample the beginning of Lyn Andrews' compelling new saga, LIVERPOOL LAMPLIGHT, now out in Headline hardback . . .

Chapter One

July, 1938

'Mam, our Joe's at it again! I saw him up the road.' Katie Deegan slammed the shop door behind her, her brows drawn together in a frown, her lips set in a line of annoyance.

'Oh, Jesus, Mary and Joseph! That lad will be the death of me, and me with the shop full! Get back behind this counter, Katie, quick as you can while I go and see what's up now.'

Molly Deegan took off her flowered print pinafore and handed it to Katie. Since Molly was a big woman, and her eighteen-year-old daughter had a different build entirely, it rather resembled a tent on Katie and she pulled a face as she wrapped it around her, wishing now she'd never opened her mouth. 'Where's me Da?' she called to her mother, who was apologising to her customers while making her way towards the door.

'He'll be in soon and so will our Georgie. This is just what I don't need right now! God stiffen him! Where exactly did you last see the little get?'

'Running out of Coyne's Undertakers with that gang of hooligans he calls "me mates". They all ran off together. Now, what do you want, Mrs Maher?' The question was asked in a quieter, more respectful tone.

Mary Maher pursed her lips and nodded in Molly's direction. 'I don't know what's gorinto kids these days.

Only last week you had to cart your Francis off to Stanley Hospital, didn't yer, Ellen?'

Ellen MacCane nodded her agreement. 'If I've told 'im once I've told 'im an 'undred times about climbing on the jigger walls. Still, a broken wrist will keep him out of trouble for a while.'

Katie hoped they weren't going to engage in a long catalogue of the faults and misdeeds of Vinny Maher and Franny MacCane. People at the back of the shop had started muttering and were getting impatient. Mam would have her life if she came back and found the shop still full of the original customers.

'What can I get you?' Katie urged.

Mary turned her attention to her shopping. 'I'll take three of your mackerel, a pound of soft cod's roe, and has yer Mam any fresh rabbits left? We'll have a pie termorrer. I'll cook it tonight, the kitchen mightn't get so hot. God, it's murder havin' to keep the range going full blast to cook stuff in the oven, especially in this weather.'

There were nods of genuine agreement.

'I think so, I'll have a look in the larder.' Katie leaned across the white marble slab behind the glass of the shop window where early that morning Molly had arranged the fish she'd brought home from market. It was always so tastefully done, Katie thought, with sea shells and parsley and crushed ice which was replaced at dinner time. Somehow the striped canvas awning outside, that protected the window and its contents from the sun, gave the shop a professional air others lacked. She picked out three of the fish, their silver and dark gun-metal scales shimmering, trying to find ones that were all the same size. It was the end of the day so it wasn't an easy task. She placed them on a sheet of paper on the counter.

'Will they do? Not much choice, I'm afraid.'

Mary nodded and watched as Katie weighed out the pound of soft cod's roe.

'Thats great, luv,' she said approvingly.

In summer the rabbits were kept in the dark cool larder off the back kitchen, which meant Katie had to leave the shop unattended. It didn't worry her, she knew nothing would be stolen in her absence. Molly Deegan's regular customers weren't like that. Of course you got the odd 'chancer' but there was always someone like Mary Maher there to confront the would-be thief.

As she walked into the living room, Katie saw Georgie hanging up his coat. At nineteen he was the eldest and worked for the British and American Tobacco Company, or the B & A as it was known locally. He earned good money, most of which he saved, and got cheap cigarettes which he sold because he didn't smoke, adding the profits to his savings. Mam often asked him what he was saving it all *for*? So that when he died he could get his name in the paper as a millionaire?

'Oh, do me a favour, Georgie – get a rabbit out of the larder and bring it into the shop for me,' Katie wheedled. 'There's a crowd out there all waiting to be served, and our Sarah's still bad with that migraine headache.'

He looked at her, annoyed. 'I've only just got in from work. Where's Mam?'

'Gone out looking for our Joe again. Oh, come on, please?' she sighed. 'I don't know why Mary Maher and the like don't shop earlier. Mam's up at the crack of dawn to get to the market.'

'They're all looking for something cheap, something that won't keep until tomorrow.'

'Mam doesn't have stuff like that ... You know as well as I do, Georgie Deegan, that she's famous around here for her good, fresh fish. Everyone knows they'd have to pay twice as much if they went to the likes of Coopers or the big shops in town.'

'Well, things she'll let them have a bit cheaper then, because she's soft-hearted and tired,' he answered

377

belligerently. 'It's the end of the day and I'm worn out.'

Katie glared at him. Worn out. Him. He might not be very tall but he was broad and fit. She was the odd one out; very slightly built, unlike Sarah who was quite tall and sturdy too. Sarah hated her build which she'd inherited from her Mam, but whenever she complained about it, Mam would say she should thank God she hadn't been born afflicted or deformed in any way. She was a fine strapping girl. She hated being called 'strapping', too. She said it made her feel like a cart-horse.

'I'm just as worn out as you,' Katie insisted. 'I've been working too and our Joe's taken the deliveries instead of Sarah.'

Some of her mother's customers were infirm, and would send a shopping list with a neighbour. Sarah would then wheel out the old bike from the back of the lean-to in the yard, put the order in the basket on the front and deliver it. On Saturdays when she served in the shop all day, her younger brother Joe earned his pocket money by doing the deliveries. He didn't mind. None of his mates had bikes and he often gave them rides on the crossbar or let them sit behind him, legs sticking out dangerously.

'Well, it's part of her job, not mine.' Georgie sat down at the table, opened the *Echo* and began to scan the pages, completely ignoring his sister.

Katie unceremoniously shoved past him towards the larder. 'Oh, I'll get it myself! There's half of Chelmsford Street out there in the shop and Mary Maher wants a rabbit, but don't give it another thought. Read your paper.' She shot a scornful look at Georgie. 'I should know better than to ask you to lift a finger. Lord Muck thinks that after a day's work it's his right to be waited on hand and foot.'